The Indispensable Julian Rathbone

A paperback original.

First published in Great Britain in 2003 by
The Do-Not Press Limited
16 The Woodlands
London SE13 6TY
www.thedonotpress.co.uk
email: IndJR@thedonotpress.co.uk

Casebound edition: ISBN 1 904316 12 3
C-format trade paperback: ISBN 1 904316 13 1

British Library Cataloguing in Publication Data. A catalogue record
for this book is available from the British Library.

1 3 5 7 9 10 8 6 4 2

The Indispensable
Julian Rathbone

THE INDISPENSABLE JULIAN RATHBONE

Contents

EDITOR'S NOTE

Julian Rathbone's work has appeared in many publications, journals and books over the years. Wherever possible we have kept to the original style except in rare cases where the meaning has altered – variations in punctuation and style are to be expected.

ACKNOWLEDGEMENTS

The Do-Not-Press and Julian Rathbone are grateful to the publishers for permission to print extracts from the following titles:

Blame Hitler, Trajectories – Victor Gollancz (Orion)

Joseph, The Last English King, Kings of Albion, A Very English Agent – Time Warner Books UK

Homage, As Bad As It Gets – Allison and Busby

The extract from the film script of *The Last English King* is reproduced with the kind permission of Geoff Reeve Films.

The extract from the script of the *TVM Dangerous Games* is reproduced with the kind permission of Westdeutscher Rundfunk and Winkelmann Filmproduktion.

1. INTRODUCTION

by Mike Phillips

Julian Rathbone belongs to a tradition of English writing that has always been consistently radical, thoughtful and endlessly inquisitive about the world. During the last couple of decades we've become accustomed to the categories imposed by the book trade, where the pressure on authors is to be one-trick ponies, confining themselves to one genre or the other. In much the same way, the commercial marketplace has little patience with authors' tendency to experiment with changes in mood or style; and this has generally narrowed writers' perspectives, imposing a parochial tone on much of contemporary English writing.

In contrast, Rathbone has maintained his desire to explore the limits throughout a lifetime of work. *The Indispensable Julian Rathbone* offers up a wide selection of his work – crime, science, erotic and historical fiction, short stories, extracts from his novels, autobiography, poetry, critical essays and screenplays. The book gives a unique insight into the mind and methods of a bestselling writer, especially for readers who have come across Rathbone's work before, but there's a great deal more in this volume. *The Indispensable Julian Rathbone* is real entertainment – a dazzling variety of stories, characters, landscapes and reflections. Rathbone displays acute observation of detail, how people dress and eat and behave towards each other, the way that places change or develop over time, and a strong feeling for the enigmas of identity. Linking all this together is fundamental curiosity about who people are, about how they interact and about the structures that govern their lives.

It's no surprise when he invokes the names of Graham Greene and Eric Ambler, because he shares with such writers a fascination with the inner working of power, and with its effects on individuals. All these qualities are on show in the complete novel in this book. *Lying In State* is an absorbing mystery, but it's also a commentary on Franco's dictatorship, an exposé of the dictator's methods and, by extension, a reflection on the effects of totalitarian rule on individual behaviour. The story is focused around the complex character of Roberto, an Argentinian historian and bookseller, who is recruited to authenticate a tape of Juan Perón, in which the dictator discusses his relations with former Nazis. The events take place during the week between the death of General Franco and the accession of Juan Carlos, and the narrative twists and turns, building up to a surprising and satisfying climax. It is a classic mystery, one of the best works of crime fiction in existence. Rathbone's brilliance, however, lies as much in the incidental detail, which sets up a sober and convincing satire about the workings of a totalitarian state, and about the relationship of its citizens to Franco's all-pervasive presence. In the present day, *Lying In State* has a completely authentic topicality, prompting an immediate recognition of decaying states and dying dictators in various parts of the contemporary world. Another layer of the narrative is a sly and penetrating mockery of the publishing trade itself and its relationship with a corrupt financial establishment. The mogul of the story, enormously rich but mean enough to share a hotel room, has all the features of a number of personalities in real life.

Lying In State is a pipe opener to a selection of Rathbone's fiction, followed by a pile of non-fiction essays, whose titles alone demonstrate the breadth of the author's interests – *The English – Who Are We? Los Ancianos, California, Kenya, Eros and Thanatos (Bonking 'n' Clog-Popping)*. Taken together, T*he Indispensable Julian Rathbone* symbolises an impressive body of work – entertaining, instructive, illuminating.   Above all, here is a writer in all his shades of mood and temperament.   More than interesting – I'm glad to have read it.

Mike Phillips, London, July 2003

2. MY LIFE AS A WRITER

I was born on the tenth of February 1935 in Stonefield Nursing Home, Kidbrook Grove, Blackheath, London. My cot had a blanket with appliqué-ed snowdrops on it. When she remembered my mother sent me or gave me snowdrops on most of my birthdays until she died. The day before I was born her brother, who lived in south London, decided to help matters along by taking her to see John Gielgud in *Hamlet*.

We lived in Liverpool at the time. I was born in Blackheath because Stonefield was part owned and run by my Aunt Helen and so it was free. She soaked the rich but gave her services away to relations, battered wives, unmarried mothers, and so forth. She even had a house in Bognor in which mothers whose circumstances meant they had nowhere feasible to take their newborn offspring were persuaded to stay for what they could afford until their circumstances were sorted out. Like most Rathbones, Aunt Helen was a very good person indeed. Her story was a not uncommon one: her fiancé was killed on the Somme, she never married and devoted her life, which was a long one, to good works instead.

The first recorded Rathbone was a carpenter from Macclesfield who moved to Liverpool to build ships around 1700. He prospered. Rathbones were always anti-slavers and in the 1780s refused to build for owners who were slave traders, and even refused to supply their builders with timber. They continued in the forefront of the campaign against slavery and in the nineteenth century feuded with another Liverpool family, the Gladstones, over the latter's refusal to free their sugar plantation slaves.

The family maintained its shipping connections well into the twentieth century, building ships, owning them, trading in and out of Liverpool, branching off into things like maritime insurance and so on. They were also philanthropists, Unitarians (which was as near as you could get to being an agnostic without losing respectability), independent politicians with a markedly libertarian, even socialist bent, patrons of the arts, and so on and so on. We include a founder member of the Communist Party of Great Britain who did time for agitating against British intervention in Russia after the Great War, and a conservative MP with a social conscience which kept him out of office until he died in 2002. Eleanor Rathbone sat as an independent MP for

Combined English Universities from 1929 until her death in 1946. She was responsible for getting the Family Allowance Act through parliament shortly before she died; throughout the thirties she constantly badgered the appeasers in the House of Commons; she fought for Indian independence, and so on and so on. James Gunn's portrait of her in the National Portrait Gallery says it all, and is one of the best pictures there.

I could go on and on. I'm really proud of being a Rathbone, though a touch bored with Basil. People do tend to ask me if I am related to Bas rather than if I am the Rathbone who writes books. Still, he was a great actor, ruined by Sherlock Holmes when he should be remembered for playing Karenin in *Anna Karenina* with Greta Garbo and Frederick Marsh. And who can forget his limpid perfect enunciation of the line 'You have come to Nottingham once too often...' in *The Adventures of Robin Hood*?

My favourite Rathbone is my great grandfather Philip, son of the William who worked with Florence Nightingale and founded District Nursing. Philip was fun-loving, independent, a hedonist, a patron of the arts. When a young man and only just married, he felt the press was not reporting the Crimea War properly so he went to the Crimea to see for himself, reporting back to a Liverpool newspaper. And, boy, could he write!

I should make one thing clear at this point. I do not believe genes influence how we turn out much beyond the colour of our eyes or a susceptibility to certain illnesses, whatever, basically stuff to do with our physical make-up. I believe almost passionately that psychological traits, bents, abilities, and everything that's important, are passed down through families, through the way parents bring up their children, and where the characteristics of a particular generation are particularly strong, they can last through many further generations. I have never met a descendant of Philip, and his equally wonderful wife Jane Steward, who did not have the same easy-going, happy-go-lucky attitude to life; an ability to work hard combined with a refusal to be bored; a lack of ambition combined with a quiet dismissal of the rewards of recognition or pre-eminence for their own sake; an immense and embracing ability to respect the good in anyone from anywhere balanced with a deep hatred of any sort of social or economic injustice. We don't tell others how to live and we don't expect others to tell us – which means we are bad at joining things or belonging to organisations. And so on. And this is NOT in our genes. It's because that's what our parents were like, right back to Philip and beyond. And that's why I'm rattling on about it. I believe I am the writer I am in considerable measure because of the way I, my father, and my grandfather experienced the first years of our lives.

My cousins to the nth degree include other writers, musicians, painters, potters, artisans, freelance photographers, quilt-makers, actors and so on. Not many of us work happily for someone else. We freelance if we possibly can. One cousin lives in one of the most inhospitable parts of Canada where he has a filling station. He serially marries Native Canadian ladies from the local tribe, of which he is a member, and has repopulated the area. His half brother is a freelance program writer who could be a multi-millionaire but who prefers to work only when his purse is empty. They're pretty typical by being as untypical as can be.

My father made a seriously bad career move by marrying a woman who has been excoriated and damned by everyone I have ever met who knew her, including her daughter, my half-sister. He left her. She would not divorce him, and in those days the only way you could get divorced was by being divorced by the guilty party. What was annoying was that my grandfather Oswald, who had made a substantial fortune in marine insurance (but sticking to Rathbone principles: for instance, he refused to insure a cargo of wood chips which were to be used to simulate raspberry pips in jam) tied up the capital to his grandchildren's generation but excluding illegitimate children or their offspring. I have heard it said that he had his own personal reasons for doing this. Whatever. Dad's wife latched on to it, so, no divorce, thus ensuring my illegitimacy and a substantial load of dosh for my half-sister and her son in the long run.

Never mind. My Mother and Dad lived as man and wife for thirty years, and not many people ever knew or guessed that they weren't married. I cottoned on when I was thirteen or so: my birth certificate has my mother down as Decima Lawrence née Frost. Didn't bother me, it's not the sort of thing that would. Well, not until I worked out the inheritance angle, and in the end I didn't do too badly out of that. Aunt Helen left me a bit, and there were other odds and bobs that came my way, and besides all that I can't really accept a system that allows more than a modest sum to be passed on.

Decima Doreen Lawrence née Frost. Lawrence because, yes, she was married when Dad came along, but on that side a divorce did go through. I don't know as much as I would like to about her family. Her father was manager of a chemical factory in Newport, Mon. They were Baptists, and I still have a bible that was given by their congregation to my grandmother, a useful bible with concordance and maps of the Holy Land and a load of other interesting stuff at the back. They had ten children, Mother being the tenth, and therefore Decima, generally shortened to Dess. She was a stunner. Rathbones have huge noses and baggy eyes. Mum in her adolescence and early womanhood was ravishing – what good looks I have I got from her. She was an infant teacher, trained at Homerton (founded for the offspring of dissenters) according to Montessori principles, but packed it in on marrying Mr Lawrence who was on the way to being a successful if fairly minor entrepreneur. She played the piano and sang very well, and she read a lot. Financially, going off with my Dad was a disaster.

Right. That's enough of all that. You'll find more, told in a more entertaining way, in Blame Hitler, *published by Gollancz and Phoenix and still, as I write, in print.*

In the early thirties the family virtually gave my Dad a small prep school in Liverpool. The war came, the school failed, Dad joined the RAF and, although he was too old to be a combatant, saw and was involved in horrors in the Desert which marked him for the rest of his life. After the war and a couple of really daft business ventures, we were broke and Aunt Helen let us live rent-free in the Bognor house she had kept for distressed mums. Dad became a mere prep school assistant, supplementing his income as paid secretary of a private social club and working illegally as a street bookmaker. Mum did that too, working from a garden shed on the local caravan site. All this was so I could be sent to the prep school on the Wirral Dad had gone to and then a minor public school in Dorset. The first was horrible but taught me a lot in the academic line, the second was jolly and untaught everything I knew. I knew more Latin when I was twelve than I ever have since. Dad was so upset when I failed Latin school certificate that I cheated in the retake.

I failed to get to his Oxford College, took a year off helping him look after Mum who was getting over a serious attack of TB and, after taking tuition by post from a friend who was already reading English at Cambridge, took the exams and got in to Magdalene. I skipped National Service because I too had had TB and anyway was stone deaf in one ear… still am.

Cambridge was OK. I read English which was a dolly: all you had to do was read a few books and comment on them fairly sensibly and that was enough for a 2:1. Lord knows what those who did worse were up to. I did a bit of acting, in fact I quite wanted to be an actor, but blotted my copybook by turning down a major role in an ADC production. They gave the part to Derek Jacobi instead. There you go. I was published in Punch, the first dosh I earned as a writer, thirty guineas. Dad had said he'd match the first money I made by writing and this nearly broke him. He was already subbing me fifty quid a term for books and living which was perfectly adequate in those days. Bamber Gascoigne, with whom I shared a lot of supervisions, said the only other guy he knew who had been paid for writing was a chap called Michael Frayn. I met Sylvia Plath three or four times, of which more later.

Aged twenty-three I had never been abroad so I tried for a posting and a career job with the British Council. I got it, but when they learned I had had TB, they took it away again. So I got an independent three-year contract teaching English in Ankara, Turkey. The most significant thing I gained from this was a sudden and really disturbing insight into third world poverty. I had not given politics much thought before then, but this revelation meant a sharp left turn.

Back in England in 1962 the only thing I could do was supply teaching. I went even further left after teaching in the new comprehensives in north London and a particularly hairy secondary modern in Camden where I eventually got a proper post, ending up head of both English and Art. What a time that was. That winter that went on and on, Profumo, Private Eye, Aldermaston, the last London Peculiar and then the two general elections. For me it became what 1968 was to a slightly younger generation.

My Dad was killed in a road accident while I was in Turkey (see *Blame Hitler*) and I felt I should be nearer Mum so I took a post as head of English in West Sussex, moving a couple of years later to Bognor Comp. I loved teaching, especially I loved directing school plays and even acting in joint teacher-kids productions, eventually doing Fagin in *Oliver!*. I did my damnedest to sound like Ron Moody, but hearing a tape of it played back could still hear that dratted Cambridge drawl or twang behind it. But the stress! Guys not much older than me were getting cancers, going mad, having heart attacks. I was rescued by Alayne (Laney) an ex-pupil who came back to a sixth-form reunion disco. Outside afterwards, in pouring rain, she suggested I pack it all in and run off with her. By then I'd had four thrillers set in Turkey published, and they weren't doing that badly, so... Well, like I mean I was thirty-eight, she was twenty. See *A Last Resort*... If you can find a copy!

The four Turkey thrillers were Diamonds Bid, Hand Out, With my Knives I know I'm Good, *and* Trip Trap. *I was writing the fifth,* Kill Cure, *at the time.*

I had a newish VW camping van, thanks to Aunt Helen's bequest. We took a little tour round Spain and Laney decided to drop out of university for a year. We'd go and live in Salamanca. First, in Blackheath again, we found a VW dealer called Churchill and Looker. Looker was an Aussie who knew all about it. He took one look at us and said: You are dropping out. You want me to take that newish VW and give you an unconverted van plus a thousand quid. I'll give you nine hundred. And he did, in used fivers, on the spot. The unconverted van was from Holland, and had a wooden floor. It was resprayed dark blue and you could see a decal or whatever of the Dutch royal coat of arms under the paint.

Salamanca was heaven. We made lots of friends. I directed a Midsummer Night's Dream for the English faculty: the yokels used the proper text, the fairies and Court a Spanish translation. There were weekly demos against Franco; the IRA, acting on behalf of the ETA, blew up the prime minister at Christmas and we got checked out by the real police and then by a shady, creepy character who, so a bar-tender told us, was a secret policeman. All very Ambler, very Greene. I got stuck on *Kill Cure* and had to bin two hundred pages, which meant pigs' trotters for supper from the market. From then on I have been over-meticulous about plotting everything before I get down to writing. We really were quite poor, especially once that nine hundred, which lasted about seven months, ran out (we had an unfurnished flat which meant having to buy some furniture and we'd bought a record player and a fridge before leaving), but we loved it.

Meanwhile I wrote *Bloody Marvellous,* the first of several books set in Spain, and ran into my first confrontation with the book trade. Anthea Joseph (of Michael Joseph) said you can't do this! You are our Turkey writer! But she took it. Back in England in September 1974 we got a basement flat in Southampton and Alayne returned to university. I had a look at Booker prize winners and wrote *King Fisher Lives* which contained incest, oral sex, and cannibalism. It was shortlisted. If Lady Wilson had not been on the committee it might have won. She made it clear to the other judges that a book as filthy as *KFL* should not, could not be a winner. Harold, who made a brief appearance at the dinner, gave me a very dirty look. An odd repercussion came from the fact that the book attacks weirdo gurus with poorly formulated libertarian philosophies which meant that a handful of right-wing litterati including Francis King and Auberon Waugh thought I was one of them, whereas the underlying message was really much more on the lines of Workers of the World Unite, we don't stand a chance if you won't.

We had a year (1975-1976) partly in France where Alayne was *assistante* in a lycée and partly in Spain. We were back in Salamanca just after Franco died (see *Lying in State,* really, you can, it's right here.

What a bargain!). Out of all this I wrote *Carnival!* (Good!) and *A Raving Monarchist* (not so good!) which was probably the worst in the uhvre. One reviewer began 'I doubt if Rathbone can write a bad book, but...' Again it was an exciting time: which way would Juan Carlos go? There were demos and marches, and five people got shot in Vitoria on a pro-Basque march when we were half a mile away wondering where the demo was.

> *The books set in Spain were* Bloody Marvellous, A Raving Monarchist, King Fisher Lives, Carnival, *and* Joseph, *which I worked on for four years while doing the others.*

Back in England for Laney to finish her degree at Southampton, we rented rooms at a riding stables in the New Forest. The snag was they did residential holidays for children in the summer so every June we had to find somewhere else to live until the landlord let us back in September. We stuck this out, because it was cheap and a beautiful place to be, for six years. Some summers we lived in a beat up camping van but for three of them we lived in my agents' Regent Square, Bloomsbury house while they took themselves off to their Normandy cottage.

I've tried to keep personalities and personal things out of this note, but I must say a word or two about Charlotte and Johnnie, C and J Wolfers.

Johnnie knew everything and everybody. He'd read all of Marx and Engels, Balzac and Dickens and a hell of a lot more too. He played the piano but because, I believe, of a weakness in one hand, was never the concert pianist he wanted to be and never played when he thought anyone else could hear. He was wicked and he was loveable. He was a hell of a good teacher. He rarely read the books he handled, but he knew a lot of what was in them by some sort of osmosis or just listening to the authors, though I did hear him once tell another author, an academic, that *King Fisher Lives* was about peasants. No, it's not, I said. Perhaps not, he replied, but So and So is very interested in peasants. He was a great person to get drunk with. He was endlessly witty, could be charming, had loads of girlfriends. Even now, nearly thirty years later, I meet persons of a certain age who come up to me at parties and say: You were one of Johnnie's clients weren't you? I was his girlfriend for a time.

His marriage to Charlotte was open. As open as a five-storey house in Bloomsbury could allow it to be. Generally he lived in the lower half, she in the upper floors. Charlotte was clever, and well-off and sort of beautiful in an individual way. She was CP and sold the Daily Worker, later the Morning Star, to the commuters on Paddington Station. What's a nice girl like you doing that for? they'd ask. She had as many boyfriends as he had girlfriends, and she didn't always pick them too well. Poets would ring her up in the night from New York and talk to her for hours. As time went on she drifted out of the agency becoming a scout for publishers in Europe and America. She and Johnnie agreed that they shouldn't buy and sell in the same market which meant in spite of everything they had a commercial honesty which I suppose most business people nowadays would find risible. Most of Johnnie's clients were academics, but his other fiction writer was Jim Ballard. Charlotte once won me for ever, or would have done had she not died a few months later, by saying Jim and I were her favourites amongst their authors, and on the whole she preferred, as an author that is, of the two of us, ME! Johnnie passed on to me a lot of her collection of Marxist texts and several years of back numbers of the New Left Review.

Enough! Johnnie retired a couple of years later and went to live in France. At his farewell party he said I could have the table on which I write, on which I am writing this, six feet by three, hard-top white formica, with the words: At any rate, no one can say I ever made any money out of you.

Partly, but always discreetly, never overtly out of the Wolfers' influence, my books were becoming more self-consciously leftist, Marxist. The turning point came not from Johnnie and Charlotte but from reading Lukacs' *The Historical Novel*, and Marcuse's *The One Dimensional Man*. Furthermore Laney, by now doing post-graduate research, and another close friend who had also been a pupil when I was teaching and was now at Oxford reading English under Terry Eagleton, were soaking up a lot of left-leaning, deconstruction theory and so forth and this all helped to shape the way writing was developing. The first result was *The Eurokillers* in which Argand, an honest conservative policeman in a Holland-like country, finds himself trying to bring polluting industrialists to book. At the end they seem to drop him into wet concrete. It did well, especially in Europe and even Japan. Along came André Schiffrin then of Pantheon Books in New York, a friend of Johnnie's, who said I'll buy *Eurokillers* but I want two more with the same policeman. But he's dead, I cry. No. You only imply he is about to be dropped in cement, you don't actually do it. So along came *Base Case* and *Watching the Detectives*. The last is the best, though they are all OK.

By now I had, what shall I call her? an adversary at my English publisher, Michael Joseph, who held the English paperback rights, and

I was no longer getting paperbacked in England. I was too sexy and too left wing for this person, apparently. I'm not making this up. I heard it from two different sources. This meant that it was some years before Peter Ayrton paperbacked the Argand books for Pluto.

It also meant that *Joseph,* which came out at last in 1979 and was also shortlisted for the Booker, remained unpaperbacked until 2000 when Abacus finally did it. It's been selling well ever since.

The Booker dinner was a laugh. Apart from me, Keneally, Naipaul, and Fay Weldon were shortlisted with fat major books. And Penelope Fitzgerald's *Offshore* which was, well, slight. When *Offshore* was announced as the winner a silence spread over the crowd like a pall, and then one voice, not mine, said quite audibly: Oh, Noooo! It was all part of what the Eye came to call the Penelope Effect. *Joseph* is a historical picaresque early nineteenth-century pastiche set in Spain between 1808 and 1813, the Peninsular War. The central character is a rogue, English and Italian by birth, but the hero who makes occasional and stirring appearances is Arthur Wellesley, later known as Wellington.

Meanwhile, however, the Blunt Affair had hit the news and André came to us with a simple proposal: write me a book about a Blunt-type character, but sympathetic and seen from his POV. The result was *A Spy of the Old School* which, with *Lying in State,* I reckon is as good as I get as a thriller writer.

1980 and Arthur arrived. Named for the Duke of Wellington for whom I have a possibly irrational but deep admiration on my side, for Arthur Scargill on Laney's. Meanwhile I wrote *A Last Resort* which was the first non-genre novel I had done (*King Fisher Lives* was described by Francis King as a philosophical thriller and *Joseph* was a historical) and the first with any real autobiographical content. Miriam in it is Laney, and, dare I admit it now, Brinshore is Bognor. I got the title from a graffito in the Southampton University Library loos: Bognor Regis, I read, whilst having a shit, is the Last Resort.

With Arthur kicking up a storm it was time to move to something a shade more permanent, though we didn't manage it for two more years. My mother in a bungalow near Bognor was developing Alzheimer's, though in those days it was still called senile dementia, that is if you were lucky enough to be able to get a doctor or social worker to pay enough attention to give it a name. She'd ring me up to get me to drive a roundtrip of a hundred and thirty miles to relight the pilot light on her gas fire, because she reckoned I was just down the road. We sold the bungalow and bought the house where we still live, because it was near enough, just, to Southampton where Laney was by now a part-time lecturer. It had a downstairs bathroom and lavatory and a room Mother could use as a bedsit. It didn't work out too well.

She hated the move and the Alzheimer's went iris. She'd try and get into the wardrobe at two o'clock in the morning, saying she was late for work, and this from a woman who had not been in a proper job for sixty years. She thought I was her husband, Arthur her son, and Laney my bit on the side. The only time we could contain the situation was when Laney's Mum came to stay and sat with her or went on short walks with her. Then, after just over two years, the social arranged for her to go in a home for a fortnight while we had a holiday. In the home she caught a chill and they let her die. I took her ashes back to Bognor and they were interred next to Dad's in Pagham churchyard.

Anyway. The Falklands, Las Malvinas, happened during the move, and the next summer the 1983 general election. We spent it with mates knocking up in the Southampton marginals and friend Danny got in a fight with some Lib Dems in an Indian. We came home just after dawn, both marginals lost, one to a Lib Dem, to have the full English breakfast, and while I was cooking it up some berk on Radio Four was asked and what are these new Tory MPs like? The answer was thrusting innovators and entrepreneurs, the sort Mrs Thatcher loves, and at that moment *Nasty, Very* was born, the last book of mine done by Michael Joseph. It's the life of Charlie Bosham from when he cheats at Monopoly on Coronation Day to June 1983 when he cheats his way into the House of Commons. As a book it was ahead of its time – a failing of mine. Critics in 1984 said it was too bleak, too black. Since 1990 there has been a raft of similar.

> *The start of the overtly leftish books and the last done by Michael Joseph, between 1976 and 1984 were the Argand books*: The Eurokillers, Base Case, Watching the Detectives; *the spy thriller* A Spy of the Old School; A Last Resort *and* Nasty, Very. *I also finished* The Princess, A Nun, *for Henry Ross Williamson who was dying of cancer, and put together an edited collection of Wellington's Peninsular War despatches, with my commentary, called* Wellington's War. *Johnnie, who hated Wellington and completely misunderstood my admiration, commented on this: Julian's arse is up for anybody, supposing I was going to make some money out of it. Well, I did. But not a lot.*

Margaret Hanbury was now my agent and she got Amanda Conquy, then a commissioning editor for Heinemann, to meet me, and the result was a two-book deal for more money than Michael Joseph were paying. The first book, which was already under way (it might actually have been commissioned by Michael Joseph and was bought out by Heinemann, I really can't remember) was *Lying in State*.

Lying in State was the last book I wrote for C and J Wolfers, in fact Johnnie retired before it was published. But it was he who gave me the idea, based on his own experience of trying to buy the Perón tapes from the actress the exiled dictator had left them with in Madrid. It's a great book and you are about to enjoy it enormously. Anyone who has read much of what I have written must guess that Graham Greene, especially from *The Quiet American* onwards, has been an enormous inspiration. I sent him a copy not seeking an endorsement but as a way of acknowledging that what was good in what I had written was good because, in part, of what I had got from him, and I wanted to thank him. He wrote back, the letter is dated 10 February, by coincidence my birthday, from Antibes saying, amongst the rest: I think your book a good one! Well, that's framed and hanging on the wall behind me...

The second book for Heinemann arose out of Conquy, following Hanbury's idea, of simply commissioning a book on the basis of a one-line sentence. Write a thriller set in a rainforest, she said. I think they wanted something ecological. What they got was *Zdt*, known in the US by the title I wanted which was *Greenfinger*. The idea behind the book was given to me by the director of the herbarium at Kew: scientists working in Mexico had found a wild form of perennial maize. The discovery, which would have thrown the whole agribusiness of maize production and processing into total confusion was suppressed. So much is fact. That, and a dream-like waking vision I had of a beautiful black girl with a newborn baby on her back fleeing through rainforest from a psychopathic killer, were the inspirations to a whizz-bang roller coaster. Plebeian writers and Americans say, stupidly, so stupidly, write what you know. *Zdt* is set in Costa Rican rainforest and the nearest I got to it was the tropical house at Kew. But, at the same time I felt almost guided while doing the research: I found all I needed – from a sociological study of poverty in San José to a botanist who had done several seasons of field work in the Costa Rican rainforest and much else in between.

The baby in the pouch was Nina, who arrived two months after my mother died. Laney struggled on at Southampton for a few months but gave up, not so much out of the pressures of double motherhood as disgust and ennui at academic life. We needed more money than I was earning, and a combination of events provided it. Hanbury knew a couple of journos who had, they said, researched cocaine dealing in Britain from all angles, but the papers wouldn't publish for fear of libel actions or reprisals. Write a novel, Hanbury told them. We can't, they said. I know someone who can, said Hanbury. We want half, they said. Hanbury told Heinemann who agreed with her that a larger than usual advance was in order. I said: I'm only getting half for this one, I want a three-book deal with the same advance for the two I do on my own. Done!

Well, to be honest, I didn't get an awful lot about cocaine which wasn't already in the public domain from the journos though they did answer a lot of questions for me on things like money-laundering and so on. Incidentally I was sworn to secrecy about their identity, so I'm not revealing it now. At the time I thought *Crystal Contract* was rather glitzy and meretricious, but I have just re-read it, and I now think it's pretty damn good, and should have done a lot better than it did, although it did reasonably well, getting to number ten for one week. *Crystal Contract* was followed by *The Pandora Option* which was centred on a US plot to poison Iranian wheat silos. It has a great main character, and it's a good read; however, the end was set in (don't ask) still divided Berlin and East Germany. The Wall came down in the week it was published thus turning a contemporary thriller into a historical novel.

The third for biggish bucks was *Dangerous Games,* which was to be set in 1992 during the Barcelona Olympics. In the event the climax was set in Barcelona but I missed out on the games. What happened was another stroke of luck just when we needed it. By then we were living in Orgiva in the Alpujarras, south of Granada, heaven on earth, just for a year, basically so Laney could get her Spanish back before setting herself up as a translator. A German producer, Alexander Wesemann, working for Westdeutscher Rundfunk in Cologne, had read *Grünfinger (Zdt)* and liked it so much he wanted to see what else I had to offer for a TV mini series. He came out to Orgiva, and agreed to take the plot of *Dangerous Games* and commissioned me to write the script. He came out three more times and taught me a hell of a lot about script-writing. There then followed the usual three years of messing about before it was filmed, but it was done in the end, both in English and German, and has been shown all over the world including on Sky but not on English terrestrial. Considering the rubbish there is around I can't see why not. I've written two more scripts for WDR which will probably never get done, too expensive for TV. But they paid, they paid.

But now I had to write the novel. I did it off the script, as a novelisation really, and it didn't do too well. Heinemann changed hands and I came back to England to find, along with nine out of ten of their authors and most of their staff, they had, um, let me go.

Books published by Heinemann between 1985 and 1991:
Lying in State, Zdt, Crystal Contract, The Pandora Option,
Dangerous Games.

Quite quickly Hanbury, who was now, but only for a short time, no
longer independent but managing the literary side of Casarotto, got a
two-book contract with Serpents Tail for two thrillers. The first of
these was *Sand Blind*, a pretty brilliant book, scary and funny, and now
again rather topical, about the Gulf War. Basically the plot is that Bush
One wants the war to happen, so they have to convince Saddam that he
can win. They do this by letting him have an air defence system which
he thinks can shoot down Stealth bombers. Then came *Accidents Will
Happen* and *Brandenburg Concerto* both set in Germany with a police
person called Renata Fechter who is in charge of an Eco-Squad.
They're a bit like the Argand books, but sexier.

Actually I did the deal for *Brandenburg Concerto* myself because by
now I had parted company with Hanbury. I won't say why because I'm
sure she'll have a different version of events. I've managed without an
agent ever since and have no regrets. I don't say this in order to
disparage agents in general or Hanbury in particular, but I will say that
the rights department at Little, Brown, which includes Abacus, has
done as good a job for me and the arrangement allows me always to
talk to and work directly with the firm who is publishing me. In practical terms this cuts out an irritating dog-leg and on a personal level it's
much better. And I have now been in the book business for nearly
thirty-five years, and not many agents can say that.

But first I had an urge to write a novel involving mother-son incest
in which the son's brothers finally castrate the son and murder the
mother. Wow! The main events happen in the run-up to the Spanish
Civil War but are set within a frame in which the castrated son is now
an elderly man who has had a great career singing castrato roles and is,
in the 1990s, teaching an aspiring female singer how to sing them in his
place. The book is called *Intimacy* and is the best book there is with
that title. It was published by Gollancz, was very well reviewed, and
sold poorly. Many people, including Sean Rafferty on Radio 3, have
commented that it would make a great film, and they're right. Sample
a chapter later in this book and see what you think.

I did two more books for Gollancz: *Blame Hitler* and *Trajectories*.
Blame Hitler is sort of autobiographical but at its centre is my Dad and
what the war did to him. *Trajectories* takes some of the same characters into 2035, though kills off the one who represents me in 2007, and
describes an England falling apart under an elderly Prime Minister

Booth and a whole new climate both political and meteorological. I like all three books but none sold too well, though the last two are still in print. I have to say, and I think most who know will agree with me, that after the death of the brilliant and wonderful Liz Knight, the spark went out of Gollancz.

> *Books published between 1993 and 1998 include* Sand Blind, Accidents Will Happen, *and* Brandenburg Concerto, *published by Serpents Tail, and* Intimacy, Blame Hitler *and* Trajectories *published by Gollancz.*

A long time ago Philippa Harrison, once my editor at Michael Joseph and much later the Publisher at Little, Brown commissioned a sequel to *Joseph*. The money was awful, and considering a couple of years research as well as a year writing the thing were called for, uneconomic for me. So I forgot about it and hoped she would too. But three years later she, or her accountants, remembered, and she asked for a book or her money back. Hey, I said, how about taking a book on Harold and 1066 instead? Think about it. You can fill libraries with books on England from 1815 to 1853, a shelf with Harold. Philippa, a wonderful publisher and person, said OK, and handed me over to the very nearly as wonderful Richard Beswick at Abacus (only less wonderful because he's a bloke), and a year or so later *The Last English King* reached the light of day. It sold, sold well. Film rights. A continuing most rewarding in every possible way relationship with ace film producer Geoff Reeve. *Kings of Albion* as a follow-up and now *A Very English Agent* which is actually the book Philippa had in mind. And another on the way. As Laney says: No one can accuse you of peaking too soon. And also my very own private eye, Chris Shovelin, who, under the flag of Allison and Busby, debuted in *Homage*, follows up in *As Bad As It Gets*.

That's it so far. I reckon I'll really peak round about 2008, watch this space. And in case you've missed it let me make what can be learned from this biographical note crystal clear: the two things a writer, no matter how good or bad s/he is, needs for success are… luck and vanity. Talent? Well, look around, not many as talented as me. Forget talent. I've been as lucky as I want or need to be, and, as one of the journos involved in *Crystal Contract* once said to me, Julian, you are *so* bloody vain!

May

On a hazy day
In May
The cuckoo called
Two beats of bliss
Life's kiss

With apples on its breath
Apple blossom fell
Death's knell

3. LYING IN STATE

I have already described how this came my way and how Graham Greene commended it. I don't think it needs any further introduction.

1

The sky was metallically yellowish, modulating to bronze where snow-cloud gathered over distant mountains, the air cold, very cold, and the city unnaturally quiet. The queue, eight files wide, nudged its way down one side of the Plaza de España and into the Calle de Bailén. Its sound was eerie – thousands of feet shuffling, thousands of whispering voices like a forest of aspens when the wind first stirs. The frenzied clatter of sparrows in a berry-filled tree was an impertinence.

The faces were frightening, macabre: beneath fedoras, Homburgs, glossy feathers shaped like the wings of crows, behind black mists of lace, were white masks, eyes tearful or rheumy with the cold, with black scarves pulled up to lips that were mauve or slashed with red. There were few who were young, few who were poor, almost none you could look at and say he's a labourer, she's a factory hand.

A man, elderly like the rest but with a trimmer figure, seemed almost to have been extruded by the revolving door on to the top step of the Hotel El Príncipe. He pulled on black gloves, settled his hat. About sixty-five with a white, neatly cropped moustache above a generous mouth, gold-rimmed bifocals, he could be, you might think, a doctor, a lawyer, a conservative academic. The Príncipe is a very good, if conservative hotel. But the leather on the black shoes was cracked, the hems of the trouser legs frayed, the nap on what had once been, say twenty years earlier, a very expensive Scottish topcoat, a Crombie, was now worn smooth, to a shine in places. And his eyes, a pale blue, almost grey, were not lugubrious or mournful, and lacked the self-congratulatory sureness of most of those in front of him. They all knew they were doing the correct thing, were in the right place at the right time, were assisting history to mark the passing of an epoch. The elderly man, however, lacked all pompous certainty and his eyes, true windows of the soul, betrayed a terrible anxiety – terror even.

The queue filled one side of the carriageway. The other was kept open for traffic, little of it now, mostly black cars with flags or badges denoting importance which whispered, as such cars do, to and from the Palace. Police and Guardia Civil stood at intervals – the police in grey and red with peaked hats pulled over their eyes, black accoutrements, the Guardias in green and shiny black. As always they looked more relaxed than anyone else. Some of them, and it seemed a sort of sacrilege, smoked. But then they were the favourites, the ones who had wrapped up the Civil War in a terrible nationwide purge and been awarded from the lips of the Caudillo himself the title *Bienméritos* – the Well-Deserving.

As always someone wanted to talk to them – colleagues in plain clothes, informers, *agents provocateurs,* the political pimps on the fringes of repression. In this case two men, thirtyish, dressed in immaculate jeans with short black leather jackets, longish black hair, stood with one black-cloaked, black-hatted moustachioed Guardia on the corner opposite the hotel. They looked the sort of touts, part gypsy, who hang around the bull-rings, even occasionally appear in borrowed finery as *peones* to the less fashionable *espadas,* and they smoked with the Guardia, chatted quietly, snickered.

But one had his eye on the hotel steps and as the elderly gentleman moved forward he nudged his companion. Briefly they stood on their cigarettes, touched hands with the Guardia, and moved away back up the queue until they were close.

The elderly gentleman's frightened eyes watched them; absurdly his bottom lip trembled and he had to hide the weakness with a gloved hand. Then with the determination of a suicide on a cliff-edge he stepped down out of the hotel entrance and with a murmur of apology slipped into the ranks of the mourners. None objected, though the faces of those immediately behind him expressed disapproval: if gentlemen from every hotel they passed did this instead of joining at the end, they'd never get to the Palace. The elderly man settled himself in the middle of the eightwide file and let his poorly shod feet whisper along the cobbles where once the tram-lines had been. Slowly they wheeled into Calle de Bailén and the two followers stood by a lamp-post. Insolently they watched him pass, and, when he had, casually they moved on to the next lamp-post to wait for him.

Barely half a kilometre away a gun began to thud again, and just out of time with it a church bell bled out a muffled clang.

Remorselessly the icy black lava flowed on, carrying the elderly gentleman with it between the gardens of the Plaza de Oriente and the side wall of the Palace. As it moved, in spite of the fear he felt and because of the dreary slowness of it all, he remembered the only other time he had done this – attended a lying-in-state. That time it had been for Evita. Eva Maria Duarte de Perón. The rite, he mused, is well named, the embalmed body being the final lie in a life of lies. A few tiny snowflakes no bigger than midges and as reluctant to settle danced a pavane above. The stream began the slow wheel into the Plaza de la Armeria and the huge façade of the Palace came into view. *Tu seras mieux logé que moi,* Napoleon had said to his brother. A tiny smile lifted the corners of the elderly gentleman's mouth as he remembered this, then the terror flooded back. The marshalled queue of mourners was passing into the Palace by the large door used by tourists on the ground floor beneath the long balcony. Discretely it drifted out again by the two doors to either side of it beneath the criss-crossing sweep of marble balustrades. Two doors, two hunters, who had only to wait for him outside. What he had thought might be an escape was a trap.

He scarcely took in the red and gold banners trimmed with black bows that hung from the windows, the giant laurel wreaths that hung between them, the lines of troops in black and scarlet with silver helmets that looked as if they had been borrowed from the fire brigade. But he felt clearly enough the change in the temperature as they passed into the building and ambled slowly beneath the black-trimmed chandeliers towards the magnificent staircase.

Four men stood at the foot of it – and his fear tightened even further, for they appeared to be scrutinising each file as it passed them. One was a general in uniform, the others were middle aged, in suits, with hard grim faces. As the elderly gentleman raised his foot for the first step two of them raised their right arms, casually it seemed, bent at the elbow, the palms flat, the fingers stretched. The man beside him returned the salute, as if acknowledging a wave from a friend. Only then did the elderly gentleman note the tiny enamel black, white and red swastika in his neighbour's buttonhole. The sight of it spiced his fear with nausea.

The underlying hysteria of the occasion began to cause cracks in the stucco façades of those around him. Old ladies with sticks paused and gasped on the steps, shallow though they were; the elderly gentleman noticed a flow of tears that ran gently as if from a partially opened faucet down the face of the yet more elderly gentleman on his other side. Black-edged handkerchieves appeared and carried with them the odours of cologne. Two files above him, just at the top of the staircase, perhaps just as the catafalque and casket came into view down the vista of state departments, or at any rate the candelabra at its corners, another old man paused, choked, sank to his knees, and toppled over; uniformed attendants came to his side, lifted him skilfully, carried him gently, off, out, and away.

It was a sign.

The terror faded a little. An excitement, perhaps even an elation replaced it. His gaze flickered about now, relishing for a moment Tiepolo's *Apotheosis of Aeneas,* and then at last they were there. A waxy face with rouged cheeks, eyelids not quite tight shut so you thought they might open, a well-clipped moustache not unlike his own, a nose beakier than he had expected jutting up from a cocoon of white satin, ribbons of red silk and gold, gold epaulets, a uniform black or deepest blue, and all concealing the awful ruin beneath. Inexorably the elderly gentleman was moved on and perhaps it was not so difficult after all to stumble and sink to the floor in a faint as convincing as any the attendants had yet seen.

Smelling salts and cologne were not enough – he saw to that. Oxygen he felt would do and when that was administered he opened his eyes to find himself in a small room lined with cased bookshelves, and old sepia photographs from the nineteenth century set on ugly tables, one signed *Victoria R,* leather chairs. Two nurses fussed over him, helped him to his feet. Carefully he let his knees relax. He lived, he said, in Recoletos, just off Velázquez, had come by Metro to Opera, but it was too far to walk, and the Metro was hell, so many people, so many people. They were concerned. If he would wait, they said, ten minutes, they would find a car, a vehicle of some sort... Too kind, too kind. *De nada, de nada,* so many brave old people have come, the nurses murmured, and the weather so cold.

It was a lie that he lived in Recoletos, just off Velázquez. Intelligent assessment of his shoes and cuffs would have made that clear. A large number of the people who had queued with him had come from that quiet expensive area of Madrid, but he had not. When the grey Land-Rover of the Municipal Police, threading its way through the disconsolate city, reached Puerta del Sol the elderly gentleman asked the driver to bear left to José Antonio. The policeman was puzzled. 'It's quicker by Alcalá.'

'Of course. But...' the elderly gentleman prevaricated, '...I have a sister. I should visit her. She is older than I, she will be distressed.'

He was dropped where he wanted, just by the Telefónica Building. The policeman obsequiously accepted his thanks, accepted his apparent status as one of the conservative well-to-do citizens he was paid to protect. The elderly gentleman watched the Land Rover turn, took in the fact that people were still drifting up Gran Vía towards what must be the end of the queue for a view of the cadaver in the Palace, then he was gone – up the alley by the side of the splendid, neo-baroque Telephone Building, Madrid's first sky-scraper.

This took him into a short, narrow street with high nineteenth-century tenements on both sides... Calle del Desengaño, the street of the Disenchanted Gentleman. It was almost deserted – no sign yet of the hunters. Briskly he crossed the road, entered a door which advertised a *pensión,* then climbed, with breath beginning to be a burden, heart pounding but forcing himself on for he knew he might be late, too late, up four flights of stairs. The steps of the first three flights were brass edged, the walls papered in raised acanthus design, purple flecked with gold. But the last flight, which climbed beyond the domain of the *pensión,* was plain, grubby but lighter. There was a skylight at the top.

He fingered his latchkey into the lock just to the right of the pale patch in the brown varnished door from which he had removed an image of the Sacred Heart, and pushed.

Darkness and no sound, except that of trickling water.

He cleared his throat.

'Ramón?'

No noise, except trickling water.

'Ramón? Are you there?'

He took a deep breath, fumbled for the light. It clicked, but nothing happened. He went on in, found a second switch, and again nothing. Back at the door he groped for the electricity meter and junction box. Its cutout button was out. He pressed it in. Something cracked and flashed to his left and the button jumped out again.

'The Devil!' he said, in English.

He moved to his right, pushed open a door. Grey, dim light. He opened a second door and a little more light from the windows of the Telefónica almost opposite filtered in. Now he could see a thickish old-fashioned grey flex snaking from a porcelain two-pin power socket and on into the room to his right, the bathroom. He pulled out the plug, returned to the cut-out switch, and pressed it. Two lights came on – one in the hall and one in the bathroom.

The bathroom was tiny – one small window venting the gas-heater into the *patio de luces* – the centre well of the building – a bath, a basin, a lavatory, a terrazzo floor that cunningly sloped to a small hole in the wall. If the floor got wet you could push the water out through it and it splashed down four storeys into the area below. It was needed now. The small bath was gently overflowing, a slow trickle, the cold tap had been left on.

In it was the appliance that ended the flex, a small, round, electric fire of the sort poorer Madrileños use under a table. The table is draped with a cloth that reaches to the floor, and you sit with your legs under it and your feet possibly touching the rim of the fire. In the old days the bowls were filled with charcoal instead of an electric element.

With it in the small bath was the body of a tallish man. His feet were submerged, his knees were bent above the level of the water, and his head lolled back over the rim. The body was thin, ascetic, an El Greco Piéta. This contrasted with the face which was solid and heavy, the lips thick and brick-red. Glossy black hair was slicked back from a broad forehead. It all had an eerily exact appearance of Juan Domingo Perón, the President of Argentina who had died sixteen months earlier. But this face, which was a latex mask, did not look dead, not as dead even as the rouged Caudillo in the Palace, not as dead as the body on which it sat.

The elderly gentleman gasped, retched violently from an almost empty stomach over the lavatory bowl. His spectacles dropped in. He retrieved them, wiped them, and his face, on a small towel, and then staggered into the tiny and very dirty kitchen where he found a bottle of Osborne brandy. It had that wretched device on top that can limit the rate of flow and he shook it twice before he had as much as he wanted in a tall, straight Duralex glass. He drank it off, shuddered, nearly vomited again, then, recalling his situation, moved quickly back into the hall to check the door was locked. With his chest heaving as if air were coal he dragged and pushed and dragged an enormous wardrobe that stood against the back wall of the tiny hall until it was across the doorway. Metal coat-hangers jangled inside.

He then went into the one of the two living rooms that was his and slumped into a low basketwork chair and waited until he had his breath back.

The room contained that one chair, a table improvised from composition board placed over a frame made from metal strips, book-shelves made in the same way, and a narrow bed with iron ends. There were also a small radio, two tape-recorders – one spool-to-spool, one cassette, and under the bed there were three battered suitcases. Two of these were filled with paperback books, and one with clothes – clean at one end, soiled at the other. The table was littered with books, tapes, and papers that almost buried a small typewriter. On the walls there was only one small decoration – a poster for a play – *Los Peroles* with caricatured portraits of Perón and Evita.

He hoisted the heavy grey tape-recorder on to the table, took off its lid, threaded up six-centimetre spools, and plugged in a large, stand-up microphone. He counted aloud, checked the bobbing needle for level, took a breath, and began.

'*Yo, Roberto Constanza y Fairrie...*'

There was a knock on the front door, then a pounding. He froze for a moment, switched off the tape, crossed to one of the bookshelves and from behind the third volume of the collected works of V. I. Lenin took a very small silver .22 pistol. He pulled back the breech to cock it and then took up a position in front of the barricade he had erected. But the pounding stopped. Then footsteps, two pairs, receded down the wooden stairs. Roberto looked down at the pistol in his hand and sighed as if a burden of guilt and shame had suddenly fallen on his weary shoulders. He crossed the tiny hall to the other living room – the same as his, furnished in much the same way, but with one feature different – where his had a table used as a desk this had a dressing-table with a triptych of mirrors and drawers beneath. On the top were sticks of stage make-up, false hair, spirit gum, powder and so on, rags and vanishing cream.

Roberto sat in front of it, looked at his reflection in the centre mirror, and the doubled reflections of his profile in the side mirrors, then sat back to avoid them. Tears suddenly flowed. He waited until they ceased, wiped his eyes on one of the rags, then wrapped the pistol in it before slipping it into the top left-hand drawer. Again the sigh.

He stood, looked out of the window. He could just see the street corner below. A man in a leather jacket, collar turned up, was lighting a cigarette. The elderly gentleman returned to his own room, switched on the tape-recorder and began again.

'I, Robert Constance Fairrie...'

Distantly the guns banged away for the last time that day as darkness slowly thickened outside and the tiny snowflakes that would not settle danced like fireflies in the light from the Telefónica, and beneath the street lamps.

2

'I, Robert Constance Fairrie, feel I need to make a statement. A statement about who I am and about how I came to be in the situation I am now in. My life is in danger. A very dear friend of mine has been murdered, yet in circumstances which could be interpreted to show that I was the murderer. Similarly a respected colleague was gunned down on my doorstep less than twenty-four hours ago and people malevolent towards me as well as towards him could uncover a credible if false motive that might indicate that I was the culprit. Most easy of all I suppose would be for them to contrive my death to look like suicide and then make sure that blame for the two previous murders was lain, laid, at my door. So. I have good reasons to make this statement. Which will be as full and accurate as I can make it'

He pressed the stop button, returned to the kitchen, shook more brandy into the glass, peeled open a small tin of sardines, and ate them with a piece of stale bread cracked from a stick loaf. Then he drank the brandy and returned to his room.

'My name is Roberto Constanza y Fairrie, Robert Constance Fairrie, and I was born in Buenos Aires in 1910. My father was an insurance underwriter and a well-to-do, even wealthy person. He sent me to a refined and progressive public school in England, St George's, Harpenden, and from there I went to Cambridge...'

Again the stop button. Roberto waited for a moment then pulled off his spectacles, wiped them, put them on again, and restarted the machine.

'But this is not biography. Merely my account of recent tragic events in which I have been involved. Not biography, but certain ... moments in my past have relevance.

'In the late forties and early fifties I was active in both the socialist and communist parties of my country and ran, not for profit of course, a bookshop where political pamphlets and books were sold. In April 1953 this shop was destroyed by fire. A fascist mob inspired by a deliberately inflammatory speech – the adjective is exactly apt – from the President, Juan Domingo Perón, was responsible. I narrowly escaped with my life and I still have burn scars. I should add that the same mob also burned the headquarters of both the socialist and radical parties as well, and made a complete job of it with the Jockey Club, the meeting place of the conservative oligarchy. Anyone who opposed Perón was in danger. Outside my shop they chanted "Jew, go home to Moscow", and, worse still, "Juden raus".

'I have a little Jewish blood. Very little by now. The Fairries were, I think, originally Portuguese Jews who settled in England in the sixteenth century. Though I have to say my grandmother insisted that the original was a good Catholic washed up on the shores of Scotland after the Armada. Her version has it that he married a daughter of the Duke of Montrose. By the nineteenth century they were sugar importers based in Liverpool. One of them came to Buenos Aires with the growth of sugar cultivation in the north of Argentina, and his daughter was my mother. My father, Giovanni Pablo Constanza was an insurance broker... this is not relevant, I will try to be relevant, from an Italian, Genovese family of bankers. His mother was Spanish Argentinian, as was the mother of my mother...

'I must keep to the point. After the burning of my shop I left Argentina and used my private means to run similar ventures in other countries. But I am an historian by training. During my exile I used my skills to research the Perón phenomenon and track the history of that man's rise and fall and extraordinary return to power. Occasionally I published articles in academic journals, though rarely, since I was not attached to any academic institution. Nor did I wish to be.

'It would not be a lie to say that I am now in impoverished circumstances and have been so for some time. My disposable capital has been exhausted to further the collapse of Capital. Ha! However, a careful grandfather entailed much of his fortune and I still receive quarterly cheques from a trust managed by what has now become the Bank of London and South America. These, the cheques I mean, are meagre. Perhaps my grandfather should not have invested quite so heavily in Anglo-Argentinian Tramways.

'Sixteen months ago Perón died. I felt I was in a position to prepare and produce a biography. I worked on a synopsis for some months and tried to sell it to various publishers, both Hispanic and English. Although I had taken pains to make the work one of objective history it was always refused... I sensed for political reasons.'

Just the pause button this time, held down while he collected his thoughts.

'I have, for a long time, admired the journalism, the "in-depth" journalism, of Steve Cockburn, formerly of the *Sunday Times*. I have read his books with enthusiasm, and often wished that I had been in a position to see his television series on South American dictatorships entitled "Where Next will the Lightning Strike?".

'Not only is he very well-informed concerning South America but clearly too he has connections in the media world of the United Kingdom. And so, about five months ago, I sent him my synopsis of a life of Perón. After five weeks or so he answered, not too encouragingly, but raising points of criticism that I felt I should answer. A sporadic correspondence ensued, which, a month ago, I believed had been terminated on both sides with mutual respect.

'I was therefore rather surprised when I...'

The stop button again. The elderly gentleman stood up and lurched out into the hall, hand groping for the bathroom door. He stopped, swung instead into the kitchen, unzipped and peed into the oily sink. He then made himself black espresso coffee, using a hand-grinder and a small pressurised pot. While the process went on he found a pack of Peter Stuyvesant on one of the shelves, shook one out, lit it from a screwed spill of paper pushed into the gas jet, inhaled deeply, coughed rackingly and threw it too into the sink. He poured his coffee into a green octagonal cup, added a small amount of Osborne, and carried it back to his room. There he wound the tape back a metre or so, listened to his own voice, nodded to himself, drank *café y coñac,* and reset the machine to 'record'.

'I was therefore rather surprised when I received a cable from Steve Cockburn. It ran as follows...'

Again the stop, and a search lasting four minutes over and under his table before he found the right piece of paper.

'It ran as follows...' The paper crackled as he spread it out. '"Urgentest we meet. Arriving Barajas *11.45. 11.11.75.* Cockburn."...'

3

On 11 November Roberto took the bus to the airport. It was a bright, dry day trying to be warm, the frost reluctant to leave the shade, snow twinkling in the violet Guadarramas. He enjoyed a trip out to the airport, took one occasionally if funds allowed, just for the hell of it, to sit in the lounge and sip cold beer from the self-service, or dry sherry with manzanilla olives. There he would watch the big jets storming in and storming out, the sad departures and passionate arrivals, would guess 'What's My Line?' for the silver heads with gilt locks on their briefcases and male secretaries in tow. Once he too had travelled in style, and while he had no hankering for it now, or regret that his money had gone (apart that is from feeling unused without a radical bookshop to run), he liked to remind himself of it all.

So that day in November, and very much aware of an extra *frisson* of excitement, very conscious that in an hour or so he would be taking a step into the unknown, into a situation which was unclear to say the least, he arrived half an hour early – which, allowing for passenger clearance, was a good hour early, and ordered himself a *coñac*. Brandy for heroes. The plane was late – fog at Heathrow – and by the time Cockburn came through the gates into the arrival area at one o'clock, Roberto was a little tipsy.

Cockburn was drunk. He came through the doors like a bull out of the *toril* and paused four yards out, blinking and tossing his head. He was tall and thin, not really bull-like at all, with very coarse hair nearly grey, a face a bit jowly and running to seed and at this moment very dissipated, with a sheen of alcoholic perspiration across a brow whose hue would not have disgraced a lily or a morgue. He was dressed in a white shirt, open at the top with a gold Christopher peeping through white and black hair, an expensive soft leather jacket in Cordoban red, tailored stretch jeans and shin-high cowboy boots that matched the jacket. A porter behind him pushed a trolley on which were two battered hide suitcases. With the arrogance of a media person he had not bothered to send Roberto any means of identification, but Roberto clutched a copy of *Up the Plate without a Paddle* which had a large Jerry Bauer portrait of Cockburn on the back, and it was accurate enough.

'Mr Cockburn?'

'Yes?' Puzzled.

Together: 'I am Roberto Fairrie...' 'You must be Roberto Constanza...'

'Yes indeed. But actually I usually drop the Constanza.'

Muy bien. Bueno. ¿Que tal, Señor Fairrie?

'Very well. But it is not necessary to talk in Spanish. My English is adequate.'

'Better than mine, old chap.'

'Did you have a good journey, Mr Cockburn?'

'Horrible. A nightmare. Call me Steve. Which way do we go?'

'You would like a taxi?'

'You don't have a car?'

'Actually no. I find the traffic in Madrid too daunting at my age.'

'Well then a taxi.'

They trundled out into the acid sunshine and blinked like bats. The taxi-driver wanted to know where he was to take them.

'You have an hotel?'

'Not booked.'

Silence. The taxi-driver waited. 'I usually stay at the Príncipe.'

'I am sure they will not be full at this time of year.'

They began the bleak descent into the piny suburbs of north Madrid and the jets thundered across the blue sky above them.

'I am sorry you had a bad journey.'

'Well. Had a bit of a party last night, and, I tell no lie, I wasn't too sure what plane I was on or where it was going. This has happened to me. I have one of these credit cards just for air travel and once, you know, I damn well woke up in Tokyo.

'Anyway, there I was, the stewardess prodding me and giving me coffee and these mountains below, a bit of snow on them, and we were coming down. Ankara? Santiago? No, the trip hadn't lasted long enough, there had been no stops on the way. Then just as I was about to make a fool of myself and ask, there was one of those great black Osborne bulls in a field, and, do you know, it all came back to me in a flash, just like that.'

Roberto was curious.

'That's most interesting,' he said. 'You really got on that plane without knowing what you were doing? What about your luggage?'

Cockburn leant forward, elbow on knee, rubbed his forehead between forefinger and thumb.

'Well, yes. I suppose so. Must have packed or Sarah packed for me. Sarah's the living-in girlfriend of the moment. Then gone to the party. Dash it, I don't normally go on business trips in gear like this. I do hope the dear girl had the sense to put in a decent suit and a tie. Probably not. I do rather feel she wanted to come and I wouldn't let her. Hopefully, there's nooky waiting for me in Madrid. Then she must have bunged me in a taxi with a label round my neck and told the cabbie to pass me on to Iberia reception at Heathrow. Jolly decent of everyone to get it right.'

The black and yellow Seat cab continued past the ugly new ministry buildings and Generalísimo became the Paseo de la Castellana.

'Business?' said Roberto.

'Eh?'

'You are here on business.'

'Yes. You could say that. Christ. I haven't told you, have I? I mean I haven't told you why I'm here, why I asked you to meet me.'

'No.'

'Christ. Jolly decent of you to turn up then. Just on spec.'

'I rather hoped... that my history of Peronismo, my biography synopsis...

'Well yes. I mean actually in a way it is to do with that. But not quite. I mean I would not want to raise your hopes at all, but at the same time I do rather think you can do me a favour in that line, and well, I might be able to offer you a quid pro quo. Perhaps even more than a quid...' He stopped, glanced sideways at Roberto. Had the old geezer understood the joke? Christ, yes. And by golly we are not amused.

The taxi halted, then inched forward in a long double queue of jammed traffic. The cabbie swore – the rebuilding of the square at Colón was the reason, a crazy enterprise full of underground shops, theatres no one would ever use.

'Look. It's quite a complicated matter. It really is. And quite honestly I don't feel up to explaining it to you yet... Goodness. Did you see the graffiti on that hoarding? *Viva El Rey*. Long live the King. Is it that close?'

'Very close. Tomorrow, the day after. No one expects it to be much longer.'

'What then?'

Roberto shrugged but said nothing. He thought: *Operación Lucero* was spoken of. The night Franco died it was said all dissidents, lefties, Basques, communists, whatever, would be rounded up. Put in the bull-rings. The football stadia. Pinochet had shown the way in Chile. He spoke at last.

'*¿Quién sabe?*'

Cockburn nodded: 'Who knows?'

The taxi broke out of Colón at last and the traffic streamed on to Cibeles with its extraordinary statue of a pagan goddess and wedding cake joke of a central post office. Shortly they were in Gran Vía, or, as the street signs called it but almost no one else, Avenida de José Antonio.

'Anyway. As I was saying. It really was jolly decent of you to meet me. I'm really not up to explaining it all to you now. But I do think you should know there really will be something in it for you – I mean, I'm pretty sure you can be of real service to me, and of course I'll pay the going rate.'

Traffic lights again.

'Listen. Are you free this evening?'

'Yes.'

'Well. Let's see. Why not meet me for dinner? By then I should be feeling a bit more up to it.'

'All right. If you say so.'

'I can see you're a bit peeved. Quite understand. But just as of now I'm not up to it.'

'All right. Dinner.'

'Yes. Um Do you know a restaurant called El Cid? Not far from the Opera?'

'I know it.'

'Nine o'clock there. Then.'

They were outside the Callao Metro station – not far from Desengaño.

'I'll get out here.'

'*Hasta la vista.*'

'Yes.'

4

THE TAPE RAN ON:
'I must confess my first meeting with Steve Cockburn had been something of a disappointment. It was not just, or indeed mainly because my hopes had been raised of a contract to continue my work on Perón, but that he seemed to be more in the mould of the conventional British journalist – a drunk in short – than I had expected. His reputation as an acute observer of our times, particularly well-informed about Latin-American affairs, had blinded me to the possibility that his actual character, his personality, might lack weight. Though reflecting on it during that afternoon, and indeed dipping again into the three books of his I have on my shelves, one could not help noticing now a certain superficiality in his approach to, say, Argentinian politics. For instance, in *Up the Plate without a Paddle* he ascribes too much importance to

Perón's dalliance with nubile girls following the death of Evita. Perón's fall was due far more to historical objective circumstances and his own bizarre failure to read the way history works.

'With these reflections and others like them I amused myself for the rest of that day, and of course speculated too on what had brought Cockburn to Madrid and on what way he believed I could help him. And, I must confess, just what sort of fee he would be paying. More than a quid. A silly joke.

'I must say, too, I looked forward with keen anticipation to a meal at El Cid. It is not in the very top rank of Madrileño restaurants, but perhaps deserves a higher reputation than it has. One should not be put off by all the Hollywood-style decorations, accoutrements and so on that fill the walls: shields, lances, and even suits of armour, that sort of thing. The food is good and contrives, without too much neglect of decent kitchen practice, to retain an authentically Spanish style. In short, it is not international cuisine.

'Cockburn, I was glad to see, had found a reasonable suit in his baggage...'

'Fish soup for you then, followed by the broiled lamb. You're sure? First day back in Madrid I tend to go for the fishy specialities. You know, one of those towers piled and hung with Dublin Bay prawns, crabs, crayfish. But they never do them for one person only.'

But Roberto was determined. Quite often he bought fish in the market behind the Plaza Mayor, but hardly ever meat, and never the larger cuts – with only two gas rings he lacked the means to cook them properly even if he could have afforded them.

'I think you will find the lamb equally typical, indeed more typical of Castile. And as you see, for two people we can share a leg.'

A whole leg of lamb – tougher, smaller, and leaner than you buy in England – but marinated for at least two days to tenderise it, then spit roast...

'Well, I'll leave it to you then.' This said a touch petulantly. 'And the wine?'

Roberto looked over the wine list.

'Castillo Sant'Simon from Jumilla is not as well known as the Riojas, but I think you'll find it acceptable.'

'It's dearer than the Riojas.'

Roberto shrugged. 'Let's have a fino to begin with. Manzanilla de San Lúcar for me, if they've got it.'

Cockburn crumbled snow-white powdery bread and leant back, eyeing Roberto over the candles. After a long afternoon sobering up, bathing, shaving, he looked now more of a personality. His face had lost its pallor, had the sheen one associates with a combination of evil living and healthy exercise – no doubt he swam and played squash in a club like the RAC. Roberto himself had been able to do just that during the three years he ran a bookshop in Rathbone Place. The suit was dark charcoal, flared jacket, two vents, the waistcoat a Liberty damask – much the fashion of the late sixties but it had style still and did a lot for a man of Cockburn's age. Roberto estimated him to be just about fifty. The Englishman's eyes glittered in the light which added something a touch Mephistophelean to his expression.

'I imagine you'd like to know something of what this is all about.'

Roberto assented.

'Well. It's a longish story, but it starts with Juan Domingo Perón in exile in Madrid from 1960 to 1973. He was made welcome here and the first years were much eased by the presence and renewed friendship of the actress Nini Montiam. You have heard of her?'

'Of course. I actually saw her perform in Buenos Aires in the early fifties. She was a good friend of Perón's and Evita's. Here in Madrid she has run, used to run a rather good little theatre where one could sometimes see pieces not usually permitted by the regime. She enjoyed the protection of a general I believe.'

Cockburn frowned slightly. 'All right, you know who Montiam is.'

He drank some soup, picked a tiny shellfish off his spoon, sucked out the meat and dropped the shell on the side plate.

'Well, while Perón was here, he was bored for much of the time, especially early on, and he amused himself by recording his reminiscences on tapes. In the end there were over one hundred and forty hours of them. Apparently he just sat there and rapped...'

'Rapped?'

'Improvised – made it up as he went along. And they contained amazing stuff, were entertaining, revealing. Never intended for publication, he was just having a ball. And when he left in '73 he just gave them to Montiam, a thank-you present not to be used until he was dead. And of course back in Buenos Aires he barely lasted a year.'

'Just over.'

'Eh?'

'Just over. About fifty-five weeks.'

'Ah. Anyway he died. Not long after that, six months or so, Montiam put them on the market, just about a year from where we are now, in fact told Becky Herzer that she had them and that they were up for sale...'

'Becky Herzer?'

'Well, I don't suppose you'd know of her. She's Czech by birth, family got out in '48, she's now French. Most of her life she's spent in France, first as a journalist, then doing TV work, now operates as a freelance independent producer, wrapping up deals with publishers and newspapers too. Very international. She knew Montiam, Montiam told her about the tapes, and Becky got in touch with me. Old pals, often worked together, and she felt she needed someone on board with a bit more spic clout than she had. Latin-American.'

'I know what "spic" means.'

'Quite. I say this wine is jolly good. Almost porty. Let's hope the lamb lives up to it.'

'I'm sure it will.'

'Where was I? Yes. Becky then called me in. I came over, we went to Montiam's and heard some extracts from the tapes and I realised we were on to something really big. Yes, very big.'

Cockburn smiled, almost coyly: like a spoilt boy, Roberto thought, a spoilt boy admitting to over-indulgence in candy but knowing no one will really mind.

'Why *big?*'

'Why not?'

'Because most politicians' memoirs are a bore. Anything Perón ever wrote was plagiarised or ghosted. He was not renowned for his ability to tell the truth.'

'Oh quite, quite so.'

Cockburn seemed disposed to sulk at this rebuff, drank soup noisily, until the leg of lamb, a rich dark brown and spitted on what looked like a medieval poniard, arrived. Brandy was heated, slopped on, lit. The head waiter held the flaring limb aloft.

'I rather like my lamb well done,' Cockburn said nervously.

'Then you should have the knuckle end,' said Roberto with something like glee. The other end was meatier.

By the time it was all done, and all the trappings served too, and Cockburn had pronounced himself very well pleased, he was ready to take up his story again.

'You see, there was no question of ghosting this time. It was Perón's voice all right, and much of what he said was sensational.'

'Really?'

'Really. On Evita's morals. US intervention in Latin-American domestic affairs. The imbecility of every politician who ever opposed him...'

'That at any rate was to be expected.'

'Of course. Also a do-it-yourself kit on how to turn a radical union into a bunch of *lazzaroni*. And there was other stuff too.' Cockburn slipped a morsel of lamb between over-white teeth that Perón himself would have been proud of, leant forward and tapped the side of his nose. 'Nazi *émigrés* in Argentina.'

Roberto's face remained expressionless. 'Did you hear any of that?'

'Not actually. But Nini said it was there.'

They ate on, Roberto drank some of the Castillo Sant'Simon, and said: 'So?'

'Well. All this you understand is preamble as to why you and I are here as of now.' Again, already, Roberto thought, he is tipsy. 'So I will move as quickly as I can through the ensuing sequence. Which won't be difficult since it definitely left me with egg on my face and that is not something I like to dwell on. Montiam wanted two hundred grand, dollars, down, no frills. For that we could have the tapes and do what we liked with them. I realised she'd got it about right. With translations, serial rights, maybe a TV spin-off, the whole shoot, I could see the project netting about two million. Becky and I reckoned we should take about fifty grand each.

'We started off, Becky and I, doing it the conventional way. We took it to a mainline Latin-American/Spanish publisher, of high repute but with a bit of devil in him. He has a fat rich business, comics and girlie magazines at the base, Althusserian Marxism at the tiny tip. He was enthralled, but nervous...'

Cockburn too was enthralled by the magic of his tale. He leant back, leant forward, flourished a fork, then a knife, swigged from his glass and ordered another bottle.

'Enthralled but nervous. He decided to set up an entirely new company to handle the merchandise, keeping himself in the background. Nervous but ready to put up a very handy lump sum... A handy lump sum,' he repeated with relish. 'We really thought we were laughing. And then...'

'And then?'

'Just two days later he pulled out. No reason. He just rang up and said no deal. This happened two more times. I won't give you the details but one drama-doc producer we're both very friendly with, said he'd actually been leant on by some very nasty characters indeed.

'That happened in Geneva where our search for finance had taken us, and that brings me to Peter Clemann. Clemann is a US exile: won't make the necessary statements about his political associations to get back his US passport. He is also a multi-millionaire. About seventy million the last time he had it counted. And he lives in Geneva, and he is a very old and dear friend of mine. How that came about I'll tell you another day. Not too relevant just now. Well, since we were in Geneva, where we had drawn a blank, I went to see him, told him what we were up to and he said he'd back us. So we all met up here in Madrid, which Peter hates, for him Spain is the arse-hole of Europe, Madrid the... We all sat down in the Príncipe, and it really did seem that this time we were OK. No one leans on Clemann. He's fireproof. Again we were laughing.' He leant back, drank deeply, refilled his glass. His dark eyes glittered. Then he swung back to what was left of his lamb.

'Even so,' – waving a fork so Roberto feared a blob of gravy in his eye – 'there were unbelievable difficulties. Becky turned out to be against Jews and millionaires and hated Clemann on sight. But the main thing was Nini seemed terrified we were planning some fiddle – like walk off with the tapes leaving her with a rubber cheque, that sort of thing. It got to be very complicated indeed. But in the end we had it right, notorised cheques for Nini, arrangements to everyone's satisfaction for transfer, deeds drawn up ready to be signed. Of course we knew there were people in the background who were trying to ditch us. I'd even thought heavies in macs were tailing us, but never managed to prove it. Peter heard from Geneva that shady characters had been trying to pry into his affairs. But he was determined. He had machines flown in from Geneva that would duplicate the tapes, transfer them to miniature cassettes as soon as we had the title. Then each of us was to take a copy and fly out by different routes. We had thought of everything. And then literally at the last moment everything went wrong.'

'I know.'

'Know what?'

'Everything went wrong. It's public knowledge.'

'I'm sorry. I'm really not with you.'

Roberto sighed, pushed his crumpled napkin on to the table. Cockburn allowed himself to be aware of the waiter at his elbow.

'Afters?'

'I think I do dare to eat a peach.'

'Very droll. I'll have a rum baba with a dollop of chantilly. Now tell me just what is public knowledge.'

Roberto took off his spectacles, gave them a polish on the napkin, slipped them back on.

'I have,' he said, 'a friend who reads *ABC*. I'm afraid I don't. I'm sure you know it is a right-wing monarchist review. But my friend knows of my interest in Perón and he drew my attention to an announcement that was made in *ABC* some time ago. The magazine – or I suppose we must say its bank or whatever – had bought from an unnamed party tapes of reminiscences left here by Perón. No reason not to suppose that they were referring to the ones you were negotiating for. Planeta, who have connections with *ABC*. will publish sometime next year. There is to be a small team of editors supervised by

Señor Luca de Tena who is the editor of *ABC*. I imagine that at the last moment they made Señora Montiam an offer she could not refuse.'

'Well, I'm damned. Of course we knew it was *ABC* who was fronting for whoever bought the tapes but we never expected them ever to publish. Quiet suppression is what we expected.'

'Oh yes. They'll publish. Under the title *Yo, Juan Domingo Perón.*'

'But edited.'

'Of course.'

'So all the dirt cut out.'

'You don't have to assume that. Listen, Mr Cockburn, Perón was bombastic, conceited, a congenital liar... it would be easy for any slandered person to shrug off what he said. Only very hard, verifiable, yet previously unknown fact would do anyone any real damage.'

5

Cockburn suddenly contrived to appear very serious indeed. 'Hard, verifiable, previously unknown fact.'

'Yes.'

'Like the whereabouts of Martin Bormann?'

Roberto nodded slowly, began slowly to peel his peach. 'Yes,' he said. 'That would have impact.'

'The exact details of how the US State Department engineered the ouster of October '46 and then bungled the aftermath so Perón was elected?'

'Rather old hat now... but people do like reading about proved instances of American intervention. Especially when they are incompetently executed.'

'How about this: the sexual relationship between Evita and her brother Juan. How brother Juan gave her the syphilis she really died of, and thus why Perón countenanced or ordered his murder.'

'Oh come on. Come on.' Roberto's incredulity seemed for a moment forced, but the laugh that followed was clearly unfeigned. 'And that's hard, verifiable fact?'

'Perhaps not. But if you heard Perón himself say it, you'd be ready to believe it. And there are millions both of the right and the left who would love to hear him say it, and pay to hear him say it.'

Roberto drank the last of his wine. 'And you have heard him say it. This is what you heard on Montiam's tapes and what you believe *ABC* and Planeta will suppress.

'Oh no.' Cockburn's face swam further into the candlelight. 'Oh dear me no. You see, old boy, it's not that first lot of tapes that brings

me to Madrid. Not at all. What brings me now to Madrid is the existence of a second lot of tapes.'

Roberto sank back. His head was swimming. Though he was used
to drink he had had a fair bit, and a long heavy meal. It had not been
easy, either, listening to Cockburn's drawn-out tale, waiting for the
punchline.

'A... ah-h.' It was more a sigh than an exclamation. 'A second lot of
tapes. And where have they sprung from?'

'That I'm not quite sure of. But of course I know who has them now.
Roberto waited.

'At this point I must introduce one of the main characters in the
whole episode.'

Roberto looked round nervously, but it was a figure of speech
merely.

'Pepa. Josefina González. Pepita. She, believe me, is something else
again.' The relish that infected Cockburn's voice when he spoke of
large sums of money, was there again – a mixture of schoolboy wonder
and greed. 'She calls herself an actress. She is, was a friend, perhaps
rather a close friend, of Nini Montiam, but I gather they see less of each
other now. Argentinian. And close for a time to the Perón household in
Madrid. About thirty years old. Perhaps a touch more. Anyway she
was around a great deal during all the negotiations and I got to know
her very well. Very well indeed. Expensive of course. She expected
presents. But. Well. My goodness.'

Roberto found it quite difficult to avoid showing his distaste for
this, but he managed.

'Anyway, a month ago she rang me up in London. A second lot of
tapes has turned up. Far hotter, far more sensational than the first lot,
and it's darling Pepita who has them. She has them in a vault of the
Banco de la Victoria de los Angeles, in Velázquez, and she wants me to
hear them. Tomorrow at one o'clock. And I want you to come along
and hear them with me.'

'Why?'

'You are an expert on Perón. I've made enquiries. You are the best
Perón expert in Madrid. Coffee, I think. And what do you say to a
brandy?'

Roberto waited while the table was cleared, brandy and coffee
served. Then slowly he shook his head.

'They must be forgeries, Mr Cockburn. I am sure they must be.
Someone has set you up. You are about to be the victim of a hoax.
What do you call it? A con. From the French?'

'No. From confidence trick. I don't see how you can say all that. I
don't see why you should. Sight unseen. You haven't heard the

evidence. You're prejudging the case.' Cockburn was no longer Mephistophelean or coy. More a spoilt boy told after all to lay off the candy.

'But it stinks of it.' Roberto was emphatic. 'You've burnt your fingers once. Spent time and money on a wild goose hunt. You want to recoup your losses, regain your lost face. You're ripe to be the mark. And this González woman knows it.'

Cockburn's face flushed. Roberto sensed he was not only a spoilt boy, but a spoilt boy with a temper.

'So you won't do it?'

'Do what?'

'Come tomorrow to hear these tapes. Authenticate them.'

'Oh, I'll come. It will be an interesting experience. Oh yes, I'll come. But Mr Cockburn?'

'Steve.'

'As you wish. Steve. I must ask you this. Do you want me to give my real opinion of these tapes, once I've heard them? Or merely authenticate them? I mean, quite clearly, what you want is to have them authenticated.'

'I'm sorry. I don't quite see the... Yes, I do. See the difference, I mean. I don't suppose you intend to be impertinent. But I am quite serious about this. I want your honest professional opinion. That is all. And I shall pay a fee. A professional consultancy fee. Would a hundred dollars be about right?'

'No fee, Mr Cockburn, Steve. No fee. Well. I'll take ten dollars as a symbol, as a sign that we are keeping the matter on a business footing. All right?'

'Fine. And do please try to come tomorrow with an open mind.'

'Of course. You can count on that. I shall be entirely unprejudiced. I shall assess these tapes on grounds of sound, voice, speech mannerisms, and so forth, and of course, too, on grounds of content. And you shall have my absolutely professional, unprejudiced, and candid opinion.' Roberto's smile was open, jolly. 'What a very pleasant meal it has been.' His glasses twinkled in the candlelight. 'And so interesting too.' He raised his globe of brandy, savoured the fumes that came off it. Not often did he drink really good Spanish brandy, made in Jérez with as much care as the best of sherries.

6

S TOP.

'Is that right? Have I got it right? Done justice to myself and to the facts as far as possible? I think so. That damned gun. That *damned* gun. If I had not taken that gun would Ramón have been able to defend himself? *¿Quién sabe? No sé.* I don't know. Doesn't bear thinking about. Mustn't think about it. Must get on. Time? Ten o'clock. Near enough. What next? That first visit to the vault of the Banco de la Victoria de los Angeles, just off Velázquez in Recoletos. That was an amusing occasion in many ways. And one which... I can simply tell exactly as it happened. As indeed is the case so far.'

PLAY AND RECORD:

'So. Next day, after a late breakfast – after such a large meal I had not slept well – I set off to meet Steve Cockburn at the place and at the time appointed.'

STOP.

'I'm cold. Very cold. But not as cold as the Caudillo. Ha! Where's the electric fire... Oh Jesus.'

PLAY AND RECORD:

'I took the Metro from José Antonio, changed at Alonso Martínez...'

The Recoletos branch of the Victory of the Angels Bank was comfortable. Very comfortable. It resembled the lounge or cocktail bar of a very expensive, very modern, very chic hotel. Dotted like islands in a dark green sea of deep pile carpet, heavy black glass tables stood on satin steel legs with deep leather chairs that soughed when you sat in them. A curved counter with a rounded satin steel edge was also upholstered with black leather, of just the right resistance to make writing cheques or deposit slips a pleasure, not a chore; it swept round two sides and took the place of the bar one expected. Only the *caja*, the *caisse*, gave the show away – a toughened glass cage enclosed the cashier – a man with satin steel hair in a midnight-blue suit, who looked more like a prosperous brain surgeon than a teller.

There were not many customers. Three or four ladies dressed in black but with discreet touches of colour here and there, and hair blown into pastel confections, sat at one of the tables. The bank had even provided them with coffee. They gossiped intimately, faces very close, claw-like hands jangling with chains and jewels, gesturing neatly, sharply, in time to their hard, clipped Madrileño consonants and flattened vowels.

Roberto sat in a corner near the door and waited. He was very conscious of the tiny shabbinesses in his clothes, cursed Cockburn for being late, wondered how long it would be before one of the flunkies asked him his business, asked him to leave. Hardly though, he thought to himself, will they take me for a Basque bank robber.

Then through the tinted glass of the door he saw Cockburn's backside as he stooped to pay off a taxi. The tall Englishman strode in as if he were a shareholder, glanced round, found Roberto in his corner. He wore the same suit as the night before but with matching waistcoat this time, beneath a short, dark, velvet-collared topcoat that he had left unbuttoned. Very English.

'Pepa González not here yet?'

Roberto bit back the negative that flew to his lips, glanced around and shrugged.

Cockburn took in the company and half-smiled. 'No. None of those is Pepita.' He took a red and gold cigarette pack from his pocket, lit the Dunhill with a gold lighter. 'You don't, do you?'

Roberto touched his chest in polite refusal.

'Well. I wonder what we'll hear. What she'll choose to play us. Listen. I hope you don't mind my saying this. But play it a bit close, won't you. I mean, don't let on in front of Pepa what your opinion is.'

Roberto gave the tiniest of shrugs.

Then there she was. Dark red hair shot with gold, eyeshadow and rouge reddish brown, green eyes, a long straight black sable, black court shoes. A single strand of large pearls glowed round her very white neck and a diamond winked on one finger. She was beautiful with that exact beauty that beautiful women discover in their thirties – not the ripe allure of adolescence, nor the thin grandeur some older women achieve – but that perfection that says that nothing of importance has been lost since the first glamour descended, and much has been learnt.

'Pepita querida,' breathed Cockburn, kissed first her fingers, then her cheek. Roberto hung back and took in, as Cockburn had not, the presence of a man and a woman behind her. The man was fortyish, perhaps more, not tall, no taller than Señora González in her high heels, but solidly built. He was well-groomed, had sandy hair, a little whitened, brushed thinly over a large round head, strong hands, small feet. He wore a coat that was camel-coloured but made from something more expensive. His small eyes were alert and wary, feral. Roberto did not much like the look of him, but was aware that ancient prejudices were at work. Especially he did not like the way his bearing towards Señora González subtly expressed ownership. Although not obvious it reeked of machismo, the arrogance of the Latin American with the woman he uses as his mistress.

The woman behind him was more interesting. Dressed in a plain brown tailored suit she was tall with very short white-blonde hair. At first glance she could have been as young as Pepita, but then one realised she was much older, perhaps fifteen years older. Her face was lined, wrinkled even, and her fingers long and thin – most extraordinary was the colour of her skin which was very brown, but sun brown not racially brown.

'Steve, I must introduce you to my friend. Enrico Gunter. Enrico is also a businessman and will advise me on the business side of it all. And Becky Herzer you already know of course.'

Cockburn was clearly shocked by the presence of the tall middle-aged lady, and barely acknowledged Gunter.

'Becky. Damn it. What the hell are you doing here?'

Herzer smiled. 'Ever the dashing charmer. Much the same as you, I suppose.'

'Listen, I hope this doesn't mean an auction situation. I mean, damn it, we were on the same side last time.'

'And can be again this time. We must talk about it.' She had an accent, not a real one, a Berlitz one, just a hint of something American over carefully Europeanised vowels.

González indicated Roberto. 'And this is your expert?'

'Roberto Constanza y Fairrie.'

'Ah. I think I know the name. You are, like me, a Porteño, yes? From Buenos Aires.'

Roberto bowed acquiescence.

'And you are an expert on *El Conductor, El Líder?*'

'Yes.'

'Not as expert as I. I knew him. Rather well.' She clicked a finger at one of the clerks behind the counter. '*Oiga. El director y ahora.*'

This was rude and the old ladies stopped their sibilant clatter, looked up. Djinn-like the manager appeared. He was a tall, cadaverous man with eyes deep-set in sockets of mauve tissue. Long fingers and wrists flopping from the cuffs of a light grey suit welcomed them, gestured them through a gap in the bar that had miraculously swivelled open. Buttons were pressed, plastic cards threaded through electronic devices and a section of wall, also upholstered in leather, sighed open. The manager, González, Cockburn, Gunter, Herzer and Roberto descended steps beneath a small chandelier set beyond the opening.

The ambience remained much the same. The carpeted stairs led to another upholstered door that also whispered open, obedient to the sesame of finger-tapped buttons. Beyond was a square room, quite large, with chairs and tables the same as those above. Three walls were lined to shoulder height with lockers much like those one finds at railway stations, but finished in satin steel. Above them on the wall facing the door and filling almost all of it was an enormous canvas. In blues set against browns, muted reds, greens, or lightning lit so they appeared to flash, twisting in perfect parabolas of flight and energy, a hundred handsome good angels put to flight a hundred handsome not so good angels, banished them to Erebus. San Miguel reported back to God's Mother who signalled her approval.

Roberto almost fainted at the wonder of it. '*La Victoria de los Angeles,*' he murmured. '*De Jacopo Robusti Tintoretto.* The Devil!'

No one else there seemed much bothered.

Señora González walked to a locker beneath the painting, fed a card into a slot. The manager handed her a small key, the door, far thicker than one finds on railway stations, swung open.

Cockburn's gold lighter rasped again. The cadaverous manager was politely terrified. '*Señor, no fumar, por favor!*'

'What? Oh, sorry.'

Gunter pulled a Philips tape-recorder from the locker, and then a smaller cassette player. In the space at the back Roberto could see a stack of cased spools and cassettes. Gunter released a flex and fitted it into a power point. González selected a cassette, uncased it, and handed it to Gunter who slotted it in. She looked up at the manager.

'*Déjenos, señor.*'

Reluctantly he went.

'*Sientense, por favor.*'

Gunter sat back, ankles crossed, hands clasped on his stomach. Cockburn was less relaxed, propped his head on one palm and with the other hand pushed fingers down on his unlit cigarette, reversed it, repeated the movement for as long as the tape played. Herzer sat next to him, knees together, back straight but leaning forward slightly, head on one side. She really was very thin, very brown, and very fit for her age. Roberto felt a tiny stir of desire which rather surprised him. He polished his glasses.

González kept the player on her knee, one finger resting on the stop button.

'What you are about to hear,' she said, 'was recorded by Don Juan Perón at his weekend residence in Olivos, a suburb of Buenos Aires, some time after he was re-elected President of Argentina in October '73, just over two years ago.'

She pressed the play button. Tape hissed. Then a click, a tiny cough. The voice was quiet, confidential, a little throaty, fluent, at ease with itself.

7

'Don Martín, Ricardo Bauer, he likes to be called, but for me he will always be Don Martín, came over from San Isidro this afternoon. His first personal call. I teased him about his *estancia* there. El Brujo has told me about it. Fortified. Barbed wire. German shepherd dogs, the lot. Why bother, Don Martín, I asked him. I'm back. You have nothing to fear in Argentina now I am back. "It's to be like the old days again, then, is it, Don Juan?" Yes, I told him, like the old days.

'Poor man. He has aged. Aged a lot. And of course he's five years younger than me, but I swear he looks ten years older. He's lost weight. His eyes have that old look... senility. He is as old as this tired old century, I, five years older than that. But I think I've weathered our difficult times better than Don Martín.

'We reminisced. The old times...

'El Brujo tells me Don Martín went to Dr Ciacaglini, the rejuvenation expert. Because he has a new girlfriend. Perhaps he'll bring her too next time. Anyway. He can't get it up for her. So he went for the monkey gland bit. Ha! Ha! Ha! Always there has been something, what's the word? *simian* about Don Martín.

'We reminisced. Old hands. Good times. He always hit it off with Evita. With Evita... he got on well.

'I must say, in some respects, I found him... overbearing. Pompous. In the past. And now, he is a bit of a bore, the way old men are. He expects me to be grateful. For what? That a few of the millions he and Eva put on one side were spent on keeping me and Isabelita comfortable, tolerably comfortable, during my years of exile? Come on, Don Martín, I said, you know it is not as simple as that. He shrugged, conceded. Martín and I are a mutual protection society. He sometimes forgets this: I, never.

'Of course it was not only Don Martín. There were... thirty thousand?

'They came to Argentina. That is well-known. We welcomed them.

Why not? They brought with them much that would help the development of the organic society that it has ever been my wish to create. Industrial know-how. Wealth. Technological advances were possible because of their presence, though not as many as one might have expected. The real brains were siphoned off through us to Uncle Sam.

'Many of them have done much for the growth of our cultural traditions, particularly in the sphere of music. As they have become part of our organic society and married into some of our best families, they have added a useful strain to what is already a valuably heterogeneous gene pool. I am indebted to the writer Robert Ardrey for this perception. One can see this brought to fruition in the performance of our boxers, tennis players, scientists and so on, with each succeeding generation.

'So. I have no regrets about this. Nothing to be ashamed of. After all, Don Martín never personally killed a man, woman, or child. I have his personal word for this fact. Not even a Jew. Of course, he signed papers. But if that is murder then all rulers are guilty. No one rules without signing pieces of paper.

'Anyway, crusty old fool that he now is, with his new girlfriend, a Chilean I understand and only in her forties, I welcome him. He is someone from the past. An old friend. Someone who knew Evita. The real Evita.

'And certainly, it's true, where would either of us have ever got without Don Martín?'

CLICK.

8

Five seconds of silence, then Cockburn murmured: 'Don Martín?' Herzer recrossed her long legs and looked up – puzzled at his uncertainty, then very definite. 'Bormann. Of course. Martín Bormann.'

Cockburn hissed: 'Shit.'

All shifted in their chairs and the leather creaked and soughed again. Cockburn shrugged and with a Byronic determination to do as he liked put his cigarette in his mouth. Herzer, very quickly, twisted her thin body towards him and snapped a tiny lighter cased in tortoiseshell. Cockburn inhaled, breathed out, an alarm bell rang, and rain began to fall. It increased in intensity. Gunter made for the door but it had bolted itself. The rain became steady, needle-sharp and inescapable. A steel screen dropped over the *Victory of the Angels*. Everyone except

Roberto was suddenly rather angry. The skins of furry animals may have been waterproof for them, but Señora González was not entirely sure they would not be ruined on her. Cockburn dropped his cigarette near Roberto, who picked it up, sodden and dead as it was, and put it back on the carpet near where Cockburn had been sitting. Herzer unplugged the still live recorder, picked it up and carried it towards González, but caught her shin on the corner of the glass-topped table. She dropped the recorder. Gunter helped her to retrieve it, and the spilled cassette. They handed both to González. With backs pressed against the walls they waited for the downpour to cease. Pockmarked puddles began to form in the carpet.

At last it stopped. The door clicked open. The cadaverous manager, as minatory as Tintoretto's St Michael, stood on the threshold.

'There is a fixed charge for the offence committed,' he said, 'regardless of the damage caused, which may well exceed the indemnity. Five hundred thousand pesetas. I will respect a note of hand to that sum before I release you.'

Cockburn was angry.

'Aprés vous le déluge,' murmured Herzer. Roberto remembered it was the tall Czech girl who had lit Cockburn's cigarette and he thought Cockburn might hit her.

Wet though they were they went briefly to Pepa's apartment which was nearby. It was furnished in that brand of bourgeois good taste Roberto most hated. The curtains were velvet, the clock on the wall was a gilt sunburst, the carpet was apple green, white and pink with a raised pattern of flowers, the furniture was upholstered in cream hide, on the walls were very competently painted views of the Spanish Pyrenees done in exaggeratedly bright colours – violet, red, emerald, orange. There were no books, not even a leather-bound set of Baroja. But there was a very new Akai music centre – gleaming matt steel finish, stereo radio, double tape decks, record player, the lot, but only six records as far as Roberto could see. Julio Iglesias, Jacques Brel, flamenco, James Last, Argentinian tango. He shuddered. A maid, an old woman dressed in black, brought them coffee and brandy.

'Well,' asked Cockburn, 'what do you think?'

Roberto took off his spectacles, polished them, put them back on. It was important, he knew, to get the next bit exactly right. He was careful not to look at Señora González.

'Not too much.'

'Eh?'

'I don't like it. Frankly I don't think it's Perón.'

'On what grounds?'

'It's very difficult to say. I should like to hear more.'

'Wouldn't we all!'

'I need to spend some time on analysis. At the moment it's mainly a question of feel. It just doesn't feel quite right to me.

Cockburn turned to González who had been listening to this with a very slight smile flickering round her lips. It made her more enchanting than ever.

'I must say, Pepa, it didn't sound quite the same as the other tapes.'

She offered the tiniest of pouts, a hint of a shrug. 'These are later. The cassettes at any rate. Done not long before he died. He was ten years older and a sick man. And then, too, they were done on equipment which was both more modern and yet in some ways not so good. On a modern, portable cassette machine. Of course they sound different.'

Enrico intervened: 'There is of course no need for us to get into an argument about this. I'm sure Mr Cockburn understands that he is not the only interested buyer. If he chooses to believe that what he has heard is some sort of forgery then that is his affair.'

Cockburn looked bewildered, even angry. He turned back to Roberto. 'Let's get this straight. You are talking about feel, hunch. You have not one single specific reason for supposing that what we heard is not Perón.'

Roberto thought for a moment, then pulled at his nose between thumb and finger. 'You could say that.'

'Will you stand by that?'

'On what I've heard so far, I'll stand by that.'

Cockburn insisted: 'There is no reason for supposing that what we heard is a forgery?'

'No.'

Herzer intervened: 'Fine, fine. But there is another factor, that I really do think should be cleared up.'

'What?'

She pulled her tweed skirt over her brown knee. She was suddenly very intent, as if the question was a matter of great importance to her. 'Provenance. Where did these tapes come from? How did Pepa González come by them? Can she show title?'

They all, Enrico Gunter included, looked at González.

She dabbed a cigarette out in a cream-coloured marble ashtray.

'That,' she said, 'is something I will not disclose at the moment. When an offer has been made, a cheque signed, then I will reveal both how these tapes came to be in Madrid, and why I am entitled to dispose of them.'

'Right.' Cockburn was brisk now. 'I've heard enough to convince me I should contact Peter Clemann again. If he is as interested as I think he will be, I'm sure he'll fly out directly. Of course he'll want to hear

plenty of the tapes himself. And I've no doubt he'll want Roberto here
to continue checking them out. You'll be able to arrange that, Pepa?'

'Of course. If you promise not to smoke in the bank vault.'

'I promise.' He turned to Herzer. 'I really do think we should work
together on this.'

'Oh yes. So do I, Steve. That is why I am here.'

'Quite. I can promise you I would have been in touch today, just as
I will be with Peter. I had no intention of cutting you out.'

'Oh quite. Mind you, I must say this. I think you are unduly excited
about the Bormann connection.'

'Really?'

'Really!' Her smile was conciliatory, that of a mother to a child
whom she is about to disappoint. 'I think almost everything anyone
could want to know about Bormann was on the Sassen tapes.'

'The what?'

'Come on, Steve. The tapes Eichmann recorded for a journalist
called Sassen. Not long before he was kidnapped. Eichmann hated
Bormann, you know? He said it all.'

'But that was ten years ago. This is virtually yesterday.'

Somewhere in the room a fly kept wakeful by central heating buzzed.
Roberto was aware of silence, that Señora González was looking intently
at Madame Herzer, intently but without expression. He wondered why.

González intervened, quite sharply: 'This is irrelevant. We are not
concerned with these… what do you call them? Sassen tapes. I have for
sale tapes made by Perón himself. Some made not long before he died.
Why bother with Eichmann and Sassen when you can hear from
Perón's own lips what Bormann personally said to him, and some of it
less than eighteen months ago?'

Herzer looked at her. 'Very well.' Her tone was entirely equable.
She turned back to Cockburn. 'Anyway, Steve, I think we should work
out just how we are to work together.' She maintained a coolly
humorous tone, which again Roberto found appealing.

Cockburn blundered on: 'Well. Shall we have dinner tonight?'

'If it's somewhere reasonable and you are paying.'

'El Botín?'

The best. Better than El Cid, thought Roberto.

'All right.'

'Half nine. You are in your studio flat? I'll call for you. I shall have
heard from Peter by then.'

In the lift going down Cockburn said to Roberto: 'You know, old chap,
I think you went a wee bit over the top, knocking that tape. It was
pretty sensational stuff.'

'I gave my considered opinion. As I said I would. I was not swayed one way or another by what you said either last night or this morning.'

'But still no real reason for saying it's not Perón.'

'No real reason. But those tapes need to be analysed. Scientifically.'

'Well. We'll get to that once we've pushed on a bit with the deal. By the way. On that tape. The… voice mentioned someone called El Brujo. The Wizard. The Warlock. Who he?'

'Nickname for José López Rega.'

'And?'

'Member of the Perón household.'

9

On the way back Roberto felt mildly depressed. His clothes, in spite of the ancient topcoat, still felt damp; the streets, in spite of continuing bright sunshine, struck cold, and the Metro was draughty. He feared sciatica more than anything. *Viva El Rey* sprayed everywhere. Why? Juan Carlos had shown no particular ability or strength of character. For years he had been a puppet, an appendage, standing behind the Caudillo at army parades, tall, slightly absurd, not unlike that English comedian with the same initials… John Cleese, was that it? … who, like Juan Carlos, did funny walks. Perhaps the graffiti writers meant Don Juan, the prince's father, and the rightful ruler. What a mess it was all going to be.

There were frightful stories about Franco. Ramón heard them in the cafés he frequented. How below the thorax gangrene had set in. How the people who monitored the machines that kept the cadaver clinically alive could scarcely bear the stink. And when they finally switched him off what then? It wasn't even certain the royal princes wouldn't compete for the crown, father against son, the Spanish disease.

And the same now in Argentina. Isabelita, Perón's third wife, would not last in power much longer. A few months at the most. Then what? A Pinochet or worse. Civil war with a Pinochet at the end of it. No doubt who would win. The United States would see to that.

The anxiety was twisted further towards fear when he changed at Alonso Martinez. The Chilean assassin was a hero not only in Argentina – he had his followers in Madrid too. A young man wearing a long leather coat aerosoled the walls of the tiled tunnel between platforms: *Del Bosch – Nuestra Pinochet*. Two soldiers and a businessman stood by and watched with approval. Others, including Roberto, hurried on down the echoing passage, eyes averted, pretending not to have noticed. General Milans del Bosch fought for Hitler on the Russian Front with the Blue Division – the swastika with which the youth completed his artwork lay well alongside his name.

Roberto struggled up the steps at the José Antonio Metro, and then up the four flights of stairs past the *pensión* in Desengaño. The unillusioned one. The one who knows it all and doesn't like it.

Ramón was in the kitchen burning a potato omelette. Taller, thinner, about fifteen years younger than Roberto, but a good friend, a very good friend.

'How did it go then?'

'All right. Much as I expected. But there was one very funny moment...' He went on to describe how Cockburn's cigarette had set off the sprinklers.

Ramón unfastened most of the omelette from the bottom of the pan, cut it in half, poured cheap red wine from a starred litre bottle into two tall Duralex glasses. They sat, knees almost touching, at either side of the tiny kitchen table.

'I should tell you. Juan Evita has been hearing things.'

'What things?'

'That some very nasty characters know about these tapes. And they don't like what they know about them...'

Roberto remembered. Martín Bormann is alive and lives in... San Isidro. A posh resort up the Plate from Buenos Aires.

'Where did he hear that?'

'Come on. You know Juan. He leads a double life. For a lot of people he's a well-to-do, right-wing student from Buenos Aires, doing medical research on pain thresholds at Madrid University. OK?'

'All right.' Roberto pulled a lump of bread off the small French-shaped loaf they shared and pushed it round his chipped plate. 'Ask him what he can find out about Enrico Gunter.'

'Who's he?'

'I don't know. That's the point of asking Evita to ask around about him, isn't it?'

'Come on, Roberto. Don't be grumpy. Who is Enrico Gunter?'

'A smooth character who hangs around Señora Josefina González. An Argentinian. A businessman. And he claims he is offering her business advice on how to sell the tapes.'

Ramón agreed that Enrico Gunter needed looking into.

Roberto sneezed. 'I told you I got wet. Can I have the fire this afternoon?'

'Of course.'

They collected up the plates, washed up ineffectually, made coffee.

Ramón smoked and Roberto, who had been a non-smoker for less than two years, envied him.

STOP.

But though Roberto's tape ceased to turn his voice went on.

'The fire. I cannot go to the bathroom. I cannot face that in the bathroom. But I'm cold, very cold. Eight, nine, ten, eleven o'clock. I don't suppose I could get the fire to work anyway. Probably I'll kill myself trying to. May not be a bad thing. I did not kill Ramón. Not actually kill him. But oh, dear Lord, he'd surely be alive now if I'd never met him.

'If I can't keep warm I'll die anyway. No snow outside. And he's still there, or another very like him. He'll be even colder than I am. There'll be fog at sunrise. Freezing fog. I should have a hot drink. That's it.

'What's that noise? A rattling engine with a squeak, a squeal. Dear Lord, of course! Tanks. Tanks in the streets.'

He shuddered deeply. He'd seen tanks in the streets before. And dead bodies.

'Swearing in tomorrow. The new king. He'll make a speech to the Cortes. Are the tanks on his side? Probably they'll make up their minds when they've heard the speech. Tanks in Gran Vía. Round Cibeles, Sol, and Canovas. Blocking off the Cortes.

'Coffee or tea. Tea would be better. But you can't put brandy in tea. Any more coffee though will make me want to shit. And there are some things you cannot do in a kitchen sink. I cannot face the bathroom. I will not face the bathroom. Lipton's tea-bags. Such thin stuff. Infusions for ailing Spanish ladies. Friend used once to send me Jackson's Breakfast. Jackson's of Piccadilly. Two bags to one cup. And if I can't drink brandy with it, I can have some before. Could always put hot water in it. Should have thought of that. But not the bathroom.

'It's a funny thing about dead bodies. Some people can't see it. I suppose most who have been going to see that gangrenous cadaver in the Palace can't see it. What they can't see is that it's just meat. Putrid meat. The man has gone. An empty house. No, that's not it. Sentimental image. A house is a house. But a cadaver is not a man. The change is swift, in the twinkling of an eye, and no matter how slow or sudden the movement towards that moment, the moment itself is complete, final. Yes, you are. No, you are not.

'So that's not Ramón in there, and that's why it is so hateful. If it were Ramón I could do something for him.

'Brandy first. Then tea. Then back to the tape. Something I owe

Ramón. Something I can do for the real Ramón, not the obscenity in the bath…'

10

PLAY AND RECORD:

'I met Ramón Puig quite by chance in the Prado. It was autumn, just over a year ago. When I come back to Madrid I go, as soon as I can, to the Prado, to meet again old friends. Charles the Fourth and his family. Those peasants pushing their way through a blizzard with a pig. Poor pig. La Maja with and without her clothes.

'Cockburn goes straight to a restaurant and has a *torre de mariscos*. I go to the Prado and meet old friends again. Always I leave to last the best. I expect Cockburn leaves the largest crayfish to the end as well. Sometimes in the summer there is a queue. Japanese. Arabs even. In September it's not so bad. Just five or six people – serious people who know why they are there.

'It… you cannot say *it*. They – the dwarfs, the princess, Diego himself, and that magical figure in the lit doorway – have a little room to themselves. Often the leaded window is open; there is quite a fuss on at the moment about the way the Prado is run, and no doubt it will be improved. But September a year ago, with bright sunshine, the leaded window was open, and I liked that. It put the painting in the context of our lives, made it a real thing. Paintings are no more immortal than we are. Traffic fumes spoil their health, may kill them in the end, just as they do us. So what? With reasonable care they still live a lot longer than we. And reasonable care means letting them live as part of our lives, live and die with us – not shut off in artificial climates behind glass that inevitably reflects.

'So. I liked the open window. There were other things I liked too. I liked the heavy, intricately carved black frame, and I liked the way they have put a mirror in an exactly similar frame opposite it. So you can stand and see the painting exactly framed but in a mirror image, and see the painting, and so on. I'm not quite sure why this works. Somehow it brings us into the world of the picture, we become the hidden people who are painted on the other side of Diego's canvas, Philip IV of Spain and Mariana of Austria, visited now by their daughter Margarita who wants to show off the finery her dwarfish maids have put her in. For surely she looks at them, at her parents (at us), as if at a mirror, to see from their reaction the truth of how she really is…

'I like also the small marble plaque which says: *Las Meninas de Diego Rodríguez de Silva y Velázquez... La última obra del Arte.*
'I like it because it tells the truth.
'And on that warm September day, with touches of gold in the chestnuts outside, I became conscious that the man next to me was quietly tearful too at the perfection of the greatest painting of all time...'

Roberto murmured: 'A fino perhaps?'
The stranger, taller, thinner, ten or fifteen years younger, with a black and grey beard very close-cropped so it was little more than stubble, dressed in a loosely-knit dark blue sweater, spotless jeans and blue canvas shoes, muttered assent: 'Why not?'
In a way they were like lovers, instantly aware of overpowering Eros, but knowing nothing of each other, having to explore and discover each other's personality. Except that with Roberto and Ramón the attraction had nothing to do with sex, or at any rate not in the way the word is usually understood, but rather with an equally powerful and sudden sense that they shared a similar sensibility. And the voyage of discovery into each other's life was instantly fraught with embarrassment – both were impossibly poor and, while neither was proud, neither wanted to admit it: for if one turned out to be well-to-do, then the other would be cast, would cast himself, in the role of sponger, hanger on.
So they went to the café on the other side of the Paseo, just below the Banco de España, where they sat in chairs upholstered in plastic wickerwork, beneath elaborate awnings, surrounded by potted bays, and with a spotless white tablecloth in front of them. They drank two dry sherries each and ate a handful of pistachios, and when they shared the bill they discovered that each had blown the food and drink budget for a whole day.
Ramón Puig had a sallow face, lined, with deep-set dark eyes, long brown fingers with white nails which flickered ceaselessly in tiny gestures as he spoke.
They talked about Velázquez and Goya without pretension, but with shared enthusiasm. Later they discovered similar shared obsessions with Mozart, the *esperpento* theatre of Spain, Fred Engels, Buenos Aires, Barcelona, and lost causes.
Ramón Puig's father had been a Catalan actor who had devoted the early part of his life to trying to establish a national Catalan theatre. His sister, Ramón's aunt, had married an Argentinian businessman of Catalan descent whom Roberto vaguely remembered as being a distant connection of his own wife, from whom he had been separated since

1945. At the end of the Spanish Civil War, therefore, Ramón's father had been able to take his family into exile to Buenos Aires. There Ramón, himself, made his début as an actor, as an extra, in a cut version of *Luces de Bohemia* by Valle-Inclán. This was in 1953, the very year Roberto began his wanderings.

When they had finished their finos they walked up the sidestreets near the Cortés, crossed Alcalá, and so came to Desengaño where they spent the rest of the day listening to Mozart on tapes. Ramón invited Roberto to become co-tenant, and Roberto accepted. They lived discretely, minded each other's business, but often shared long meals with little to eat but plenty of cheap red wine, through the afternoons in the tiny kitchen.

On his second day there Roberto asked what was the history of the street's name.

'Calle del Desengaño.' Ramón stubbed out and shredded the dark tobacco of his cigarette, drank more *tinto*. '1650s. Thereabouts. Two *caballeros* in love with the same woman, set off down the street, don't know what it was called then, to fight a duel.' His thin fingers flickered like rapiers. 'A dark shadow passed between them, a cloaked figure.' His hand, flat and vertical, floated across the table. 'A woman? Their woman? Perhaps. They followed. Came to the corner. The figure turned...' – Ramón's eyes went large, the whites of them glowed in the gathering shadows of the kitchen, his jaw dropped – simultaneously he was a death's head and the astonishment of the gallants –'...a *memento mori* – a skull with dried skin, rotten teeth, and...' – his little finger rose up, writhed like a tiny snake – '...worms in her eyes!' His face took on an expression of lofty disdain. 'There was a stink of putrefaction. *"Qué desengaño,"* exclaimed one of the gallants, and arm in arm, off they went to the nearest tavern.' He drank his wine, poured more for both of them, saluted Roberto. 'Friends after all...'

Desengaño.

'Not a word for which there is an exact English equivalent. The awakening, the awakened, the breaking of the spell, the unenchanted and so the disenchanted, the unillusioned.'

STOP.
Then PLAY AND RECORD:

'There was no further awakening for me with Ramón.
No disenchantment. We did not get to know each other any better after those first few days. We did not need to.'

11

'I awoke the next morning, that is the first morning after the first hearing of the dictator's tapes, in something of a quandary. Cockburn knew my address and I knew his. But since those who live in the street of the unenchanted have no telephones, well not in the despised *ático* apartments, there was no ready way he could make contact with me. I was reluctant that he should call and discover the rather reduced circumstances in which I live. Naïve people, and I rather suppose Cockburn to be naïve, tend to believe expertise is demonstrated by the trappings of success. The history of medicine alone proves him wrong – the greater the quackery, the greater the rewards.

'He had been to dinner – and possibly to bed – with Señora Becky Herzer. Or perhaps after dinner with Herzer he had returned to Recoletos and bed with González. I did not expect him to be awake early. I therefore telephoned – from one of the public call boxes outside the José Antonio Metro station – a message to the Príncipe Hotel that if he wanted to contact me during the day a message could be left at the Biblioteca Nacional.

'The Spanish National Library is not the most efficient institution in the world, but I felt an investment of a hundred pesetas in the cream marbled hall, which is the last of the many barriers that keep books and people apart, would pay reasonable dividends. I came back to it roughly on the hour throughout the day – tearing myself away from Marañón's biography of Antonio Pérez, the favourite of Philip II – and found a message waiting for me at 2pm.

'It was terribly garbled of course, quite unintelligible – Cockburn's unsatisfactory Spanish and the stupidity, or at any rate lack of interest (really one hundred pesetas was not enough) of the clerk who had taken the call made sure of that.

'I rang the Príncipe. Cockburn passed on the necessary information. Clemann and he, and, he hoped, I too, would be at the bank the following morning at eleven o'clock. With us would be Professor James McCabe of Milton University, Iowa – an expert on Perón and Argentina, known as such throughout the world. Professor McCabe would help me to authenticate or discredit the tapes.

'Known throughout the world? Not to me. I went back into the Biblioteca to find out what I could about McCabe.

'The following morning I took the Metro again to Velázquez – tedious journey since it involves a change and takes one across two sides of a triangle – and found myself, after Alonso Martinez, looking through the connecting windows between two carriages at Clemann and Cockburn. I assumed it was Clemann and it turned out I was right.

'From the way his knees stuck up I realised he was very tall. He wore glasses framed heavily in black, a dark topcoat made from blue and black tweed, dark brown gloves, a striped suit. He looked like an English academic. Cockburn and he said little as the train swayed in and out of Colón and Serrano and I guessed Cockburn was annoyed, peeved, at going by public transport. Clemann clearly had a millionaire's view of the value of money and was not going to ignore the wisdom of the City Fathers of Madrid who have set a blanket single fare on the Metro of eight pesetas with reductions if you buy a book of tickets. I wondered if Clemann had invested in a book... it would indicate how long he expected to stay.

'At Velázquez I let them move on up ahead and hung back too as they walked round two sides of a block to the bank. Thus I became aware of a man with longish dark curly hair, swarthy skin, a black leather jacket and jeans, with two-tone black and white thick-soled shoes who was walking with me. And his actions too were directed by the two people in front of us. When Cockburn paused to light a cigarette on the corner we paused together to stare, side by side, into a shop window which displayed one silk oriental rug of majestic elegance priced at my current income for one year. Then we both hurried on to the corner round which they had gone.

'Well. "Evita" had told Ramón that news of the existence of this second lot of Perón tapes, if that is what they are, was talked of in fascist circles in Madrid. While my companion did not look like one of them, he certainly did have the appearance of the sort they employ as lackeys. I have every reason to fear that sort of person. A mob of them burnt my shop off Calle Florida in Buenos Aires and damn near burned me. Jew go home to Moscow, they shouted, and *Juden raus,* and the man who poured out the demagogic bullshit that set them off was that charlatan windbag who seems to have spent most of his later years talking to himself on tape.

'Anyway, not wishing to draw his attention to me I crossed the road to a kiosk, bought a copy of *Cambio 16* whose cover announced that the nation and the world were waiting for the termination of the Caudillo. The black-jacketed lout stayed on his side, only a shop front away from the bank, and he too lit a cigarette.

'Presently another tall man, unmistakably another Anglo-Saxon, came briskly up Velázquez, head and shoulders above everyone else in the street: he wore a porkpie hat, had a yellowish complexion, a long nose, a short raincoat, brownish tweeds, carried a briefcase. Brisk, yes, and the way he sidestepped to avoid one of the elderly ladies on the bank's steps and then lurched forward put me inescapably in mind of Jacques Tati. I soon learnt that this over-tall gaucheness was the only point of similarity. I took him, correctly, to be McCabe.

'I was in a quandary. The lout remained on watch, but I had seen everyone concerned arrive except González, Herzer and Gunter, and they might already be inside. If they were then all might proceed to the vault without me. Therefore I dropped *Cambio 16* in a bin – I already had a copy at home – and crossed only to arrive on the step of the bank at exactly the same time as Señora González. She smiled most pleasantly at me as I held the door for her and I could not help noticing the exquisite fragrance of her perfume as I followed her in...

'The three tall men unfolded their legs almost like giraffes from the low chairs they must have only just sat in. Not like giraffes. More like herons or storks. For a moment I felt that Señora González and I were as vulnerable as fish in a pool...'

12

Cockburn introduced Clemann and McCabe to Roberto, and McCabe to González. Clemann was quiet, incisive, courteous. McCabe had thin gingery hair brushed artlessly to cover near baldness, gold-rimmed spectacles, mottled hands with loose skin and limp fingers.

'No Gunter then today, Pepa?' asked Cockburn. It was a crow, betraying that for him Gunter's absence was good news.

'No, Steve,' Señora González replied, 'Enrico has a business appointment he could not postpone. It's of no importance. He has already heard the tape I intend to play today and anyway, as I told you, he is to advise me on the actual terms of the sale, and I do not expect to make too much progress in that direction right now. Señora Herzer also phoned me. She too has an appointment she could not break but I gather your dinner date went well with her and she will work with you again.' Roberto thought: so Herzer was bedded by Cockburn who would rather have bedded González who was being bedded by Gunter. Then he shuddered at the multiple idiocy of this reflection and the inner confusions it revealed. 'Gentlemen, shall we go down? And this time, please, no *fumar*. All right?'

Again there was the rigmarole of opening the door to the vault and then that of Señora González's locker. She took out the cassette recorder at the front and then signalled Roberto to come forward and help her with the far larger and heavier spool-to-spool machine. He dragged it out, set it flat, discovered some difficulty in finding how the catches on the lid worked, and the hatch behind in which the flex was stored, but he managed it all to her instructions. She then handed him a six-centimetre spool and asked him to thread it up. He fumbled this and Cockburn, with brusque impertinence, intervened.

'Here, let me.'

Roberto stood aside.

Señora González, her eyebrows slightly raised, said: 'Set the counter to zero.'

Cockburn did so.

'Now wind forward until the counter reads 068.'

Certainly he was more adept with the machine than Roberto had been.

'Good. Now before I play this extract I think I should provide a little historical background. It will be familiar to Señor Fairrie and Professor McCabe if they are as expert in the life of *El Conductor* as they claim. But it could be useful for Mr Clemann.'

'I don't think that will be necessary,' said Clemann. 'I pay to have experts decide for me what I cannot decide for myself. If they understand the background of what we are about to hear, then there's no need for you to fill it in on my account.'

Señora González thought for a moment. Then: 'Nevertheless. What you are about to hear is sensational. It would not be believed by you for one moment even if your experts accepted it, unless you heard some of the background, the circumstances that make it credible.'

Clemann had manners as well as intelligence. With an odd movement of his head, not a shake or a nod but something in between, he gave her the floor.

She took it with presence. She was dressed much as she had been before – the sable, which she now took off, the black dress. But this time, instead of the pearls she had a small emerald brooch above her left breast.

'You are,' she said, 'all more or less aware of the phenomenon known as Evita. The second wife of Juan Perón. Of how she came from humble origins – the details of which are still disputed – became an actress on the Argentinian radio, in Argentinian films. The mistress of Perón shortly before he became the Vice-President in the mid-forties...

Indeed Roberto was familiar with all this. Momentarily he lost himself in contemplation of Tintoret's *Victory of the Angels*. It was lovely. Presumably belonged to the bank. Did the bank take its name from the painting? Or had the bank bought it because it already bore that name... the whim of a director? The St Michael especially was very fine – admittedly owing something to Michelangelo's Christ in the *Last Judgment*, but none the worse for that...

McCabe, however, did take an interest in what Señora González had to say. He leant forward over a small scribble pad held on his knee, and jotted notes with a gold-cased ballpoint loosely held between white and orange fingers.

'What few people outside Argentina know much about,' Señora González was saying, 'and not many people in Argentina for that matter, is the nature of Evita's relationship with Juan Duarte, Juancito, her brother. He had few talents but was personable, even charming. From the moment Perón had patronage Evita assured Juancito's advance. He even became Perón's private secretary. He was basically a wastrel, a nonentity, a nobody. During the last years of his life, and Evita's, the dissipation that had always been an obsession became a habit. Several sources assert that he was syphilitic. Perón himself is on public record as to this, and there are people alive who claimed that Juancito admitted the disease to them.'

Somehow, from somewhere, she had arranged to have available a glass and a small bottle of Perrier. She poured and sipped.

'Nevertheless. Evita adored him, and did so from adolescence or earlier. While she was alive, he was indestructible. Once she was dead he was useless, an embarrassment. Just nine months after she died, on 6 April, 1953, he resigned his post as Perón's secretary. Three days later he was found dead, shot, in his apartment. He had taken off most of his clothes, which were folded neatly, and was in pants, vest and socks. He was on his knees by the bed, as if in prayer. There was a note, hand-written, that certainly reads like a suicide note, and contains the phrase: "I came with Eva, I leave with her."

'At that time he was being investigated by a commission of army officers who were inquiring into a meat shortage that had arisen because of speculation by government officials.'

Roberto remembered: a week later Perón incited the mob to burn... lots of things. Him. His shop. *El Conductor* had a lot of troubles just then. Fighting for his political life, as they say. But he damn near killed me as well.

González's voice went on: 'The joke everyone told at the time was "Everybody knows he committed suicide. Nobody knows who did it."'

Cockburn snickered. González again looked at him with slightly raised eyebrows. McCabe frowned, pulling sandy, almost invisible brows together. Clemann remained motionless as he had throughout, left ankle on his right knee, held by both hands, head a little on one side, alert. Señora González sipped Perrier again and the cunning light from above found spun gold in her hair and flashed fire from her emeralds. Roberto pushed the memory of the other fire to the back of his mind, and she went on.

'There is one more piece of this particular jigsaw to be fitted before I play the tape. It is still not certain, not publicly certain what

Evita was suffering from, what killed her. Certainly for several years before her death she suffered increasing spasms of pain in the region of her groin and almost continual vaginal discharge. She was anaemic, so much so that leukaemia was spoken of. Her skin took on an unhealthy, coppery glow. She suffered almost continuously a low fever. In November '51 she at last consented to a hysterectomy, cancer of the womb having been suspected for some time. There is no public certainty that the operation discovered a malignant growth. Her condition continued to deteriorate until her death nine months later.

'Now I shall play the tape. It was recorded early in Perón's exile, perhaps even before he came to Madrid.'

13

All, even Clemann, shifted and the black leather creaked and sighed, but they froze as the voice, that voice came again. It sounded different. Of course this recording had been made at a quite different time, on an older machine, perhaps more like the one used on the tapes bought by *ABC* and Planeta. That, at any rate, was what they had been told. The tone of the voice was different too. Meditative, slow, with long gaps between phrases. One sensed that the speaker was close to the microphone, on his own, talking to himself at night, perhaps in the early hours of the morning.

'I know what they say. That I ordered the death of Juan Duarte *Juancito*.' (The last two syllables came in something between a spit and a rasp.) 'Certainly I had good cause to. But my record... I stand by my record as a man of peace, a man who hates violence. Twice I have turned my back on my destiny to avoid inevitable and unnecessary bloodshed, and have been called a coward when the gratitude of thousands was my true desert. But Juan, Juan, Juancito.' (This time he drew out the whole word – starting with a guttural consonant, breathing the second syllable, and again spitting the *zeeto*, relishing his hate for it.) 'Yes. I had good reason to order his death. Those who say that are right, but little do they know how good the reason was. All right...' (The voice quickened a little.) '...he was a waster, a scoundrel, an idiot even. These are forgivable crimes. He was an incompetent. He botched all the work he ever did for Eva or for me – irritating, yes, but no reason for killing him. He abused his position, made money from it, a fortune... well, these are crimes

– but not punishable by death. A good spell on Martín García, perhaps, but not the pistol to the head.'

At this point McCabe looked up, his glasses flashed. Then he scribbled busily, but briefly.

'But how about this. Suppose… suppose the First Lady's infatuation with this booby went beyond a purely sisterly affection…'

There was a long pause on the tape, the rasp of a lighter. Cockburn's hand too went to his pocket and froze there as González, basilisk-like, glared at him.

'It's been said,' (the voice went on – still meditative, still very much as if speaking to itself) 'it's been said Juancito and I had much… in common. Certainly Evita doted on him. As she did on me. Yes. He had charm. Looks. Anyway. Supposing his disease. Had been transmitted. In whatever ways such diseases are transmitted. To his sister. My wife. And she died of it. Then would I not have every reason in the world to order his death?'

CLICK.

They all stirred, coughed, sighed.
Clemann spoke. His voice was serious but polite, just coloured with a New England accent.
'Señora González, is that all we are to hear today?'
'Yes.'
'I doubt it's enough for our experts.' He turned enquiringly first to McCabe, then to Roberto.
McCabe flipped over the cover of his scribble pad, parked the gold ballpoint. He cleared his throat.
'No, Clemann. Not enough.' His accent, a mid-West drawl, nasally delivered, was far more marked. 'No way can I make a sound judgment on what we have heard. An informed guess at best.'
'I have of course heard an earlier extract,' Roberto spoke, as Clemann turned to him, 'but there are very many questions to be asked. And answered.'
Cockburn could not restrain himself. 'But that was pretty sensational stuff. You must admit. I mean if that is real, if that is Perón, we have a very saleable commodity here. Damn it, it's worth a bomb.'
Roberto chewed his bottom lip, then: 'Perhaps, Mr Cockburn, your Spanish isn't quite up to the nuances, the tenses; he never actually says that

Eva slept with her brother, that she died of syphilis, that he, Perón, killed Juancito. All the way it is conditional. If this, if that, then would I not...'

Cockburn's laugh was brusque. 'Come on. It's dynamite. You know it.'

'Come now,' Clemann intervened, 'it's not the saleability we're concerned with at the moment. It's the authenticity. How far are our experts prepared to go in that direction? Señor Fairrie, I gather you said of the first extract you heard that you had no reason to say that the voice was not Perón's. Do you still stand by that?'

'Yes. No. Yes.'

'You have reservations. I should like to know what they are.

'I'm not happy about the voice. It's too... imitable. The genuine Perón, I mean. While I don't deny for one moment that it does sound very like him, I could not swear to it without scientific, electronic analysis.'

'But for that we would need not only the necessary machinery and an expert to operate it, but an accredited sample of Perón's voice for comparison.'

'Yes.'

'And where will we find that?'

'ABC?' suggested González.

'Of course, ABC has one hundred and forty hours of accredited tape,' – Clemann's voice took on an edge, something stronger than mere ruefulness – 'but I doubt they'll let us borrow a sample so we can authenticate a set of tapes that will blow their product into limbo.'

'We can try,' said Cockburn.

'Sure. We can try.'

'And I don't think you need go to Geneva for an electronic voice analyser.' This was Roberto. 'Such equipment is in use in Madrid University. I have a friend who does not actually work with it, but his own line of research is related and he knows people who do.'

'Thank you. And what about you, Professor? What's your view?'

'Much the same as Señor Fairrie's. I have not heard enough to say definitely one way or the other. Not enough to assert categorically that it is not Perón. But...'

'You too have reservations.'

'Yes. But unlike Fairrie, I'm not too bothered about the voice. That can be tested, as he rightly says. It's the content that bothers me.'

'The content?' Roberto's voice fluked up.

'Nothing specific. A feeling, not much more. As Cockburn says, it's dynamite. But dynamite to Peronismo. To the present government there which is toppling anyway, of course. But to the very survival of Peronismo after it's gone.'

'Why do you say that?'

'Look. Every conceivable slander, including this one, has been thrown at Evita from both the right and the left – and for the *decamisados* it just proves what shits they all are. But to hear something like this from the lips of *El Líder* himself... that would be pretty destabilising of the Evita image, which is central to modern day Peronismo.'

'Perhaps. But that doesn't necessarily cast doubts on the authenticity of this tape.'

'I think it does. Whatever Perón personally thought of the matter, he knew the absolute importance of the Evita myth. I just don't think he'd put something like that on tape.'

'What about Nixon? What about the White House tapes?' Cockburn again.

'Sure. That's a precedent. But,' – McCabe stroked his chin – 'whatever you think of Perón, he had something tricky Dicky just did not have. You could call it... class, I suppose.'

'Gentlemen. We're getting no further. Señora, you are adamant that you won't let us hear any more tape on this occasion?'

'Would there be any point? You want voice analysis. You set it up, and I may or may not allow it. I'll see.' She twisted the ring on her finger. 'But... I don't wish to be impertinent. But you have been in this market before. You lost out. There are many potential buyers, who may not be so choosy, so fussy as you.'

Clemann grimaced, unfolded himself from the low leather chair, moved towards the open locker. González followed him, placed herself just ahead of him.

'Four spools of tape. Thirteen cassettes. Not as much as *ABC* bought. The spools look the same sort of thing as they've got. Really, Señora González, I'm interested, I wouldn't be here if I were not. But that last trip cost me a lot – and before I spend any more money, I do need to know just a little bit more of what we are into.'

They faced each other. She barely came up to the top pocket of his jacket. She was aware of it, refused to look up at him, returned to her chair, sat forward on it, legs to the side and crossed at the ankles. She smoothed her skirt.

'The spools were done, we think, in Madrid during the same period as those *ABC* bought. But Perón kept them separate from those precisely because he knew they contained very sensitive material. He had been more than usually indiscreet. They went back to Buenos Aires with him. In the baggage of one of his entourage. It's possible he thought they had been destroyed. Eight cassettes were made in the presence of the same companion during the months preceding Perón's death. He knew he was dying. Discretion was no longer important – only self-justification and an old man's desire to have some influence on history after his death. He was a vain man.'

Cockburn crowed: 'Surely that takes care of the Professor's quibbles about content?'

Clemann ignored him. 'And the other five cassettes?'

Roberto, confused, looked at Pepita with serious but expressionless eyes, and waited.

González looked at her immaculate fingernails, then, her eyes still cool, directly at Clemann.

'They are nothing to do with this. They are tapes I choose to keep here, but they were not made by Perón.'

Clemann nodded, apparently satisfied.

'All right. But you must realise that before we have a deal I must know where the Perón tapes came from, and what right you have to dispose of them.'

'I think you already know that I shall reveal that when a deal is struck. If then you don't like what I tell you, you will still be able to draw back.'

'And you want…?'

'Two hundred thousand dollars – and you get the tapes to which I shall renounce all title.'

'A similar deal to the earlier one.'

González said nothing.

Clemann turned away, looked up into the *Victory of the Angels* for nearly two minutes. The others sat on, avoiding looking at each other for most of the time, though once, briefly, Cockburn's eyes met González's, and a ghost of a smile crossed both faces. Then Clemann turned back.

'Frankly, I don't like it. I'm not going into why right now. You can work it out for yourself. However, I've sent for a lawyer, Henry Swivel. I wish I'd had him here before. Becky Herzer – who somehow heard of all this already and felt she was entitled to get in on the act again – is also around. They'll both be at El Príncipe Monday evening. Steve. You'll be there too. At the Príncipe, 7pm. We'll have a conference about it all and go on from there. Right?'

'Right.'

'Fairrie, McCabe. Thank you for your help so far. I can see difficulties about this voice analysis procedure, so I think it likely I'll need further help. I'd like you two, both of you, to be in Steve's room at the Príncipe at eight o'clock on Monday. I'm paying you expenses, that's right? And professional consultancy fees. Fairrie, Cockburn tells me you won't take more than ten dollars a throw. That's a gesture. You get a hundred every time I ask for you... we do things properly or not at all.'

He turned back to González.

'Thank you, Señora. I appreciate your impatience with me, but today is Saturday, the bank closes in ten minutes and nothing much is going to be done by either of us until Monday. I'll be in touch.'

14

'I was followed from the bank.

'Not by the black-jacketed oaf I had spotted before but by an older man – fat, he looked like a minor clerk, a shopwalker in an unfashionable shop. His clothes were too small, did not button up properly. I imagined that he had been brought up by a hard-line Falangist and recruited or pushed into JONS in his adolescence. Probably, I thought, he spends his evenings and weekends harassing intellectuals and left-wingers at the behest of the Secret Police. Or fulfilling duties like the one he was presently engaged on. There is a vast pool of such people who can be relied on to turn out for anyone whose credentials declare them to be pillars of the regime.

'I wasn't that far off the truth. The only thing is, his duties go beyond mere harassment.

'All of which suddenly seemed fanciful as I watched him stumbling and gasping on to the platform at Alonso Martinez as the Línea Cinco train I had just managed to slip on to as the doors closed, pulled away from him.

'However, when I got back to Desengaño, it seemed likely my paranoia was justified.

'Evita was there.

'I don't think it's necessary for me to justify my friend's attachment to Evita. He is handsome, dark, thin, fit, intelligent, capable of affection and passion. If he were a girl no one would think twice, except possibly her parents who would not want her chances on the marriage market spoiled by a liaison with an impoverished actor twice her age. That their relationship is ... was...'

STOP.

'Can I go on?'
'I have to.'

PLAY AND RECORD:

'That their relationship *was* often stormy, had as much misery in it as bliss, is neither here nor there. That sort of thing can happen, too, in heterosexual relationships. Indeed it can. Anyway, Evita was there.

'We call him Evita because he once... achieved an amazing impersonation, and the nickname stuck. He claims to be a Montonero in exile. Perhaps he is. But it is a claim that gains him status in the *ambiente* in which he and Ramón move. *Moved*. And perhaps for that reason he keeps it up and it cannot easily be refuted. Certainly he comes from a well-to-do Buenos Aires family, and is doing research at the Madrid medical school. I need a drink.'

STOP.

Roberto moved like a zombie through the tiny, literally freezing flat. There was ice on the inside of the kitchen window. A nearby clock struck once, which was annoying. It struck once for half-past twelve, for one o'clock, and for half-past one. Without turning on the radio he had no idea which it was.

He suffered pains now in his lower abdomen – crablike clutches at his gut, and his concentration was drifting more and more frequently.

Absurdly he thought: I will blindfold myself, go, as they say, to the bathroom, come out, take off the blindfold, then wrap myself in every blanket I can find and go to bed and sleep...

But he heated water, slopped brandy into it and fought one foot in front of the other back through the hall where he noticed a line of dust and dead spiders marking the old position of the wardrobe he'd dragged in front of the outside door, and so back to his room and his tape-recorder.

PLAY AND RECORD:

'"Evita" was there. And Ramón of course...'

Ramón called from his room as he heard Roberto's key in the door. He was sitting at his actor's dressing-table slowly painting his face into a likeness of Richard Nixon whom he was to portray for the first time that night in a *café-teatro* off Barco. Juan 'Evita' Castillo was lying back on the narrow bed with his head propped high on the pillows. He was idly fingering a small silver pistol – snapping back the breech, clicking the trigger. The air was thick with cigarette smoke.

'Yes?'

'Evita's got news for you.'

Evita pointed the gun. Roberto flinched. Click.

'I wish you wouldn't do that.'

'Enrico Gunter.'

'Yes?' Roberto sat in the spare cane chair and it creaked. The room was so small and so cluttered his knees touched the bed. It stank too – of unwashed clothes and weeks of strong, cheap cigarettes. But at least it was warm – the round electric fire, set on its back under the dressing table, saw to that.

'Enrico Gunter. Buenos Aires businessman. You could say cosmopolitan. He's been helping Astra to expand in South America. Has worked on links between Astra and Beretta. Has German friends, and relations, in Argentina.'

'An arms-dealer.'

'Not *dealing*. Manufacturing. But he's just a businessman. With a businessman's skills. He's a consultant. Advises firms who are thinking of working together but are suspicious of each other. Paves the way in little countries who want arms made on their own territory. Knows his way round the bureaucracies – who needs a kickback and how much. OK. It's arms he's into now, but it could be anything – agricultural machinery, he's set up a Mengele factory or two in his time, rainforest clearance, hydro-electrics. What comes out at the end is fees and commissions, the product is no concern of his.'

'How did you find out all this?'

Evita shrugged. 'It's still a small world – the South American bourgeoisie in Madrid. You know that. They like to gossip.'

He snapped the breech, pointed it again. Click.

'How long has he known...?'

'Señora Josefina González?' Evita's tone was sarcastic. 'I really don't know. Hey. Ramón? How many rounds do you have for this toy?'

Richard Nixon swung round. The swooping nose, like a phallus with a grooved glans on the end, wobbled and fell off. Ramón said: 'Six. A magazine full.'

'This?'

'Yes.'

Evita slotted the tiny case up into the butt.

'It's not really enough you know. You should get some more. I mean it's only small calibre, utterly ineffective over ten metres – unless you get lucky and hit someone in the eye. To be sure of that you need to be able to spray the landscape.'

Ramón turned back to the mirror, manipulating the putty between his fingers. 'Difficult. It's old. German. Pin-fire two two. It's all rim-fire nowadays.'

'I'll get you some. Pepita. And Enrico. Difficult to say. He's been around in Madrid for more than a year. That circle being what it is he would have met her pretty soon. How long he's been fucking her is anybody's guess.'

He snapped the breech, pointed, and Roberto grabbed. The bang – short as a whiplash – was utterly shocking. They all looked at each other. Was any of them hurt? Apparently not. They began to giggle, then roar with laughter, and Ramón indicated the tiny hole in the ceiling. The smell of cordite spiced the other odours.

'I told you it was harmless,' heaved Evita, thrashing on the bed.

'And now there's only five,' shouted Ramón. 'There's something else,' he added.

Evita tried to wrestle for the gun but Roberto was firm, acting the role of the benign surrogate uncle.

'One lucky escape was enough. Something else?'

'Tell him, Evita.'

'A top German Nazi, he's called Hans Adler, flew into Madrid three days ago. To honour the Caudillo and assist in the obsequies to come, he told the press. He's second generation, so can move about as he likes. But he called on an *ex-Azul* in the Security Police who told him where to find La Aguja.'

'The Needle?'

'The Needle.'

'Who is…?'

'A hit man. A contract killer.'

Roberto felt cold in spite of the fug in the room. 'Fat? With glasses?'

'Yes. But he's over forty, a Cuban by birth. So, he has spectacles and he's fat. He is said to be SS trained.'

STOP.

A deep sigh.

PLAY AND RECORD:

'So I kept the pistol in my pocket. After that sort of news I would have been stupid not to. Later I hid it amongst my books.

'I asked: "Can you connect Gunter with these Nazis?"'

'Evita replied: "Yes. Of course. I already have. He has German connections, he's in business. Do I have to make any other connection?"

'"But nothing concrete. Nothing firm."

'Evita, not able to give a concrete answer, feigned boredom. He swivelled on to his hip and groped for another cheap black Canaries cigarette from the packet under the bed.

'"No."'
'That was Saturday afternoon. Two days before the meeting at the Príncipe. No reason really not to continue with one's established routines. These, however, were interrupted. I was warned. Warned off. I should really have taken my cue. Of course I should. Ramón…'

15

S unday morning. An elderly man struggled up out of the La Latina Metro, struggled because the crowd was quite dense although it was November, struggled because he was carrying two battered suitcases which had once had quality but which were far too heavy for him. A young boy, about twelve years old, his clothes patched and clearly handed down or bought on street kerbs, waited for him at the turnstiles.

Roberto straightened, gasped for air, rubbed the palms of his hands into the small of his back, then put his hand on the boy's shoulder. The boy put down the cases, which he had already taken, and waited.

'*Momento. Por favor.*' A little colour came back into his cheeks. He shook his head, wiped his hands then his face on a handkerchief. '*Buenos, Jaime, y gracias. Arriba. Vamos.*'

The boy hoisted the cases and followed Roberto up the last flight of stairs into the cold winter sunshine of the Plaza de Cascorro.

The Rastro, the flea market of Madrid, is for real. In summer the poverty is diluted by the tourists – Americans, Japanese, Arabs come in coaches, and the middle, even upper middle classes come down from Chamberi and Recoletos to pick up bargains: Castilian furniture made from hide studded on to black frames that weigh lighter than you expect when you pick them up, three-legged stools that weigh heavier; fans which claim to be hand-painted – and so they are, in sweat shop assembly line done by numbers, Talavera pottery, ditto; Toledo swords six inches or six feet long, all bearing the name of the sword of El Cid; antique pistols made the day before yesterday; all the paraphernalia of the Corrida from a full suit of lights to a paper-knife made like an *espada* and therefore impractical because of the bend at the tip; paintings of soulful virgins, and of soulful Virgins, of chubby Christs and of chubby little boys who wink over their shoulders while weeing in the gutter; paintings of Don Quixote and Sancho Panza done in the good old *costumbristic* style, ditto done spiky and modern with impasto inches deep; paintings there solely to advertise the ornate frames they are in. And, mostly at the top end of the area, not far from La Latina, books.

In summer the poverty is real, in winter it is obvious. A thin man sells an empty gas cylinder to buy food he will no longer be able to cook. An old man sells a chair because his room has no fireplace in which he might burn it. Old ladies in black, with plastic bags in yellow and red carefully saved from trips to Simago, bargain at the vegetable and fish stalls for produce gone limp and unwholesome since Friday morning when they first arrived in town.

And the books. Apart from a few second-hand bookshops in the narrow alleys off the Ribera de Curtidores these are mostly sold from trestled tables at the top end of the market: stacks of illustrated *folletines* and *novelas por entregas,* simplified translations of everything from *The Wandering Jew* to *War and Peace,* and none of them complete; similarly incomplete book-club sets of Pérez Galdós and Baroja; stacks of children's encyclopedias produced alphabetically as weekly magazines whose publishers went bust at *Manila-Mexico.*

Roberto took his usual pitch under a plane tree, little more than a sapling; Jaime took the *duro* he was paid for carrying the suitcases and promised to be back for another at two o'clock – assuming the elderly gentleman had not sold off his stock, ha, ha. Roberto unfastened the catches, undid the straps and spread his wares on the cobbles and the tiny scrap of earth under the tree. He sat on a tiny camping-stool. He was cold. He wore his black Homburg, his ancient Crombie, a grey muffler and woollen gloves cut down to make mittens, but still he was cold. There were very few buyers about and he wondered, as always, why he bothered. Out loud a Municipal Policeman wondered the same. Roberto shrugged, said nothing.

His life would have little purpose if he did not do it – that was why.

The policeman, a robust fat man, peered down at the books. He did not like what he saw. Most of them were paperbacks with rough edges where the pages had been cut. Some had fawn-coloured covers printed boldly with striking designs in black and faded red. Was that not a hammer and sickle? Was that not a clenched fist? And were not many of them printed in Barcelona and in a language that was not Castilian? A week ago Juan Carlos, as acting head of state, had signed an edict permitting Catalans to speak Catalan. But that surely did not mean that books in Catalan could be sold in the streets of Madrid. He wondered if he should use his lapel radio and consult his superiors, but he feared that he would be told off for being a fool. Anyway, the elderly gentleman looked very respectable with his close-clipped white moustache like the poor Caudillo's and his gold-framed spectacles.

Half an hour passed and the cold began to bite. Roberto stood and banged mittened hands together, then sat down again on his camping-stool. Two students, a girl and a boy, dressed in imitation of American students in donkey jackets, sweaters, jeans, and sneakers, but all, because they were Spanish, pressed and spotless, stooped and poked about in his pile and whispered with awe to each other at what they found. *The Civil War in France. The Origin of the Family.* 'Jesus,' muttered the boy, 'it's dangerous to own even the *Origin of Species.*' And they passed on.

Three more youths arrived, not too different from the students in appearance but with boots instead of sneakers and leather instead of duffel. They too poked about in Roberto's stock for a moment or two, peered into his face, checking they had the right man. Then they closed in and the one in the middle unzipped himself.

For a moment that seemed like a minute Roberto, on his stool with his head on a level with the uncircumcised, slightly tumescent prick, waited. Then the manipulated foreskin slid back and the stream, directed at his books, began. He snatched off his hat and swatted.

The other two lads moved in. They backhanded him across the face and his spectacles scuddered away across the cobbles. He groped after them. Then, not wanting to mark his face, they came in with their boots. They knew their trade. They aimed for the soft parts. There would be no broken bones, no blood. No external blood. When they had finished they lifted up the suitcases and tipped the books and pamphlets over him. The whole episode lasted two minutes at the most.

Roberto clutched at his heart. Or so it seemed. In fact he was protecting his spare, and now his only, pair of spectacles, kept in an inside pocket, in an old-fashioned strengthened case.

Jaime, the street boy who earned ten pesetas every Sunday carrying Roberto's cases to and from La Latina had been told what was happening. Just as the other sellers and buyers were on the point of deciding that really it was no longer dangerous to see if the elderly gentleman needed help, he arrived. To everyone's relief the old man was persuaded to sit on his righted stool; he allowed Jaime to repack his suitcases; he allowed him to lead him back to the Metro.

16

The second warning came on Monday. Roberto, who had been beaten in the street twice before, recovered quite quickly. The actual injuries were painful enough certainly, but had left no internal lesions or haemorrhage. The worst thing about such events is the shock, the sense of outrage, the feeling of helplessness in the face of hostile forces one can do nothing about...

One reaction is an almost overpowering desire to stop in bed, to stay away from it all, keep out of sight. Roberto resisted this by giving himself a treat: breakfast in the Nebraska *cafetería* in Hortaleza, where he blew half the day's food and drink budget on chocolate and *churros*. After all, he was already two hundred dollars ahead of the game, and would presumably earn another hundred that evening. Three hundred dollars was a month's income.

So there he sat beneath warm spotlights, in a black leatherette chair watching with pleasure a pretty girl with a low-cut shirt which exposed deliciously the swelling creaminess of her breasts as she stooped to wipe the tables nearby. He listened with delight to an exchange between the older lady, fat and jewelled, who managed the Gaggia, and the tall, sallow barman. Prime Minister Carrero Blanco, blown up two years earlier while leaving a brothel now claimed his position in heaven would be senior to Franco's for he had left only a leg behind. While it seemed Franco would be bringing only his head...

A young man, expensively dressed, immaculately groomed, came in, interrupted their snickers, asked a question, ordered a *café solo,* and, to Roberto's surprise since the *cafetería* was almost empty at this hour, came and joined him.

'*Se puede?*'

Roberto signified assent. The young man placed his octagonal green cup on the table and distributed around himself a collapsible umbrella in a leather case, a pair of gloves, a scarf, and a soft leather purse with a wrist strap. Then, seated at last, he pushed long hairy fingers through wiry black hair (a gold ID bracelet glittered in the spotlight) and came finally to rest with his chin on his hands, and his elbows on either side of his coffee. He fixed Roberto with dark eyes, serious, concerned.

'Señor Fairrie?'

'*Sí.*'

'I am Private Secretary to the Marqués of Boltana, Don Antonio Pérez y Mendizábal. He is a director of the Bank of Corpus Cristi.'

'Really?'

'If it's no trouble for you, he would like to speak to you this morning on a matter of some importance.'

Roberto attempted to make a show of looking at his watch, a gold Rolex twenty years old, but he had sold it, and it was no longer there.

'Finish your breakfast, of course.'

'I intend to.' He dipped the penultimate *churro* in the thick, cinnamon-flavoured chocolate, sucked appreciatively at the grooved, drooping length of fast-fried doughnut paste, before relishing the crispness at the undipped end.

The Secretary sipped his coffee, grimaced. He had taken neither cream nor sugar, and clearly it was far too bitter.

'How did you know where to find me?'

'Your friend in your apartment said you might be here. The head office of the bank is in the Plaza de España, as I'm sure you know, opposite the Hotel El Príncipe. We can take a taxi.'

Roberto refused to be hurried. He slipped a couple of tissues from the dispenser on the table, wiped fingers and mouth with exaggerated care, took two more tissues and slipped them in his top pocket. Then he picked up the unused, still-wrapped sugar lumps the Secretary had left. Remote cousins in England had done very well manufacturing little cubes of sugar. Through some commercial quirk these still carried his name on them.

The Marqués, seated at a desk that would not have disgraced an emperor, beneath windows which, had they been stained, would have graced a cathedral, welcomed, or at any rate acknowledged his presence, across half an acre of Aubusson. Roberto, bred into and by the upper bourgeoisie of Buenos Aires, was up to it. He stood in the doorway through which the Secretary had announced him, slowly took off his hat, gloves and muffler, and dropped them on a nearby chair, straightened one of the Nebraska's tissues in his breast pocket so just a dot of a white triangle appeared above the hem, and set off on the journey to the desk.

The Marqués leant back in his throne to watch his progress which was stiff, painful and slow. Roberto did his utmost to disguise the pain, but it was not easy, and he felt he was not doing well.

Then he stopped. He couldn't help it. On the panelled wall, half-way down the room, was a very large painting of an elegant eighteenth-century grandee dressed in scarlet and white with a blue and white sash. He was surrounded by *objets d'art* and in the foreground a smaller, darker figure held up a painting for the grandee to inspect. He, however, had eyes only for his portrait painter.

Roberto, arrested at first by sheer surprise, took the opportunity to stay where he was and thus forced the Marqués to make the first move.

He cleared his throat. 'There is, as I am sure you know Señor Fairrie, a similar painting in the Urquijo Bank.'

'No better than this, Marqués,' said Roberto. 'And it was very rare indeed for Goya to do more than one version of a painting. Velázquez, on the other hand…'

'Well,' the Marqués was expansive, 'they both ran studios you know. Not quite factories perhaps, but they had assistants and so on. The Urquijo Bank's version is better known than ours, and they are much bothered by people asking to see it.'

The Marqués offered him a seat in front of the desk. There were three chairs set there round a low table. Roberto pointedly remained standing and eventually the Marqués came round the desk and took one of them. It was now possible for Roberto to see him properly. Until then his second pair of spectacles, not quite the same prescription as those smashed in the Rastro, together with the light flooding in behind the Marqués, had left his perception of the man vague.

What he now saw was not interesting. A well-set-up man, about his own age, with a figure once trim going to fat behind a perfectly cut silver-grey suit, a tanned face that shone, hair silver, wiry and brushed back, eyes and mouth mean, suspicious and bullying in repose, but capable of instant charm.

'It was good of you to come at such short notice. I will return the favour by coming straight to the point. You are an expert on the life of President Perón.'

'Yes.'

'Not well known as such. But still an expert.'

Roberto remained mute.

'And as we, I, understand it, you are at present employed by an American with Swiss nationality called Clemann to authenticate or otherwise a set of tapes that are on sale as the uncensored reminiscences of Perón.'

'Yes.'

'I take it that you know that a large set of tapes made by Perón here in Madrid were bought a year ago from Señora Nini Montiam, the actress, and will be published next year by Planeta? Possibly *ABC* may serialise some of the transcriptions.'

'Yes. I know that. That is public knowledge.'

The Marqués leant back, his eyes glittered narrowly over clasped fingers.

'Tell me, Señor Fairrie, you have heard some of this second set of tapes?'

'Two short extracts, yes.'

'And they are forgeries.'

This was said with finality. Roberto took his time.

'I have not yet made up my mind.'

'But I think you will say they are forgeries.'

'I doubt if I shall ever make a final assertion on the matter. Without scientific electronic voice analysis involving similar tape known not to be forged, no one is ever going to be able to say definitely, without a shadow of doubt one way or the other. What I have heard of the tapes so far is near enough like Perón's voice, near enough the sort of thing you might expect him to say, to make such analysis a necessity.

Without it, one can only express opinion. Informed, expert opinion. But only opinion.'

'And your opinion?'

Roberto repeated: 'I have not yet made up my mind.'

The Marqués got up, moved behind his chair to the side of his desk and so to the tall window furthest from Roberto. His head sank a little between his shoulders, his podgy fingers were clasped behind his back where they fidgeted and flexed.

'I gather you had an unfortunate experience in the Rastro yesterday morning.'

The Marqués's eyes remained fixed on the Cervantes monument below.

Roberto's gut shrivelled with fury and fear.

'And I suppose your permit of residence must run out some time in the next few months. I imagine you will not find the regime in your own country very congenial. And when it falls, the sort that will take over will be not so much uncongenial to you as positively dangerous. Really, Señor Fairrie, it does seem to me, on the face of it virtually certain, even without scientific analysis, that these new tapes are forgeries, and your duty is to expose them as such. Well. I mustn't keep you. You are, I am sure, a busy man.'

This was a sneer. The podgy Marqués, framed in the window, drew out a long thin cigar, and snapped a flame at it. Sweating with rage, chagrin, and terror, Roberto stumbled and limped back to the big door, collected his outdoor garments and went.

The Marqués did not move, did not acknowledge his departure.

17

Again Roberto stopped the tape. This time what was happening in his lower gut would not be denied. The only bucket in the attic flat was overflowing with garbage. Later he realised he could have tipped this into plastic bags but with his head swimming with brandy and sleeplessness, his limbs almost paralysed with cold, it did not occur to him. And so he blundered at last, eyes averted, into the bathroom but was forced to turn round to sit on the bowl. He evacuated evil-smelling diarrhoea and waited to enjoy the release from pain. Inevitably he looked at the obscenely masked cadaver of his friend. He had never seen the body naked before – he regretted this deeply, to the point of renewed weeping, that the wholesomeness of familiarity with the living flesh of a man he had loved had been denied to him by the absurd restrictions of a 'civilisation' he had devoted most of his life to trying to undermine, subvert. He should have known better. That was the trouble. No matter how hard he had tried to reject all that he hated, it was congenital, introjected, inescapable. Marcuse and Lukács, and many others, in very different ways, had written about this. It was something he had not given enough thought to.

Then something horrible happened. His friend was gone, but movement, even life went on, though no longer the life of his friend. Hair and nails grow after death. Less pleasant things happen too.

The cadaver farted. The bubbles burst in discoloured water above its crotch.

Roberto vomited – everything, it seemed, that he had eaten and drunk since he came in. Then he managed to get to the kitchen where he boiled a saucepan of water. This he emptied into a jug, and from the jug he poured the hot water into a litre-sized Casera lemonade bottle with a porcelain and wire top. He closed the top. Then he collected every blanket he could find, using Ramón's as well as his own, and, stripped to his long underwear, with his improvised hot-water bottle, rolled himself up on his own bed. The clock struck twice just as he was sinking into a short but very deep sleep.

Later he woke and half dreamed, half dozed, half consciously recollected a variety of things. Buenos Aires – wide streets and high buildings, acacias and plane trees, drums remorselessly beating in tango rhythm to punctuate the flow of speeches mouthed from a balcony, hideously amplified by loudspeakers. Evita – pale hair, skin glowing unnaturally, driven through the streets at Perón's second inauguration, with, they said, a steel ramrod up her back to keep her upright.

He dreamt too of, or remembered, a wife. A lovely woman. She had come to his arms with glee and together they made a child as beautiful as she. But she had not liked his bookshop, his friends, above all she had not liked the raids the police occasionally made on them. They separated. And confused with her he dwelt on the sudden totally unexpected bliss of bed with Becky Herzer – and here something niggled, worried, nagged. Why had she done it? Why? Though not a vain man, Roberto had his share of masculine vanity, and only now did it occur to him to ask: why?

He twisted and turned, forced himself a little more awake, and acknowledged as the memory of it all became sharper, that of course he knew why. It had been quite clear. And in gratitude he had made her a promise, a promise he would no longer have to keep. Nevertheless, something nagged again. If Cockburn had not asked Herzer to come back to Madrid, had not told her about the new tapes, then who had?

He dozed on, woke in a dim light filtered between the slats of the

built-in roller blind that covered his window. Not bright enough to
wake him, so what had? The guns and the bell. The monotonous thud
of the field guns in the Parque del Qeste took up again their dreary
salute to the dead dictator, and the nearer, muffled clang of the church
of San Martín a couple of hundred metres down the road.

The security, almost a numb sense of contentment, that had built up
with his body warmth evaporated as quickly as the warmth itself.
Anxiety, as sharp as fear bit into him, and for a moment or two he
sucked and chewed on his thumb and whimpered.

But he got up, attempting briskness though his bruised organs
would not allow it, put on trousers, a cardigan, a long flannel dressing-
gown, his muffler and mittens. Then he made himself coffee again, and
finished the stale bread. Back in his room he sat himself in front of the
tape-recorder, pressed the play and record buttons, then stopped them
again.

He reached for the radio and caught the end of an announcement.
Don Juan Carlos de Borbón will be sworn in as King and Head of State
in front of the Cortés at noon. He will then address the Cortes and the
nation. Roberto thought – well, if nothing has happened here by then,
I'll listen to that. Meanwhile news bulletins will follow every hour on
the hour, and in between solemn music…

The Eroica! The Eroica symphony for that cadaver in the *Palacio
Real*, and all the man had been and done! Napoleon even was a more
suitable dedicatee! Still, not too often did one hear Beethoven on
Spanish radio, it was an added bonus when evil men were allowed at
last to die.

Could he continue to tape his version of the events that had led to
two murders with the music on too? Well, he had a small set of headphones, and he could try, with the volume turned low.

PLAY AND RECORD:

'I arrived at the Príncipe at eight o'clock on Monday evening,
sparing a curse for the Banco de Corpus Cristi on the other side of the
Cervantes monument.

'Professor McCabe was sitting in an armchair in the foyer and he
rose to greet me.

'"I thought I'd wait for you. We can go up together."'

'In the lift he asked me what I thought about the whole business. I
was non-committal. He said he was inclined to think the tapes were
forgeries and that the swindle had been set up by Señora González
and Cockburn. Nevertheless, they were good forgeries, other people
must have been involved as well. He added that he was talking about

no more than inclination, instinct. He'd have to hear a lot more tape.

'I agreed: that from my point of view that was a necessity too – without electronic analysis, which I still hoped would be forthcoming, I should want to hear a lot more tape before offering a firm opinion.

'We knocked on the door of Steve Cockburn's room, and he let us in.

'The room was of course relatively small, and, to my dismay, thick with smoke. The two twin beds had been pushed together against the wall. On them sat Swivel, an American-trained Swiss lawyer, and Becky Herzer.

'Swivel is podgy, indeed fat. He was in his waistcoat with shirt collar unbuttoned above a loosened tie, one of those striped ones the English wear to show they belong to something. He has thick, moist lips, sharp eyes, and is no more than thirty years old. In answer to a nod from Clemann he went out into the corridor and came back with two upright chairs.

'Herzer, Becky, on this occasion wore a white blouse with expensive lace beneath a black velvet pinafore, black court shoes, jet necklace, and carried her glasses suspended from a silk noose.

'There was a bucket of nearly melted ice and a litre bottle of duty-free Glenlivet three-quarters gone. McCabe and I were offered a meagre finger each in hotel toothmugs.

'During the discussion that followed Swivel took notes, in a small hard-backed notebook. He did not use shorthand. Lawyers learn to take very complete notes in longhand. I felt I should be careful, anything I said was being taken down, and …'

'I think I should fill you in on what has happened since we last met,' said Clemann – leaning forward over his knees so his face, with his large glasses framed in black, rocked between McCabe's and Roberto's in a way that Roberto found too close for comfort. 'Briefly, aware as I am that Señora González would like us to think that she has put us in a privileged position because of her relationship with Steve, and her knowledge through the last set of negotiations with Señora Montiam of his connection and friendship with me, and that this privilege has a limited date set to it, I used my influence with, and knowledge of, Spanish finance to make contact with the owners of the *ABC* tapes during the afternoon and evening of Saturday, although of course business houses were officially closed.'

The brisk but complex way this was put indicated to Roberto a little more what sort of man Clemann was. Not a fool, except in so far as he believed that those he paid would respond with the sort of intelligence he had to whatever he said.

'I asked them to release ten minutes of their tape so we could use it as a sample in an electronic voice test. Late on Saturday evening I received a very firm refusal. Henry was about to give his assessment of this when you arrived.' He swung his head towards the fat lawyer. 'Perhaps you'd like to take it on from there.'

'Sure.' Swivel was smoking a small cheroot and he now ground the end in the glazed pottery ashtray that bore the arms of the nineteenth-century Bourbon prince whose palace the hotel had once been. He spoke with an accent that very nicely blended Swiss-German with American law school. 'There was no way the owners of the ABC tapes would let you use a sample in that way...'

Clemann: 'I did not mean them to know how it would be used. I just offered a large sum for a small sample.'

Cockburn: 'That's not exactly how it was. I was the one on the blower. First they refused outright. Then I offered the top fee you would be prepared to pay. They came back three hours later and suggested that we wanted the tape so we could compare it with other tape. I have to say, I believe they had somehow found out why you, we, wanted that sample. I suspect that my denial was half-hearted.'

Roberto thought: So the street beating and the Marqués of Boltana happened because of Cockburn's clumsiness.

Swivel, meanwhile: 'So. As I said. No way would they give you a sample. Consider. If the voice test proved your tapes the same as theirs, they are blown. Yours are far more sensational, you'd take the market, no one would buy the ABC tapes once yours were out.'

Clemann: 'They don't know ours are more sensational.'

Cockburn: 'Not ours yet.'

'Anyway,' said Swivel, 'they'd sense competition they had no reason to welcome. On the other hand, if the analysis showed a mismatch the way would be open for you to say yours were the right ones and theirs the forgery. All of you heard some of the tape ABC now has. Or the people ABC are fronting for. You say the quality of recording was awful. On grounds of voice alone there was no way of asserting they were authentic. There was background noise, hiss, distortion. It could have been Charlie Chaplin doing the Great Dictator.' He lit another cheroot taken from a tin with a picture of Tom Thumb on it and blew a cloud of new smoke through the layers about his head. 'OK. You accepted their authenticity, and so did the ABC buyers. For why? Because Nini Montiam's credentials were impeccable, and because the content fitted. McCabe here was sent transcriptions and he agreed the content...'

McCabe nodded slow agreement.

'Now, however, you have a set of tapes, one of which at any rate dates from the same period as the first ones, but a very good quality recording, the voice apparently accurate, and the content though sensational, apparently credible. At least not to be thrown out of court. If, as I say, there was a mismatch, and no foolproof scientific evidence available, and if it came to a legal dispute, the owners of the *ABC* tapes might well lose. And for sure they'd have to spend a lot of money. And, too, they know that for as long as Clemann is buying the second tapes, there is an awful lot of money if he chooses to use it to go on fighting court cases for ever. No. No way are *ABC* going to lend you sample tape for comparative analysis. No way.'

Clemann turned to Herzer.

'Is there anyone else we can get an authentic sample from?'

Herzer leaned forward and her glasses swung beneath her chest. She clasped her fingers in front of them and made brisk double-fisted gestures. To Roberto it seemed as if she had managed somehow to unsex herself.

'Not easy,' she said. 'The regime that ousted Perón in '55 tried to destroy the Perón myth. All recordings of his speeches, together with a mass of other material, were destroyed or hidden. The recent stuff is controlled by Isabelita. She is not going to release anything without very firm assurances that it can't be used in any way to damage Peronismo or her.' She recrossed her ankles. 'But there are agencies and privately run archives – firms that keep sound, video and film stock to hire out. I know of a couple that might have some Perón and one is in Barcelona. They know me. I'll be in touch with them first thing in the morning.'

'That sounds hopeful,' said Clemann.

Swivel shook his big head morosely.

'I don't see it,' he said. 'ABC or whoever is behind them are on to you now. They'll have leverage in Barcelona. Any firm, any private firm that has Perón tapes will be strongly pressured to deny it for the next few weeks – you'll see. You should have gone to the libraries first, not alerted ABC.'

Cockburn, his arm up on the high-backed chair, said: 'So. We're back with our experts. At least that's what it looks like. And if we don't buy by the end of the week González will go elsewhere, and I don't see us getting a voice test off the ground by then.'

They all looked at Roberto and McCabe, neither of whom seemed ready to say anything. Then McCabe cleared his throat: 'If you mean you want us to give a guaranteed certificate of authenticity or an equally firm thumbs down, then I for one, and I think Señor Fairrie agrees with me, I am just not going to be able to do that.'

Cockburn was insistent – face serious, dark eyes intent: 'But surely the more you hear, the more certain either way you can become.'

'Oh sure. Give us a matter of some hours, preferably listening to the lot, and I reckon I could then give a pretty definite assurance one way or the other. Pretty definite, and subject only to being proved wrong by an objective scientific test. You see, when the chips are down, it's content that counts. Could a forger go on for some hours without dropping into some crass and entirely provable error? I doubt it.'

'Señor Fairrie?'

'Up to a point, Mr Cockburn, Steve, I agree with Professor McCabe. I'm not too sure though about his emphasis on fact. Apart from anything else Perón was an inveterate liar. If there were no lies at all in the tapes, then I might doubt them quite seriously.'

McCabe was edgy: 'There's fact and fact, content and content. I accept what you say about Perón's veracity. What I shall be looking out for rather more carefully is little errors about *him*. For instance in that last extract we heard him apparently light a cigarette. But was he a smoker?'

While Roberto was still reacting, McCabe cut him off and went on: 'Yes, he was. Fine. But if he had not been a smoker, then those tapes were blown. That's really the sort of content I'm looking for all the time. And that's why I want to hear a heck of a lot more tape.'

Clemann: 'Steve. Do you think González will go along with that – give McCabe and Fairrie a chance to hear the lot? Eight cassettes, supposing them to be fully used C90s is twelve hours plus, leave alone the spool-to-spool stuff, which could be recorded double for all we know.'

Cockburn shrugged. 'We can but try. But there will be problems with the bank. I suspect they might not like us taking out squatters' rights on their vault.'

'She could try asking them to let her use it after hours. Or she could take the goddamn things out and play them here or at her flat. I would pay for some goons to guard them.' Clemann suddenly stretched his arms above his head, then stood up. Coming from a low chair in a small room, Roberto thought the process would go on for ever. The tall American exile moved through the chairs to a marble mantelpiece above what was now a filled-in fireplace with an electric fire. He turned, rested his elbows on the high shelf, and looked down at them all. 'I think that's as far as we can go tonight. Becky. Tomorrow morning you use the phone here on my account to get round any of those agencies or archives you think might have tape. Steve, you get González to give us a proper audition of a substantial section of tape. Professor, Señor Fairrie, Cockburn will be in touch with you as soon as he's fixed that up. Your fees are a hundred dollars for the first hour and a further hundred for every part of an hour thereafter. Henry will pay you cash at the end of every session. At the end of the whole business, whatever the outcome, you give him a digest of your expenses with receipts for bills above twenty dollars.

'Now. I want you all to understand that my initial reaction to these tapes remains the same. The set-up stinks. On the question of their authenticity I fear both our experts have got it a bit wrong, and Henry has got it right...'

Swivel smirked.

'...If I buy a Monet, I don't go to Clark or whoever, I check out the provenance, a family tree of who owned the picture right back to Claude's studio. So. Steve, you have to go back to González on this question too, with Henry, and tell her she comes clean about provenance, and title, before we move a step further. As Henry says, the provenance of the *ABC* tapes is impeccable. That for these has to be at least as good. She's said she wants money before she reveals provenance. OK. The first thing that happens is this. She explains the provenance to us, to all of us. If our experts agree it looks good, then, there and then Henry gives her $2,000 and we go ahead and hear more tape. If our experts don't like her story, then we give her $1,000 for the trouble we've caused her and we all go home. Henry, I leave it to you to set this up, with Steve liaising between you and González, or whatever representative she chooses to appoint. I imagine we might meet again at this stage the Gunter character you told me about.

'But even if provenance looks good, I'm still not at all sure we shall be able to publish. Clearly a lot of people are going to go to considerable lengths to stop publication. And I am absolutely not interested in the tapes for any other reason than to publish.

'Worst of all, it all feels to me that Señora González is using us precisely in the same way as we were used before – using our interest and the clout of my money to jack up the price to buyers already in the market.

'So. Unless our experts agree on the authenticity of these tapes, and unless we are satisfied as to their provenance and González's title to them, by two o'clock Wednesday when the banks close, I'll be on the evening plane back to Geneva. Right. Any brief comment or questions?'

McCabe cleared his throat. 'I find your consultancy fee fine in itself. But I do not take it that you expect for that for me to be on call in Madrid until this affair is settled.'

'I do. You want a retainer fee? Five hundred dollars a week.'

'For the first week. After that...

'Professor, I pay people to bargain for me. See Henry about it. But I would suggest you recall that I do not intend to be in Madrid beyond Friday. Señor Fairrie. Do you want a retainer?'

Roberto thought, then said: 'No. But I should like you to understand that I entirely accept the importance of provenance; if Señora González can convince me in that respect, I shall feel far readier to endorse the tapes.'

Becky Herzer unharnessed her spectacles and folded them away into a soft leather purse: 'Of course. Señor Fairrie is right. It is the question I asked at the first meeting at the bank. Where did these tapes come from?'

Swivel closed his notebook, snapped an elastic band over it. All stood up, stretched, brushed off tobacco ash, bumped into each other. Cockburn held the door open for McCabe and Roberto. 'I'll see you to the door. Organise a taxi.'

In the lift he went on: 'I don't think you should take too seriously Peter's threats about pushing off on Wednesday. Pepita is pressing him. So he's pressing back. Standard business practice.' He asked where they could be found the next morning. McCabe would stay indoors at his hotel, the Wellington. What else was a retainer for? Roberto was going to the National Library in the morning. But first he would phone in between ten and eleven to see what was happening.

18

Roberto had a large Mahou beer and a toasted ham and cheese sandwich at the Nebraska in Hortaleza to celebrate the increase to his exchequer. As he came out into the cold, frosty, starry night he could see beneath the street lights Richard Nixon and his wife coming down the pavement towards him.

Tricky Dicky was in front, walking briskly, head down, with thinning sleeked black hair, the nose swinging like an ant-eater's, almost, it seemed, sensing the scraps in the gutter. His wife, on high heels, clacked behind and was screaming at him in furious Spanish...

'It's always the same. You take on too much. You're a fucking Utopian. A Quixote. When you run out of giants, you look for Turks. It was crazy to do this at this time. I'm through. If you think I'm staying...'

Nixon stopped in front of Roberto.

'Roberto? You shouldn't be on the streets at this time of night. They're not safe.'

Ramón pulled the nose off, rolled it into a ball, took his friend's elbow. Nixon's face, with Ramón's nose.

Mrs Nixon came up on Roberto's other side, pulled off the ash-blond wig, revealed Juan Evita's sleek, short, black hair.

'What happened?' Roberto asked. 'I did not expect you home so soon.'

'Fucking police raided us,' cried Juan Evita. 'Just before the end of the first performance. Paulino bundled us out through the window of the ladies' toilet, as the pigs came in the front.' He stopped, twisted, lifted his skirt. '*And* one of my stockings has run. Ramón, you'll pay for this. You really are a silly, silly cunt.'

'You didn't have to...'

'Didn't have to? No. I said I wouldn't. But that wasn't enough. You pleaded. You wept. And silly cow that I am, I gave in. But that's it. I'm through now.'

They swung into Desengaño and Juan Evita's foot twisted on the kerb.

'Shit and fucking hell!' He hobbled, stooped, plucked off his shoes and trotted after them, skirts swinging, beads clacking, catching them as they turned into the *pensión* entrance.

'You know, Ramón, I could brain you with these shoes. I could have your balls off...'

Ramón turned on the stairs.

'Jesus, Evita. Shut up. Go home. Piss off. I've heard enough.'

'Go home? In these rags? Just let me remind you there's a law against female impersonation in this arsehole of a city. I've got clothes up there and I'm going to change into them, and then take everything else you've got of mine, what you haven't sold in the Rastro...'

Smack.

Ramón hit him. Not very hard, but very definitely a very significant gesture. For a moment their eyes blazed at each other, seething with energy and emotion, then they went on up the stairs with Roberto panting behind.

'I went to my room, Ramón stood in the kitchen doorway, Juan Evita stormed about in Ramón's room banging drawers and then the wardrobe in the hall. The one I've pulled in front of the outside door...'

'Don't expect me back. I've left the dress and wigs and all that crap. But I've taken everything that's really mine.' He hesitated for a moment, perhaps waiting for Ramón to climb down, apologise for the slap, take responsibility for the whole scene. But Ramón, still for the most part Richard Nixon, glowered above the cigarette he'd lit. Juan Evita turned on his heeled boot and the flares of his low-slung trousers swung like a flamenco dancer's. He went.

Ramón stubbed his cigarette on a dirty plate and went to his room.

Roberto waited a moment and then followed him in. Ramón was sitting at his mirrored table cleaning Nixon off his face. Already the toupee had gone revealing his *en brosse* grey hair with the hairline shaved back to match that of the ex-President. His eyes watered – with sadness, not the peeling away of gum arabic.

'He's right, Roberto. Not only female impersonation, but also impersonation of the head of a friendly state even when he is a crook, a war criminal, and no longer head of state. And this is not the time to be in a Spanish jail on charges that smack of deviance and dissidence. I should never have done this act. And I certainly should not have dragged him into it.'

'I think you worry too much about Evita.'

'Not so. I still have a Spanish passport. But he, like you, can be deported. And in Argentina he may be wanted as a Montonero. And that means death. The Pinochets are taking over. Have you heard of General Videla?'

'Of course.'

'When Isabelita goes, he'll be in. And it will be worse than Chile. Anyway. How did it go with you?'

'All right. There's a problem or two, but nothing we can't deal with.' Roberto's voice was a touch plaintive. 'We thought this might happen, you remember?'

Cotton wool tossed into the tin waste-paper basket. 'I need a wash.'

Ramón got up, went to the bathroom, peeled off his shirt, dipped his head above the running taps. Roberto stood behind him. Ramón scrubbed at his face and swilled. The gas-heater banged and flared, and the fumes swung round them. Then he grabbed a threadbare towel, dried face, neck, hairy forearms.

'And I need a rest. I'm upset, you know?'

'Of course.'

'Tomorrow, eh? After all it seems I'm out of work again. In the morning, if you like.'

'In the morning. Later if you like. I'll leave you a draft, we can work on it in the evening. There's time.'

Ramón turned, patted Roberto on the shoulder, went through to his own room. Then called: 'Oh yes. Before Evita and I started shouting at each other he told me something you ought to know. You won't like it though.'

Roberto came to his door. Ramón was already on his bed looking up through the smoke of the cigarette he'd lit.

'La Aguja. Francisco Xavier Betelmann. And Don Martín. You know, so far eight people have died trying to prove Don Martín is alive and well and living in Argentina. Or Paraguay. Or Chile. Or wherever.

And three of those times La Aguja, the Needle, was there or there-abouts. That's the gossip anyway. The sort of gossip Evita hears.' He stubbed out the cigarette, turned on the tiny unmade bed so the springs rang, pulled up the covers, and reached for the light switch.

Roberto went to his own room, but heard Ramón call: 'And he's fat, middle-aged, and wears spectacles.' Nevertheless, he pulled paper towards him and began to write, quickly, with confidence, only occa-sionally pausing to check with a reference book. Like many Spanish and Hispanic brain-workers he did his best work between midnight and two in the morning, and, provided he did not have to get up too early, felt none the worse for it.

19

PLAY AND RECORD:

'The next morning at about half-past ten I phoned the Príncipe and was told by Cockburn that hitches had occurred. Herzer was trying to find sample tape, had had no luck with the Barcelona firm, and, more important, González had said there was no question of playing the tapes that day. She was booked, he said, to give another prospective buyer a hearing. Clemann, far from pleased, had agreed to attend, with his experts, on the morrow at noon, on condition that she revealed the provenance of her tapes and established title under terms agreed between them.

'I confess this was a relief in a way. After so much excitement I was ready to spend a relaxing day at the Biblioteca with Marañon's biog-raphy of Antonio Pérez. But of course that sort of plan or expectation never falls out. First, when I got off the Metro at Colón, I suffered a disagreeable experience.

'The Colón station is a terrible mess at the moment, because of the massive alterations going on both above and below ground. To get from the platforms to the surface one has to brave long, narrow tunnels with board walls, the infernal racket of construction machinery, and the rudeness of harassed officials and overstretched workmen.

'The boarded walls are an irresistible temptation to the agitprop activists of both left and right, and on one corner I found myself jammed in a small knot of people watching a young girl and boy, students perhaps, aerosoling out a message from the *Partido Español Nacional Socialistica* much decorated with swastikas which they clev-erly and neatly converted into the Anarchist 'A' in a circle. But then there was a clattering of boots down the long passage and four or five hooligans burst through us – I received a savage blow in my still bruised and painful chest. They were ruthless and the scene was ugly. I hurried as well as I could up the slopes and steps to the chill daylight but the screams of the girl, amplified by the passages, almost drowned out the machine-gun fire of masonry drills, rang in my ears for most of the rest of the morning.

'I was ashamed too. Twenty, thirty years ago when that sort of incident occurred, I was not afraid to join in, and was sometimes beaten for my pains. This time I lacked even the courage to report the incident to a pair of Policia Armada who stood at the exit to the Metro. Not that that would have done much good. Probably they would have added arrest and another beating to what those brave children had already suffered.

'The library was warm and a temporary comfort. After negotiating the tedious checks and double-checks I at last reached the reading-room – a pleasant hall, well but not garishly lit, decorated in cream marble and with bronze embellishments on the cases and reading lights, and they kept me waiting for less than twenty minutes before the book was brought to me.

'The tale, however, now lacked charm. Antonio Pérez had fallen from favour through his connection with the disastrous Princess of Eboli, was a wanderer now through Henry IV's Béarn, Elizabeth's England, and Paris – an ageing man without glamour or influence, constantly afraid of assassination from his old master Philip II. Philip III turned out to be no better. Not long before he died he refused to see a fashionable rope-dancer, saying: "I have danced on the rope myself, and I have seen dancers fall to the ground with their limbs broken. I broke my back at it, there is too much danger and I am afraid." It all reminded me too vividly of my own situation, and at a little after midday I decided after all to go for a walk. Since the Bank of the Victory of the Angels is scarcely six blocks from the library it is not surprising that I found myself in its vicinity...'

Anyone observing Roberto's progress from the library to the bank, and there were in fact two men following him, would have detected nothing casual in his movements. He walked directly and briskly and only when he came in sight of the bank did uncertainty creep into his manner. For a time he hovered between two small plane trees, hung about the newspaper kiosk but did not buy anything, and finally walked fifty metres or so to a bus-stop where he waited, though he did not board the buses when they came. He remained there for over twenty minutes until at about ten to one a small party appeared on the steps of the bank. They included Señora González, Enrico Gunter, two middle-aged men in dark overcoats, and Becky Herzer. González and Gunter turned up the street, away from Roberto, towards González's apartment. Herzer and the two men in overcoats came towards Roberto but stopped fifteen metres before the bus-stop in front of a Mercedes and a Renault 12 with French number plates parked in echelon. The men shook hands briefly with Herzer and let themselves into the Mercedes. Herzer stooped, with her key feeling for the door of the Renault, straightened, face pale and blank, then suddenly smiling.

'Señor Roberto?' She came towards him. 'What brings you here?'

He explained: he had been to the library, felt he had needed a change and had gone out for a walk, found the air more chill than he had expected, and was now waiting for a bus to take him back to the city centre where he had some shopping to do.

'A coincidence, merely?'

'Hardly. The library is very close.'

She laughed. 'Come. I was curious too, so why not admit it yourself? When Steve told me Señora González was entertaining further prospective buyers this morning, I discovered an urgent need to change some traveller's cheques.'

Her candour was disarming, the openness of her smile, creasing the soft brown skin round her eyes and wide mouth, enchanting. She had dropped the severe, executive appearance of the previous evening, was dressed in a long brown soft leather coat, with fur-topped boots that reached almost to its hem. Her near-white short hair was fluffed up beneath a Balmain scarf, and her cheeks glowed – with the cold after the warmth of the bank, perhaps.

'Don't you want to hear what I discovered? Of course you do. Well. The answer is… not much.' She laughed again. 'Of course it was embarrassing. They came up from the vault just as the cashier was giving me my pesetas. Nothing for it but to face it out. Introductions. Not all necessary, for I already know one of the men. I can give you a lift to Sol if you like.'

She unlocked the Renault, leant across to release the catch on the passenger's door. Inside Roberto was immediately conscious of the sharp and faintly feline pungency of her perfume. As she reversed the car into the carriageway she twisted to look over her shoulder and her face came very close to Roberto's. The sudden intimacy quite shook him. No doubt at all, she was a very attractive woman, and her age was an irrelevance.

'Well. Surely you wish me to tell you who he was?'

He agreed awkwardly that yes, though it really was no concern of his, it would be interesting to know.

'His name is Franz Rudel – I believe a connection of the *Luftwaffe* ace – and he is a banker in a house that has a lot of South American business. Clearly he knows Gunter well.'

'And the other?'

'Him I did not know previously. Herr Adler.'

She coped with the Madrid lunch-time rush-hour traffic competently, even competitively.

'If I have this Adler placed properly in my mind he has a Bolivian passport.'

Roberto surreptitiously felt for the tissues still stuck in his top pocket and wiped perspiration from his palms. 'How do you know all this? All this about people like that?'

She shrugged without taking her eyes off the road. 'I am what Steve calls an international media person, you know? At bottom I am a journalist. I have been around a long time and it is the sort of area I specialise in. I think we should talk a little longer if you are not in a hurry. The shops will be open for a little longer yet.'

'All right.'

She turned down the Paseo del Prado, took a left turn, and parked near the Naval Museum. As always her movements were brisk, decisive, efficient. He was disappointed though when she shook out a cigarette and lit it with her tortoiseshell lighter.

'I cannot understand' – smoke streamed from her nostrils – 'why such people should be interested in the Perón tapes.'

'I suppose because of the bit about Bormann coming to visit him after his return to power.'

'Perhaps. But the rest… poof! Oh, it's all very interesting, perhaps will sell, make us all, as Steve would say, a bob or two. But I cannot see why people like Rudel and Adler should be here. Unless of course it is not the Perón tapes they are interested in. There are five cassettes that have nothing to do with Perón, according to Señora González. What is on those tapes, Señor Fairrie? I am sure you know.'

'No, indeed I do not.'

'You surprise me. For I think you know more about these tapes than you are prepared to say. Is that not the case?'

'No, really, Madame Herzer. You do me an injustice. I am simply, fortuitously, an acquaintance of Cockburn's, and I happen to be the expert on Perón he needed in Madrid.'

'So he says. So you say. But, forgive… you are hardly known widely as such. You are though known amongst the older generation of South American exiles as a staunch, indeed devout socialist, anti-fascist and life-long opponent of the Peróns.'

This was all said lightly, even teasingly. Roberto was able to shrug off any implication that he had been less than frank.

'That is entirely true,' he said, 'and I have made it my business, the business of a lifetime, to understand what I so strongly oppose. I really doubt if anyone knows as much about the Peróns as I do. Not even the egregious Professor McCabe.'

She laughed. 'All right, Señor Fairrie, I must believe you. Now. Shall I take you to Puerta del Sol?'

'Please.'

Once there he groped for the catch on the door, could not find it, and she reached across him, her shoulder brushing his chest, her hair his cheek, and he felt again the sharp urgency of desire.

As she straightened she said: 'And you really do know nothing of these five extra cassettes?'

'Nothing. I assure you.'

This was said with entire frankness…

'Rudel and Adler. Adler – what did Evita call him? A top Nazi. It was the third warning. Dear Lord, I should have realised then, my very hormones, glands, whatever, if not my addled reason, were telling me. I was frightened when I got out of Becky's car. Very frightened. And with good cause, dear Lord, with good cause…'

20

At twelve o'clock the following day, Wednesday, they were all again in the vault of the Banco de la Victoria de los Angeles. All – Señora González had Enrico Gunter with her; Clemann had Cockburn, Herzer and Swivel in tow; and the experts – McCabe and Roberto. It made the room very crowded, extra chairs had been brought in. The cadaverous manager was clearly edgy about it. The most he would allow them was the hour and a half to closing time, and if any other customer wanted to use the vault during that time then they would have to clear out and move back later.

González, not in black this time, but in dark green wild silk with black star sapphires at her neck and in her ears, looked round them all slowly, fixing her gaze on Clemann with eyes that picked up the colour of her dress.

'First,' she said, 'you want provenance. I have agreed terms with Mr Swivel. Four thousand dollars now, in cash, if our experts are happy with what I say, and nothing at all if they are not. You have the money here?'

'Er, yes.' Swivel shifted uneasily, tapped a black document case that stood on the floor at his side.

'Señor Fairrie. As one of the two entirely independent people here, will you check the case for me?'

Roberto, surprised, but pleased to be singled out, stood up. The operation was not easy. Swivel had fastened the case to himself with a thin but clearly serviceable tungsten chain, and the keys to the case and chain were in the trouser pocket on the same side. Embarrassed, as embarrassed as Swivel himself, Roberto retrieved them. The case was opened.

'Señora, the money is here. I am not of course qualified to assess...'

Clemann was angry. 'Come *on*. This will not do. I am not the sort of person to give short change or pass forged bills.'

'Of course not.' González was soothing. 'Well then.' She paused while Swivel and Roberto returned to base. 'Well then. Provenance. You have already heard in this room the name López Rega mentioned. Someone described him as a member of the Perón entourage. He was a lot more than that. Perhaps Professor McCabe would like to tell us just who José López Rega was.'

'Me? Sure. Yes. Why not?' McCabe snapped shut his notebook, passed a mottled hand across his thinning hair, recrossed his legs. 'Yes indeed. He was far more than that. Really I don't know where to begin.'

Clemann: 'Keep it short. Just what is relevant.'

'Right.' McCabe made a church of his finger tips, thought for a moment, then: 'José López Rega was a police corporal, and for a time one of Perón's bodyguards during the second presidency. After the ouster of '55 he disappeared from the scene. Apparently he resigned the police force, and attempted to make a living as a spiritualist, a medium, that sort of thing. Then in 1966 Isabelita, Perón's third wife, now the President, went to Argentina...'

'Sixty-five.'

'Yes?'

Roberto insisted: 'She left here in '65, came back in '66.'

'Yes, yes. You're right. Anyway. While she was in Buenos Aires this López Rega got on to her staff as a baggage-handler, bodyguard, that sort of thing, and she brought him back here. Somehow or other, some would say by occult means, he gained a very complete ascendancy over her, and, either on his own account or through her, over Perón as well. Before they left here, he, López Rega, was running the household. He was nicknamed "Daniel", and was also known as El Brujo – the Wizard, the Warlock. When Perón came to power again in Argentina, López Rega was given various cabinet posts, including Commissioner General of Police. When Perón died and Isabelita, as elected Vice-President, automatically took over, El Brujo's power and influence became enormous. He embarked on a purge of the Peronist left, including the Montoneros, using a para-police force of death gangs called the Triple A. But he upset the right too. Probably because sensible government, government which would allow the ordinary continuance of business, was impossible with him around. July this year the generals felt strong enough to throw him out – though Isabelita's popularity with the unions left her safe still. He came to Madrid. Was seen here I believe. Then disappeared.' His long fingers fluttered like prehistoric birds, then flopped to his thighs. 'In a nutshell that's José López Rega, known as Daniel and El Brujo. Any questions?'

Silence.

Clemann: 'Thank you, McCabe. Neatly succinct. Señora?'

González shifted on her chair which sighed.

'Yes. Very succinct. And accurate. He was a very strange man. In some ways a buffoon, a fool... but occasionally impressive things happened at his... behest. He had... hypnotic eyes.' She shuddered, looked up, above their heads, then at them, and smiled. 'Since 1968 I was quite intimate with the household, and I met Daniel often. It was therefore natural that he should come to me four months ago. He was frightened. With cause. But he had insurance. He thought. He gave me these tapes, told me to put them in this vault. He paid me a quite large sum. The understanding was that, should anyone ask me if he had given me these tapes, I should say that he had, and say how they were stored here. He hoped this would deter his enemies. I believe he was over-sanguine. I have not seen or heard of him since the third of August this year. I now believe him to be dead.'

Silence. Swivel again: 'Even if he is dead, this does not amount to title to these tapes.'

González delved in a soft leather purse that matched her dress. 'I think this does.' She read from a small piece of notepaper. '"In the event of my death, or in the event of my failure to communicate with the manager of the Velázquez branch of the Bank of the Victory of the Angels on the tenth of two succeeding months, the contents of my deposit box in that bank and control of that box shall pass absolutely and without prejudice to Josefina González, whom the manager of the said bank will identify. Signed, José López Rega, at the bank, and in the presence of the manager and Señora González, this fifteenth day of July, 1975." Now, gentlemen, Señora,' – a slight bow towards Herzer – 'you may dispute the authenticity of this document if you like. But the manager of the bank does not.'

Slowly Clemann tapped one finger on the low arm of his chair. Then he looked up, first at McCabe, then at Roberto.

'Well, gentlemen.'

McCabe cleared his throat again. 'López Rega brought you eight tapes. Five spool-to-spool. Three cassettes. And he said these were all recorded by Perón.'

'Yes.'

'Did he bring any other tapes?'

'Yes.'

'What were they?'

'You are going to bid for them?' Before he could answer she shook her head abruptly. 'Yes, Professor, he brought the five other tapes in the box, but as I said before, they have nothing to do with... at any rate they were not recorded by Perón, and they do not concern the present circumstances. As of now they are not for sale. Please forget them.'

No one but Roberto noticed how Gunter's body had gone rigid – like a large cat surprised by an unidentified noise, he was suddenly wary.

'To the point please, McCabe. Do you believe this account of the provenance of the Perón tapes with which we are concerned?'

'If the manager of the bank accepts that piece of paper, then, yes, I accept it.'

Swivel: 'There is still a very large question mark.'

'Yes?'

'Señora González has unlimited access to this deposit box. OK. Maybe once López Rega's tapes were in it. They don't have to be now. Or others could have been added...'

'That,' said Cockburn, speaking for the first time, 'surely brings us back to the real reason for our presence here. Let us accept González had tapes from López Rega. We can't seriously challenge that. Nor can we challenge the possibility that López Rega had access to tapes recorded by Perón. We are back where we started. All that remains is the authenticity of the tapes she proposes to sell to us. *Let's hear some more tape.*' He emphasised the last sentence.

Clemann: 'Señor Fairrie?'

But Roberto seemed to have drifted into another world: right elbow on the chair arm, cheek supported on his hand, he was staring with fixed, worried intensity at a point in the *Victory of the Angels* slightly above Señora González's gorgeous head.

'Señor Fairrie. Please.'

'Eh? Ah. Yes?'

'What do you think of Señora González's account of the provenance of her tapes?'

The glazed look leaked out of his eyes, then he pulled his body back into the chair, sat upright.

'Yes. I go along with what, er, she has said.' His voice became firmer. 'Knowing some of the background, the character of López Rega and so on, I am convinced of the provenance of these tapes, that is that Señora González's account of how she came by them is accurate. But their authenticity is still in doubt. López Rega himself might have arranged a forgery.'

'Right,' Clemann sighed. 'Henry, you may give Señora González her money. Señora, we are ready to hear what you have to play us today.' He looked at his watch. 'I fear that the manager will not give us more than another hour, so we had better get on with it.'

21

González chose one of the spool-to-spool tapes and again called on Roberto to set it up. The voice was more vivacious and energetic than on the ones they had heard earlier, more confident, more public, but the quality of the recording was poor: there was background noise, traffic, a bell that tolled the hours and the angelus.

'I got back from Europe at a moment when as usual the political battles were being rigged, the rules fixed to help the oligarchy. The socialists, intellectuals mostly and divorced from the working people they claimed to represent, and the radicals to the right of them, were all determined to maintain legality in the contest for power, and so were hamstrung from the start. I asked myself therefore, what would happen if someone began to fight for real and announced they were going to play to win.

'Nevertheless, my injection of myself into this unclear, turbulent, unresolved situation was not the unprincipled, opportunist action that many of my detractors have claimed it to be. I had learnt much in Italy, I had seen the way fascism, National Socialism, could be made to work to transform society. I had spent many hours in conversation with *Il Duce,* and some of the greatest thinkers in his movement. I had too seen the dangers, the unprincipled and often unnecessary violence, the often unattractively and unnecessarily brutal way of dealing with the Jewish problem, and so on, and I had already thought deeply on these matters. I do not say that the historic formulations of Justicialismo and the Third Position were already clear in my mind, but they were certainly there. I had a vision for my country, for my continent, for the world even, that motivated quite trivial, or laughable actions. I remember how we pulled

President General Rawson to a window of the Casa Rosada and said: We'll throw you out if you don't resign. He resigned.'

The voice chuckled, a little huskily, and then resumed its serious but dynamic note. It went on to expound the theory of Justicialismo, the Third Position, the social contract Perón wanted between the classes and the non-aligned position in foreign policy with a wealth of name-dropping: Popes, world-famous philosophers, senior statesmen of international repute, all agreed with him. It was all done with conviction and disdain for logic. After ten minutes everyone in the room except Señora González, Enrico Gunter, who occasionally nodded in wise agreement, and McCabe, who continued to make notes, began to fidget.

Then suddenly, at the back of the tape, two female voices could be heard. They were, of course, indistinct, but it seemed one voice was welcoming an unexpected visitor who refused coffee and cakes. González pushed the stop button. 'That,' she said, with a sort of modest glee, 'was me. Isabelita welcomed me and suggested we should have coffee together. But I could see that *El Conductor* felt he was doing well and preferred to go on, so I refused.' She smoothed her skirt. 'Eight, no seven years ago. I was still quite pretty then.' Considering the near magnificence of her beauty now, this seemed a silly thing to say.

Indeed the flow went on, the voice becoming more and more pompous and inarticulate. At one point there was a short break, and clearly everyone could hear the clink of glass and the glug of liquid. Meanwhile, in the bank vault, glances were exchanged, eyes raised in mock horror, yawns suppressed.

Roberto looked slowly and carefully at each of them, trying to make some sort of assessment.

Cockburn he spent least time on. He had his number. A whizz-kid on the skids, seeking desperately to re-establish himself in the media world. The opportunity to present and edit the Perón tapes in newspapers, books, magazines, on TV and radio, across the world, was just what was required. He needed the tapes to be authentic, which was probably why he had been clumsy about setting up scientific voice analysis.

Swivel. Not a pretty sight. Plump. Even fat. Sweating and mopping up with a silk handkerchief. And bored to hell. Has reasonable Spanish, it had been said, but probably not up to unravelling the Voice off the cuff as it were. Well, thought Roberto, he's being paid a fee, and there'll be more fees if Clemann makes an offer for the tapes, but law is not like the media. Law is for real and for ever. The Spanish say no one ever saw a dead donkey or a poor lawyer. He'd like the tapes to be real

– still young enough to get a kick out of first-class hotels, first-class flights. But really, he's not bothered.

> 'Of course the Third Position was one of my greatest contributions to the continued existence of the human race. Oh yes. I know it has been scorned by the Western Bloc and rejected by the Communists. But tell me. Would there have been conferences of the non-aligned nations if I had not made my initiative…?'

And Herzer, Becky, she seems withdrawn, intent, preoccupied, has hardly acknowledged my presence. Who is she, anyway? The media person she claims to be? Was she really here yesterday out of curiosity, or is she involved more closely, did she perhaps come *with* Rudel and Adler to hear… what? That damned second lot of tapes? Roberto shook his head, felt tightness in his throat, a creeping sensation at the back of his neck. She is, after all, German Sudeten by birth and fled the Czech revolution of 1948. And how did she get to be here? Cockburn was surprised, annoyed when she turned up the other day. So did the Señora ask her? Possibly. The more keen potential buyers the better. Yet she remains an enigma. And enigmas frighten me.

> 'That this concept, the Third Position, solidly based in the philosophical tradition of Justicialismo, was never properly understood was entirely to be expected. Though, of course, at the time, I was too optimistic, too thoroughly convinced of the wisdom of the human race, of the workers – my *decamisados* – of the intellectuals, to realise I stood no chance of persuading the world that I had been granted, *gratia Dei*, a vision of the salvation of civilisation. What I had realised was how deeply implanted pure self-interest is in those of us who lack the gifts of seeing beyond…'

That, thought Roberto, was a shade over the top. And there's that bell again. Have we been listening to this bombast for a full half-hour? González, Gunter and Clemann appear to be almost asleep. A moment of fear! Is there proper ventilation? Did the architects envisage so many people shut in the vault for so long? Are we all suffocating? Roberto yawned, and the yawn spread round them.

Gunter, Enrico Gunter. Stocky, solid, well-kept body – probably the Señora finds that very attractive at her age. Beautiful women in their thirties, of uncertain means, don't want penniless, spindly adolescents. They want solidity and experience. And wealth. And

Gunter is wealthy. His shoes alone must cost ten thousand pesetas. So what's he doing here? Is he really just doing the Señora a favour, looking after the business side for her, making sure Swivel doesn't pull a fast one? Or is there more to it than that? In arms' manufacture. Astra in Madrid, Beretta in Italy, factories in the Argentine. With a name like that, in that business, he has to be in with people like Rudel and Adler and the Argentinian Nazis. And he really took note when she said those five extra tapes came from López Rega. What the devil are those five extra tapes? Did López Rega really bring them? Are *they* the great attraction, not this Perón *stuff* at all? Gunter frightens me. He can smile, slash with lethal claws, and smile again. His eyes tell you that. And I am frightened because there is more going on here than I know about.

Clemann. An oddity, a freak. His disconcerting height, his with-drawnness, but too his occasional flashes of toughness. When he says 'go', people go, when he says 'come', they come. No doubt seventy million dollars are a consideration, but it's the personality that does it. Mind you, thought Roberto, the personality must owe something to the fortune. It's like the British Queen. You're born to it. Like Juan Carlos...? We'll have to see. And he gave a little shudder at the thought of what the next few days would mean. One thing. I am not about to be deported during this period – every policeman of every police force in Spain, and every connected bureaucrat is going to have his hands full elsewhere, once they pull the plugs on that bag of shit in the La Paz clinic...

A buzz near the armoured door and a light above it flashed. Gunter leant forward and tapped the recorder into silence, stood up, went to the intercom by the door, tapped another button. The manager's voice. A customer wanted to use her safe. Everybody out.

They rose, stretched, sighed, grunted – generally the feeling was of relief. Ushered, no, herded up into the main hall of the bank they stood around awkwardly while a small lady dressed very expensively in lace-edged black, chiming and glittering with jewellery, was bowed by the now obsequious manager down the deeply carpeted stairs beneath the chandelier.

Cockburn, already smoking, suggested: 'A countess at least. Checking up her tiara is *in situ.*' He offered González a cigarette.

'Thank you, I prefer my own.' She gestured to Gunter, who flashed a gold case on a level with her very slightly plump tummy. She breathed out smoke – very strong Virginian. 'Actually she is a dowager marquess, and a very good neighbour of mine.

Cockburn looked mortified, as well he might, thought Roberto. Was he not, had he not too been Pepa's lover, as well as Gunter? And today she was making it very plain that of the two of them she favoured the Argentinian entrepreneur...

STOP.

With hands blue with cold, Roberto lifted the headphones off the close-cropped white hair of his head, pulled the jack from the radio and let Mozart's Requiem, which had followed the Eroica, sound out loud and clear. He rummaged in his clothes suitcase for a second pair of socks, found only dirty ones but pulled them on, padded out again to his icy kitchen. For a time he contemplated the double gas ring and its rubber tube that led to a red gas container. Could he dismantle it all and then get it together in his room without either blowing himself up or losing the use of the gas ring? Probably not. He could move the tape-recorder into the kitchen and turn on the gas where it was. But better not. It smelled, gave off fumes, there was something wrong with the burners. Anyway, in the kitchen he was too near La Aguja... He looked down and across the *patio de luces,* at the window opposite. Still no sign. But that meant nothing. Best of all to put up with the cold and go on giving himself hot drinks.

He waited for the saucepan to boil and remembered how he had stopped listening to all the junk about Justicialismo and had tried to make up his mind about them all. Since then there had been betrayal and two murders. And at least one of them... dear Lord, let it not be Becky. Dear Lord, let it not be Pepa, Pepita.

Tea this time. Coffee could produce a bowel movement. Back, then, to Mozart. At least with the phones on, I can't hear those damned guns and that awful bell.

Sunny morning, now the fog's gone, but not sunny enough to be warm. If no cloud builds up I should get direct sunlight in at about half-past ten.

Outside?

Lord. A tank.

Roberto clutched his heart as the spasm of shock and fear surged through his torso. He'd forgotten he'd heard them in the night. Of course they'd be here, behind the Gran Vía, out of sight but ready to move down if necessary. And also they'd be guarding the Telefónica Building itself. No leather jackets, but that means nothing. They're probably on the landing outside the door, the other side of the wardrobe.

No use dwelling on it. Get back to my memoirs, *apologia pro mea vitae!*. My cleaned-up slate for posterity. Ha! Only thing to do really until... someone comes. And someone will come. No doubt of that at all. La Aguja. With a bare bodkin. Who is behind him? Who betrayed us?

The jack back in the radio. The headphones on. *Agnus dei qui tollit...*

PLAY AND RECORD:

22

Back in the bank, Cockburn had shown signs of impatience. 'Will we have to go on listening to that crap?' he asked. González looked up at him, her eyes serious but mouth in the slightest way possible pursed as if to push back a smile. Momentarily Roberto felt a terrible nostalgia which he instantly suppressed.

'You would like something a little more... sensational?'

'Christ, yes. Something any publisher in his right mind might want to print.'

'We'll have to see what we can find.'

In spite of the differences in their heights she dominated him.

'Here we go,' breathed Swivel, as the door to the vault sighed open. Then he spluttered, turned dreadfully red as he tried to suppress mirth. Indeed of all of them Clemann alone was not amused or mastered the urge to show it.

The lady, the dowager marquesa had removed every scrap of precious metal and precious stone from her head and body, and even the lace edgings and her mantilla.

González's party again descended into the vault. As they did so McCabe, taking up the rear, remarked from on high: 'I noticed too how there were queues at the grocery stores.'

'Eh?' said Swivel. 'I don't get the connection.'

'Really? You *don't?*' McCabe was incredulous.

'Let us see,' said Señora Josefina González, 'if this will amuse Mr Cockburn.'

This time the voice was intimate again, as it had been on one of the earlier tapes.

'The most beautiful thing in the world. Is a young girl. Mind you, she must be fit, though not excessively so, not like those Russian monsters fed on steroids in the Olympic Games, but properly, as a young woman, a girl on the point of becoming a young woman, should be. With a bloom like that on a peach the day before it should be picked. I remember many girls like that. Mind you Eva was never like that. Not while I knew her. Except perhaps after Doctor Ara had finished with her. Nelly Rivas, however, was exemplary. There were others. I remember Pepita then. She's a fine woman now, make no mistake. But Pepita aged fourteen, playing volleyball with Nelly who was a year or so older. How they rose to the net like swallows! And while Nelly did allow a gentleman of a certain age certain very harmless little liberties, Pepita, who did not, had style. An aloofness. Not that she could not be playful if the mood took her, and would if pressed, offer me harmless caresses. She never let me touch her. And she could fence. God, she could fence. She really could use a foil...'

CLICK.

This time Pepita González touched the button, not Gunter. Her face was expressionless as she looked up at Cockburn.
'We can do better than that.'
Recrossing his legs, he shrugged.
'I'm sure you can,' he said.
She ran the tape on for several metres.

CLICK. The voice still intimate.

'Well. She's back. Upstairs. Mario himself brought her back. He took her away. He brought her back. In a van. With two army jeeps as escort. Thank you, Paco...'

CLICK.

Señora González pulled the hem of her green dress over her knees and looked around.
'I can,' she said, 'see puzzled faces. Perhaps as we go along Professor McCabe and Señor Fairrie too if necessary will tell the rest of us what it is all about.'
McCabe looked up from his notebook, set as usual on the high platform of his knee. With the hand that held his gold ballpoint, he pushed a strand of ginger hair across his freckled scalp.
'Frankly, ma'am, I'm as much in the dark as anyone.'
'Señor Fairrie?'
Roberto shrugged.
'Well then, I'll give you a hint. The date of this tape is 22, possibly 23 September, 1972.'
'Yes.' Recall with the scholarly Professor was at last instant. 'I'm with it now.' He looked around. 'At that time Perón, with a small

entourage, was living in a villa in Puerta de Hierra, a select suburb on the north-east boundaries of this city. With him were his third wife Maria Estela Martinez, known always as Isabel or Isabelita, and several other hangers-on, including López Rega, who, we are asked to believe, is the source of these tapes. At that time intense negotiation was under way to arrange Perón's return to Argentina. Civil war threatened. The Peronists were taking over. All that was needed was the return of *El Líder*.

'On 22 September, Eva's embalmed body was flown from Milan, where it had been buried under a false name, to Madrid. It was delivered in the way the voice we have been listening to has described. There's more background I could go into...'

Clemann raised a hand. 'That'll do for now, McCabe.' He made a slight gesture towards González, but was interrupted.

'OK. I'm the thick one,' said Swivel. 'But who is Paco?'

Roberto spoke: 'Francisco Franco. He provided the two army jeeps as escort. Perón's gratitude is expressed, I think, with sarcasm.'

'And Mario?'

Roberto looked blank.

McCabe half-raised a couple of fingers. 'That would be Colonel Mario Cabanillas. In 1956, not long after the ouster that sent Perón on his travels, he became director of Army Information. He discovered Eva's body in a box labelled "Radio Equipment". He sent that too on its travels. There's an interesting story in this connection...'

'Another time, Professor.'

'Surely. But it is a grotesquely interesting story.'

CLICK.

'Upstairs. I really don't know what these people think they are doing to me. Well. They can't know.

'Daniel. El Brujo. Opened the wretched thing. There were five... six, no, seven of us. Two fucking monks! Who asked them? And the room dark, black, just candles. Why? I can't stand all this mystery, this rubbish. But Isabel, she likes it. Black box, candles at each corner. Of course it was sealed. Tight. With a metal seal. You know the sort of thing. Cunningly arranged so however you fiddled the seal the screws that held the hasps in place were masked. What to do?

'Daniel knew what to do. El Brujo. He went down to the garage below and found a blowtorch. One of those things you pump paraffin into under pressure to produce a hot flame. And he melted...'

'Jesus,' said Swivel.

CLICK.

'Yes?' González was impatient.
'They're talking about an embalmed body in a coffin?'
'Yes.'
Swivel shook his head slowly. 'They were crazy.'
'Why?'
'Formaldehyde. Ethyl alcohols. Compressed in a possibly airtight box. Quite simply the embalmed body of Evita could have blown them all to kingdom come.'
'Apparently it did not.'
'I'm not sure I want to hear any more of this,' said Herzer, again clasping her hands in front of her to make the odd chopping gesture.
'You can leave if you want to.'
'I'll stay.'

CLICK.

'...the seal. It hissed, spluttered, became incandescent. Dropped away. Well done, Daniel. Paladino opened the box. It needed a lot of self-control on my part to face the next moment. Twenty years... Well. I looked in. That, I said, is Evita. Mind you her nose was squashed, but Doctor Ara who lives here now, has come over since and put that right. Isabel has given the corpse a wash and a hairdo, and my dear sisters-in-law, Evita's sisters, harpies, are here too with a new shroud, the old one having fared less well than the corpse. They want to put her in a tomb here. No chance. The Montoneros and the lefties who call themselves Peronistas want it in Argentina, and that's where it'll have to go.
'Silveyra was there...

CLICK.

McCabe was brisk. 'Argentinian ambassador to Madrid.'
'And Paladino?'
'Respected politician of the centre-left who was working for Perón's return.'

CLICK.

'...and he told me how she had travelled. It. Asked me to sign a receipt. I did. I had to say something, it was expected. I said: "I spent many happy years with this woman." Ha!'

This time the click was on the tape itself. González let it run and then it came again and the voice.

'They tell me El Brujo has been doing magic. Isabelita lies naked on the coffin and he conjures Evita's spirit into her. As well try to pour a litre of cognac into a half-litre milk bottle.'

CLICK.

'I think,' said González, looking squarely at Cockburn, 'you'll find that printable. In, say, the London *Sunday Times*.'

The buzzer went again. Gunter answered it.

'More clients need access to their strong boxes.'

Clemann unfolded and re-erected himself. 'Tell the manager we'll be finished presently.' He looked down on them all. 'That must surely be enough. McCabe, Fairrie, I don't expect you to give me an answer immediately. Originally I said by two o'clock this afternoon. Now I give you until the same time tomorrow, at the latest. I should add that I expect you to agree on your verdict. When I pay experts for their advice, and they disagree, then clearly one of them is not an expert and does not deserve to be paid. Since I don't know which, neither gets paid.'

McCabe turned to Roberto. 'In that case clearly we must consult. But first I should like to go over my notes.' He looked at the gold watch on his thin freckled wrist. 'Shall we say eight o'clock in my rooms at the Wellington Hotel?'

Clemann instructed Swivel: 'Pay McCabe and Fairrie what we owe them so far. Include a hundred each for their deliberations tonight.'

Three more old ladies dressed in black and jewellery were waiting at the top of the stairs.

23

Clutching his five one-hundred dollar bills in his coat pocket, Roberto walked a block to the next bank, a branch of the Banco Central, where he managed to change them just before it closed. He then entered the Metro at Serrano instead of Velázquez, and possibly for this reason was not followed by a black leather jacket or anyone else. Thus his irritation was all the more sharp when, emerging at José Antonio, he found Cockburn waiting for him at the top of the steps.

'I thought we might have lunch together.' Cockburn took Roberto by the elbow. 'Where do you usually go?'

Not – I would like to buy you a lunch. Roberto, realising they would be going Dutch, said: 'On my own I use a small Galician restaurant near the top of Barco.' It was a lie. On his own he usually bought a snack at an Asturian delicatessen nearby.

'Galician? Not all octopus I hope. I can't take octopus.'

'No *pulpo en su tinto*, I promise you.'

Roberto took the turn by the side of the Telefónica, used Desengaño to cut the corner into Barco.

'Don't you live round here?'

'Very near.

Cockburn was contemptuous. 'I suppose it's convenient.'

'Very. And cheap. I am not a rich man.'

'So I had really rather begun to gather.'

They turned into Barco – an older street for some of its length than Desengaño. Many of the narrow houses had wrought-iron balconies, and dark bars on the ground floor or in the basement. In the summer the ladies – many of them Blacks or Philippinos, dressed in bright reds and some with fans, sequins and so on – sit on the balconies. In winter you find them in the bars. When they're not working they wear jeans and look like students though fatter and with elaborate earrings, and they queue up with the old women in the tiny grocery shops. And that day there were queues. Cockburn almost knocked over an old lady who was carrying two string bags in each hand, all four filled with tins – sardines, mussels in *escabeche*, Asturian *fabado*.

'It's almost as if they expect a war.'

'They do.'

'Do you?' asked Cockburn.

Roberto shrugged.

'And why now?' Cockburn went on. 'I mean the old bandit's been on the machines for a month. The healing process stopped completely ten days ago. But those machines can bleep for a month more if those in charge want them to. So. Why today rather than yesterday? Why today are the duchesses locking their jewels up in the Banco, and the retired whores in Barco stocking up with tins?'

'Turn right here.'

The restaurant was small, clean, and if you got there early enough to be near the stove, warm. If you were not there by two you kept your coat on, which was what Cockburn and Roberto did.

Cockburn ordered spinach broth, Roberto broth with noodles. He knew which would have more nourishment in it. Cockburn ordered *filete*, Roberto hake. It was a long time before they were served. They drank their wine allowance and crumbled their bread away on the damp tablecloth.

'They know,' said Roberto. 'It's really very simple. I mean the duchesses and the housewives.'

'Yes?'

'Tomorrow is 20 November. At dawn on the 20 November in 1936, José Antonio Primo de Rivera, the founder of the Falange, was executed by a legal firing squad in Alicante. The moment is remembered annually by all the Falangists in Spain at dawn ceremonies. They'll declare Franco dead tomorrow morning. Possibly, if he'll co-operate, at exactly the same moment, at dawn.'

'Only one shopping day to Christmas.'

'Precisely.'

Cockburn rolled a pellet of bread until it was grey and compact and then flicked it across the floor.

'Why are they so long about serving us?'

'We are not regulars.'

'I thought you said you came here often.'

Roberto shrugged.

Another pellet of bread was launched into space. It travelled further, into the gravitational field of an Asturian warehouse clerk, who looked up from his copy of *ABC* with disdain.

'I was followed from the bank,' said Cockburn. 'He is sitting at the small table by the kitchen door. Black leather jacket. Funny thing. Swivel, who, believe me, is a creep of the first water, was always convinced he was being followed when we were here before. I think I told you he bought a bullet-proof vest? And we all laughed like drains when he told us. But this time round I think he's right. I wonder why that should be. Ah. At last.'

His broth had eighteen shreds of chopped spinach floating on the surface. In Roberto's there were eighteen small noodles. Neither was hot. Cockburn wanted more to drink, tried to hold the waiter's attention long enough to say so, but failed. The restaurant was very busy.

'I think,' said Roberto, trying to choose his words carefully, 'perhaps more people are in the know this time. Word has got around. Been put around.'

He recalled his street beating, his interview with a Marqués, and the presence of Rudel and Adler at the bank. He shuddered. Perhaps after all it had not been Cockburn's clumsiness in asking *ABC* for a voice sample... for indeed yes, word had got around, had been put around. A top Nazi, Evita had said, was in Madrid, investigating the tapes, co-ordinating a response. Rudel and Adler, at the bank, were part of that response... The sinking feeling returned as Roberto wished, not for the first time, that *he* knew what was going on.

Cockburn leaned forward, waved his soup spoon.

'You could be right. I think Montiam was very discreet. She needed only one rich and unfrightenable buyer to get the ante raised. Really this broth is rather disgusting. And that was enough. But Pepita does seem to have let this lot be known about... I'm thinking of that Gunter chap. Who has he been in touch with?' The thought of Gunter produced a grimace. He looked around. 'I can't say I'm entirely happy with this place.'

Roberto's turn to be apologetic: 'Three courses. With wine. And the present uncertainty has depressed the peseta. It'll hardly cost us a pound sterling each.'

'All the same. So. Interested parties keeping a watch on us. Who?'

Roberto shrugged.

Cockburn pushed back his chair, palms on the table edge, and his eyes widened. 'At least it shows these tapes are being taken seriously. Someone believes they're genuine. Even if you don't.'

'I have not made up my mind yet.'

'But you must lean one way or the other?'

'Perhaps. But I take Clemann's point. I should like to agree with McCabe. And if I find we differ I should like to debate the differences with him until we agree.'

The waiter brought about thirty grams of thinly sliced *biftec,* eight chips, and twenty hard green peas for Cockburn, and the same for Roberto except that a thin slice of hake, bone in, took the place of the meat. Again Cockburn's request for more wine was resisted.

'Clearly,' said Cockburn, after his third mouthful, which left his plate nearly clean, 'you are in need of a bob or two... I won't press the point. You are going to McCabe tonight?'

'This evening.'

'What time will you be finished?'

Again Roberto shrugged.

'Well. I shall be at Pepita's from about nine o'clock. It's two or three blocks from the Wellington. I'd be grateful if you'd drop by when you leave McCabe and let me know the result of your deliberations.'

'Should I not report to Clemann first?'

'Why?'

'He's paying me.'

'You can phone him from Pepita's if you like. That's as much of this place as I can take. I don't want half a stewed pear for the next course. Where can we find a decent drink?'

'The Nebraska in Hortaleza.'

'Come on then.'

He put down notes, did not bother to ask Roberto for his share.

At the Nebraska Cockburn had a toasted cheese and ham sandwich, a coffee and a large brandy. Roberto had just the brandy and the coffee. Leather jacket took a booth four tables away from them. With the warmer and fattier food Cockburn at last drew towards the point.

'Clemann and I are close,' he said. 'Very close. I'll tell you why. We were at Bedales together and thence to Queen's College, Cambridge, both read History, trod the gowans fine, tell the truth, he helped me over an embarrassing entanglement. So, if the tapes are authentic, he'll buy, and he'll set me and Becky up to look after publication. And this is what I have to say, and it is this. When that happens we'd like you to be on board, as our in-house Perón expert. Peter is tight over small things but he likes big things to be done well, so there'll be plenty of money. You get my drift?'

'I suppose so.'

'Of course you do.' He knocked back his brandy, stood up. 'Right then. I'll hear from you tonight when you've seen McCabe. *Chez* Pepita. *Ciao.*'

Leather jacket followed Cockburn. Roberto gave them a minute then followed them out into the street. The cold pinched like a crab.

24

As he turned into Desengaño the Renault 12 with French number plates pulled away from the pavement a hundred yards or so away and came to a halt on the opposite kerb. As the driver's window sank Roberto felt an excitement entirely inappropriate to someone of his age. He could see Becky Herzer's short soft hair lit like a nimbus against the early dusk by the flow of light from the Telefónica.

'Señor Fairrie?'

'Madame Herzer?' Embarrassed he realised that even in those two words he had revealed a little of what he felt.

'You must call me Becky. Can we talk? Do you mind?'

Not wanting to invite her to his awful rooms, where, in any case, she would surely discover things he would not want her to see, Roberto crossed the road, passed behind the twirling exhaust, found the passenger door already open. He got in.

She made no move to set the car going, instead shook a Kaiser loose in its packet, offered it to him. He refused and she lit it for herself. The harsh smoke smote him across the forehead like a blow, and brought nausea with it.

'I think,' she said, 'I should come to the point straightaway. Really, you should declare those tapes to be forgeries. As Clemann says, the whole set-up stinks. And. Even if they are forgeries they are dangerous too.'

He was startled, looked across to her. She was staring straight ahead, with her glasses on, the silk cords looped below her ear. Her hands were clenched tight on the steering wheel, the cigarette clamped between whitened knuckles. Then she turned to him, and said, with a smile that was gentle and even alluring: 'You cannot believe I am here at half-past three in the afternoon by accident. I have been trying to make up my mind to come and see you for the last hour or so.'

'I was having lunch with Mr Cockburn.' He paused, went on: 'Believe me he would be surprised, even more surprised than I to hear you say this. He expects you, and I too it seems, to assist him in their publication.'

She shrugged. 'Well, it will cost me to be saying this. It really will. Steve, you, and I could all make a lot of money in this situation. So. Now you will want to know why these tapes should be damned and their publication stopped.'

'Of course.'

She twisted so that her back was almost against her door, put her arm, with the cigarette along the back of the seat. To avoid its fumes Roberto also twisted away so that, as near as possible in the small car, they were facing each other.

'You are a socialist. You must realise these tapes will be very damaging to the Peronist movement and therefore to the causes you believe in.'

'Peronismo is no friend to socialism. The reverse. Roberto was earnest. 'It drew off, still draws off the revolutionary spirit of the Argentine working class and pours it into a leaky bucket.'

'I think you are wrong. I think you are out of touch. What you say was true of the Peronismo of the fifties, of Perón himself, even Evita. But since then it has been appropriated by the revolutionary cadres of Argentinian labour and is the vital ingredient they need to inspire the masses in the struggle that is about to begin.'

'That sounds like opportunism. In any case this is hardly a judgment you are qualified to make.'

'It is not my judgment.' With a sharp gesture she inhaled smoke, blew it out through her nostrils. 'Señor Fairrie, I am a member of the French CP. I have made reports about your tapes, and have received instructions, arising I believe from consultations between...

'I don't believe this, I really don't.' Roberto's right hand again searched ineffectually for whatever catch or handle would let him out. Exhaustion, anxiety, the cigarette smoke in the tiny cabin of the car all combined to produce an almost pathological sense of unreality, but too he was conscious of the voices of reason and experience. He really did not believe a word of it.

Herzer twisted back to face the steering wheel, dabbed out the cigarette in a shower of tiny sparks, shifted the gear, revved the idling engine, then let it die. 'Don't go,' she said.

They sat in silence for a time, then: 'You were quite right not to believe a word of what I said. Though I am a Party member. And it is true, very true, that I want your tapes suppressed. That I want to prevent their publication by Clemann and Cockburn.'

'They are not my tapes. Why?'

'It is not now that I think I am going to tell you why.'

He shrugged. She fidgeted, drummed fingers on the wheel. Then she lit another cigarette and smoked it ostentatiously, like Ingrid Bergman or Lauren Bacall in a classic movie, demonstrating tension, creating suspense, perhaps, thought Roberto, trying to place the film he had in mind, hinting at duplicity.

'Roberto, I may call you Roberto...?'

'Of course.'

'Forgive me. But I must say this. I sense affinities between us. We have perhaps much in common. We could... understand each other... rather well. Your family were well-to-do bourgeois. Yet you are a man of the left. Why? '

A note of sincerity had been struck. Roberto strove to preserve it, spoke slowly, and simply.

'I hate privilege. Not the privilege of the very rich over people like us, which is not important. But basic privilege. I hate to think that the people who produce the rice, the lentils, the beans I eat may be poorly fed. That the people who made this shirt may not have enough clothes. That the people who mine and process the chemicals and minerals that keep me comfortable may die from enforced overdoses of dust, gases, side-products. That sort of thing.'

Now he felt embarrassed though what he had said was true, perhaps, stripped of theory and rationalisation, for him the only real truth.

Herzer apparently approved. She stubbed out her barely-lit cigarette, and her hand dropped to rest on his knee for a moment.

'I understand,' she said. 'I was born in 1927. In a family, to a background not unlike yours.' She looked at him, head turned, pale brown eyes serious and haunted. 'Solid bourgeois, you know? A small grand piano. Servants we treated like poor relations unless they got puppy... no. Uppish. Both my parents were doctors. Good doctors. They worked for anyone and charged only according to what the patient could afford. Often nothing at all. Of course this was not universally popular…'

She was interrupted. A Municipal Policeman was edging along the pavement recording licence numbers. She restarted the engine.

'Would you mind coming to my place? We could talk more freely there.'

She let out the clutch, swung through the alleyways on to José Antonio, crossed Cibeles into Alcalá. She drove slowly, but very competently, and talked on.

'We were, are Sudeten Germans. Glad, when it happened, to become part of Germany again, whatever we thought of the regime. That did not last. My father was drafted to the Russian Front, not as a doctor but as an orderly. Nothing have we heard of him since. My mother practised a year more, to 1943, then she was ordered to join the medical staff at Birkenau. You know? Under Herr Doctor Mengele? I was fifteen, sixteen years old. My brother was eleven. We were in a home for war orphans. My mother did not know where we were. Whenever she refused to do the things Mengele asked her to do, she was threatened that one day she would find us at Birkenau with her, but on the wrong side of the wire.'

This was all said coldly, recited, like lines repeated too often before.

'After the war she returned to her practice and we were reunited. But although we were liked and respected in what was left of our little community it became clear that Czechoslovakia was no place for us, and we moved, fled, not far, just to Regensburg, in 1948. My mother joined a practice there and our German nationality was established. But I rejected my German past, studied at the Sorbonne, and married a Frenchman. That too is over, but I remain French. Meanwhile my mother has done well, is now much respected in her region, although of course she is by now retired apart from committees and so on…'

'Go on.'

'Well. Four times now, this is the fourth time, I have been asked to do things, not difficult or dangerous, or even criminal, but not always to my liking, to protect my mother from exposure and public trial for what she assisted in at Birkenau. This time I have to do what I can to establish that your tapes are forgeries…'

'They are not mine.'

'That these tapes are forged. That is all. We are almost there.'

They were off the main road now, threading through narrower streets not far from Las Ventas, the bull-ring. She parked neatly in front of a narrow block, more modern than its neighbours.

But Roberto was not ready to get out.

'Listen,' he said, 'everything you have said indicates... that you were not at the bank yesterday merely to change traveller's cheques. Those German businessmen...'

Her head fell forward to rest on her knuckles which still clutched the top of the steering wheel. Then she raised it, shook it, and sighed.

'Of course you are right. But I really was changing my cheques.' She said this firmly and then gave a short laugh. 'But yes, I was asked to be there, first to ask Señora González, Pepa, if I might be there. She agreed.'

Roberto's pulse quickened. 'What did she play? Was it the other cassettes? Not Perón's?'

'No. The same as the first time. The one about Bormann coming to visit. She let it run though. There was something about, oh, I don't know. Money. High finance. Now that really is all there is to say. Perhaps I should take you back to Desengaño. Unless you would like to come up. I should like it if you would.'

'I should like that.'

'Look at me.'

He did. Her eyes were glowing wells of unshed tears, yet they smiled.

'Kiss me.'

'Soon I shall have to go.

'Yes?'

'To see Professor McCabe at the Wellington Hotel.'

'I know. That's at eight o'clock. It's not quite six. It's not far. I'll take you.'

Her thin brown body pressed warmly into his back, her knees were at the back of his, the delicious difference of her pubic hair nestled near his bottom, the softness of her breasts below his shoulder blades, and her arm curled round his tummy. Kissing surfaces parted, but gently.

Roberto turned on his back, looked up at the coloured glass light-fitting in the form of a bell-shaped flower, which hung above the centre of the small studio flat. As he moved the saggy, put-u-up bed creaked. Their love-making in it had been scarcely competent, comic rather, with a brief shared ecstasy followed by sleep and a waking euphoria that was almost the best part of the whole business. Roberto felt fine. His joints were soft and relaxed and only one thing bothered him. Shortly he would have to wee.

She touched his mouth with a finger, ran it along his trim white moustache.

'And what will you agree with the Herr Professor? That these tapes are forged? I think they are.'

This produced a jerk of irritation.

'Why do you say that? I understand you would like it to be true, but why do you believe it?'

'Well!' She gave a short laugh. 'As Clemann says. The set-up stinks. After the first one.' She was dismissive, swung on her side, her back to him, fumbled for cigarettes.

Gently he got off the awkward bed, glad she was turned from the sight of his sagging bottom and skinny shanks, and crossed the short space to the bathroom. Like the rest of the apartment it was carpeted in brown. Inevitably he left three dark drops, scrubbed at them with toilet paper, made them yet more evident with shreds of tissue.

Back in the room he sat on the edge of the bed, felt the pressure of the tubular frame in his backside.

'Who is threatening your mother?' She said nothing.

'Who is doing this?'

'Die Spinne, I suppose. You know?'

'And Adler and Rudel are part of the Spider?'

'Part of? No. They are businessmen. Rudel anyway. Adler I'm not so sure of.' She kept her back to him. Smoke hung in layers above her. 'Listen,' she went on. 'The information about Nazis in South America on these tapes may well be accurate. These things can be found out. But if when they are published they are shown to be forgeries, not really recorded by Perón, then no one will believe it...'

Roberto scarcely listened. He was almost overwhelmed with compassion for this thin, brown lady, not so very much younger than he, who had treated him so sweetly. He felt gratitude as fierce as a passion, and guilt too.

He squeezed her shoulder, kneaded it. 'Your mother must be a good woman. A good doctor.'

'I believe so.'

'And what you want is assurance that these tapes are forgeries, and will be revealed as such after publication. I mean, you are not so concerned with stopping publication as that they should eventually be shown to be forged.'

At last she turned. Her eyes were now wary, suspicious, pleading too, but she said nothing.

'Well, really, I can assure you of that. That they are forged.'

He told her exactly why he could be certain that this was the case, and why he would still have to try to convince both Clemann and McCabe that they were genuine. She pulled him back into bed and cajoled him, old and tired though he was, into a longer and more perfect ecstasy than the one before. Then, still with no clothes on so he could continue to enjoy the thin if wrinkled all-over brown athleticism of her body, she busied herself about the tiny flat, and produced for him a French omelette with a bottle of Rioja dry white.

25

'I think I should say at the outset,' Roberto said, as he accepted a pleasantly upholstered Oxford chair at a table not so low that you couldn't write on it, 'that I have been subjected to pressure both to declare these tapes forgeries, and to pass them as the real thing.'

'I, too.' McCabe took his place opposite. On the table there were the then very few reliable texts on the life of Perón, most of them concentrating on the years up to 1955; also books of reference – the *South American Handbook,* the Maria Moliner Spanish dictionary, the Larousse English-Spanish, Spanish-English.

'I, too,' McCabe repeated. 'And since pressure has come both ways we have really no choice but to give our honest opinion. Not of course that we ever intended to do otherwise.' He leaned back, blinked owlishly through gold-rimmed spectacles over long pale orange fingers clasped beneath his chin. 'Still it puts us in an invidious position. It seems one way or another we have to displease powerful interests. Isn't that so?'

Roberto agreed that it was.

McCabe went on. 'Well, I'll be frank. I am protected. I have tenure in an academic post which pays a quite disgustingly large salary. And I have other connections as well. In short, I don't need money, and I don't think I need fear physical violence. But can you say the same?'

'Certainly not.'

'So, I'm suggesting that since the whole question of the tapes is going to remain unresolved, I would not like to come to a decision, or recommendation on them, that would put you to personal inconvenience, harm, loss.'

Roberto looked back across the table and tried to weigh up McCabe's motives for this apparently considerate offer, and decided that if there was a trap he had better not fall into it.

'That is kind of you. But it is not a consideration at all. Shall we begin?'

'Right. I've drawn up certain headings. I suggest we take each one in turn and see how we go.'

They discussed the sound of the recordings, the voice and delivery of whoever was on the tapes – they were careful never to call him Perón – and the content, for an hour. At the end of it they were broadly in agreement that they had no very good reason for saying the taped voice was not Perón's. But McCabe had serious misgivings which he finally reduced to three or four concrete points.

The quality of the first spool-to-spool tape they had heard was too good since it was supposedly done in Madrid during the same period as the tapes *ABC* had bought. Those, they had been told, had been distorted, there had been background noise, the whole effect was amateurish. And so the sheer professionalism of the recording of that particular tape made it suspect.

'And then,' McCabe went on, 'there is the inconsistency. The second spool-to-spool tape we heard, the one about Justicialismo and so on, did have traffic noise, a church bell…'

'How good is good?' Roberto asked. 'I mean are you implying a professional technician was present? That it was done in a studio?'

McCabe deliberated. 'Not necessarily. But certainly someone who knew a bit more than your average home enthusiast, who knew how to position a microphone, get voice levels right. And all the evidence suggests that that was beyond Perón.'

Roberto, head twisted away, finally nodded.

'All right. What else?'

'In terms of factual content only one very minor point in the whole lot. The Voice says that Juan Duarte, Eva's brother, should be sent to Martín García for corruption. Now Martín García is, as you know, an island in the Plate estuary, only really used as a prison for political reasons – dictators ousted, leaders of failed coups. It is not a state penitentiary for ordinary criminals. As I say it's a minor point, and since Perón himself spent some time there in October '45 at a very crucial point in his career, it's not perhaps surprising the name came unconsidered to his lips. No. These tapes consistently get facts right. And in a sense that is against them too. Perón was lazy about facts, and what he forgot he made up. That is something you yourself have pointed out. Yes?

'Then again, I was puzzled by what we heard first this morning. All the Justicialismo bit. In the first place it came very close to a section of the earlier tapes, and, as I've said, from the technical point of view it was almost as bad, but not quite to my ear, the same. For instance, there's no church bell near enough to the villa in Puerto de Hierra…'

Roberto had reacted, he couldn't help it. His head swung back and their eyes met across the table. Empty, both refusing to register anything in case either gave something away. McCabe stood up, moved to the curtained window, pulled the drapes slightly apart.

'There are military vehicles parked in the gateway to the Retiro.' He turned back. 'Remarkably similar in style and content to a section of the *ABC* tapes. Why should he record that twice?'

The moment of doubt and emptiness, the moment when pretence had almost given way, was gone.

'Perhaps,' said Roberto, 'he wasn't satisfied with the quality of the recording the first time.'

McCabe came back to the table. 'Personally, I've come to the conclusion that that tape at any rate is a forgery, and a rather hurriedly botched-up one. Señora González's intervention, coming for coffee or whatever, indicates she's a party to it. Perhaps the one genuine voice, playing herself, we've so far heard. Finally, I'm not happy about the overall tone of it all.' He drew out the word 'tone' to give it a steady emphasis. 'There is a consistent thread, a common factor that links all we've heard apart from the Justicialismo bit. Perhaps you've spotted it?

'No? Well, it's this. Everything we've yet heard, if published and accepted as authentic, will seriously damage the Perón image and therefore the afterlife of Peronismo: closer links with Nazis than anyone expected; Evita branded as an incestuous syphilitic by no lesser person than Perón himself; a near confession that he ordered Juancito's murder; his callous treatment of Evita's remains and readiness to use them for political gain, his libidinous liking for pubescent girls... and so on. I just can't quite believe he'd so expose himself. Even to himself.'

'Surely that is why these tapes were kept apart from the others, and not left with Señora Montiam.'

McCabe shrugged. 'That's the line taken by González. And Cockburn.'

'So you really do think Señora González is acting in bad faith. That she knows these tapes are forgeries.'

'Yes.'

'A conspiracy to defraud.'

'To defraud. And to inflict serious damage on Peronismo. Undermine the workers', the *decamisados'* faith in him and Eva. I suspect Cockburn is a party to it. I imagine it was he who pressured you to declare the tapes authentic.'

Roberto said nothing for a time. Then: 'So. Your report to Clemann will say that while you have no firm or conclusive reason for saying these tapes are forged, you have serious misgivings. And you will outline these misgivings in the way you just have to me.

'That's about it. Now. How about you?'

Roberto took off his glasses, gave them a polish, put them back on. Both frames and vision were still a touch unfamiliar, and he blinked a few times.

'I can go along with some of that, some of the way. However, I think your last point, that the tapes are too overtly damaging to Perón's image, carries no real weight. At least until we know the content of the whole set. I imagine Señora González has been playing the more sensational stuff to stimulate Clemann's and Cockburn's interest. There may be hours of Justicialismo all as boring as what we heard this morning. No one's going to put up two hundred thousand dollars for that sort of stuff – especially when there's already an awful lot of it in what *ABC* and Planeta are going to put out. And I really don't think your other points amount to a great deal.'

McCabe's sandy eyebrows were raised in an expression that was both quizzical and threatening.

'So you think these tapes are authentic after all. I understood you previously to be very sceptical.'

'I still am. But I still have no real reason for saying so. Nor really do you. And there is another possibility we have not considered at all. That some of these tapes are authentic and some are not. Really, to give a soundly based opinion we still need to hear a lot more tape. Don't you agree?'

'Sure. Yes. I'd go along with that. Though Clemann is not going to be pleased.'

For half an hour they worked on an agreed form of words that disguised their lack of unanimity. Then McCabe rang up Clemann.

As he put the receiver down, he said: 'No, he definitely was not pleased. But he will try to arrange for us to hear more tape tomorrow morning. You're to ring him at ten o'clock, and he'll let you know if Señora González will set it up. Would you like a drink before you go?'

McCabe dropped ice from a small fridge into glasses, added Seagram's. Roberto took an opportunity: 'What exactly was the grotesquely interesting story Clemann would not let you tell this morning?'

'You don't know? Why should you. It was well hushed up. It goes like this. Colonel Cabanillas, you know, who discovered Evita's coffin in a warehouse, was at a loss. To gain time he moved it to the apartment of a Major he felt he could trust.' McCabe warmed to his anecdote, relished it. 'This Major had a wife. Pregnant. The coffin was in the spare bedroom. The Major slept in the living room with a loaded pistol. In the middle of the night a sheeted figure drifted across the open door and then back. Evita's ghost? The Major thought so, and without pausing to consider what he would achieve by the action, he snatched up his pistol and fired.'

'It was his wife,' said Roberto.

'Precisely. Shot dead. In the head.'

'Not the happiest of tales,' said Roberto, and finished his drink in a gulp.

26

It was about a quarter past nine when Roberto left the Wellington. On the steps of the hotel he reflected, in slightly tipsy amusement (Rioja and a stiff Seagram's), how in one evening he assured first one person that the tapes were forged, and argued very convincingly to another that they were not.

Glancing down Velázquez Roberto could see the line of jeeps huddled under the wall of the Retiro, the black silhouettes of giant cedars behind them, and he remembered how McCabe had admitted to *hearing* the *ABC* tapes, when Clemann had only sent him transcripts. How? When? What did it signify? Clearly, if nothing else, that McCabe was not simply an independent expert, but was playing some game of his own as well.

He turned away, set off up Velázquez, turned right into Jorge Juan, and left into Nuñez de Balboa. On the second corner he was almost knocked down by four tall, lean soldiers in immaculate combat dress with red berets. Paras with battle experience in the Sahara, guns and grenades hung about them, but laughing and clutching parcels of huge *bocadillos* – sandwiches made of whole loaves of French-style bread stuffed with potato omelette. *Santiago y Cierra España* on their shoulder flashes – St James and pull up the drawbridge. Whoever they stayed loyal to would win.

As he walked up Balboa Roberto recalled one of the jokes Ramón had told him. Doña Carmen, Franco's wife, tearful at his bedside, says: 'They are even taking the Sahara away from us.'

'They can't,' says the dying Caudillo. 'I have already given it to Villaverde.' The Marques of Villaverde, Franco's son. Rumours everywhere that as he died the family were plundering what they could before it was too late.

Roberto identified himself through the intercom and the toughened glass door clicked open. Nevertheless, the uniformed *conserje* looked up through the window of the *conserjería* and followed his progress across the marble floor to the lift with obvious suspicion. With a fattish oval face and a trim white moustache he looked astonishingly like the already putrefying if not actually dead Generalísimo whose portrait hung on the wall behind him. Roberto shivered as he turned and took in the resemblance before the lift door closed.

A desperate, alcoholic and erotic confusion filled Josefina González's apartment. She was back in black again but this time a shortish dress of crêpe de Chine with a plunging neckline that exposed the inner sides of her small, wide-set breasts; her amber and gold hair

was wild, Medusa-like, and her long fingers flickered and sparkled with
frenetic agility. Gunter was there as well as Cockburn and both men
were not far off drunk. Roberto glanced round, took in each and
decided that the problem was that neither of them knew who was to
receive the lady's favours that night, and that it was possible that she
had not made up her own mind. Momentarily a heavy sadness formed,
as solid as a tumour, behind his breast-bone. He accepted a drink from
Cockburn who seemed determined to register his claim on Pepa by
assuming the role of host. It was a daiquiri – tall, and long, and very
strong.

'I wanted champagne tonight,' Pepa cried, 'but do you know there
is not a bottle to be had? Extraordinary.'

'Every left-winger in Spain,' said Gunter, 'is waiting by his TV with
a bottle chilling in the fridge.'

'So,' said Cockburn, 'you and McCabe are putting in the boot.'

'The boot?'

'Thumbs down to these tapes.'

'Not at all. But how do you know…?'

'The lady just had Peter on the phone. He was not pleased. He will,
he says, pay for you and McCabe to hear one more lot of tapes, then, if
no reversal of your misgivings is about to forthcome, he'll piss off back
to Genéve.'

'Steve. You must try not to be so boorish. Roberto, I may call you
Roberto? Please come and sit here.'

'You may call me Roberto, if I may call you Josefina.' Said with the
old-world gallantry of an elderly don.

Her green eyes were for a moment warily defensive, then flashed
with coquetry.

'I shall be mortified if you do. No one I like calls me Josefina – Pepa
or Pepita, please. And perhaps because I like you I shall call you not
Roberto, but Papa. Papa Roberto. You are old enough to be my father.'

Roberto realised that she knew she was nearly drunk.

'Now, tell us what has gone wrong.'

The immaculate white hide of the armchair creaked beneath him.
He looked up and around at the sunburst clock, the new music centre,
a tall vase made out of an incandescent glass, blue like lapis lazuli, and
filled with scarlet gladioli flown from Seville.

'Nothing has gone wrong.

'I should think not.' Enrico Gunter, holding a cigarette just below
the tips of his index and middle fingers, drew in smoke, breathed out,
gave the tiniest of shrugs – all gestures that seemed oddly effeminate in
a man of such solid build. 'I should think not. There are other potential
buyers. I personally know of interested parties.'

'Nothing has gone particularly bloody right either.' Cockburn's face flushed darkly, his eyes were almost savagely angry.

'Calm yourself, darling, and let Papa... Roberto speak. What has this tall yellow professor got against our tapes? He reminds me of a stick insect.'

Roberto repeated how McCabe suspected the technical soundness of the first spool-to-spool tape and that the one that was badly recorded had been botched up in a hurry to correct that impression; that every extract they had so far heard appeared to damn Perón out of his own mouth in a way which he could not credit. 'That's it in a nutshell.'

Cockburn took it badly. 'Just a moment. Hang about. If he's saying that that tape about Justicialismo and so on was put together since Monday, because on Monday Swivel queried the good quality of what we'd heard, he must be implying this was done in response to that. In other words, that one of us who was in my room at the Príncipe that night is party to the fraud.'

Roberto kept his face and voice as bland as he could.

'Precisely. He thinks you and Pepa are in a conspiracy.'

'He thinks *what*? All right, I heard. Jesus. I'll break his fucking neck.'

'Steve. Steven. You really are being boorish tonight. All right. The man's an idiot. How can we persuade him he is wrong? How can we drown these misgivings of his, Roberto, Papa?'

Roberto put down his glass, now almost empty. In spite of the crushed ice he had been drinking through he already felt a warm elation that had dissolved his earlier moment of sadness. He thought: I must not speak or act irresponsibly. Cockburn refilled his glass from a jug, knobbly, decorated, pink – a grand thing but a bad pourer. A splash fell on Roberto's knee.

'I think, Señora...'

'Pepa, please, Papa.' She dabbed at his knee with a tissue taken from a silver dispenser.

'I think... Pepa, you forget my position here. I am, you know, an independent expert like McCabe.'

'But you think my tapes are genuine. Steve, get me a drink please, but weaker than before.'

'I am still open-minded. I must say I was most impressed by your account of their provenance. I cannot doubt any of that. Therefore I must assume that if these tapes are not genuine then it was López Rega who forged them.'

Cockburn stooped over her and his dark eyes tracked down the plunging dress. He set her glass on the marble table. Roberto noticed the beginning of a round belly pushing over the tailored hipster slacks he was wearing.

'Which reminds me, my dear, of what Peter thinks of your account of how you got those tapes. Like Roberto here, he was impressed. Even Swivel couldn't find much to pick holes in. But. Dear Swivel is still not sure, in spite of that document you have, that López Rega will not reappear and claim title after we've paid up.'

Gunter shifted forward. He spoke with finality.

'López Rega won't come back.'

'How can you be so sure?' Cockburn swung to face him, the movement aggressive.

'Because he is dead.'

Pause.

'How can you be so sure?'

The Argentinian businessman placed his broad hands on his spread knees and looked up with a sharkish smile.

'Because a contract to kill was given to the most reliable operator available to those who wished him dead.' He looked at them in turn. 'You don't believe me? Why not?' He pulled a snakeskin wallet from an inside pocket, slipped out a photograph, leant forward and handed it to González. 'Is that El Brujo?'

She took it between finger and thumb. Then paled and choked. 'A handkerchief please, please.'

Cockburn and Roberto pushed handkerchieves at her. Cockburn's was first, Roberto picked up the photo. A flashlit Polaroid of a heavy face with mean lips, parted in what looked like surprise. Eyes small, open, shocked, sightless. The high dome of a balding forehead was marked by a black hole in the centre from which a tiny dribble of blood had begun to leak before the heart which pumped it stopped.

'You never told me of this!'

Gunter looked at his squared-off fingernails and again something menacing that yet could be called a smile twisted his mouth.

'And you did not tell me until this morning that López Rega gave you tapes.'

Gunter sat back in the sofa and silence settled across the room. Distanced by the double glazing and the heavy curtains a police-car sirened down the street.

Cockburn too had lost his high colour. Perhaps out of fright, perhaps because he had reached that level of alcohol poisoning where the skin goes waxy and one perspires lightly.

'It's not easy… to copy a Polaroid print,' he said. 'I mean – that has every appearance of being the top copy, the actual photograph. Where did you get it? How long have you had it?'

Gunter did not stir. Cockburn went on: 'It's altogether a bit much. Contracts to kill. Why kill López once he'd been thrown out? Never mind. Really, I think I'd better get back to Clemann with this. And McCabe.'

He straightened, swayed a little, laughed. 'Poor old Swivel will be scared shitless. He'll be on the next plane back. Contracts to kill.'

'You're not going to stay then.' Pepita held out his handkerchief to him.

'No. Not much bloody use, really. But listen. Can't you find one more bit of tape that will satisfy him? Something straightforward, factual, checkable, and sounding right? McCabe has a point. Too much self-exposure. Psychic flashing. That's a criticism... I am impressed with. But, please, find something Roberto here can be positive about, something that will box McCabe in and make him admit there are no real grounds for doubt.'

'I'll see. I think I can. I must admit I have not yet heard more than half the tapes myself. But I'll do my best. Now. I'll ring for a taxi.'

While she organised his departure Roberto and Gunter sat in silence for a few minutes, then Gunter threw a swift, sidelong glance at Roberto.

'Are you shocked?'

'Even after living for sixty-five years in the twentieth century I am still shocked by murder.'

Gunter shrugged: 'El Brujo killed, ordered the deaths of many. He had it coming to him.'

'But it was not done legally. Or even out of a sense of justice. He must have had many enemies. You have this photograph. Did... did you organise this contract?'

'Or did I borrow it to impress people? Does it matter? Do you think I'll tell you? Listen, a lunatic crook should not hold the positions López Rega held. He had access to too much. Perón himself was discreet. In exile he kept to himself the knowledge he had, did not make the mistake of threatening people with it. If he had, the same would have happened to him. If... the existence of these new tapes, and how they differed from the ones *ABC* bought, had been suspected...' Gunter pouted and shrugged.

'You think they are genuine?'

Gunter's eyes narrowed a little.

'As I say, it was known El Brujo had tapes with him. They disappeared. Here they are. I did not know until today that it was from El Brujo that the Señora got these tapes. All of these tapes. She never told me. Now she has told me... many things will be different. I think.'

'She is in danger then?'

'Not while they are in a bank vault over which she alone has control.'

'And if she sells them?'

'Then the danger goes with them.' Nevertheless, Roberto remained deeply uneasy.

Which tapes was Gunter talking about? The ones that purported to be Perón's second lot of reminiscences, or the five others López Rega was said to have brought, which, presumably, were not Perón at all?

González came back. The frenetic flamboyance had gone. Violet shadows had appeared round her eyes, her gorgeous hair had begun ever so slightly to droop. She collapsed into her chair again, fumblingly lit a cigarette.

'I should like a Perrier,' she said. 'With ice.'

Gunter stood, busied himself at the drinks cupboard, loped through to the kitchen – a buck asserting his privilege in the place of an ousted rival.

'I think,' – and she let out a long lungful of smoke – 'I should sell those tapes as soon as I can.'

'Yes.' He handed her the water. 'The people you met yesterday will pay for them. But not as much as Clemann might. I doubt if they will go above ten thousand...'

'Ten thousand? But that's...'

'That is what it costs to take out a contract. I know.' They knew he did. The Polaroid proved it. She grimaced, hugged herself, looked terribly vulnerable.

'Your people will try to stop me from selling to Clemann.'

'I do not see how they can. The tapes and money change hands in the bank vault.'

'I shall pass on the risk to Clemann and the others.'

'Clemann knows his way around. He can look after himself. Better than you can.'

'But will Clemann buy?' asked Roberto.

Gunter looked at him with curiosity. 'Yes. If you and McCabe tell him to.'

Roberto shrugged, refused to commit himself. He thought furiously. Forget the mysterious second lot of tapes for the moment; remember that Clemann was there to buy Perón's tapes, the dictator's tapes. That was the thing.

Roberto shrugged, refused yet again to commit himself.

Then: 'I too think,' he said, 'McCabe has a point. There is too much in these tapes that is damaging to Perón and Peronismo. No doubt, Señora, you have played only those bits that are most sensational, most likely to catch the appetite of people like Cockburn?'

She frowned, passed a hand across her forehead. 'I think I'm hungry,' she said.

Again Gunter padded towards the kitchen.

'I have not heard all of these tapes. But I would suppose El Brujo concealed only what was most dangerous when they left Madrid, and brought back only what was most saleable when he left Buenos Aires. Amongst what I have not played you is a detailed account of Nazis in Argentina. I cut that tape just as it became interesting.'

'I remember. Go on.'

'Then. There is a detailed, indeed, in a mild playboyish way a rather endearing account of his relations with Nellie. His favourite from the Union of Secondary Students. Apparently she would not go down...'

'All right. What else?'

'A rather witty and amusing account of how a trade union can be subverted, bought, threatened, generally coerced to do what Peronismo demands. I rather liked that bit.'

'And?'

'Let me think. An account of what he knew of Pinochet, of ex-Nazi, German research into torture, of a village in Chile where Nazis develop techniques of repression, interrogation and so on, funded in part by the CIA.'

'So. Most of it, as McCabe says, guaranteed to blacken Perón and Peronismo.'

She fixed him with a blank, indecisive gaze. Gunter watched them from the kitchen, sharp knife in hand. 'Yes. If you say so.'

Roberto took off his glasses, polished them.

'And you have heard about half of these tapes, Señora... Pepa?'

She looked at him carefully. 'Yes.'

'Well. I suggest you listen to a lot more tomorrow morning, until you find material that will assist McCabe, and myself, to decide that the apparent bias to improbable self-revelation is not so obvious as it now seems.'

Again she spoke very carefully.

'How long do you think I should spend on that?'

'How should I know? Until one o'clock? Tell Clemann and McCabe to be at the bank at one o'clock. I'll come at about that time. Or...' He took a chance. 'A little before. I can see myself out. No need for a taxi.'

As he stood up Gunter returned, with a plate of paper-thin country ham, a sliced tomato, olives.

27

Roberto was high again as he returned to the street – high on alcohol, fear, exaltation. The momentary exhaustion that had fallen across his shoulders like a load had slipped away again.

The night had gone chill, frost glittered on the pavements. Three or four specialist shops glowed like Aladdin's caves, the moon hung above the canyon of the street as if supported there by levitation or a conjuror. He walked a block almost to Alcalá then turned right, listening to the smack of his thin leather soles on the paving, relishing the slight sting that came with it. No one followed. Of all Madrid this part was most like the Buenos Aires he knew, and even after thirty years hankered for – large blocks, stone-faced, built on a ruthless grid system, with expensive shops, restaurants, smart cafés on the street, the offices of top professionals above – lawyers, doctors, dentists – and then huge apartments, like the one his wealthy underwriter father filled with children, an English governess, two other servants, and which his mother, who claimed Castilian hidalgo forebears, ruled with elegant benevolence.

But Buenos Aires was rarely as crystal clear as this, as clear as Madrid on a smog-free frosty night. Always there had been the presence of a great port, the hint of sea mist between you and the stars, the smell of the ocean. And still to Roberto the stars of the northern hemisphere were wrong, made a pattern strange and untidy.

Four more blocks took him across Velázquez and down the side of the Biblioteca Nacional to the Paseo de Recoletos. He paused for a moment under the trees looking up to the devastation of the Plaza de Colón – skyscrapers, terminals, a vast underground complex of theatres and restaurants now being hewn out of the rock beneath and sweeping away one of the best of Madrid's nineteenth-century squares. From where he stood he could see on the giant boards that masked much of the site new graffiti aerosoled perhaps only minutes before – *Abajo Franco, Amnestía, Poder al Pueblo,* and *Vivan los Reyes,* except this last had been done by an illiterate and read *Biba los Reyes.* There were others too: JONS, the Falange sign of yoke and arrows, *Muerte al Rey,* signs of a nation deeply divided. As indeed was his own. As is everybody's in the West.

He crossed the first avenue, stood on the kerb of the dual carriageway as if on the edge of a swollen river. To the right it was a river of red tail-lights pouring up through Colón to the northern suburbs, and of white lights coming the other way out of the darkness and into the city. The nearest traffic lights were a block away at Recoletos. He waited for the gap and jaywalked into it. Horns blared and the traffic policewoman up at Colón saw him and her whistle screamed, but he got through, stood panting on the kerb, panting and laughing.

He crossed the east side outer avenue and walked straight into a restaurant bar of a sort he never normally considered. First he used the payphone and rang González.

'You understand what I was saying?'

'Yes.'

'It's going to work you know. We're nearly there.'

'I hope so.'

'I always said it would be difficult. And dangerous.' Pause.

'Where are you now?' she asked. 'Give me the number. I might ring back.'

He did.

She rang off.

He chose a small table still free or just vacated by the enormous expanse of the single-pane plate-glass window that looked back on to the avenue, and ordered a plate of *jamón serrano,* a half bottle of Manzanilla de Sanlúcar de Barrameda, the dryest and lightest of sherries, and a grilled grey mullet. Then he sat back and let his mind dwell expansively and glowingly on what had been done, and what was still to be done. When it came he attacked his thin ham with gusto, relishing its denseness, its darkness, its salty richness, so much better than that of Bayonne or Parma.

By the time the fish was brought, the Manzanilla, not as strong as fortified sherry, but stronger than most table wines, had again sharpened his vision, as if it were mescalin, and he looked about the restaurant with a high, happy feeling of camaraderie. Not that the people were those he most approved. There were three or four couples from the quarter he had walked through – doctors perhaps, senior civil servants or traders in oriental carpets in their heavy winter suits, their wives in fur. Three businessmen wrapped up a deal and two colonels ate steak: possibly they were from the Army Ministry just up the road, perhaps they commanded the troops Roberto had seen earlier.

Yet they were the sort of people Roberto had been brought up amongst in the Buenos Aires of the twenties, the sort of people he had married back into in 1940. He could not help feeling at home with them near, could not suppress a warm feeling of familiarity. There was even a priest, a Monsignor judging by the flash of purple on his chest, entertaining with ease and dignity a fine old lady in black, his mother perhaps. He pulled the last flakes from the bone, tidied up his plate, left prongs of fork and blade of knife neatly resting on the plate edge, finished his wine, wiped his mouth and leant back. He anticipated coffee and cognac with pleasure.

Then he looked up and out.

Perhaps he had been prompted by the primitive instinct that we like to believe tells us we are being watched.

Outside the enormous plate-glass window which placed between Roberto and reality the reflections of globe lamps and white-coated

waiters moving amongst the Madrid bourgeoisie, stood the fat man
who had followed him through the Metro after his second visit to the
Bank of the Victory of the Angels.

He was not more than a yard from Roberto. This time he wore a
black belted coat with shoulder flaps and a black hat pulled over his
small bespectacled eyes, eyes that stared intently at Roberto, met his
through the glass, and it was Roberto's that flinched away. A Nazi had
hired La Aguja, the Needle. López Rega died from a bullet in the head.
Gunter had the photo of López Rega dead, perhaps the proof the
customer requires of a contractor that the job has been properly done.
Street murder was not the most despicable, not the most horrible
means by which the people in this restaurant, the people he had rejected
so long ago, maintained, albeit at several removes, their property, their
privilege, their hegemony. Was Gunter merely just a part of that amor-
phous conspiracy, or, as now seemed probable, nearer the sharp end of
it?

How had La Aguja known where to find him? He could have been
following him all day. To the bank. To the Galician restaurant. To
Becky Herzer's tiny flat... Or had Pepita given Gunter the phone
number of this restaurant?

The euphoric high did not exactly evaporate – it very definitely
changed colour. Roberto rose with dignity, called for his bill, left a
large tip and paid at the bar. Good of Clemann to have paid up
promptly: at least, thought Roberto, I have spent my last hours in style.

28

THE TAPE RAN ON:

'It seemed as good a moment as any to go. I was well fed. That
has not always been the case. I was a little drunk – that happens often
enough but not on the very best white rum, the very best dry sherry.
That day I had made love with a woman. At my age, in my circumstances, I could not expect that to happen again for a long time, if ever.
The stars, the moon, the night, the frost. Go on, I said. A bullet now in
the back of the neck. I'll even pause *here* and let you do it. *Here,* I recall,
was outside the Lottery for the Blind Building. A few weeks ago
walking from the Biblioteca I saw two blind ticket sellers returning to
base, storming down the street, the one behind with his hand on the
shoulder of the one in front, goose-stepping they were, white sticks
held high, unsold tickets blowing in the autumn breeze, and as they
marched they counted – fifty-five, fifty-six, fifty-seven, LEFT TURN –

and faultlessly they marched through the open door of the building. Such courage. Such *élan*. Such a defiant Bronx cheer at the malign universe that had deprived them of sight. So. Remembering them. I stopped at the very same place, wished I had a cigarette to light, but refused the blindfold and waited for four-eyes in the black hat, La Aguja, to end it for me. But he did not.

'I walked on. Paused at a small art gallery and peered in at faintly luminous canvases. Stopped at an exotic pet shop where tiny monkeys huddled up to each other in wary, watchful sleep, much disturbed by a nocturnal cousin who swung about a larger cage behind them. Still no bullet. I pushed on to Desengaño.

'Why was I so certain this really was La Aguja? I had looked into his eyes through that restaurant window, through my glasses and through his, and I had seen... emptiness. Not the emptiness one assumes when one knows someone is searching you out, trying to read your mind, the emptiness Pepa and I had once or twice assumed in her apartment, the emptiness that came into McCabe's eyes when he had let slip he had *heard* the first tapes, not merely read transcripts, but the permanent emptiness of the permanently immoral, the emptiness of the eyes of the man who has nothing to hide.

'Since very clearly all concerned knew where I lived, there was no point in going into gross antics to shake him off. At the pet shop window I looked back, and there he was, a hundred metres or so behind. He made no attempt to conceal himself from me, that he was following me. He just stood there on the pavement, legs slightly apart, hands in the pockets of his belted coat. His head shifted slightly and moon-or-street light lit his glasses, turning them momentarily into ghoul-eyes.

'I pressed on and La Aguja came too down the almost empty streets, but always he kept his distance. In a way it was disappointing – I had made up my mind to it, my mind being high on drink, tolerably good food, and frosty starlit, moonlit night. But I must confess I felt relief too as I slotted my key into the keyhole of our door. I paused. Listened. No feet echoing up the deep well of the staircase, then yes. But they stopped at the second landing, and I heard the bell of the *pensión* peal.

'The landlord is a mean man. He sleeps, but his wife does not. She opened the door on a chain – I heard the conversation. Black Hat wanted a room. She doubted if she had one so late at night, and certainly not if he had a girl with him. Gravely he assured her that he was alone. He passed in his identity card, no doubt wrapped in a five hundred peseta note. She acquiesced and the chain jangled. I moved to our kitchen from which I can look down into the *patio de luces*. A pause. Then a light came on on the floor below ours, on the opposite side of the well, which is a wide one, this being a nineteenth-century building, perhaps its shell is a hundred years older than that. So I could see clearly how she showed him the room, left him. How he shed his black hat, his black coat, then came to the window, put his hands on the sill and looked up at me. Then he turned away and turned out his light. The moon, reflected off his window, concealed whatever he did next, and I turned away too.

'Ramón was not in. And he should have been. The *café-teatro* where he and Evita performed had been closed by the police. He had nowhere else to go. Never did he spend the night with Evita in Evita's flat. It was shared with four other students. When they spent nights together they spent them in Desengaño. So. Where was he? I needed him, I needed him here.'

STOP.

The horrible crescendoing clatter of a helicopter swiftly filled the room until it seemed the walls would burst with the noise. Hands over head-phoned ears Roberto watched it come between him and the sun whose first warm caress he had hungrily sought as it fingered its way into his room. Dust and litter, an old nest, whirled away as the monster shifted, swayed, and slowly dropped on to the roof of the Telefónica Building. Below, a white-helmeted soldier also watched it from the turret of his tank.

The noise leaked away and Roberto returned to his cane chair, pulled flannel dressing-gown closer around him, reached for the buttons, then paused. He pressed the rewind, let it run for five seconds, then pressed the play. His voice sounded dry, squeaky, breathless, tired. He let it run on until the roar of the helicopter again began to fill the room. He made silence, sat and thought. Then sighed very deeply, very heavily, took off his spectacles, rubbed his face and scoured his eyes with his knuckles.

PLAY AND RECORD:

'I think I have blown it, have I not? I am too old, too tired to think straight anymore. Or rather… to think crooked. I think I might almost pride myself on my failure as a crook, even though the motive was sound. To begin with I told it well – the truth, the right amount of truth, hardly any lies at all. But that was last night. I am sick and old and the best friend a man ever had is dead and still I don't know why. All I know is that whoever killed him must kill me. I should like to think the killers might face some sort of justice. Even Spanish justice. So why not tell the truth, as much of it as I know.

'Barclays International Bank, New York. Pay Roberto Constanza y Fairrie. Ten thousand dollars. Account of J E McCabe. And another. Pay Josefina Constanza González. Ten thousand dollars. Considering the payer is blasted apart, and the payee likely to be... Both payees? Oh God, or, if not God then the dialectical process of historical materialism, spare Pepita. Even if La Aguja is there because of her. She should have told me the truth about Gunter. But we agreed to keep well apart. I'll know soon. Meanwhile, press on...

'That night, Wednesday night, always hoping Ramón would return while I worked, I started to write a script. Yet another script. It was to be a detailed account of how there had been no hoarding of money or gold or diamonds by either Perón or Evita. Surprisingly enough it started well. Less surprising was the fact that soon I could go no further, I was falling asleep as I wrote. It had been a long day...

Becky! Well. At my age.

'I fell asleep but woke at about three o'clock or just a little after. Perhaps the church bell brought me to...'

He went to the kitchen for coffee and looked out to see if he could make out anything of La Aguja. More sober now, the presence of a killer after him seemed unreal, an alcoholic hallucination. The window was black, like a deep pool. He breathed in icy air and thought of champagne, and then he knew. Ramón *was* in Vellas Vistas, in Evita's apartment. The only times he spent the night there were when there were parties – and tonight there would be a party. With champagne.

He had to see him if he was to record this last tape in time. Was La Aguja a problem? No. For three reasons. La Aguja could have killed him already if he was going to. La Aguja could not, from his room, see Roberto leave the building. La Aguja was not La Aguja but a commercial traveller arrived late in Madrid.

29

Coat on again, muffler, black Homburg, still, at night, very much the professional man, Roberto walked down to Gran Vía and hailed a taxi. He gave the road and number of Evita's apartment in Vellas Vistas and sat back amongst the warm odours of cigar and cheap eau de cologne. The cabbie's radio was playing dance music.

'No news yet?'

The cabbie shrugged. 'They'll tell us when they're ready to.'

They passed across the top of the Plaza de España leaving the

Príncipe, the Corpus Cristi Bank and the Cervantes monument behind.
The wide avenues were now almost empty. Though white-helmeted
soldiers and police crouched round clusters of jeeps and armoured cars
at major intersections, they were not challenged.

'Historical moment,' offered Roberto.

'Of course.

Suddenly he wanted to be there. An historian by instinct and education he had often tried to get near the centre at turning points, nodes in
the process.

'Señor?'

'¿Qué?'

'Would you mind? But I think... why not? I think I should like to be
at the La Paz clinic. You can take me to Vellas Vistas later.'

'I'll take you as close as they'll let us.

They took the next major turn to the right and to the east, cut across
the north of central Madrid, back to that part of the central artery that
was still called Avenida del Generalísimo Franco, and turned north
again. Just as the apartment blocks began to give way to villas set in
bare frozen gardens, the hospital came into view.

The forecourt was floodlit, there were many more soldiers, Guardia
Civil, police. The cabbie pulled his Seat off the carriageway, parked at
a point from which they could just see the gates. He turned the radio
down but left it still clearly audible, twisted over the back of the front
seat and offered Roberto a Ducados. Roberto refused, the cabbie
shook one out for himself, snapped a Zippo. Surreptitiously Roberto
edged his window down, felt the bitter chill of the air and closed it.

'What time is it?'

The cabbie, a large man, black hair, dark rings round his eyes,
gestured with his cigarette at the illuminated clock on the dashboard.
Three forty-five.

They sat in silence. The music, distant it seemed, became a wordless
tango. Roberto's fingers tapped on his knees and he thought of the
Plaza de Mayo in the bright spring sunshine of October – Perón's
weather – and he remembered the big bass drums the lazzaroni carried
and beat in tango rhythms to excite the thrilling energy of the enormous crowds.

Lights behind, down the hill, bounced off the mirrors round the
inside of the cab. Three large black cars with motorcycle escort
sounding sirens came racing up the wide road from the city, ignoring
the traffic signals, moving with power, purpose and disregard for
anything that might be in their way, like powerful jets on a radar-
controlled flight plan. They slowed only to swing through the high iron
gates. Floods brightened and the top of an RTVE camera swung

towards them. Silver hair burned above grey suits that shone like silver.

'Ministers. Either it has happened or it is immediately about to happen.' The cabbie stubbed out his cigarette – as a mark of respect?

Orders were shouted, heavy diesel engines coughed into life, tracks rattled and squealed. A line of white-helmeted troops goose-stepped out from an intersecting alley, and, fussed over by a gander-like sergeant, deployed across the forecourt of the hospital.

The cabbie turned up the radio, searched for another station. Still dance music.

'Yet,' he said, 'I'm sure he's gone. It's all over.'

'They'll wait till dawn.'

'Why?'

'To coincide with José Antonio's execution.'

The cabbie lit another cigarette and his fingers drummed nervously on the rim of the steering wheel.

Two military policemen, hung about with guns, grenades, truncheons and whistles came across the road. Roberto wound down the window, said in Spanish but using the German word, 'So. The Führer is dead. Is he not?'

He sensed the deepening of their menace. The larger of them waved, swung a huge fist in front of the windscreen.

'Lárguense o ya veran.'

The cabbie turned the key and the engine fired.

'Vellas Vistas?'

'Please.'

He turned right into Avenida del General Perón, followed Roberto's directions across Bravo Murillo into the warren of smaller streets above the university.

'This is it. Please wait.'

The cabbie fiddled with his radio.

Roberto climbed stairs to the apartment Evita shared with other South American students. There was indeed a party, with dope as well as champagne. Ramón was unconscious in Evita's arms. Roberto wrote a note pleading for his presence at Desengaño as soon as possible, pinned it to his shirt and left.

'Listen,' said the cabbie. He had found a French station. There was static but the voice was clear enough. '*Le Général Francisco Franco, Caudillo d'Espagne, est mort. Un conseil de regence...*

They drove back to Desengaño in silence. Why? Perhaps neither quite dared to express what he felt – elation? grief? fear? hope? – in case it would not be shared by the other. Roberto paid off the cabbie with pesetas changed from Swivel's fistful of dollars, and got back into his flat, for the second time that night, without being pounced on by La Aguja.

He was now entirely ready to dismiss the fat man who had followed him from the restaurant near Colón as... just a fat man. A commercial traveller perhaps, arrived in Madrid late at night, perhaps from Barajas or the Chamartín railway terminal, coming from the Recoletos subway railway station, looking in at a restaurant too expensive, and then wandering into central Madrid looking for a cheap *pensión*. As he slopped brandy into a tall glass he accepted that high as he had been on alcohol, exhaustion, excitement, and Gunter's Polaroid photograph of the murdered López Rega, he had been too ready to believe what now seemed palpable nonsense.

At his desk he pulled paper towards him, set his glass at his side, switched on the radio which still played wordless light music and, with the electric fire between his feet, began to write.

There had been (and it seemed the ghost of Perón stood behind his shoulder and gave dictation) no hoarding of money, gold or gems by either Juan Domingo or Eva. Oh yes, he engagingly admitted, a certain rechannelling of state funds, and yes, there had been personal extravagance. There had too been lavish generosity – to friends, family, supporters, but also to the poor, the needy, the underprivileged who had been so remarkably championed by Eva, and so scandalously neglected since 1955.

But no massive movement of funds to Swiss banks, no hoards of gems smuggled abroad in the false bottoms of suitcases.

It was a creative flow, Roberto scribbled as if possessed. He had felt the possibility before, had distrusted it, rejected it. But now... why not? For thirty years Perón – plump, jolly, toothy (at first they called him Colonel Kolynos, after the toothpaste) – had been there in his life. Three years of hope and trust, two of hope, and twenty-five years of hate, confusion, and now, lately, a sort of understanding. Trying to get the tapes right he had learnt even a sort of affection for the charlatan, the rogue. Not a mass murderer (how could he be when his central power base was the masses?), a physical coward, perhaps, who certainly side-stepped and lost whenever he was faced with violence, he had been no Pinochet, no Nixon, no Kissinger.

And now, prompted by the necessity of producing a tape McCabe would unhesitatingly accept as genuine on all counts, he wrote as Perón would have wished it, recreating a Perón more like what Perón wanted to be than ever Perón himself had achieved on the *ABC* tapes.

At six in the morning the dance music stopped and the regular first newscast of the day began. Incredulously, flooded suddenly with weary despair, Roberto heard that the Caudillo, though worsening, was still alive. Other items followed. Then silence. Then the Minister for Information was announced, and at last it was official. Spain was allowed to know what the rest of Europe had known for two hours. Franco was dead.

Roberto raised his glass, drained it, and rolled, still dressed, into his narrow bed, and slept, again.

30

He awoke at ten and panicked. At ten he was meant to phone Clemann. There was still no sign of Ramón, he had not finished his script, there was no chance of getting the new tape to the bank before one o'clock. Clearly he had to make contact with Pepita, though the agreement was that this should never be done unless there was an emergency. Any evidence of collusion between them, however slight, would be the end of everything. But this surely was an emergency.

Roberto pulled on his outdoor clothes, found a handful of pesetas for the public phone boxes, and slithered and clattered down the stairs past the *pensión* entrance and out into the street. He hardly gave a thought to the paranoid delusions he had entertained about the traveller, no doubt Galician, who had arrived behind him the night before.

Outside the José Antonio Metro each of the phone boxes had a queue of at least two people. As he joined one of them the user, a large working man in donkey jacket and jeans burst out, swearing – nothing but engaged tones and crossed lines. The lady in front of Roberto shrugged – 'The Caudillo is dead,' she said. 'The whole world phones Madrid, and everyone in Madrid tries to phone everyone else.' She turned away and Roberto took her place. It was all true. He replaced the useless handset, scooped up his returned pesetas, thought of the Metro, rejected it, sighted a miraculously empty taxi and flagged it down.

He had time now to take in the city on the morning of Franco's death. It was, as the bulletins said, calm, and, with the news still little more than four hours old, unchanged. Shops and, Roberto noticed with despair, banks were open.

Outside Pepita's apartment block he pressed the buzzer three times, got no answer, and at last resorted to the keys she had given him but told him never to use unless the success of their scheme was under terminal threat.

The *conserje* had draped the portrait of Franco with black.

The locks in Pepita's door opened almost soundlessly, and as he let himself in he heard her cry – a moan, a sob, a gasp, something of all three, and then repeated, once twice, rhythmically. He was standing in a tiny hall off which three doors opened – the living room, bathroom, and bedroom. The bedroom door was ajar. Two steps only took him to the gap. It was not a room he had ever looked in before. There was a small bright chandelier, a lot of quilted leather and yellow quilted satin, and many mirrors. He took it all in in less than five seconds and the images he left with were confused but vivid.

Pepita was kneeling on the bed, her body very white in contrast to the yellowish gold of Gunter's. He was standing behind her, thrusting at her from behind.

Roberto fled – out of the door, ignored the lift, stumbled down three flights, across the marble hall, out into the cold bright air. He leant against the bronze door jamb and heaved and coughed, even let his knees sink a little before pulling himself together sufficiently to stagger down and across the street to a bar where he drank, because he could not think of anything else to ask for, coffee and brandy.

Twenty minutes later he went back to the street door and again pressed Pepita's buzzer. This time she answered, said she would join him in the bar as soon as she could.

'You came in an hour ago. You saw.'

'Yes.'

She was in her sable, her hair was wild, thrown up like a mane above her forehead, her face white but bruised on the left cheekbone. Her top lip was swollen. Roberto longed to take her in his arms, comfort and caress her into some sort of quietness. She shook out a cigarette, lit it.

'I think he saw you. In the mirror.'

'So?'

She shrugged. 'I don't suppose it matters. Too much. He knows... suspects or has guessed what there is to be known. Why did you come?'

Her anger was manifest – he sensed she wore it like a mask to cover... what? Shame. Humiliation. He wanted to tell her that it did not matter that he had seen what he had seen, but he could not.

'I can't get a new tape to you by one o'clock. Ramón is up at Vellas Vistas with Evita. Lord knows when he'll come back. Lord knows if he'll be in a fit state to do anything when he does come back.'

She stirred sugar into her espresso, flung back her head and her angry green eyes glittered at him.

'It doesn't matter. It doesn't matter at all.'

'Why not?'

'Listen. Haven't you heard the bulletins? Don't you know what's happening?'

'Not since six o'clock this morning.'

'Three days, full mourning. He lies in state from tomorrow morning through to the funeral on Sunday. The King will be sworn in at the Cortés on Saturday. The banks are due to close at any time and will not open again until Monday. You've got four days. Four whole days.'

'But Clemann...?'

'Clemann can't get in touch with me, nor I with him by phone. They are jammed, or I can pretend mine is. He won't seek me out in person. Nor even send Steve. That would be a sign of weakness. So. He'll sit it out until I ring him. Anyway,' she gestured a little wildly and gold chains chimed and flashed as they slipped down her thin veinous arms. 'He can't leave.' She drew in smoke, breathed it out with flared nostrils like a dragon. 'The question is. Can you get together a tape that really will answer that orange lizard's bizarre objections?'

Roberto remembered the creative flow, the sense of Perón himself giving dictator's dictation at his ear.

'Yes.'

'Well then. That's fine.' She shrugged the sable about her, drained her coffee, stubbed out the cigarette, pressed a precise finger and thumb into the corners of her mouth. 'His lordship thinks I have gone out for eggs. I had, I suppose, better find some. Somewhere. Oh yes. Last night. After you phoned me from that restaurant at Recoletos he asked me who had rung and where from. He had seen me take down the number. I told him.' She touched her bruised cheek. 'Why not? Then he rang someone else. Called Betelmann. Who is he?'

Fear and despair rose like vomit.

'He is,' said Roberto, 'sometimes known as La Aguja, the Needle. Probably he killed López Rega...'

Her anger dissolved. Her face dropped into her hands and she sobbed. He came round the table, put an arm round her, and twisted his fingers into hers.

'Oh Papa, Papa,' she moaned.

'Pepita. *Querida,*' he offered. 'I always said it would be difficult. Dangerous. I always said so.'

Nevertheless, as he strode through the chill streets back to Desengaño he found her breakdown, her tears not quite convincing. Or rather, though genuine enough – she really would be sorry if he came to harm, he was sure of that – he felt that in her scheme of things he was not the most important thing of all. Before his skin she would certainly put her own; for less, for certain luxury and security, she might well sacrifice him. She was, after all, part of *them,* part of the corrupt conspiracy of the rich and the would-be rich; she lived off and at the mercy of people like Gunter. In short, he did not believe that it had been absolutely impossible for her to withhold the restaurant phone number from her Argentinian lover.

Obeying the traffic lights he began the crossing of the Paseo del Prado at Cibeles, and in the middle found himself caught in a jostling but silent and surly queue that was forming round the kiosks. The first papers printed since the announcement of Franco's death had appeared on the streets. He allowed himself to be pushed forward to the vendor, found there was as yet no new edition of the new liberal paper *El País,* to avoid argument bought the popular *Ya.*

Scarcely bothering to look at it he hurried on. The giant electric clock and thermometer above the junction of Gran Vía and Alcalá registered 3 and 11.55. He was surprised. It felt colder. And then he saw a man banging helplessly on the glass door of the Banco Hispano Americano, and he realised with a touch of panic, that Pepita had been right – all round him shops, businesses, banks were closing, shutters going up. Had he enough food? Enough money? Yes, of course. He certainly had enough money.

He shrugged. There were always wine, brandy, coffee and tinned sardines at Desengaño.

He walked the last couple of hundred metres more slowly and brought himself to face one of the questions he had been avoiding. What was Gunter up to? *No sé.* I don't know. Gunter had known Pepita for many months. As far as the tapes were concerned Roberto had no reason to suppose that Gunter thought of them as anything but genuine. *Unless Pepita had told him otherwise.* The man was a bully, a moral degenerate, a fascist. He was also rich and unscrupulous. Why had he sent La Aguja to follow him to Desengaño, to take a room from which he could watch Roberto's attic? Because, in spite of whatever Pepa had told Gunter, Gunter believed there was still more to know.

There was some comfort in this thought. As long as Roberto knew something (though Lord knew what!) that Gunter wanted to know, then presumably his skin was reasonably likely to stay whole. At least as far as La Aguja was concerned. And meanwhile, there was still just a chance that a sale could still be agreed with Clemann. The danger would pass with the tapes to him – and they might yet make the sort of money they hoped for.

Roberto laboured through the later afternoon and as he did, the script became sluggish, nasty, dead. No longer did Juan Domingo Perón strut about the room behind him, no longer did he feel the power all but the most self-denying historians feel as they mould and shape the clay of fact into the subtle pottery that those who pay them will accept as true.

His mind was poisoned. By fear: the fat commercial traveller who rented a room below his own and across the *patio de luces* dealt after all in death; by the wretchedness of knowing that Pepita would never quite forgive him for having actually seen her at her trade. By guilt: he had promised Herzer he would expose his tapes once Pepita had sold them – now he doubted he would have the courage to do so. By guilt again: if he did not expose them he would have put lies on the market and profited from them. I am, he thought, an old-fashioned bourgeois at heart – my word is my bond.

Not long after darkness fell there was a knock on the door – knuckles against the whitened patch where the Sacred Heart had once been nailed. He peered into the ineffective spyglass and saw McCabe. Terror subsided. It could have been Betelmann, La Aguja, the Needle.

31

'**M**ay I come in?' McCabe did not wait for an answer but stepped forward. Roberto moved to avoid the humiliation of being pushed.

He panicked. There was nowhere to put the tall gangly American except the kitchen or bathroom, nowhere, that is, where there was not evidence of some sort or other that the apartment was a factory for the production of Perón tapes. He tried to shepherd him into the kitchen.

'I'm afraid we're rather unorganised.'

'So I see.'

McCabe stood in the doorway, his thinning gingery hair almost touching the lintel. He surveyed the filthy cooker, the crowded sink, the narrow white-topped table stained with rings of dried red wine. 'You must have a living room.'

He turned up the short narrow passage.

'The further one.' Roberto indicated his own room with a sinking feeling that all was now lost. 'More a bed-sit really.'

He pulled himself together, made a last effort, drew on resources provided by an English public school, albeit progressive, and Cambridge.

'I say, you know. I do think you've got a nerve. Barging in like this.'

'Really?' McCabe folded himself down on to the cane chair, looked around slowly, nodded to himself. 'Really!' He mimicked Roberto's Englishness back at him. 'I say, be a fine fellow and get us a cup of coffee, and we'll talk it all over, shall we? Black. One sugar.'

Humiliation continued. Roberto, agitated, found he could not unscrew the top section of the espresso coffee maker, and there was no Nescafé. He had to take the pot in to McCabe who twisted it apart with ease, in spite of the thinness of his wrists and fingers.

Worse was to come. When the coffee was made and he carried it through McCabe was, of course, reading the script Roberto had been composing. He glanced sideways as Roberto placed the coffee at his elbow.

'I have to say,' he said, 'I rumbled Josefina Constanza González quite early on. Who, incidentally, I take to be your daughter. Yes?'

Blankly Roberto assented.

'But I didn't too quickly see how you fitted into the act. Clearly these tapes were forgeries. So the lady had to be fronting for someone.'

Chagrin bit. 'Clearly?'

'Oh, don't misunderstand me. The quality of the performance is exemplary. It might not get by an electronic analysis, but then that's not going to be that easy to set up. And it's a game lawyers and experts love to play. They could keep the thing going for a year or more, cost a million.

'Content-wise there are problems – but nothing insurmountable. Mainly, as I said last night, they're too anti-Perón. That guy wore a mask all the time. He never let it drop. Not even to himself. And now I see you are attempting to adjust that bias.' He tapped Roberto's script. 'The actor of course is Ramón Puig.'

To deny this too seemed futile.

'He's very good. You see, when I came over to help *ABC* with the real tapes, I saw that poster' – he pointed to it on the wall: *Los Peroles* – 'and of course I had to go along and see it. Great. I liked the script. But Puig *was* Perón, and that Castillo as Evita was something else again. But that's by the way. I had no reason to make connections then and your name did not appear in the publicity. No. The first reason for suspicion was the whole set-up, the ambiance of it all. It was too like a re-run of the Montiam episode. And then I have my contacts in the Perón household too, you know? And they were as certain as could be the Montiam tapes were the only ones Perón made. And so on. As for you, I began to ask myself and others questions about you the second time I saw you set up a tape-recorder. The first time you were a bumbling old fool who did not even know where the flex was housed. The second time you ran it like a disc jockey. Well. I'm in touch with resources, databanks and so on. You have left-wing affiliations for half a century you acquire a file or two, you know?'

He finished his coffee.

'I've still not figured how you got in on the act up front as a Perón expert in Clemann's pay. I guess it was through Cockburn, but I don't think he's in this with you.'

'He is not. Early on, six months ago, I wrote to him saying I was an expert on Perón and Peronismo with a book I wanted to publish. He came to think of me as an independent expert who happened to live in Madrid.'

'Neat. In fact all in all it's been quite a neat little operation. The question is, where do we go from here?'

'Yes. Indeed.'

Silence lengthened between them.

McCabe pushed out his long tweedy legs, folded his fingers together under his chin.

'Whoever,' he said, 'acquires these tapes of yours will in one way or another publish them in an edited version. The point is to what end will the editing take place?'

'But if you say they are forgeries, who will want them?'

'Come on. Any buyer, Clemann or anyone else who actually buys them, will find experts to say they are good. You know that. To what end the editing? Clemann would cut out repetition and ennui. He would not respect certain perfectly legitimate interests that could be inconvenienced, at the very least, by publication. That would not be a consideration for him. And I think it should be. It is not only legitimate, it is essential, *pro bono publico,* that responsible persons, with clear guidelines, should handle material as sensitive as this...'

'You go on talking as if the tapes were genuine.'

'Saleable. Which is genuine, real. Definition of reality – you can exchange it. So. I conceive it as a responsibility to make sure these tapes do not fall into Clemann's hands, that they should be properly... sanitised before going out into the market-place. In point of fact it is not merely a responsibility. It is in this case a commission.'

'I don't follow you.'

'Well, we'll see. Is there any more coffee?'

Roberto reheated what was left in the pot, and in the kitchen remembered La Aguja. Was he still sitting on the floor below, across the well, looking up at the lights in Roberto's apartment? He shuddered, stared at the frosted glass of the closed window with a sort of fascinated revulsion, then turned away. He took the pot back into his room, refilled McCabe's cup, set the pot on the table at his elbow.

McCabe drank, dabbed his lips on a large blue handkerchief.

'Just let us continue to temporarily hypothesise that your tapes are genuine. As I say, if that were the case, I would have been commissioned to make sure they fall into responsible hands.'

'Whose?'

McCabe made an odd little pout – half grin, half grimace. 'Those of the Great and the Good. Whose else? Whose servant I am. As the one politically reliable, academically accredited expert in a very important area of Latin American studies, I naturally do not withhold my services when the State Department asks for them.'

'Clemann knows nothing of this.'

'No.'

'And he employed you before?'

'Indeed yes.'

'And sent you transcripts of the Montiam tapes?'

'Yes.'

'And later you *heard* those tapes. You admitted as much.'

'That's right. Once *ABC* had them I got to hear the lot.'

'Assisting them in the process of sanitisation.'

McCabe shrugged. If he was on the defensive at this point he hardly showed it. 'That was perhaps the idea. It was scarcely necessary. There was very little of interest in them. They were boring and repetitive. And downright inaccurate. They were the almost mindless wanderings of an old man rewriting history to justify the mess he'd made of it when he was in a position to do so. Let me tell you, Fairrie, your tapes are a heck of a lot more interesting. I'll come to the point. I want to buy them.'

'Oh dear Lord.' Roberto struggled to his feet, pushed across the table at the window catch, knocked the espresso pot so it fell across his papers spilling a dribble of grainy brown, got the window open. A gust of freezing smog blew in on them, and the subdued traffic noise from Gran Vía. Then he shut it again, subsided back on to the bed. The room was very small, and he had to twist his knees away from McCabe's to avoid contact. 'Why?'

McCabe was brisk now. 'They are like a palimpsest. Under layers of other stuff they actually do contain real information that is not available elsewhere. You had your sources close to Perón, like Señora González who no doubt gave you the details of how the old lecher carried on with his nymphets. Then there is the stuff about Nazis and their immigration into Argentina. Martín Bormann is alive and well...'

'You weren't there when that bit was played.'

'You can be sure I heard of it.'

Who from? Roberto struggled to disentangle the web of possibilities.

'And checking back it was accurate, very accurate. Source?'

'A friend of Evita's. Castillo's. Another Montonero. He came from a family that had married... been married into by... *émigrés*. I never met him. They judged it would be safer if I did not. Ramón and Evita came home with the facts, and I wrote them up.'

'Do you mind telling me just about when this source of information did materialise?'

'Why should I mind? July this year. Early August.'

McCabe nodded slowly, owlishly wise.

'You see? I really do think your tapes have real value. And I, or Milton University, Iowa, which I represent, is, are, ready to... to take them off your hands.'

Roberto was now deeply confused. Not least because McCabe had guessed quite wrong where Pepita was concerned. The bits about Perón and his nymphets, including Pepita, had all been invented by Roberto. For all the *demimondaine* aspects of Pepa's lifestyle, she had been brought up an ultra-Catholic in an ultra-bourgeois (once Roberto had left it) household. It was unthinkable that she should talk to her *father* about such things. And now, educated twentieth-century man that he was, he guessed he had projected his own desires concerning his daughter on to Perón, who was, of course, a father figure... Stop. That way madness lies. Or sanity.

He was shocked too, in spite of himself, at the duplicity of this academic, this representative of the liberal, humanist tradition, the tradition that had created such fine and independent temples to science and the arts as Milton University, Iowa.

All he could think of saying, after a long pause was: 'What, if we sell, will you do with them?'

'They will go into Milton University archives as the real thing. With my say-so pinned to them there will be no questioning of their authenticity, no way will an electronic test be thought necessary.' There was an appeal here to Roberto's vanity. 'It will be announced that they will be a major source for a definitive biography that I am working towards. Meanwhile, however, they will be available to other researchers, and even the media, as and when the other people I work with see fit.'

'The State Department?'

McCabe assented. Was there something again almost coy in this admission? If so, why? Was he checking a tendency to show pride in his connection with real power? Or was there a residue of guilt that he thus compromised the always dubious independence of Academe? Perhaps an uneasy mix of the two.

'Sure. The State Department.'

'And what criteria will determine how they use the tapes?'

'What do *you* think? They will use them, quite rightly in my view, according as to how they will perceive, in the constantly dynamic situation that always pertains in Latin America, they may best assist the execution of State Department policies in that area, at any given time.'

Roberto took breath. 'You cannot imagine it was ever any part of my design that they should serve the interests of the State Department.'

'No. I cannot say I imagine that. But. You and the State Department do have a lot in common. A deep dislike of Peronismo. To that extent your tapes will be in good hands.'

It could have been a cry of pain, but it came out like a squawk: 'Doctor Kissinger's!'

Again the coy shrug. Roberto guessed that McCabe rather liked the idea of Kissinger – the academic who'd made it so far outside Academe that he could drop bombs on a genocidal scale.

'I have to think about all this.'

McCabe looked at his watch. 'Five minutes. Right?'

In his squalid kitchen Roberto drank brandy and tried to arrange his thoughts – and all, finally, he could think of was the danger, and the money, and then again the danger. Ramón and Pepita remained at risk while the tapes were in Pepita's possession. All very well to knock the liberal humanist stance – but this was his daughter, his only child, and the other his best friend. It was time to call it off. They had intruded themselves into a thoroughly nasty world – children floating paper boats amongst crocodiles. Perhaps there was still time to paddle back to the edge.

'How much?'

'A hundred grand. Dollars.'

'Ramón and Pepita may not agree.'

McCabe said nothing. Roberto pushed on: 'I think a deposit would help. Ten thousand dollars for each of us.'

McCabe pulled out a cheque book, wrote, tore off, went through the action three times.

'You have dated them the twenty-fifth. Tuesday.'

'That's right. Earnest of my good intentions. You get the rest in cash, Monday, at the bank, at two o'clock precisely, where and when you hand over the tapes to me. But if you don't come across, these cheques will be stopped. I'll leave it to you to make sure González gets it all properly set up. I'll see myself down.'

He unfolded himself, reconstructed his spindly height, reassumed his herring-bone tweed top-coat, brown scarf, leather gloves. He took his hat, which exactly matched his coat, and said: 'Perhaps too you'll consider an option on the next instalment?'

'I don't follow you.'

'I mean, we might want to give you a scenario for some more tape. You and Puig could then…?'

Roberto was suddenly very angry, but he concealed it. 'I don't think so.'

McCabe shrugged. 'Think about it. Oh. And by the way. I want all the tapes. All thirteen of them. Is that understood?'

'Thirteen?'

'The eight, no nine, you made, so it is fourteen *in* toto, and the five you did not make.'

Roberto opened the door, standing aside as he did so. It was as well he did. One bullet at least passed right through McCabe, and ended up in the ceiling. The body was thrown against the door jamb, but then toppled forward, loose limbs at last definitively unhinged, down the narrow flight of stairs towards where his killer had stood.

32

PLAY AND RECORD:

'Ramón came back an hour after McCabe was shot. Before I could tell him about that, he told me that a man in a leather jacket was standing on the landing below ours. Ramón was not in good shape after twenty-four hours of champagne and dope, and was in worse shape after I had told him that a murder had been committed on our doorstep. The body had been taken away of course. Blood and things nastier wiped up, by, I rather think, the Galician landlady downstairs. Not long after the noises of swabbing and so on I saw her from my kitchen cleaning out a bucket in hers. There was no sign of La Aguja, but that meant nothing.

'For an hour we debated what was to be done, and concluded we could do nothing. Neither of us was ready to go out into the streets, not even as far as a call-box, in the middle of the night. Neither of us was ready to go to bed. Ramón told me of demonstrations near Vellas Vistas, of Falangists returning from the dawn ceremony at the tomb of José Antonio in the Valley of the Fallen, where Franco will shortly be put, returning and chanting *Muerte al Rey*. Others, or the same, had cheered Pinochet's arrival at Barajas, thus signalling support for any Spanish general who might be making up his mind to do to Juan Carlos what Pinochet did to Allende. He showed me a PCE leaflet urging the workers to strike, to form soviets, to march on the prisons and begin the final battle for democracy.

'Definitely there were plenty of reasons for staying indoors. I have experienced similar situations in Barcelona in 1936, and in Buenos Aires. All street murders are deemed to be political and none is investigated. People settle scores.

'Neither of us wanted to sleep, but in the end we had to. In bed I tried to forget McCabe's body smashed with heavy bullets, tried to remember Becky's warmth and tenderness the day before but that pleasure was vitiated by the stupid promise I had made her. Bone and blood splattered across the door intervened, and in the end I had to take some of Ramón's Seconal.

'At dawn or not long after we listened to the radio. The night had been quiet and Franco's body was already in the Palace. We drank coffee, wondered again what was to be done. I explained to Ramón that we had already made ten thousand dollars each, showed him McCabe's cheques, and argued that for the sake of our own safety, and Pepita's, we should call it a day, hand the tapes over to whomever wanted them, and explain they were forgeries. Get back to terra firma before the crocodiles snapped again.

'He shrugged, said an odd thing: "Not bad pay really, since, when all was said and done you and I were little more than bait."

'How to get out without being murdered or kidnapped, how to get to Pepita or Clemann was the problem. Intermittently we listened to the radio and it provided an answer. An enormous queue was forming to view the cadaver, already it stretched up Bailén and into Plaza de España. People were advised to approach its tail via José Antonio, Gran Vía. Ramón insisted that the fascist propaganda machine was exaggerating the numbers, but looking out of the window and into the street we could see a steady flow of say ten at any one time of people in mourning moving towards Gran Vía. If there were so many in Desengaño, there must truly be a vast crowd coalescing in Gran Vía.

'Ramón's Thespian instinct asserted itself. He insisted I should dress the part. While I searched out clean linen and black tie he brushed my suit and cleaned my shoes. Soon I looked the very model of a modern bourgeois gentleman in mourning.

'Bravely he went ahead of me down the stairs and shortly I heard him asking leather jacket for matches. I moved quickly past them as leather jacket cupped his hand round Ramón's cigarette. He followed me of course but I made it into Gran Vía before he could get at all close to me. The wide pavements were indeed crowded and there were police everywhere. The general movement was towards the Palace, but the smaller streets on the left which would have led there more quickly were blocked off. The crowd fed into the tail of the queue just short of the Santo Domingo Metro and I found myself in a file which, it appeared, contained two duchesses, without jewels, a retired surgeon and a retired general. For a time I assumed with them the upright bearing, the eyes glassily fixed on an imaginary point six inches above the head in front, and shuffled along thus to the manner born. But I was anxious too to see what had become of leather jacket and soon I was committing the solecism of peering all around me. Garish and bizarre, the several cinemas clustering round Santo Domingo displayed posters that would not change for a week or a month, no matter who died, whose funeral it was. *American Graffiti, Clockwork Orange,* and, live on stage, *Jesus Christ, Superstar.*

'The queue occupied one half of the carriageway. The pavements were now almost empty except for the *policia armada* at intervals and intersections. And sure enough, before long there he was, in front of me, on the pavement scanning the files of mourners as they passed him. He spotted me and flashed white teeth in something like a grin – I did not smile back.

'Five minutes later we rounded into Plaza de España, and, to my relief, the queue moved along the south side. A minute or two later and we were passing the steps of El Príncipe. I murmured apologies to my duchesses and generals and trotted up the steps into the congenial warmth of the foyer…'

33

Cockburn's room was less congenial. As he let Roberto in, Swivel podgy, with a towel round his waist, came out of the bathroom, rubbing his sparse hair with another. Clemann, fully dressed, was sitting at a table in the window watching the queue. The remains of a large Spanish hotel breakfast were scattered over the room.

'Come in,' said Clemann. 'You are lucky to find me here. Thanks to this… *show,*' he gestured scornfully at what was happening below – 'flights from Barajas are all delayed or cancelled. Well, what have you come to tell me?'

This was indeed the question. Should he tell the whole truth, some of it, none of it even? The important thing was to persuade Clemann to take the tapes off their hands and take on the danger that went with them. But could he do that? No doubt Clemann could take care of himself. No doubt McCabe had thought the same. And there remained the crisis of conscience he had felt at McCabe's cynical readiness to use the tapes even though forged. Clemann's use would be conditional on his acceptance of them as authentic and it would not be cynical. But could Roberto now allow him to market them in that way, write into history a falsehood?

Dumb with all this in his mind, he removed gloves and coat, groped for a chair.

Clemann, with compassion that was both Olympian and reproving relieved him of the necessity of making a choice. 'We know you forged some if not all of your tapes. Señora González made one quite serious mistake. She underestimated Steve's attachment to me and the extent to which he was upset by her association with Gunter. He returned the night before last drunk but coherent with a tale of intimacy and collusion between you and González. I spent most of yesterday making enquiries, as far as the log jam on the Madrid telephone system allowed, and it now seems Josefina Constanza González is your daughter.'

This made an act of confession, if not contrition, easier. Roberto nodded his head emphatically, fingered a broken madeleine on the table in front of him, rejected it. 'Yes, yes. That is all just so. But there is something else you should know. McCabe came to my flat last night, having come to a similar conclusion, in spite of which he made a private bid for the tapes. He was shot as he left. Shot dead...'

'Jesus,' cried Swivel, and edged further into the room, away from doors and windows. Fat and wet, he looked very vulnerable.

'Oh shit!' hissed Cockburn, who was sitting on the edge of one of the beds.

Clemann was brisk. 'You had better tell me the whole story as briefly as you reasonably can.'

It was a brief account. Roberto quickly outlined how he had written a satirical play about the Peróns for Puig and Castillo; how Pepa had seen it and been impressed by Puig's impersonation; how she had approached them and revealed that she was Roberto's daughter whom he had not seen for twenty-five years and told them of her peripheral involvement in the sale of the first tapes; how Cockburn had been set up to believe Roberto was an independent expert on the Peróns. He skipped through the events of the previous week, but gave them a fuller account of McCabe's visit and murder.

Clemann asked: 'Why did you do all this? You do not strike me as greedy or ambitious. I should have guessed you were too sensible to be merely a meddler.'

Roberto explained how for thirty years he had devoted his life and money to running radical bookshops. Life remained but the money had gone.

Clemann turned to Swivel who was now clothed in a scarlet silk dressing-gown.

'He should go to the police,' said Swivel. 'Immediately. And if he doesn't we should. We are in possession of facts the police should have. No doubt of it. No two ways.'

'Steve?'

Cockburn leant forward, passed fingers through the tarnished silver of his curly hair. 'No doubt from a narrowly legalistic point of...'

There was hysteria in Swivel's voice: 'Christ, Cockburn, it's not narrowly legalistic to suggest murders should be reported to the authorities.'

'All right. But I do rather take leave to wonder what will be achieved.'

Clemann: 'I take your point. This was the murder of a man working for the US State Department, possibly with a CIA control. On the State Department's behalf he was apparently conspiring to commit a fraud. Fairrie indicates it was a contract killing set up by one of the agencies the Nazis use to protect themselves, the sort of people who had López Rega shot. If that is the case the Spanish police will be totally ineffectual, their hands tied twice – by the CIA, and by the tolerance of fascism in the ruling cliques. The law may be served by reporting this to the police. Justice will not.'

Swivel shook his fat head in exasperation, unknotted and reknotted the silk belt round his waist.

Cockburn: 'And if this murder is reported we, you Peter, will be subjected to a lot of inconvenience. Form at least will require that we be asked to stay in Madrid at least during the preliminary enquiries. I imagine that would be a nuisance for you. It certainly would for me.'

'Hang on.' Swivel, on one side of the bed, twisted his head to bring part of Cockburn in view. 'I do find I have to ask myself this. To what extent is Cockburn's position one he has taken up out of undeclared motives of self-interest?'

'What the fuck are you talking about?'

'I imagine Josefina González's interests will also be served by hushing this up.'

'Oh come on. Come *on.*' Cockburn appealed to Clemann. 'You can't imagine I've got any thought of that in my mind. She set me up for this. I was the means through which she was to get her grubby fingers on your lucre. Anyway, Gunter is screwing her on a regular basis, he's a hell of a lot richer than I am and better at it too, I dare say.'

Roberto detected real spite directed at him behind this outburst. The whole business indeed was distasteful, like some sultan's divan where advisers vied with each other to offer what would best protect their favoured positions at the Sublime Porte. Except, he thought quirkily, in this case it's not the Sultan who is on the divan, but the advisers.

'Which brings us back to Gunter. What do you know about him, Fairrie?'

Roberto recapitulated what he had heard from Juan Evita Castillo.

'Clearly,' said Clemann, 'there is every indication that he is a link between your tapes and Die Spinne.' He stood up, peered out of the window and down into the square. 'In the last decade lines have become very blurred in these areas. Nazis, financiers, arms-dealers, drug operators, the banks, the hierarchy of the Church, the Christian Democrats – one used to know one area from another, though recognising that an evil symbiosis existed between them. But now they're more locked together, tangled, as if disparate parts have come together to make – a monster. Your leather-jacketed friend is still there, and indeed there are now two of them. What we have to decide is what *do* we do. No, Henry, I am not going to the police.'

'In that case sit tight, and get the hell out as soon as we can.'

'Which won't be for several hours yet, if not days.'

'So. Sit tight.'

'Yes indeed. I heard you. *We* have little option. What I meant was, how can we help Mr Fairrie, for it was, was it not, for help that he came.'

Silence. The murmur as of a sea distant and calm, of ten thousand well-shod feet shuffling, moving like a single organism.

Swivel let out air. 'Peter. This man tried very hard to sell you fraudulent goods. For one heck of a lot of money.'

'Yes, Henry. But his motives were not dishonourable. One may question the means, but that's an old question which no one has answered without being guilty of either blatant hypocrisy or overt brutality. So. How can we help him? It might be helpful to see if we can't put together a clearer picture of what he's up against. Many people might have an interest in suppressing or getting editorial control of these tapes. As was the case with the first lot. But most, CIA, *ABC*, even Peronists would murder as a third or fourth option. But I suspect Nazis alone would choose that option first. Now. At the first hearing of these tapes Cockburn tells me González played a tape cutting it off immediately before apparent revelations about Bormann. I imagine, Fairrie, you had a lot more of the same sort of thing.'

'Yes. A whole cassette. Ninety minutes.'

'But invented.'

'No. I believe not.' Roberto tried to master the agitation he felt. 'The chief source, I believe, was a Montonero exile in Madrid, in touch with Montoneros in Buenos Aires, Córdoba and so on. As you know, most of that movement are middle-class, or higher. Many families have been married into by Nazi *émigrés*. There were, after all, ten thousand of them or more. The Montoneros have built up a large, and I believe accurate dossier. What they lack is a means of publishing it. No one would touch it without adulterating it. Our tapes seemed a good outlet, and they gave us the information.'

'But no one heard that cassette beyond the introduction, apart from González, Puig, yourself and the Montonero source.'

'No.'

'Unless,' said Swivel, 'González played it to Gunter on the qt.'

'She did play some tape to him, but not that one I'm sure. We made her very aware of the danger of it, of what might happen if anyone got wind of it apart from you.'

'Why play even the introduction then?' asked Cockburn.

'I'm sorry.' Roberto now sounded desperate. 'It was my idea as far as I remember. I wanted to impress you. I wanted to give you something that you would expect *The Sunday Times* to pay well for. Thus, to make sure you would get in touch with Mr Clemann.'

'Certainly that was well judged.' Clemann was dry. 'And no one else heard the rest of that tape?'

'No. I am certain of it.'

Clemann moved back to the window. 'Not even the Nazis would have committed murder on the strength of that small extract. Someone has leaked the rest of that tape. I suppose it has to be the Montonero who supplied the information in the first place.' He moved across the small room to the chimney breast and again perched his elbows on the high mantel. 'If, and it seems very likely, we are up against Die Spinne or some other Nazi agency, with the added possibility that they have infiltrated the very people you most trust, there is very little we can do about your safety until you can satisfy them that these tapes are destroyed. Except offer you asylum here.'

Swivel looked up sharply. 'Peter, I have to say this. If you do that you book a second room. Three in here is bad enough. Four would be impossible.'

Clemann appeared momentarily embarrassed. 'Well, I don't see that as entirely necessary.'

'Come on, Peter.' This from Cockburn, who turned to Roberto. 'Peter has strict ideas about what is money well spent, and what is not. This room is booked for one person, but three of us are living in it...'

'That will do, Steve. I spend my money as I see fit. If you want me to pay for your accommodation in Madrid, and Henry's, you accept what I offer. Well, Fairrie?'

'There is Ramón to think of. He is still in Desengaño.'

'You got out. Using that show out there. You can get back the same way. You can come back with Puig too if you want.

'I think,' said Roberto, 'I shall have to try something like that. I must first get back to Ramón. It was silly to leave him.'

He stood up, reached for hat, coat, muffler, gloves, put them on slowly. As he did he reflected that it had been a wasted visit. He was not quite clear about what he had hoped to achieve from it. Perhaps instant deployment of Clemann's wealth and power, US Cavalry-style, to get Ramón and him out of Desengaño, safely guarded in armoured limousines. Clearly such an idea was pure fantasy. There was quite a lot to be said for Clemann. He used his wealth for broadly progressive causes, and rather more wisely than Roberto had used his. But he was after all Peter Clemann, not Clark Kent.

Clemann stood up too. 'Before you go I would like to return to one other matter.'

'Yes?'

'López Rega. Your daughter used his arrival and disappearance in Madrid to give her an explanation of the provenance of your forged tapes. This was an opportunistic device prompted by his arrival after your plot was under way?'

'Yes.'

'His arrival was reported in the newspapers?'

'Yes.'

'But do you not think it possible that he really did come to see her? We checked out that document giving her title to the contents of the safe deposit box, and the manager of the bank was adamant that it was genuine. So she really did see López Rega, who really did put something on deposit in that bank, or if not López, then someone else. Do you have a view on any of this?'

Roberto felt the grip of cold doubt and fear.

'I don't know. I really don't know. You see, for very obvious reasons we have kept as far apart as possible once things got under way.'

'I understand that. Now it appears there are five cassettes in that safe that have nothing to do with you and Ramón Puig. Is it not possible that those are what López Rega brought with him?'

'I don't know. It's possible. But I don't know.'

Clemann turned back to the window. 'Mr Fairrie, *if* those tapes, five of them, are what I think they are, I would be very interested, very interested indeed in acquiring them. Please bear that in mind. Steve, show Mr Fairrie down. I hope we'll meet again. Perhaps later today if you can manage that without undue risk.'

34

On the way down Roberto felt impelled to say: 'I am sorry, you know. Sorry for many things. Not least my daughter's behaviour towards you.'

Cockburn continued to look grim as he strode, chin up, dark eyes glittering, towards the lift. He jabbed the call button.

In the lift Roberto went on: 'I see now it was a very silly caper to invent, to involve others in. Very silly for amateur conspirators. My heart was never quite in it. I did not like the element of deception, the distortion of history. And now it has ended in tragedy. I find I can describe the murder of even a man like McCabe as tragic.'

They came into the warm, silent foyer, walked to revolving doors.

'I am horribly afraid the tragedy is not over. I only hope it will not involve Pepita.'

Cockburn stopped, hand on the door.

'She has Gunter to look after her.'

As Roberto entered the revolving door he felt it suddenly impelled from behind so he was almost ejected into the cold air.

Momentarily furious he almost said aloud: 'You *bastard!*'

Then he glanced down the steps, saw the leather jackets talking to the Guardia Civil on the other side of the road, and fear clutched again. Muttering *'Perdón señor, señora perdón'*, he slipped into the river of icy privilege.

Nevertheless, it moved slowly, far more slowly even than before. For five minutes or so his mind juggled aimlessly yet fearfully with all the disparate elements in the mess he now saw himself to be in. He could not make them fit. Basically it came down to this: everyone, even apparently Gunter, from what Pepita had suggested, now seemed to know that the Perdón tapes, his and Ramón's tapes, were a hoax, a fraud. Yet still McCabe, and now Clemann had been, were ready to buy if the five other cassettes were included in the bargain. And someone was ready to kill, had killed to make sure they were not sold. Clemann had suggested that the information, which Evita had brought them, concerning Perdón and the Nazis, was accurate and that that was what lay behind it all. If that was the case then Evita or his source had betrayed them... or, there was no one else, Pepita, coerced by Gunter.

These were thoughts not to be faced and Roberto consciously pushed them from his mind, deliberately set out to recall the only other occasion he had attended a lying-in-state – though such is the way the unconscious mind works the choice of distraction was dictated by the fear that prompted it.

27 June 1952. Driven by a complex of emotions almost as unravellable as those he felt now, he had joined that particular queue at about half-past three in the afternoon and then shuffled for two hours beneath his umbrella, in torrential cold rain, before reaching the portals of the Ministry of Labour.

That queue had been very different. It had been poor. Rain-soaked, it smelled – of wet heavy cloth, of unwashed armpits, of onion and garlic, above all of work. There had been some resentment at his presence: an Italian-looking docker from La Boca had suggested that those with their coats on, that is those who were not *decamisados,* had no business there. Someone else had told the docker to be quiet: Roberto must be sincere, one of them, for all the real bastards were being driven in in large American limousines or the new Mercedes. If you had money, if you were a general, above all if you were a crook you did not queue.

Half-hearted bickering broke out about this but was silenced by the angry wailing of a nearly blind old woman, who claimed Evita had cured her eyesight just by touching...

Roberto had been accompanied by an acquaintance called Alfonso, about five years his junior, a law student from a poorish background – his father a modest wholesale dealer in vegetables. Alfonso, a member of the Argentinian CP was there, he said, because it was important that all cadres should understand the nature of the Evita phenomenon: only from a basis that included true comprehension of its nature would it be possible to build up objective class consciousness in the Buenos Aires proletariat.

Nevertheless, after they had climbed the long staircases of the Ministry building to the columned rotunda of the auditorium and had at last seen the white, tilted casket, and peered through the reflecting glass at the painted doll framed in orchids, it was Alfonso who wept. Not Roberto, because for him a spell had been broken, the spell that had captivated Argentinians of every class apart from the oligarchy, the landowners, and the grandees amongst the generals. The doll was part of the myth and, whatever had been real in Eva had nothing to do with the myth, and it was the reality that had died. The doll and the myth remained – to be refuted, defused, exorcised.

And then something extraordinary had happened, for at that precise moment a corner of the curtain of the myth was tweaked, and a touch of reality showed past it. Just as he and Alfonso were moving on, impelled by the spaces in front of them and the solid thousands behind, the whole slow movement stopped, as it had a hundred times during their wet wearisome progress to this point, to allow some dignitary or whatever a privileged minute of farewell.

Three men in leather coats, with soft hats pulled over their faces, were let through a tall, white door to one side, and were ushered by a functionary to the front of the casket. They removed their hats. One, the shortest of them, took a step forward, and stood for a full minute with head bowed, only a yard from the doll so it seemed he could lean forward and kiss her back to life. He had a plump but strong face, receding black hair, thickish lips: so much Roberto clearly saw before he snapped back to join the men behind, and with both hands pulled the hat back firmly over head and face. Like a gangster in a film he twitched up the collar of his coat. They turned, did not exactly march, but walked swiftly, and were gone.

Alfonso's tears were gone too. He was white – with terror? Rage? He said nothing until they were in the rain-drenched street again, anonymous particles in a vast but disintegrating crowd.

'That,' he said at last, 'was Martín Bormann.'

This second queue moved on, wheeled beneath the tiny dancing snowflakes – the very old and the very sick always die when the weather is bad, thought Roberto – into the Plaza de la Armería, and the huge, ornate façade, one of the last and most assertive monuments in Baroque art, spread and climbed above them. Momentarily a tiny laugh bubbled in Roberto as he recalled those earlier and on the whole more likeable gangsters in history, the Bonaparte brothers. Napoleon, handing the palace over to his elder brother Joseph, had said wryly: 'Tu seras mieux logé que moi.' Then he realised how the crowds leaving the palace by only two exits dissolved instantly, just as that leaving the Ministry of Labour in Buenos Aires twenty-three years earlier had done, and the two leather jackets had only to wait at those narrow exits to pick him up.

35

An arrangement for military band of the slow march from Chopin's B flat minor sonata was, for Roberto, an act of vandalism. He silenced the radio, looked sightlessly out of his window at the corner of the Telefónica opposite.

PLAY AND RECORD:

'I suppose it has to be someone among the Montoneros. It could be Evita. Why not? He's the only person apart from Ramón, Pepita and me who knew what was on the Nazi tape. He could be playing a double game. He generates the information from his Nazi friends and relations, then, through our tapes sells it back again. And Nazi friends he certainly does have. He slips like a snake from the *ambiente* of the exiles into the bourgeois world of Gunter and South American business with all its shady associates, and then back to the exiles. And he has money from somewhere. He supported Ramón as far as Ramón would let him.

'They quarrelled bitterly. Violently at times. He could, yes I believe he could, when drunk or doped or angry, permit Ramón's death... I think so.

'And he knew all about La Aguja. The Needle. Why is he called the Needle? Perhaps I'll know soon.

'Of course he may not be doing it for money. Like poor Becky he might very well be caught in some dangerously ambiguous position. A relative under threat, something of that sort or evidence of terrorist activity strong enough to make the authorities here frightened enough to deport him.

'Becky. Poor soul. And... how lovely in her way. She was kind and warm to me. If, if, when La Aguja comes for me, and takes me, dear Lord... not too painfully, and not blasted to bloody pieces like McCabe, please no, I must try then to remember Becky, her long fingers caressing my neck, the warmth of her brown breasts...

'La Aguja.'

STOP.

As a very small boy, playing with friends whose father owned a hacienda in the Tucumán, he had poked with a stick into a hole where they knew a giant spider was lurking. They called it a tarantula, though in fact it was one of the *aviculariidae* or bird-eaters. With just the same horrid fascination he now moved wearily into the kitchen and pushed open the metal-framed frosted glass.

He should not have done it. The shock was almost a death blow.

They were framed by the lower window like puppets in a booth, a family group in a photograph frame: La Aguja standing, and Gunter too, both looking over Pepita's shoulder as she sat at the table and wrote something with a thin gold pen.

He closed the casement, and as he moved back, shaking his head with despair like a caged animal, his ears were mind-shatteringly assaulted with what sounded like a short burst of heavy machine-gun fire followed by a longer, continuing burst which became a deafening roar. For a moment the pale lemon sunlight on the corner of his desk went out, then the monster, black against the sky, a giant metal dragonfly, canted and, moving obliquely, soared briefly across his field of vision, and was gone. The dreadful clatter of its engine diminished, receded, became at last just another element in the subdued rumble of the expectant city.

Against it the nearness of a breath pulled in behind him, a yard behind him, had the force of an electric shock. Every muscle in

Roberto's body tightened, including his heart, and terror rinsed his mouth.

'Where's Ramón?'

Roberto twisted, the cane chair creaked. Juan Evita Castillo was in the doorway, dark hair swept back, face pale, anxious, above a denim jacket over a blue shirt with mother-of-pearl buttons, immaculate jeans, repeated: 'Where is he?' He still had his latchkey in his hand.

Roberto struggled to speak, half rose, twisting, pushing back the chair. Evita gave the key an impatient shake.

'He's in the bath.'

'What?' Sharp black eyebrows drawn together in a frown.

'Dead... in the bath.'

The youth turned on flamenco heels, two, three steps across the hall brought him into the bathroom door. Roberto followed, just had time to take in the wardrobe, angled back from the door, then...

'Christ! Jesus fucking Christ,' and Juan Evita went at him, hand drawn back,. and then, bang, bang, slapped the old man hard, twice, across the face. Roberto turned, tried to get back to his room, but was caught by the collar, twisted and hit again. His glasses, already askew and slipping, went with the backhand to the wall, to the floor.

'How? HOW?' Juan's voice a scream and a shout.

'Yesterday. Morning. I don't know...'

Juan pushed Roberto into his room, tumbled him on to the bed and sat on the cane chair. Piecemeal and confused some of what had happened during the previous twenty-four hours was dragged out. When Roberto came to describe how he had got past the leather jacket to get out of the house and into the street, into Gran Vía, Juan suddenly smashed his fist into the confusion of papers, pencils, tapes on the desk.

'You bastard sons of donkeys...' Hands shaking he found a pack of Chesterfield in the breast pocket of his jacket. He struggled with a lighter, then: 'Shit. Get me a brandy.'

Roberto, dabbing a nose that bled and a bruised lip, groping almost sightlessly in the dark passage, but able to see in the kitchen, poured out the last of the Osborne, gulped back one for himself.

'Those leather jackets as you call them are mine. When I knew La Aguja was around I found them, and paid them to keep watch on you. On you and Ramón. And when you went out they both followed you. They must have thought Ramón would be... safe... here.' And suddenly he broke, his hands went to his face, seemed almost to be clawing it, and he sobbed and sobbed, gasping for air between each spasm, and rocking from side to side in the creaking chair. Roberto watched, then stubbed out the smouldering cigarette, put an arm around the boy, he was no more than that, and beneath the jacket bird-thin, tried to get him to drink brandy.

Juan shrugged him off but took the brandy, looked up at him. 'Did they torture him?'

Roberto's eyes flinched away.

Juan nodded. 'They'd want to know… all about the tapes. Jesus, I hope he told them quickly.' It seemed the storm of grief would return but he bit his lip, clenched fists, pushed himself upright, ran hands across his face, through his hair.

'We must do something for him. How could you leave him?'

He went back into the bathroom. Roberto, reluctantly, followed. Juan stooped, knelt, tenderly peeled the obscene Perón mask from his lover's head, then kissed his lips.

'Get towels. Spread them on his bed.'

Sick at the horror of it all, but now deeply ashamed that he had done nothing, Roberto stumbled blindly about the flat, did as he was told. He found four largish towels, all already damp and threadbare.

'You must help me. He is too heavy. And he is still stiff, though beginning to give. We'll manage.'

He had his arm round Ramón's back.

'Take his legs. Under the knees.'

The body was icy, the cold a shock. Roberto felt a wave of appalling pity, followed by a terrible determination not to slip, not to drop him, not to inflict further humiliation beyond the humiliation of death on his friend. Even if it meant ruptures, or a heart attack.

The foul cold water cascaded as they lifted, splashed on and about them. Almost he slipped.

The body would not straighten, would not lie easily on its back. Tenderly they allowed it to go on its side. Then Juan wiped it clean with the towels, took them back to the bathroom. He took a sheet from Roberto's bed and draped it over the body. For a moment they both looked down at it. In spite of the intensity and depth of what he had felt, Roberto's quirky sense of the rational reasserted itself in a corner of his mind. The hair in the beard had grown a little. Ramón never let it get beyond a stubble. And the eyes, like those of the dead Caudillo, were not quite shut. It was, when all was said and done, a corpse.

Gently Juan drew the sheet over the head.

'In the bath he looked like a dead dictator. Lying in state. This is better.' He breathed in deeply, let out a long sigh, and said, peremptorily: 'Leave us.'

Roberto, gratefully, went.

Brandy, a beating, the effort of moving Ramón threatened to finish processes begun forty-eight hours or more earlier. The worst of all was the vision of Pepita with Gunter and Betelmann in the room below. All part of Clemann's monster, part of the same organism. What romantic nonsense had led him to believe any otherwise? Nausea which retching would not relieve, a sandbag heaviness in every limb and joint, tunnel vision that flickered, and an evil weariness of the soul that would have led to suicide if he had the strength to do it descended upon him. He heard Juan moving, then a door clicked, and he believed he had gone and was relieved. At least La Aguja would have to look for him. Presently he pulled his legs up, sank back, and thumb in mouth, eyes open, waited.

Twenty minutes later, perhaps, he heard again the click of a key in the outside door, steps, then his own door opened. Pepita, and behind her La Aguja. She dropped to her knees beside him, tried to cradle his head in her arms. She wept. 'Papa, Papa, what have I done to you? What have we done to each other.' La Aguja took the cane chair, twisted it so he could see them. In podgy white hands he held, across his knees, the large automatic pistol he had used to kill McCabe.

After a time Roberto pulled himself up into a sitting position with his back against the bars of the bed, his head on the wall, and took Pepita's head in his lap. He stroked her gently and peered at the indistinct figure that blocked out the light from the window. With an effort he focused. Without glasses his vision was long, nothing nearer than two metres was distinct.

A fat pasty face, bad teeth which occasionally their owner picked, a suit that was overfilled, a black tie. Many people wore black ties during those days after Franco's death, but Roberto felt La Aguja wore one all the time.

'You are going to kill us?' Then, as the horror became more certain: 'Both of us?'

'Sí.'

Beneath his hand he felt Pepita's spasm, and he stroked her more urgently. Crazily he relished the fineness of her disordered hair and the warmth of her head and shoulders in the pit of his stomach, the fragrance of her perfume and body. At least it was clear the betrayal he had feared was not as complete as he had thought. Perhaps there had been no betrayal at all.

'You should not keep us waiting.'

'I am not to do it until this business in the Cortes is over and the streets are open again.' The voice was squeaky, almost unbroken. 'Your bodies and the one in the bath will have to be moved.'

'What will you do with them?'

'One of the contractors for the development at Colón owes us. Ten cement tankers go into the foundations on Monday. Should have been today.' He now began to bite the nails of one hand. Then he giggled: 'You'll have good company. López Rega, El Brujo, is already there.'

Roberto blinked, closed his eyes, clenched his whole body except the hand that stroked his daughter, tried to force himself out of despair and into thought, action even.

'You must kill me because I saw you kill the American. But why her?'

The fat man shrugged. 'I do what I am paid to do.'

'I think you should at least contact your employers and allow her to question... She has assets they are interested in. I think they must in fact be tapes López Rega brought with him. Everything dangerous that López was to your employers still exists on those tapes.'

Pepita moaned, twisted a little. 'It's no use, Papa. No use. Together they made me write an authority for Enrico. So he can collect the tapes from the bank. He did nothing for me, nothing...' Again she began to sob. Outside, the bell down the road slowly tolled twelve. She continued to sob. Clearly the noise irritated La Aguja. He reached out, dabbed a finger at Roberto's radio.

A measured voice, pitched a little higher than its normal level, filled a round space, terraced seats beneath a small dome, silent except for a distant cough or two...

'La justicia es el supuesto para la libertad con dignidad... Insistamos en la construcción de un orden justo, un orden donde tan to la actividad público como la privada se hallen bajo la salvaguardia judiccional.'

In spite of everything Roberto's back stiffened, a light began to glitter in his eye. With his head almost jauntily set on one side he strained to catch the words. As if sensing it was what he wanted, Pepita fell silent. And what was this? Public activity, that is the activity of the State, should be as subject to the law as private activity? But that is openly acknowledging that under the old regime that was not the case!

'A just order allows the recognition of regional differences... The King seeks to be King of everyone, and that means each one in his own culture, his own history, his own tradition.' So, an end to Castilian cultural hegemony over Basques, Catalans, Andalusians.

'Una sociedad libre y moderna requiere la participación de todos en los foros de decisión...' Was it imagination or did the hush deepen over a parliament packed with Franco's henchmen? Certainly, thought Roberto, there is no likelihood of rapturous applause... the participation of everybody? That's democracy, of a sort. And now... He's Catholic, respects the Church. But respect for the dignity of the person

implies the principle of religious liberty... *Libre*... *Libertad,* come on,
Júan Carlos, that's no sort of language to use with that old monster still
above ground.

Roberto felt a lightening of his soul as the speech moved on, a
pricking of tears. Was this the suppressed bourgeois in him, the unre-
constituted liberal humanist that was moved thus by the voice of a
king?

Click and silence. La Aguja killed the King, or the voice at any rate.
There were two blobs of colour on the assassin's cheeks, and savagely
he pulled back the breech of his gun, cocked it. 'King?' It was almost a
squawk. 'I give him six weeks.'

Roberto slumped back, resumed his weary stroking of Pepita's hair,
felt the stupid tears on his cheeks – 'Wipe thine eyes,' he murmured,
'the good years shall devour them, ere they shall make us weep.'

La Aguja stirred, glanced at his watch, felt in his pockets. Metal
clinked, through Roberto's broken vision something glittered,
flashed in the space between them, landed chunkily on the bed.
Handcuffs.

'Fasten one cuff of one pair to your left wrist, let the other cuff hang.
Then use your left hand to fasten the second pair to your right wrist and
the other half to the woman's right wrist.'

'Is this...?'

The gun lifted. 'Do as you are told. This will be painless and clean.
No mess. Otherwise I shoot you, and no matter what you see at the
cinemas that is not always quick, and is always dirty.'

Ratchets snickered. The metal was not cold, had been in the fat
man's pocket. Roberto's nausea returned.

Suddenly, so it made him jump, renewed the flavour of fear in his
mouth, the assassin moved – he snapped the remaining cuff on to the
metal upright of the bedstead. Roberto caught the sourness of his
breath. La Aguja, back at the table, placed the gun carefully at his
elbow and took two packets from his coat pocket. Working briskly he
peeled oiled brown paper from them, opened the lids of dark blue,
solidly made cardboard boxes, disclosed a phial and a hypodermic
syringe. He pierced the rubber seal on the phial, held it up, sucked a
colourless liquid from one to the other.

'Pentobarbitone,' he said. 'Vets use it for killing unwanted or
suffering pets. It is very quick and there is no pain.'

Roberto strove to gentle Pepita, but found the most he could do was
lace his fingers with hers.

'I shall struggle.'

'That would be foolish. For if you do I shoot you instead. Perhaps
in the stomach.'

He withdrew the needle from the phial. He was breathing faster now, almost panting. The cane creaked as with his left hand he pushed down on the arm and his body again began to fill the light. The right hand held the loaded syringe point up, like a torch. Perhaps, Roberto thought, someone will listen to my tapes. All of them.

And there, as the door opened, La Aguja froze, his grey face suddenly ashen, his mouth dropped open, the bottom lip quivering. As if, as they say, he had seen a ghost.

Which, in effect, he had.

Eva Maria Duarte de Perón, blonde hair swept back to a bun, rhinestones flashing beneath her ears, a rose-coloured ball-gown that glittered with gems and sequins except where a blue and white silk sash covered them, faced him, and pointed the small silver pistol at him. Still holding the syringe La Aguja sank to his knees crossing himself repeatedly with his free hand. An Act of Contrition, or a superstitious attempt to placate the powers of evil? Eva shot him, through one lens of his glasses, in the left eye. Death was not quick. Three more shots, placed behind the left ear were needed before the terrifying pumping of blood ceased.

36

Juan Evita Castillo had not only resource, but resources too. On Saturday, the day of Franco's funeral, when Pinochet was again cheered by the *Azules*, the veterans who had fought for Hitler on the Russian front, and Falange hymns in the Valley of the Fallen drowned out the speakered order of the service, Roberto and Pepita were driven from Vellas Vistas where they had spent the night, to Salamanca.

It was a good place to hide: one of the most right-wing cities in Spain, it had been the rebel headquarters in 1936 before Franco moved to Burgos. Bormann stayed there off and on between 1945 and 1948. Perhaps for this reason the IRA bombers who blew up Carrero Blanco for the Basques in 1973, also lay low here before crossing into Portugal.

Roberto and Pepita stayed with a part-time teacher in the English Department of the University who frequently lent her spare room to transient refugees of one sort or another. She was writing a thesis on Arnold Wesker, a leftish British playwright of the sixties. She had a son, aged two and a half, who walked about the flat without a nappy and was pursued by a maid with a potty. Roberto helped her with the thesis, Pepita with the little boy, therapy for both of them. There was a husband, also an academic, but not much in evidence, except at nine

o'clock in the evening when he came into the living room to listen to the
BBC World News in Spanish, and everyone had to keep quiet.

It was a domestic time. Roberto and Pepita got to know each other
and planned to pool all their resources: $20,000 from McCabe, over
$4,400 altogether from Clemann, and another $17,000 from the
surrender of the lease on Pepita's flat and the sale of jewellery and furs
she no longer much liked, and so restart yet again a Fairrie Radical
Bookshop. They rather hoped it might be somewhere near the Rue de
Rennes in Paris.

Snow fell. Freezing fog descended. Christmas came and they were
feasted by their host's family through midnight on shellfish, sucking-
pig and a Christmas pudding sent by one of her English friends. At the
end Roberto accepted a *Romeo y Julieta* from Havana, enjoyed it enormously, and regretted it for four days. It took that long for the flavour,
growing steadily nastier all the time, to leave his mouth. He had his
revenge. He taught the infant to chant *Juan Carlos, Juan Carlos, Juan
Carlos* and *Viva El Rey*.

On the day before New Year's Eve, in the late afternoon with dusk
gathering, Roberto and his daughter wandered through the snow-
clad city, came to the small square where a bronze philosopher tried
vainly to stride off his plinth. Unamuno, Rector of the University. As
a writer and thinker he was by no means a leftie, but when Franco
came and made his university the headquarters of a rebel army,
Unamuno made a public attack on the rebellion and the morals of
fascism. A little later he died. Some say that he fell asleep over a round
bowl of glowing charcoal, that his feet were burned, and he died from
the gangrene that followed. Others of course said Franco did it. Who
knows?

Roberto told the story to Pepa as they sat on a bench from which he
had cleared the snow.

'I think,' he said, 'my moustache is icing up.'

'It is.'

So too were the plane tree saplings. The bobbled seedcases that
hung from their twigs looked like Christmas baubles.

Suddenly, without immediate premeditation he took a plunge he
had been fearing to make for a week or more.

'López Rega, El Brujo,' he said, 'really did come to you?'

'Yes.'

'It must have seemed a heaven-sent opportunity.'

'Hardly heaven-sent.' She laughed a little. 'Opportune certainly.'

'And he actually did give you tapes of his own. Those five cassettes.
And you put them in the vault with ours.'

'Yes.' She had stiffened, was defensive. 'I'm cold. Let's go back. Or to a café.'

They trudged through snow to one of the grand cafés in the Plaza Mayor – the loveliest square in the world, a rococo glory in rose and peach coloured stone, made yet more magical by snow. They sat in a window, ate cinnamon-flavoured biscuits with espresso coffee.

'Did he say what was on the tapes?'

'Yes.'

He waited.

She went on: 'They were copies made from the Sassen tapes.'

He looked out. Bronze lamp-posts stood black against the white and rose. Windows glowed beneath the arcades. Children threw snow-balls.

'Dear Lord. The Devil.'

Pepa's face was white above the sable she had kept, white but made-up, and so clownish, a tragic clown.

'Do you know what the Sassen tapes are?' he asked her.

'I didn't then. I know a bit more now.'

'They were tapes made by Eichmann not long before he was kidnapped. They were recorded by a Dutch Nazi journalist called Sassen. Transcripts went to Israel. They were a very full account of Eichmann's part in the Holocaust. The tapes were sold, to *Time-Life,* I think. But not all of them. Sassen refused to part with five of them, the last five, which gave a very full account of Bormann's association with the Peróns, between 1945 and 1955, and went on with the story of the German emigration to our country, right through to 1960. They very possibly indicated where the Nazi treasure was realised and invested. If that is the case, then with those tapes you could trace the assets of a hundred apparently reputable concerns back to Bormann and Hitler, and show that bankers, company chairmen and the rest may often know even now the ultimate source of their wealth. Sassen never sold those tapes. And anyone who ever got close to Bormann, or the secrets of the finances of the Fourth Reich, got killed. That is why Sassen kept those tapes.'

Roberto looked out over the square, and picked at imaginary crumbs.

'I suppose,' he went on, 'López Rega, a Chief of SIDE and the other security organisations, got his hands on them. No doubt he thought they were insurance. But always with Bormann that sort of thing becomes a death warrant. Damn near ours.'

Pepa looked down. 'I'm sorry.

Roberto let out a sigh full of heartache. 'Ramón's death warrant.'

She looked up, eyes suddenly flaming. 'All right. But don't blame me, or yourself. He knew what he was doing.'

'He did?'

'Of course. Everything about the Nazis in your tapes that he recorded, came from the Sassen tapes. Not from Montoneros, or Evita, nothing like that. We listened to the Sassen tapes, fed the material to you, you rewrote them as if Perón was speaking, and Ramón recorded them. He knew what he was doing.'

'But why did you not tell me?'

'First, because you would have suspected that we did not have the same confidence in your forgeries as you had. Second, because we knew you would say it was too dangerous, that you would stop us from going ahead. So, don't blame me. It was, in any case, an accident.'

'An accident?'

'Gunter told me. La Aguja broke into the flat. He was to persuade Ramón, or you if you were there, to tell the truth about the tapes. He had heard... something, I don't know what, that finally convinced him that what we... I was really selling was the Sassen tapes. Anyway, when La Aguja got in he found Ramón already in the bath, with the fire beside him...'

'And the Perón mask on?'

'You know he liked to fool with that mask. Probably he was about to record your new script. He was being Perón as part of his preparation...

'In the bath?'

She flashed back at him: 'Yes. Why not? Whatever else, you must admit Ramón was a bit *weird*. Anyway La Aguja threatened to drop the fire in if he would not talk. But far from talking he tried to resist, to fight for it, and La Aguja dropped the fire in, and that was that. It gave La Aguja a scare, what with the wet floor and everything he got quite a nasty shock himself. Which was why he left.'

Roberto crumbled his biscuit and looked out at heavy flakes of snow floating like feathers into the beauty of the square.

'It makes no difference,' he said, 'how he died.'

On one day in the first week of the New Year an Argentinian student they knew, a friend of Juan's, came for them. He had a Seat 127, quite new, and told them he was to take them to the French frontier. They were as safe now as they were likely to be.

'How so?'

The youth unfolded a newspaper cutting from his wallet.

Roberto read it. Enrico Gunter, Argentinian businessman, Knight of St Columbus, pillar of Hispano-American society in Madrid, had been shot dead in the street outside his office in Arguelles. The police were concentrating their enquiries amongst the communities of left-wing exiles... Roberto made an effort and became shocked. After sixty-five years living in the twentieth century he was still determined to be shocked by murder. But his main feeling was of relief.

He passed it to Pepita. To his consternation she went pale, her eyes filled, her body was racked with sobs. For two hours she was unconsolable. He remonstrated. Gunter had been a thug, a bully, a cheat, a criminal – perhaps he had ordered their murder, certainly he had countenanced it. But... 'He was my lover,' she moaned.

By morning, when they were to leave, she was recovered. She had had, Roberto reflected with pompous wisdom, sufficiently few lovers for the act of physical union still to create deep bonds, leave its mark. But enough lovers for the bond to be a pretty flimsy business.

They left Salamanca before dawn, were driven in the Seat through the persisting freezing fog at alarming speeds with visibility often less than ten metres, up the Great Road through Valladolid, Burgos, Vitoria, and at nightfall over the Tolosa pass where the fog turned to rain. In a hotel in Irún they spent their last night in Spain.

The trains north were packed with migrant Portuguese and Spanish workers returning to industrial Europe after the Christmas break. No bookable seats were available until three o'clock in the afternoon. They took a taxi to Fuentarrabia and had a seafood lunch. After the awfulness of freezing fog and snow the Atlantic weather was mild, almost balmy.

Pepita left Roberto on a bench from which he could gaze across the estuary, and went off to do some last-minute shopping. The atmosphere was pearly. Why go further than St Jean de Luz, or Biarritz? Basques buy left-wing books. But through the haze he could see the gabled villas painted red and green, and saw them as suburban, provincial. No. It would have to be Paris. At thirty-one Pepita was not ready for the provincial life. Nor perhaps was he. But it was a good corner of the world to settle in, no doubt of that. Restlessly he recrossed his legs, and questions reasserted themselves that he had not dared face for weeks.

Pepita came back. She carried two plastic bags. Vichy cosmetics, made under licence in Spain where they cost just over half what they cost in France.

He asked her: 'Gunter and McCabe knew more about that first tape we played than just the extract they heard. How?'

'Do you think I told them?'

Pretty as ever. His daughter – newly discovered. King Lear and Cordelia, or rather Pericles and Marina.

'No.'

'You would rather that I had not?'

'Yes.'

'It would have been sensible of me to tell them what was on that tape.'

'Not sensible. Very dangerous.'

She tossed back the auburn hair that reminded him of her mother.

'Listen. You remember when we played that tape in the Banco de la Victoria de los Angeles?'

'Yes.'

'Think back. Visualise it.'

'I am doing that.' Prawn fishers were pushing complex rafts or rigs into the estuary of the river that separates Spain from France. The tide had changed. Cirrus overhead promised cold weather even here, tomorrow perhaps. The atmosphere had cleared a little and La Grande Rhune, a volcanically shaped peak to his right, to the east, the first of the Pyrenees, loomed a little through the haze.

'Well?'

'Tell me.

'Herzer lit Cockburn's cigarette.'

'Yes.'

'And… the rain fell.'

He laughed – why not?

'And we all rushed about, and she picked up the tape-recorder.'

'And the tape?'

'Yes.'

A long pause.

'Did you see her do this?'

'No. But I realised someone had taken it, and she only really had the opportunity.'

'And you said nothing.'

A glassy wave from the Atlantic nudged the ripples of the river. Raucous seagulls wheeled and dived.

'Why not?'

'Papa. We had to *advertise*.'

'And she brought it back the day you played it to the Germans and through her the world and his wife knew what we had. And those really in the know would have pieced together that what we were really advertising was the Sassen tapes.'

'That's right.'

And, he thought, the one doubt in their minds was resolved when I convinced Becky that the 'Perón' tapes really were forged. Up until then it had always been possible that the detailed information on how the money of the Third Reich has been set to work like a virus throughout the financial centres of the West, with the declared purpose of creating a Fourth, came from Perón himself. But once those tapes were known to be forged, then the question became – where had the accurate and lethal information on them come from?

The most likely known source was the five tapes Eichmann recorded for Sassen that Sassen never sold. And one man had briefly held the sort of power needed to get hold of them and use them for his own ends: López Rega.

'It must have been a shock when Beck… Madame Herzer mentioned the Sassen tapes in your apartment. After the rainfall in the vault. I mean… at that point no one was meant to know they were what it was all about.'

'Yes. Yes, it was.'

'Do you think she knew… even then?'

'I don't think so. They would have moved more quickly, with more certainty, if that had been the case. But for them it was perhaps already a remote possibility and she was, what do the English say?'

'Flying a kite?'

'Flying a kite.'

He reflected. 'You did well then. You covered up… bravely.'

She squeezed his hand. Slowly she was learning to forgive the father who had deserted her when she was four years old. Deserted? Her mother's version. He was a nice man. They could get on.

Meanwhile Roberto continued to dwell on Becky Herzer's role.

As soon as Herzer reported to whomever was directing her, that the Perón tapes were forged and that person redirected Gunter, presumably sometime early in the night Franco died, then everything changed.

'That night I was at your apartment. Did Gunter receive a phone call?'

'I think he did. Yes.'

'Before he phoned Betelmann, told him to contact and follow me?'

'I think so.'

He watched the gulls, the sea, and the mountains, looked nervously at his watch. A train, after all, to be caught. Becky, warm, brown, deceiving, welcoming, lovely. Deceiving and ultimately, though she could not have known how things would turn out, murderous. He felt disenchanted. *Desengaño*.

'She was controlled by the Nazis. Not Gunter. Someone above both of them. But McCabe too?'

'I think so. She had this background. Something in her past. Just as likely the CIA knew about it as anyone else.'

'Yes.' A thought occurred to him. 'Did *you* ask her to Madrid? To advertise?'

'No. I think Enrico... Gunter must have done. Or perhaps this person you go on about who you say was behind Gunter.'

He shuddered. Die Spinne. The Spider. Stupid, ugly, melodramatic name.

'What's the matter?'

'Nothing.'

He stood up, picked up the Vichy bags. They would be hunted for what they knew. Pepita had heard, actually heard the Sassen tapes. Roberto knew their contents in detail.

'We don't,' he said, 'have to go to Paris.'

'We don't have to open a bookshop.'

'We could make it a sweet shop... a *con fiserie,* in Biarritz.'

'Or a boutique.' Then, suddenly excited: 'Both perhaps. A *con fiserie* on one side, silk scarves on the other.'

He looked back at the ocean and the estuary, sat down again and she sat beside him.

'Why not?' he asked. 'Why should anyone look for us in Biarritz or St Jean de Luz? I think perhaps, I prefer St Jean de Luz. But will it make money? Harrogate Real Old Toffee. Barker and Dobson humbugs. *Spécialités de la maison.'*

'Yves Saint Laurent. You can sell Chanel dresses off the peg now, you know. At any rate it will do better than a *bookshop.'* This said with a touch of scorn. Then she turned to him, greenish eyes above the sable, finding his, holding them. 'And never need we be broke. We have insurance.'

'We have?'

'Sure. Of course. *Bien entendu. Claro.* I copied the Sassen tapes. It's very easy now, you know. Well within the capabilities of my Akai music centre. I have them in this handbag.'

'You do?'

'And Clemann will buy. If we want him to.'

'Oh... The Devil!'

Blank with the never-ending horror of it all he watched herring gulls dive and scoop at the shifting flotsam where tide fought river.

He squeezed her hand, sighed.

4. TRAVEL

I love travelling. When the fell sergeant fingers my collar, whether it's tomorrow or in twenty years' time, my one regret at the end of a very happy life will be that I have not travelled enough. And I'm not pompous about it. I don't care whether it's a short walk in the Hindu Kush, or a fly and drive organised by Thos Cook with four star hotels, whether it's living for a year or more in another country with no money, or a two-nighter using the Eurostar to Brussels or Paris, just so long as I'm on the move and seeing new places, ways of living I've not seen before, landscapes and seascapes that paint new pictures for the galleries of my mind. We had a fortnight, most of it with a hire car, in Morocco this summer, and as I write this, we're just back from two days in Liverpool. I'd not been to Liverpool since the day war broke out apart from passing through on the way to boarding school or on my one visit to Aintree back in 1954. And Liverpool was as exciting in its way as Marrakech.

My goodness, the travel writers have it made! I reckon I can do a darn good travel piece and, since most of the novels I've written have been set in foreign parts, and I have slotted the odd bit of travelogue into them, I'm hoping now, as I organise their reprinting here, some travel editor will read this and say: Rathbone's the man, let's pay him to do a series on... India! Or Oz! Or Japan! Or New Orleans! Or Rio! Or... just about anywhere we haven't yet got to.

As I've already said I didn't get across the Channel until I was twenty-three, but then it was Turkey via Venice and the Corinth Canal. And almost straightaway in Turkey it was the south coast and camping rough in a huge ruined city round the tiny village of Sidé. It was almost untouched then. Just a tiny museum and a fish restaurant on a bamboo pier, a tiny mosque and maybe forty single-storey flat-roofed cottages and ten fishing boats. Now I'm told there are hotels, the ruins have been tidied up with gravelled walkways, and official guides, coach parties from Antalya shuffle through, all that diesel-tainted jazz. I shan't go back, but here is how a bit of it was in September 1959...

I Turkey

Sidé, from *Hand Out*

Roderick was trapped. His feet were on a fallen lintel, an entanglement of thorns behind him contrived to fasten in his back and push him forward at the same time. In front of him but three feet beneath him stretched a treacherous area of rubble and briars. He could not turn round to go back and he did not dare to jump forward without testing the ground he was going to land on. His rather fat thighs below his shorts were torn and bleeding, his finger had been stung by a very large wasp-like insect, sweat was blinding him and his nostrils were filled with the foetid smell of the ugly yellow flowers that bloomed behind him. Being thus totally absorbed in the present of his physical situation, he was very happy.

After some consideration he forced his behind downwards towards his feet against the pull of the thorns and heard, with some satisfaction, his shirt tearing into shreds. He winced with scarcely less pleasure as some skin went off his back too. Now he could prod with his feet beneath him and then gently ease his whole body into the rectangular shallow pit. He reckoned without much certainty, for he was no expert, that he was in the atrium of a Roman town house. Thinking vaguely of the Locri Faun and delicate garden statues from Pompeii, he pushed his way forward over the cracked boulders of brown concrete and sharp slivers of veined facing marble. A sweeter scent came to him and he found its source in a clump of Madonna lilies nodding above the stones, more luxuriant than those carefully cultivated in England. The air was heavy and filled with the deep rumble of gorged insects.

He crossed another barrier of fallen stones supporting a stunted wild olive and found another, wider court which would be the peristylium. Three broken columns in polished dark stone with a blue tinge lay across his path and the foliage shone more green and lush.

Conscious always of a spice of danger, at any moment the ground might open beneath him and drop him into a cistern or well, the tiny scuttlings ahead of him might betray scorpions or snakes, Roderick pushed and pulled himself across the shattered gardens towards a still-standing wall on the other side.

In the wall was a wide niche, partly roofed, the rubble beneath it not entirely overgrown, though flanked by low bushes of thyme, aromatic with tiny purple flowers. Here Roderick sat and lit a cigarette and then idly started to turn over the stones around the roots of the bushes. The third stone was shapeless marble, three inches long and two wide, and it seemed firmly settled in the crumbled mortar and the loose earth. He scrabbled with his fingers and prised it up. Adrenalin flooded his blood, cleared his vision and the sudden joy he felt was physical.

A small epicene face looked up at him from his palm, the curves of lips, cheeks and eyelids softly but clearly defined, a melancholic smile hovering in the corners of the mouth and in the sightless eyes. Above the wide brow the ridged stone signified braided hair beneath a sort of snood. Was this not a Phrygian cap? Roderick gazed wonderingly. Did that not make this discovered face a bacchante? He turned the stone over and let his fingers run over the rough texture of the flattened back and decided that the head must have been part of a frieze in deep relief, but speculation faded into another burst of satisfaction at his luck. He lay back, holding the object in front of his eyes, letting the deep mystery of the ancient smile wander in the dark passages of his mind.

He became aware of the heat and the discomfort of sweat and drying blood. He took his clothes off and lay back, his head in shadow. The sun relaxed him like a gentle masseur and unordered day-dreams played behind his closed eyelids, day-dreams of goddesses, goddesses graceful yet maternal, remote yet overshadowing. Led by these visions of a lost age his self-awareness receded and consciousness became for a short time a simple matter of earth, sky, sun and the distant murmur of the pregnant sea.

Roderick reached the restaurant just as the others were picking the last slivers of flesh from Davut bey's bony fish. With a distant modesty which went strangely with his forceful bulk and florid face, he watched them hand round the small stone head and listened to their exclamations and congratulations. At last it lay in Bella's hand. She looked up at him, her face in shadow, but lit from beneath by the wavelets of light from the water.

'I'd like to come exploring with you,' she said, 'but in the evening when it's cooler.'

Nomadic Kurds, from *Kill Cure*

*During the time I lived in Turkey (1959-1962) Kurdish
nomads could be seen both in the mountains and the eastern
plains although the government was already making vicious
and stupid attempts to settle them in hideous prefabricated
villages.*

That evening Claire sat on a boulder at the edge of the camp and felt better. Below her were twelve or thirteen large black tents, woven, she had learnt, from goat hair. Redolent smoke drifted from fires into the clear sharp mountain air, mixing with the odours of pines, cooking, and goats. Further away from her the flocks were grazing on a wide water meadow; she could hear the dull chiming of their bells, and a gentle murmur from the tents, pierced by an occasional laugh or the cry of a child. A small river meandered through the meadow; beyond it trees marched up to scree, and then the mountains – enormous cliffs which darkened from pale grey to blackness except where the invisible sun still shed a rosy glow on the highest peaks and warmed the icy purity of the perpetual snows.

Robin had told her that up there was the small glacier that fed the river, even at the end of the long dry summer. The whole scene was about perfect and she could not help thinking that the nomads fitted into it, were part of it, not alien intruders. As if to point this thought a reedy pipe began to play on the far side of the encampment: a haunting melody, rising and falling and marked by the brittle snap of cane stick on goatskin drum. Only the vans jarred, bringing a touch of 'Le Camping' into the scene. Like all tourists who seek out the strange, the unusual, or the unspoilt, Claire was facing the dilemma that her very presence, which was giving her so much pleasure, was an intrusion and possibly a hostile one. But then she wasn't a tourist, she remembered, and certainly the Panmycin had been welcomed and there seemed to be some need of it.

Their welcome in the defile had not been hostile, merely exuberant. Once Robin and Jack Dealer had identified themselves a calm had fallen and the Expedition had been welcomed with a strange, serious formality, by each of them. Communication had been difficult and remained a problem, although they discovered that the son of the chief had attended High School in Damascus and spoke French well; but for the rest, the Kurds' Iranian dialect remained quite unintelligible – though odd words from both Turkish and Persian phrasebooks got through.

A journey of three hours followed at a pony's pace. They left the track and soon entered this second valley – broad and almost park-like in its lush pastures, light woodland, and pine forests. Claire had had plenty of opportunity to study the six Kurds with them. They were tall thin men, weather-beaten but not dark skinned, heavily moustached with deep set eyes and bushy eyebrows. Their clothes were an odd mixture: four of them wore black, robe-like garments, faintly Arabic in appearance but shorter and less voluminous, over huge baggy trousers which ended just below the knee. Three wore leather gaiters, and the others woollen stockings and army boots. From under the robes heavily embroidered waistcoats glinted with tarnished silver. All were armed – with silver-mounted knives, heavy revolvers, rifles thirty or forty years old. Their horses were shaggy, ill-kempt by Claire's suburban standards, but well-fed and hardy. The men looked fierce when they were at all preoccupied, but often they relaxed into shouts of laughter or broad grins which revealed strong teeth.

At last they had come to the yayla or summer pasture. The rest of the clan turned out to meet them – perhaps eighty all told, counting women and children. In the midst, in front of the largest tent, stood a very old man, supported by two equally old women – the Sheikh Ibrahim himself, and to him the members of the expedition were presented by his son, Barzani. They were served with thick coffee in tiny cups with heavy silver cup holders. The coffee was drunk with the heavy formality of the first introductions; then, Sheikh Ibrahim, who said little and was obviously on the edge of senility, bowed and was led into the great tent, leaving them with Barzani. The formal welcome over, the atmosphere changed. The whole clan had gathered round them, the children gazing with wonder, the youths exclaiming over the Volkswagens, the men, led by Barzani, opening and examining the cases of Panmycin with restrained wonder, questioning Booker with eager seriousness about the mysterious vials of white crystals.

Two women – tall, straight, unveiled like all Kurdish women, with chains of gold coins like little suns gleaming across their foreheads – led Claire and Donna around the camp, and at last into one of the tents. Inside, Claire was surprised at the number of partitions, cubicles, rooms there seemed to be. The atmosphere was black, heavy with the smell of goat hair, but the furnishings were rich: tiny silver lamps swung above tasselled cushions, rugs and chests. Copper and silver utensils hung from the posts; there were richly inlaid stringed instruments, guns, embroidered robes, and everywhere the dull gleam of oxidised silver in fine filigree. It was like a strangely authentic Aladdin's cave. Claire and Donna were seated on cushions and offered mint tea, hard, dry biscuits, and soft Turkish Delight stuffed with hazel-nuts.

As they sipped and chewed in a rather embarrassed silence Claire became aware of an intermittent moaning and whispering from some-where at the back of the tent. She must have glanced towards it for after a time one of the Kurdish women rose and touched her on the shoulder, beckoning to her and Donna. They pushed through woven hangings into the furthest recesses in the tent, to the darkest enclosure of all, a tiny cell lit by only two pinpoints of flame on miniature oil lamps. In the gloom they made out three figures stretched out on palliasses. One was a youth of about twenty, very pale, his eyes gleaming in a face darkened by stubble, sweat standing out on his head, with one leg heavily bandaged in stained rags. It was he who was moaning. The other two were children, asleep, but obviously in high fever. There was a smell of stale vomit and something else too – not unlike putrid meat. Their guide stooped over the youth and wiped his brow with a cloth before cradling him in her left arm and offering him water from a wooden cup. She straightened and smiled at Claire.

'Ilatch,' she said, and pointed at her. 'Ilatch.'

Claire had bought more of the pills Booker had prescribed for her three days before in Ankara, and she recognised the Turkish word for 'medicine'.

Opium Fields, from *Trip Trap*

This is the opening of the best of the Turkey novels.

Augusto afternoon. A gusty, hot breeze stirred dust-devils down the long straight furrows; the foot-hills were silvered and shim-mering; the distant peaks – massive, snow-capped, cracked and fissured – stood clear above the haze. Women, shapeless in shawls, smocks and baggy trousers, heads swathed in white scarves, moved silently down the long lines, snapping the seedcases from the brittle stems, their feet shuffling through white papery petals stained with purple at the roots and browned at the edges. (THE GLOBAL REQUIREMENTS OF OPIUM FOR MEDICINAL USES DO NOT EXCEED FIVE HUNDRED TONS A YEAR.) The pods fell dryly in their baskets. A man, a city man, watched them. He wore a dark suit but no tie, his head was balding and he was fat. Occasionally he wiped sweat from his face and from behind his large black sun-glasses and once he coughed and spat into the dust at his feet. A heavy, sweet smell, faintly foetid, seemed to lie across the fields in front of him.

A donkey clopped along the long white road towards him. The rider was tall and his legs, cased from the calves down in leather, might have met beneath the donkey's belly or his feet trailed in the dust. He rode upright, carrying a stick; his face was hard and lined, covered with fine white bristles; his eyes were clear beneath a peaked cloth cap. (EVEN IN THE OPIUM-GROWING AREAS OF TURKEY ADDICTION IS ALMOST UNKNOWN.) He saluted the city man.

'Merhaba.'

'Merhaba. Nasilsinis?'

'Iyi, teshekur ederim.'

'It looks a good crop.'

The farmer shrugged. 'If God wills.'

(ONE HECTARE CAN PRODUCE TEN KILOS OF RAW OPIUM.)

'You will sell to me?'

'Attila Gokalp is paying his grower twenty liras in the hundred more.'

'This year. It will not last. He is dealing with new people. From Izmir. The police will stop it and he will go to prison. Perhaps you too.'

'I shall sell to you. This year.'

'On Thursday then?'

'Inshallah. If God wills.'

(THE TURKISH PEASANT CAN SELL RAW OPIUM AT FIFTY DOLLARS A KILO.)

The grower kicked and his donkey moved off the road and into the field. The stick-like stems rattled along its short-cropped flanks. The city man nodded, satisfied, a doubt erased, and walked slowly over to the fifteen-year-old Pontiac parked beneath a stunted acacia tree which grew by a deep well with a long, curved, wooden derrick. He swung the beam and hauled on the rope to lift a five-gallon oil drum to the low parapet. The water was tepid and brackish. He drank a little from one cupped hand and dried himself on his handkerchief, and then straightened his jacket with the tiny tug of a fat man who likes to be neat.

The road passed through four or five miles of poppy fields, before climbing into stonier foot-hills. (TWENTY SQUARE MILES CAN PRODUCE FIVE HUNDRED TONS OF RAW OPIUM.) White dust streamed behind the car, as if pumped from a CS gas grenade, across tall outcrops of rock, dry water-courses, thorn bushes. The road began to wind. Pitch-black shadows thrown by the jagged crags lay across the road junction like broken panes of glass. As the car decelerated the offside rear tyre burst, and then the front one. It slewed to a standstill and the dust settled yards from the metalled highway. The city man eased himself from his seat and stood beneath the hot sky, feeling the sun sinking into his broad back, and he gazed at his shredded tyre. A glint of steel caught his eye, he knelt, his fingers plucking the cloth loose over his knees, and cradled in his hand a six-pronged claw, so designed that however it fell, three points would stick up. In the silence he shrugged, without turning. Inshallah. Five shots shattered the stillness. He fell, pulled himself up, hands groping blindly, the iron taste of blood welling in his mouth from the numbness in his chest, and finally rolled forward against the post of the road sign. (PROCESSED HEROIN IS WORTH TWO HUNDRED AND TWENTY-FIVE THOUSAND DOLLARS A KILO IN NEW YORK.) A shadow fell across his body, and the stillness was broken by the scrabbling of hooves in grit; a horse whinnied and silence closed again over diminishing hoof-beats. The signpost read 'Afyonkarahisar – 20 kilometres'. Afyon is on the northern slopes of the south-western range of the Taurus Mountains in Turkey. 'Afyonkarahisar' means 'the Black Castle of Opium'.

Constantinople, from *The Last English King*

Although Istanbul is the background for much of Diamonds Bid *and some of* The Pandora Option, *I can't find a chunk about it long enough to stand anthologically on its own, so here's Constantinople before the Turks arrived. Its not actually changed as much as you might expect.*

They passed between the huge towers of the gate and, leaving an inside line of smaller, older, crumbling walls on their right, now converted into caves and hovels, began a steep zig-zagging climb up cobbled, narrow streets between buildings taller than any dwelling places Walt had ever seen before. Most were faced with grey plaster, sometimes moulded or carved into fantastic patterns. In places this stucco had fallen away, exposing walls of narrow bricks.

The streets here were less busy than on the other side of the horn-shaped estuary but not much; there were many priests and monks, but in robes and cloaks quite different from those worn by the clerisy of his own country. There were soldiers too who guarded the greater doorways of the bigger buildings, or strolled with a martial gait beneath plumed and gilded helmets. There were many pedlars like the women who had crossed in the boat with them, who shouted their wares to the blank windows or set up stalls on the street corners. As well as fruit, there were men who sold fish from the crowded sea. Mackerel, sardines, grey and red mullet, anchovies, octopus and squid filled shallow baskets scattered with salt. Others carried huge trays on their heads filled with crisp loaves covered with seeds, tiny and black or white like fresh-water pearls. A large cart passed, pulled by a glossy mule and filled with amphorae containing oil or wine. The seller exchanged full amphorae for empty ones with money added for the contents. The people who bought from this perambulatory market were, from the clothes they wore, servants at best but more probably slaves. Some were black, some had high cheek-bones and ochre complexions.

About half-way up the zig-zagging stopped and a street on their left ran straight to the crest. Here on this corner the traveller paused, slipped his gourd from his staff and offered it to Walt, first removing the bung.

'You look thirsty, tired too. Drink – it's water, spring water.' Indeed Walt, perhaps because he was, he thought, coming to the end of his quest, was now shaking as if with a fever; and sweat, more than the hot sun might have caused, streamed down his cheeks and neck.

They toiled on up the slope until it opened out into a wide, uneven space, flagged with striated marble, white, cream, rose-pink and black, flat and smooth enough to dance on. In the middle was a lofty column supporting a huge equestrian statue of a bearded emperor or warrior, bronze but gilded. Behind it there stood a big building with a portico of six noble columns with acanthus fronds decorating their capitals, and to the right a great gateway sumptuously carved with emperors in their niches, their armour not the chain- or ring-mail of the times but clad in the shaped breast-plates and crested helmets of another age. The gates themselves were bronze, also moulded in relief with the stories of ancient wars. They were guarded by tall soldiers, many fair-skinned and blonde, whose freshly cleaned and polished mail glittered in the noonday sun.

Walt rode waves of dizziness, vertigo. He was bewildered, confused.

'What is it all for?'

His new friend shrugged.

'Monuments of their own magnificence?' he suggested, with dismissive wryness.

But most magnificent of all, to their left as they entered the square, were the domes and half-domes climbing like foothills to the huge domed drum in the middle. Walt seized the traveller's thin, freckled bare arm.

'What is that?' His voice was now a hoarse whisper.

'The Church of Holy Wisdom.'

'Then that is where I shall find what I seek.'

Walt turned and headed across the marble towards the big, black, round arched door, open like a whale's mouth. As he approached the steady beat of a repeated note sung in a deep bass voice came to his ears, and the tinkling of bells.

Once inside he knew he was in heaven. The huge interior was far brighter than it had seemed from across the sunlit square. The base of the central dome was ringed with forty arched windows, and beneath it four more arches, the east and west ones themselves half-domes, also pierced with lights. Below these, four galleries, each with fifteen columns, were supported by forty taller and larger columns rising from the floor. No two capitals were the same but all intricately and fantastically carved.

Everywhere there was light and colour. The dome and semi-domes seemed to float on light or on the smoke from countless thuribles and candles. Every wall was revetted with marbles of various hues and patterns, often cut in veneers that echoed each other in mirror fashion. The columns were all of marble, save for the largest eight on which all else rested. These were a deep-striated, glimmering red porphyry, from the Temple of the Sun in Baalbek.

Weaving between them or grouped around altars a hundred priests and acolytes, all in vestments and copes studded with jewels, embroidered with gold, some wearing high hats that swelled at the crown beneath jewelled crosses, sang masses in a language Walt did not recognise, swinging gold and silver thuribles and chanting in the long, deep repeated way he'd heard from outside – a quite different chant from the undulations of the one used by the monks at home.

More wonderful still were the mosaics which filled every space available, but especially the curved three-sided spaces where three circles or semi-circles touched. In most the background tesserae were gold. In the four spaces below the dome there were colossal cherubim; round all the walls angels, prophets, saints and doctors of the church. On the circle of the apse the Virgin sat enthroned, flanked by archangels with banners inscribed in an alphabet Walt could not read.

But the greatest of all, filling the inside of the great concave semi-globe of the central dome, was the Pantocrator Himself – the creator of all things, He who made Heaven and Earth and all that therein is, the CreatorRedeemer, throned against a lapis lazuli heaven studded with gold stars, the Judge inflexible yet compassionate, his complexion the colour of wheat, hair and eyes brown, grand eyebrows, and beautiful eyes, no beard or moustache, clad in gorgeous clothing, humble, serene and faultless.

II *France*

This is the only travel piece qua *travel piece I've had printed.
It was published in the old, original* Literary Review, *in
autumn 1980. Interesting to see what has changed since
then and what is still* la même chose.

Allonging and Marshonging

'LITTLE Arthur,' we said, 'the time has come to go amongst the
Allongers and the Marshongers.'
Little Arthur smiled and dribbled.

At Passport Control (Southampton) the Pakistani official in his
glass cage also smiled. 'There are three of you?' he asked, and we indicated Little Arthur, a mini-traveller nearly buried by life-support
systems in the back of... a Mini Traveller. Behind the Pak were three
Special Branch men, mimicking exactly their counterparts on Telly.
They frowned and one made sure that the third boarding ticket really
was for Little Arthur and not an Irish Bomber cunningly hidden
beneath one hundred disposable nappies.

France! – easier to enter than England was to leave, one bored official hardly lifting his hand to wave us on – and straight to the
Cherbourg *hyper* (say: eeepair), pick up a *caddie*, and see what's new
after two years away. Well, what's new is that only lamb is still much
dearer (which is just as well, since we've smuggled in a New Zealand
gigot for the friends we'll be staying with), just about everything else is
the same or cheaper than in England – even the things like clothes and
beer – which one tended in the past not even to look at. And there's
style, and variety, and choice, and colour and lights, and it's clean and
fresh and not scuffed or scruffy – in short, for an hour or so my chronic
but mild francophobia is quite suppressed. Some things of course are
always arranged better in France: by evening Little Arthur is pushing
out his lips and waving his arms to the manner born: *Vive la belle
France et les PETIT'S SUISSES*, he seems to say, and I should think so
too. Why on earth we don't have these tiny slightly sour cream cheeses
or cheesy creams which all French babies thrive on, I just can't imagine.

The euphoria wears off. Our route takes us away from the glossy
dual carriageways which, wherever you are, lead from everywhere to
Paris and nowhere else, and soon we hit the *chausees déformées*, the
gravillons, the *virages sur 5kms*, and the *circulation dangereuse*. Yes,

one sign actually says that: dangerous traffic!... as if we needed to be told. Once in the south-west we saw a sign on a main road that announced *degradations importantes*. We never discovered what these were, but we speculated...: And then there is the countryside, so pretty for the first twelve hours or so but *bocage* after *bocage* after *bocage*, and always on the horizon the barbaric water-tower, and the grey villages with off-white shutters strung out along the road, *messes à 7hs, à 8hs, à 10hs* – messes any time of the day if you ask me, and the brutal concrete telephone posts, the lavatory bowls that have never seen bleach or cleaner... Little Arthur dribbles. Will there be *petits suisses* for tea? Of course there will be, so *he's* all right.

We are heading for Brittany – Douarnenez, where our friends, teachers of English (persistent readers of TLR have met them already), have rented a farm cottage for ten months of the year. It turns out to be a nice place – modernised, modestly but comfortably furnished, all done under a system that is explained to us as follows: the peasant farmer no longer needs full-time assistants; the agricultural ministry lends him money to modernise his outlying cottages to standards of comfort beyond those appropriate for a farm labourer; for ten months a year he lets them to students or young teachers not yet qualified to have secure tenure in one place and for the other two he quadruples the rent for summer visitors. In ten years the rents have paid off the loan and the farmer has a nice place to retire to. This system is, of course, subsidised, and we, angry and bewildered as we are with common agricultural policies, the UK contribution, mountains of this and lakes of that, and VAT at 15 per cent, we are pretty sure we know just who it is pays the subsidy.

Entente cordiale is restored by the New Zealand *gigot* – cooked French style, i.e. on the outside only – but none the worse for that, well, it makes a change – and the holiday develops, in spite of the rain.

Cue for Song.

*Le Dernier Tango en Breizh**

The rain in Rennes
Is raining yet again,
In Quimper
It's definitely damper
(You'll need your *imper*),
In Douarnenez
The rain is here to stay,
For on the Breton coast

It rains the most...
(Reprise: You'll need your *imper*)

*Breton for Brittany

Quimper is the only town I have ever visited to have a large and expensive shop selling raincoats (*impermeables*) and nothing else at all. Frankly, I'm surprised there weren't *queues*.

When we get back the *très sympa* farmer's wife wrings her apologetic hands, and says by way of consolation that the weather is just as bad in England. She knows because the fishing fleet has just returned with empty holds, it was too rough to put out the nets, *and they always fish in English waters...*

June 18th. The French press makes a fuss about the fortieth anniversary of de Gaulle's Free French broadcast (never mind it's the 165th anniversary of Waterloo), and we go down to the harbour where a restored tunny-fishing boat is to repeat its historic journey to Penzance with four of its original heroes on board. Two of them arrive – nearly elderly, with the smooth well-groomed look English business men never quite achieve, one with a *Legion d'Honneur* rosette. The local radio interviews them, the rain thickens, the wind rises, and by evening the trip has been called off. The weather was better in 1940.

Back at the farm we play Brubeck tapes. *C'est très cool, ça, très cool*, says our friend. Then pauses. He is about to ask what the English say for 'cool' but thinks better of it.

We go to a *crêperie*, drink too much cider and eat too many buckwheat pancakes. An odd couple sit near us, the man lean, dark, small, a sort of gone-over look to him, the girl wild, long-haired, hippyish. My companion brings up Polanski who has just finished making *Tess* nearby. Loudly we say what we like about Polanski and what we don't. The couple watch us, listen. The man puts on a long black leather coat, and they depart. Later we see them at a bar on the water-front. Later still my companion says 'you know that man in the crêperie? That was Polanski. Didn't you realise?' Now if only she'd said earlier I could have chatted him up, told him about *King Fisher Lives* and *Joseph*... Oh well. Probably it wasn't Polanski. But it *was*, she says, it was.

Franglais is everywhere. Baby clothes especially go in for it – *Little Boy, Yacht Club, Sailing* embroidered across chests and on pockets. We buy a warm, hooded garment, very good value, *pour le bébé*, and stand corrected when the shopkeeper says *pour le baybee*.

Midsummer's Night, miraculously the weather clears, and we go to a *Fez Noz*, a fete. I adore *fêtes* and *ferias*. This has an ethnic band, tents selling *crêpes* and *sistr mad* (which is Breton for 'good cider' – there can't be much wrong with a language where the word for 'good' is 'mad') and a giant bonfire. The sun sets perfectly over the fiord, the bonfire is lit, and the Bretons dance a maze dance solemnly around it. Later the younger ones will jump over the dying flames but little Arthur, although snug in his *Snugli* (unsolicited testimonial for the best baby-carrier) should, we suppose, be in bed. In spite of the Snugli he won't sleep here… *sistr* is flowing like water, and already four boozy Bretons have kissed him.

One last superb memory of Brittany – a gannet cruising off the broken cliffs of the Pointe du Raz, sailing on six feet of effortless wing and too concentrated on the waves a hundred feet below to bother about the planned *nucléaire* down the coast.

There are things to hate in Western Europe and travelling in an unfamiliar part helps one to focus on the general sickness a little more sharply than one does at home. Here are three or four symptoms that struck us this time.

The ten franc piece: one side symbolises industrial energy, the independent deterrent, satellites; the other has a stylised map of France with Paris as a radiating sun – a coin apt for state regulated monopoly capitalism with no patience for devolution or any other such democratic nonsense. It's the only current French coin that does not carry *Libertè, Fraternité, Egalité,* the last not to do so were minted by Vichy and carried instead the slogan *Travail, Famille, Patrie.* The attitudes behind this ten franc piece recall those times more effectively than the nostalgia mongers in the media.

Our friend has applied for a posting abroad. He is assured that the appointment is his… *so long as the police check on him is clean.* He has a record? Of course not. But he reads *Libération*…

At Plogoff, near the Pointe du Raz, a *centrale nucléaire* is to be built. 100,000 demonstrated against it and there was massive and violent reaction from the state. In June three people from Plogoff were arrested without trial for allegedly beating up a policeman; they are on hunger-strike as are five members of their families. The local paper made no connection between these incidents and the anti-nuclear campaign – *Libération* printed a fuller story: the policeman had been recognised as one of those who had acted violently at the demonstration, and the incident is thus put in its anti-nuclear context. For most Frenchmen, as it is for us, the self-censorship of a docile, conforming press, both local and national, means that only the sensational side of events is printed – and the background that gives them significance is ignored. We could do with a daily like *Libération* here.

In the last days of our holiday we attended what should have been a massive demonstration at La Hague, a nuclear reprocessing and research plant near Cherbourg. Appalling rain ruined it and the whole thing was shifted to a small town twenty miles away. Many, many thousands of mostly young people attended from all over France. Inevitably there were isolated incidents of bad manners and minor vandalism, but in fact the ambience of sustained serious gaiety is what most impressed us. Again the press reporting was superficial – at best it patronised, at worst exaggerated the incidents.

Throughout, the forces of order (I will *not* call them the forces of *law*) kept a very low profile. Few saw, as we did, by accident, the deployment of many hundreds of heavily armed police between the main body of demonstrators and the site of a nuclear power station at nearby Flamanville.

Near Flamanville we spent three sunny afternoons on a beach of great natural beauty and watched ten huge cranes, and listened to the thunder of heavy lorries in narrow lanes preparing the site. One slogan at the demonstration read: 'Nuclear power stations are clean, but would you like your sister to live near one?' No. Nor will we take Arthur back to that beach once the power station is operating.

In Brittany we saw artichokes dumped by the road-side, in Normandy potatoes. In the south Spanish lorries carrying cheap tomatoes were burnt. Can we really trust governments whose current policies produce such, tragic, silly waste to be right over nuclear power?

And so the ferry again – to Portsmouth this time. We pass our navy and it looks tatty – apart of course from the Britannia and the Victory, both in as good nick as ever. A cigarette hoarding announces Mozart for the Throat, and the notice on the side of the gangway reads 'Welcome to Guernsey'. After France everyone seems to be sleep-walking. Still, it's good to be back. Of course Little Arthur (*Ahrcktewer* to the Allongers) blows noisily through his lips – French baby talk for *Ou sont les petits suisses d'antan*. He really enjoyed his first experience of allonging and marshonging. Come to think of it, we did too.

Walking in the Pyrenees, from *A Raving Monarchist*

Paco, a Basque, has asked the narrator, a middle-aged lecturer and his young partner Maurice, a rather louche not to say camp youth, to help him walk illegally into Spain.

Paco had called the next day, and surprised me, actually caused me some disquiet, by producing a wallet containing at least a thousand new francs with which he took us shopping. I know it held that much because that's what it cost to fit the two of us out with basic *randonnée* gear – fell boots, stockings, knickerbockers, anoraks, and rucksacks.

'Not only for your comfort,' Paco announced, 'but because we must be authentic if we are to outface the pigs.'

Now, as we struggled up the last and steepest slope to the Refuge des Oulettes I felt grateful – especially for the boots which were thick-soled with deep treads and heavy padding over and above the ankles; consequently my feet had suffered least. For, though in good condition – I hate to see a man of my age flabby and there is no excuse with the facilities that are available in the university – I was conscious of aching muscles in calves and thighs, and of the Col still far above us – a further twelve hundred feet.

The halt at the refuge was therefore welcome and not only because we needed the rest. The view was now quite magnificent: the Vignemale, the highest mountain in the French Pyrenees, stood across the valley floor in front of us, three huge pieces of rock – or perhaps one piece that had been split by aeons of frost – with a Y-shaped glacier separating the two smaller fragments from the larger; and then the sweep of the massif, a giant arc on either side of those giant peaks, like battlemented walls branching out from a keep or citadel. It was disconcerting to stare at such an immense object, and impossible to ignore it, even if one looked directly away, turned one's back on it; disconcerting because the mind refused to accept its size and weight – it *had* to be two-dimensional, a backdrop, an ephemeral projection merely on a screen of air or mist. To accept it as solid was to be forced to face up to volumes, surface areas, adamantine hardnesses and brittle cold, forced to accept sheer *weight* in thousands upon thousands of megatons, and then relate that weight to the whole globe it sat upon, smaller even than a blackhead on the back of Gargantua.

We sipped ice-cold beer from cans at fifty francs a throw, gazed at all this and now particularly at the col to the right, lower than the rest, and listened to the Refuge Keeper talk about the afternoon of storms ahead. Indeed, as we watched, the white cap of cloud I'd noticed earlier inched itself higher into the sky, began to show its grey and purple-black undersides suggestive of volumes of space even greater yet than the mountain it was drifting towards.

We were not alone. A group near us, two women with children, watched the rock-faces a mile and a half away through binoculars, and muttered together monosyllabically. My eyes could not make out their men roped and nailed to vertical granite, but Maurice said he could see them. A little later, just before we left, another group of four men and two girls came across the valley floor towards us from the glacier's foot and flopped with a ringing rattle of pitons, crampons and picks at our feet. One of the women lowered her glasses and asked them how it was.

'Wet,' came the reply. 'Very wet. Slippery.' And the speaker returned to his boots which he unlaced with slow care, savouring the release as if it was a drink.

'Three Spaniards fell a month ago,' said Maurice in English, 'halfway up the glacier. All killed.'

Paco upended his can and lobbed it into a bright blue plastic sack left out for rubbish.

'If we are to be in Torla by nightfall we must go,' he said. 'Don't worry. This is not a climb we are going on, only a walk. There is no danger at all.'

As if to prove his point, two figures appeared silhouetted on the very col we were to make for, stood poised for a moment, one foot in Spain and one in France, and then began the descent towards us. Paco was right – it looked steep, rocky, but walkable.

After twenty minutes Maurice complained. In that short time we had gone up perhaps five hundred feet and left the grass, indeed all living things except lichen, behind us. The path was no longer a path – simply a succession of widely spaced stones splashed with the red and white insignia of the *Parc* zig-zagging loosely up the steep slope of scree and rock above us. Looking back, the view down the valley had already opened up as if we were climbing in a helicopter, the folds and ridges flattened so that one was conscious now of space, the emptiness between us and the nearest similar height two miles or more away the other side of the refuge, and nothing, not even a bird, between.

'I don't like this,' said Maurice.

'It's tiring, no?' said Paco cheerfully. 'But in less than an hour we will be at the top, and then it is downhill all the way. A long way but downhill.'

He had not even looked round.

A little later the two we had seen on the col met and passed us;

impassive and bearded with huge rucksacks, they tramped dourly by as if they carried the Tablets of the Law and were not yet too sure they would add to the sum of human happiness.

'*Diás,*' they muttered, and were gone.

I realised Maurice was lagging; for a moment or two the problem – whether to remain in contact with Paco or linger for Maurice – had an almost intellectual feel about it: one weighed up the alternatives as one weighs up some minutiae of literature, the possible meanings of a quibble in Donne, say, then Maurice's voice, more urgent now, brought the problem into sharper, more personal focus.

'Archie. Please stop.'

I turned and something near my heart melted. The poor boy was white, had gone forward on to his hands though from a purely physical point of view there was no need to at all, and was gripping the stones in front of him as though if he released them for a second he would go spinning out from the mountain-side like a space walker whose line is cut. I say "out" and not "down" for the gradient we were on was not as steep as a flight of stairs, and if he or any of us had taken even a nasty tumble a slither of more than ten feet was impossible. Enough to twist an ankle, take a nasty bruise or scrape, but no more. Yet the poor boy was obviously terrified out of his wits.

'I don't think I can go any further.'

'Paco? Paco!'

'Yes?'

'Something's wrong with Maurice.'

'Something's wrong? What's wrong?'

'I don't know.'

'Let's see what's wrong,' and the *soi-disant* Basque came clumping back down towards us, dislodging a stone which, through an unlucky bounce or two, carried quite a long way before coming to rest. Maurice's eyes watched its course with widening horror.

'I'm frightened,' he moaned.

'But look, there is no danger. No danger at all. This is walking, not climbing. No ice; no snow even.'

'I'm sorry, but I'm frightened.'

'Why are you frightened? You are not sick are you?'

'If you mean do I feel as if I might heave up, the answer is yes. And dizzy too.'

'Perhaps he has vertigo,' I suggested.

'No, that is not possible. How can you have vertigo when there is no drop? Did he have breakfast?'

I thought back. Coffee with a lot of milk and sugar, hot bread with butter.

'Reasonable, I should have thought.'

'Has he got a hangover? Did he drink much last night?' Again I remembered. 'Yes,' I had to admit. 'We had half a bottle of *Izarra.'*

'*Joder,* that's it then. *Izarra* is strictly for the tourists. No Basque ever touches it. His stomach is upset a little, that is all. We shall have a rest, a little to eat, admire the view, and then we shall go on,' and he pulled bread and hard sausage from his rucksack and hacked out a rough sandwich with a clasp-knife.

With dreadful reluctance Maurice began to eat. I noticed that his eyes now never left the immediate foreground, our faces, his own hands; it seemed he would not even let them wander to his feet or the rock he was sitting on without their flinching away.

'Good. Now he feels better and we can go on.'

'Would you prefer it if you came between us?' I asked.

Dumbly he nodded.

As we continued to climb, I noticed that he was using his hands almost all the time and really it was almost never necessary. Also he dislodged a stone or two, one of which bumped against my shin.

'Watch it,' I called, and again he froze.

'Archie, I really don't think I can take any more of this.' Again Paco galumphed back to us.

'Maurice, you must tell me what is the matter.'

'I'm bloody scared, I'm scared out of my mind, I think I'm going to slip.'

'You will not slip. You cannot slip. But you are far more likely to slip if you lean forward into the slope, and that is why you keep dislodging stones. Look. It's a simple matter of gravity.' He demonstrated. 'If you are upright, your weight pushes the stones down to the centre of the earth, not to the valley floor. But if you lean, the line of force is parallel to the slope and so of course you slip and make the scree move too. Now take my hand and stand upright.'

'Sod your lines of force. Leave go. For Christ's sake, leave me alone.'

There was a moment's silence. Dimly I was aware of more passion beating around me than I understood.

Then there was a new noise, a sudden splatter of heavy rain drops and a gust of wind. Distantly thunder rumbled. I looked up. The sky immediately above was black, though there was still plenty of blue elsewhere, even behind the peaks of the Vignemale itself.

'Come,' said Paco. 'We shall get a soaking else.'

'Archie, I don't have to, do I?' The plea was agonising, though incomprehensible.

'No, of course you don't if you don't want to,' I replied.

'But I think he does,' Paco's face was more blank, the eyes harder than I had seen before.

'Why?'

The argument had shifted: it was between the Basque and me now, with Maurice watching helplessly. The rain began to fall steadily – cold, on a wind, and thunder barged about the peaks behind us, already closer.

'Why? Because I need someone who will speak Spanish if I am stopped; so I can maintain the pretence that I am Irish. I explained all this.'

'But it doesn't have to be Maurice.'

'Doesn't it? I think so. Maurice knows why.'

We turned back to him. Rain was streaming down his ashen face mixed, I suspected, with tears. He had begun to shiver.

'I can't, Paco. I can't go on.' He was shaking his head with an emphasis one could not possibly ignore. 'You just don't know how frightened I am. I don't think I can get down, let alone go on. Do what you like, I can't go on.'

Again the rain and the thunder. What did he mean by 'Do what you like'?

Paco resolved it at last. 'All right. All right, I shall chance it on my own. You shall have to get down as best you can, but I am going on.'

He gave his rucksack a hitch, thrust his hands into his pockets, and stumped off up over the rocks and scree. In a moment or two he was out of sight and the thunder crashed suddenly right overhead. The rain became a torrent, the upper slopes of the Vignemale to our right disappeared behind cloud, though the glacier still gleamed whitely through.

Going down was a desperate business. For most of the time Maurice insisted on clutching my arm or shoulder which made balance difficult on the now wet stones; hysteria is catching – I began to share his sense of the emptiness in front of us, the horror of the chasm of air and rain between us and the mountain opposite. At least I now had an inkling of the state he had got himself into – an inkling, too, of what you must have suffered here in Santiago, dear Maurice, on the roof of the Cathedral.

III *Spain*

La Corrida, from *A Raving Monarchist*

What better introduction to Spain can there be than the Corrida? This is a real one: the last day of San Fermín in Pamplona, 1976, the first San Fermín since the outbreak of the Civil War exactly forty years earlier. Peñas are fan clubs, not of any particular matador, but of la Corrida in general. I've heard and read the spoonerism at the end three or four times since I invented it.

The bullring filled quickly and early. One by one the *peñas* marched in, climbed out of the arena, and up into the sunny cheap section which is entirely sold out to them. Here they made a dense mass of white, broken only by two blocks, one of grey and one of black – clubs that wore Basque smocks. The giant hollow cylinder began to roar, almost vibrate to the noise; anticipation sharpened; ring attendants in red shirts and black trousers came out with sprinklers and rakes to lay the sand – miraculously it hadn't rained since Sunday – and then at exactly six twenty-five the confused babel of shouting, dancing, singing, *riau riau riau-ing* fell quiet for a breathless second; the *peñas* rose together, perhaps ten thousand of them, fists in the air, and again the Basque hymn *Euskal Gudari* rang out, the anthem we first heard at the demonstration, ending in wave after wave of cheering that drowned the sound of the hooped cornets and kettle drums that signalled the entry of the *Alguaciles* with their white panaches and curvetting horses.

As bullfight critics, the *peñas* of Pamplona are not generally noted for their discrimination. This is a mistake. Granted they thunderously cheer any matador who tries to enliven the proceedings with the more showy ornaments; granted they go ecstatic over unnecessary risk; and granted they abhor the fighter, however good, who kills on the shady side of the ring in front of the most expensive seats. But they do know a sham when they see one and will whistle and hoot him out of the ring and all the way back to Seville; and they also, and most greatly to their credit, recognise what is true and genuine.

Nearly twenty years ago they made up a chant which has since been adapted all over the country to fit any popular hero at any time – for footballers, tennis players, I've heard it sung at a wedding for the groom. Not all Spaniards know that it originated on the sunny terraces at Pamplona and that it was first sung for one man only.

In Spanish it goes:
¡El Viti! ¡El Viti! El Viti es cojonudo
Como el Viti no hay ninguno.

El Viti is the greatest
There's no one like El Viti.

Not the greatest *copla* in the language – but the jingle they sing it to has something of the opening bars of 'see the Conquering Hero' and sung *con brío,* by thousands, for the man it was first invented for, it is quite powerfully affecting.

And they would not have sung it that night, not even for El Viti himself, if he had not deserved it.

Santiago Martín Sánchez – yes, Santiago – known as El Viti because he comes from Vitigudino near Salamanca, is pushing forty which is old for a matador. In 1974 he went into semi-retirement to run his bull-ranch; in 1976 he came back to fight a full season: I don't know why – it is as likely that he returned because he felt or was persuaded he still had something to offer *Toreo,* as that he needed the money. He is lantern-faced, tall, lean, pale but not at all swarthy: very much a Castilian – there is nothing of the gypsy or Andalusian about him. His style of bullfighting is the purest that has been seen for many decades: he never ornaments, he never cheats, he is never even showy. With an ordinary bull he can therefore be dull. With a bad bull – a coward or a weakling – he is far better than most because he is quick, skilful, decent. With a good bull – well, with a good bull – *Como El Viti no hay ninguno.*

He almost never smiles and so another title he has is *La Trista Figura* – borrowed from an older idealist who also refused to compromise. Because of his dignity, his poise, his authority, and the respect given to him by all other *toreros,* he is also known as *Su Majestad.*

On this occasion his suit was bright crimson – as royal a red as one could imagine – and gold.

His first bull was weak. By the *faena* it was too far gone, and he killed it quickly and cleanly.

His second bull was strong, and brave, but unpredictable: a lesser matador would have ruined him by tiring him, by over-dominating him, or even by exaggerating the danger to justify an early kill. But after some awkward moments El Viti achieved exactly the right level of *mando;* when *the faena* came the bull was fixed in the lure, and ready to charge again and again until he dropped; between them they thus achieved five minutes or more of perfection.

If the kill had been flawless – and the reason it wasn't was a combination of El Viti's integrity taken with a last second return to unpredictability on the part of the bull – if the kill had been perfect the *peñas* would have gone up to the Cathedral and brought him San Fermín himself, gold mitre, crozier, jewels and all. As it was he received – two ears, three red scarves tied lovingly round his neck by worshippers who eluded the police to get to him, a black Basque smock, two live sucking pigs, and all the more conventional offerings a successful matador gets on his lap of honour: flowers, wallets, hand-bags, boxes of chocolates, cigars, wineskins, hats, and so on. And above all the song:

¡El Viti! ¡El Viti! *El Viti es cojonudo* and at last he smiled – he smiled quite a lot. Not many people see Santiago Martín from Vitigudino smile.

The other bulls, the other matadors were good, even very good but *Como El Viti no hay ninguno.*

At the end, with dusk gathering, *the peñas* flooded down from the terraces and into the ring, formed behind their banners and their bands, and headed out through the big gate, club by club, for their last procession round the town. As each approached the exit the upflung hands twisted yet again three times: *riau, riau, riau,* and out they danced. The later ones carried large, lit candles.

As we left I noticed that Maurice's grin, the silly grin one can't help wearing after a perfect occasion, had taken on a level of smug inanity that had to be explained.

He tried but spluttered, tried again. At last, with eyes beginning to water, he managed to articulate: 'I know it's silly. It's daft, it really is. Oh Archie, please forgive me... I just couldn't help thinking, when all the *peñas* were trying to get out of the ring at once, well, when there was a bit of a jam, and no one seemed to want to go first, I couldn't help thinking, I'm sorry, but it just came to me: *That's an awful lot of Basques in one exit.'*

Las Batuecas

*This is a lost valley, a Shangri-La, in the mountains south
and east of Salamanca. Friends from the university took us
there just before Christmas in 1973, and I've used that trip
three times in novels since. This extract is taken from* King
Fisher Lives *and is part of a letter sent from Nadia, the main
female characer, to Mark, her half-brother.*

Now we climbed up into the mountains proper, the western end
of the Gredos they'd be, and everything got bleaker until at last
we were above the tree-line and there were patches of snow.
Then quite suddenly we were going down and down and down and
down for ever it seemed. F had told me what to expect but I haven't told
you to surprise you. It surprised me even though I had been told. At first
there were views for a hundred miles over range after range of wild
wooded mountains, much woodier than on the way up. We were going
south and down, you see. Then they closed in a bit, but still you could
see miles down into a system of dark green valleys. The road was now
unmetalled and hair-pinned dreadfully and there was no wall or fence,
just chicken wire. There were streams gushing down the mountain-side
and waterfalls on the other side of the valley. JL said he could see eagles
and F said they were vultures. There were tall trees with red trunks and
these were cork trees where the cork had been stripped off but it was all
wild and uncultivated.

At last, and I think we were now about four thousand feet below the
pass, the road met a river and there was a track up to the right. We
drove up it and came to a little clearing where cork had been stacked in
front of a wall with a gate. The river was still there, and there we were
in the Valley of the Batuecas. We got out and it was so warm, you've
really no idea, warm like July in England and it was sunny and the
mountains floated away above us. When your ears popped for the tenth
time you could hear nothing but silence and the river which was really
only a mountain stream and chattered and gurgled all the time round
stones and rocks. That sound was there all the time – quite unlike the
muddy gurgling I can hear now as the rain drops out of the sky.

The wall belongs to a monastery of discalced (shoeless, in case you
didn't know) Carmelites and we had quite a tricky time of it getting
round it as it is built right down to the river and along the river and
blocks off the valley. But we managed, with only one wet shoe, mine,
and then it was easier. At first it was like walking though an English
wood but much wilder. There were tall trees, fern, bracken, butterflies

(in December!) and dragonflies. Once we could see a bit of the monastery garden with orange trees in fruit, black cypresses, and a palm tree, but soon we left all that behind and the valley got wilder and wilder, with the path disappearing sometimes and patches of scree to cross.

There were so many plants and bushes – such a paradise of abundancy. There was a whole grove of strawberry trees (arbutus, I think is the proper name) like big laurels with waxy white pendulant flowers and, at the same time, red, squashy fruits like strawberries but bright yellow sweet and fragrant inside. I can't begin to tell you what else. Larches, pines, willows, hazels, rowans, juniper. And what flowers there must be in spring. I could see primrose and violet plants and various sorts of lily which I couldn't identify.

A mile or so and it began to feel more mountainy and F kept stopping and looking up at craggy bluffs above us – the rock was all sort of hard-edged and fissured, and brown and red, except where bright greenish-yellow lichens were growing on it. He was looking for the cave but it was five years since he had been there and he wasn't sure he could find it. But he needn't have worried because the path more or less led to it. We had to cross the river (big, flat boulders, and pools – I wanted to swim but I think the Dagos would have been embarrassed) and then the only path left was up, very steeply and brokenly, towards one of those rocky cliffs. At the top there was a sort of ledge we had to get round which would have terrified you with your vertigo but was quite safe really and there we were.

Well the cave was a bit of a disappointment at first. It wasn't really a cave but just a large space under a high overhang. F said it had been a cave once but the roof had fallen in and rolled away down to the river. Then, would you believe it all that way from anywhere, there was an eight foot high spiked railing cemented into the ground and padlocked together in front of the rock face. And thirdly the paintings weren't much, being signs really, circles and dashes, not figurative apart from one which could have been a goat's head. F and JL got over the railing and spat on the marks which made them show up better. F said they were for magic probably, or maybe for astronomical calculations, who knows. Anyway the place was probably a sort of shrine.

But the view was marvellous. Below us was the river, in front the other side of the valley, to the left it wandered on further and branched away into ever wilder areas – no more paths, until it climbed into mountain faces over which we had come in the car. To the right the woods we had come through and the monastery which we couldn't see but we could see their wall climbing over the crags like a miniature Great Wall of China. And it was all so peaceful, so empty.

JL was looking everywhere through glasses, but there were few birds about because it was hot and midday, but he said there could be wild boar and even bears and wolves above us, and certainly cats, pine martens and deer. But we never saw anything like that.

Going back was almost more beautiful because now we were going into the sun and it reflected off the river and off the millions of leaves so that if you half closed your eyes it was like walking though a shower of sunlight. JL had a camera, quite a good one I think, and he said he'd make sure I see them when they come out.

Well, that's about it for the Valley of the Batuecas. It really is paradise though. The nearest village five miles down the stream, a few monks, and nothing. But so warm, friendly, pleasant. Now I look back on it it's like those lovely rich paintings by Breughel, I think, in the Prado, of paradise with lovely spotted pards lying down with deer, and fruit and flowers dense everywhere, and peacocks, and humming birds. I feel about it the way people do who have been to a super place for their holidays and dream about retiring there one day.

Los Ancianos

From July 1989 to July 1990 we lived in a semi-modernised small-holder's cottage by the river Guadalfeo a mile below Orgiva in Granada. It was the wettest autumn in living memory and the track from the main road to the cottage was washed away three times. When this happened we had to park our Renault 5 (called here Blanca) a quarter of a mile up and across the hillside outside the cottage of Los Ancianos, the Old Ones. We got to know them well. What follows are extracts based on various sections of the diary I was keeping and starts here in November.

On the morning, a really beautiful hot morning, of Sant'Antonio's Eve we took Amalia up to town. The almond blossom was beginning to spread up from the valley: opposite the electricity sub-station there was a small grove of the pale dusty pink variety: once they were in full bloom, it looked like fairy land.

Amalia was excited – Sant' Anton was the patron saint of Torviscón, the village where she was born, seventeen kilometres up the Guadalfeo, and she was going to buy six big rockets to celebrate. Seventy-seven, her white and iron-grey hair held off her face with a solitary kirby grip, her stoutness beginning to shrink beneath her quilted black dress, her face brown and wrinkled, yes, just like a walnut, with eyes as alive as Mrs Tittlemouse's in spite of incipient cataract, she was, as Laney used to say a 'dear old bean'.

It was a job to get her into the front of the car – 'La pena, la pena', she'd cry, not at the physical pain though that was real enough, but at the misery of being old. She'd broken a hip falling off a donkey seven years before, and more recently done something crucial to her neck falling from a chair while white-washing her ceiling.

'We'll give you a lift back,' Laney said, handing in her thick, knobbly, shiny stick, 'but we may be some time.'

'I'll sit in the sun on the church-steps and wait for you – I won't be bored, because I have my radio...' and from her basket she took an ancient transistor radio – it was a stream-lined hoop of bright yellow plastic, narrow at the top to make a handle, thickening at the bottom where the works were. And sure enough there she was, an hour or so later, sitting on the steps beneath the orange trees, with her hanky spread over her head, her stick between her knees and her radio blaring out Andalusian pop from Radio Alpujarra.

Next day, the actual Saint's day, at about half-past four, there were six enormous, wide-spaced explosions – Amalia celebrating. And on the following cloudless morning, deep frost, perhaps the deepest we'd had, the children struggling to keep their hands warm, steam rising from the river, Arthur fantasised about Amalia while they waited for the bus: her radio, he said, was two-way; her rockets were missiles; the handkerchief she put on her head was a parachute.

The twentieth of January was both fiesta and a Saturday.

At about eleven o'clock we went round to Los Ancianos to find them already sitting out in bright sunlight on the bench by their front door.

Amalia was in cheery mood.

'The frost,' she said, 'was like the old days in the Vegueta. One of those days when we had all washed our sheets and spread them on the bushes to dry.'

Their cortijo, like José Luis's just down the hill, had a small second storey, a square block with shuttered windows over the main door, possibly originally used as a small hay-loft or a place to cure tobacco or dry corn-cobs. Roses and a vine framed the square entrance, which looked out over the river to the Sierra Lujar and the Contraviesa, on which there was a high pall of snow. Although they could not have been more than twenty feet or so higher than Tío Mateo, and a hundred yards further north, the visual ridges fell away for them and they could see the mountains beyond.

In front of their door was the small paved yard where Blanca was parked, a pile of firewood and caña, and built into the side of the house, hutches for hens and a couple of ducks. The paved yard had once served as a threshing-floor for the rye which in earlier times had been the favoured cereal crop.

Amalia embraced Laney as she always did, kissed the children's cheeks, then fastened her strong if arthritic brown hand on J's wrist, shaking her head at the foolishness of a man who couldn't speak Spanish even though his wife and children could. Behind her Don Francisco wheezed and puffed. Once a big man with big shoulders and a big chest he was now a near ruin, his back slightly hunched, his breast-bone pushed out like a bird's above a waistline that was no longer robust enough to fill trousers which sagged. He suffered badly from chronic emphysema and fits of dementia – both the result of working for twenty years in the lead mine over two thousand feet above us on the Sierra Lujar.

They had two dogs: one, pretty with hints of a King Charles spaniel was called Duque (Duke) the other, Lucero, was more nondescript, a dachund crossed with a Jack Russell. These now made a very big fuss indeed, managed somehow to scramble into the back where Don Francisco had Nina on his knee and J had Arthur. They had to be hoicked out by their collars and firmly shut in behind the high gate – the trouble was that it was very unusual for both Amalia and Francisco to be out together at the same time and the dogs were clearly distressed to be left on their own. Indeed it was unusual for Don Francisco to come up to town at all, and we wondered why he was making the trip.

At last we were off, down the bumpy track and over the broken sewer. With the extra load the back of the car clanged on a rock and we prayed it was the tow-bar and not the transmission.

As soon as we opened the gate at Los Ancianos, Amalia was out in the forecourt. No, today she did not need a lift to town, but as usual she wanted a chat. Her hip was bothering her more than usual: the trouble was of course that when the accident occurred, her stupid son had insisted that she go to Barcelona to have it fixed. He had been adamant that the treatment she would get there would be better than anything she could get in Granada. In fact it had all been a ruse to persuade her and Don Francisco that they would be altogether better off living in Barcelona. They had hated it. They hated the journey, hated the hospital, and hated the city. They didn't even want a flat in Orgiva, let alone Barcelona. They were tranquillo where they were, warm, had everything they needed. Only the sewer was a disgrace – she had had to paddle through again yesterday to get to the Venta for her lift in the baker's van – yes she'd been to the town hall about it, even spoken to the mayor. Oh yes, he's a nice young man, but...

'We would like,' said Laney to Amalia one day, 'to buy a ham. But we do not know how to be sure we are getting a good one.'

'Don Francisco is an expert. We will come with you and you can be sure he will choose you a good one.'

So, Thursday 15 February, we set out a bit earlier than we usually did on market day, picking the old couple up on the river bank, beneath José-Luis's twelve-foot hedge of caña. On the way up we pulled in on the outskirts of town, and J got out, opened the boot, took out three or four supermarket bags filled with rubbish and hung them from the hooked arms of the three thin metal rod crosses that stood in a gap between modern apartment blocks. Don Francisco was amazed.

'What are you doing that for?' he asked. 'Why not use the river? We always do.'

Laney was tactful.

'We have so much more rubbish than you do.'

The old man went on about it.

'I've never noticed those hooks before. What a clever idea, they keep the rubbish out of reach of dogs and rats...'

We remembered how Jeff (our English landlord) railed and stormed against their practice of dropping rubbish bags into the irrigation over-flow that ran under his road. What he had not realised was that it was neither peasant ignorance nor peasant malice that led them to do this but centuries' old tradition. And not a bad tradition before food came in cans and bags were made of plastic and not paper. The rubbish they threw in when they first came to a cortijo in the Vegueta in 1940 was very little less biodegradable than it would have been if they had moved in in 1840.

Don Francisco rumbled on about it until we had parked beside Nina's school in front of the Guardia Civil, by the big frondy pepper tree. Its sprays of tiny white and yellow flowers were just coming into bloom with a strangely sweetened scent of black pepper. Although its seeds look and taste like black peppercorns and are sometimes harvested and used as such, it is an ornamental originally from Persia. True pepper corns come from a tropical vine. All of which shows that learning can destroy pleasant illusions – ever since he first saw pepper trees in Majorca J believed that they were the source of black pepper: now checking back to Guillaume de Rougemont's splendid *Collins Guide to Crops of Britain and Europe* he found he was wrong. End of digression.

Los Ancianos led us round the top of the municipal market and into the alley that led down to the Roxy Disco. At the top was the only large grocery store left in Orgiva that had not adopted supermarket proce-dures. Amalia told us that this steep and slightly serpentine alley was once a barranco (probably used as an open sewer) and that when it was first surfaced it was where people bought and sold piglets. Often she used to bring her piglets here to sell them.

Inside the shop, basically a high marble counter ten feet long, with shelves all round, Antonio, 40, iron grey hair, lean, efficient, but solid and nice, did his best to cope with a cohort of iron-clad, black-clad grannies. His buxom straw-blonde wife, and two girls, one blonde and probably their daughter, the other dark, assisted.

'I am taking you in the right order,' he shouted. 'You'd have real cause for getting angry if I didn't.'

But one very old man, sitting on a stool at the back, *was* getting angry. He was smaller than Don Francisco but his eyes were slightly protuberant in the same way, his chest stuck out, his colour was high and he was clearly enfeebled both in body and mind: symptoms often seen amongst the older men in the town who had worked the lead mines. He was sure his tiny but tough looking wife had not been served in order, and he began to shout and protest, although she took Antonio's side.

On the marble counter there was a tall spike with a hook from which hung pigs' tongues, hearts and lights. Antonio sliced off bits with a knife ground through the years to stiletto thinness and sold them for pennies.

'How do you cook them?' Laney asked Amalia.

'Fried up with onions...' she answered, and politely swallowed back the natural 'of course'.

There were several grannies ahead of them, and J spent some time marvelling at the difference between these ladies over fifty and their counterparts in England. These were tough, purposeful, and basically happy. Although they all dressed the same, in black over the armour plated corsets that gave them such queue-cred, they were all deeply convinced of their own individuality, of their own presence and purpose. They were proud fighters, but good laughers too... yes, come down to it, what made them so different from the fifty- and sixty-year-old ladies in Britain was, quite simply, happiness.

Meanwhile, prompted by the large framed colour photograph that hung above Antonio's head as he wielded his stiletto, Amalia was telling Laney about Orgiva's Protector and Guardian – the splendid larger than life-size baroque image of Christ on the Cross at the moment of death, El Expiración. For three hundred and sixty-four days a year it stood in a deep recess behind the high altar in the church. Its picture was in every shop and bank, and most pubs; smaller versions, playing-card size, were in every wallet and purse, and in thousands more across South America as well as in Madrid and Barcelona. It was,

Amalia said, the town's treasure, paraded through the streets with a lot of fireworks on the Friday two weeks before Good Friday. She told of how church authorities had wanted to clean it, but the town would not let it out, barricades constructed from farm-carts were put up, manned by men with shot-guns, so in the end a special warehouse was built in the precincts and the cleaners came from Granada to do the cleaning.

While all this was going on more and more grannies and grandads, and some younger ones, dropped by to greet Los Ancianos. Clearly it was not often that both were in town together. There was a lot of joking and back-slapping, especially of Don Francisco, whose appearance was more of a novelty than Amalia's.

At last it was our turn and we looked up somewhat apprehensively at the row of hams hanging from the ceiling. They all looked the same – a pig's trotter circled with coarse white string, and looped to a hook hanging from a bar eight feet high, then a shank of chestnut coloured dried skin dropping to the knee and the thigh and the hip which swelled out in a flattened irregular oval, now a sort of subdued buttery colour, which they knew was packed with dense, salty purply brown meat. The whole thing was the rear leg of a porker, hopefully fed on corn and maybe acorns, severed from the animal, left in strong brine for a month or so, then taken up to the highest village in Spain, Trévelez, just up the road, to be cured for a year in a warehouse carefully constructed to allow a controlled amount of dry, cold, mountain air to drift around it. If the ham was acorn fed, and cured for more than a year then it doubled in price, was labelled 'añejo', mature, and probably ended up in Madrid.

There are two areas in Spain that produce these hams – the other is Salamanca. Having lived in Salamanca as well as Granada we were prepared to accept what is generally accepted – that the Salamantine ones are better – mainly because there is more chance that they have come from pigs free-ranging through oak forest.

In both cases the meat is dense, dark and tough, and worth what you pay for it, which is more than one can say for Bayonne or Parma ham.

'How big?' Antonio asked.

Laney suggested: 'Six kilos?' This being the smallest one was likely to get, and since while we were a family, we were not an extended family, it seemed the best idea was to go for small. Kept in a cool dry atmosphere these hams will not go off, but once cut into you want to get through them in a month or so.

'Sorry,' said Antonio, 'everyone's been buying the smallest. Because of the wet autumn, they're afraid the bigger ones might not be properly cured. I've got nothing under seven kilos. Well-cured or soft?'

Laney hedged: 'Middling?'

Antonio fixed on one in the middle of the ceiling and hooked it down with a pole. Antonio and Don Francisco then stuck the beast in the four joints with a white, hard, plastic needle, grooved, with a little cup, like a mustard spoon at the end. No fluid ran off – a good sign. They offered us the needle.

'Smell it,' they said.

We all smelled it.

Laney said: 'What should it smell of?'

'Ham.'

Antonio slipped the monster into a coarse muslin stocking, and gave us a card – a sort of receipt and guarantee.

'When you get home take off the stocking, that's just for transporting it, and hang it up where the air can move around it and where it won't ever be in sunlight. If it's not right, then bring it back with this card and I'll give you another. I don't want to sell people anything bad. It should last two months though if you keep it that long it will get a bit dry and tough.'

The card said the pig came from Murcia, north of Almeria, but was guaranteed cured in Trévelez. We paid 6,416 pesetas, about £34, for nearly eight kilos. Bought in the Granada Hipercor it would have cost eight thousand; in Madrid, twelve. Within six weeks, with a little help from our friends, we ate every last edible scrap.

Amalia bought a pig's tail to add richness to her stew pot, and we went out at last into the warm sunlight and put our ham in the boot of the car.

'We'd like to buy you a drink.'

Amalia looked relieved. She wanted to look round the street market, but not with him.

'Francisco will take you. He knows a nice place up at the top of the market.'

'You come and find me there later then,' said Francisco.

Amalia was firm.

'NO!' she said. 'I'll be at the flower stall in the Municpal Market – you find me there. And while you're up at the far end take them to Don Antonio's mother-in-law's flat.'

We walked through the lower part of the market then up side streets parallel to it, into the new area near the Health Centre – a magnificent building of glass, stainless steel and white concrete. The bar was on the ground floor of an apartment block and was also new: lots of chrome, mahogany counter, computer game and pinball machine, there are thousands like it all over Spain but they nearly all carry some touches of individuality, knick-knacks, pictures, a colour combination, that express the personality of the owners, who are almost always a couple. In this case the female half was a lady in her late thirties to early forties, once pretty, now hard and tough. Her husband was a little man with balding hair and neat moustache. Her daughter took after her. It was clear who was in charge.

It was very busy, all sorts came and went, not many stopping for more than five minutes: a mother with a little boy of four, both smartly dressed, she with a coffee, he with a chocolate batido and buttered toast. Mum was almost desperate in her desire to make him eat every crumb although he was already quite porky. Next to them a little old man with a Soberano brandy, and then a handful of stall-holders drinking cañas of beer while their wives looked after the stalls. No two orders were the same. The noise was terrible – Radio Alpujarra, the coffee machine, the pin-ball machine, and everyone shouting.

Continuing our search for the perfect Vino de la Costa we ordered a demi 'jarra'. It was drawn from a barrel into a clay jug which the owner covered with an orange fringed napkin, putting three small straight glasses beside it, and then three tapas of delicious stewed pork. With the second jug we got three dried anchovies: we'd often seen these for sale in both markets but had not quite dared. Don Francisco was delighted with them, but we found them strong tasting, good to have tried once, but not twice.

'Are they dearer than the fresh fish?' Laney asked.

'Of course,' said Don Francisco, smacking his lips and then wiping them on a paper serviette taken from the counter dispenser.

He talked to Laney about the Civil War. They already knew that for two years the front line had been the Guadalfeo with the Falangists holding the Orgiva bank and the Republicans on the southern side. There was a lot of shooting and shelling across the river, and the well-to-do of Orgiva retired to Lanjarón. But the ordinary people had to stay where they were. Amalia's brother was killed in the fields very close to the cortijo they were now in. Don Francisco himself was conscripted by the Falangists, the rebels, because in the first weeks of the war they got control of the whole of Granada province except the coast. Although Don Francisco did not actually say so they knew that if he had resisted conscription in any way he would have been shot instantly, thousands were. He was at the siege of Málaga where there were a lot of Germans. If you asked the Germans for cigarettes they gave you whole packets. When World War II came he and his friends were asked to join the German army, but he had had enough by then, and worked in the lead mines instead.

The Vino was good, very good, and they asked if they brought a bottle or a demi-arrobia would the Landlord fill it.

'Of course.'

'How much?'

'Two fifty a litre.'

That still seemed too much. Ordinary commercial table wine could be bought for as little as eighty, and the really good stuff, Jumilla for instance, was no more than one thirty – seventy English p.

Laney reminded Don Francisco that Amalia had asked him to show us Don Antonio's new flat. But now he was tired, and his mind was wandering, he'd had a bit more to drink than was usual for him. Suddenly old and confused, out in the street he had to think for a moment to remember where he was. Often Amalia accused him of being 'loco', mad, and he replied by saying jovially that she was the one who was 'loca'. But the truth of it was on her side: he had worked the lead mines and would never be the man he should have been.

He wandered into the entrances of two or three new apartment blocks, but clearly could not tell one from another. They walked up a stairwell to the first floor – and he pushed the spy-holes set in the doors instead of the bells. Eventually they persuaded him to give up and they took him back to the street market. Halfway down he seemed to come round again.

'Ah, now I know where I am,' he beamed and struck his forehead.

'And do you remember where you are to meet Amalia?'

He thought for a moment.

'In the flower shop in the Municipal Market?'

'That's right.'

'That's where I always meet her. The lady there lives at the Venta and she'll give us a lift home.'

Amalia and Francisco had seen some changes, and one long evening they told us a bit about them. It happened like this. Towards the end of January J rang up Gina, our landlady, living at that time in Tower Hamlets, and said, 'Hey, what about the road?'

'What? Hasn't he done it yet? I'll ring him tonight!'

'No, we'll do it, save you the international call.'

And ringing Paco Ortíz, Construcciones, Motril, Laney cleared up the misunderstanding. On 30 January he delivered five big concrete tubes, one metre in diameter, one and a half long, to where the bar had been, and a week later a labourer appeared and began to dig out a trench for them. Next Saturday Paco turned up with his plant, laid the tubes in the trench, and cemented them in. The irrigation waterfall dutifully deviated from cutting canyons into the bed of the track, gushed through the tubes instead and into the river. A week later Paco came again but this time with his big open truck and his grown-up son, as well as his JCB. First they shifted great shovelsful of gravel and earth from the river bed into the truck, then the truck trundled up from the river bed like a great rhinoceros from a water hole onto the road, along to the bar, and whoosh, out it all tipped. Back again for the next lot. They did this four times, then the JCB, like a big yellow dinosaur, rumbled and ground itself out of the river bed and with earth moving blade to the fore this time rather than the shovel, graded the tips. It took twenty-eight loads and most of the day.

Just in time for our first fair weather visitors, due in the middle of February – English half-term – and just as well since they had accepted the necessity of a hire-car at Málaga. Which was also the reason why, on that Saturday morning, Laney did not come up with us for the weekend shop-up and churros and hot chocolate: she was busy white-washing out the black mould, and putting down red floor paint where it had blistered into a messy cement powder over much of the kitchen and sitting-room floors, jobs that took a couple of weeks.

'It's only the Ruffs, for Chrissake,' cried J, meaning no disparage-ment of the Ruffs, just that they weren't like the pope or something.

'It's not for the Ruffs. It's for us. I'm sick of squalor.'

That was laying it on a bit, J thought. But in a way, no, utterly, she was right – the cobwebs and mould, the red-hot stove, the dust collecting on the drying peppers, the disintegrating floor had seemed not inappropriate to our Hobbit-like existence through the rains and then the January frosts – but now, early in February, the weather was bright and warm, it was spring...

So it was just J and the children who turned up at Los Ancianos early on the Saturday Paco put the road back.

It was still frosty, and their gate still cold to Arthur's hands as he swung it open, but already the sun was on their little patio, and as they started the business of opening the bonnet and taking out the blanket inside, Don Francisco came out, just in his trousers and a vest, and put his head under the tap that stood by their doorway. Now, why he did this they don't know for sure, since they had a tap inside, and, almost certainly, a hot water system, but the answer might be that it was what he had been doing for seventy years, ever since his mother stopped doing it to him when he was old enough to manage on his own.

Then Amalia came out and had a lot to say.

'Arthur, what's she saying?'

'I think she's saying it's cold and would we like something hot to eat.'

'And would you?'

Arthur shrugged positively – a lovely person, always ready to say yes, give it a whirl.

Amalia brought out a white plate with three small omelettes. They had been cooked firm, not leathery but so we could eat them in our hands, like thick pancakes. They were salty, and made the children thirsty, but they tasted... of egg. Amalia's hens, who had never ever tasted a processed poultry food, squawked their appreciation of our approval.

But now came the moment of truth for we were in the middle of a saga that had yet to reach its end. For three or four weeks it had not been easy, in fact generally it had been impossible, to get Blanca to start. We blamed the damp, we blamed the cold. We covered her with rugs both inside and outside her bonnet and that seemed to help. It was just the first start of the day that did not happen – the others were always all right. So what we did was push-start down the hill towards the river, and that was OK if Laney was there. On this occasion it was just the children and emphysemic Don Francisco.

Amalia said: 'No!'

J said: 'We'll go back and get Laney,' but probably Amalia didn't understand him.

Arthur translated.

Don Francisco said the Alpujarran equivalent of: 'I'm fine, Amalia is a silly old cow, come on I'm going to have a push.'

And he did, and as they trundled down the hill firing on two, then three, and finally all four cylinders, J was left with the impression that Amalia was very annoyed, even angry.

At about five o'clock Arthur and Nina came back to the house to tell us that Paco Ortíz had almost finished – they had had a lovely afternoon sitting in the earth-mover's cabin, in the cab of the truck.

'It was wicked fun,' cried Arthur, and then added, somewhat disloyally, 'more fun than digging out boulders with Jeff.'

And a grand job he had made of it – the track, sorry, road, was now about three feet higher than it had been before it was washed away, and he had pushed a water-break of really huge boulders across the river bed to protect the curve where it was most vulnerable. But he reckoned there was still an hour or so to do.

He was not alone. Don Miguel, his wife, Don Antonio, José-Luis, and sundry goat herds had all turned out to watch a free Saturday afternoon's entertainment, better than the telly, and of course Don Francisco was there too.

'You won't be needing to park your car with us any more.'

'No. But we're so grateful, it would have been an awful worry...'

He batted aside Laney's thanks. 'Come up and have a coffee with us.'

They followed his slightly hunched back up the track to their cortijo and Duque and Lucero gambolled at his heels.

Arthur and Nina had already been inside, more than once, called in by Amalia to keep warm while the grown-ups struggled to get Blanca to start, but it was the first time for Laney and J. First they passed across a rather gloomy windowless kitchen. There was a basin with two taps, so there *was* a hot-water system, a tall fridge-freezer, and a washing machine which stood like aliens from outer space against undressed stone and mortar walls. There was also a conglomeration of kitchen implements, cooking vessels, plates and pottery, some covered in dust, a few gleaming because they were still used.

How did the hi-tech get there? Amalia and Francisco had four childen, all now with families, one in Granada, one in Madrid, and two in Barcelona. They had insisted on putting in all these gadgets, most of which Amalia never touched, though she did use the fridge-freezer to cut down her painful trips to town.

We all crowded into their small sitting room. A big open fireplace in which a couple of big olive logs smouldered filled one corner. It had a wood mantel of undresssed timber about four feet from the floor, and the domed chimney piece narrowed into the ceiling above it. The ceiling was beams and exposed, unplastered caña, painted ochre or dyed by smoke. And here maybe was something to be learnt or re-learnt – the dampness that had so afflicted us in a similarly built cortijo might not have been a problem if the caña had not been plastered or boarded in. Left exposed it would have given the roof a much better chance to breathe out.

Below the ceiling the walls were freshly white-washed. There were lots of old photos, mostly faded black-and-white or sepia though Amalia proudly showed us colour snaps, recent, of huge family groups at weddings and baptisms. Knowing Arthur did karate she made a particular fuss of one of her grandsons in Barcelona, much of an age with Arthur and like Arthur a karate adept: the picture showed a dark-haired well-knit flashlit lad doing a round-house kick.

Many of the old ones were of young men in uniforms, with the tasselled forage caps and German-style helmets of the rebel army.

On the walls there was also a fascinating collection of implements and utensils varying from what looked like an old cast-iron pepper-box with a holder for a small pestle and mortar to a brand-new cheese grater. In the deep hearth, behind the smouldering logs, there was a forged iron triangle with short legs for cooking pots. The floor was untreated cement. There was one small square window like the ones in Tío Mateo and beneath it an oval table with a cloth. Arthur got one of the very low leather chairs, with old cushions, in front of the fire, and soon Lucero, the white Jack Russell-ish dog, put its head on his knees and slept or enjoyed his fondling. We disposed ourselves round him and in the other old leather armchair or on the four wooden ones.

Coffee seemed to be a problem, so Amalia got out a box of mantecados which had come from Barcelona, she proudly assured us, or at least from one of their children who lived in Barcelona. Actually, like most shop-bought mantecados, it came from Estepa, halfway between Seville and Granada. Neither Amalia nor Francisco were much good at reading, neither letters nor numbers. One of their family had insisted on putting in a telephone after her most recent fall, so they could ring up the Centro de Salud in the event of another emergency, and had written out the number on a card very boldly indeed, but even so she wasn't confident she or he would get it right. But they loved it when any of the family rang them up.

She chatted away with Laney, indeed took a delight in telling her about things in the far past. Francisco kept on interrupting.

'She doesn't want to know about all that old stuff,' he kept saying and tapping his head to show Amalia was a bit touched, but in the end it did get through to him that we really did indeed want to know about all that old stuff and he began to join in.

Amalia was born in Torviscón, probably in 1913. She did go to school for a couple of years, but at the age of ten went into service in the big house in Orgiva.

'The big house? Do you mean the Palace of the Counts of Santiago, on the corner opposite the Café Santiago?'

'That's it. It didn't have shops beneath it then, and it was very big and very grand, and the people owned a lot of land round here.'

When she was fifteen or so she switched to agricultural labour in the fields on the other side of the bridge which were owned by the same family. The main cash-crop then was tobacco. She and Francisco were *novios* for fifteen years before they were married – a common arrange-ment in rural Mediterranean areas, especially where some form of land tenure was possible. If you owned a small patch of land you didn't want too many children splitting it up or fighting over it when you'd gone, so you married late. If you didn't have land of your own then you had as many children as possible in the hope someone would be in work some of the time somewhere. Land tenure has always been the best contraceptive in rural areas – hence the declining birth-rate in France right through the nineteenth century.

The first cortijo (by which they understood not just the building but the land, the small-holding, that went with it) was her mother-in-law's. The implication was that she married Francisco either when his father died or became too old to farm the land.

The one she was in then was her fourth cortijo and only her youngest son was born there. The lady who owned it before was killed in the fighting, she was actually sitting outside in the little patio peeling potatoes when it was machine-gunned. Amalia had already shown us the bullet-holes above the lintel, and there were many more in the walls of the venta which of course had been fortified as a block house guarding the bridge. The bridge itself was blown up and rebuilt after the war: many of the bridges in the area were of the same date and style – a frame-work of hard grey stone from the Sierra, filled in with a softer redder stone from the closer Contraviesa and Sierra Lujar. Francisco's kid brother, only seven years old, had also been shot running from one cortijo to another across open ground, trying to warn his family that an attack was on its way.

But one small small-holding could not generate enough income and after the war Don Francisco worked in the lead mine – from 1940 to 1968. It was an appalling business. From her cortijo you could still see the buildings of Las Minas de San José twelve hundred metres above sea level, nine hundred (more than three thousand feet) above where they were. The ore, blasted from the rock, was shovelled into steel gondolas which then swung from pylon to pylon down to Los Tablones where it was dumped and the first extraction processes were carried out. The flat-topped pyramids of spoil that these created now provide the hangliders with launching pads for beginners and landing points for the experienced who fly down from the mountains.

Francisco left the house at five o'clock in the morning and clocked on at eight having climbed three thousand feet (the height of Helvellyn in the Lake District). He then shovelled lead-laden rock for twelve hours, before walking back to get home at eleven o'clock at night. Amalia used to stand outside and watch the procession of torchlights coming down the mountain. In the morning, especially if it was raining, she'd plead with him not to go, but he would always reply: 'It might be worse tomorrow.'

Clearly it was a hell of a hard life. Don Francisco took it for granted that that was the way things were and they got the impression Amalia was more angry about it than he was. But he had been subjected to four years' intense indoctrination in Franco's army, and he knew that communists, trades unions other than the official Francoist ones, and all socialists and anarchists were devils incarnate. Nevertheless, Laney once asked him what he thought of Felipe's socialist government. He thought for a moment, then replied: 'We eat.'

Hard, but without slipping into pastoral fallacies, it had its good sides. Amalia started talking about them, prompted by a question from Laney.

'I haven't kept a pig for six years. Not many do now. Not many round here used to cure their own hams but Don Francisco did...' The tradition she was referring to, still extant in many parts of rural Spain, was to rear or buy a pig in spring, keep it in your ground floor front room and feed it up on scraps all through the year. Then on St Andrew's Day, 30 November, you slaughtered an animal which had more than doubled in weight since you bought it and probably not cost you a penny to feed. No freezers, so nearly all of it was cured or made into sausages of many different types, and would provide animal protein through to the spring and early summer when you bought another one... Once, driving through central Spain at the beginning of December, in bitterly cold, freezing fog, we actually saw the moment of truth – a porker held upside down against a board by three strong men, while the owner whetted his knife. Needless to say, the EC is putting the boot in and such harmless customs will soon be eradicated by statute and promulgation, even from the few remote areas where they are still part of rural life.

Pastoral fallacy? Surely a decently regulated slaughter-house is vastly preferable to cutting the throats of pigs in the open air, and prepacked, heat-sealed sausage is surely far safer than the home-cured variety? Wrong. First: a pig reared as a member of the family in the room that most occupiers of desirable terraced residences in Andalucian villages would now call their living room, fed on the scraps from the food you don't want (recycling – yes?), has a happier life than almost any commercially reared pig in Europe.

The only pigs we have ever even seen, from the Baltic to Gibraltar, have been in English fields, in English and Spanish oak forests, or Spanish front rooms. When you consider the importance of pork that's an awful lot of pigs who are born in prison, live – if you can call it that – in prison, and die in prison. The few moments longer a pig might suffer when actually slaughtered with a knife rather than with a stunner', and then a knife, are immaterial – against the better life that preceded it. Home-cured hams and home-made sausages taste better, and do you more good than factory-produced ones from factory-produced meat. And a society that has lived with its meat before it eats it has more respect for it than one that hasn't.

Amalia went on, heedless of the train of thought she had produced in what passes for J's mind.

'Your cortijo,' she said, 'had a big fireplace and a big bread oven. The fireplace was for when they killed the pig – big pans for the blood to make black pudding, to cook the chops and joints that were not going to be preserved. The big ovens were domed – they were for bread. Everybody knew everyone, and everyone was related one way or another to everyone else...' She put her hand on Laney's knee. 'You know Juan and Luis, your children go to school with? I'm their Godmother. They're good lads. It was like that all over.' Big, deep sigh. 'And whenever there was any reason for it at all, an engagement, a wedding, a baptism, a Saint's day, we'd all get together in one of the bigger cortijos, and there'd be music, and dancing on the threshing floor, and lots of good things to eat and drink, just the moonlight and some oil-lamps...'

And such dancing – to guitars and fiddles and hand-clapping, sevillanas, whirling, and windmilling, brushing the cobwebs from the corners of the sky.

Presently J slipped away, and reported back that Paco Ortiz had finished the road. At last after six weeks we would be able to drive Blanca back into Tío Mateo, into her snug, and fairly weather-proof garage. He went back to Don Miguel's, and drove the short distance to Los Ancianos. Warm hugs and kisses all round. On the way home Arthur was in tears because we wouldn't see them any more and we explained they should go back whenever they wanted to.

Nina, with doubt in her voice: 'On our own? Without you?'

The main reason for seeing them and talking to them had gone once Paco Ortiz had mended the road and the rains ceased and we made only one more visit to their cortijo. We felt a little guilty about this. We loved their company, we loved them, and we knew the old people enjoyed the connection with us. But several factors were at work. First of all, quite simply, work. J had his film script to work on and a novel set in Orgiva. With the children now very much full-time at school Laney was spending a lot of time servicing their Spanish for them, taking Arthur through each day's work before it happened and after it happened, keeping Nina in line with her English reading and number work as well as sorting out the Spanish side of her education and doing most of the housework. And of course – the visitors. But then there was also a reticence on our part, an unwillingness to intrude now there was no excuse to do so.

That one further visit was memorable. Years ago J's agent was Ian Gibson's agent and over the years he and his family became casual acquaintances and finally very good friends indeed, although they actually met each other only very rarely.

Ian Gibson? That such a great name should be not instantly placed by most of our readers is not to be wondered at in this day and age. Brownie points for those who do recognise it. Ian, like J and Laney, is a drop-out, but has made a better job of it. Once an Irish exile lecturing at Birkbeck he is now THE authority on Spanish cultural life in Spain

1920 to 1936, has written THE biography of Lorca and is now working on THE biography of Dalí, lives in Madrid, has Spanish nationality and a lovely wife, Carole, who has taught English to countless students over the years, supporting Los Gibsones when the advances on the Lorca biography had been spent and the book still five years from completion. She once said Ian and J were Beta plus as writers, maybe Alpha minus, which hurt at the time, but is fair enough really.

But this is Amalia's chapter not theirs. On 25 February they drove over from Granada where they were on a visit, that is Ian, Carole and Carole's mother who was staying with them, and we all had a splendid lunch. Prawn soup, barbecued pork chops with *el condimento*, strawberries and cream, and El Vino. All this in February, out of doors. Ian did a big number on El Vino saying, often, how no one in Madrid believed him when he told them how good it was, the best wine in Iberia. After lunch he borrowed Arthur's keyboard and played us a piece or two written by Lorca who was not only Spain's Shakespeare, but was a marvellous painter and a very good musician too. Manuel de Falla said so. And during all this merry rout we talked about Amalia, and how she had said the frost reminded her of the days they used to spread sheets on the bushes to dry, and of course Ian insisted we should all go round and see her.

They were in, with the family from Granada. Her son recognised Ian, had seen him on TV, so that made us very welcome indeed, and he and Amalia chatted away for an hour or so while the children played with the cats and the dogs, and the rest mumbled along amongst themselves as best they could. We hope Ian has remembered Amalia, and can tell the world what they talked about.

The last time J saw her was in the middle of April. He was walking round the block one afternoon, that is up the track past Antonio's, then left past Don Miguel's cortijo and then the Cuñado's, before heading on past Amalia's and the spur that led down to the Waterman's. It was an afternoon of cloud and mist with warm gentle hazy rain. There were flowers everywhere, and the figs were in bloom, tiny green flowers that filled the air with a sweet vaginal smell like hawthorn. Because of the rain the birds were singing up a storm, the orange blossom came like a warm spicy wave off the Waterman's orchard and there were banks of periwinkle and white bluebells in the eucalyptus wood. And through it all, rocking on her bad hip, came Amalia, her grey hair wet with the rain, lolloping down the track from the village, her stick in one hand, her basket in the other.

'Hola,' J cried, as she went past, 'buenas días...'

But she did not answer, hardly paused, but limped and stumbled on down to her house as if he had not been there at all. And then he realised: the look she had given him was almost sightless – the cataracts she had always complained of had clearly got the better of her, and she was virtually on automatic pilot.

Several times after that we passed their cortijo and it became apparent that they were no longer there. But they had been to stay with their children before, especially the Barcelona family, for quite lengthy spells and that was what we assumed was happening now. But by the middle of June, when we were already beginning to pack up, we wanted to return the wine carboy she had lent us six months earlier, and still the cortijo was deserted. At last on the thirteenth of June we met the sister-in-law, tiny, wizened and birdlike, still with her aluminium crutch, in the supermarket by the Post Office. With her free hand she took Laney's arm and the story poured out. Six weeks earlier Amalia had a fall, a bad fall. At the time her Barcelona family were staying there. Sister-in-law said, 'Look what local hospitals did to me – I need a crutch all the time.' So they took Amalia and Don Francisco to Barcelona, which already she had been to for medical treatment and hated.

There she fell again and was now in her son's flat in bed paralysed and either refusing or unable to speak. Worse yet Don Francisco's madness had taken a turn for the worse: he had walked out of the flat and wandered the streets for days, trying to find his way home, and that probably meant Orgiva, before the police picked him up. He was now in a mad house (her term), also in Barcelona.

That evening J made this entry in his diary.

'There's too much to say about all this but it makes me cry now to look at the hills and mountains, at the flowers and the river into which she threw her rubbish for so many years, and all the things she knew so well and loved and refused to leave, even for a flat in Orgiva, and think of her and him dying in Barcelona. And he mad because he worked in that obscene mine.

'Clearly they should have stayed here. But Barcelona has a better hospital than Granada, and a mad house to shut people in. I find it very difficult to bear looking out on all that is around us and know they are cut off from it almost certainly for ever. When, if ever anyone could say this beauty is mine (yours too of course) but mine, they could – they worked to make it what it is, their work and lives subtly contributed over seventy years to every bit of it, and they loved it so much nothing would make them move – and now so stupidly they are cut off from it when its presence could have crowned their last days together. They could now be sitting in the red and gold setting sun with their dogs and cats and their roses and geraniums – in pain perhaps, and in Don F's case through no fault of his own a bit touched, and with some relation or other around or even a state-subsidised nurse, instead of... the unthinkable. She in her mutinous silence only longing to be here – the one thing they won't allow her – he estranged in a modern citified psychiatric ward.'

La Expiración del Señor

You can't do Spain without joining in in the fiestas. We've done the big ones: Santiago Compostela when the King was there in 1976, San Fermín in Pamplona, Alicante, and Corpus Cristi in Granada; the middling ones like Carnival in Ciudad Rodrigo and Saint Teresa in Alba; but the best are the village ones and especially when you live in the village. During one year in Orgiva there were at least six: some secular or secularised like New Year and Carnival; others jolly excuses for a family knees-up like los Reyes, when the Three Kings paraded the streets and every child in the village was given a present on the steps of the church. But, when all's said and done, it was the religious ones that really got to you, for they had all the drama or jolliness of the others undercut with a numinous mystery far older than Christianity.

J was not too happy about it. His early adolescence had been marked by a nasty attack of religiosity, anglo-catholic style, during which he had really believed that he was truly and deeply responsible for Christ's Passion, that it might not have happened if God had not foreseen that a really substantial sacrifice would be required to wipe out J's sins committed two thousand years later. These were almost entirely confined to the usual sins of adolescence: sloth and lust. It all finally ended on a frosty autumn morning, when he was twenty-four. He was cycling across a park on his way to teach at a secondary modern, his first real job. It was a lovely morning of golden chestnut leaves and air like ice-cold champagne and suddenly it came to him that when he was dead he was dead, and that was it. At that moment the whole baggage of senseless superstition slipped off his shoulders like the Albatross, and left him with one regret. For ten years the pleasures of sloth and lust had been compromised. He resolved that from then on he would do his best to enjoy both to the full.

So, would it be possible for him now to be moved by the parade of a life-like image of a dead man? Would his dislike of the Nazarene get in the way of the experience, a dislike that could turn to angry hate whenever politicians trundled Him out of his charnel-house to justify killing Serbs, Croats, Arabs or whoever it was just now happened to be sitting on a bit of land or oil you thought was really yours? Were not Arthur and Nina perhaps already at an impressionable age?

'It says here,' said Laney, 'that there will be mucho pulvo.'

'What does that mean?'

'Fireworks.'

'Can I wear my flamenco?'

'Mmmm, I don't think so. I don't think this is really a flamenco fiesta.'

Got that right.

They got up into town at about half-past five, and the first thing they found was that the square had been closed off. They had to park well below it and walk up past the usual fiesta stalls selling nougat, cheap toys, and so on, and even, on a patch of waste ground, a small octopus and bumping cars. None of which seemed to chime well with the occasion nor with the way people were turned out. Everyone was in their funeral best. Dark suits, caps and hats, even ties on many of the men – which in Orgiva was not usual. Not even the bank clerks wore ties to work, not even the Head Master. The women with bourgeois pretensions were dressed in tailored black suits (oddly sexy for the occasion since the skirts were fashionably short and slit at the back to reveal black nylons with seams) and wore black veils. The less pretentious and younger women were in their cleanest newest jeans, and sweaters of sombre hue. And of course the grannies wore the black they always wore, but the best black. Yet there was a difference. This was no ordinary funeral. There was a touch more jewellery about, and the women had taken a different sort of care with their make-up: one began to feel that they had dressed a touch more theatrically than they did for the real funerals, for the real thing they were not so grand, not so... presented.

The crush barriers, borrowed from Motril, were in place just above the lower end and the crowd was already thick in front of them, in the narrow gap between the barriers and the main road which had to be kept open until the last moment, so we threaded through the back alleys and got to the top instead. Here too the crowd was already thick but because of the slope beneath the town hall they could see quite well down into the square even though they were nowhere near the front.

And what filled the space, maybe eighty metres downhill and sixty across, between the two rows of barriers? It was almost empty – of people and the seven or eight who were there wore builders' helmets. But it was filled with racks and racks and racks of fireworks and there were only, at this stage of the proceedings, two sorts. Thunder flashes and whizz-bang rockets. Two thousand? Three? And who paid for all these fireworks? For the last four weeks or so every bar and bank and shop had run lotteries to raise the money; no doubt every individual and certainly every business, and anybody with pretensions to be some-body in a town of somebodies had contributed. But there was the diaspora too. For a hundred and fifty years Orgiva has been exporting the labour its own fields cannot support to Barcelona, Madrid, Bilbao, and all of Latin America. And every exile carries a picture of the Image in his wallet or purse, every home has its framed photograph, and they all send money for the Friday two weeks before Good Friday.

All the shop, bank and café windows had been criss-crossed with brown parcel tape, which put J in mind of a childhood at war, but above them the balconies were filled by the families and friends of the flat owners.

The big church bell had been tolling – the way it did for a funeral. It stopped. The church clock began its pre-hour chime. The big doors of the church opened – two lads carrying big lanterned candles had appeared beneath the orange trees. Then the clock struck, the first stroke of six, and there He was. Twelve feet high on his cross and...

As near as could possibly be arranged they all went off at once. Incredibly fast fuses linked each rack and they were lit at the same time. Almost instantly the whole scene was blotted out with flash-filled smoke and the noise settled into a steady unbroken roar that literally made the ground shake. You could even believe that your lungs and your liver were shaking inside you. And the explosions went on for a full five minutes.

When the smoke cleared you could see them bringing Him down the steps into the Square. Then came Sorrowing Mum, high up between her candles, and when they were both safely down into the square, why then the next lot went off, and nearer us this time, the unused racks at the top of the square between us and Them. We squeezed down through the crowd to the corner where the procession turned up out of the square and started its trek through every barrio, and practically every street and alley of the town.

Close up, J felt his reservations crumble. There was really nothing there at all of the New Testament. It went back a long way, a lot further than a mere two millennia. The crowned sacrifice and the sorrowing woman – not his mother, she's not a day older than he is. Ah well. The beans and lentils were already in pod, being picked. Next week they'd plough them in, organic nitrates for the barley and maize that follow.

Most small-holders in the Alpujarra get three, sometimes four crops a year off their land, as well as olives and oranges, and they don't use nitrates or plastic the way they do on the other side of the mountains. Well not much anyway. Just good husbandry, the sacrificed King, and the Goddess who mourns her son and lover.

Every barrio and street? Each one had its own firework display, now vying with each other in elaboration and beauty. Catherine wheels, miniature castles, fountains of light and delight. Violet, rose, emerald green, and azure as well as silver and gold. And one amazing thing was this. They had all been set up hours before and left untended or only partially watched over, waiting for Her and Him to arrive. And was there a single naughty boy in Orgiva who felt the urge to set them off prematurely? If there was he resisted the temptation. And that of all the many things they saw and heard and joined in with during the year demonstrated as efficiently as anything else the glory of Orgiva then. It was a community.

We followed Them through three or four more streets then made our way back to the square where we picked up a pinchito each – the skewered pork doused in *el condimento* – and Arthur engaged fey Emilio in a Two Musketeers swordfight in the colonnade of the town hall. Swords? Fallen rocket sticks, of course.

'We're going to the Molino.'

'Can I stay with Emilio?'

'Yes. But come and see us in half an hour just so we know you're all right.'

We didn't see him for an hour and a half, and began at last to be worried. But he turned up.

'Emilio took me to his flat. It's above the Post Office. And we watched the fireworks from his balcony and they gave me supper.'

'What did you have?'

'Oh, prawns and things. Big ones. And lots of other stuff. Ham and chorizo, the usual things.'

La Virgén de Fatima

El Cerro Negro, the Black Mountain, which of course was not black at all, was a big round lump of a thing to the east of Orgiva. It stuck out from the general system of barrancas and crags that lay between Orgiva and the Sierra Nevada, and rather annoyingly blocked off from Tío Mateo views of the actual Veleta and Mulhacen. Driving up to the mountains the road passed behind it before running along the side of the Poqueira valley. Road signs indicated that there was a silver mine called 'Las Minas de la Virgén de Fatima', and occasionally one heard blasting from the back of it. But there was no indication that there was a chapel, a shrine.

On Sunday 13 May, Radio Alpujarra announced there was to be a *romería* and to be sure that no one would have an excuse for not going, the school buses would be laid on to ferry the car-less as far as the Eterne Padre. This was also a shrine, a hamlet, a restaurant and an artesiana about halfway to Pampaneira and that was where the sign to the mines was.

A romería? The countryside is dotted with little chapels, especially near natural springs, and each has its día when the local villagers walk, ride or drive out to the shrine, give the Image an airing, let off a few fireworks, and have a picnic. Some of these are famous – especially the Whitsuntide one to El Rocio in Las Marismas near Seville, attended by thousands of gypsies, and the one at the end of July near Santiago, which is also a horse-fair, where the stout Galician ladies ladle huge helpings of octopus out of seething cauldrons.

'Can we go in the bus?' asked Arthur. 'All my friends are.'

'But then we might take seats from those who really need them.'

'But we might miss it, or lose our way…'

All through Sunday lunch in the patio, the centrepiece a magnificent paella, Laney's best ever, which meant shrimp-shells and fishy rice for the cats, and another scratched nose for Nuca (a sort of sausage dog from up the lane who often visited us), the anxieties rose, indeed had to be quite rudely suppressed if we were to get any fun out of the meal.

No chance of not finding it: setting off shortly before five we were soon part of a procession winding up the mountain-side. This was no longer quite the embarrassment it had been back in August: by now we knew the road well, and generally managed to urge Blanca on at a speed those behind could tolerate.

Two big buses were already parked in the Eterne Padre car-park, but cars went on further down a winding track towards the mine. Soon though more and more were parked, and since the track was getting rougher we decided to park too. In fact many, many cars went the whole way, but that would have been a mistake.

For a start it was a gorgeous late afternoon, early evening. With EC summertime in force it didn't get dark now until nine o'clock or later. The sky was unblemished apart from a rag or two of cloud in the highest valleys; it was balmy warm but not hot; we were walking through a wild garden with huge views across the valleys and right up to the great white lump of the Mulhacen, and best of all there was the feeling of being part of something. Family parties with friends were ahead of us and behind, a long chain winding across the slope, round the bluffs, chattering, laughing, occasionally overtaking a familiar granny pausing with her grand-children to get her breath, often over-taken by scampering children: '*Hola Arturo. Hola Nina, Neena, Neena, Neena. 'Turro, 'Turro, 'Turro.*'

A wild garden? As Evelyn *(friends – Evelyn and her daughter Katherine were visiting)* pointed out it was amazing how these hill and mountain-sides looked just sort of patchy green and ochre from a distance but when you walked through them the flowers were every-where and in wonderful variety. There were thymes in all sorts of shades from nearly white through mauveish blues to bright pinks, and including lemon thyme, and the rosemary was enjoying its spring flow-ering. The Spanish word for rosemary is *romero* which also means pilgrim, which is why what we were on was a *romería.*

But apart from the aromatics there were masses of other flowers too. The brooms were getting underway though not yet covering the hillsides with gold as they would in a week or so, the rockroses were not quite over, the vetches and peas up here were as profuse as they had been lower down a month before, hounds' tongue, alkanet, bugle and viper's bugloss, and there were big patches of wild antirrhinum with flowers as large as the cultivated varieties in England. Indeed one of the things we noticed at this time was how the flowers that had been in season at the bottom of the valley and in Gina's wilderness a month or six weeks earlier, were now out fifteen hundred feet higher.

As we approached a shoulder of the steep hill-side a little flurry of rockets popped in the sky above it. Arthur and his mates adopted combat-mode, scurrying from rock to rock along the ditches, making out they were under fire, and they all quickened their pace. The track wound round the bluff and we could see how the hillside now opened out into a wider, but still very irregular and hummocky plateau, with, across one ridge a little higher than the rest, a little hamlet of four or five cottages, and amongst them, nestling in amongst them with a sort of sunken patio in front of it, a tiny white chapel with a pitched red-tile roof. A large crowd was gathered round them, with a lot of cars parked any old how over the hillside. There were streamers of little flags, Spain, Andalusia, Granada, and all nations, strung from the one soli-tary telegraph pole and from trees and shrubs; the sun flashed from the silver instruments of the band, which, just as we approached began its stately oompah, pah pah; a serious salvo of rockets whooshed up into the empyream, and a string of firecrackers set across the track bang, bang, banged above our heads.

And there She was. Not a gorgeous baroque doll like the Lady of the Head at Capileira, nor the sorrowing Mother in deep purple velvet, embroidered with silver, which is generally the gear She favours in

Andalusia, nor the blue and white she wore for Soubirou at Lourdes, but the simple figure in white with a cowl or hood, as seen by the Children of Fatima, not far from Lisbon, on 13 May, 1913. One cannot help remarking that when She puts in these occasional appearances She does tend to dress for the times. And indeed, why shouldn't She? Plain She may have been, but the flowers that surrounded and decked the little float she was on were not: there were roses, arum lilies, tiger lilies and madonna lilies, sheafs, bunches and swags of them. And in front of her came a Clown, Penitent, Joker – we're not sure what, but mad anyway. He was wearing an ordinary brown jacket and old trousers, but what looked like a tin hat painted bright green with yellow flowers as well, and he carried a sack of rockets and a smouldering match. Every now and then he would stop, turn and face Her, take out a rocket, light its fuse, and hold its stick in front of his face until it roared away from his hand and into the sky. And these were not titchy whizzbangs, but quite big ones with proper star-bursts.

They carried her, censor in front, band behind, the rest of the way along the track to a little copse of willows at the end, where the slope of the mountain took over again and tumbled down to the confluence of the Poqueira and the Guadalfeo and the big valley was spread out beneath her; and then they took her back again, and we followed, some way behind the rest, so we could see above her head and the heads of the huge jolly crowd the thorn of the Veleta and the snowy lump of the Mulhacen above.

The band played on, a stall sold beer and soft drinks, the bocadillos of ham and cheese people had brought with them appeared. The children queued for free handouts of boiled sweets and chewing gum, and we all bought raffle-tickets. Presently we looked in the chapel itself to which She had already been returned. It was very small, very simple, with cheap prints of holy scenes on the white-washed walls. But the altar was set in an arch decorated with a yellow diamond pattern, and with all her flowers around her She looked very splendid.

We walked back to the car, still in a rambling informal procession with all the people we knew so well, through the warm gloaming and the flowers, and picked our rosemary like the others on the way. The only gloomy thing was the mine itself, up a short spur to the left. J went up and had a look: it wasn't large, but still it was an intrusion: piles of spoil, sheds, untidy machinery, it seemed to have little connection with the lovely metal it produced, and none at all with the jolly pilgrimage we had been on.

IV California

A sudden flow of dosh in 1999 bought the four of us a hire car holiday in California, our first trip to the New World. Straight away San Diego got to us in spades. It was the light, it was the feeling that Americans can do anything: man on the moon obviously, but build and plant with flowers a huge city and naval base out of desert, a bridge two miles long and high enough for the biggest aircraft carriers in the world to go under...

These extracts are from Homage, *the thriller that came out of the trip. We start in La Jolla, home of Raymond Chandler, no less, and the scene of much of* Jim Thompson's The Grifters, *book and film.* Homage *is hommage to both those authors and Californian noir in general.*

La Jolla

We stood side by side, my hands clasping the cast-iron rail, his left hand loosely lying in the crook of my right elbow. Together we looked down into one of two small coves on a headland sixty feet or so above shingle and sandy beaches and watched the rollers heave themselves out of the deepest purest blue I had ever seen, before rumbling over brown rocks and breaking into sierras of white, whiter than any snow. They scurried up the sand which turned the water emerald, and finally, like children using a playground slide, they hurried gleefully round to the back again for another go. On their way they pulled the kelpy hair of mermaids, just for fun.

'I have never seen light like this,' I said.

'Light anywhere else is merely virtual. This is the real thing.'

On the surface his voice rasped a little. But underneath there was always a bass note, not unlike the one you can hear on a beach where the surf thunders in for forty miles in either direction.

'Why?'

'The Ocean of course. You are looking at more unbroken water here than almost anywhere else in the world. It is a huge mirror. It reflects the light and the sky back into the light and the sky, and back it bounces again. Ad infinitum. Anyway, until sunset.'

Taxi Downtown

H alf an hour? Tall order to get from La Jolla to downtown San Diego in that time unless you knew the best route. I didn't, but I found a cabbie who did, with a fat five-year-old Merc. Early evening so all the traffic was coming out of town. Usual catechism. I'd had it once already coming up from the airport.

'First visit? How long you staying? Limey are you? We get Aussies but not many Limeys. Business? Buying or selling? Ain't it just always one or the other…?'

I looked out the window. Wonderful. Totally wonderful. Freeway. Clear sky just purpling up but the tinted windows may have had something to do with it. Flat land below La Jolla and land-locked water as we came rushing down the long curve, marshy some of it looked and the long line of Pacific Beach between us and the Ocean; then the sweep of the bay, almost black now with an aircraft carrier the size of a small city inching towards the open sea. Finally downtown, wonderful skyscrapers of glass and steel, blue, bronze, gold, flashing back the sun which still had an hour to go, and the Stars and Stripes here, and here and there again, sometimes as big as a tennis court, and with just enough breeze to lift them from the flag-poles. And trees and shrubs and flowers, oleanders, jacarandas, giant begonias, strelizias, plumbago in flower-beds and baskets…

'Not a tree do you see,' carolled the cabbie, who was Hispanic from his accent but with quite a lot of Afro from his colour, 'but it was planted and watered by man's almighty hand. A hundred years ago, this was desert, man. Pure desert. Just sage-brush and a little cactus. Ain't those sky-scrapers just beautiful? The newest, see, because only in the last fifteen years have they been able to build real high on sand prone to earthquake. So they are the newest dee-sign. And look there. The Coronado Bridge. Ain't she a joy…?'

On the far side of the skyscrapers a long rollercoaster of narrow white concrete snaked an S out across the bay.

'…high enough to get the biggest tallest ship in the world out of harbour and two and a half miles long.'

A proud man, proud of his city. He dropped me in a street that just about lay on the boundary between downtown and the old gaslamp district, an ordinary sort of street with office blocks that weren't that high, predating, I supposed, the new technology.

Tijuana

The main drag in Tijuana, Avenida Revolución, is a wide street of mostly two-storey buildings stretching for a mile or so down a gentle slope. Almost every joint on either side, and that includes side-streets and covered arcades going back a hundred yards or so, target over-the-border tourists, mostly on day-trips. Which is not to say by any means that they are tourist traps. From cat-houses easier to find, less inhibited about what they're selling and cheaper than San Diego's to fake Tommy Hilfiger T-shirts there are bargains. Especially if you're prepared to bargain. I have a technique.

'How much for these shades?'

'Sixty dollars.'

Walk away.

'They're 'Ray-Ban'. It says so.'

Keep walking.

'Hombre, how much will you pay?'

'Ten dollars.'

'Twenty.'

'Fifteen.'

'OK.'

Wearing my new shades I glanced up and down the sidewalk. How to find the Farmacia San Cristóbal?

The problem was every tenth shop was a chemist. Large, neat, spotless. White-overalled shop assistants watched over stacks and stacks of proprietory medicines in gleaming white packs with embossed labels, sealed openings and tops, with placards announcing names and prices, and, in case you hadn't guessed, 'No scrip necessary!'. Border-line hard drugs like methadone and codeine; viagra, cortisone, fifty-seven varieties of antibiotic, beta-blockers; and the latest cocktails of HIV controllers were all stacked up with offers, buy thirty, get ten free, a free packet of multi-vitamins with every pack of Viagra, and so on. I remembered Harry Lime and watered-down penicillin but these places wouldn't stay open if they sold placebos or duds. San Cristóbal, I argued, must be here: with its answerphone message, cool and professional, it wasn't going to be a backstreet apothecary selling snake-venom and mescalin.

And sure enough I found it, on the corner of one of the arcades. Closed but about to open. I took a saunter down the passage: big spaces, many of the stall-holders unlocking their lock-ups, setting up their stalls. One specialised in dreadful plastic kitsch; another toys, ten thousand Micky Mice. Watches, sunglasses, pottery crudely painted with busty flamenco dancers. Guaranteed silver jewellery, filigree and rings. Pointless knick-knacks, joke or macho key-rings, cigarette lighters with nudes on the barrels, bottle-openers ditto, packs of cards, roulette wheels and those pocket torches that throw a red dot of light a couple of hundred yards or more so kids can think they're laser-equipped snipers. I bought one for my twelve-year-old son. Didn't tell you I had a family, did I? Well, I don't really but there's a family live a mile away from me in Blighty where the kids still call me Daddy, though their mum kicked me out five years ago. Make a mental note. I've bought Richard something he'll like, now I mustn't forget little Rosa.

I waited on the corner for the lights but still got caught by a cab taking a right. Yes, a Merc, but ten years older and ten feet longer than the ones from La Jolla and painted red and black. I got the full Hispanic open-palm-above-the-forehead chopping gesture that signals you are a *hijo de puta*, but escaped without injury. From the middle I walked in the shadow of a very old man in a Calvin Klein T-shirt and very old very distressed Nike trainers. He used a stick, had a back hunched by age and arthritis, pendulant ear-lobes and a charmed life. I still had a side street to get across but it was narrower and all I scored was a bull-roarer from a bus. The final obstacle was a shoe-shine stall, the full monty, fifteen brass-topped bottles in racks, sixteen brushes, and a Fagin-sized bundle of rags – the matériel of a small, energetic, muscular Indian who had no intention of letting me get past once he had spotted my tan Oxfords.

He sat me on his leather upholstered throne, pulled my right foot onto a thin, worn brass rail, slipped oval guards into the sides of the shoe so no polish would get on my sock, spat on his hands, took a swig from a tequila bottle and got on with it.

I guess reflexology has its roots in the ministrations of shoe-shine boys. You come out of it not only with shoes that look as if they have been french-polished but in a relaxed and altogether happier frame of mind which is not entirely dispelled by the shoe-shiner's insistence that one five spot is an insult that can only be removed by a second. Which is fair enough when you think about how much a reflexology session can cost.

La Cantina was *tipico* and had had the sense to do little more than exaggerate or point up what it already had to make it tipico plus. Almost everything was wood – the floor, the ceiling, the walls, the tables, the bentwood chairs, the long bar down the inside wall, the six-foot long blades of the ceiling fan. The jukebox was not wood, looked old but was probably repro. There were bullfight posters, also old. El Cordobes for Christ's sake. And high up in a corner, near the ceiling a framed and faded newspaper photograph of a square-headed guy, crew-cut, granny specs, military-type top – none other than Leo Trotsky himself. The whole place smelled of black tobacco, garlic, re-fried beans, overcooked tomato and coffee.

There was one barman, six customers and a waiter. I ordered a cortado, an espresso with a splash of hot milk, and then went to the caballeros for a slash. It was small but as clean as cracked lino, and cracked porcelain would allow. As I zipped up and turned away from the urinal two men came in. The first, a big man with Mediterranean features and colouring smashed my face with his open palm so my head cracked against the wall behind me, and the second, who had the bony nose, high cheekbones and parchment skin of an Indian, like the shoe-shiner, round-house kicked me in the stomach. Fortunately I'd pocketed my new shades out on the sidewalk.

That was enough kung-fu fighting for me and I sat down.

San Francisco

I took the road east out to Salinas, where Steinbeck was born and where I joined the one-oh-one. The self-scanning radio found a local rock station celebrating Mick Jagger's fiftieth birthday so I sang along to all those early numbers Jefferson and I had bopped and even jived to. Ruby Tuesday, Little Red Rooster, Satisfaction. Don't go much on the later ones, but that's middle age for you, I suppose. Then there was a news bulletin. A nutter in Atlanta, Georgia, who played the stock market on the net and got fed up losing, took three pistols into the office he used, killed a dozen or so and then offed himself. By now Kennedy Junior, as a news item, was well over the horizon, an axman who beheaded girls in Yosemite National Park hardly rated a mention.

I crossed the Bay Bridge about an hour before sunset under a perfect sky spoilt only by vapour trails. Ahead the skyscrapers of downtown San Francisco were a cluster of light pillars climbing towards Nob Hill; as I crossed Yerba Buena Island, the bay stretched like a polished flat plate of pale turquoise right past Alcatraz to the orangy-red of the Golden Gate Bridge. Then the piers of Fisherman's Wharf and the Embarcadero together with the World Trade Centre closed the view down.

Thanks rather to the map than their instructions it all worked out for once as it should. I dropped the Grand Am off at the Alamo on Bush and Powell, more Bush than Powell actually, and walked down the two blocks to Union Square. Then I walked back up them and retrieved the Wells Fargo bag from the glove-locker just before a mechanic got there first. I was lucky – Jefferson's Soul Compilation had gone from the tape deck.

Already I was liking San Francisco very, very much. Apart from occasional shafts high up on the skyscrapers the sun had gone but the clear sky was still bright, the big buildings were lit up and glitzy, and by a happy chance I was on one of the three cable car routes still left. A couple rumbled by, one up, one down, packed to the gunwales with waving youngsters standing on the running boards, the bells clanging like musical fire engines. The hill dropped as steeply as all the films one has seen said it should past the ornate frontage of the Sir Francis Drake Hotel. That reminded me that he, we, actually got here two hundred years before the Spaniards founded their Mission. He called it New Albion and claimed it for Queen Elizabeth I.

On I went, carrying my old holdall, past a Borders bookshop that announced it stayed open late and which I promised myself I would visit, into Union Square with its own delicate, almost rococo statue of Liberty, so much prettier than the monster on the other side of the continent. There was even a permanently parked red London double-decker bus now used as an information centre. With Macy's facing me I took the right into Geary. By now I was humming the Gilbert and Sullivan standard 'He is an Englishman' and nearly gave a beggar a heart attack with the five dollar note I gave him.

I wasn't sure why I felt so elevated: partly perhaps because I'd got shot of the Pontiac, the Duchess, the Grande Dame which, though in every respect a fine car, had always made me feel a touch uncomfortable, we just weren't made for each other; perhaps I had a sense that here was where everything would be worked out and this whole wretched, not to say tragic, episode would burn itself out; but mainly I suppose, well, San Francisco.

I didn't actually have flowers in my hair, but I felt as if I did.

From Homage, *published by Allison and Busby, 2000*

V *Kenya*

Finally Kenya. It was such a thrill to see, from the airplane, the dawn come up over Africa. We've been to Egypt and Morocco since but that first landing in Jomo Kenyatta, coming in over the Nairobi National Park and arguing with Laney as to whether or not those really were gnus beneath us, was magic. Nairobi itself was something else.

Nairobi

I strolled down Kenyatta Avenue, with the park I had seen from my window on my left and another on the right, to the big intersection where Uhuru (Freedom) Highway crosses it. Downtown Nairobi now rose in front of me in the shape of the usual gleaming forest of banks, hotels, and regional HQs of the bigger global corporations that you see at the centre of every major conurbation the world over. But first there was a maelstrom of flesh and storming metal to get across. Police whistles shrilled, brakes screamed, distressed engines spewed black smoke, women who appeared to be moving house with their belongings on their heads sailed past like clippers, sumps clanged as vehicles were squeezed by their neighbours into potholes at least a foot deep. I hovered on the edge like a cowardly swimmer, braving not cold rapids but the possibility of being mangled alive between hurtling hunks of hot metal. Somewhere a light changed, or a policeman blew a whistle those around me understood, and I was almost carried to a central reservation marked by broken kerb-stones. The flow of metal resumed in front of me but now, by and large, going in the opposite direction. Again an almost momentary pause in the screaming cascade of rusty metal, peeling chrome, whirling fumes, allowed a surge across; as part of it I was buffeted by the crowd coming from the other side. Sidestepping, weaving, challenged and knocked sideways by a shoulder charge I tripped on a loose lump of concrete and almost fell on to the sidewalk as a *matatu* clipped my heels.

Well, I was in culture shock and maybe it wasn't quite as bad as that. Invigorated rather than intimidated, I made my way on up Kenyatta, past the new General Post Office, and almost immediately I was brushing aside just about every blandishment and threat aimed at getting anything valuable I might have on me, off me. Babes wrapped tight and lying in the crooks of the arms of healthy, indeed beautiful young girls could win a fifty shilling note off me so long as they looked happy and smiled, the maudlin ones I rejected. Small boys, dragging at my sleeves and gawping up at me with tragic eyes imbued with suffering, I could handle. I made myself a rule: if I could get that soulful look to change to a complicit grin I was prepared to part with ten Kenyan shillings, ten p. Older hustlers I tried to ignore, kept my eyes fixed above their heads, shrugged off any physical contact with unaggressive determination. But once or twice I was frightened: a young man would try to engage me in conversation: Where you staying, man? You English, man? And so forth while others slowly closed in round me, one or two on each side, a couple behind, edging up closer. I began to feel glad I'd taken those rings off, that I wasn't carrying a camera. All I had was a wad of K shillings, about thirty quids' worth, held in a roll in my jacket pocket, and I was quite ready to part with them if things began to look seriously physical. I'm a coward. Believe me.

Then suddenly they were gone, melting away like scavenger gulls behind a ship that has crossed an invisible border. I glanced over my shoulder. A family maybe twenty yards behind me, two adults, two adolescent kids, clearly looked likely to provide better or easier pickings. And suddenly it really hit me how we stood out, me as well as that family, how we were different, how we were the ethnic minority now, this was their city, not ours.

Less bothered, I began to take in something of my surroundings. Above me the sky was now almost clear of cloud, the sunlight was hot if you stood in it, black kites swirled like those paper planes one used to make, not the darts but the delta-shaped ones with tails, at five hundred feet or so above the avenue; then came the big blocks, some upended shoe-boxes, several newer, post-modern – ziggurats or with curved, bent frontages of coloured mirrored glass: Barclays, Deutschebank, AFI with its corncob, green and gold for the I, the Mercedes star, BA, the logos one sees in every developing conurbation from Lima to Macao, from China to Peru. The contrast came at street level. The pavement was cracked, the kerb stones fell away round deep holes, some with a snakepit of cables at the bottom, gaping without warning or protection. The trees looked as if they were dying and the flowers in the neglected beds rattled in the fumes and slipstreams of the traffic. Shops were boarded-up or half empty, often they were just open spaces between concrete piles filled with litter, trash and garbage. Every now and then pedestrians were forced into narrow files where an older building was being demolished in a confused racket of falling masonry, drills, bulldozers and dumper trucks. The big glass doors of the corporations were inches thick, with uniformed police, paramilitaries and security guards on both sides, the harsh black hardware of H and K MPs or Berettas swinging at their sides or from their belts. But between blocks sidestreets ran into areas where the buildings were lower and older and at the end of one on the far side I could see a sunlit square with palms and the impressive frontage of a mosque. There were market stalls too.

Street markets don't vary any more than downtown skyscrapers, yet they all have their own quirks and even if the aubergines glow as richly purple in Cape Town as they do in Cairo, and the heaped chilli peppers and judias beans are as lushly green, the music blaring from sound-systems varies, and so do the knick-knacks for tourists, and anyway, they're always fun and every now and then you have to stop and look, usually at a food-stall, and ask yourself: What the hell is *that?* And while the Calvin Klein knickers, Tommy Hilfiger tops and Reebok trainers are the same, the local clothing is not.

From the street market I strolled into a big oblong, partly enclosed, galleried courtyard filled with the tourist stuff, everything you could possibly make from ebony, ivory and soapstone, from troupes of serried elephants to beetles, from chessmen to crocodiles; there were baskets made from sisal, jute and cane, and decorated with African motifs; masks, feathered head-dresses, assegais, elliptical shields, fly whisks made from the tails of colobus monkeys or antelopes (bone-in), knobkerries and huge collars consisting of thousands of bright beads. If you stopped for more than ten seconds the cry went up: Seeing is free, come in and look, you are my first customer today, kind sir, I can see you are a connoisseur, have a shufti, but all done with an open friend-liness, cheery fatalism, and little apparent resentment when you moved on with a shrug and a dismissive wave of the hand. There were so many tiny shops, so many potential customers – you might buy elsewhere but the next one along might buy here.

But then I found myself in the meat and fishmarket. This was some-thing else. All right it was nearly lunch-time, the best produce no doubt had gone while I was still having my breakfast, but what was left, offal, heads and tripes, attracted flies like William Golding never imagined, the smashed remains looked like Waterloo two days after the battle, the smell was something Dante never thought of. I staggered out into a sidestreet, handkerchief to my mouth, on a corner by a cinema (Tom Cruise, Mission Impossible 2) and made it back on to Kenyatta.

Never mind that market, I was peckish by now. I looked up and down. Behind me a cyber café, but not the sort that actually sells coffee, just rough plaster walls, flaking paint, tatty posters, a booth where you got your ticket, and stalls set up on tables with screens and keyboards.

The latest thing? Yet somehow it contrived to look older and shabbier than the professional letter-writers with their typewriters it no doubt replaced. But across the road, in a gap between two blocks, there was a space, a rectangle of sunlight with tables and chairs and a glass frontage set back on the side – Simmers Restaurant. Again I crossed the cataract, quite the old Nairobi hand by now.

Simmers was what I wanted. The Answer on a Plate was its English slogan. Not smart, not a McDonald's either, but an ordinary place where the local office workers were already having their lunches. The tables outside were all taken but I found one inside. OK, it was not a diner, it was grubby and busy, but cheerful too with a counter at one end where cooks fried and grilled and big pots, yes, simmered on bottled-gas rings. The menu was in whatever brand of Swahili was the common language but English too. I chose Kuku Chomas fried chicken – and out of the choice of manioc or chips, chickened out and went for chips. It was OK, you know? And with a Coke cost about one pound fifty.

What now, I thought, as I pushed back my chair and stood. The national museum seemed worth a visit, according to the Lonely Planet guide. Huge collection of stuffed birds. Casts of footprints made by our ancestors four million years ago. But again I remembered the warnings. So… go back to the Serena, get them to call up a taxi. And maybe use the swimming pool first. I made my way back on to the main drag.

They closed in round me straight away. Perhaps, I thought, one of them had been in Simmers and had seen the wad of shillings I peeled notes from to pay.

There was one on each side of me, and I sensed another behind. But it was the one in front I had a proper look at. Black baseball cap with the white NYPD logo, pocked skin, yellow teeth, breath like sewage overlaid with garlic and raw spirit. Shabby black leather bomber, GAP T-shirt, white on black. Big boots like DMs. I took a step forward, hand in front.

Don't be raising your hand at me, Mister, and he lashed out with his right boot at my left shin and then took advantage of my reaction to knee me in the balls. As my head came forward his hands came up in a double-fisted blow that caught my upper lip and nose. I sat down, very heavily, on a corner of broken concrete. All four began to kick me. I blacked out. My last thought was, hell, I'm no longer just a tourist, I'm a victim.

From As Bad As It Gets, *published by Allison and Busby,* *2003*

VI *Morocco*

Six Songs

1. Before Departure

Where do you come from
Bright red rose
Burning under the holly?

And where do *you* come from
Silent, sibilant lily?

They nod at the Earth
And gently sigh:
She knows.

2.

Follow on Moroccan faience
An endless track
Over and under
Away and back.

This ludic science
Spells no history
But maps
A mystery.

Time's not an arrow
It's a maze
No sequence
But a nest of days.

3.

On the road from Fez to Marrakech
I met a man who had to preach
About the mountains and the haze
That hides them from our mortal eyes
Til evening rends the veil
And all can see them as for real!

God's like that, the preacher said,
He's always there just hides his head.

You are, I cried, a silly sod
Those mountains are more grand than god.

4.

*The Man who is in a Hurry is already Dead
(Moroccan proverb according to our taxi-driver)*

We sit on the edge of the pool, on a step,
Water up to our shins.

Cold! you say.
I say: Only where the surface laps your skin.

No hurry, you say. Plenty of time.

For you, I think, inshallah,
But not for me, God knows!

And I launch myself in.

5.

Do I feel the weight of
Juggernauts and cargo cults?
Of mosques, cathedrals, temples?
Do I feel the weight of god?

Do I hear the cries of
Starving children?
Of all those hedged by wire and terror?
Do I hear them cry for god?

I feel the pressure of a cat
As she purrs below our feet
And I warm with love and gratefulness
As I give her lamb to eat.

6. A Solipsist on Essaouira Sands

No one makes things live the way I can
My eyes and head alone can see three lines
Of surf between the islands and the sand
Or how the brown boys make a football climb
To reach its apogee against the sky
And hang like a moon beneath the sun.
The sounds are also mine, the cake-boys' cry,
The water-sellers' bell. Above the crowded hum
The call to prayer like a swallow's flight
Swoops on my ears. There is one God and his Name
Is Allah. Not so. In a trillions' sight
A trillion worlds exist and none the same
But where there is no eye, nor ear, nor head
The world, the heavens, even god are fled.

*That's it for Travel. Cuba, Egypt and more from Morocco
are in the pipe-line, and many more after them, I hope. As I
wrote earlier: travel editors please note. Expenses plus a
modest fee will get us almost anywhere.*

5. HISTORY

History is an inescapable part of reality, though the past remains unknowable. History is a toy the writer of fiction can play with. Pity the poor historian who is noosed with facts.

I Damned Spot

This, together with its introduction, was first published in Past Poisons, An Ellis Peters Memorial Anthology, *edited by Maxim Jakubowski, published by Headline. It was shortlisted for the CWA Short Story Silver Dagger in 2000.*

Introduction

ALL historical fictions, including mystery stories, invariably betray and portray the time they were written in as much as or more than they accurately present the time in which they are set. This is a) inevitable, b) generally not openly acknowledged. No matter how well we do our research we experience our sources through twentieth-century sensibilities. One cannot, for instance, examine a piece of coarse worsted worn next to the skin from the point of view of a medieval peasant – inevitably, however hard we strive to fight it, awareness of Marks and Spencer's lingerie remains indelibly at the back of the mind and elsewhere.

This is just as true when we consider works of fiction written in the past but adapted or dramatised, and even more so when we read modern sequels to, say, *Emma* or *Frankenstein*. No amount of care with historical reconstruction of costumes, manners, etiquette, horses, carriages and the rest can hide the fact that we are looking at or reading a construct made by contemporary minds for contemporary consumption. All this is all right if one accepts that a historical fiction is a straightforward commercial venture designed to sell to a substantial and paying audience a product it will enjoy and from which it may even learn something about our times, here and now. But let us not imagine that the experience has opened up to us an understanding of the real Jane Austen or the real nineteenth century.

It may serve to remind readers (though not without providing some entertainment as well) that historical fiction wittingly or otherwise reflects the way we are now far more than the way we were then.

Damned Spot

Tall windows, leaded in diamond patterns, looked out on a knot-garden of box. Around it gravel walks were edged with formal borders of gillyflowers and tulipans...

Hang on! Already I am performing one of the tricks of the history fiction writer's trade. You, dear readers, well, some of you anyway, have no idea what a gillyflower is and you're guessing hopefully that a tulipan is a tulip. But because I have used these unfamiliar names for common flowers, I have won your trust. I have disarmed any suspicion of anachronism, and if you have no idea at all of what you are meant to be visualising, no matter – you have been transported into the past. Whereas if I had written wallflowers and tulips you would have suspected a historical solecism and seen, in your mind's eye, a modern municipal garden.

You would, however, have been right to think late April-early May – especially as I am about to describe the cherry trees in full but falling blossom beyond the knot-garden. Not, of course, your flamboyant vulgar Japanese ornamentals, possibly pink, but a decent modest, fruit-bearing English tree. The merry month of May then, the first week, and the year is 1593.

Tall windows and two men looking out of them – one of them old, very old for those times, already in his seventies, supporting himself on an ebony stick and occasionally dabbing with a lace edged linen hand-kerchief at a drooping lip which leaked spittle, the other middle-aged, sturdier, a coarser version of the older man who was his father. Both were dressed soberly in black velvets trimmed with fur and enlivened with discreet flashes of gold and polished gems – nothing flashy, you understand, but not mean either.

There was a large oak table behind them, with bulbous fluted legs, covered with papers and some parchments, the latter fastened with red tape and heavy seals. There was also a posy of spring flowers – not there particularly to give pleasure but to ward off plague. 1593 was a bad year for plague which was why all this was happening well away from London.

I nearly wrote 'dark' oak, an epithet which I thought would also do for the oak panelling decorated with fruits and flowers carved by... but no, Grinling Gibbons came a century later, and even worse, as we well know if we think about it, new or newish oak is pale, honey-coloured, it darkens slowly with age, and the oak furniture and panelling in Hatfield House in 1593 would have still been pale.

But we don't imagine our Tudor grandees surrounded by pale oak, do we? And now, damn it, I find Hatfield House did not belong to the Cecils until ten or so years later... but it was a royal residence in 1593, so without laboriously checking the fatter history books I think we can say that the Cecils were there not because they owned the place but because that was where the Queen was. And the Court. Yes, why not. And in fact a meeting of the Privy Council has just taken place, most of the members have withdrawn, leaving William and Robert behind to set in train the execution of the results of the council's deliberations.

There was, however, one other person hovering in the shadows at the back of the room, furthest from the window. Not, yet, a member of the council, though he thought he should be, a prim, pompous man, lean and hungry, with permanent five o'clock shadow, already noted for his cleverness and lack of humour. He was a cousin by marriage of the Cecils and could not quite understand why he still lacked preferment beyond the Bar where he practised his trade with a punctilious observation and knowledge of the law which annoyed judges but which they could not gainsay.

The older of the two men by the window held a piece of paper under its cool light. That was why they were by the window – not to admire the wallflowers and tulips or even the cherry blossom, but because the old man especially was suffering from failing eye-sight.

'This confession,' he wheezed, he had been suffering from a rheumy chest since Easter, 'that Thomas Kyd is supposed to have made, what's it worth? I mean, will it hold up in a court of law?'

The younger man in the background uttered a different sort of cough.

'Oh, I think so, my lord. Fear of hell-fire produced it. Hell-fire following whatever unpleasant death is now deemed suitable for heretics.'

He looked smugly at his nails.

'You mean he wasn't tortured?' The old man's son, Robert, sounded incredulous.

'Well, of course he was tortured. Enough for recollection of the experience to make him vow that this confession was offered freely.'

'Even the bit involving this blighter...' William peered again at the close written italic hand, '...Christopher Marlowe? Is he really going to shop him?'

'Certainly. For heresy. Marlowe is an atheist, and an antinomian.' No need to say Marlowe was a secret service asset who betrayed us. 'We'll get him on a heresy rap.'

'I don't see how he can be both,' Robert chipped in again. 'Both atheist and antinomian.'

'Personally,' his father commented, after giving the matter some thought, 'I prefer atheism. At least an atheist might recognise the importance of moral imperatives. An antinomian has carte blanche to do what the hell he likes. If he's one of the chosen he'll get to heaven anyway, however evil his life; if he isn't chosen he'll go to hell anyway, however worthy his life. Such a doctrine is not conducive to good order in the state, observance of the Commandments, and it undermines degree. Untune that string and all you get instead of harmony in the general polity is pandemonium...' As old men will, he was off now.

The young man behind him tried to dam the flow.

'There are, my lord, examples in Holy Writ, especially in Romans four and five, which being interpreted by over-cunning and zealous minds...'

'Francis, I have managed this kingdom for its monarch for more than three decades and throughout I have been guided by one principle alone. Whatever threatens the stability of the state must be contrary to Holy Writ – and there's an end to it. I leave others, clerics, theologians and the like, to find the bits of Holy Writ that will serve. And they find them. Or else they lose preferment. Ask Richard Hooker – he's not yet forty years old but on the back of that book he's writing he should make Canterbury before he dies. Now, where were we?'

'Christopher Marlowe.'

'Off with his head! He always was a pain, a threat. Double spy, taking Dutch gold for spying on us as well as our gold for spying on them, totally immoral, a jerkin-lifter from all accounts, writes lewd poetry, thinks a great deal too highly of himself, and then there are those dreadful plays...' The old man was beginning to spit properly now, and his colour had risen, rouging the soft wrinkled old skin on his cheeks. 'Openly seditious as well as lewd. I mean, come on, that Edward the Second piece, grossest disrespect for the Crown. Of course he was protected by that toad Walsingham, to whom he was I believe related, but Walsingham's been pushing up pied daisies and blue violets these last couple of years. Off with his head, I say.'

'Problem, father. Walsingham's gone, yes, but Marlowe's got other friends... scholars, scientists. William Harvey...'

'Tush, man! Whoever heard of a scientist who wouldn't perjure his learning for the sake of a good seat in a university or to escape burning? Give them enough carrot and stick and they'll tell you the Earth's flat, or goes round the sun, any nonsense they think you want to hear...'

'Sir Walter Raleigh is also an intimate.'

'That's not, just now, in his favour.'

He was referring to the fact that Sir Walter was at that time in internal exile in Sherborne having seduced and later married one of the Queen's Ladies in Waiting without asking her first. The Queen, that is.

'There is one other problem.'

'Yes?'

'Marlowe's in hiding. We don't know where he is.'

Francis Bacon again cleared his throat.

'But he is also penniless. He's got to come out, show himself, if he's going to eat. If we approach his actor friends, and people whom he owes money to, and promise them he's in the way of getting some money, they'll lead us to him.'

'That's that settled then. You find out what Marlowe has he can sell and who will buy it, get them together in some tavern or dive somewhere and we'll move in on him.'

William Cecil Lord Burghley dropped the small sheet of paper he was still holding and reached towards the table for the next. Then he paused. 'He's not worth a trial and all that fuss, you know? Flush him out and have him skewered in a brawl over a bummer-boy, something of that sort.'

Some tales based in the past are *quotha* tales and some are not, and some fall between two stools – not aping the speech of the time, but maintaining a spurious dignity that chimes with our perception that people spoke with more weightiness and less forcefulness than they do now. The problem is particularly acute when dealing with the Tudor period. So much of the literature purports to represent spoken language there is a temptation to pastiche it. Some have managed successfully – one thinks of Robert Nye or Anthony Burgess, but Burgess or Nye I am not, so I must ask you, dear reader, to accept some dialogue at least transliterated into modern. You can waste a lot of time checking the N E D to see whether or not a particular word was current in the 1590s, and if you're not going to be thorough about it, you might as well take the modern option. And having, um, grasped that nettle, you might as well go the whole hog. Enough. Let us get on with it. More matter, less art, I can hear you saying.

What, Francis asked himself as he trundled down what was later to be the A1 towards London, has Marlowe got that other people might want to buy? His art. His ability to turn out copper-bottomed, sure-fire, theatrical hits, the like of which no one has ever seen before. Tamburlaine. The Jew of Malta. Dr Faustus, for Christ's sake. He'll be working on something right now. Because he's in the shit he won't be able to get it put on. But he can always sell it to someone else who can have it done under their own name or a pseudonym or whatever. But who? To whom? Thomas Kyd's Spanish Tragedy was much in the same style, and he won't be writing anything on his own account again, not with his thumbs in the state they are in now. But, since he's just shopped his old mate on an atheism-heresy rap, which was why he was in hiding in the first place, it isn't likely they'll get together amicably to do a deal. Who else? Well, the players will know.

Thus the wily lawyer as his cumbersome cart climbed the hill towards Highgate. He'd make the rounds of the companies, buy the right people a few drinks, even a square meal... kill two birds with one stone, he might even get a line on where Marlowe was hiding out.

Problem. All the London theatres were shut and had been for a year. First there had been riots, now plague.

It took him until the end of the month to set it all up. And though the fact the theatres were closed did make it harder to track down the sort of people he wanted to meet it did also mean that once he had found them they turned out to be more than usually hard-up and susceptible to bribes, or the promise of getting their hands on a box office hit to put on as soon as the theatres opened again. The competition to find a really hot script was fierce – whichever company scored with the sensation of Christmas '93 or the '94 season would make a killing. Indeed the rewards seemed so promising that he began to think he might try his hand at this play-writing lark himself. He'd already circulated a few short pieces he called essays which were quite highly thought of by those who hadn't read Montaigne.

The upshot was, you might say, satisfactory. A whisper here, a clandestine meeting there, money passed beneath a table in a tavern, a promise offered in one of the Inns of Court, all led to an understanding that Chris Marlowe did have a script he was willing to sell and that he'd be at a certain lodging house cum tavern cum brothel in Deptford on the twenty-eighth of May shortly after dusk. He'd have the play with him and he'd only part with it for twenty pounds. Lot of money in those days. The party of the other part was quite happy too. The play was apparently very much in the Marlowe mould, a rampaging piece about a Bohemian duke who murdered his way to the throne of

Wenceslas, taking out young princes and raping the widow of one of his victims on the way – the usual Overreacher Theme that had done so well for him in his other plays. The only stipulation the buyer had apparently made was that the play should be re-jigged to round off a trilogy he'd already had performed, based on the Wars of the Roses. It had been pretty tedious stuff and the players he had worked for weren't at all sure that they wanted any more in the same vein. The guy was a poet really, not much of a dramatist at all. Lousy actor, too.

And he it was, rather than the lawyer, who turned up at the Deptford house of ill-repute to buy a play and lure the playwright out into the open. He ordered some cakes and ale, and waited. Then, to pass the time, he pulled out of his bag a well-thumbed copy of Holinshed's Chronicles, some scrap paper and a pen and ink-horn. He began to make notes.

Eventually, an hour late, Marlowe came sauntering languidly down the stairs from the upper room just as the serving-girls were bringing in the candles. He was tucking in his shirt and yawning at the same time since he had spent a fair bit of the afternoon buggering one of the stable-lads.

'Oh Christ,' he said, as he took in the short, prematurely balding, plumpish young man who was waiting for him, 'it's young Waggle-dagger, the Warwick grammar school boy. Little Latin and no Greek. Upstart crow who steals our feathers. Budge along, there's a good chap.'

He pushed himself onto the bench beside the scribbler and slapped down a thin folio tied with ribbon.

'There you are then. It's all good stuff, I promise you. Got the chinks, have you?' He rattled the bag the man he had called Waggle-dagger had put on the table next to his book. He picked the book up and sneered again. 'Don't shade your eyes, plagiarise. It's still your shout so I'll have a pint of sack.'

And he signalled to the landlord.

'Sack's off,' said mine host, and snapped his fingers and winked at the three ruffians who were concealed behind a high-backed settle. 'Got some good Kentish ale though. Good ale hath no fellow.'

'Stratford actually,' said the aspiring playwright, and began to undo the ribbons.

'Eh?'

'Stratford on Avon. Not Warwick.' He smoothed out the title page. The Troublesone Raigne and Lamentable Death of Sigismundo, King of Bohemia... except the words Sigismundo and Bohemia had been crossed out.

Marlowe laughed, the high bray of an Oxbridge graduate.

'The Bard of Stratford on Avon,' he crowed. 'Got quite a ring to it.'

At that moment the three ruffians jumped out from behind the settle, armed with daggers and clubs. Marlowe also had a dagger, but he fumbled the drawing of it and poked his eye with the point. Thus incapacitated he could not defend himself from the one lunge a man variously named as Archer or Ingram managed to get on target. At this point the landlord, seeing the business was done, and mindful of his reputation, began to holler for the constable and the ruffians legged it.

Marlowe fell to the floor. The Warwickshire Bard placed a handy cushion under his head and examined the wound.

'It is not,' he said, 'as wide as a church-door, nor as deep as a steeple but...'

'What the devil are you talking about,' Marlowe groaned. 'How in blazes can a steeple be *deep*?'

And died.

While waiting for the constable, the bard could not help congratulating himself on how things had turned out. He had, of course, had his suspicions about the whole set-up. Dick Burbage had told him he thought something fishy was going on, especially when that lawyer chap volunteered to put up the twenty pounds in gold himself. Putting two and two together he had guessed it was a ruse to get Marlowe to show himself. Well. Serve the bastard right. Always putting on airs with his university ways. 'The name's Marlowe...,' that smooth drawl, 'Marlowe with an e.'

The way looked pretty clear now. Seven or eight actors' companies around and with Kyd out of the way and this bleeding lump of flesh shortly to be laid to rot in cold obstruction... Obstruction? What did that *mean*? Never mind, it had a ring to it... he was the only one left with any sort of half-way respectable track record. He'd soon show them who was the king shake-scene on the block.

Meanwhile he couldn't resist turning the title page. 'Now is the winter of our malcontent made glorious...' He frowned, picked up his quill, crossed out *mal* and wrote in *dis*.

There was a splodge of Marlowe's blood on the top of the page. He used his penknife to scratch away at it but it wouldn't shift.

'Damned spot,' he muttered.

I doubt if there's a single indisputable fact in any of that.
There certainly aren't any in the next bit.

II *The Battle of Hastings*

These are a couple of scenes taken from a screenplay of The
Last English King *which I wrote for Geoff Reeve Films. The
option on the book was renewed three times; I wrote (and
was well paid for it) three versions of a screenplay; Jude
Law, Sir Michael Caine, and Jean Reno were talked of, and
so on... But you know what the film industry is like and the
whole project went somewhere behind the back burner. But
now, as I write this, it could be moving forward again. It
would make a hell of a good film... so if there's anyone out
there who thinks they could get together fifty million
dollars, do drop us a line.*

129. EXT. OUTSIDE DUKE WILLIAM's TENT. DAY.
*DUKE WILLIAM, ODO, LANFRANC, FITZOSBERN, A VALET.
MONTGOMERY waiting to get a word in edgeways. With the
VALET's help DUKE WILLIAM has just put his hauberk of mail on
back to front, so the fastening and the Norman lion are on his back.*

DUKE WILLIAM
Aaarrrgh! Bloddy fool!

The VALET clearly expects to be beheaded on the spot. LANFRANC
intervenes.

LANFRANC
What a good omen, Sire.

DUKE WILLIAM
What the devil do you mean?

DUKE WILLIAM and the VALET struggle to get the hauberk off, and
on again the right way round.

LANFRANC
Surely this changeabout signifies how today you go from being a duke
to a king.

DUKE WILLIAM

I'm king already, damn you. Roger! What's that bast... bugger up to on that hill.

MONTGOMERY

He's waiting. Good troops in front, more coming in, and up to five thousand levies.

DUKE WILLIAM

All the more reason for getting at them as quick as we can. Men lined up and ready to go? Right we'll be... hang on. Historic occasion. I'll say a few words first. Get that fellow Taillefer to write them down. Be part of our heritage. Our English heritage.

130. EXT. THE BATTLE-LINE OF THE NORMANS BELOW TELHAM HILL. DAY.

The Normans are drawn up in three divisions, each having three lines several files deep with a gap between them. First lightly armed ARCHERS and CROSSBOWMEN, then FOOTSOLDIERS, finally HORSEMEN, the latter armed with lances, carrying axes, swords or maces as side-arms, helmets with nose-pieces, chain or plate mail, huge horses. It is to these that DUKE WILLIAM addresses his speech, riding up and down the front rank. He is now fully armed like them, on a white horse. He is followed by a mounted SQUIRE carrying his standard. The SQUIRE gets in a muddle with DUKE WILLIAM's frequent changes of direction. TAILLEFER is also there, on a donkey perhaps, attempting to scribble down DUKE WILLIAM's speech. FITZOSBERN, ODO, MONTGOMERY are also mounted and each in front of their divisions of HORSEMEN.

DUKE WILLIAM

Normans, countrymen, and other chaps too. We are not here to praise Harold but to bury him. We'll fight him on the beaches, on the hillsides, wherever. Mind you, he's no push-over. There'll be blood, toil, sweat and tears before bed-time. Some of you today will fall and not get up again. Never in the field of whatever will anyone have owed so much to so few. Apart from anything else, their share of the loot and booty to come will fall to those of us who survive... If you can't keep that fucking standard upright I'll have your balls off. Where was I? Today this little off-shore island becomes part of Europe. Today the poor buggers who live here begin a thousand years under the Norman yoke, the Norman heel. The Pope has blessed us. Harold has broken his word to me to be my vassal. Right is on our side, might is on our side. Cry God for William, England and Saint... Saint... Odo! You're a fucking bishop, who's the patron saint of England?

Cut to ODO. He pouts, very gallic shrug, puffs his lips, plucks a name out of nothing...

ODO
George?

Back to DUKE WILLIAM.

DUKE WILLIAM
Never heard of him. God for William, Normandy, England and Saint George!

DUKE WILLIAM spurs his horse which takes off down the line, almost dumping him and frightening TAILLEFER's donkey. He loses pen, ink-horn and parchment which blows down the battle-line. Drums and trumpets, then just drums in a steady marching beat as all three lines of all three divisions move forward... and up the hill.

145. EXT. THE TOP OF TELHAM HILL. DAY (AS BEFORE).
The ARCHERS are shooting arrows at the circle of HOUSE-CARLS. The arrows either hit their shields or pass over their heads. DUKE WILLIAM rides up amongst the ARCHERS. Behind him ODO and a line of HORSEMEN, some of them carrying burning brands and torches, the DARTH VADERS in front.

DUKE WILLIAM
Shoot upwards. Up into the air.

146. EXT. THE CENTRE OF THE HOUSE-CARLS CIRCLE. ALMOST NIGHT.
HAROLD in front of and between his standards. A slow creaking beating noise. He looks up. Three swans flying in formation low over the hill and out towards the sea.

HAROLD
Tostig. Leofwyne. Gyrth.

A fourth swan, behind the others. Screen goes black (or white? Or red?) Sudden camera movement and from now on sudden burst of rekindled furious action. Very fast pull-back to DUKE WILLIAM's POV. The Fighting Man of Cerne standard is down as SHIR tries to hold

HAROLD. One of HAROLD's eyes is black, streaming blood. Everything in the centre of the circle is turbulent, chaotic with shouts of despair, dismay, but orders too. But all heard from the fifty or so yards that separate them from DUKE WILLIAM. Arrows continue to fall.

SHIR
The king's hurt. He's down. God help us now. He's still alive. Fight on you bastards, the king is still alive...

DUKE WILLIAM
We've got him, we've got the bugger, come on!

But ODO leans out of his own saddle and manages to catch DUKE WILLIAM's bridle as he surges forward.

ODO
Hold on, Billy boy. We need you alive if you're going to be king.

And it is the five DARTH VADERS who gallop into the centre, two holding torches which they thrust into the faces of the HOUSE-CARLS then laying about them with all their might with axes, maces, swords. SHIR goes down quickly, then WULFRIC. WALT tries to shield HAROLD but as the first axe blow falls he flinches sideways (maybe freezeframe or slow motion on the falling axe) and we hear Who do we die for? We die for the Chief, then...

ERICA V O
You'd better not make me cry again, ever. Promise?

And he deliberately takes it on his arm which is sliced off below the elbow. He rolls away howling with agony. Maybe we see his hand, still holding the sword, with the owl ring his father gave him still on its finger, then the axe blows smash into HAROLD's body... fade to black.

147. EXT. THE CIRCLE ON TELFORD HILL. DAY.
Dawn actually. C U on the old scar on HAROLD's chest. The finger of EDITH SWAN-NECK tracks along it.

EDITH SWAN-NECK
This is him.

Slow pull back to show HAROLD's body hideously and unrecognisably maimed, then the bodies of WULFRIC, SHIR, HOUSE-CARLS around. EDITH SWAN-NECK kneeling, GYTHA, QUEEN EDITH cloaked, behind her. Behind them WALT (arm bandaged crudely with blood-soaked rags) and DAFFYDD. Long shadows fall across them. Some yards behind them WILLIAM THE CONQUEROR, DARTH VADERS, ETC silhouetted blackly against the rising sun. ODO leaves them, comes forward to the women, looks down on them.

ODO
Harold?

EDITH SWAN-NECK
Yes.

ODO
(Over his shoulder to WILLIAM) It's him. He's dead.

Without a word, just a jangle of harness, WILLIAM THE CONQUEROR and his entourage, wheel away and trot off over the visual ridge of the hill.

GYTHA
We must bury him.

ODO
Not in church ground. He broke his oath and was unrepentant.

GYTHA
Then we will do it the way it should be done.

148. EXT. A TRACK HEADING TOWARDS CLIFF-TOPS, THEN DOWN A GROYNE TO THE BEACH. DAY.
Four ENGLISH PEASANTS carrying HAROLD's body on their shoulders. It is now shrouded in the blood-stained Fighting Man of Cerne. Behind come EDITH SWAN-NECK, QUEEN EDITH, GYTHA arms round each other supporting each other. Behind them a small line of MOURNERS, some wounded, including WALT with what is left of his right arm bandaged and in a filthy sling, and DAFFYDD.

WALT
(Weeping, struggling with the words) I should have died with him. I should have bloody died.

149. EXT. A BEACH BENEATH CLIFFS. DAY.

The body still in its shroud on a funeral pyre made from a wrecked ship. EDITH SWAN-NECK takes a burning brand from a MOURNER and lights the pyre. It catches and begins to burn. She and QUEEN EDITH and GYRTHA put small posies of flowers in the flames. Mix to dying embers. C U on WALT and DAFFYDD.

> **WALT**
> What will you do now?

> **DAFFYDD**
> Back to Wales bach. I've done my bit for England. You?

> **WALT**
> I've got to pay. Somehow I've got to pay. I don't know how. I can't stay here. I can't stay in England.

> **DAFFYDD**
> It's not your fault, boyo. They'd have killed him with or without you. You know that.

> **WALT**
> *(He hasn't really heard)* I've got to go.

They watch the flames, and we do too.

> **DAFFYDD V O**
> You'll be back.

Hold on flames. Mix to rain on Hambledon. Perhaps show title over TWO YEARS LATER.

150. EXT. THE TURFED RAMPARTS OF HAMBLEDON. DAY.

In silhouette against sky, no need for dialogue, WALT talks with gestures to FRED, who turns away to go down the hill. Time passes. WALT shelters from rain, or just hides beneath the hawthorn tree, in one of the turfed fosses in the spot where he and ERICA picnicked after their betrothal. Looking up with him we see ERICA holding an eighteen-month-old baby, standing on the rampart above him, wind blowing her hair and clothes. He gives a low whistle, she turns…

151. EXT. THE VERY TOP OF HAMBLEDON. DAY.

WALT and ERICA, his arm round her waist, hers over his shoulder, the infant sitting on the turf picking at a flower or playing with flint stones.

> **WALT**
> It's been bad?

> **ERICA**
> Very, very bad.

Pause. They drop their hands, hold hands, C U on the tightening grip.

> **WALT**
> We've got to get the bastards out. Even if it takes a thousand years. We've got to get them out.

Their POV. The landscape of the Vale of the White Hart opens in front of them. Some curtaining rain, some very bright sunshine.

> **ERICA**
> We will. We will.

Hold on the view. Very quietly at first, distantly, but building to a climax, heard over, choirs singing…

> Bring me my bow of burning gold
> Bring me my arrows of desire
> Bring me my spear, O, clouds unfold
> Bring me my chariot of fire
> I shall not cease from mental fight
> Nor shall my sword sleep in my hand
> Till we have built Jerusalem
> In England's green and pleasant land…

Slow fade to final title sequence. Then, as this gets under way, again starting distantly, using the full stereo effect from behind, the Yaa-taa, ya-ta-ta rhythm of the England football chant (as heard before when the English marched from Stamford Bridge to London) ending, full volume…

> ENGLAND.

Repeat through remaining titles, fading towards

The End

Sound of a cold wind gently blowing, fade to black.

This is not how the book ends, but now I rather wish it did!

III *Kings of Albion*

The driving force behind this was the idea of turning King Solomon's Mines *on its head and having three highly civilised Indians and one Arab (the main narrator) visiting Ingerlond during the Wars of the Roses, much in the way Sir Henry Curtis, Captain Good, and Alan Quartermain penetrate darkest Africa in the earlier book. Although* Kings of Albion *doesn't echo* King Solomon's Mines *slavishly, here is one moment where it gets close. The scene is the Battle of Mortimer's Cross, where, historically, three suns appeared and won the battle for Eddie who was Edward IV and Duke of York.*

Three Suns

Once back in his tent all this weighed heavily and Eddie said: 'We need a sign. An irrefutable sign that we will win and win because god is on our side. Only that way can we be sure that chaps will realise their oaths to Henry were falsely sworn and that I am rightfully king.'

He turned to our prince.

'Hurry-hurry,' he said, 'you oriental chaps have a reputation for magic and so forth. Could you conjure something up for us? An eclipse, perhaps. Put the sun out and say the sun is Henry?'

I've had occasion, once or twice, to mention the Fakir who

attached himself to us right from the start. He came and went like a shadow, a not very familiar familiar. Tall, dark, a Mussulman godman, he was, I sometimes thought, my other self, my similar, my brother, the ghost of the man I might have been had I not been mutilated as a child in the way you see before you. Indeed at times I was none too sure in just what dimension he existed, for it seemed to me none saw him or was aware of his presence but I. He was often there, a flicker in the corner of my eye who was gone when I turned; a presence between the sun and a wall which faded with the light whose rays it interrupted.

It's a trick fakirs perfect, often by the simplest of means. Appear in a locked room? Simple. Hide there before the room is locked. Manifest in a crowd? Easier still. Arrive in disguise and when there is a distraction, throw it off. They have garments that look coarse and poor through cunning weaving and painting but are made of silk so fine they can be crushed and balled away.

They can swallow almost anything and so their bodies provide hiding places that walk with them; they can get their fists up their rectums and leave there a king's globe, cross and all.

They also know substances with strange qualities, unlikely powers, that can turn metals into ashes; they can make a rope stand on end with no apparent means of support and encourage a small boy to climb it. Lying on the ground they make six people each put a finger under them and, lo, they rise into the air and none of the six feels the weight. They work with mirrors. And… they understand how the track of light can be concentrated and bent by passing it through cunningly shaped lumps of glass.

I had seen him quite frequently on the way from Macclesfield Forest. Once walking towards us through the rain up an unusually straight track (unusual, that is, for Ingerlond where all but the Roman roads wind like corkscrews), climbing a hill. But he crossed the ditch when he was still a couple of hundred paces from us and strode away into the mist that came down over the moor. On another occasion he sat opposite us in a tavern, went out as if to take a piss, and never came back. Three times he walked just beside and behind me for an hour or two, and then was gone.

Peter insisted that he was a figment of my imagination, that he had heard of such manifestations appearing to people suffering from extreme physical exhaustion and mental distress. Christians even identify this presence with the risen Jesus.

Considering what we had all been through my response was to ask him: 'Why then, Brother Peter, are we not all suffering the same hallucinations since we have all suffered in similar ways?'

At all events, having heard this plea from the youth we still thought of as Eddie, this Fakir came up behind me and whispered in my ear: 'Do you still have the kurundams in your bag?'

'Yes, indeed I do.'

'Let's have a look at them then.'

I pulled them out and laid them carefully on a table, beside the candles that lit the tent. The others were still in the doorway, watching the torches of the Welsh, drinking wine and eating pork. Two good reasons why I was already hanging back behind them.

Have I described these stones, these crystals, before? Well, I will do so again but in more detail. They were six inches long, shaped a little like a weavers' shuttle, that is pointed at both ends, and about one and a half inches in diameter at the thickest point in the middle. They were multi-faceted but basically hexagonal, the points at each end being six-sided pyramids. They were perfect, unflawed rubies and even in the dim candlelight on a simple small black oak table, they gathered the light and glowed with it.

'We shall,' said the Fakir, 'need the brightest mirrors that can be found. Not polished steel or silver, but glass ones, the backs coated with an amalgam of mercury. Such mirrors are made in Nuremburg and Venice but can be found in the houses of the wealthy almost anywhere in the known world.'

By now those who had remained in the doorway of the tent had turned back in and were listening to us.

'It would help too, if we had someone with us with a proper knowledge of the science of optics.'

And of course, Brother Peter cleared his throat.

'I am not myself an adept,' he said, 'but I have here,' and he tapped the bag he had been carrying since Easter, 'the investigations the great Roger Bacon made on the subject.'

Eddie turned to the other Roger, Sir Roger Croft.

'Get us a couple of mirrors, of the sort the chappie wants, there's a good fellow.'

'I know just where I can lay hands on a pair,' said the knight. 'There's a cloth manufacturer in Hereford who trades with the Arnolfini family in Bruges. They sent over a pair as wedding presents when his son got married.'

'While we are waiting,' the Fakir went on, 'we could initiate some simple experiments as precursors,' and he picked up one of the kurundams, held it point first towards one of the candles and moved it further and nearer. Presently we all gasped. From the pyramidal point furthest from the candle a narrow beam of bright light, not red as one would expect, but green, appeared, and, with almost no spreading at all linked the stone to a tiny spot of light six feet away on the canvas wall of the tent. Which began to smoulder.

'Light amplified by stimulated emission through a ruby,' said Peter, with awe.

The Fakir frowned, as if the Friar had got something slightly wrong.

It took some doing, but it worked. It had never been done before. There was no possibility of a rehearsal or a trial. At sunrise the next morning it would have to work. And Nature too would have to co-operate. A river, a low hill to the east, which was behind us, they were given. What was not given but could reasonably be expected was a mist. At that time of year, on nights when there was no wind, there was almost always a mist, a fog even. And if there should not be, or if it was not of the substance the Fakir wanted then fires burning green wood and wet dead leaves would be lit on the other side of the rise, to create a false mist. These too were prepared but in the event not needed.

But all this was as nothing compared to the calculations and brain-racking that the Fakir and Brother Peter put into the application of the theories of optics Bacon had adumbrated in code, based on but taking far further the discoveries of his Arab predecessor Abu Yusuf Ya' Qu Ibn Ishaq ul-Kindi. Worse still was calculating the exact point at which the rising sun would be at the right height to make the projection they desired.

All was done in time, but only just. The mirrors, which were small, scarcely eighteen inches across within their carved and gilded frames, but very bright, were placed on scaffolding made from lances and ashpoles found in a nearby farm. The kurundams were mounted in front of them and tilted to what the Fakir and Peter calculated would be the correct angles. Once all this was done, there was nothing left to do but wait.

'Why three suns?' asked Prince Harihara.

'To represent the Trinity. The Three in One, the One in Three we are stupid enough to insist represents the godhead,' Brother Peter replied.

'How,' asked Eddie, 'will the sun shine on two mirrors at once, filling both with its light at the same time?'

This gave one or two who were there a moment's doubt – we could see it in their faces.

'By the same means,' said the Fakir, with weary patience inflecting his words, 'that it casts a shadow from your body at the same times as it casts one from mine.'

'Ah. Yes. Of course. I see.'

But I doubted that he did.

It worked all right. It worked. There was a mist. It hung in the tree-tops, grey like a wolf's pelt in the pre-dawn light. It became rosy then golden and… began to shift. But then the sun a red disc beneath a bank of cloud, rose above it and the illusion was there, there for perhaps two minutes, but long enough.

The sun's rays hit the mirrors, were reflected back into the kurundams which projected them as beams which spread enough to form red circles of light on the mist, just below the sun itself, giving an illusion of three suns not one. The army cheered, they'd been told to. Two lords who had been about to lead their men across to the other side, reined in their horses and rather bashfully waited Eddie's command to charge. It came as the two lower suns faded. Pausing only to announce that from henceforth the sun in its glory, this sun of York, would be his personal badge and that he wanted a shield with the three suns on it prepared immediately, Eddie touched spurs to Genêt's flanks and trotted across the bridge to lead his men to victory.

The Fakir looked around, touched finger tips to the bottom hem of his turban in the Allaha Ismahrlahdik.

'Light Amplified by Stimulated Emission through *Radiation,*' he said, over his shoulder as he walked off down the reverse slope, away from the battle. We never saw him again.

IV *Englishness*

Englishness became an over-arching theme in these two books. Here is the end of Kings of Albion. *Mah-Lo, a Malaysian merchant who trades in information as well as goods is telling the Grand Chamberlain of China what he has learned in his travels about the English.*

Mah-Lo Reports

Looking further afield, to the other side of the world, it was his conclusion that none of the European kingdoms need be considered an immediate danger to the Chinese apart possibly from the

Portuguese. And even the Portuguese, it seemed, were more interested in building up a maritime trading empire based on enclaves of merchants than military domination.

However, in the long term, he had no doubt that eventually the Inglysshe could become a problem. If Ali was right in his depiction of this island race, once their internal disputes were settled Mah-Lo feared they could well become a problem for the whole world.

'They are,' he told us, 'a nation of individuals who yet can combine and behave with ferocious bravery under leaders they respect; they are skilful and ruthless traders with few natural assets of their own to exploit; they are foolhardy sea-farers; they are inordinately arrogant; they are ruthless, unforgiving, cruel enemies. Unfettered by morals or a common religion they take an empirical, pragmatic view of life, adapting their beliefs to circumstances, though always favouring an approach which leaves each individual the captain of his own soul.

Ali once heard an Englishman say: 'I do not tell others how to live and I do not expect others to tell me.' Mah-Lo continued: 'They enjoy and even live for camaraderie, the company of their fellows, physical prowess, hedonistic if simple enjoyment shared with others, strong drink and rough, speedily concluded sex. They have an incredible capacity to suffer pain for a short term, and will face death willingly. But they will not put up with pain or toil as a life-choice. They hate boredom.

'They will cheerfully accept individuals of other creeds and races as individuals, especially if they take a personal liking to them, while continuing to despise all foreigners in general.

'They are mad,' Mah-Lo concluded. 'One day they will conquer the world.'

There was a moment's silence, then the Grand Chamberlain made a dismissive gesture with his long-nailed fingers.

'But not China,' he said.

The English – Who are We?

Back in 1999, I was asked to speak at a conference on Englishness organised by the British Council in conjunction with the History faculty at Warwick University. Here is an edited version of what I said.

I am not a scholar or an academic. I am not a historian, sociologist, ethnologist, anthropologist... or even a cultural critic. I am an un-disciplined creative artist, more specifically a writer, a novelist. I am also emotionally if not intellectually a Romantic – as will become apparent. I'm here because I have written two books that, amongst other things, explore my ideas of Englishness, *The Last English King* (1997) and *Kings of Albion* which will be published by Little, Brown next summer.

A general assertion: a culture is self-perpetuating as long as nothing intervenes to change or destroy it. At a micro-level you can see this in schools where the entire pupil population can change every five years but traditional patterns of behaviour repeat themselves over decades, even centuries, without being codified or imposed – the songs sung at the back of the bus that takes teams on trips to away matches, initiation rites, and so on. There's a Phd thesis waiting to be written about back-of-the-bus sub-cultures. Therefore my thesis that what is English has its roots in pre-conquest culture, though warped horribly by the Normans, is not vitiated by the thousand years that separates us from that terrible date.

The English. There are two strands in Englishness that I believe achieved a sort of uneasy meld, uneasy because of the basic contradictions between them, by about 1450, and remain dominant right down to present times. They derive from two cultures.

First, the Anglo-Saxon Danish. The Anglo-Saxons were Teutonic, Germanic. When their conquest of what we now call England began they were a split culture – the males were warriors and focused on their leader or king. Women lived in an almost separate realm where they were powerful and respected. It is arguable that the Freudian conflict between war and work on one side, and hearth and sex on the other, was not entirely resolved. On the male side obedience and loyalty were the most highly-rated virtues.

The Danes, whose more or less assimilated descendants amounted to at least a third of the population by 1066 but had their own traditions and laws, the Danelaw, were also a warrior culture but perhaps based on smaller units whose size was circumscribed by the number of men in a long-boat. They valued individualism and individual feats more then the Anglo-Saxons did, individual pride over-rode a loyalty that could become servile in the Anglo-Saxons.

The political organisations of both retained strong traditions of a democracy an anarchist like Peter Kropotkin would have found congenial. A sort of mutual aid ran through village-based society, moots or meetings at all levels took decisions after endless discussion, all principal offices including kingship were elective, and so on...

Then came the Normans who were, and are, like their leader, bastards. It is true that they were descended from Norsemen who had arrived in northern France a hundred or so years earlier, but during that hundred years they had lost their language and most of their way of life. If I may interpose a thought here, I think historians generally have failed to make enough of the effects of intermarriage between conquerors and conquered. Conquerors rarely bring their women with them and certainly never enough women. The Danes arrived in England and intermarried into a culture that in many ways was significantly similar to the one they brought with them; they thus retained much of their own identity. The Normans, from the same roots, arrived in a France where the culture was very different, and within a hundred years no longer lived, nor even looked much like the Norsemen they were descended from.

Following 1066 the Normans imposed a rigid hierarchical, ethnically-based authoritarian bureaucracy on the anarcho-democratic systems they found. They were anal, dull, cruel. They practised ethnic cleansing in the West Country and South Yorkshire, in the latter case reducing a well-populated, prosperous area to what the Doomsday book itself, twenty years later, called a barren wasteland. They did not assimilate. Laws were not written in English until the 1390s, and the first post-conquest king to speak English easily was Henry V. Imagine Germany had won the last war. It is as if the official language would not revert from German to English until 2300.

However, the Normans were few in number, not more than 10,000 initially, maybe less, and they brought few women with them. They therefore relied on Anglo-Saxon collaborators to fill the minor posts of government and the lower echelons of the church, and to some extent they interbred – initially by rape.

The result of 1066 is the English: two, possibly three, conflicting strands that I believe are with us today and make us what we are. On the one side individuality and the rights of the individual are more highly valued here than almost anywhere else in the world. Most of us object to government, do not respect politicians, hate and fear bureaucratic interference. We are hedonistic, pragmatic, empirical, pluralist, hate dogma. We like a good time. We do not understand spirituality because we reject the duality that is a precondition of the concept of spirituality. We are Roger Bacon, William of Occam, John Wycliffe, Jack Cade, Wat Tyler and the Lollards; Langland, Milton and the Levellers; Blake, Tom Paine and the Chartists; Turner and Darwin. We are lager louts and we hate the French. We are adventurers. We believe a change is as good as a rest.

On the other side we are Normans. We are superior, we rule by right, we obey the rules though we congratulate each other when we get away with breaking them. We are one of us. We are control freaks. We are bossy. We like systems for as long as we are in charge of them.

We march, we do not amble, we fire as one and not at will, and we take our hands out of our pockets when we speak to me. We tabulate, order, divide. We are deeply prejudiced (God is an Englishman – a Norman actually) and intolerant.

And worst of all, somewhere in between, we are collaborators. In exchange for security, a certain status, we will keep order for the Normans; we fear change, we are tidy, we clip our hedges, we keep off the grass (pun intended), we do as we're told.

With these contradictory strands, no wonder we don't know who we are, but I believe, in spite of 1066, we are at best Vikings with some of the stolidity, reliability, even dullness of the Anglo-Saxons, and, well, pardon my Anglo-Saxon, fuck the Normans and the collaborators. I really do believe that at last, like the House of Lords, they've had their day.

V *The Duke*

Ever since a school teacher who was a touch besotted with me when I was an attractive fourteen-year-old gave me Arthur Bryant's The Age of Elegance *and Philip Guedalla's* The Duke, *I have suffered sporadically from an obsession with Arthur Wellesley, Duke of Wellington. A Freudian might say he was a father-figure. At all events he figures large in three books:* Joseph, Wellington's War *and* A Very English Agent. *If he had been English he would have run Darwin and Wycliffe, Blake and Turner pretty close for my Greatest Englishman. Though he himself, when asked was he not Irish, replied, magnificently, considering who else was born in a stable: If I had been born in a stable you would not have considered me to be a donkey. Joyce, an even greater Irishman, referred to him in* Finnegan's Wake *as 'stableborn'.*

Why this obsession? He was clever, sensitive, incredibly hard-working and conscientious, indomitably brave, a dandy, a womaniser, a wit, yet utterly honest throughout his public life. Having seen the effects of war and civil war in

Spain he made sure England would not suffer the same fate between 1815 and 1848 even at the expense of his own principles (distrust of the Catholic Church and belief that a stable society depended on the sanctity of private, especially landed, property). He was also far more inspired as a general than is generally allowed. And has there ever been another general who could say, at the moment of his greatest triumph: Nothing except a battle lost is half so melancholy as a battle won?

Wellington's War

Wellington's War *is an edited selection of Wellington's dispatches and letters from the Peninsula between 1808 and 1813 with a linking commentary. It wasn't easy to pick a sample passage for a general audience, but the following catches the flavour of much of what is typical. After winning the battle of Fuentes de Oñoro in May 1811, the French garrison of Almeida were allowed to blow up some of the fortifications, their magazine, and escape – through the incompetence of one of Wellington's generals.*

P ossibly I have to reproach myself for not having been on the spot; but... haying employed two divisions and a brigade, to prevent the escape of 1400 men... the necessity of my attending personally to the operation, after I had been the whole day on the Azava *seeing Masséna across the Agueda,* did not occur to me...

I certainly feel, every day, more and more the difficulty of the situation in which I am placed. I am obliged to be everywhere and if absent from any operation, something goes wrong. It is to be hoped that the General and other Officers of the army will at least acquire that experience which will teach them that success can be attained only by attention to the most minute details; and by tracing every part of every operation from its origin to its conclusion, point by point, and ascertaining that the whole is understood by those who are to execute it.

To his brother William he added: I was then quite sure of having Almeida but I begin to be of opinion, with you, that there is nothing on earth so stupid as a gallant officer.

There is a sort of comedy in all this, but as we have noted before comedy or farce in war nearly always end with bitterness. Erskine, dining too well, stuffed Wellington's order in his pocket and forgot it.

Later he proposed sending a piquet of a corporal and four men to the bridge, but his staff prevailed upon him to send a regiment. Nevertheless, Bevan, Colonel of the 4th, did not get the order until midnight when he took his officers' advice and decided to wait for daylight. Erskine lied when he said the 4th had received the order earlier but lost their way. Bevan was to face a Court Martial which would probably have exonerated him. Rather than face it he blew his brains out.

One other result of all this was that Liverpool did not recommend Parliament to move a Vote of Thanks for the Battle of Fuentes de Oñoro.

To William, 2 July: Lord Liverpool was quite right not to move thanks for the battle at Fuentes, though it was the most difficult one I was ever concerned in, and against the greatest odds. We had very nearly three to one against engaged; above four to one in cavalry; and moreover our cavalry had not a gallop in them, while some of that of the enemy was fresh and in excellent order. If Boney had been there we should have been beaten.

And to Prime Minister Spencer Perceval, 22 May: My soldiers have continued to show the Portuguese nation every kindness in their power, as well as the Spaniards. The village of Fuentes de Oñoro having been the field of battle the other day, and not having been much improved by the circumstance, they immediately and voluntarily subscribed to raise a sum of money to be given to the inhabitants as a compensation for the damage which their properties had sustained in the contest.

Attention to the most minute details... Did Boney look to it when his army got the shits? Welly did.

G.O. Cuellar, 1st August, 1812.

1. The Commander of the Forces requests that (all) officers will take measures to prevent the soldiers from plundering and eating the unripe grapes.

2. The followers of the army, the Portuguese women in particular, must be prevented by the Provosts from plundering the gardens and fields of vegetables...

3. ...to each soldier daily one eighth of a pound of rice, if it can be procured; if it cannot, the same quantity of wheaten flour, or of barley, or of wheat, which the officers are requested to see that the soldiers boil up with their soup. If barley or wheat should be issued, the husk should be beaten off before it is boiled.

5. As much of the sickness of the troops is attributed to the use of

raw spirits by the soldiers in the hot season... the officers will see that the men of each mess in their companies mix their spirits with four times the quantity of water as soon as the spirits are issued...

All of which may seem quaint, but the advice about rice, or de-fibred substitutes was sound – no doubt something Arthur Wellesley had learnt in India. And the situation was serious. To Bathurst, 4 August: I am sorry to say that the British troops are by no means healthy, notwithstanding the pains which have been taken to make moderate marches with them, and to encamp them in healthy situations, and they have never failed to receive their regular food... The soldiers are not able to bear the labour of marching in the heat of the sun... *(some)* officers have disobeyed orders... to have their men supplied with blankets... and they are consequently very inadequately protected, in comparison with the other soldiers, from the sun in the day time, and from the dews at night... it is melancholy to see the finest and bravest soldiers in the world falling down, owing to their own irregularities, and the ignorant presumption of those who think they know better what is good for them than those do who have been serving so long in this country.

Welly makes several appearances in A VERY ENGLISH AGENT *and not all of them to his credit, but the book almost finishes with his funeral, still, especially considering the difference in populations, the state occasion which drew the biggest crowd in our history. It's odd how he has dropped out of favour in the last fifty years or so: think of all the Wellington and Waterloo pubs, squares, stations, terraces, roads and streets there are all over the country; the number of families who, following Victoria herself, called their boy children Arthur after him. What happened? What put the one-armed, one-eyed sailor boy on a pedestal in his place?*

Wellington's Funeral

Charlie, who is really Joseph from Joseph, *is being temporarily employed by the Frankfort (sic) police to spy on German exiles living in Soho. Thirty-six years earlier Wellington tried to tip him sixpence but had no change on him. A running joke from then on is that the Duke always remembers the incident but always finds an excuse not to pay up.*

Of course I'd seen the black bunting go up everywhere, and I knew there was a lying-in-state at the Chelsea Hospital, in the Great Hall, but I stayed away. And on the morning of the funeral itself I turned up in the boarded-up doorway of the house almost opposite number 28, as per usual, with my coat collar turned up against the rain, and was quickly aware that all was very quiet, none of the shops or pubs open, very few people about and those that were hurrying down towards the Trafalgar Square and bit by bit it dawned on me that this must be the day. There were muffled bells tolling, the nearest was St Martin's, and some way off, in one of the parks I suppose, a minute gun was being fired.

I was just beginning to feel a touch of regret that I was rooted as it were to the spot and would miss the big occasion when the door opposite opened and on the stoop the prosperous looking gent from Manchester, all done up to the nines in full black mourning, with a black silk scarf round the base of his topper and a black cane with a silver top and, coming out with him the two kids of the household, my friend Edgar and his sister, three years or so older, they all called her Jennychen. Pretty little girl she was, most attractive. Their Dad, big man with a huge mop of silvering black hair, huge brows, big black beard like a pirate, in his waistcoat and shirtsleeves with a pen stuck behind his ear like a bank-clerk, was inside the door, wishing them a good day of it. So it was clear he was staying behind to get on with his scribbling. He was a journalist, I'd learnt, writing for a New York newspaper, as well as being a socialist or anarchist or whatever. Which is why the Frankforters wanted an eye kept on him. And while he was working his friend was taking the children... well, to see the Funeral, obviously. So I felt I had my excuse, and followed them.

It occurs to me now to wonder why he was so poor if he was a newspaperman. I mean, like the Spanish say of lawyers, who ever saw a dead donkey or a poor journalist?

We were early. We would not have seen a thing if we had not been. The crowd was already four or five deep and the windows filling up, and a couple of hundred on the raised plinth of the column. Our prosperous Teutonic Mancunian succeeded in getting us into the portico of the National Gallery, but those already there occupied as tight as may be the gaps between the columns so we headed to the east side and got on to the lower steps of St Martin's which wasn't bad at all as it gave us an uninterrupted view right down the Mall. Jennychen stood in front of her guardian whom both kids called 'Uncle Fred', and so shall I from now on, while Edgar, sharp as ever, winkled himself through the crowd, slipping like a sheet of paper through gaps where no gaps were, and got himself to the very front next to a Special, one of thousands who lined the route.

We still had a couple of hours to wait before the first of the bands reached the plaza during which the crowd became more and more dense until it was like a sea of black on either side of a causeway, and every window, every roof, every tree was filled with black too, black hats both tall or, on the women, confected out of piles of black velvet above white faces. And there were all sorts in there, believe me. Gents and their ladies, working men, shopkeepers, barrow boys and coster-mongers, and still after thirty-five years a good sprinkling of the old men who had fought with him, wearing one or both of the medals, the medals I should have had by rights. They were the ones that cried, even more than the women.

But there was a fair sprinkling of foreigners and colonials too. Hindus, Arabs, and Blackies, for had he not made the French give up the Slave Trade, and had he not spoke for emancipation? In short, there was a unity of disparate parts there, a readiness to forget conflicting interests, an acknowledgement we all belonged to something bigger than we could fully understand. A brotherhood, Mr Elliott? An Empire? Well, whatever. I flatter myself I have made my contribution one way or another in its creation.

There was intermittent sunshine out of a cloud-filled sky and occasional squalls, enough to make some attempt to put up umbrellas which their neighbours then made them pull down. There was a constant susurration of speech, rising and falling, even occasional bursts of laughter or song, especially from those who remembered the old ones like The British Grenadiers, and Rule Britannia, and even, a touch ironically, for he'd fallen victim to the one enemy none can defeat, See the Conquering Hero Comes; but then, as the first band wheeled in slow march into the Mall, a half-mile away, and began its slow advance towards us, the silence spread in front of it like a dark wave.

Behind the first bands came the coaches, most of them open, filled with the highest dignitaries of the land, the nobility, the Commons, the bishops and archbishops, the Lord High Chancellor, the Lord Chief Justice and all the other justices in their wigs and robes, and then bands again and more bands. The Funeral March by Chopin, and the Funeral March of Beethoven and most often the Dead March from Saul by his favourite, George Handel. He liked a good tune, did the Duke. Next came the heralds in their splendour, and all those more closely connected to the Deceased than those who had gone before, including Prince Albert himself in a coach and six (the Queen maintaining the protocol that says the Monarch attends funerals of family only, though there were those who said an exception should have been made), and a Lord carrying the Duke's baton, the first a British general ever carried. And then at last the Funeral Car, and the second duke, on his own, trailing a long black velvet gown.

The car was beyond everything. How big was it? Twenty-one feet long by twelve feet wide, made out of moulded bronze, decorated with a hundred allegorical figures, a great moving pyramid or Juggernaut weighing eighteen tons and pulled by twelve giant cart-horses decked with nodding black plumes that did not disguise the fact that they could only have been borrowed from a brewery. The coffin on the top looked tiny.

And there, right in front of us but maybe two or three hundred yards away, while it still had a third of the Mall to go, it stuck, stuck in the mud where a gas main or whatever had been recently laid or repaired and sixty stout men from the crowd were called for to get the thing moving again.

It made no difference to the occasion. Indeed it added to it, for now the Common People had had a hand in it.

Across the bottom of Trafalgar Place it all came and off came all the hats in front of it, person by person in a concerted flowing movement that was strange and moving to see, like a huge flock of black birds rising and settling, so I wished I had a hat too I could have lifted as the old man went by. And then came his horse, not Copenhagen who died some fifteen or more years earlier, but a black beast he'd hunted on and ridden on state occasions, led by his groom and with his own boots, yes, those boots, hung reversed from the saddle, a sight that brought a long strange whisper from the crowd as if at last they fully realised they'd never see him again in Rotten Row, or riding to the State Opening of Parliament or at the Trooping of the Colour.

And so on to St Paul's

Let the long long procession go,
And let the sorrowing crowd about it grow,
And let the mournful martial music blow;
The last great Englishman is low.

And Edgar is lost, and not long after Jennychen too who breaks free from Uncle Fred's hand and wiggles through the crowd like an eel or a baby dolphin, looking for him. Uncle Fred is distraught, as well he might be. He pushes through the slowly turning tide of the crowd calling their names, and 'Has anyone seen a small boy?' or 'Has anyone seen his sister?' He pushes along the Strand one way then back to the Square again, and there I leave him, alternately wringing his hands and waving his hat in the hope the missing children might see it above the crowd.

He is, I know, reputed to be a clever man, but like all clever men lacks sense. We are what, a scant halfmile from Dean Street? Those kids know where they live, especially street-wise Edgar. I slip away and get back to my doorway just ahead of them. I slip out as they turn the corner and by the time they have reached the door I am between them and holding their reluctant hands. Edgar bangs the knocker and their father, our bearded friend who looks more like a Moor than ever, stands in front of us.

'Herr Marx,' I say, 'your children were lost—'

'We were NOT,' cries Edgar.

'...but I recognised them and here they are.'

He looks down at us, shrugs, his hand goes to his pocket, he sighs, for it's more than he can afford, and he gives me... sixpence. A tanner.

I have it still, Mr Elliott. It's a pretty coin, don't you think? The young Queen on one side with her hair pulled back beneath her crown and a spray of oak leaves on the other. True silver, all through.

VI *The Spanish Civil War*

As I have said elsewhere, the two books I have written which I feel should have done better are A Last Resort *and* Intimacy. *So I hope readers will not mind too much if I include a rather large lump from the latter. Apart from the obviously fictional characters the public events are as they happened and most I obtained from Ian Gibson's wonderful biography* Lorca, *published by Faber.*

I am in a long narrow room, ill-lit with unshaded bulbs of low wattage and it is filled with women, mostly young or at the most middle-aged, though there are a few old ones in black. The lucky ones are sitting in collapsible wooden seats, the ones in the front are on the floor with their skirts pulled over their knees. At the back behind the seats there is standing room only and also down the sides of the hall. I am standing near the front on the side, with my back to the wall which is streaming with moisture. It is very very hot, and nearly all the women are fanning themselves with pamphlets, newsheets, and, especially the older ones, fans.

At the front there is a slightly raised daïs with a trestle table, and behind it six women amongst whom is my mother, still, as always when in Madrid, dressed in black, but again with the red scarf wound high round her neck, but fastened now with a small brass safety pin, not a diamond. She asked me to fix it for her before we left the apartment.

Me? Yes, I am in woman's clothing again. A long cotton chemise, dark grey, over a full black cotton skirt, tennis shoes, no socks or stockings. Oh, yes, and next to me is Mother's friend Mad Juana. She is wearing her usual mannish clothes which this time include a leather helmet of the sort aeroplane pilots wear, and large round goggles pushed up on her forehead. Yes, I suppose she must, must know who I am, that I am Dolí's son.

A woman is speaking. She is beautiful, with high cheek bones and large eyes, some five or ten years older I should guess than my mother, with black hair already lightly streaked with grey pulled back in a bun. Oddly, she has the same Christian name. She is coming to the end of her speech, her voice is like a trumpet, and like a trumpet it can by lyrical as well as abrasive.

'Comrades. The assassination of comrade lieutenant Pepe Castillo yesterday was an act of despicable barbarity. My blood freezes at the thought of it, and all our love and tenderness overflows for the suffering of his poor wife, a bride of less than a month. Nevertheless, the execution last night of that arch enemy of freedom and the working class, the most excellent (said with terrible scorn) Deputy Calvo Sotelo, carried out more as reprisal than an act of justice, was ill-judged and is also to be condemned. Ill-judged because it will provoke a crisis we are not yet ready to meet, a crisis that will be upon us perhaps as soon as tomorrow. Indeed even as I speak it may be that the generals are on the march. So, ill-judged and to be condemned. I say so, I, and partly I say it to scotch the foul rumours which already circulate the rich men's clubs that I threatened him with death in the Cortes only two days ago.

'Sisters, this fatal act of reprisal, born of unconsidered emotion, is precisely an example of the sort of failure of discipline, an example of the unbridled individualism which will destroy our movement just as we approach the threshold of revolution and triumph which, however strong the temptation to break ranks in conspiratorial acts of terrorism, driven as we may be by feelings almost uncontrollable, we must resist. And discipline, the iron discipline which is the only force that can bind us in the truly united front that is necessary to overcome the enormous forces of evil that are marshalled against us, can only come from the Party. Comrade sisters, join the Party if you can, travel with us if you would prefer, but above all let us remain united, cohesive, and always ready and willing not just to die for the Cause but to serve it in the ways your democratically elected leaders will indicate. Heroism, yes. Sacrifice yes. Force and violence where they are the only way forward. But above all Unity, Solidarity, Obedience, Discipline. Long Live the Republic. Long Live the Party. Long Live the UGT.'

Storms of applause, many fists raised to echo her farewell salute, an attempt in some sections, which include me and Mad Juana, to sing the Internazionale, but all dies quite quickly as this stormy passionate lady leaves the daïs and the hall by a side-door. There have, I have to say, been some boos and jeers too.

'She has four meetings to address this evening,' Juana shouts in my ear, 'and I wish I could be at every single one of them.'

But now my Mother is on her feet, and the hall falls still again, and I feel a surge of emotion: admiration that this small beautiful lady should have the strength and the conviction to place herself in this situation, tremendous pride that she is my Mother and my Friend and my Lover, and an awful tender anxiety that she might bruise herself or be bruised by what might well become a confrontation.

'Sisters,' she says, and her fine gentle voice immediately suggests song, the sweet song of reason, after the passion of the lady who went before, 'the work we are taking on today and in the coming months is nothing less than Social Revolution. And I do not believe that this can be carried out by a central government, or a ruling party. It requires the knowledge, the brains, the willing collaboration of a mass of local and specialised forces, none of which alone can cope with the diversity of problems such a revolution implies. If we sweep away that collaboration and trust and bow only to the ukases of party dictators we will destroy all the independent forces for progress to a better world that already exist, each in its own way expert in the areas they were born to cope with. Trades unionists, teachers, scientists, artists, co-operatives of producers and distributors will never serve us, serve the whole of humanity in the fullest way they can, if they are dominated, as they have been in Russia, by the bureaucratic organs of the Party. That is the way to undo the Revolution, the way to render its realisation impossible...'

And at that moment the big double door at the back of the hall is burst open by a phalanx of ruffians in blue shirts and black breeches. One lobs a smoking bottle into the air which crashes spreading flames that catch the skirts of one of the older women who has been less nimble than her sisters in getting away from it. Others, three or four, loose off pistols, for the most part into the ceiling though one bullet smashes one of the light-bulbs. And through them, and then through the scattering screaming women comes an unmistakably familiar sight:

Ariel, baying in short deep howls, leaping across upturned seats, and panting madly. Miraculously, considering the confusion and the noise, she has picked me out almost straightaway and is soon pawing my chest and licking my face in excited recognition. Fighting his way through from the back of the hall comes her legal owner, my brother Miguel, and it is horribly apparent that in spite of the clothes and make-up I am wearing Ariel has betrayed me. Miguel's face twists with fury and pain. He levels his pistol in my general direction and fires, and the top of a woman's head which rises between us explodes in a spray of bone, hair, blood and brain, much of it slashed across my shoulder and face. The deflected bullet smashes into the wall above me, Ariel drops to a cringing crouch, and her baying becomes a whine.

'Dolí, Mama,' I scream, desperate now to get to her before he can do either of us any harm, and Juana too turns me towards the daïs and herds me towards it and the other door. I glance over my shoulder to see what Miguel is doing, just in time to see him collapsing beneath blows struck by two of the women nearest to him, one of whom I know works in the vegetable market and can lift a sack of potatoes more readily than most men. They are beating him with the collapsible chairs which are folding up like traps in front of the falangists. The noise is indescribable. Screams, the chanting of rival hymns: *History is on our side...; Tomorrow belongs to me...; Arise battalions and conquer; Arise ye starvelings from your slumber...* the smashing of furniture, cries of pain, and still, occasionally, shots.

Pushing and shoving, both with and against the tide, for at least as many women want to get down into the front line as are trying to get out into the street, we at last manage to link up with Mama and spill outside into the heat which sits on the pavement like a fat cat.

'Juana, *querida*,' my mother cries, as we storm down the sidewalk, 'I am done for unless you can get us back to the apartment and then on to Atocha railway station.'

We swing round a corner, and there, parked where she left it, is Juana's motor-bicycle, a British Norton with side-car. Juana buttons the leather strap beneath her chin, pulls down her goggles, Mama and I, first Mama, then me, but that won't work, first me and then Mama perched on my knees, pile into the sidecar. Juana rises in the saddle and kicks down, kicks down again and again, her strong bottom and thundery thigh close to my face. At last the engine fires and roars as she twists the hand-grips which are high and spread like the horns of a bull. The cobbles beneath us judder like bullets fired from below, a tram-driver frantically sounds his bull-roarer and rings his bell as we shoot beneath the curved prow of his vehicle, the wheel of the side-car brushing it and shedding a gleaming chrome hub-cap which spins away. Above us, beyond the crackling sparks on the tram-wires, the hot sky is shredded with crimson cloud like the banners of evil armies...

The same evening? Certainly. We are in the apartment, I am stripped to the waist, and Juana has my head over the bathroom basin, is dousing me with water... to wash off the blood and tissue of the poor woman Miguel killed, I suppose. Mama is rushing about the apartment, piling clothes into a big leather bag with straps, its twin already full stands in the hall. Suddenly a huge pounding on the big internal front door, and shouts, enraged shouts: 'Ma-a-adre, you cow, let us in, you bitch!'

Juana seizes my shoulders, spins me round, thrusts the chemise I had been wearing before into my hands, yes, I am still wearing the skirt, and pushes me towards the kitchen and the fire-escape. There is a crash behind us, and I see the varnish or paint on the outer door star, and then again it comes: they are using the fire-ax taken from its glass case on the landing. Mama with an unclosed bag shedding underwear and stockings is behind us as we spill out on to the clanging stairs and stumble and hurtle down through three right-angles to the area below.

The three of us sprint across it, out through the service door and on to Ayala where once again the Norton awaits us. Mama in a gesture of magnificent despair hurls the bag from her, turns to Juana: 'I've got no money,' she screams.

'I've got some.'

'Enough?'

Juana shrugs broadly, swings her leg over the petrol tank, and again we pile into the side-car.

On the concourse of the station there are enormous queues at the ticket kiosks, arched holes framed in wood like dove-cotes, crowds of people of all sorts fleeing Madrid, heading for relatives in the country, home towns, places where they, like us, might feel safer when the catastrophe comes. Clearly we are going to be part of this log-jam for some time, and with that innocent blend of boredom and curiosity which I now sense is typical of thirteen-year-olds, I get to looking around me, picking out the details. Much of the huge hall we are in is decorated with turn-of-the-century art nouveau: swirling flowers and foliage, with allegorical ladies draped in flowing garments representing the virtues and attractions of Andalusia and the South. Here and there a naked breast peeps out. None is as beautiful, as full and rounded and perfectly shaped as Mama's.

Juana has left us to keep our place in the line while she has gone to the front to make enquiries. Now she returns.

'It's no good,' she cries. 'The Granada train is fully booked in the first class, if you get on at all it will be standing room only, but it leaves in half an hour and anyway I am eight pesetas short of the fare. There is a later train, not fully booked, for Badajoz and the Portuguese border. Won't that do?'

'No,' Mama cries, and stamps her foot. 'Granada is the nearest large town to Don Gabriel's villa, and he promised he would shelter us if ever we got into the sort of trouble we are in now. It has to be Granada.'

'I may have some more cash at home,' Juana chewed her lip doubtfully. 'Or I could borrow some from a friend. Should I bike back to Desengaño? I could probably be there and back before you get to the ticket window.'

'But not before the train leaves. Oh, I don't know what to do. Juana think of something. You saw what happened. That brute Miguel tried to shoot my David. If we fall into his clutches shooting will be the least unpleasant thing he'll do.'

I shudder now, for two reasons. First, because in all the excitement and noise, and the adventure of the meeting and then the bike ride, it has not dawned on me that our situation is indeed that serious. It is only, I realise now with hindsight, in the light of later events, that I know for sure that that shot was aimed at me. Personally. But a worse consideration crosses my mind: if Jorge is around, things will be ten times worse than if we have to deal with Miguel alone. But just then Mama lets lose a high cry filled with surprise and hope.

'Federico! Federrreeeee-co!'

Twenty paces away two men are crossing the concourse towards the departure platforms. Both are suited in double-breasted dark grey, and wear wide-brimmed fedoras, and they are followed by a porter with three large suitcases on his hand-cart. The shorter of the two men stops, as if shot, turns, and gazes in our direction with large eyes beneath thick eyebrows wide, yes, with fear. Mama waves frantically, then breaks ranks and swoops across the space between.

'Who is it?' I ask Juana, who is frowning, possibly sneering.

'Federico García Lorca.'

I sense her disapproval.

'But he's all right, isn't he? Mama is always talking about him and we've read all his plays and poetry...'

'Oh, he's fine.' She attempts to sound bored. 'Spain's greatest playwright and poet. And about as politically useful to us as Shakespeare was to the English revolution. But...' she pauses, and her face lightens, 'he comes from Granada so that may be where he is going...'

I see a long railway carriage, the corridor. Everything is wood. Hard dark wood. Not only the door frames and the window frames, but the panelling between, above and below. The fittings are brass, and the windows are raised and lowered by thick, heavy leather straps which have holes that can be buttoned over brass nipples.

I see a girl, tall and thin, with large bony hands and large feet, with close-cropped black hair, wearing a dark grey chemise, damp and stained about the neck, above a full black skirt. The top part of her back is leaning against the wood panelled space between two compartments, her feet which are shod in un-blanco-ed tennis shoes, no socks, are thrust forward, her head and shoulders hunched over above them. Behind her cupped right hand she is surreptitiously smoking a cigarette, black Canary tobacco. A black, jet-beaded purse dangles from her left wrist. It is empty apart from the cigarettes and matches. Seven or eight other passengers are in the corridor, migrants from the third class, waiting to be shooed back into the sardine cans they have left by a railway guard who is armed. Knowing they have no right to be where they are they ignore the girl and she ignores them.

Outside the interminable cliché of the interminable Spanish meseta rolls by beneath a sky that is not quite dark. Indeed, as s/he watches, the last sliver of a water-melon sun sinks below a distant low escarpment and the clouds of black smoke, belched from the smoke-stack ahead to spew across the campo merge with the white smoke rising in fog-banks above the streaks of red flame where labourers are still burning off the stubble.

Three hours later s/he is there again, for the grown-ups talk and talk and talk in their compartment and though it can be converted into a sleeping chamber with four couchettes, the offer of the conductor to do so has been refused, twice. Mother and the Poet gossip on. So bored and weary, s/he is out here again for her third cigarette.

The throb and racket of steel wheels on steel rails slowly drops in beat and tone, and finally even in volume, and at last comes to juddering rest. Outside a small signal box, yellow stucco framed in grey cornerstones carries the name of the station they are approaching but have not quite reached: MANZANARES. *Manzana*: apple. Town of apples. Name of a river too, Madrid's river. But it means more than that. This, s/he remembers, is the small town where Lorca's great friend, the torero Ignacio Sanchez was fatally gored not quite two years ago, inspiring the Lament which, long though it is, he knows by heart and now recites to himself.

At five in the afternoon, at exactly five in the afternoon a boy brought the white sheet at five in the afternoon. A basket of lime was already bespoken, what followed was death, just death. At five in the afternoon.

He could hear the engine wheezing and clanking in front, like an

iron bull panting, hauling in air over its grey swollen tongue, still trying
to shake free from its withers the papered darts that torment it. He
hauled on the leather strap, unbuttoning it, and let the window drop.
The air outside was cooler than the air inside but heavy with the deep
odour of coal and hot metal.

When the sweat streaked the bull like snow, when the bull-ring was
covered with iodine, at five in the afternoon, then death deposited eggs
in the wound, at five, five in the afternoon, precisely at five.

Something sets them off: a sudden storm of frogs croaking in a
nearby marsh, and then the crickets roar too.

The door by his elbow drags open, he drops his cigarette and tries to
cover it with his tennis shoe, but it is the Poet, not his Mother.

'Where are we? Why have we stopped?'

Proud that he can provide the answers to both questions, knows
things this most charismatic (apart from his Mother) of adults does not
know, he speaks with elaborately nonchalant ease.

'In a siding, taking on water, and waiting for the express from
Seville to come through. We are just outside Manzanares.'

'Manzanares.' The Poet pushes his hand across his forehead and the
widow's peak of his hair-line, and sighs. He steps to the half-open
window and places his elbows on the ledge.

'But now his sleep has no end. Now the moss and the grass open
with sure fingers the flower of his skull. And his blood comes singing,
singing through marshes and meadows, sliding along unfeeling horns.
Soulless, its way lost in the mist, it stumbles into thousands of hoofs
like a long dark sad tongue beside the Guadalquivir of the stars.'

'Now the mosses and the grass… Not *the moss.*'

'Really?' The Poet turns, leans his back against the door, the
window. 'The mosses? The moss?' He smiles. 'Yes, you are right.'

'I know I am. I learned it by heart.'

'Well, that was a task I did not feel I had to undertake. It was
enough to write it. But why *the mosses*, and not *the grasses*?'

'Too many 's' sounds? And perhaps you were thinking of the
different types of mosses, and that interested you, while the fact that
there are different types of grass did not.'

'Of course.'

The Poet pulls a cigarette packet from his jacket pocket, pushes up
the inner casing, offers it. The girl/boy hesitates, throws a swift glance
at the compartment door. The Poet smiles.

'She is getting ready for bed.'

The girl/boy takes one and the Poet lights it for him, with a tiny gold
lighter, and then lights his own. The boy gags on the smoke which is
acrid and harsh, American, an instant sore throat.

When he has recovered, he finds the Poet's smile is now, through the blue smoke, a touch devilish.

'She knows, you know.'

'Knows what?'

'That you smoke.'

'She does?'

'There are two things no man can hide, and you are almost a man. Love and smoking. You are in love and you smoke.' He sighs. 'One of them will kill you, but which first?'

A distant train whistle, a banshee in the faraway night. Disconcerted, the almost fourteen-year-old boy reasserts adult equality.

'That will be the express from Seville. Soon we will be moving again.'

'Yes.' The older man draws on his cigarette, then removes it from his mouth with his left hand. His right reaches out, strokes then cradles the boy/man's cheek.

'Soon… you will have to shave.'

A huge deep sigh, drowned in a shudder.

The metal roar rushes closer, and The Poet just manages to hoist the window in time. Nevertheless, the pandemonium of the passing train rocks their carriage and its sulphurous heavy breath fills the narrow corridor they share.

VII *Blame Hitler*

I used to think that, going backwards, history began in 1900, or say 1902 with the death of Queen Victoria. Later I was ready to move the date forward to 1918 or anyway the October Revolution in 1917. But now my daughter, who is eighteen and will shortly go to university to read history, tells me that the day before yesterday is about right. So while I still feel a touch uncomfortable about accepting events that occurred well within my lifetime as history I take it that most readers won't be bothered.

My father volunteered for the RAF in 1940 at the age of forty. Since this made him too old to fly or do combat duty I believe he had no expectation of anything more exciting than a desk-job in Blighty. However, after some preliminary training he was made adjutant of a mobile radar station initially based in Egypt, and therefore the officer in charge of the men's welfare, emotional as well as physical, and their entertainment. To begin with the experience exhilarated him. It ended badly.

I tell the story in Blame Hitler. *I have called myself Thomas Somers and my father Christopher Somers. Anything that purports to be written by him, was written by him. On his return from the East in September 1943 he was made adjutant of a large air-base near Melton Mowbray and that's where these selections start. I was eight years old then but I am recounting the story to myself in 1994 while on holiday in Biarritz, staying in a friend's house, and suffering from an unspecified but alarming bowel complaint.*

D ad had a huge Smith and Wesson revolver kept in an RAF pale blue webbing holster. He also had lots of bullets for it. He kept the bullets separate from the revolver, though one night he and mother had a terrible row and Dad tried to shoot himself with it. Thomas heard the row but did not know that the gun had been out and loaded. It was only after Dad died that mother told him about it. Died? Was killed. Killed himself. In effect he really did will the kill, if not actually killed himself, fifteen years later.

Anyway, Thomas loved that gun. It was heavy and solid and smelt of fine oil and when you pulled the trigger (almost too stiff for an eight year-old) the chamber went round and the hammer, which had a pin-head on the end of a curved beak, came back and then click! and it slammed forward. Thomas used to put Swan Vestas matches in the groove which the hammer entered on its way to where the base of the chambered round would be, and the match would flare and fill the air with sulphur. Was that happy? Certainly it was fun.

It was fun too on the rare occasions when Dad took him up to the airfield, especially the day they let him sit in the cockpit of a Mosquito. He would have liked it to be a Spitfire, but Dad explained how the Mosquito was just as good an aeroplane in its own way, had cannon like the Spitfire but could carry small bombs too and go almost as fast.

Thomas rolled on to his back. The woman had stopped washing her balcony and a slight haze of rain was curtaining in the space that separated Moni's shoe-box block from the next one. He thought of them all on the beach. Perhaps they'd be back early because of the rain. He turned back from the window, went back to Melton Mowbray and a sky filled with the thunderous roar of Flying Fortresses. He remembered a summer's day, early summer perhaps, a cricket field, a cricket match. Dad a flannelled fool, slow off-spin, occasionally with a chinaman or a googly thrown in. Which? What was the difference? Thomas had no idea then, and had no idea now, but he remembered he enjoyed the camaraderie of the men, the way they treated Dad, well, each other really, with a sort of mutual respect. They called Dad 'Pop'. Which meant Dad. Why did they do that? He was Thomas's Dad, not theirs. For the rest of his life the family called Dad 'Pop'. Thomas never did.

When she was washing-up Mrs Warner always insisted on leaving saucepans to the end on the principle that God might call her away to higher things before she got to them. Also she often left them to soak and for years after all of them, that is Dad, Mum, and Thomas would say when faced with a particularly recalcitrant saucepan: 'Give it a Warner'. Of course in those days detergents, washing-up liquid, plastic scourers and so on were uninvented, and metal scourers were not available because – there's a war on, you know? Vim was around, or perhaps came back. It was at Melton Mowbray that Thomas had a banana again. He'd forgotten what bananas were like. It was like your first ejaculation – the pleasure such an enormous surprise. Subsequent bananas were just as good, but never again would there be that shock of delight.

All of which was displacement activity, if lying in bed trawling your memory can be described as activity. Dodging the issue, the one memory of Melton Mowbray that troubled.

His mother took him to the pictures. They walked there, hand in hand. She was wearing white gloves. Women wore gloves a lot in those days. They were not going to the pictures to see what they often jokingly referred to as a flim because that's what his half-sister had called them when she was five. They were going to see the newsreels, because Mummy thought they ought to.

What they saw was the opening of the camps.

A learning experience. Thorough too. It lasted, in memory at any rate, all of an hour. All the images which are now as much part of the baggage our minds carry with us as, say, the Dome of St Paul's, were there – unheralded, unmediated. New. The piles of white bodies, skeletons with skin on; the survivors like ghosts with hollow eyes; the guards forced by the British and Americans to load the bodies into the backs of lorries; the huge grave, with the bodies tumbled in anyhow. The plummy commentator, original Mr Voice-Over Man, explaining how many of the survivors had been killed by the liberators who gave them food straightaway, food their stomachs could no longer cope with… and so on, and so on. Not believing she could have wittingly inflicted this on him, Thomas turned and looked up at his mother's face, flickering in the light reflected from the screen. She sat up very straight, chin up, and tears were tumbling down her face. Aware he was looking at her she took his hand in her white gloves and held it in her lap.

Thomas in Biarritz did not think he had been harmed by the experience. Scarred, yes. He knew from then on what fascism is, and why his Dad had had to go off and fight it. He knew because that is what his Mum told him when they came out of the cinema. It was knowledge that he built on for the rest of his life. It underpinned many things he would later become and believe – attitudes that by now, almost sixty years old, had hardened into atheism and hatred of all power structures.

That summer, before they caught the boat to Caen, they had gone to see *Schindler's List*. Well, Katherine and Richard had. It was a multi-screen cinema, so while they saw *Schindler's List,* Thomas and Hannah-Rosa went to *Sister Act 2*. He reckoned seeing the real thing when he was ten was enough, and besides Hannah-Rosa was way under age. Richard too, but only by five months.

There was another difference. Back in 1945, in the newsreel, there was no mention of the word 'holocaust', nor, Thomas was pretty sure, of the word 'Jew'. Just that these were ordinary people the Nazis had taken against for no good reason. This still seemed right to Thomas. To him the point was not who these poor people were, but what had happened to them. Later he found it repugnant the way people and particularly Jews referred to the holocaust as an event that had been suffered solely by Jews. Sometimes repugnance became resentment – he felt the holocaust had been hijacked.

On the way back to Mrs Warner's digs Thomas and his Mum passed a large dead dog lying in the road in a large pool of blood. Its body had been crushed by a lorry. She pulled him in into her side, and covered his eyes with her hand in its cotton white glove.

'Don't look,' she said.

The worst time poor Christopher Richard Somers had was on the retreat from Benghazi. Though it was years after the event before Thomas found out just how bad.

His mother had not kept any of the letters his Dad sent her from the Middle East and Ceylon and only one survived. However, he did have a score or more that Christopher had sent to his mother and sisters

(Thomas's granny and aunts), and a diary he had kept on official Signal Office Diary paper from 22 December 1940 to 8 August 1941.

Pilot Officer, later Flying Officer and finally Flight Lieutenant Christopher Richard Somers had been adjutant of a mobile radar station, a unit with two officers and fifty men. As adjutant his particular duty was to look after the men's needs as best as he was able. And, from the letters, it was obvious that he was very able and his best was, as he would have said, a damn good one. Before the retreat from Benghazi there was the advance to it.

P/O C R Somers
216 M R U
8/1/41 C/0 A.P.0. 590

Dear Ma & Family
At last a little time to write a proper letter. Within the limits of censorship regulations, I'll try to give you some idea of life out here.
First of all, for me, as far as the work and conditions are concerned, this is the happiest time of my life. The roughing it is just enough to make you feel you're doing your share, and just enough to be called hardship. And the work is just what I love: I do all the 'administering' and organising; getting rations, sanitation, camouflage, defence, welfare of men etc: (It was still sound othographic practice in those days to mark an abbreviation with a colon.)
For about 3 weeks after landing we simply made preparations and sorted out equipment. Then a long journey with a convoy of vehicles: a few days round about Christmas at a desert station, and then several days' more journey, pitching camp each night at about 4 o'clock and getting off next morning by about 10. On January 2nd we reached our site, and I only hope we stay here. We are quite on our own, living under canvas, and it's pleasantly warm in the day but very cold at night. At night I wear winter under-clothes (that meant woollen vests to his knees and woollen long-johns – what you wore in winter in the north of England with no central heating), pyjamas (flannelette), a pull-over, & sleep on a camp bed with four thicknesses of blanket & a greatcoat all tied up with the covering of my valise! In the day-time khaki shorts and a shirt.
Water is generally a bit short, and as a rule we can only allow one gallon per day per man for all purposes: but we manage quite well & I can arrange a 'laundry' day about once a fortnight. At present we are getting no bread or vegetables, but the cooks and I have invented a large variety of ways of dealing with bully beef and hard biscuits. Anyhow I'm trying to arrange a trip of fifty miles twice a week to a

place (Sidi Barrani – seventy or so miles from the frontier between Libya and Egypt) *where we hope to get 'soft' rations.*

On our very first day here (the diary identifies the Halfaya Pass, twenty miles from the frontier) *we had to put up a Group Captain and a Squadron Leader (= Colonel and Major in Army) for a couple of nights. The other officer & I slept in a dug-out & gave them our tent: they seemed to be quite pleased with everything, thanked us for the good food they had had, and left us both a bottle of whisky!*

The men are marvellous. Three of them are from Liverpool – one a reception clerk at the Adelphi. The way they settle down & start making the place habitable and comfortable, with a little encouragement, is lovely. Now that we have all our essentials well organised, they spend their spare time making little paths round the camp & sticking up notices. I only hope we don't get orders to move from here, as we're all beginning to look on this place as our 'home'.

There isn't really much more I can say. I was hit by a bullet 2 days ago! Some damn fool engineer started firing an Italian rifle, and as I leapt out of my tent to shout to them to stop, a bullet ricocheted (don't know how to spell it) off a rock and grazed my throat. It didn't hurt but I managed to swear at them for about ten minutes without repeating myself once. Our only other casualty was caused by one of our men picking up an Italian hand grenade in disobedience to orders. He blew his hand to bits, poor brute. I hate to see a man have his whole life ruined for one damn silly mistake: and it was the result of the one bad bit of discipline we've had the whole time.

I hope you're all right at home. I'll be glad when letters start arriving. Being cut off like this is the only snag in the life out here. In all other respects it's a damned good life. I hear it's pretty cold in England. Has Wilf: got his commission? Tell him that if not I'll expect him to pull out the hell of a salute when he meets me. (Wilf was his brother, ten years younger.)

The Group Captain has just been along and told us where there is a canteen: so I'm going to lay in a stock of beer, chocolate, tooth-paste, soap etc: and start a canteen of our own in the camp. Profits will go to our 'Comfort Fund', and we're hoping to get a wireless set. At present we depend largely on rumours for any news.

Love to all,

Christopher

Life is likely to go on much as usual until we move from here, so I won't write often. There will be nothing to say.

The diary entry for the same day reads:

Better rations this morning: potatoes, onions & tinned sausages.
Sent Martinson to 2/7th Australian Field Ambulance with otitis media (Inflammation of the middle ear, something Pop knew about all too well). *Strength now 43 O.Rs.* (other ranks)
Found Naafi & opened credit a/c.
Some bombing during the night, but nothing very serious.

The radar station travelled in lorries and cars from Mersa Matruh via Tobruk to Benghazi in the successful campaign against the Italians and then back again rather more quickly, with Rommel and the Afrika Corps up their arses. Through it all Pilot Officer Christopher Richard Somers made sure the rations and water got through, that the accounts were kept, that petrol and paraffin were available, that the men's health was looked after properly, even that they washed their clothes (dhobi duty) when water was available, every thing you could think of. He organised entertainments, quizzes, whist drives, censored their letters, sorted out their emotional problems... and all this through sand-storms, periods from Benghazi onwards when they were bombed and machine-gunned from the air, while all the time the lorries and cars broke down or got bogged in the sand. He was a father to those men and he loved it when they accepted him in turn, even though he was a toff (they called him Toffer, short for Christopher, but toff as well. Later they acknowledged how well he looked after them by calling him Pop), and even though the other officers rather disapproved or envied his easy bonhomie. Much as, two decades later, Thomas was proud of the rapport he had with deprived inner city kids, a rapport that proved elusive to his more experienced colleagues. It was, he later realised, a belief not universally held, though every Somers he had ever known held it, that all youmens are worthy of precisely the same, that is total, respect.

Unit 216, mobile radar unit, based at the top of the Halfaya Pass near the Egyptian/Libyan border remained relatively inactive for the first three weeks of 1941 while the army under Auchinleck pushed the Italians back to Tobruk and then further west towards Benghazi.

23/1/41
2 teeth out at Bandia and had boil on my bottom lanced (all without anaesthetic). *Returning found that immediate move to T: likely. Got ahead with arrangements for move.*
24/1/41

Indications now are that move to Tobruk will be delayed.
PM. Took party for bathe and got 96 bottles of beer.
25/1/41
Received orders to move up to Tobruk tomorrow. Men worked well and preparations well forward by evening.
26/1/41 From Halfaya pass to 80 km E of Tobruk.
Convoy moved off at 1100 hours. Considerable delay at FSD (Forward Supply Depot) as rations, ordered yesterday, not ready. Further delay at Capuzzo where we got more water. PM. Splendid progress: better roads than further East: went straight on until 16.15. Total mileage about 45.
Leaves broken in Stamp's lorry & defect in brake drum of water trailer.
28/1/41 Fort Acroma
E and I again went ahead in clear weather & found the site without difficulty. We decided to use Fort Acroma as billets although it is 1¼ miles from the site. The billets are filthy but can be made satisfactory.
Cook's in a bad flap. Otherwise things going well.
29/1/41
Billets now v: g:. Spent AM making clearly marked road between billets and site. Two men in small tank turned up. They had spent 8 days on 2 days' rations, but were cheerful and optimistic.
PM. Went into Tobruk (25 miles) in Humber with Cpl Waite & Humphries. Nothing yet organised, but managed to scrounge some rations – including lemons and Vichy water…

The first two weeks at this new site went well enough, but then things began to go wrong. There were serious difficulties over fresh supplies and there were frequent sand-storms…

7/2/41
Men cleaned billets etc: of sand. Wind still high but no sand blowing.
Food situation now really bad. No bread, no potatoes, no oatmeal, no jam & only one tin of cheese, no bacon, sausages or beans. Sugar getting very low. But we have stacks of tea & the water supply has been good.
8/2/41
Returned from technical job & found Edgley had run over an Italian landmine 7 miles away. He was stone deaf, badly shaken & exhausted. Took him to hospital in Tobruk.
Rain fell heavily PM.

The next week was grim. Lorries broke down, telephone communication broke down, the technical side failed to work possibly as a result of storm damage and possibly because the absent Edgley was the officer in charge of it. But meanwhile Benghazi fell – the final achievement of what had been a startlingly successful campaign, overshadowed by the terrible retreat and then by the even more successful campaign that started at El Alamein.

15/2/41
I was just setting out with ration party at 0730 when a signal arrived ordering immediate move to Benghazi…

In spite of the usual mechanical failures with the lorries, and having to be re-routed when it was discovered a bridge had been blown up, it took them only three days to get the three hundred miles from Tobruk to their next site near Benghazi. And they found time to have a bathe at Derma – a place and experience so beautiful Pop talked about it many times in the years after. They were now well into Cyrenaica, the ex-Roman province expropriated by Mussolini and colonised by Italians during the previous decade or so. Orchards flourished, the roads were good, there were new comfortable buildings…

19/2/41
Perfect site from domestic point of view. Large, clean ex Road House with beautiful gardens and useful outbuildings. Said to have been favourite haunt of Graziani (who was, I believe, the marshal or whatever leading the Italian army they had just defeated – or maybe the one who conquered Libya in the first place).
21/2/41
Most successful day – except that Carter had to be taken to hospital – probably appendicitis.
Found ration depot, Australian unit for drilling picket holes (I think there's a joke here – against Australians – but blest if I know how it works) – & remarkable opportunities for scrounging.
PM. Drew rations including bread and vegetables and won about 100 bottles of chianti, 2 cases of milk and one of fruit: also quantities of jam & marmalade.
Meanwhile men blacked out airmen's mess & cleaned place up.
Good progress technically.
11/3/41
Fairly heavy raids in evening & night. Unit congratulated on work.

This is the beginning of Rommel's offensive, which drove the Allies back into Egypt though clearly Dad had no idea of what was about to happen. The euphoria was sustained right up to the nineteenth when he wrote this letter to his sister Olive – the one married to the Liverpool haemorrhoid specialist.

19.3.41 P/O C. R. Somers
216 M.R.U.
A.P.O. 590

Dear Olive
Many thanks for parcel posted Dec: 8th. You asked what we needed most. It is: News from home, Reading matter, Chocolate, Darts. Old Penguins would be much appreciated by the men.
  I've been writing letters to 'Family' so I hope you've had a few of them. In case not, I'll say that for several weeks we were in the desert, living in tents, generally miles from anywhere: toughish sort of conditions, but not too hard except during sandstorms, and for one short period when the only water obtainable had been salted by the Italians. Now we are in fertile country again & billeted in a large building: however I've got used to being out of doors & don't like sleeping in a house, so I've fitted up a box lorry with a good bed ('won' from an empty hotel), table & chair & telephone & use it as a bed-sitting-Orderly Room. Very pleasant. It's lovely to have a real bed after months of a camp species.
  Also it's marvellous to see trees & and even a little grass after nothing but sand and stone. Trees here are chiefly palms, oranges & lemons. The orange trees are in blossom & and the lemons are ripe. There is also lots of cactus and mimosa & that beautiful purple stuff that you've probably seen in the S of France (Bougainvillea? Jacaranda?).
  The natives remind you of pictures of Biblical times & have probably remained at about the same stage of development. We buy eggs off them and I can count up to 20 in Arabic now which makes it easier than it used to be at first. I run a canteen for the men, selling everything at 10 per cent profit: then spend the profit on buying extras like eggs to add to the normal rations.
  Rations, by the way, are quite good here. For weeks & weeks we had no bread, no potatoes or vegetables, no fresh meat & and no fruit either fresh or tinned. Now we get all these things. The men were amazingly good during our harder times, held sing-songs in the Mess Tent etc: & were always quite cheerful. They're a good crowd. By the way we have a piano and an excellent wireless set. The piano was rather funny. When we first arrived here things weren't organised & the

ration arrived back with all sorts of things they had scrounged. I went out to them and said jokingly, What! No piano! And they said, Yes sir, we can get one if you'll sign a chit for it, & we thought, sir, if you'll let us take one of the big lorries, we'd get it straight away.

A few nights ago we had a Unit Concert & asked officers and men from other units. It was really very good & included Exhibition Waltz by Sgt Stephenson & AC Ross (!) (The exclamation mark because the name and rank are the same as the ones adopted by Lawrence of Arabia when he joined the RFC after WWI), *tap-dancing by a youth from Croxteth Road, the usual songs and dirty jokes etc: and free beer (from last month's Canteen profits)…*

Thomas remembered snatches of them that he had heard his father sing: *Oh what a pity, she's only one titty to feed the baby on, Poor little bugger he'll never play rugger, he's not sufficiently strong, dadadadaaah, dadadadaah, He's the Queen of the Fairies* and a routine that began *And you Corporal Smith will carry the drum. Not me, Sir, I'm in the family way. You're in everyone's way, you Smith will carry the drum…* and so on.

…I've been quite fit out here, except that my teeth started to go on the hard biscuits and I've had 3 out – and a boil on my bottom. We've had bombs near us on a few occasions: I don't mind them as much as I thought I would, but have a couple of seconds of intense fear when I hear the whistle of them coming down. However that hasn't happened often.

I like the life here. I think it's what I always wanted to do, but we feel very cut off from home & and all hope it won't last too long. I think that if the war's over in about a year I shall be damn glad I did this: but if it's much longer than that I get very home-sick and Decima-sick. If only Dess could come & live in Cairo or Alex: & I could get a week's leave occasionally it would be grand! Certainly as far as work's concerned, I like this better than any job I've had except perhaps for my 2 years as headmaster in Liverpool.

Love to all of you
Christopher

Please send this on to Ma.

21-23/3/41
Conflicting orders over possible move to Escarpment. Eventually move postponed, but all domestic equipment packed and ready.
1/4/41

A few bombs. S/L Barclay asked if everything ready for immediate move. General flap increasing.

2/4/41

Hostile plane intercepted and almost certainly shot down. Unit congratulated.

3 & 4/4/41

0830. Received orders to move at once. Good progress with packing & all ready by 1230.

*Made towards Benghazi aiming to strike main B – Barce road but within a few minutes of our start dumps of It: ammo began to be blown up by the road. Flames and shrapnel across road, terrific explosions. Commer (15cwt van) hit twice. Managed to turn vehicles round & then made for escarpment via Benina. – Further destruction there, but no danger to us (*The pencil P/O Somers normally wrote in is crossed out here. Above the deletion he wrote in the fountain pen ink used in some later entries.) *Although we had been warned not to take this road as it had been mined.* The entry continues in pencil. *Expected to find considerable defences on top of escarpment, but found place deserted. Reached Barce 1830 & told by G/C Brown push on. Refuelled beyond Barce and had late meal. I suggested driving on till moonset & parking at cross-roads,* (underlined words bracketed in ink) *but E decided to go on through the night. All well for 100 miles, then the Commer ditched and turned over. While we were waiting on pass down to Derma lorry of another unit let 2 wheels over dip opposite one of our vehicles. Bowman's lorry sent down hill to turn: when opposite ditched vehicle had head-on collision with yet another vehicle coming down with no lights & apparently out of control. B's lorry now U/S. Consequently left* (written over in ink with: had to leave) *much camp equipment behind...*

And so it went on as they got themselves back through, behind, and occasionally in front of a retreating army, right back to Halfaya Pass where it seemed they might stop and begin to operate again as a radar station from the same spot they had left six weeks earlier. On the way tow-bars broke, were repaired, broke again. The men got dysentery. All Edgley (E) could think of was saving the radar masts. The men were Pop's responsibility.

8/4/41

Situation now as follows: Men have little but what they stand up in: Commer and one Crossley (destroyed) in enemy hands: one mast trailer cannot be moved: Ford U/S.

By the thirteenth they were right back in Mersa Matruh well inside Egypt and there at last the retreat halted – mainly because Rommel had extended his supply lines far too far and had to wait for supplies and support to catch up. On the way they lost more vehicles and equipment, but not men. And at one time they had to drive through detonating petrol dumps. It was either during this last phase, or the earlier one outside Benghazi when the ammunition dumps were being blown up, that it happened. Probably it was outside Benghazi – however, the diary was re-written for the later part: the pencil entries are very scant but are supplemented by ink entries obviously filled in after the event. This possibly suggests the horror occurred in the last stages.

During the two years after his Father was killed Thomas's Mother sold the Wroxham Way bungalow and bought one very similar close to the Bay Estate. It was there, in October 1962, that Thomas had his first opportunity to spend a few days with her on their own. The reason for the gap was that he had been teaching English in Ankara University, Turkey.

They spent the evenings in what she called the front room, and what the estate agents called a lounge-diner, drinking g and ts after a supper of poached egg on toast.

Most of the furniture was not what had been bought for Wroxham Way – she had thrown all that out apart from one armchair and one small sofa. The rest was all from Aunt Helen's including a grandmother clock made in Scarboro by an Italian called Vasalli, a walnut veneer wall-table which could be pulled apart and the top folded out to make a square green-baized card-table, a gate-leg table and an elegant rocking chair.

The card-table was what she called a boon. The Widows who came to play bridge with her were all enormously more wealthy than she was, but none had a card-table to match it. Nor did they have Real Old Willow Pattern, in that inimitable blue with the gold leaf rims, a set still complete enough to lay on a Bridge tea for four without showing a chip. Several of Aunt Helen's ornaments had resurfaced too. Thomas wondered about this. Mum had resented not being able to furnish Seventy-One with stuff of her own, but now seemed content to use some of the leftovers, though really she didn't have to. Was it because she now had title to them? That they were of a quality that would impress the Widows? Or had they after all, over the years, become not only familiar but actually liked?

There was a small coal-fire set in grey glazed tiles. Another decade had to pass before fitted carpets and modern genteely designed gas-fires came in.

Thomas sat in the rocking-chair and occasionally rocked. His Mother sat opposite him, with the low gate-leg table between and to the side of them, the anthracite glowing hot in the small grate. On the table there was an ashtray, small, silver, inscribed:

To
C. R. Somers
Master at
Sutton Court School
1947-1954
From all the Boys

...which she had to empty into the solid basket-work waste-paper basket at her elbow about once every half hour. Instead of Weights she now smoked tipped Senior Service through a short silver and amber holder he had bought for her in Turkey. He smoked Camel – the only cigarettes readily available in England at the time which had some Turkish tobacco in them. She used a tiny chrome lighter, he a Zippo. They drank very strong g and ts without lemon or ice out of cut-crystal whisky glasses which she must have bought herself. And why not?

'No point,' she said, reaching for the Gordon's, 'if you can't taste the gin.'

Her hair was stylishly permed with a hint of blue rinse. As ever she smelled of Côty's L'Aimant. She was wearing a mottled green and brown pleated Crimplene dress, and a necklace of silver and silver gilt filigree flowers. Delicate, perfectly proportioned so as to be noticeable not showy, it was lovely. Pop had bought it in Jerusalem, the major city of what had been a Turkish colony called Palestine, inhabited by Arabs, and was then a British protectorate.

And, Thomas remembers, as he briefly opens his eyes, just before Alzheimer's got a serious hold on her, she freely and unprompted gave the necklace to Katherine. It was a gesture of sublime magnanimity, incredible. It was without doubt her most treasured single possession. It was perhaps a gift to her son who, obviously, would never wear it himself, but when Katherine wore it he would look at it. It also demonstrated faith: Thomas had cocked up before. With Katherine, Decima realised, he quite probably would not cock up again and the necklace would remain in the family. There was another dimension too. Through the twenty-three years or so Thomas and Katherine had lived together he had tried again and again to give her gifts as precious, as good (forget commodity exchange – this necklace we're talking about has no serious monetary worth at all) but had never found anything as lovely. So there you go. The best object signifying love your partner has was given by your father to your mother who gave it to your partner. Something to be celebrated.

'There are things, I should tell you about your poor Dad...'
'Oh? Yes?' Wary now of possible embarrassment, he lit another Camel. Really, his Mum was, he thought, in pretty good nick. Probably more in charge of her own destiny than she had ever been. Sixty-four years old, left tolerably well off with half the income from Dad's share of Grandad's estate (the other half going to the execrable April), she still worked for twenty hours a week in Bob Murfett's Pagham branch office and she was having a whale of a time planning a decent bit of garden the way she wanted it. A Romneya and a purple small-flowering hardy hibiscus, a hedge of mallow and a bay tree in the front, some good shrubs and trees including a eucalyptus at the back, a hedge of roses, and a vegetable patch behind it. All of course immature as yet, but ready to flourish in their own good time. Sixteen years yet for her to enjoy it before the Alzheimer's set in.
'Like what?'
'He was sexually very repressed.'
And you weren't? Already his toes were curling, his scrotum contracting, but if this was something she wanted to talk about, so be it.
'When we first began to sleep together he was terribly nervous. He came out in a sort of nervous eczema. Like measles.'
Psoriasis, I bet, murmured Thomas to himself, thirty plus years later.
'But he got over it. Often it was very, very good for him. He said so.'
She smiled, a touch grimly, not at Thomas, but at the cigarette holder as she used her thumb-nail to lever the Senior Service filter out of it and insert another. He wanted to ask her: And how was it for you?
He should have asked her. He'd never know now. At the time the implication he had received was that she had done her duty and made her bloke a happy man, all that people of her sex, class and age were meant to do, but perhaps that was quite wrong. Maybe she'd had a ball. But he couldn't, couldn't ask her. In 1962 you'd only just begun to talk openly about sex, and then not with much knowledge and certainly with no wisdom, to one's partner. But not with one's parents. And certainly not about *their* sex lives.
She looked up, eyes expressionless behind her new bi-focals.
'Earth moved and all that, you know?'
For Whom the Bell Tolls had meant as much to her generation as *Lady Chatterley's Lover* had to his.
He recalled his father at prize-giving during those two years he had been head-master of his own school and the photograph there was of

him doing it. Lean, yes, but robust in a way he never had been later, and confident too, even saturnine. The point was that at thirty-eight he had been his own boss, had sired a son on a woman reputed to be sterile and the earth moved... quite often.

'But he'd lost it when he came back.'

'Oh?!'

'He was a mess.'

'Really?'

'I don't mean just in bed.'

Thomas then, back in 1962, recalled the rows heard through thin walls during the hols, the despair. How, almost as soon as they were in Seventy-One they had slept in separate bedrooms. Why? Daddy snores was the answer given.

'Three times he threatened to shoot himself. Once he threatened to shoot me. He got very drunk you see. And then, far later than I should have done, I got him to tell me all about it. You see... I thought he'd had an affair with someone, I don't know, a tea-planter's wife or sister in Ceylon. A nurse in the hospital he spent three months in in Gaza.' She giggled a little. 'You know, he wrote to his family that he was eyeless somewhere and at the mill with slaves. The censorship wouldn't let him say the real name. They were worried out of their minds, thought he had been blinded and was in some frightful concentration camp. Of course I could tell them he meant Gaza. Milton.'

She smiled with satisfaction at the memory. They'd always looked down on her – but she knew her English Literature better than they did.

'Anyway, that's what I thought was the trouble. He had a mistress somewhere he wanted to go off with or back to, and she was in bed with us every time he tried to... Another little drop, eh? Dead Man. There's another in the cupboard.'

Thomas did the honours.

'Where was I? Yes. So eventually, not till after we had been at Seventy-One a year, I got it out of him. What the matter was.'

'And?'

She shifted a little, spread her knees, angled herself towards the fire, and talked to it rather than to him.

'The retreat from Benghazi. He never expected to be in that sort of business. He was forty when he joined up. Yes, he'd volunteered for overseas – we needed the money and you got extra. But he thought that even abroad he'd only have a desk to fly. Anyway he was adjutant to this radar convoy, looking after the men, and they had to get out quick. Convoy of lorries and he was in the one in front. And they started blowing up all the ammunition dumps and the petrol dumps just as they were going past them, and they were being bombed at the same time. The lorry he was in was hit twice with shrapnel, and the second time... he was sitting beside the driver, you see?'

'Yes...'

'And either from a bomb or the explosions all around them the driver got hit. In the head. Badly. Fell forward over the wheel, couldn't steer... Or drive at all. And all these explosions going on all round them...'

She looked up at him, now almost over her shoulder she was so hunched forward, took a drag on her amber holder. Then she turned back to the fire, looked into the glowing coals.

'He, the driver, was bleeding terribly, the side of his face and head caved in. Imagine. Poor Pop. He didn't know what to do. The men at the back were shouting, screaming at him to get a move on. Several bombs fell straddling the road in front. Blocking it. The next ones... He leant across the driver, opened the door, and pushed him out. Then he took his place and turned the lorry round, in a tight circle, and the ones behind followed him. They said later he'd run over the driver...'

'Later?'

'There was an enquiry. Most of the men believed he'd saved their lives but two or three of them were friends of the driver and said he probably wasn't dead. They said Pop could have pulled him into the passenger seat then gone round and got into the driver's seat from the outside. They said Pop was frightened and had done it all to save himself. The enquiry found for him, said he'd done the right thing. The important thing after they had been hit twice was to get out as quickly as possible. And that's what he did. He saved the rest of the unit and the driver was to die soon if he wasn't already dead. But Pop *was* frightened, terrified. Even so he did actually try to pull the man along the bench seat, but he was all tangled up with the steering wheel and the gears and his feet with the pedals, so he gave up and leant over and got the door open and pushed. But he could never be sure that the decision was not made to save his own life as well as, or even rather than, those of the men he was meant to look after. That's what ruined him. That doubt.'

She leant forward, picked up a small poker and gave the coals a rattle they did not need. Sparks flew upwards.

'All that time he couldn't tell me about it, just the horrible nightmares he had, waking up in a sweat and drinking, and wanting to kill himself. He should never have been there. It... stained the rest of his life.'

Blame Hitler.

Blame fucking... no, he didn't do a lot of that from all accounts, just Hitler. Blame Hitler.

VIII History, Pre- and Post-

That's enough history for now, though even without mining the history novels I could probably fill a book with history bits from the rest. Like I said: you can't do real without including the history. So let's finish with a spot of really ancient history, or pre-history, and then the future, both from the same book – Trajectories. I wanted to call it Tragictories, and I think I was right.

Since I first came across it back in the late sixties I have been completely captivated by the Aquatic Ape Hypothesis and the books its chief partisan Elaine Morgan has written. I'll resist the temptation to ride this particular hobby-horse right now except to say that the arguments for supposing that we went through an aquatic phase somewhere in the Horn of Africa and the Rift Valley are, taken together, insurmountable and the failure of the establishment of Evolutionists to even give it the time of day is an execrable example of entrenched academia refusing, as it usually does, to admit it has been stupid.

Trajectories takes place, for the most part in 2035, and involves the same characters, suitably aged or dead, as Blame Hitler. This extract purports to be part of a scenario about the Aquatic Ape Theory that Thomas is supposed to have written three decades earlier.

Tragictories

And now, growing from insubstantial ghosts into real presences, first manifested to us by their multifarious chatter, mammalian, primate, almost human, we become aware of creatures who lounge, play, sleep, and squabble along and among the lower branches of the spreading tree.

At first it seems there are two species involved – one much larger than the other, at five feet nearly twice the size of the smaller ones. But their physiques are very similar. The larger ones are male, the smaller female.

They have hairy heads, the hair quite long, and shaggy round their genitals. The rest of their bodies is covered with a fine, short, but patchy pelt, streaked in some cases with sweat. The bigger adults are males, the smaller female. At first sight we forgive ourselves for taking them for apes, or even monkeys. They have long arms and short splayed legs, long hands and feet, with long phalanges or curved toes and fingers. Their chests are pear-shaped, conical, and they have pot-bellies. And, in so far as they are active at all, for it is early afternoon and the hottest part of the day and most are inactive, even somnolent, they are behaving like arboreal apes.

Those who want to move about the big tree do so by swinging from their hands or curling their prehensile toes over the curved branches. Others are grooming their neighbours, worrying especially in the longer head hair for ticks and lice, and a couple of mothers are suckling their young on skinny small nipples placed almost as high on the pectoral area as those of an adult female chimpanzee.

But the older youngsters are behaving quite differently. They are playing in the pond. Some are splashing each other with their hands in a playful, indeed comforting, way, for the water they splash on each other is keeping them cool. But one of them, a male, a little older than the rest, attracts the disapproval of all of them and they chase him across the pool, yacketing more loudly and splashing with more ferocity. Thus ganged up on he uses his greater height to wade into the deeper part so the water reaches his chest, and what had been an ungainly gait when the water was between his thighs and pelvis, now becomes smoother, and he sweeps the water away from in front of him with half circular motions of his hands, holding his head higher and his chin, for yes he has a chin, clear of it.

Damn nearly he is swimming.

Indeed the last yard or so take his feet off the bottom but a kick or two brings him to the dam of branches and mud and he clambers on to it.

We get sight for a moment of his bottom. His rump is rounded, more hairless than the rest. It is not a bit like the flattened bottom of a baboon or chimp. It is… fat. Well, fattish.

He hauls himself up on to the top, turns on his tormentors with a snarl, revealing large canines, and pulls handfuls of mud and the odd large pebble from the top of the dam and hurls them back at the littler ones, who anyway have not been so ready to venture out of their depth. But he is over-excited, carried away by what he is doing and slipping a little pushes a larger lump off the parapet and into the water where it swirls, in a sandy-coloured cloud of fine grit, before sinking. However, it has left a gap and the water now filters across the top, runs faster, becomes a rivulet, a tiny waterfall.

This excites one of the largest males in the tree. The alpha male? Perhaps. Hand over hand he swings himself out to the periphery, drops to the ground, and with a loping awkward but definitely bipedal gait covers the ground to the end of the dam. Chattering vigorously he launches himself along it, pushes the younger male off it, not into the water but down the slippery wet slope on the other side. The adolescent is now contrite and obedient and he helps Dad, or Grandad, to replace the mud and stones he has thrown or dislodged, scooping up debris around the brook and filling in the gap he made. It's not easy for him – the parapet is above his head and on a level with Dad's face.

Suddenly a commotion behind them. More screams and chattering shouts from those who have remained in the tree. A big black cat has been spotted weaving its way through the undergrowth on the far side. The adult males pick up sticks and rocks and make an untidy line between it and the tree. The alpha male leaves off repairing the dam and rushes round to lead them. They snarl and shout at the cat who, ears laid back, alternately snarls and spits, her long tail lashing behind her as, belly to the floor, she edges forward, occasionally tightening the springs of her thighs for the pounce that never quite comes for the males know precisely how far her leap can take her and they stay just out of range.

Meanwhile the females with their suckling babes have abandoned the tree and are now in the pond, up to their waists, their breasts, in water. The cat breaks through the line of males and, for a minute or so, stalks the edge of the pond, angry, tail lashing, snarling with frustration but refusing to get her paws wet and knowing a leap on one of the females would bring her into water far deeper than she can cope with. The alpha male now comes up behind her and beats her rump with his stick. Defeated at last, the cat makes off back into the forest, where, as soon as she can, and with the tone of the chatter of the now distant hominids shifting from fear and threat to laughter, she begins to wash. When in doubt, wash.

The adults and babies slowly return to the boughs of the shady tree. Let us fix on the face of one suckling infant. Attracted by the disturbance she comes off the nipple and stares out of dark eyes with solemn interest at what is happening. Something in her expression appeals to us: an intelligence, a brightness, an awareness, a kind of beauty even. Her mother cups her round head in her palm and gently eases her back to the nipple. She resists for a moment. Her mother makes a soothing di-syllabic noise through lips pushed out. Looseee, looossseeeee, she murmurs, and the infant returns to the breast.

A time-shift now of ten, twelve years perhaps, suggested by a soft-focused merging of images showing a speeded-up change to the environment. The forest has shrunk further; the banks of the river are closer to each other leaving a narrower, deeper channel between; the pond with its dam is much the same but only because the hominids have kept it in a good state of repair. Even so the water level has dropped by a foot or so beneath the parapet. The big spreading tree is still there but has fewer leaves. In short there has been a prolonged drought or at any rate a continued gradual drying up of the habitat, which has had consequences for the clan of hominids we have been observing.

The nursing mothers and infants still gather around or in the tree, but there are fewer of them and they do not look as healthy as they did before, thinner perhaps.

Once all this has been established we see a group of adults wending their way through the forest bearing fruit they have gathered – nuts, plantains, custard apples, but not much, not enough. The females and children squabble over what there is and one, Loooossseee, let us call her Lucy, is left with just one very small red banana. She gives it to one of her infant siblings and wanders off on her own, on her own two feet, into the forest. Her gait is still awkward and frequently she reaches up to the boughs and strap hangs her way along, so her arms take the weight.

We follow her as she pushes through the etiolated forest screen and on to the sandy bank of the river. On her haunches now she pokes about with her long fingers in the sand, reading the tell-tale signs, until she finds a clutch of turtle eggs. She tears one open and sucks down the contents, smacking her lips. But she has disturbed a crab, quite a large one, and crab meat she knows is even tastier that turtle egg. It scuttles sideways away from her towards the river, she snatches up a flat plate-sized pebble whose top she has already stubbed her toe on, and chases it with her awkward stride towards the water's edge: she cannot run, her legs are not adapted for fast forward motion.

Yet, excited now, she splashes into the water, attempting to strike through it at where she thinks the crab might be. And now, gifted with the sight of an under-water camera, we see but she does not, how the sand she is on suddenly shelves sharply into much deeper, murkier water and through it we see how her long phalanged toes slip on the edge of the shelf and suddenly she is slipping down through the water, arms flailing, long head-hair streaming behind her. Her arms and legs kick and windmill, and for a moment we feel certain that she will make it, for, yes, she is, sort of, swimming. Shoals of fish and a crocodile, disturbed by the commotion dart or cruise away from her. The crocodile, surrounded by a lavish supply of food, is more frightened by her wild movements than attracted by the idea of a possible meal.

She gets her head above water and breathes in, but through her nose only, not the huge life-saving gulps of air available to fully human swimmers or divers, or seals and aquatic diving birds. Under water again, strength failing through lack of oxygen, her cheeks swell, bubbles balloon out of her mouth and nose, and, driven by reflexes beyond her control, she sucks in water through her nose, once, twice, three times and, drowning, dies.

She drowned because her larynx was still basically that of an ape, that is it was high, at the back of her throat, acted as a valve, and, while she could breathe out through her mouth, she needed her nostrils to breathe in. Worse still, and far more significant, her breathing was controlled by unconditioned reflex – it speeded up when she exercised, slowed down when she slept, driven by impulses beyond her control. In short, she lacked the ability to control her breathing consciously – she could not hold her breath. Maybe in the last seconds her head was above the water she forced some breath through her mouth down into her lungs even though her physique rendered this almost impossible. Perhaps, even, for a few moments she did hold her breath. If so, the adaptations that would make her descendants more fully human, had already started – but too late for her.

Three and a half million years later a man called Donald Johanson found her fossilised skeleton, embedded in the sand, and gave her a number: AL-2881, and the name – Lucy.

She was bipedal, an *Australopithecus afaransis*, and lived by water a million years before the savannah habitat became prevalent anywhere near where she died. Thus she is chronologically the first indisputable argument against the hypothesis that bipedalism developed as a response to a move on the part of our ancestors from arboreal habitats to grasslands. She also proves that bipedalism preceded the development of the much larger hominid brain.

> *And finally, to take us out of the past and into the future, another bit from* Trajectories. *2035. UK-ania is in the process of falling into a sort of Balkanisation, the big cities have fragmented into largely lawless ghettos or are run by liberal anarchists. The countryside is occupied by non-workers and the extremely wealthy who live in gated enclaves or sub-enclaves. Southampton is under siege: threatened by red-neck non-workers and government forces. Massacre of ethnic minorities is talked of. In fact it all looks like Bosnia and Kosovo in the nineties. The point is: given the right conditions, it can happen anywhere.*

The Siege of Southampton

T om, a white teenage lad studying Digitalised Surveying at the Institute in the hope of breaking out of inner city status and into the ranks of sub-enclavists, went with them and told them what had been happening as they walked up the hill.

'It started three weeks ago,' he began, 'with a non-worker march of Afros from Northam. They were protesting that the repatriation programme which is meant to be voluntary was being forced on them. It began peacefully but the protectors called in the regional reservists who opened fire as the procession came across the public garden out of St Mary's. They drove them back across the ring road but left about twenty dead and sixty who had to be taken up the hill to the hospital.'

He paused, lit a cigarette with a disposable lighter. Hannah-Rosa wondered where he had got them from, illegal as they were, and how old they were.

'After that, things got confused. About three hundred red-necks from east of the Itchen came across the bridges or down the railway line and attempted to fire the whole of Northam, Portswood, Bevois Valley, all that area. The City Council met and voted, by a quite large majority, to protect all citizens regardless of colour. Arms were taken from the City Police who refused to carry out the Council's orders, from the Territorials, and from a couple of Navy ships that were visiting, and a voluntary militia was formed.' He touched a red arm-band improvised from a scarf on his left arm.

'Things quietened down for a day or two but then we got orders from Winchester to surrender all arms and open up the city to the reservists. We were going to obey but then we heard the reservists and the original white rioters, working together now, were back in Northam, working their way street by street, raping and burning, towards the city centre. The Council met again, pulled the ethnics in from the threatened areas and set up militia guard posts to protect the inner streets. And that led to an ultimatum. Pull back the militia or be cut off from the outside world. The Council refused to pull us back.'

By now they were picking their way through broken glass. The only street lights on were over the major road-junctions. But for the rest everything seemed fairly normal though most ground-floor windows in shops and pubs had been boarded up. But it smelled – of drains inadequately flushed, burnt houses, and worse. Tom chucked his cigarette, kicked an empty plastic bottle into the gutter.

'Just how many… combatants are involved?' Hannah-Rosa asked.

'Not a lot. So far it's a very small war. There are about five hundred of us under arms. The reservists out there probably don't have more than a couple of hundred, but are much better armed than we are. And by now they have maybe a thousand or so white non-workers ready to move in if they get the chance.'

He walked on.

'Seems silly really, doesn't it,' he added, 'that so few people can cause so much trouble? Southampton still has a population of more than half a million in spite of everything, but until someone with proper authority gets involved it'll go on. You see if we don't stop them, with the weapons they've got they can simply massacre whoever they've a mind to. One problem is that we have no idea who knows about what is going on. Is central government involved or just ignorant of it? Clearly the regional government is in the know – the reservists wouldn't be here if that were not the case.'

'How close are they?'

'We've managed to hold them on a line from where the old football ground was through the south boundary of the Common, to the old hospital in Portswood, and then down the inner ring-road. But they have occupied and looted and fired the low-lying ground between the ring-road and the Itchen. And apparently interned or possibly murdered any ethnics who chose not to come up into the city. We sent a small party out with letters and so on saying what was going on and asking for help. We don't even know if they got through the first pickets.'

'Some got through.' Deep in her skull she saw again the dying, black woman reaching out to her for comfort. 'But they were being hunted through the countryside. Partly, that's why we're here. We met one of them. But she died. She'd been napalmed from the air.'

'The air force? That's bad news.'

'Why? I mean why especially?'

'Well. We thought we were up against the reservists, and a raggle-taggle of white non- or under-workers. But if the mili are against us, we've not got any hope at all. Trouble is we just don't know what's happening in the rest of the country. All the comms lines have been broken or switched off. Radio is jammed. Like I said, we don't know what the government is up to, whether they're turning a blind eye or what. But one thing's for sure. We'll have to give in in a week or so, whatever happens.'

'Why?'

'Food's running out. Ammunition as well. The regional water supply has been cut off, but the Council opened the old city wells, and the city engineer has managed to convert the power units on the four big ships in the docks to generate electricity. But only one of them is nuclear, and the diesel has almost run out on the others. We were just hoping to hang on until the government sorted it all out. After all, it's the other side are the rebels, the law-breakers. Not us.'

Suddenly he sounded bitter, tired, dispirited.

'This all happened before, you know? In Bristol. They put out that plague broke out there and they had to quarantine the port and the ethnic area round it. But I met a black who got out, and he said there was no plague at all. Just repatriation for those who'd take it, and internment, which probably meant massacre, for those who didn't.'

They walked round the Bar, the Norman gateway which had been a traffic island since the old city centre had been levelled by the German Blitz of 1941. Here the damage, the signs of a bombardment, were more evident. The shop walls and the boarding in the windows were pocked with what looked like bullet-scars, and there was blood on the paving. Still, nothing yet comparable to the barbarities of the 1940s.

'Cluster bombs, fired from a mortar, or maybe even a howitzer,' he said. 'It's the biggest thing they've been able to throw at us yet and the most disturbing. You just don't know where the next is going to go off.'

He led them off to the left past the old HMV shop, through the city wall and up to the entrance of a multi-storey car-park. He had a few words with a small group of red-scarfed militia like himself.

'I'll leave you here. You should be OK.' He turned to the twins. 'Your mum's in there somewhere.'

And so on... Could it happen here? You'd better believe it.

IX Unkind Cuts (1985)

Down empty corridors when school has closed
One hears a young lad climb a rising scale
Then blow the theme of Haydn's Anthony Chorale.
His teacher, one to one, hears between the notes,
The shade of Brain, Tuckwell's more abrasive call,
Murmurs encouragement and suggests he keep it up,
Might join a band.
Last lesson done he takes the golden coil and lays it in green baize,
Folds down the coffin lid and carries it away —
From L E A it came, to L E A it will return.
The boy forlorn goes home,
Picks Lemmings from the rack and slots it in,
And thinks that this is it
There is no band to join,
They closed the pit.

6. BITS AND BOBS

I am a non-aligned party un-member, materialist, coarse Marxist, coarse Darwinian, coarse Freudian, libertarian anarchist of the old school. Coarse? Yes, because although I have read a fair bit of all three and a fair bit more in the way of commentaries and updates, I cannot claim to be any sort of an expert in any of them. I am not any sort of an academic, and I do not have the sort of mind that takes easily to intellectual, analytic, clever-stuff discourse. I am Old Labour. Very Old Labour. Jack Cade and Wat Tyler Old Labour. A from the bottom up revolutionary. A When Adam delved and Eve span, who was then the gentleman sort of a bloke. And all of that runs like a thread of twisted black and red through the tapestry of what I have written. I nearly wrote the rich *tapestry,* you know, *like* Life's *rich* tapestry, *and thought that that was a touch pretentious, but, hell, why not. This is not the time to assume a false modesty I do not feel, so* a thread of twisted black and red through the rich tapestry of what I have written.

I Nasty, Very

Charlie Bosham (not the only Charlie Bosham in the uhvre) is the nastiest of many nasties I have put together. I have already described how he was invented or discovered, like under a stone, on the morning after the 1983 general election. While I was cooking up breakfast some berk on Radio Four was asked 'and what are these new Tory MPs like?' The answer was thrusting innovators and entrepreneurs, the sort Mrs Thatcher loves. In other words... Charlie!

At this point in the book, twenty years earlier, the late spring of 1963, he is twenty-three years old, but already married to a druggy society dolly who has ten thousand pounds in the

bank (lodda money in those days) and she has told him he
can use it if he can come up with a copper-bottomed scheme
for making it grow, fast. If he can't, well, she'll just spend it.

For days, weeks, he kicked round the old question. How do I get rich? Really rich. How do I convert the assured income from eleven grand – which is about one grand – into eleven grand a year? What makes money make money? What is at the bottom of the heap?

He answered these questions on his own, without any help at all from books, education, newspapers, Teach Yourself, the BBC, ITV, anything at all. It was not surprising that he had to do it on his own, since the culture he was a part of, however disparate, contradictory, conflicting, competitive, greedy and grasping, was unified at one point: it would conceal from itself, from all its disparate heterogeneous parts the one great secret of all – the source of capital. Perhaps one in ten thousand knew, but they weren't going to tell Charlie. Why not? If you had the secret of untold riches, would you tell the rest of the world? Of course not. So he had to find out for himself.

Here is how he did it.

First he obsessed himself with products that sold nothing for something. Particularly he doted on those firms that sold air. Aero chocolate. J cloths. Polo mints. Corrugated cardboard. All ways of packaging air and selling it. The one he liked best was aerated water. To package air in water, chuck in a squeeze of lemon and a drop of quinine, and get a man with a cut-glass accent and a funny beard to advertise it – and make… MILLIONS.

So, for a week or two he was obsessed with this idea – or rather lack of a new idea – a new way of selling air. He thought of, or stumbled on, many more ways of doing it.

Foam rubber in all its forms from mattresses to shoe-liners. Mousses, lemon or chocolate flavoured. Bubbles – yes! Those little pots of liquid detergent with a plastic ring you dipped in and blew through… Christ! In that version you even conned the punter into providing his own air. But, they were all thought of already, patented, tied up, shares quoted on the Stock Exchange, no chance now of getting in on the ground floor.

'Why was I misguided
I wish I had decided
to buy elastic-sided
…bootees.'

So carolled Bernard Cribbins all through the winter, mocking winklepicker shoes, the last fad of the Teds before Mods and Rockers took over the scene. And Charlie had done just that: bought a pair of very expensive Italian, elastic-sided bootees. By March the appalling winter had torn a neat little hole in each sole, and he took them to a tiny cobbler's shop in one of the alleys between Earls Court and Cromwell Road.

A day later, on his way to pick them up, he had an odd but total recall of very early childhood, sitting on Aunt Elizabeth's knee while she read him *The Elves and the Shoemaker*:

'The same morning a lady came into the shop to buy a pair of shoes. The Shoemaker showed her the pair he had found on his bench. She said, "I have never seen such well-made shoes." The lady tried on the shoes, and they fitted her perfectly. She was so pleased with them that she paid the Shoemaker twice the usual price. With the money the Shoemaker was able to buy leather for two pairs of shoes... That morning, a man came into the shop to buy some shoes. The Shoemaker showed him the two pairs of shoes he had found on his bench. The man said, "I have never seen such well-made shoes." He was so pleased with them that he bought both pairs of shoes. He paid the Shoemaker twice the usual price... And so it went on. Many rich customers came to his shop to buy these perfect shoes. So, in time the Shoemaker and his wife became very rich indeed...'

And where did the wealth come from? The story had a surprisingly convincing, not to say honest, if you could read the code, explanation.

'In came two tiny elves. They were dressed in old clothes and their feet were bare. They began to stitch and sew and hammer. They did not stop for a moment until all the cut shoes were finished.'

'That'll be ten and sixpence please. Sir. Ten and six.'

Charlie snapped out of his dream, looked around, took in the tiny dark shop with its single unshaded light over the workbench, its grinding wheel, heavy sewing machine with thick bent needle, the lasts, hammers, pliers, the stack of skin-shaped leather, the smell.

'Ten and six?'

'Yes, sir. It sounds a lot, the price of leather these days is something chronic. But see. We done a good job.' He pulled one of Charlie's shoes out of the bag he had already put them in, and went on with perky cockney obsequiousness. 'Good as new they are now. Lovely pair of shoes. Italian. Lovely craftsmanship there, pleasure to work on them. Cost you a bob or two, I expect.'

'Five guineas.'

'There. I thought so. And they'll last you another twelve months at least.'

This man, thought Charlie, is an idiot. I have spent ten and six and saved myself the cost of buying a new pair of shoes. I have made a profit of four pounds, fourteen shillings and sixpence.

He picked up the bag and began to walk very slowly back to Bannington Gardens, but he was still thinking it all out when he got there, so he went on, walked in circles for another half-hour until he was certain he had it worked out.

What had he bought for his ten and sixpence? A pair of shoes worth five guineas. No. That's not it. That's the way his bankrupt father thought, the way most people thought. They see an article, a product, a commodity at one price and they buy it, and then they try to sell it at a higher price. But what have I *really* bought? Two small pieces of leather. What else? How long did that idiot work on my shoes? Twenty minutes. So for twenty minutes I bought his shop, or rented it, paid for his electric light, the power of his machines, the machines themselves in a way (he wasn't too clear about this, but sensed that the machines had cost, were perhaps still costing, the cobbler whatever he had had to lay out or borrow to provide himself with them), his rates, and even the stale steak pie which his breath demonstrated had kept him going since lunchtime, his taxes, the rent on his house... What else? His skill, and a portion of what it had cost to give him that skill. Not only his skill. Everything he is. Everything he will be. Even his obsequious, dull, idiot mind that was happy to charge ten and six for something worth five times as much, and then apologise.

For twenty minutes I bought all that. But none of that put two new soles on my shoes. Those were all static, preconditions for the process, the activity, the... work.

I bought his labour.

Not treasure to be found, which is dead, but a transforming agent, the thing that actually changes one thing worth so much into another thing that's worth a fucking sight more, that secret little grub... is labour. Other men's work. Not a thing you can touch or feel, but an action; not an abstraction even though you can't get hold of it, because it is movement, energy, something after all real, concrete, something you can buy as easily as the electricity through the meter.

What I need, thought Charlie, is a load of elves. Preferably in old clothes and bare feet: they come cheaper like that.

But what should his elves do. What form should their labour take? At least this second insight had given a sharper logic to the first one, the one about packaging air. The reason why he had been obsessed with that was now clear: it was the simplicity that attracted him. Labour was the source of wealth, but most of the time there was a whole heap of complications on top of it, obscuring the simple fact that, by and large, the elves who provided the magic ingredient were screwed rotten by everyone else.

His mind felt the presence of these complications, secondary worlds he named them as, like dark, impenetrable mountains – for few of the perceptions that were now blossoming in his mind were fully articulated – many felt like physical presences bumping around in his head. A larger part of the heap he sensed sat almost literally on top of the secret, obscuring it, making it into a mystery, above all controlling it: governments, police, armies, school-teachers, vicars. Another lot controlled and regulated it in an entirely different way: banks, accountants, insurance, building societies, laws, regulations, customs. Yet another consisted of those systems like the one he belonged to, that lived off old labour, the centuries-old labour that had built houses like the one he lived in, on land that had not belonged to the elves, with tools and bricks that had not belonged to the makers of those tools and bricks, and now it was all sold, and resold, and sold again, to be bought and bought again, and rebought by people who had gathered in to themselves the profit to be made from someone else's, some other elves', labour somewhere else...

Charlie felt all this like a sickening weight in his mind; he realised it was far beyond his capacity to manipulate it on his own, to cream the profits of labour at seven or eight removes from source. You needed to be a Cotton or a Clore, a Rockefeller or a Getty or a Gulbenkian, to do that. And if you couldn't do that, then you were just stuck somewhere in those black lumps, the secondary worlds, as a cog, an employee, albeit well paid, salaried, but in someone else's bank, insurance company or property firm. And Charlie, a loner, did not want that. He would rather make a meagre ten grand a year out of directly employing his own elves, rather than the same sums or even more servicing the employment of someone else's.

But he knew his limitations. It would have to be simple, dead simple, for him to manage it on his own. What he wanted was a way of owning *air*, of hiring a few elves to package it, make it saleable, and then he would sit back and let nature take its course in the very simplest way possible.

Summer came. A bad summer after an appalling winter. The West Indians set about thrashing the daylights out of everything that came their way. But what was worse than a load of niggers playing cricket better than anyone else was that Lissie had started spending money again – on clothes, on a Centre Court ticket, on a share of a box at

Ascot, and, what was worse, he found himself excluded from both. When he remonstrated, she declared that his three months were just about up. If he was going to make a fortune out of her ten grand, he'd better get a move on.

On one of the first days of June, he got another letter from Aunt Elizabeth.

Dear Charlie,
I think you should know that your Father has finally gone bank-rupt. Also he is not very well. Alderson has agreed to take over the stock that's left – about five hundred pounds' worth, I understand – at cost, which is a very fair offer. However, he has nowhere to put it, so it must be stored for a few weeks at least.
I have found a place which will look after it for a not unreasonable fee – Williams's Storage in Mottingham – but it must be moved there quickly and at as little expense as possible. The bank has agreed to let us keep the van until next Monday. I calculate three trips will be suffi-cient. I should like you to come over and help us to move the stock, as above, to the warehouse, since it is out of the question your Father should do any lifting or carrying. On completion of this small service, I will give you five pounds.
Your affectionate aunt,
Elizabeth

Which must be at least two pounds less than any quote she's got from anywhere else, thought Charlie.

His first instinct was to refuse, but then he thought about it, thought about how he would be assisting in the final toppling of his father's empire, the end of all the pretension, the bullying, the self-congratula-tion, the self-righteousness, that had been built on his father's apparent ownership of a rotten little business with a shop on the High Street. So he went, having first squared it with Aunt Elizabeth, by phone, that he would not actually have to see either of his parents.

Williams's Storage was a bomb-damaged cinema – not a large one, but the sort that used to be called a flea-pit; now the seats had gone, it was nothing more than a large shell, with corrugated-iron roof, a dais at one end, and an upstairs office in what had once been the projection room. It was three-quarters filled with a miscellany of furniture and packing cases, with here and there a real absurdity sticking out from the rest: an invalid chair made out of basketry, a stuffed tiger and thirty-six *black* lavatories.

When Charlie dropped the first load – six tea-chests filled with nails, screws, broom-heads, paint, brushes and gallon tins of turps – two men, one old, one a Negro, helped him carry them in on trolleys, while a little Welshman – your actual Williams, Charlie presumed – told them where to stack them.

'Short term, is it? Less than one month? Right, boyo, we'll keep it all up front, then, all right?'

As he drove back to Woolingham for the second load, the significance of all this dawned on Charlie with organic slowness. It was all so simple. Williams – who wore a good lightweight tweed suit, had a gold watch on a chain, and smelled of whisky – owned *air, air* enclosed in a shell. To make it pay not just a little but a lot, he bought the labour of two elves. No doubt he could have managed without them, but, if he had, eighty per cent of the air would have remained unsold. To maximise the profitability of the air he owned, it was necessary to have elves to stack the objects people displaced his air with in the most efficient, the most profitable way possible. The long-term stuff at the back and at the bottom, the shorter-term stuff in the middle, the three-, four-week stuff in the front and on the top.

And so these two elves converted the air into wealth by their labour. It was better than Aero chocolate. It was better than Ssssch... you know who! There were no materials to be bought once you had the shell that enclosed the space, the very minimum of overheads and upkeep; it was the divine reduction to its absolutely barest essentials of the process of wealth creation. Two elves, for whom you did not even have to provide shoe leather, whose skills did not have to be paid for since no skill was involved, provided, for absolutely the lowest wage that one could get away with paying able-bodied men, the labour that converted air into wealth, and Williams – at least until Charlie bought him out – took the profit, the loot, the riches.

The elation grew like a lovely crimson flower in his chest, in his throat, in his head, all through the afternoon – a prize won by a knight for his lady, a gift brought by a small boy for his mother – and was just about unfurling its velvet petals, releasing its gorgeous perfume, as he trotted up from Earls Court tube, along the alleys and ringing pavements, past the newsstands (MINISTER RESIGNS), through the warm lovely air of a June evening, down the steps and into the basement flat.

'Lissie, I've cracked it. We can do it. We're made.'

'With love from me to you' came bouncing off the Dansette, instead of the usual Vivaldi or Telemann.

'Have you?' she said. 'If you could buy a piece of that sound, I'd believe you.'

Considering how he had come in, with the whole sweet secret of success buttoned in his mouth and ready to spill it out before her, it's a wonder he didn't brain her on the spot, not surprising the fathomlessly deep disappointment he felt.

Ten years later Charlie is doing well. He's married to a childhood... no, sweetheart is not the right word, has acquired step-children, and is on holiday on Majorca.

Another day, the last coach trip – Thursday, 13 September: the fag-end of the holiday, the fag-end of the season, the fag-end of the world. The coppery haze was back: flat, right across the sky it seemed to hold down beneath it the stale, nicotine-laden, exhaust-heavy, fart-filled air. An afternoon trip, depart after lunch, the usual buffet down by the pool: eight salads, prawns in mayonnaise, rings of fried squid, sliced roast of beef (guaranteed *toro bravo* and tough as old boots), cold paellas with langoustines and mussels, gateaux piled with cream but oddly unsweet to the British tooth, bunches of giant grapes, water melons and honeydew, and as much sangría as you could drink.

Really, thought Charlie, I'd as soon as not go on a coach after that lot, but it was the last trip, musn't miss the caves, and the *barbacoa* on the way back.

'What the fuck is a *barbacoa?*'

'Barbecue, silly.'

A slight delay waiting for the coach to leave, Charlie and Bob in one seat together, Jane and Connie in front of them, the children in front of that.

'You've got to hand it to them, my son,' said Bob.

'Hand what to who?' asked Charlie nervously.

'The dagos. Look at that.'

They looked. A block of flats going up on the other side of the narrow pot-holed road, a shell of empty boxes without ends, the concrete floor/ceilings supported on wooden poles, ladders between the floors, and men shovelling concrete up in steady rhythm from floor to floor, stoop-scoop-heave and a twist of the shovel at the top of the movement and then down again, stoop-scoop-heave-twist and hardly a handful of cement dropped or spattered. A small concern, no cranes, no swung buckets or hoists, but every shovelful shovelled from the mixer on the ground floor to the sixth floor above. The men were naked to the waist, had backs like polished leather, and as tough.

'A floor a day over the last week. You don't see blokes working like that back in Blighty.'

'No. Indeed not. Oops. Pardon.'

'Must have done once. Think of all the building done in Victorian times. Canals, railways. The navvies. They worked like that then. Made us great. Not now, no more Victorian virtues, see. It all depends on the system. Strong government. No to socialism and that. I reckon Franco has it about right.'

If what Bob Dobson was on about was clobbering the elves then I'm right with him, thought Charlie, but Connie had intervened before he could make the point. She was having a good old giggle in front of them. Laughing. At him? Perish the thought.

'What's the joke, Connie?'

'Not for your ears, sweetie.'

'Come on. Share the joke. What you say, Charlie? Can't let the girls keep all the fun to themselves.'

'No, indeed not.' Poor Charlie had begun to sweat, sweat olive oil it felt like. Why didn't the coach move? They were frying in their own juices, waiting.

'OK, sweetie. Jane and I were just wondering which of those backs we'd like to get our nails into. She fancies the one on the third floor, I fancy the one on the top. He looks better hung.'

'Bloody women,' said Bob.

The doors hissed. The diesel engines coughed, settled, and at last the air conditioning began to work. 'When Irish Eyes are Smiling', 'My Old Man', 'I Say Hello, You Say Goodbye', 'Tambourine Man', 'Blowing in the Wind'.

A long hot drive across the yellow burnt plain, stubble burning, a glimpse of the airport, wind pumps, fields of sunflowers, heads old, brown, dropped on their chests like geriatrics waiting for the grim reaper.

Charlie found he had the *English Language Daily,* where from he had no idea, but he was glad to have his mind taken off the dreary drive.

Dr Salvador Allende suicides in Santiago, Chile. Seventeen bombs dropped on Presidential Palace as Army take control. Salvador Allende was reported to have killed himself with the heavy automatic machine gun his friend Fidel Castro gave him...

'This is out of order,' said Charlie.

'Eh?' said Bob.

'This is plain out of order. It says this dictator in South America shot himself with a heavy automatic weapon. Well, that's not on. You'd have to be a contortionist to bring that off,' Charlie knew it all from the glossy books he took such pride in.

'Which dictator was that then?'

'Allende.'

'Got his comeuppance at last then. Commie bastard.'

Charlie read on. A report from the legislative branch of the Chilean Constitution had recently arraigned Allende for stealing farms and industry, for setting up a programme of indoctrination.

'You're right. He was stealing farms and industries.'

'They're all the same. Cut them how you like, they taste the same.'

'Nevertheless, he couldn't have suicided with that gun. Not possible.' He'd been assassinated with it. He speculated – probably it was an M60 Castro gave Allende. Even the IRA had M60s.

He read on. Egypt, Syria, Jordan hold talks to co-ordinate the war effort against Israel. War, a war that could spread, seemed inevitable. Charlie felt a hot tightness in a circle round his head, above his eyes, and could feel the turbulence in his upper gut. Things were falling apart, nothing was secure, safe, not like it used to be twenty years ago. 1953. Jane. She'd been thin then, a stomach like a smooth china plate, dropping and gathering to that haze of fine curly hair. And here she was now, the same person in front of him, her hair, darker now on the anti-whatsit on the seat in front, with a tummy that sagged to a swatch...

'Nothing about the cholera, then?'

Christ. I'd forgotten about the cholera. Naples. Rome. Sardinia.

'Two years back we were in Torremolinos. It was admitted to be in Cadiz and we knew it was in Malaga. Just eight miles away. Their sewage on our beach.'

Las Cuevas del Drach. The Caves of the Dragon. A seedy, bunker-like entrance, concrete, dust, tatty gift shops, dying cacti. Abandon hope. Oh, it was extraordinary enough, the fluted columns of greyish stone, the greasy sheen on everything, the strange shapes weirdly brought to life and a sort of prettiness by the cunning use of coloured lights. A stalagmite dripping on to a stalactite, or the other way about? 'In eight millennia they will be united.' In eight millennia I will be blowing in the wind.

Charlie hated to be herded, and to be herded with however many thousands of tons of rock and earth above his head was terrifying, herded down steep, twisting, wet steps, along narrow galleries above spaces which might well be bottomless, across pools and rivers that looked black as ink, and try as he might he really could not make out the likeness in the formations that the guide claimed were there – the Penitent, the Column of the Dragon, Charon's Skiff and Shrouds.

They were put into boats. The seats were too narrow, the level of the water horrifyingly close to the gunnels, and then when they were well out into the middle the fucking lights went out.

A moment of the worst panic he had ever felt, and of the pitchest darkness he had ever experienced, the after-images and the swimming cells of his own plasma garishly spread across the darkness wherever he looked; then, just as he was sure he was dying of speleophobia and cholera he knew he was dead and ushered into the underworld with music and a dim light.

De dum, de dum, de-dum, de-dum *de-dum*. De dum, de dum, de-dum-de-dum-de-dum. Dum dum, da-da-da-dum dum...

The light grew stronger, began at last to illuminate some of the rock ceiling above it... a barge, much like the one he sat in, propelled as if by magic, moved across their front, and on it five men with stringed instruments and candles that barely flickered in the motionless air.

'The Arriaga Quartet are playing for you the acknowledged masterpiece of Wolfgang Amadeus Mozart – *Eine Kleine Nachtmusik*. The acoustics of this cave are acknowledged to rival those of La Scala, the Royal Festival Hall...'

Connie murmured, 'I've never known anything so beautiful...'

Next stop a bodega. A barn-like place that tried with roughcast plaster, fancy brickwork and wormy beams to disguise the fact that it had been built out of breeze blocks and steel girders. All round the walls there were hundreds of barrels, some huge and standing upright, other big-bellied and on their sides, most tiny, the size you could tuck under your arm like a piglet and carry off. These had taps, drip-catchers, and everywhere there were trays of disposable drinking vessels, each about the size of a *petit suisse* container.

'You taste everything,' the couriers insisted, 'and you buy what you like. Do remember your duty-free allowances, and please take my word you will buy nothing cheaper on the island, nor on the plane home.'

'I'd like a nice sherry, like an oloroso, you know?'

'Try this peppermint, not that it really seems great to me.'

'Oooh, they do have Benedictine.'

'This white rum is not bad at all, I mean it may not be Bacardi...'

'But it is Bacardi.'

'Golly, so it is.'

'I wouldn't mind taking home a bottle of sangría mixture.'

'I wouldn't, old love. It never tastes the same back home. Remember the Robinsons tried it at their Guy Fawkes party, and you were sick...'

All aboard. Back in the coach. That's better. That settled the old tum and chased away the blues. Maybe I don't have cholera after all.

'I was right about the peseta.'

'You were?'

'One three four. Saved you a bob or two there.'

'You did indeed.' But he felt queasy. Still over a hundred quid stuffed in the toe of his shoe, in the wardrobe back at the Sol y Sombre, and even if they didn't get stolen there was now only a day and bit to spend them in. Mind you, there'd be a bit on the top at the hotel... he had signed for a few things and breakfasts in their rooms were an extra. Dear God, perhaps he wouldn't have enough!

Bob now had the paper. Charlie tried to peer round his arm. Bombs. At Euston. Kings Cross. Thirteen injured. Bang! That's an eye gone. Or a hand. Or your balls. Ship the Micks and Paddies back. Tell the Prods they can come over. We let in those Indians from Africa, surely we can find room for our sort. Then those that stay can get on with blowing each other up, and leave us alone.

George Brown. Seventy-five pounds, banned for a year, two hundred and fifty pounds. Lucky bastard didn't kill anyone. Charlie's stomach heaved again, burping back the caramelly odours of cheap brandy, and he saw again the blood on the road, the broken dentures...

Bob leaned forward, tapped Connie's elbow.

'It's to be on 14 November.'

'What is, sweetie?'

'Anne's wedding. To that Mark Phillips.'

'How nice! But November. Odd time for a Royal Wedding, I should have thought.' She giggled. 'I hope she's not in a hurry.'

At least the *barbacoa* was in the open air, to begin with at any rate. Ushered in to the usual glasses of sangría, they were shown to tiered benches round a sand-surfaced paddock and treated to a brief display of Spanish dressage. The young girls at least enjoyed this: the trim ponies, mostly pie or skewbald, the exotic, western-style tack with inlay of silver and mother-of-pearl, the handsome if pompous young riders.

It was all rather spoiled when a green Land Rover drew up at the far end of the paddock. Four Civil Guards got briskly down – cloaks, shiny black hats, moustaches, all a bit comic except that two had carbines. They knew the man they had come for, so did he. A waiter, standing near the rail and apparently at his ease smoking a cigarette and watching the display before going back to serve the meal, suddenly bolted up a slope of dry grass and immortelles towards a low dry-stone wall and a neglected olive grove. The guards shouted. Then one barked an order, the men with carbines crouched, the guns clattered with appalling noise, the waiter's body was scooped in the air as his legs were shot from under him.

They had a stretcher up to him in no time and one of the guards stuffed a handkerchief in his mouth to cut off his screams. All bundled back into the vehicle, which swung away down the dusty drive and under the arch that separated the *finca* from the main road. A siren diminished slowly in the thick air. The whole incident had lasted scarcely two minutes.

The French pulled down the corners of their mouths, pouted and shrugged. The Germans peered with expressionless blue eyes out to the coppery horizon and drummed nervous fingers on the cases of their cameras. Only the British seemed to have felt that something terrible had happened. The whole coachload from the Sol y Sombre suffered a wave of collective anger, though this was caused by shock and fright rather than by any real sense of moral outrage.

By the time they had been herded into the long whitewashed dining rooms of the *finca* and fed with charred steaks and as much *tinto* as they could drink the mood had shifted to one of sturdy self-satisfaction. The uncivilised impossibility of all foreigners had been unequivocally demonstrated yet again. Nothing like that could happen back home.

Not then. Not in 1973.

And finally, 1983, Woolingham Town Hall, on the London-Kent border…

And now the apotheosis approaches, although the group of Tory supporters in the middle of the stage has shrunk. Mrs Grosscurth has gone home, so has Mrs Armstrong and so has Mrs Goulden. Amongst those left, the two lads from the British Movement who suggested Charlie should give them a tenner each to make sure no Labourites tried any aggro on him, loom more obviously. But there are still Labourites and SDP supporters in plenty. What once had been a safe Labour seat goes Tory with the SDP ex-Labour candidate coming a goodish second, and one of the SDP side makes the mistake of offering a cheer. A dark-haired man in a leather jacket, whose pinched face and frayed jeans declare him to be one of Maggie's Private Army, bursts out of the Labour camp, heads straight for the SDP man, a youth, a student, and thumps him heartily on the nose.

Ken Langley follows to pull clear his overenthusiastic supporter and Old Bill lumbers up from the back of the hall. Apart from the punks on the balcony, who cheer and whistle, as the dark-haired unwaged character is frogmarched out, order is restored. The punks, it seems, are actually card-holding members of the SDP – a fact that becomes apparent when Charlie asks to have them ejected.

The count is almost over. Scrutineers have a last poke or two at the bundles of votes. Totting-up commences. Thousands, hundreds, tens, units. The Returning Officer, who is also the Chairman of the Borough Council, gives his chain a premonitory hitch. Almost as if he is drowning Charlie suffers recall of the campaign:

No man is an island. Entire of itself.

Bosham's gotta lotta bottle.

What is needed is not consensus, not compromise, but conviction, action, persistence, until the job is well and truly finished.

There is a new way, a classless way. Let us end the class war, let us break the mould.

The emancipation of the workers from trade union exploitation is our aim and purpose.

1980 saw the greatest ever one-year decline in British output. Deindustrialization, a massive increase in unemployment, a surge in the export of capital, decrease in real wage incomes, tax concessions to the rich... those, brothers, are the figures for 1980. They will be worse in 1981 and 1982 and 1983.

Bosham's gotta lotta bottle.

America, Ronald Reagan, means to win the Third World War in Europe. That's what Cruise means.

What is needed is real British Government, a return to home-made leadership that bears the once formidable impress of equal... I mean quality: Made in Britain.

Bosham. Charles. Edward. Twenty-two thousand and forty-three votes. (Four thousand *less* than Terry Mead scored in 1979.)

Langley. Kenneth. Twenty-eight... Sorry. Eighteen thousand four hundred and twenty-eight.

Murdish. Thomas. Twelve thousand, eight hundred and sixteen.

I hereby declare the above Bosham, Charles duly...

May God the Master bless our fare
And give those here the lion's share
As gathered here in friendly glee
We share it round quite equally
Hurrah!

'Charlie.'
'Yes, pet?
'You owe yourself a holiday.'
'Yes pet. But where?'
'Grenada?'

From the tiered gallery a chorus breaks out; to Charlie, it seems as if, absurdly, they are singing the words of a commercial for the high-fibre breakfast cereal Jane now makes him eat instead of muesli.

Tasty, tasty, very, very, tasty... He's tasty!

Then two of the punks moon – that is pull down their jeans and expose their bums over the rail, and the words come through more clearly, loud and clear:

Nasty, nasty, he's very, very nasty...

The lads from the British Movement flank Charlie and Jane as he moves to the front to make his speech of acceptance. The chant ends on a shout:

HE'S NASTY!

II To Teach or Not to Teach

During the early 1980s I wrote several pieces for the then new Literary Review. *In those days it was A4 format on cheap paper and included long articles on generally literary or philosophical themes and extended reviews. Broadly speaking it was left-leaning. The editor, Dr Anne Smith, eventually had an editorial crisis with the owner and resigned. In sympathy for the stand she'd taken I, along with some other regular contributors, dropped out too. Auberon Waugh took over and it became more or less what it is now: an entertaining and useful magazine but lacking the weight and clout it had. The following is a shorter version of the first piece I wrote for the* Literary Review.

Gradgrind, Alive and Well

FOR fifteen years I was a teacher of English in secondary moderns and comprehensives in Camden and West Sussex. When I gave up I was head of department in a school of over 2,000; the next step in my career would have been either into the LEA advisory service, or into a deputy headship; I was on an LEA working party on language learning, and I was a committee member of the local branch of the

National Association for the Teaching of English. I enjoyed much of what I did in the classroom, had few problems; I enjoyed the prestige and responsibility of guiding a large department of dedicated teachers; in the year I left our English Language 'O' level pass rate was over 80 per cent; our successes in other examinations were comparable. I mention these facts to dispel any idea that I gave up through incompetence, or because I had no further prospects in education.

The reasons that pushed me into giving up are simple enough though they interrelate in a way that is complex. I shall start with the simplest – a not unnatural desire to survive.

In 15 years' teaching, mainly in three schools, only one of which could be described as 'difficult', five colleagues died prematurely, six to my knowledge became seriously ill with diseases associated with stress (ulcers, heart, gall-bladder, cancer), and five had serious nervous breakdowns. All of these colleagues were competent, sensible, industrious people; all were in positions of responsibility comparable to mine – heads of department, senior teachers, deputy heads, heads. I was aware that I was suffering from stress; it seemed likely that I too would become seriously ill within, say, 10 years.

The reading load alone of a specialist teacher in English in a large secondary school is impossible, amounting to over five million words a year, mostly handwritten, all to be read with care and discrimination. When I gave up I reckoned I could mark a 600-word composition at 'O' level standard in five minutes. All this means that an English teacher should expect to spend over 700 hours a year reading, nearly all of which will be outside school hours – that is 17 weeks' work at 40 hours a week. He will be working in school for 40 hours a week. This includes, besides 25 hours actually in the classroom, lesson preparation other than text reading, dinner duties, playground duties, pastoral care, administrative duties if he is above scale one, clubs, parents' meetings, attending meetings at year, department, school and county levels. He will thus be properly working, working hard, not sitting around gossiping as the clerks are in every government office I ever go into, not combing his hair or polishing her nails, but properly working for 2,300 hours a year. Add on the time when he has to be somewhere waiting for something to happen (though there is very little of this in teaching, less I should imagine than in any other non-manual job) and you arrive at something like a 52-hour week, 48 weeks a year. Of course it doesn't work out like that – preparation of texts can be done during the 'holidays' and the marking load caught up with at half-terms, but in full term a 65-hour week is normal.

I believe English teachers work harder than others – but only English teachers will agree with me.

A desire to reach 60 with health unimpaired was not the only reason for giving up, simply the easiest to explain. There were other reasons more deeply related to the ends of teaching English, and finally, awareness that I was doing less and less of what I believed I should be doing in the classroom became insistent and inescapable.

What is wrong with the teaching of English is that it happens at all. A hundred years ago it did not; or only in a very limited way once basic literacy had been achieved. More recently, at the private school I attended between the ages of 8 and 13 we had only two English lessons a week, and they were 'soft'. Later, when I was 18 the classics teacher at the school I was then at saw it as a sign of a decadent civilisation that I was going to study my native literature at university. Then I thought she was potty; now I am sure she was right. None of which means that English should not be taught, but that it is a symptom of our sickness that it is necessary. Teaching English is not just necessary – it is a crusade or it is nothing. I found I could no longer believe in the crusade – and I had begun to believe that the nothing I was left with was worse than nothing. English teachers are asked for bread and can only offer stones, sometimes what they must offer is nastier than stones.

Before I go any further, I must ask to be understood. 'Creativity', 'discovery learning' and so on, are abused, misunderstood words for abused and misunderstood ideas. Consequently they tend to express attitudes and approaches to teaching which are now unpopular, and which are to some extent discredited. If what I say next is not properly understood it will put me in that discredited camp. Well, if I have to be lumped with one or the other, I should rather be there than with the cost-effective, rational, 'technicological' Benthamites.

Yet the 11-year-old who has drawn on all his ability to use language to produce a working account of how to make a paper glider, without using diagrams, wins more of my approval than the one who describes a sword ripping a knight's armour as being 'my pen nib tearing the paper I am writing on' – though I admire both. The point I am making is that application, awareness of rules and how to keep and break them, the willingness to polish, to improve, with a clear-cut idea of what one is trying to say, are more essential to any user of language than an easy gift for a telling metaphor.

Having said these things – that I believe technique, practice, self-discipline are essential elements in any individual's developing capacity to use his language (to which let me add that I think comprehension is the side of language learning that is most disastrously under-practised in schools, and indeed anywhere else; and that 'creativity' and 'self expression' are a load of – well, stones – if they do not promote shared perception) – having said these let me state firmly and without equivocation that language is a limb, an extension, another dimension of the individual, that is as much a part of him, *his own,* as his tongue, or his fingers. A person's language is himself; it is not all that is himself, but it is inseparable from himself, and his language is his language and no one else's. If I touch another's fingertips with mine, mine do not cease to be mine – however intensely felt and perfectly shared the experience of touching may be, however perfectly understood the message behind the gesture. My use of words, my understanding of words is like that. It does not belong to society, it is not to be nurtured to promote what somebody else has decided society needs, my use of words (and, I reiterate, use in comprehension as well as expression) is me.

Yet we believe, probably rightly, that language development cannot any longer be left to happen on its own, although this was the case, until quite recently, at all levels of society, once literacy had been achieved. To put it crudely, neither the Duke of Wellington, nor Jane Austen, nor William Blake, nor John Clare ever had formal English lessons in their lives and all speak, to me at any rate, with a limpid subtlety and range of expressiveness that I do not often find in living writers, whether their subject is military logistics, the mores of their society, or prophetic vision. It is not my concern here to discuss why this is so, but – *so* it is. The language ability of dukes and ploughboys today, however gifted they may be with lions or guitars, electronics or genetics, just does not match that of Wellington or Clare, untutored though both were.

If what I have tried to say about the way one's native language is part of one is true, and if it is accepted that language teaching is now necessary, then it follows that the success of language teaching will depend very largely on a positive personal relationship between teacher and pupil, and on the teacher having the patience, skill, and above all the time, to give constant particular attention to the work and progress of each pupil. It will be equally clear from my description of the workload of most secondary school teachers of English that this is not possible.

But it is not only the workload that makes good English teaching the difficult, heart-sickening job one recognises it for as one becomes, year by year, more and more aware of the great slough of mediocrity around one, as the frequent glimpses of something really living, and fine and free in one's pupils' work become not noticeably rarer, but known more properly for what they really are – glimpses of potentiality for ever and tragically unused, or improperly used, and never, by any stretch of the imagination, fully used. Of course, basically what one is fighting is a culture that is, compared with anything we know much of since the Dark Ages, appallingly impoverished in its use of language and its understanding of literature. In itself this would not be too terrible – fighting the good fight does not weary the heart, however exhausted mentally and physically one may be at the end of the day; but the English teacher is carrying on this struggle within a framework created by the culture, and, whatever he may think he is doing, what he is finally doing as a teacher is supporting and sustaining the very things which have created and perpetuate the impoverishment he is trying to alleviate. He is reinforcing the tendencies in our culture which make language dull, limited, de-personalised, stereotyped. These tendencies express themselves in educational thinking through the belief 'that only what can be demonstrably shown to enhance a pupil's earning capacity, his docility and his acceptance of Britain today should be taught in schools, and that the efficacy of this teaching should be measurable'.

In every secondary school two battles are fought. The first is for order, for discipline. By and large this is achieved, whatever people may believe from what they see on the telly and read in the tabloids, in 99 per cent of classrooms for 90 per cent of the time. Once this first battle is won the second starts and for most teachers it is a far more dispiriting, calcifying, deadening struggle than the one for order was – this second battle is for 'good' examination results.

'Good' results matter: they attract a 'better' class of pupil (choice still operates in more areas and in more ways than one imagines); they attract a 'better' class of teacher; prospects for promotion are very heavily enhanced by them – especially if the teacher is making his way as a subject specialist rather than a social worker or administrator; LEAs generally favour schools with 'good' results; and so on, and so on. And of course most people, blindly unaware of what exams do to teaching, think that this is a good thing, that schools and teachers, as well as children, should be judged by examination results.

I believe it is impossible in any useful way to examine a child's ability with his native tongue and arrive at a quantifiable, 'objective', assessment. It *appears* to be possible to make an assessment of a child's ability to perform the few limited exercises in, say, 'comprehension', precis writing, short composition work, which form the pattern of most language tests. One is not impressed by the attempts to tart these up: 'Show how much you enjoyed this passage by reading the questions and then answering them' is comprehension; 'See how well you can say the same things as this in only half as many words' is précis; and so on. And when such fashionable dressing-up is more than just that, it tends not towards heightened, freer, keener use of language, but to woolliness, self-indulgence, complacency and falseness. And there is plenty of evidence to show that even these wretched, impoverished, almost meaningless little techniques which children are required to practise over and over again and which teachers have to mark again and again and again, do not produce results accurate enough to provide the basis of awarding something as important to a child's whole future career as an 'O' level pass in English Language. So now we have the multiple choice test and 'comprehension' is 'tested', not by asking a child to write a sentence in answer to a question, a sentence which could just occasionally give the child the chance to show how fully, accurately, *and* personally he has comprehended, but by putting a tick in a box.

To sum up – because of the importance of exams the greater part of language teaching in secondary schools is directed not towards helping each child to use his native tongue with more fluency, freedom, and depth, but towards passing these exams. And that means practising exercises which actually tend towards the very opposite of what language teaching should be – restrictive exercises which promote sameness, shallowness, narrowness.

It will not, by now, surprise the reader to learn that I believe the effect of exams on the study of literature is even more horrifying.

The language/literature split on the curriculum is not something I approve. The shoddy ants who did this, and also made literature an examinable subject, are, in my estimation, enemies of civilisation in the class of Attila the Hun and Adolf Hitler. This sounds joky – but it is a considered judgment. The 'men' who reduce children's response to the lifeblood of a master spirit, the best that has been known and said, to an hour's sweated banality in the girls' gym, which has been requisitioned for the purpose while the girls do PE in the sun, who make this sterile, dull agony the end and purpose of, say, a year or two's study of *Romeo and Juliet,* have done more to kill literature than any book-burner. At least the book-burners acknowledge the power of literature and burning a book does little to lessen its power. 'Give an account of the contribution made by the Nurse to the dramatic success of the play' clearly does.

Literature is the peak of language, it is language used at the very fullest stretch of its powers; literature is the record of what language is really for. A person's language should be a sort of literature, should be the person in words; literature is people striving to fulfil themselves in language. To say that language is not literature, is not people, but is simply a useful tool for, let us say, persuading people to buy things, teaching people how to do things, telling people what to do, describing how things work, and so on, even entertaining them, is like saying that people exist to advertise, to instruct, to control, to teach, to entertain (and to be advertised to, to be instructed, to be controlled, to be taught, to be entertained). And here my heart sinks, because I know that it is believed in our society that things like these *are* what people are for.

James Callaghan is, I suppose, a good, well-intentioned man with what he takes to be our best interests at heart. (And Shirley Williams worked hard.) In default of anything better (and there is certainly nothing better in sight) I voted for their party at the election, and turned up at local headquarters to lend a hand. Yet this is the man who opened the Great Debate with a speech that said first that there had been a possible failure in education to equip children with basic skills for life and work, and then went on to say: 'There is no virtue in producing *socially well-adjusted members of society* who are unemployed because they do not have the skills.'

Encapsulated here is the awfulness of what the creative, child-centred approach to education has become. The implication is that by *allowing* children to be 'creative', to find something amusing to do with empty Fairy Liquid bottles, we will do something towards alleviating the boredom, the dullness, the lack of significance that afflict our lives, that we can in fact make children into socially adjusted people. Callaghan does not reject this; simply (and the word is considered), he wishes us to emphasise productivity as well as social adjustment.

I suppose that I have made it clear that language teaching, with literature at its apex, has nothing to do with this, with social adjustment, nor with productivity. It is to do with helping people to be themselves – and, if once they begin to know what they really are they find themselves alienated from the society, the culture, we live in, then it is the society that needs adjustment. This is not a view, however radical it may sound today, that the founders of Trades Unionism and the Labour Party would have rejected.

Gradgrind Goes for It

This extract from A Last Resort, *exemplifies why I felt I could no longer teach English Literature in the ways examination boards force one to.*

Nick Green picked up the eighteenth exercise book. On the green cover: Frances King 4G1 English. He turned to the last used pages and picked up his red pen.

> Imagine You are a Neighbour of Silas's – How would You React to his Fostering of Eppie? How would you try to help him? You may imagine this story is happening now if you like.

man
slang/ large

does

> Down our road lives this old geezer and he's a right one I can tell you, great staring eyes and an old coat like a sack. Well he doesn't do proper work, I mean he don't go out to work, he sits in

his front room all day and just weaves, making
cloth like. But he does it well and the posh ladies
over on old Merriedale where the posh houses
are by his stuff and he makes a living. But that
don't stop him being a real dirty old man in all
senses if you ask me and not quite right in his
head, especially since his money was took. Well,
he said it was, he said he had tons there, all in
gold, but no one had ever seen it like, so who
knows, that's what I say. Anyway, like I said,
he's not quite right in the head and gets into like
trances all the time, when he just stands there
like a post and don't see nothing nor hear
nothing neither.

Anyway, the other day, like it was New Year's
Eve actually, and it snowed and snowed till
there were drifts all down our lane, what should
happen but what a young girl with this baby
comes stumbling along the lane and snuffs it
almost on this old geezer's, Marner's his name,
Silas Marner's doorstep. And the baby just
toddles in past Old Marner because he's like
having one of his fits.

This girl, the mother I mean, not the kid, is a
junkie, and full of opium which is like raw
heroin, well that's what comes out at the inquest,
and no one knows who she is.

Well Marner takes a shine to the kid on
account it's got gold hair like the gold he's lost,
in fact when he comes out of his trance he
reckons her hair is his gold come back, he being
what they call nowadays partially sighted, but
I'd say was nearer being as blind as a bat, but
then he reckons it's a kid, and she, she's about two
going on three she seems happy enough to stay.

But of course she can't, it wouldn't be right
not nowadays would it.

First thing is they say he oughta go to the

[Handwritten marginal notes, top to bottom:]
slang
spelling does/really taken
as
does any / any other
along
slang
I think you could have given his name earlier
slang
punctuation
cliché
Americanism Ugh!
punctuation
two words

punctuation

punctuation to

punctuation

it's not got any

lonely

Know

slang

This sentence is too long. At least you should put commas in some

than

does

quickly

as if

coal hole very

Indent for new para

council with it but he says I can't part with it, I
can't let it go. It's come to me – I've a right to
keep it. Then some tell-tale (there's one in every
street my mum says) goes up the council and
tells them and the next thing is he has the
Health Visitor there, and the social workers, and
meals on wheels and the doctor and the district
nurse, till you can't hardly get in his house and
they say the kid should be in a home. Who says
so Marner says will they make me take her? Till
anybody shows they've a right to take her away
from me ... the mother's dead, I reckon it got no
Father: it's a lone thing – and I'm a lone thing.
My money's gone, I don't where, and this has
come from I don't know where.

So they go up the court, the health visitor and
the social worker and all that lot to get a court
order saying she's got to be in an home but the
magistrate's an old-fashioned old codger and
says why should she be a charge on the rates if
old Marner will look after her so back they all
come, the visitors and social and all and they get
together all the evidence they can and it takes
them more'n a year all told.

But this is what they get.

Old Marner don't change her wet clothes
quick enough.

He ties her to his loom thing with a long linen
band like she was a donkey or something.

He lets her play with scissors and lets her get
in the Stone-pit which is dangerous and anyway
he being partially sighted he can't find her.

He lets her play in the coal'ole and she gets all
dirty.

He feeds her on nothing but brown sugar and
porridge.

He takes her on his trips with him when he goes
selling what he's been weaving.

He calls her Hepzibah which is a daft name,
even though it's what his mum and sister were
called.

But worst of all he's always cuddling and
holding her and stroking her hair and putting on
her under things <u>like</u> after she's had a bath, and
that's not right, an old man with staring eyes
and prone to fits and not related like, that's
pedophilia the <u>socials and all that lot</u> say.

So when they all go back to the court this time
the magistrate makes an order and they take this
Eppie away from Marner and puts her in a
home, and I shouldn't wonder but what she goes
to the bad, becomes a scrubber and a druggie
<u>like wh</u>at her mother was, most girls as go in
homes ending up like that if what you read in
the papers. ⅄⅄

Marner's upset at this, especially when enquiries arising reveal he's not been buying his
stamps or his VAT so now he's back at TRICE on
nights like my Dad who went self-employed
decorating but found too much paperwork and
worry attached so gave up.

[Handwritten margin notes: "Another 'chatty sentence'", "Lazy expression", "as", "This needs a bit added"]

[Handwritten at bottom:] 6/10 Quite good Frances, but try to write in a slightly less chatty way; I don't think that bit at the end about your Father was quite relevant, do you?

Two days later, when Frances got her book back, she added
the following below Nick Green's comment.

Dear Sir,

that bit that goes 'It got no Father, it's a lone
thing – and I'm a lone thing ect' I copied from the
book as Ms George Eliot wrote it. So I think you were
wrong to interfere with that bit.

III *Some Reviews and Other Journalism*

Shining Licht in a Naughty World

I think this must be the best review I have ever written. Apart from anything else it shows where Marxism had taken me. It still seems about right to me. It appeared in the Literary Review, *30 May 1980.*

Fred Licht, *Goya: The Origins of the Modern Temper in Art*
John Murray,

288pp, illus. £9.95.

THIS is a tremendously good book, one that reasserts, as most 'art' books do not, the central importance of art as activity, as inquiry, as thought, as an indispensable source of understanding. And in a quick parenthesis let us add that it is beautifully produced, that is to say the physical form of the book serves the writer's intention – the print is bold; the reproductions are copious, always illustrative of the text and always set close to the textual references; although none is in colour, all are printed with exemplary clarity (compare the general obscurity in, say, Allen Lane's *Goya and the Impossible Revolution);* cross-references forward and back are clearly but discreetly signposted; the index is thorough; and the proofreading, by today's declining standards, nearly perfect. I found an 'a' for an 'as', a couple of Spanish accents omitted, and one painting, *The Second of May,* reversed. (I should say I was told of this before I saw the book – but I think I would have spotted it: so *many* south-paw Mamelukes?)

Still, it is the text that matters – and let no one whose interest in Goya is less than thoughtful buy this for their coffee-table, nor turn to it for what a people's commissar for the arts, I mean the Chairman of the Arts Council, referred to as the consolation of art. Goya is a profoundly disturbing artist and the text is concerned to emphasise this, to analyse how and why he is; in short, it attempts to do justice to

Goya as a *mind*, a thinker, which above all else he was, just as Beethoven was or Shakespeare.

Yet I am going to be severely critical of certain aspects of Licht's text so I must insist, at the risk of being repetitive, that it is a long time since I came to the end of a discussion of a painter with such a feeling of gratitude to the author: gratitude for insights; for clarification; for expertise and scholarship always at the service not of Academe or the State but of understanding; gratitude for being provoked sometimes into recognition of my own wrong thinking, sometimes into radical disagreement, but always into a closer, stricter, more disciplined awareness of the subject matter. Above all this is an open-ended book, a contribution and a stimulus to illuminating discourse; it does not, as most academic products on the arts now do, package up the subject matter and put it on the shelf – there, that's done, no need to worry about Goya any more. It invites reply, close questioning, amplification. One feels: ah, if only one could attend a seminar with Fred, how good that would be, together we'd draw from him even more than he's so far given us.

Each chapter deals with one main area of Goya's work – Tapestry Cartoons, Religious Paintings, or with just one work or a small group of closely related works – *The Family of Charles IV*, the Black Paintings, and so on. Each follows broadly the same scheme. The works are set briefly in their historical context; then compared, always with great insight, scholarship and tact, with earlier works of similar subject matter and/or similar overt intention, and finally related to later 'modern' works. Thus chapter by chapter a picture is built up of a great artist struggling with a revolutionary situation and out of the struggle creating the 'modern temper in art'. Stated broadly and boldly this is a matter, for Fred, of accepting and depicting human activity in a universe that has, quite suddenly, ceased to be God-centred, and thus ceased to have meaning and purpose, at least in the terms that had been broadly accepted for millennia. Moreover, the light of Reason, which was to have taken God's place, has been extinguished or at least burns with irrelevant feebleness in the face of implacable, blind, uncontrollable forces. A lesser theme, though clearly related to the major, is the enforced isolation of the artist in modern times and his reaction to this – as experienced by Goya and typified by him.

The tone is therefore one of pessimism – at its best grimly even heroically stoical, at times slipping into a less appealing nihilism. Now part of what makes this book so interesting is that Fred is not quite at ease in this stance – I would guess that he is not by temperament the pessimist his intellect tells him he should be; less certainly I would suggest that a self-censorship is operating throughout – sometimes consciously, sometimes not – a censorship that saves Fred from coming to terms with the whole tradition of thought that has consistently, stringently, and unequivocally proposed a philosophic, aesthetic, and above all political road beyond the impasse of a Godless, alienated universe. Bluntly, Fred is aware of Marx. Occasionally he uses Marxist terminology (but at least once with almost abject apology); more significantly he resorts to circumlocution where a Marxist term clearly presents itself, where the thrust of his argument is Marxist enough to make the use of the vocabulary almost inevitable. And this is the point – again and again he seems on the very point of plunging in, one more step and he'd be away; but like a learner swimmer he keeps one foot on the bottom – on the shifting sand of a stoical pessimism that he suspects may be a cop-out, or, worse still, the justification of a repellent cynicism.

I can see four consequences arising from this: first, I think he fails to relate Goya sufficiently to the particular historical circumstances in which he worked, relating his 'modern' despair and alienation too broadly to the disappearance of God and the defeat of Reason and too little to the very specific context of Madrid during the period. Frequently, for instance, he compares and contrasts Goya with David, and most illuminatingly too, but fails to follow the comparison right through – to do so would be to place both artists too fixedly in their respective environments and thus destroy or weaken the idealist strand in his argument.

A second consequence is that at times he overstates his case to the point of actually mis-seeing, or misreporting a particular painting; a third is that he does at times, I think subjectively misread a painting (this is of course a matter of my interpretation against his); and fourthly, and most significantly of all, it leads him, extraordinarily fluent and lucid writer though he is, into imprecise and even self-contradictory statements, and these often at crucial points of his exegesis.

By way of continuing the discourse he invites I will try to illustrate each of these consequences in that order.

A relatively unimportant but symptomatic example of his failure to relate Goya sufficiently closely to the historical context in which he was working occurs in his treatment of *The Injured Mason* in which, ironically enough, he cites Marx in a way which I think Marx would not have approved. 'If we wish to find a gospel consonant with Goya's total lack of transcendental sentiment as he views the victim of a working accident, we must look forward to Marx and not backward to Christ.' The point is that we need look no further than the rational, enlightened, humane edicts of Goya's monarch, Charles III who, supported by a succession of gifted ministers, initiated a programme of reform for Spain that included a complete shake-up of the moribund universities, limits on the power of the Church, the centralisation of government, a road system that was the envy of Europe, canal building, the encouragement of cash-crops and so on and so on. Amongst it all were edicts protecting workers at the place of work, including building sites, and it is to these that the painting refers.

Now this programme was carried out in the teeth of an opposition made up of the Church, the Inquisition, and the feudal land-owners supported by urban mobs who depended on both for bread and circuses; it was supported by a rising but still very insecure middle class of bankers, merchants, industrialists, serviced by lawyers and doctors from the reformed universities. With this latter grouping Goya quickly identified himself, and throughout the rest of his life his closest friends belonged to it. They looked to the France of the *philosophes* and the England of Whig parliamentarianism and economic expansion for inspiration.

The French Revolution, coupled with the succession of Charles IV who was weak, vacillating, moronic and terrified out of his wits by what had happened to his Bourbon cousin, put a sudden, blank end to all this. Reform virtually stopped, the Church and Inquisition resumed their old power, censorship on all forms of intellectual activity clanged down like a steel door, and the emerging middle classes were suddenly transformed from being the leading edge of a gradual and peaceful revolution to bourgeois hegemony into a beleaguered, persecuted sect.

Goya's descent, accelerated by the terrible illness that left him permanently deaf, into what looks at times like stoical pessimism and even alienated nihilism, and which Fred finds to be the first expression of modernism, should, I believe, be far more closely related to these particularly Spanish events than he allows, rather than to the ideological shift from a God-centred universe to one of alienated emptiness, made worse by the apparent failure of reason. Moreover, Goya's situation was further worsened by the French occupation of 1808-1813, and not simply because it brought with it the appalling horrors of a ruthless war against local insurgents followed by famine, but because these were the French, the bringers of the gospel of brotherhood and reason. After 1814 came a reaction far worse than that of 1788-1808, a ruthless suppression of all freedom of thought and action under Ferdinand VII, a monarch whose vileness, cruelty, greed, and stupidity (I quote Fred) have rarely if ever been equalled.

I think Fred's failure to consider this context as specific and objective has led to many mistakenly weighted conclusions. Before examining, one instance as a typical example let me reiterate: it is his conclusions I am questioning, not his brilliant yet modest, and always exciting and stimulating discussion of the work.

His discussion of *Capricho 44,* the one of a woman beating a child who has broken a pitcher, is generally excellent, especially on the technique and composition, but comes to this conclusion: 'The total appeal made by this image is not the didactic wholesome lesson: "It is wrong to beat children". Instead we are simply told that mothers when pushed to the limits of human endurance by their wretchedness will eventually turn into animals and behave brutally to their children. It is as if Goya, in the face of the pointless misery of the human condition resigns himself to the simple statement of the facts of the human condition. Thus Fred finds wretchedness an inevitable concomitant of the human condition – whereas in the engraving it is clearly the concomitant of poverty. (Fred almost acknowledges this in the use of his word 'wretchedness' – this is part of the fascinating awkwardness of his stance.) Now the enlightened (and, in Spain, pre-1788) position was that poverty can and should be alleviated. But, in the reaction of the 1790s the likelihood of this happening had receded hideously leaving the enlightened artist filled with despair – not because wretchedness *can't* be alleviated, but because it won't be.

Fred concludes his discussion of the disorienting and illogical backgrounds to the *Caprichos* and *Disparates* with this: 'His true theme… is the inadequacy of man's intellectual and sensory apparatus for gaining knowledge of himself and his world.' Here, and in many other places in the book, Fred accepts explicitly the *rightness* of this pessimism, accepts man's inadequacy as an objective fact that Goya has pointed up for us. But I think there is a difference between Fred's pessimism and Goya's. Goya, with the removal of the enlightenment utopia of reason and education to a never-never land had cause for personal and deeply felt despair. It was a position, a state of mind a liberal progressive in the Spain of the French occupation could reasonably find himself in. But this is not so *now*. Pessimism *now* only serves as an excuse for reaction, conservatism, withdrawal. For Goya the forces of reaction were more and more deeply entrenched with every succeeding historical event of the times he lived in. But times have changed – pessimism is not now the agony of the liberal, it is the *excuse* of the conservative, his justification. Goya's pessimism was despair *at* the conservative – the ultimate condemnation of reaction.

Fred's determination to have Goya making idealist, essentialist statements about the human condition leads him actually to misread paintings. His discussions of *The Family of Charles IV* is for the most part exemplary and includes one shattering insight that seems marvel-

lously obvious once it is presented to us. Relating it to *Las Meninas,*
which we must since Goya obviously invites us to, Fred asks – where is
the mirror? And answers, I am sure absolutely correctly, we are the
mirror – that is the family, and Goya himself, are all in front of a
mirror. From this he draws several conclusions, most of which are fine,
but the one I won't accept is that this group portrait embodies 'man's
inability to rise to a higher ideal of himself, man's doubt in the significance of his destiny and in the guiding hand of an all-powerful divinity
that has ordained the course and tenor of his life'. I think it is a picture
of a specific group of people some of whom are suffering very acutely
from this inability but for the objective historical reasons I have already
suggested. Poor old Charles IV was up a creek, and he knew it. But this
alienation (it is here he uses the term) does not apply to everyone in the
picture, and Fred does indeed exclude the younger children. But he fails
to exclude *Goya himself* who looks straight out of the picture, straight
perhaps at his own reflection, but also at us with an absolute confidence
in what he is doing and in a way that invites us after all into a world
that alienation closes to most of the others. Now this not only undermines the essentialism of the alienation, it also undercuts Fred's second
set of conclusions about the painting which relate it to the hermetic
quality of *some* modern art (my *some,* not his) and the way in which
modern painters like Picasso and de Kooning 'paint themselves out' of
their pictures.

A final point in this section: Fred, in his anxiety to convince, says:
'The Queen, the Princes, and Goya do not look out of the picture. They
look *at* the picture they make in the mirror before them... The theme
is... the Royal Family looking at itself' and so on. But in fact at least five
characters are *not* looking at themselves – and one is Charles himself. I
think *he* is looking at Goya's reflection to see what the painter is up to
– and if so then this is a marvellous piece of underlying psychology. The
insecurity of the poor man, the insecurity of a particular man at a
particular time, not an insecurity that we are meant to accept as an
inevitable part of our condition.

The least successful chapter I think, the one that suffers most
from Fred's stance, is that on the Majas. Again his comparisons
(with Boucher's *Mile O'Murphy* and Manet's *Olympia)* are illuminating as ever, but again I think his theme of secularisation and
alienation leads him into a misinterpretation, a misreading. First, he
virtually ignores the clothed Maja. Unclothed he dwells on the
lubricity of the image, her icy sexiness, he remarks that the presen-
tation is 'singularly lewd', and concludes that the human figure has
'lost its rank and special dignity as the aesthetic and moral masterpiece of the Creator'.

In this I think he is wilfully refusing to follow where Goya is leading us. I am surely not alone in finding lubricity only in the *clothed* Maja. She indeed invites fantasy. But unclothed and with unchanged expression apart from perhaps the very slightest narrowing of the left eye, she miraculously becomes a person. You cannot now ignore the fact that the encounter that is implied by the setting and by the undressing is going to involve – *if* it takes place, and this now seems *less* likely – another human being. Clothed, one can imagine that her body might correspond to some engaging but anonymous ideal of erotic beauty; unclothed it belongs to *her,* it *is* her. The encounter cannot now take place without a conscious acceptance or denial of her individuality, without accepting or denying personal, human responsibility for what is going to happen. He who makes love with the naked Maja, or indeed with any woman, can no longer hide behind abstractions or mystifying ideals, whether attractive – woman as a symbol of fecundity, nature or whatever – or ugly, relating her to animality, lust, and so on.

This seems to me to be the content of the best of Goya's later work, and it is something Fred has cut himself off from by insisting that we are presented with a pessimistic, not to say nihilistic, but certainly idealist view of the universe. For instance, on *The Third of May* he concludes, following illuminating discussion of the Baroque tradition of martyrdom painting and then comparisons with Gericault's *Severed Heads,* 'Death is no longer an individual occurrence beheld and judged by an infinitely aware God. It is instead a repeatable, impersonal disruption of life devoid of special significance.'

It is symptomatic that he should have been led by the inner logic of his argument against what must surely have been his better truer judgment to deprive the execution of that agonised and entirely secular central figure of significance. In my estimation, and surely in that of all of us who willy-nilly find the painting so compulsive, significance, *human* significance, is precisely what it has. I would go on. To say the deaths of the victims Goya presents here and in the *Disasters of War* lack significance is to deprive the victims of a dignity that Goya never denied, even when the mutilations are at their most horrible.

The Third of May is not about death, nor are the *Disasters of War.* They are about killing, killing at last deprived of all theological or otherwise mystifying justification. Without God we have no excuse, the responsibility is ours. From now on when we kill, or have sex, we do so as one human being to another, unmediated by religious or idealistic flummery. What it amounts to is that in modern times the inescapable truth faces us bleakly – we, and we alone are responsible for what we do to each other. In short, man is now responsible for his own history – the era of pre-history is closed.

Whether or not this is a matter for optimism (and Goya suffered doubt on this score, doubt taken to the level of suffering expressed in the *Black Paintings)* remains highly problematical – but at least let us recognise that the horrors we have lived through since Goya, though technologically assisted, have been no more than repetitions of the horrors that man has inflicted on man since 'civilisation', or class society, began. What Goya tells us is that we have no one to blame but ourselves.

Fred's position, as I said earlier, pushes him into uneasy contradictions. At the close of his discussion of the *Disasters* (which is marred by his insistence on those plates that most terribly reflect man's 'vileness, cruelty and insanity', ignoring those with a content, however muted or problematic, of heroism, tenderness, and sacrifice) he yet has this to say:

'Goya seeks to bear witness to the fundamental nature of man's eternal warfare against himself; he seeks to bring to the attention of the fatuous and forgetful the fact that the world is divided into two races: the complacent and the wretched. Both states of mind are incompatible with the dignity man might achieve.' This won't do. He moves from an idealist position characteristic of late liberal, neoconservative nihilism – 'eternal struggle' – through a simplistic but accurate description of a world divided into 'two races', to a 'dignity man *might* achieve'.

Similar unease, or wilful refusal to follow his own insights through to their conclusion continue to mar much of what follows. Most obviously, because most necessarily, this happens in his discussion of the *Session of the Royal Coy of the Philippines* which he says is Goya's supreme masterpiece. His long and excellent analysis cites *Heart of Darkness,* Poe, Baudelaire and Kafka, and ends in one of his best descriptions: 'The demon of acedia steals all the luster from this world's sunlight; jeers at our comings and goings, and mocks all our pretensions.' Yet clearly he is unhappy with this, realises he has described the mood of the picture and not its content, so he goes on: 'Goya is the first to illustrate in his paintings the dubious nature of action when action is no longer determined by a fixed transcendental moral code.'

Which is fine but not enough, for he does not ask, as I think Goya insists we should ask, just what it is now determines action. Clearly it is not the reason and instinct of the enlightenment. The answer, and really Fred has seen it – his citing of *Heart of Darkness* shows it – is the imperative of expanding imperialist capitalism, based on the mechanism of the market, with ruthless exploitation as it means. That is what the Royal Company of the Philippines was occupied with and it is what Goya's picture is about, and it is out of it that the alienation and shame that afflict both the people in the picture and we who look at it come; and not out of some preordained human condition.

The book almost concludes with a very uneasy discussion of what Fred calls the 'Proletarian Paintings'. Again the analysis is fine, and involves a splendid comparison of Goya's blacksmiths with Wright's *Iron Forge*. But inevitably his position catches him out – he sentimentalises the workers, which Goya most decidedly does not: 'Men doing a job and doing it well, the dignity of workers caught in the performance of tasks that require mastery...', is plebeian tosh. No mastery is required by a water-carrier, and very little by a knife-grinder. It is the guilt of the exploiters of labour that ascribes dignity and skill to laborious, tedious, repetitive work. Yet again, it is Goya who gets it right and who will not let Fred off the hook, who drives him on to this: 'We believe in the existence of the water-carrier and the blacksmith because they incontrovertibly exist *in their own right.*'

That phrase (my emphasis) is vague, shifty, ultimately irresponsible in its refusal to consider its own implications. What is this *right* these workmen have that, say, Ferdinand VII does not have? It is not 'soul' for Fred has been at pains to show how Goya has destroyed that particular bit of mystifying nonsense. Could it be that Goya is replacing 'soul' with a truer if bleaker humanism, the humanism that places responsibility for the nature of our existences on us alone, the humanism that was later to identify (and not 'much later') the progressive class of our times as the proletariat – those who have nothing but their labour to support them, and so no class interest to defend, no pretension beyond their humanity, and no shame or guilt either? Is that what Fred means by 'existing in their own right'?

If it is, he ducks away again in the last chapter, the Epilogue, which concludes with this inflated peroration: 'If we are still able to feel gratitude and admiration for the artist... it is due only to the vague hope that mankind, though seemingly doomed in an impenetrable universe, cannot be quite lost as long as there remain spirits such as his: incorruptible and courageous witnesses whose passage on earth lends dignity to their race.'

Using it merely for consolation we do Goya's achievement a terrible disservice. For by it we are turning his mastery, his honesty, his dour stoicism, his insights, above all his heroic intellectual grappling with a profoundly problematic situation into sustenance for a pessimism he himself never finally surrendered to, though he had more reason than we have, the pessimism of a decadent and disillusioned liberal humanism which, before our eyes, is even now dwindling into the ugly, facile cynicism that characterises so much of politics, art and thought in western society today.

It remains to add that while statements like this do constitute the most overt, generalised descriptions of Fred's position, they do *not*, I believe, represent the underlying tenor of this book, which, through his analysis of particular paintings and particularly through his comparison of Goya with his predecessors, remains the best I have read on the subject.

Jesus Saves

I am including this, also first printed in the Literary Review, *not to take a second swipe at a fellow writer who has to earn a crust with the rest of us but because it encapsulates my deep hatred for the cynicism of all who ascribe original sin (in any of its forms) to the human race, and turn to old Mumbo Jumbo, the Juggernaut in the Sky, for a get-out.*

Piers Paul Read, *A Married Man.*
Secker and Warburg 264pp. £5.25

In January and February 1974 *A Married Man* reaches its climaxes, a winter of discontent – not the first, and, one now realises, by no means the last. John Strickland, a barrister with socialist ideals received from his father, bourgeois aspirations, and a snobbish Catholic wife, develops a middle-aged desire for sexual novelty, and a middle-aged awareness that he has sacrificed his ideals on the altar of his wife's pretensions. The results are, on the one side, a gauche attempt to seduce an adolescent member of his set followed by an affair with an heiress; on the other, that he stands 'in the Labour interest' (several of the characters use expressions of this sort) and wins his seat in the February election. However, by the following August he has chucked up politics and ditched his wealthy mistress for reasons which I shall not disclose, since the book has a thrillerish element, though this side of the plot is pretty transparent, especially given the hint in the blurb.

The telling of all this is brisk and often bright – in its observation of the petty snobberies of the main characters and in its occasional flashes of wit. It should be said though that the latter often have a second-hand reach-me-down feel about them – 'each couple felt tacitly flattered by the companionship of the others, and that in their circle was often the basis for friendship' might well have been said more sharply by La Rochefoucauld – perhaps was; and sometimes they can be a touch wild – to say a face is creased with self-pity so that it looks like Christ on the Cross is to leave open the possibility that one is asked to ascribe self-pity to Christ as well as to the owner of the face. Fair enough, you might say – except that by the end of the book it has become clear that Mr Read takes JC very seriously indeed.

The characters are from stock – telly stock, for the most part. There are amongst them a nasty working-class petty crook called Terry Pike(!); a mephistophelian banker with landed connections called Mascall(!!); a mean millionaire; a rich bitch straight out of big business soap opera and about as real as Bambi; an adolescent cock-teaser; a retired brigadier, eccentric and wearing old clothes but whose heart is in the right place; and so on. Mr Read fleshes these out to an extent – partly by contradicting himself about them (maybe Mascall's philandering has an altruistic side to it after all?), and partly through their conversation. At its best this is clever and quick, but a lot of it takes the form of Strickland's attempts to justify his political beliefs and ambitions to people for whom socialism equals satanism.

In these passages the level of political discussion is too often naïve, and sometimes ill-judged. For instance, at one point Strickland, in an argument with his high tory wife, concedes that middle-class children will always do better at exams than working-class children because middle-class children are genetically more intelligent. We may accept that this is still a view widely held, in spite of the demolishing of Cyril Burt *et al*, and no doubt it is a view that will be with us until the last high tory has been attached to a lamp-post – but surely no social demo-crat, however far to the right, would accept it so readily. That Strickland should admit that wide differences of intelligence occur, that he should find these differences to be class-based, is all credible; but that he should volunteer the idea that high intelligence is genetically pooled in the middle class, is not.

It is a truism, in some circles at any rate, that a ruling class that has ceased to believe in its moral right to rule will resort to cynicism – in its daily life, in its social relations, above all in the way it will manipulate its power more and more overtly in its own class interest. Moreover, such a class will cynically adopt attitudes to human nature in general which will justify these practices, attitudes which degrade us all to a level lower than the brutes – ascribing to our every action the basest motives of self-interest. Since a moribund but still ruling class will have effective control of scientific research, education, and the arts, these beliefs will be vigorously promoted as the received truth about mankind and will seep down to infect classes that have no need to justify their existence by holding them.

Such a ruling class Mr Read portrays – perhaps, for all I know, accurately. So far, so good. But Mr Read portrays it from the inside, and ultimately his view of human nature is no different from that of the people he describes – only his response to it is different. At one point the authorial voice declares that a cynic would say that the laws of England are framed in the interest of the ruling class – that adultery and buggery are no longer punished, while shop-lifting and brawling (working-class vices, apparently) are. One is left at that point (fairly early in the book) wondering what the author is going to offer in place of this cynicism. Indeed the cynicism becomes so complete, is so laboured (in both senses), that one becomes interested, as one is when reading a thriller, to see just what he is going to offer in its place.

Clearly socialism is out – it is a mask for spiteful envy, the resort of the residually guilty, a means to political power if you don't belong to the right clubs, the last shred of dignity for self-deceiving drunks (represented here by a journalist writing for the *New Statesman*, which seems unfair to me. I've met *Spectator* journalists who like a drop too, and who claim to be idealists, though of a different sort). There are other sorts of socialists, Mr Read concedes, but, with a smugness I find offensive, discovers them to be painfully boring and ineffectual do-gooders, and plain to boot. In fact there is a vein of snobbery in this book which denies style, good looks, and wit to anyone but the upper classes. I find this distasteful, as well as false.

So Mr Read offers us a view of human nature that is entirely pessimistic, however superficially presented. Socialism is not the panacea, and he is too earnest to fall back on the bottle or suicide. What are we to do? Well, like a good thriller writer, Mr Read has planted his clues – perhaps with more skill than he placed those that point to who dunnit – I mean who dun the actual murders that also come near the end – and so it is not a complete surprise, but still a little bit of a surprise, when he whips away the black cloth and reveals that after all the white pigeon is still alive and well. Or to be specific, when Strickland (whose name has by now taken on a slightly allegorical tinge – John = Everyman, Strickland = Stricken Land, get it?) discovers an exchange of letters between his rather lapsed Catholic wife, and Father Michael, the Jesuit priest who married them.

Everything is awful, but Jesus saves; that about sums it up.

One should not think, as has been suggested, that Mr Read is moving towards Catholic Marxism – whatever that may be. His Jesuit locks the door on that one very sharply. This is what he has to say to poor Clare Strickland: 'Would you rather I… belittle the significance of sexual sin as against the greater evil of monopoly capitalism or starvation in the Third World? (Actually, it's most unlikely that she'd rather any such thing.) The Truth is, however, that the temptation which faces you is not to starve an Asiatic child or sell goods at excess profit: the temptation is to adultery...'

At one point in these letters the Jesuit says that a woman should, for the sake of the family, submit to her husband, just as he has had to submit to his Vatican superiors. A cynic might comment that in the Church of Pope John Paul II, Father Michael looks set for speedier advancement than John Strickland is likely to enjoy.

Global Thrillers

This piece, part review, part think-bit, was published on the net by an Austrian zine, called eurozine.

Ed McBain once famously said: "Writing a commercially successful novel comes high on the list of white-collar crime." Put up Robert Harris.

Archangel is set in contemporary Moscow but looks back to Stalinist Russia and particularly the death of Stalin. Central to the plot is an oilskin-bound notebook in Stalin's handwriting, found by Beria in a Kremlin safe, hidden, rediscovered by an ex-Stalinist functionary and used by him to advance the return of Stalinist communism. The main character is an English academic who is manipulated to authenticate the notebook. The Russian background is presented strongly and vividly and convinces the reader of its truthfulness, and much of the writing is pacey. In short, it is in a tradition of English thriller writing that goes back through Hall, Ambler, Household, Lyall, Graham Greene and many others to John Buchan and beyond. Except that...

Except that it is 421 pages long instead of two hundred and fifty. Except that it is overloaded with a portentous analysis of contemporary Russian society which I imagine is accurate enough, but not in the least revelatory. Except that its central characters are woeful stereotypes. Except that the writing is sometimes clogged and lacks the clarity of Harris's predecessors. Except that the plot creaks, barely stands up, and turns on an event, a situation, that is frankly as fantastically unlikely as anything Buchan or his lesser contemporaries ever dreamt up. Except that it attempts to flatter the reader into believing he or she has been given genuine insights into the deepest recesses of the corridors of power and the minds of the giants who shape our lives. In short, it is on the way to betraying the tradition it came from and seeks to create for its author and his publisher a niche in the best-seller lists dominated by such names as Ludlum, Clancey, Higgins, the later

Forsyth, and many more.

What are the characteristics of these formulaic blockbusters? They are long. They are complicated. They are often written in a bland but opaque prose that is like wading through a stew with not much meat and occasional pieces of gristle. They flatter the reader into believing they reveal, for our personal eyes only (all twenty million of us) secrets of recent history that have been vouchsafed to the author alone. They take no account of the economic, social, and historical imperatives that shape our lives but insist that history is a matter of personality only, and generally speaking psychopathic personality at that. Contingency, sheer mischance or happenchance which in actual fact are so much part of our individual lives, are almost completely excluded unless the Author has got his knickers in a twist and needs an outrageous coincidence. At the lower end of this low market, they are generally set, at least in part, in exotic places, but not too exotic: Caribbean hideaways are common, as also are Alpine schlosses, and the villain usually has a yacht, a sadistic bodyguard and is given to unusual sexual practices.

Incidentally, let me add *Archangel* is not as bad as this but it will be interesting to see how long Harris can hold out from the worst excesses of this sub-genre, especially as the pressure of writing, of being bribed to write, one blockbuster every two years takes its toll.

Does all this matter? Yes it does. The blockbuster genre has produced very few books of any lasting value at all. They are by definition holiday fodder, to be read on long flights, or given as presents at Christmas and they have entirely ruined the market for the older sort of thriller out of which they grew and which did produce many many books that one can return to again and again, and which are now out of print or, if new, virtually unpublishable. The great English exemplar of this genre was Eric Ambler who died last year. He too had his formula and there is a fair bit of it still lingering on in *Archangel*. Basically an ordinary sort of person, a businessman, a journalist, an academic, an engineer (Ambler trained and practised as an engineer before becoming a writer) stumbles into or is drawn into an intrigue involving spying or crime and is generally given a hard time as a result. That's being very reductive, but you get the idea. What makes his books so fascinating is the interdependence that exists between the main character and historical forces of some importance. The Cold War – *The InterCom Conspiracy*; the Conflict in Palestine – *The Levanter*; Communist subversion in the Far East – *Passage of Arms*... and so on. But Ambler never makes the mistake of presenting real historic personalities, leaders or otherwise – it is at street level that the impact of historical forces are experienced and therefore understood; his prose is like the flow of spring water unclogged with neo-baroque description; sex and brutality take their proper place on the periphery of our lives though love, hate, greed and revenge may figure largely; technical know-how and hardware serve the plot but are never there to impress or flatter the reader, and so on and so on... And in England now, NOT ONE OF AMBLER's books is in print, though I believe, following his death, an English publisher is now planning to reissue some of them.

What has happened? Well the answer is clear enough and boring too: globalisation, the Market, commodity fetishism, and the ineluctable tendency of all products of capitalism to lose their individuality, to imitate each other, to become standardised. Publishers and authors may believe that they remain above all that sort of thing, but do they? Do they, hell! The first thing a publisher asks, faced with a manuscript which he hopes might be a mega-seller, is 'What do we sell this as?' And if it doesn't fit a market niche it's either dumped or rewritten until it does.

It seems to be received wisdom these days that a mega-seller thriller must be long, 120,000 words at least, it must deal with global events at a fantasised level beyond our normal reach, it must have a core of expertise presented in a way that flatters the reader's understanding without actually asking him/her to learn anything or use his/her brain. If the author has been previously published it must absolutely not in any way go beyond the readers' expectations of that author. It must not be genuinely original or personal. In short it reduces the author's function to that of the sort of tradesman or artisan who makes reproduction furniture, turning out the same chair or table again and again, and employed to do so only because 'hand-crafted' is a selling point on the label or because the computerised machine that will do the job as well has not yet been invented.

An important part of this whole exercise is the author's Name. This becomes the Name not of a person, an individual, but of a brand, the author's name becomes a brand-name. What is the difference between Addidas and Nike? The name. 'The New Forsyth' the advertisements proclaim on the posters on the Underground, next to those that announce a 'New and Improved Washing Powder With A Name We all Recognise'. So far has all this gone that it is now generally believed and alleged that Lord Archer hasn't written a book for years, but a stable of hacks turns them out for him. I am sure this is not true, but the fact that it is credible proves the points I am trying to make.

Anyway, the result of all this is that the bookshops' shelves are more and more filled with identical products, all of the same thickness, with the same embossed glittery covers and the same names on them, quite a lot of names still, maybe as many as forty... As many as FORTY? Just forty authors for several billion readers across the world to choose from? *Only* forty??!!??

When all's said and done it's not the publishers' fault, nor the readers', it's not even the booksellers'. It's just one small part of the global process that homogenises the food we eat, the cars we drive, the clothes we wear, the music we listen to, the shopping malls we shop in, even, God help us, the lamp-posts in the shopping malls.

You want a return to the good old days? You want to halt this process? You want fiction, crime fiction, that has genuine meaning, relevance, emotion and individuality? Then you will have to man the barricades and consider putting those lamp-posts to uses that were not foreseen by the programmers who wrote the software that designed them.

Get Real

A version of this was printed in the New Statesman, *Christmas number, 1995.*

Like it or not, and clearly a lot of people don't like it at all, there is swelling up yet again a feeling that the crime novel has the space and the responsibility to take itself seriously. It's happened before. At my age (60 – and that means fifty years reading crime and thirty writing it) you begin to realise that almost everything that happens in the crime-writing world and indeed in the literary world as a whole happens at roughly fifteen-year intervals, again and again and again, and the media always forget.

But before I go any further I feel I'd better clear the decks for action. There are misapprehensions abroad about me. I am not a Stalinist. I am not a Trot. Horror of horrors I am not even working class. Nor indeed do I write about the working class. Nor am I some sort of po-faced Leavis-ite. I am, and anybody who has seen me mucking about at a crime writers' conference will bear this out, a fun-loving, frivolous hedonist, occasionally irresponsible, sometimes rude, but always out for a good time. Two. Some of the jolliest moments I've had when not in a bar chatting up ladies with a similar outlook on life have been spent reading frankly escapist literature. I'll cheerfully curl up with Wodehouse – especially *Right Oh, Jeeves*, or *The Code of the Woosters* for the ninth or tenth time when I get bored with whatshisname and you-know-who, who just really don't know how to be funny at all. I love anarchic films. From *Duck-Soup* through *Airplane* to *Funny Bones*.

However, the thing that many people think is seriously wrong with me is that I have never been able to persuade myself that murder is a matter of fun, unless the fun is surrealist or satirical. Thus I can laugh in *Naked Gun 33¹/₃*, when the guy on the stage looses off his piece into the theatre flies to get hush, says no one will get hurt, and a body drops at his feet. But I do not find it fun when in chapter one a body is found in the quad so that in chapter thirteen I can be told that, from the point of view of a middle-class, tory-voting audience, the least likeable person in the book done it. I don't like it when all this happens without a single glance, or at the most a token one, at what violent death is like both for the sufferer and the doer, at the sort of things that can turn a human into a killer (and a lot has to happen before she or he will give way to greed, jealousy, revenge or any of the usual hackneyed motives), at what a person must go through at the hands of real police, or when s/he knows s/he's going to be locked up for life. Or, in the good old days, hanged.

Occasionally, I admit, I succumb, but only when the whole thing is removed completely and self-consciously from real life – as in say Suchet's Poirot, or Brett's or Basil Rathbone's Sherlock Holmes. Or in the baroque choreography of *Reservoir Dogs* and *Pulp Fiction* where, empty of content, style is king. And even then, I have my qualms. But what I truly cannot cope with is those modern mysteries that congratulate themselves on having got out of the unreal world of the country-house, the Riviera pad, the fear and loathing in Sixpenny Handley and into the real world of... of Oxbridge Quads, private hospitals, Lloyds, the Stock Exchange and the House of Commons. (The real world? Pardon me.) They make great efforts to get the forensics as blood-curdlingly right as they can, and though almost none of them can resist giving their detective a side-kick (which no real policeman ever has) instead of a team, they try to do the same with procedures. Yet, while on one side they go to great efforts to convince this is real, this could happen, on the other they still maintain that what they do is a bit of fun and nothing to do with life at all (to quote Colin Dexter in a recent interview given to *A Shot in the Dark*). Sorry Colin, but this will not be the only time in this article I shall appear to have a go at you – nothing personal, but I just have that interview to hand, and I'm sorry, again, but it really does encapsulate a lot of what I'm banging on about.

Anyway, this insistence on having a bit of fun with reality seems to me to be deeply psychopathic. If Freud had got round to it a good appendix to his *Psychopathology of Everyday Life* would have been the ditto of the detective novel and he really would have had a ball with the contortions, confusions and contradictions of the detective/mystery novel now. But I suppose the discontents of civilisation are more obvious too, sixty years on.

Having said that: 'Colin Dexter goes on to say, and many of my colleagues agree with him, the fiction writer who sets out to be morally uplifting or socially valuable soon becomes an unread writer'. You know, like Jane Austen, the Brontës, George Eliot (who didn't write crime novels), or Charles Dickens, Conan Doyle, Joseph Conrad, Graham Greene, Raymond Chandler, Dashiel Hammett, Eric Ambler, Geoffrey Household, Lawrence Block (whose moral fervour almost got me off the bottle and certainly helped to pull me back from an unacceptable brink), and Ross Thomas (who wrote Greene in the style of Spillane) and many, many, many, many more who did or do write crime novels? Let's get this straight – these are all avowed moralists who tried or are still trying to be socially valuable. The point I am making is that it is not impossible for a book that creates the 'I don't want to... turn out the light, I want to finish this' (Colin again) feeling to be morally uplifting and socially valuable as well. And if it can, it should. Especially if its central subject matter is crime.

That's the responsibility – now the space. Two of this year's Booker Prize nominees are, to some extent, murder stories. That already says something about straws in the wind. But swallows don't make summers. I don't follow literary trends very closely but I do get the impression that few literary novels face up to the realities of modern society as well as the best crime stories or any better than the worst. Am I right in thinking that many are written by people who believe their own egos divorced from any genuine social reality are inordinately interesting to us all? That there is, as my mother would have said, a plethora of books whose authors feel they must inflict on us, two generations too late, the angst of being brought up in or in exile from an ex-colonial society? That many are apparently trying to move on from the psycho-dramas of the suburbs that filled the seventies and early eighties by escaping into pseudo-fantasy or pseudo-historicism but taking their psycho-dramas with them? That by and large the contemporary English literary scene is dominated by poseurs and mincers? That's where the space is.

And never was there a better time for the crime novel to be the one to fill it. We live in a criminal society. I mean a society which is structurally criminal. If we removed from our economy every trace of exploitation of the Third World and actively worked in the opposite direction... if we wiped out all unnecessary pollution... if we removed all traces of sexism and racism... if we had a police force, a clergy, a judiciary, a parliament we could respect and trust... if we wiped out white-collar crime in all its forms and gave the roads back to the travellers... if we legalised pot... if we stopped selling weapons of horrifying destruction to homicidal maniacs... if there was one single political party interested in structural justice rather than getting their bums on the government benches... if, if, if, *then* we might say our society is not structurally criminal. It follows that a novel which reflects, portrays, presents or through satire ridicules society must be, to some extent, perhaps to a very great extent, a crime novel.

There do seem to me to be three honoured and honourable traditions in crime-writing, and none of them cosy or merely hard-boiled, that remain in place and show the way forward and up into that space vacated by literary fiction. Taking them in no particular order let's start with the genuinely psychological, the writers who really do have the ability to get inside the so-called criminal's mind and thereby reveal to us all the criminal inside each of us. The leader of the pack, and no one has touched her yet, is Patricia Highsmith, especially in Ripley mode. She has splendid apostles, Rendell/Vine and Minette Walters are two who spring immediately to my mind and that's where I'm leaving it – there are enough lists already in this article. But these two, and many others like them, often fail for me by being tied to the mystery format. Desperately fenced in by agents and publishers, or possibly by a confused idea of what they are about, they insist on a twist, a surprise at the end, even occasionally a whipping away of a mask à la mode de Christie, the answer to the puzzle and all that jazz.

We don't need it. We stopped needing it when, forty years ago and a quarter of the way through *The Talented Mr Ripley*, virtually right at the beginning of the whole monstrous Ripley enterprise, loveable Tom picked up that oar and battered Dickie Greenleaf to death on the misty Mediterranean in a little boat off San Remo. And that's where the suspense starts, not where it ends. Oh dear, how many hundreds of good novels have been reduced to mere mysteries by that fatal desire to keep us guessing? Patricia Highsmith has plenty of surprises along the way, and plenty of suspense, but above all the confidence to do away with the nasty little question that is only answered on the last page. And the metamorphosis of Ripley from a rootless, shiftless, barely educated drifter to a prosperous, middle-aged bourgeois with a ritzy French wife continues to ask, and answer, questions about the mentality of people who get to positions like that from such inauspicious beginnings.

Tradition number two: those who set their stories against real social backgrounds which to a large extent mould the personalities of their characters and explain their actions, who explore themes like social deprivation in inner cities and depressed rural areas, racism, domestic violence, drug-related crime at the petty gangster level and so on, writers who inherit in part the hard-boiled vision of Chandler, Hammett, Ross Macdonald, but who are also part of a long European tradition with roots in people like Balzac, Dickens, Dostoyevsky, Zola, Maupassant. I am thinking of people and places – the Sweden of Sjowahl and Wahloo, Simenon's Paris, Freeling in Holland and Strasbourg. And nowadays MacDermid's Manchester, Harvey's Nottingham, Rankin's Edinburgh, Timlin's South London.

Somewhere between these two areas, the inner world of Highsmith and the mean streets, lies the heart of darkness where few of us dare to go. Did Derek Raymond entertain? It's a question you hardly dare ask. But, dear Colin, Cookie kept the pages turning, and you didn't keep the light on in order to finish *The Devil's Home on Leave* or *Dora Suarez*. You kept it on and longed for daybreak *because* you'd finished them. And perhaps, dare I say it, at dawn you might have had a little more understanding of what went on at 22 Cromwell Street.

My third area of crime writing which has in the past produced fiction of genuine value and seriousness and I believe could do so again is that of the thriller/adventure story. In the hands of the masters it had the potential of exposing the realms of politics, national and international, organised crime above street level, arms dealing, mercenaries, nuclear power, the politics of oil, ecology, food production and distribution, the Third World, and so on, the list is a long one. The two great masters were Greene and Ambler. The present CWA could well remind itself that the first Diamond Dagger Award ever was made to Ambler, and the third to Le Carré. It is in this area that I claim my own humble niche (Right up there with Le Carré – *Publisher's Weekly*).

Ambler is usually credited with the rather negative quality of lifting the thriller out of the Boys' Ownish mire of Sapper and Le Queux, but what is not sufficiently recognised is that he, and many many more of us, look to the author of *The Secret Agent, Lord Jim, Under Western Eyes, Victory* and *Nostromo* as the grand-daddy of us all.

Unfortunately the adventure-thriller was hijacked by the Cold War warriors and also by the door-stoppers. Often by both at once if you see what I mean. But if ever there was a time when we needed an Ambler or Greene then this is it. Where is the writer who can do for today's arms trade or ex-colonial sub-wars what Ambler's *Passage of Arms* or *Dirty Story* did? Where is the Greene of *The Comedians, The Quiet American* and *The Honorary Consul* to give us the great fiction that could expose Bosnia or East Timor?

Well, just round the corner, is the answer one hopes for – or rather buried under fat airport novels or the tired detritus of played-out Forsyth, Deighton and, I'm afraid, Le Carré himself, judging by their most recent performances. As Gerald Seymour (along with Ted Allbeury, one of the very few genuinely worthwhile door-stopper producers) has said, 'The genre has the capability of informing an audience, giving them more insight into the problems we are all talking about, than a forest of newspapers and a cloud of newscasts'. Yes, but only if the old guard are moved over and let voices with genuinely contemporary concerns be heard.

So, Crime Writers of the World, we have the responsibility, the space and the means to take the high ground occupied by the great critical realists of the late nineteenth and early twentieth century, ground woefully abandoned by straight, and literary, authors. But, I hear you cry, publishers and critics never treat us seriously... to which the only answer is: get serious, man, and they might. Get real.

Big Brother has Your Number

(Printed as one of the Independent's *Pass Notes to the Twenty-First Century)*

Forget the miniaturised cameras everywhere, the bugs, the spotter planes, the satellites, think about computers and how they keep an eye on every aspect of our lives, and I am not thinking about the obvious things like credit ratings, insurance claims, political affiliation.

Using the details on Sainsbury's receipts over a year, a clever analysis, itself computer created, could, probably does, arrive at a remarkably detailed and accurate picture of every regular customer: how much he or she and their family drink, eat chocolate, use convenience foods, and so on; how their financial status fluctuates, whether or not they are impulse shoppers or fixated on the multi-buys and super-savers. Then add to Sainsbury's database those of every other retail outfit in the shopping mall.

GPs' and hospital records are now being computerised. Slot them into each personal file and the picture fills out that bit more: liver crisis two years ago (warning: no alcohol), high blood pressure (watch the salt intake in the convenience foods), diabetic (who's the chocolate for, then?).

All this information and much much more is scattered over several databases in which we are all logged under different numerical and alphabetical codes and which, so far, do not speak easily to each other or to any central database. But IDs and smart cards are on the way: a steady drip of speculation and discussion, nearly always presented in a way that makes the objectors look like naïve or antisocial Luddites, is already softening us up.

In 1940 everyone had a number. Those who were alive then and are still alive now still have that number on their medical cards. No problem there then. Every one of our separate personal files, including those generated by credit cards and by supermarkets, and those held by the Inland Revenue or the bank could have the same number. It could even be the number of your car or your telephone. Certainly it will be the number on a nation-wide employers' database and on your criminal record. Could be? Will be. And all that information could be, will be, available on a state-controlled database, logged under that one number. Too massive to handle for sixty million people? Ten years ago it might have been – not now. Think of the ease and speed with which you can trawl the internet for the most abstruse piece of information.

Can you imagine? A polite phone-call. Sorry to disturb you Mr R, but here at the Central Health Office we see your purchase of chocolate has gone up and is spread over three different retail outlets. Your doctor has been informed. Sorry to disturb you Mr R, Tax Control here. Your cash withdrawals over the last three months are not accounted for through normal electronic channels. We are required to remind you of the penalties incurred by those employing unlicensed builders and paying them in cash... And so on.

Marvellous. Who could possibly object? The economy will be run more efficiently, our health needs properly assessed, cheating for benefits will be a thing of the past, and cheating on taxes too... and that's barely scratching the surface. Who are we that we should worry? Potential criminals? Welfare state scroungers? Anarchists, for Christ's sake?

There's no third way. Either you believe in the State's right to run things (that is, our lives) as efficiently as possible in the interests of the multi-nationals, sorry, I mean for the greatest good of the greatest number, or you don't. Whose side are you on? How can you justify your resistance? Are there enough of us to stop the rot? Are we sufficiently upset by it all to be bothered? As a romantic optimist with anarchist leanings (i.e. English) the answer for me is yes, perhaps, maybe. Yes.

I am not Amused

For a time we were made to pay to enter our great museums which had been largely financed by Victorian philanthropists on the understanding that they would be free. This made me very angry… as angry as the cheques I have to write now to keep my son out of debt while he goes through university.

Goya's great masterpiece of his later years is *La Junta del Compañía Real de las Filipinas,* which hangs in the Musée Goya in Castres in Tarn, north of the eastern Pyrenees. It is a massive group portrait of the directors of the company that ran and plundered the Philippines through the eighteenth and nineteenth centuries. The central figure is Ferdinand VII, one of the cruellest, stupidest and most greedy despots ever to get his bum on a throne in Europe and here portrayed as such. It is an intensely awesome painting which foreshadows Conrad's *Heart of Darkness.* Fred Licht in *Goya, the Origins of the Modern Temper in Art, (John Murray, 1980)* analysed it brilliantly: 'The false foreshortenings, the unrecognizable faces, the pointless yet menacing stares out of the picture, and above all the suspension of any understandable action, give one the peculiarly Kafkaesque feeling of being on trial without knowing why… one can't help but feel oneself humiliated, isolated and insidiously exposed on all sides.'

La Junta del Museo de Victoria y Alberto placed in a similar situation and painted by an artist as profound as Goya would, I suspect, have much the same look about them, and much the same effect. Already they have left me feeling humiliated, isolated and insidiously exposed.

Not that long ago (an aeon by media standards but a few months for ordinary mortals) Daniel Feeld (Dennis Potter's Feeld, that is, Potter's Field, geddit?) condemned to death by pancreatic cancer, considered whom he might most usefully rid the world of before he himself departed. I am so angry, distressed, bewildered and bereaved by La Junta del Museo that if I were more terminally ill than anyone of my age might expect to be, and if I could arrange for it to happen, I would cheerfully sit the Junta, sorry, Trustees of the Victoria and Albert, behind a table like the one in Goya's painting and… blow them. With, I should imagine, an *Apocalypse Now* type M60.

Why? Because from the first of October there will be a five pound entrance fee though you'd never know it when you go through the portals. Like all dirty little secrets it's tolerably well kept, unless as I did you happened to catch a small paragraph in a newspaper or a five second flash on Radio 3 news. But no notices actually there invite you to make the most of the last few weeks.

I am sixty-one. I have probably visited the V & A thirty times in my life, maybe more. The National Gallery and the National Portrait Gallery and the Tate at least as often. There have been several periods in my life (and right now is one of them) when I have not had five pounds to spare to enter anything, and, thankfully, other periods when a fiver or its then equivalent was a matter of no consideration at all. BUT THAT IS NOT THE POINT.

I know these collections very well by now. And very often I go in for just half an hour, to have a chat with old friends: Anthony Palliser's portrait of Graham Greene in the NPG, Velasquez's *Immaculate Conception* in the NG, any Hockney that happens to be in the Tate, the costume cases in the V & A, the Raphael Cartoons, the Michaelangelo wax models, the Great Bed of Ware or just for a cup of coffee in decent surroundings. Five pounds for half an hour...! But that's not the point either.

The animals who have ruled us for the last two decades (I know what I'm saying – this sort of thing started with Callaghan) have been promoting a strange concept called English Heritage. What meaning can you put on the word 'heritage' other than something inherited? I do not pay to read the books I inherited from my parents. Why should I pay for this? If, for instance, I want to look at the only domestic arte-fact still extant that we know Shakespeare knew, and since it obviously made an impression on him, he probably saw it, perhaps slept in it with eleven other people, why should I have to pay? I used to look at it, and with sentimental tears glistening in my eye wander out into Museum Street ten minutes later only to find I was in Hyde Park when I was meant to be at South Ken Tube.

What do these bastards think art is for? How can people from now on build up that sort of closeness, intimacy, love for these great collec-tions if they have to hand over a fiver every time they go in? (Sure, the Tate, the NPG and the NG are still free, but for how long?) How can they become part of your very soul, a deep and important part of your intellectual physiognomy, if you have to think of each visit as a planned event, an outing, get your money's worth? How deeply absurd it is to make us even think about our money's worth – it is bound to make us wander for an hour or two, until our legs ache, instead of spending twenty minutes on, say, the Bernini, and the Bernini only so we could carry away that experience, unencumbered by the ten thousand other exhibits we've felt ourselves constrained to glance at.

And here's another thing: paying for what might be called, for want of a better phrase, a spiritually uplifting experience, debases the experience and the artefact that engenders it too. And the more you pay, the more debased it becomes. How? As soon as you put down an amount of money that is meaningful to you (and five pounds is as meaningful to me and most people as a hundred is to the ten per cent of us who are moderately well-to-do) other base factors come into the equation. People who buy the best seats at the Royal Opera House are buying self-esteem just as they are when they buy cucumber sandwiches at the Ritz or the Savoy. A cucumber sandwich will hardly suffer as a result, but it certainly corrupts what one receives from hearing *Falstaff* or *Cosi*, and similarly you will not renew your acquaintance with the Florentine silverware or the Della Robbia terracottas in the V and A with the same rapt innocence you brought to the gallery thirty years ago if you are feeling smug, or distressed, by the amount of money you paid to be there.

How can the solace such places bring, the understanding, the humanity, the things that civilise us, work their magic if you have to pay for them?

And there are other factors too. These places exemplify the real Victorian virtues – not just philanthropy, not just reform, not just magnanimity and extraordinary generosity (there were I believe no tax benefits for helping hospitals, art galleries, schools and universities in those days), splendid though these were. But too, there was the greater virtue of faith that underpinned these lesser virtues, a faith which was held through wide swathes of the non-conformist bourgeoisie, the faith that the fruits of civilisation in all its aspects should be available to everybody, whatever their degree, from the civic virtue that built town-halls to the display of a hand-embroidered handkerchief.

It was this faith that poured money into these buildings, financed much of the care of them and their staffing at all levels, and led many, many people to donate single artefacts and whole collections, or support public subscriptions when the Trustees of bygone years, people in whom one could place one's trust, felt they needed to buy a particular object or collection. Most of them, I assume, did so in the belief that the exhibits would be available to the expert, the dilettante and the ordinary lover of lovely things, free of charge and in perpetuity. I know that is the case with my own family who donated thousands to Liverpool's art galleries and university. All of these people are betrayed by this entry fee.

I visited the V&A yesterday. Possibly for the last time. The Raphael Cartoons were blocked off and will remain so until well after the buy-your-way-in date, the same for the pre-1700 English Collection though by peering over a barrier we could just see the Great Bed of Ware looming out of the shadows. Later, leaving my partner and eleven-year-old daughter exclaiming excitedly over the delicacy and beauty of Jane Austen dresses – such pleasure and instruction lies in being able to see the real thing after watching the recent TV and screen adaptations – I wandered down the familiar galleries searching out old favourites and finding new marvels until I came to the Gamble Room with its gloriously lavish glazing, tiles and all the rest, and there I pieced out for the first time the words that run round the frieze:

There is nothing better for a man than that he should eat and drink and make his soul enjoy good in his labour.

Apart from the sexism can one think of a statement that surpasses this in simple straightforward greatness of spirit? Does not this stinking entrance charge fly in the face of this and all the other noble sentiments that lie behind the foundation and purpose of the Victoria and Albert?

One last word. These entry charges are not necessary. The funding they will provide could well be found elsewhere – the lottery, sponsorship, by scrapping Trident or by redirecting the money the government spends, our money that is, in baksheesh to middle-eastern and Pacific Rim arms buyers. But no, these charges are to be put in place by the mean-spirited, vacuous, envious, soulless cretins who believe that the only good things in life are goods and goods have to be paid for. Their faces are in Goya's *La Junta*. I really would frame them in the sights of an M60, if I could only lay my hands on one and round them all up.

A last, last word. Victoria and Albert would not have been amused. Not in the least.

Lies, Damned Lies, and...

(Printed in Accounting and Business)

Statistics. There are two lots of figures that come out every year which I have a particular interest in: the Public Lending Right, and the secondary school league examination tables.

PLR. This is the system by which authors are paid a sum calculated from the number of times their books are borrowed from public libraries and where it all goes wrong is in the spin journos and publishers put on the figures. The aim is to be able to say ya boo, my authors are doing better than yours. And it's a loud of cobblers. Why? Go into any public library, take a novel off the shelf and look at the date stamps inside. You will find that each book is borrowed as often as the next, that is, about once every three to five weeks. If a book is on the shelves, it is borrowed. End of story?

Not quite. How come Catherine Cookson is always at the top or very close to the top of the titles borrowed league while I make it, almost, into the top thousand (out of nineteen thousand registered authors)? The answer is that there are more Cooksons on the shelves than there are Rathbones. And why are there more? Even though I've written almost as many titles? Because, anticipating a demand they are in effect creating, librarians actually bought more copies of each Cookson as they came out. So, what do the PLR figures prove? Simply that the authors librarians deem to be popular are more often read than the rest of us.

I don't for one moment blame librarians. Many local authorities have ceased to allow council-tax payers to request or order fiction. And librarians are committed to providing a popular service if they do not want to face further cuts. Who can blame them then for ordering books which they judge there will be a demand for in preference to those they perceive as having less appeal? One result of all this is that there are fewer readers and fewer sales for the vast majority of authors and more for those who already sell well, and fewer new authors get published since hardback sales depend on sales to libraries and most new authors do not get paperbacked. And a third is that we receive a warped perception of what is and what might be popular.

School league tables. This is more serious. Because of them conventional wisdom says selective schools get better examination results than non-selective. Selective schools tend to get 80 to 90 per cent of their pupils through five GCSEs at grades A, B, and C, while the national average hangs around the low to mid fifties. Schools select by class and background (disguised as money), or by testing ability and listening to primary school reports on attitude and behaviour. Many schools use both sets of criteria. All right, you might say, but is it not inevitable that a long-established grammar school with an academic tradition is bound to do better than the local comprehensive down the road? Inevitable? Really?

The league tables are based on the numbers of pupils entered. If all your entrants are in the top forty per cent (actually seventeen per cent in the case of our nearby grammar schools), your results are bound to be better than those of a school which enters ninety-eight per cent of all pupils. In all the furore that comes every year when the results are published I have never seen this simple fact even acknowledged, let alone taken into account.

All schools are selective. Some at the point of entry, some during or at the end of year 7 (old year 1). My daughter is in year 9 at a fully comprehensive school and has been in one of two 'accelerated' groups for two and a half years. It is virtually unthinkable that any of the fifty or so children who make up these groups will get less than eight or nine As or Bs. There are two more groups where five or six As, Bs and Cs is the minimum achievement expected. Together these groups represent about half the intake for their year. If the school was represented in the league tables by these children alone, selected as they have been in much the same way as pupils who gain entry to private or public selective schools, then… well. I don't have to spell it out.

Why do the league tables not take account of all this? Clearly the 'statisticians' who prepare the tables for the posh newspapers have to please their readers who are convinced of the superiority of selective schools and in many cases have paid to get their children into them, but Minister Blunkett? What's he playing at and why? Could it be that to reveal the huge success of the comprehensive system could be a major embarrassment? Teachers would, as a profession, have to be praised and paid properly? Or that it would mean admitting what everyone knows already, that comprehensives almost without exception are internally selective?

Interpretation of statistics is a highly fallible process in these two areas at least. What worries me, is how fallible is it in areas where I have no personal expertise and have to accept what the 'experts' say? This applies to almost everything from forecasts of a firm's profitability over the next year to an industry's over a decade. It applies to beef on the bone and new strains of meningitis, to global warming and the putative life-span of the universe. How much can I believe of any diagnoses and prognoses based on the interpretation of figures? Would I do better studying the entrails of a cow, mad or sane? These seem to me to be questions statisticians should be able to answer, but can they? And how should I interpret the result if sixty per cent of statisticians say interpretation of statistics is an exact science and forty per cent say it isn't?

Bloomsday, 2000

(*Printed in* The Times Literary Supplement)

A fortnight ago I received an invitation: Fun-loving lady (half-Irish) seeks plumpish, stately gentleman to accompany her around Dublin on 16 June, 2000. I accepted, of course. We left on the fifteenth – Ryanair from Bournemouth, a hotel opposite the school Joyce attended after Clongowes became too expensive, time on that first afternoon to do the Writers' Museum and the James Joyce Study Centre, both less than five minutes' walk away.

My first time in Dublin. A fair city, made not less fair for me by the fact that it celebrates writers in a way that implies Dubliners rate us the way the English value generals and empire builders: is there a Museum of English Writers? Can you go on a guided literary pub-crawl round Soho?

The next day, the sixteenth, was a perfect day, as was to be expected since it was by Irish reckoning, my reckoning, Swiss reckoning, and the reckoning of anyone who has half a mind to reckon things as they are and not the way spinning politicians do, the last Bloomsday of the twentieth century.

We did some of the right things. Fortified with the full hotel breakfast (but not pork kidney), we stepped out into bright sunshine at about half-nine, took a right opposite Belvedere College, and walked down the hill. A substantial crowd was already gathered outside the Study Centre, many in Edwardian costume, an Irish band played, a young fellow juggled clubs with endearing incompetence, a state coach with six fine horses was pulled up next to the mayor's limo, and clearly a jolly time was getting under way, with not a few glasses of Guinness already in evidence. We mingled for five minutes or so before hurrying on to the bus-stops on O'Connell Street.

The train from Tara station took us to Sandycove. The light was glorious, Howth a green whale back across the bay, the sea amethyst and sapphire (not in the least snot-green), gulls mewed as they kept station on a breeze that straightened the blue Dublin flag on top of the round solid tower, higher and more imposing than I had expected. The circle on top was filled with as many as could squeeze on to hear Barry Mcgovern read from Aeolus, he was doing the whole section in four parts through the morning. Down below, in the tiny shop, one could buy books stamped with the date, and having mislaid my copy of the Ellman biography some twenty-five years ago I happily stumped up a punt or so more than I could have had it for the day before in a Grafton Street bookshop.

Back to the town and on the way to Davy Byrne's in Duke Street, we paused in Lincoln Square to buy lemon soap at Sweny's Pharmacy (chemists do indeed tend not to move). Davy Byrne's was packed and the street outside: the gorgonzola had run out so we had oysters and prawns instead. The crowd was all sorts, all ages, some flashy in silks and gold, some shabby with battered straw hats and frayed trouser hems. The women especially were dressed up to the nines or thereabouts, and the talk...! We were discovering that it is impossible to sit down anywhere in Dublin without being instantly engaged in conversation.

We were there for three and a half glorious days, much of it Joycean including pub and street theatre, and the man himself everywhere... his picture cartooned, photographed, painted in ancient and modern styles, the statue, the brass inlays in the pavements. So what's to be made of it all? A tourist trap? An excuse to get a dollar or two that might otherwise have been spent in Stratford-on-Avon? Oh, go take a running jump...

On the train, coming back from Sandycove, I heard a woman say to her eight-year-old son, exactly as the thought first occurred to her, 'Today is Bloomsday.'

'I know,' he replied, 'they told us so at school.' This was so sublimely ordinary, so much an accepted thing between them, you had to ask yourself: what is going on here?

A religion? Steady now. Steady the Bays. But consider the parallels. There were the prophets that came before: Shakespeare, Balzac, Tolstoy and Flaubert; the apostles: Svevo, Budgen, Gilbert, Weaver, Beach and many others; the church fathers: Gilbert again, Ellman and... invidious to pick from the authors of more books than there are about Shakespeare; the priests: critics, school-teachers (when I was head of English in Bognor Comprehensive I requested every member of the department to wear a rose on Bloomsday); and there is the Mother, the triple Goddess, his real mother Mary Jane who was beastly dead, Nora who claimed always not to be Molly Bloom but certainly was his muse, and his adored daughter, poor mad Lucia, all conjoined in Anna Livia Plurabelle.

And what lies at the heart of the new Bloomasalem? Richard Ellman struggled like Paul in the Epistles to get his head round it, seeing in Ulysses and Finnegans Wake two points of view: one, that life is unspeakable and to be exposed, welded to the other, that it is ineffable and to be distilled, nature as a horrible document or a secret revelation. Joyce, he wrote, lived between the antipodes and above them, he rendered reality without the simplifications of conventional divisions.

For me this is where Joyce starts, and indeed where Ulysses itself starts. Joyce looked at the corrupt dualisms that have butchered humanity both physically and spiritually and he destroyed them without remorse. It is no accident (there are no accidents in holy writ) that Ulysses opens with a send-up of the Mass, exposing the con, the conjuring behind it: 'Shut your eyes, gents. One moment. A little trouble about those white corpuscles... Thanks old chap. That will do nicely. Switch off the current, will you?' A joke now, perhaps still offensive to some, but then, in 1904, seriously, perhaps criminally blasphemous, and in the twenties, when the book came out, censorable.

Denied the solace of magical religion what are we left with? An uncompromising acceptance of humankind; a humanism from within that sees the truth of our condition, that forces us to accept the spaces revealed by the Hubble telescope and the chemical and electrical impulses on the boundary, which is no boundary at all, between brain and mind.

A big achievement. But does it have anything to do with Bloomsday as celebrated in Dublin? The thing of it is (to use a phrase my Cork-born mother-in-law used a lot) the Dubliners (of whom what, one in a hundred have read a word of what he wrote?) yet know the man, the way that woman in the railway carriage and her son know him. I don't know the word to describe what they feel for him. They're proud of Yeats, Beckett, even Shaw I guess. They feel, I sense, a sort of amused affection for Wilde. Then there's Roddy Doyle whom I think they love, and Heaney, O'Connor, Kavanagh, Kate O'Brien and maybe Edna too, and many others. But love is too limiting a word for what they feel for Joyce. Even if they haven't read a word they know there was a man, there is a book, that understands and knows them in all their wonderful, terrible, terrifying, pitiable and admirable loneliness and companionship.

And what if few have read the good book from cover to cover? Not many of the old lot, in terms of percentages, read the whole New Testament, let alone the whole bloody Bible, and they were none the less Christians for all that. So let no pretentious pharisee, scribe or hack scorn the Dubliners', nor anyone else's, celebration of Bloomsday, on the mere grounds that they haven't read the book. It's a wifely, husbandly, fatherly, motherly, filial, brotherly, sisterly thing to know you're known. Worth a celebratory pint or two. And my guess is they'll still be at it in 3000 by which time nobody will be reading the book at all but happily celebrating what hopefully we will have learnt by then – truly what it is to be human.

William S Burroughs

Somehow he seemed much older than eighty-three: one felt he had lived for ever, would live for ever. Body and soul, he had passed through so much fire and ice, one believed he was now immutable and indestructible – the frailty seemed not to be that of age, but something formed and made, pared down to house a life force that would not go out.

Inevitably the obituarists have, for the most part, even the most sympathetic, hedged their bets. The life and work come with a health warning – the drug-taking, the obsessive homosexuality, the absurdity of the cut-up technique and the creation of routines, all this and much more are not the trappings one expects from a great literary figure, or if they are then not to *such* excess. There is also, let us admit it, an underlying irritation that the bastard got away with it. He did not die in the gutter; he was not often, and never for more than a few days at a time, in jail; he died loaded with medals, honorary fellowships, and so on, often from institutions which had in the past anathematised him. He was probably even rather wealthy.

And it remains true that few, even among those who express admiration, seem able to get beyond the shock-horror factor in his writing. Mention has been made, but often only in passing, of the fact that he was one of the great prose stylists of the century. His writing always has an apparently unforced limpidity, an ability to go straight to the point, or the jugular, that the neo-baroque clutter of much modern writing is incapable of. He was also a brilliant pasticheur, his guying of hard-boiled thriller writing in the Private Asshole sections of *Cities of the Red Night* an affectionate tribute alongside the more acerbic, indeed vitriolic send-ups in *The Naked Lunch*. As a letter writer he ranks with the very best.

But of course none of this would be worth a toss if it were not for the content, the project, the things he was about.

He was, his legacy is, great. First, his work was and is a hugely powerful liberating force. For generations of artists, for generations of all who value art in all its forms, he opened up spaces on whose thresholds his greatest precursors could only stand, and he found the verbal means to lead us into them.

One speaks of art in the context of Burroughs rather than literature only (I nearly wrote 'merely') because his influence stretched far beyond literature. Invidious to list the film-makers who have been freed by his exploration of the terra incognita of our psyches, or the painters and artists, even the composers, but every time one sees or hears something which shocks by its newness, its originality, every time one knows for sure that one is experiencing something that would have been unthinkable thirty or forty years ago one can be sure that Burroughs is in there somewhere, and probably now, in the case of many younger artists' work, at a second or third remove.

Second, and more important yet, as all true artists should, he resolutely and courageously, both in his life and his work, set himself against all systems, all prescriptive practices, ideologies, and any and

every form of authoritarianism. He was a polymath with an encyclo-
pedic mind: he revered the greatest of his forerunners but always and
only for the illumination they could bring – never as the makers of rules
or systems. His work attacked capitalist totalitarianism with as much
scorn, hatred, and bile as it did that of other ideologies or systems. He
taught us that in the face of the behemoths and juggernauts of bureaucracies and corporations paranoia is the rational stance of the
persecuted. Yet, he never gave up his search through all the horrors of
the twentieth century for the personal enlightenment which in a frag-
mented, warring society is the best that can be hoped for: 'You have to
be in Hell to see Heaven. Glimpses from the Land of the Dead, flashes
of serene, timeless joy, a joy as old as suffering and despair.'

As retrospection grows it may be that it will not be with the surre-
alists and other twentieth-century mould-breakers that he will be
ranked but with great individual visionaries like Bunyan and Blake.
They have more in common than one might think. With Bunyon
Burroughs saw his life as a pilgrimage and his last extended work *The
Western Lands*, from the end of which the lines quoted above are
taken, is a pilgrim's progress. With Blake he shared a hatred of the dead
hand of all those 'who know best', of systems and formulae; with Blake
he explored endlessly the contradictions and complexities of innocence
and experience. He was a prophet too. The Dantesque visions of an
apocalypse that seemed to originate in paranoid drug-induced nightmare now read like computer-derived projections of a future that
includes both global warming and genetic engineering.

The human qualities he most valued are those of the people he
mythologised as 'The Johnson Family'. Johnsons don't let you down, a
Johnson keeps his word and honours his obligations. He is not a malicious, snooping, interfering, self-righteous, trouble-making person.
The Johnsons represent an elusive, slippery sort of morality, apparently
almost grotesquely naïve, but when you look at it and live with it it
grows in your mind and, if you are like-minded, as I believe every
person who believes oneself to be an artist must be, you become filled
with a warmth of recognition. You become aware of what you really
already knew, that there exists this vast underground reservoir of ordinary people who don't shit on you, who mind their own business, but
can always be relied upon to give help, enough help, when it's needed.
They may be down-trodden but they are not meek; they are, for the
most part lowly, but they are not humble. They are lit with an inner
dignity and do not need robes, titles, or the plaudits of the sheep to
bolster their self-esteem.

Like Bunyan and Blake Burroughs may cease to be widely read, for,
like them, he is not at length, for all the purity and seamlessness of his

prose, an easy read. But for as long as the Hell we have made continues to exist and grow worse we shall need him, and through hidden channels his life and work will continue to carry their message of courage, self-respect, and unflinching integrity spiced with a sly wit, a self-mocking grin that belied any grandiose claim to an illumination that is not within the reach of everyone, should we care to look for it. Blake with laughs? We really are so lucky.

Like Blake's his vision was basically manichean – 'good and evil are in conflict and the outcome is at this point uncertain'. He goes on:

'It is *not* an eternal conflict since one or other must win a final victory. Which side are you on?'

Which, indeed.

Every Piece on Earth

What used to be called Advent, and is now called the Countdown to Christmas, brings out the best in me. Normally a pretty easy-going, hedonistic sort of chap, a Bach and Beethoven, two of Darjeeling to one of Earl Grey sort of a chap, my anger rarely lasts long, my life as a socialist activist is sporadic at best. But the Countdown penetrates the cocoon, strips off the veneer of jolliness, destabilises my self-regard, and for three weeks a year I become a Savanorola with a stubbed toe, Jeremiah with a hangover, Lenin faced with the latest from Kautsky.

It's the shops that do it: Saintroses a week before Christmas, the crunch, or pension day when the place is full of fat old people who park themselves and their trolleys three abreast across every aisle so they can tell each other about the consumerist diseases they suffer from: blood pressure, varicose veins, constipation, kidneys and bowels. And have you noticed how *rude* old people are nowadays? They used to cringe, touch their forelocks if you held open a door or offered a seat. They knew their place – that of guests who have overstayed their welcome. No more. They no longer scuttle – they are too fat. They meander. They trudge. And if they see you trying to get through a swing door with two children under six and a supermarket trolley they hold it open for you until you are almost through and then they let it go. And behind their glasses, behind the pasty pallor of their expressionless faces, they are not even laughing: they are saying – serves you right for not being old.

So. Pension day in Saintroses with Xmas Fayre on the shelves and Jingle Balls on the tannoy snaps me out of my customary haze of genial well-being, brings me face to face with reality. Turkeys trussed like senior citizens to exaggerate their plumpness convert me to veganism and Animal Lib: I buy three types of beans and wholewheat pasta.

In the good old days I used to stick my thumb into oranges whose peel glowed like vermilion plastic before I realised they were labelled Spania not Outspan; over in drinks I deliberately dropped two bottles of Chile red on the tiled floor; I bought Red Label instead of Imperial Blend and I asked the poor shelf-filler where the Nicaraguan coffee was, and I still squeeze the Zionist avocados until the pips squeak...

In the good old days when the son and heir demanded Optimus Prime – Chief Transformer, Robot in Disguise, I happily refused. Optimus Prime, being three in one and one in three, was a paradigm of the Trinity and his voice, in the TV cartoon, could have been Ronald Reagan's. Wooden bricks from Czechoslovakia for you, my boy. Once, many years ago, a Rotarian Father Christmas standing by a sound system that would not have disgraced Notting Hill before community policing ruined the place, but which was blasting out While Shepherds Scab, instead of Pressure Drop, accosted me with a collection receptacle. He assured me all proceeds would go to Age Concern. I hit him over the head with a two litre bottle of diet cola-substitute and it took three policemen exercising their hard-won rights under the new act to get me down the nick...

But that's all gone now and something has to take its place. Last year I thought I had the answer. Bum-fondling. Every time I read or heard the word *Christmas* I substituted in my mind the word, and concept – *Bum-Fondling*. It worked a treat. All those cards wishing me Merry... Christmas? The posters in the shop windows said it: Christmas Treats in Store. Christmas Thrills on TV. And it wasn't just White Christmases I was dreaming of. Of course, when all's said and done Christmas is for the kiddies, isn't it? Euphoria blossomed again, for a week at least I moved everywhere beaming with good will and relishing every piece on earth.

Of course there was a tab. The decorations came down, the bills came in, the Inland Revenue turned churlish. The son and heir went back to school which meant getting up in the dark icy rain to get him there. And whenever I turned to the blissful solace of bum-fondling for comfort, what did I think of? Fucking Chr*stm*s. It was almost enough to make a year-round freedom-fighter of me. Almost.

Easter Monday, Longleat

Behind bright faces framed by fragile ears
Their eyes twin pools of unpained night,
The rhesus monkeys flash their sunset butts.

A baby you could cradle in one hand
Clings to sienna hair beneath Mum's walnut teats.
Mum leaps the space between two cars
Inside her cage of glass
Another mum lifts her infant off her lap
And makes the introduction.

Food in the grass –
Grey pellets and halved orange skins.
A fox freeloads, catlike his long neck swoops
From roller-coaster back,
Haunches sprung for swift retreat.
Spring liveried, his ears are tipped with sable,
Nose, lips are shiny jet.
His body turns above his snowy breast,
The panache of his ginger brush sweeps the starry daisies.

He and the monkeys have agreed a five yard zone
But when a Przewalski horse tip-taps on dancing hooves
Across the tarmac
Dog fox shies, takes the higher ground, brush trailing:
Sees the red-coat on its back
Hears the Master's shout?

He'll be off now up the hill, into the trees.
The monkeys wait and watch and think:
Fox got in – can we get out?

7. A PERIODIC OBSESSION

In March 1956 I met Sylvia Plath in Cambridge. We had both been invited to join a Pooh Club. The first meeting was behind St John's on a small footbridge over a brook that ran into the Cam. We were the first arrivals. Are you here to join the Pooh Club? Yes. Shall we play Pooh Sticks while we wait for the others? All right.

As I remember, and I may have this wrong, we all know how creative memory can be, her hair was blonde (dyed, though I didn't know that at the time), her face was carefully made-up and she was wearing a flared light blue coat. Sort of Sandra Dee, but more classy.

I met her three more times, all in the University Library, and on one occasion we had coffee together in the basement cafeteria. As far as I know that particular Pooh Club did not catch on.

Pooh Sticks

Spring with daffodils and catkins
Dusting the air with gold
And the willow leaves, always the first, already trailed
Thin fingers in the brook.

Elbows on the rusty rail
We dropped our sticks
Mine bobbed through on a ripple of brown water
Yours was snagged.

Damn! And then, Who will you be?
A friend, I said. A friend or relation. And you?
Of Rabbits? Oh, I'll be Roo.

There was a Willow

A weeping willow trailed its tendrils,
Not quite fully leafed, across
A brook and some just touched the cold cast iron
Of the bridge's sides. The longest swam against
The current but made no headway. The water
Browned by the mud beneath, not deep, ran cold and clear
Between steep banks layered like a basket with roots,
Just fast enough to rumple but not break
Its surface. The space beneath the bridge
Was shadowed and prompted thoughts of graves.
The sky was white, eye-wounding, promised sun,
The air chill, with a fennish breath too weak
To bend a flame, but strong enough to kill.
She stood on the bridge, her yellow hair
Bright as a gew-gaw or a daffodil.

The University Library

Bleached beech tables beneath blue light-shades,
Chairs with seats and backs of blue.
A stack of books, a folder, a busy fountain pen.
You sensed my hesitation and you smiled again.

Your lipstick was too bright, your dress too floral,
Your speech was innocent of guile:
No, no one has that place,
But as you put your specs back on
Your lips formed mockery in a moue.
Not only me they mocked, but you.

That careful, east coast femininity
Suggested friable fragility
Made a statement: Keep off the grass,
I am a china doll in a cabinet of glass.

I ordered coffee, paid for it
Searched about and found a place to sit.

The English Gentleman, at last, you said,
I thought they all were fantasy or dead.

*But then I more or less forget her through several decades –
until the father of her children died, his last book of poems
came out and I began to read her poems again.* Ode to Ted,
*written on 21 April 1956, stuck like a fish-hook until I had
gouged out a sub-text.*

Ode for Ed

My man tramples shoots of green oats
Crushing them

By naming a lapwing
He exposes my ignorance and
Claims possession of the bird

He scares the rabbits out of daylight
Stalks a fox and stoat

He explains how molehills are made
As if I didn't know
He uses a flint-rock to smash a piece of quartz
The colours of the broken stone
Suggest bleeding flesh

He looks over the landscape as if he owned it
As if the spring-time growth happens because
He willed it
Even the birds build because he has told them to

Ringdoves moderate their song
To suit his moods

Since his words summon the whole earth
To rush to praise his blood
How can his woman be other than glad?

Envoi
The deepest saddest irony is this

She gave it to him with a kiss
Knowing his greed would render it a treasure
Not seeing how she'd got his measure.

8. IDEOLOGICAL ROUND-UP

I *Essentia non sunt multiplicanda*

(From Kings of Albion)

1460. Ali, a wandering Arab merchant and philosopher, has taken refuge in a Franciscan Friary in Oxford. He is recovering from the sort of dysentery one gets in foreign parts and during his convalescence he discusses The Meaning of Life with Brother Peter.

A week or so after our talk about Roger Bacon, we were perhaps into April by then, for I remember it was raining sweetly, gently, but enough to keep us indoors, our conversation moved on to the second of Brother Peter's great Inglysshemen. In his upper room with his cased books around us and comfortable chairs to sit in, he began with an apologetic attack on Avicenna whose version of Aristotle was based on the neo-Platonist Porphyry's interpretation of the Stagyrite. Following William of Occam, the second of our heroes, and referring to his writings and occasionally to Aristotle's Organon he demonstrated how Aristotle's speculations regarding entities, essences or universals had been corrupted by the neo-Platonists. For the latter, essences existed in the mind of God, and were presented corporeally, materially, on earth, in a corrupted, degraded way. Thus the *idea* of 'cat', for instance, and here my friend fondled the tabby beauty called Winnie who often slept and purred on his lap, existed in the mind of God as a perfection of cats before cats were created, and no cat that had ever existed was perfect cat, since corporeality always falls short of the perfection of the Idea.

'But this,' he went on, fondling Winnie's throat and forehead which was marked with a W, 'is to deny what is so markedly the most important feature of Winnie, her haecceity, the fact that she is individual, uniquely herself, unlike in every significant way, every other cat who has ever lived. And she has her own perfection – whether or not she is perfect cat is not for me to say, but certainly she is perfect Winnie.'

'Oh come,' I replied, 'all cats have many features in common. Quite apart from their appearance and their anatomy, they follow patterns of behaviour that are identical. All wash in the same way. All eat and drink alike. They all use the same techniques when hunting. I could go on and on, but you know what I mean. You cannot deny there exists an idea we can call 'catness' which includes all these qualities.'

A silence lengthened between us. Then:

'You have never been owned by a cat, have you?'

There was a coolness in his voice that irritated me almost as much as the stupid way in which he had framed the question. I was perhaps at that time more than usually easily annoyed – the way convalescents often are.

'No,' I replied. 'I like them, be sure of that, but they do not travel well, and I have never remained in the same place for more than six months since I was eight years old. Apart from when I was in the Mountain, where I learnt what wisdom I have.'

'Then allow me to speak with more certainty of being right concerning the nature of cats.'

'There you are,' I cried, and leant forward to tap his knee, at which Winnie leapt down to the floor and went and mewed at the door, 'you speak of the nature of cats. By that you surely mean the essence, the idea that informs them all.'

'No. I simply mean the characteristics we light upon to distinguish them from other animals of a similar size and familiarity. But what I am asking you to consider is this. It is in the nature of cats to be different from each other. Believe me. And not through the corruption of matter through the fall of Man or any other such cant, but because that is the way cats are.'

It was clear that if a falling-out was to be avoided, we should remove the conversation back to a higher plane.

'And you, you would apply this to everything, every phenomenon in the perceivable world?'

'I, Aristotle, and William of Occam, yes, we agree.'

A sunbeam pierced the rain-clouds and fell briefly on the table between us.

'Even to two motes of dust?'

'Observe,' said Brother Peter, 'no two motes of dust occupy the same space at the same time. In that at the very least they are different. And I believe if we could grind lenses sufficiently fine and line them up to study even the most *mikro* of particles we would find differences between them – *mikro* is the Greek word for very small.'

'I know very well what *mikro* means. What I am trying to say is we use words to define types. The word 'cat' is meaningful. Do not such words indicate Ideas, Essences?'

'Types yes. Essences no. Though I would prefer to use the words 'species' for 'types' and 'universals' for 'Essences'.'

'I am still confused. You are simply swapping terms, but you prove nothing.'

'That is because you give too great a power to words. Words are tools. Useful, but in themselves they do not contain truth. It is useful to say that beer is beer, by which we indicate a certain species of drink. It is useful so I can say, 'Would you like some beer?' and you will know thereby the sort of experience you are being offered. But this is not to say that there is an essence of beer, a perfect beer in the mind of god. Indeed not. Looked at another way, the word implies quite the opposite, for it allows us to say this beer is different from that beer, this beer is better than that beer. Do you like this beer?'

We both drank.

'Yes,' I said. 'And it is different. You are right.'

'That is because this species of beer is made with hops of a particular species. Some of our Hussite brothers from Pilsen in Bohemia sent us a sack. But we must return now to William of Occam. Let me sum up what he had to say about words. There are terms of first intention which is what we call words that are the names of individual things and which, in Inglysshe anyway, we qualify with an article: the cat at the door. This cat at that door. There is a cat at the door. And there are words used as terms of second intention, as universals, genera, or species. Cats like fish. Cats wash behind their ears when there is rain about. A universal is thus a sign of many things, in this case the many things that make up a cat. Universals do not exist. The only existence they have is as qualities of individual cats.'

'Hum,' said I.

'Words used thus are merely tools,' he repeated, 'which we resort to for convenience sake: they do not describe something which has a reality of its own. Only individual things have that reality. That is what Aristotle, properly understood, thought. That is what Occam meant when he said: *Essentia non sunt multiplicanda praeter necessitatem.* A sharp dictum that slices through a lot of cant. Essences, universals should not be multiplied except out of necessity, and ultimately the only Necessary Universal is God, the Prime Mover. And,' and here he lowered his voice for what he was about to utter was a burning matter, 'And he, or it, goes back a long, long way. Maybe all it was was a bang, a big bang like the bang of the Brazen Head, but with the motto, "Time is, Time will be, Time might just as well go on for ever."'

He had gone beyond me now, as sometimes he did when a sort of divine afflatus, an ability to prophecy, fell on him. I tried to bring him back to earth.

'Is it not the case that your Brother Bacon was kept mute in the cells of the Franciscan order in Paris for many years? That Occam was imprisoned as a heretic, that even John Wycliffe might have been burnt but escaped...?'

'But, my dear Ali... one moment while I let Winnie out. See, like many cats once disturbed she will not resume her former comfort, but not all cats reach with their front paws to rattle the latch to signify they want to go out. There. They were... gunpowder. They threatened to blow apart the whole structure of our society. They undermined the very foundations on which the authority of church and king can be said to stand for they privileged, as inevitable consequences of their thought, individual observation, individual judgment; they revealed ways to the truth that did not depend on the authority of Mother Church nor the divine right of kings, but on knowledge obtained by practical everyday experience, as it was said those doctors of antiquity who relied on experience and observation did, the ones known as *empirici*. What gives a Pope or Emperor the right to rule? Why, if you take away frail and unsuited authority of custom, of the opinion of the unlearned crowd, the display of apparent wisdom; if you take away the idea that a Pope or King embodies, albeit corporeally and with earthly corruption, the Essence or Entity of Priesthood and Royalty as conceived in the mind of God, you are left with two things, two justifications for investing certain individuals and institutions with authority over the rest of us.'

'And they are?'

'The power to command and unleash force, death, torture and deprivation on those who would gainsay you...'

'That I understand. But brute force is scarcely justification.'

'Quite so. Nor, really, is the other.'

'And that is?'

'The willing consent of the ruled.'

'But,' said I, 'that does seem a justification. Better anyway than brute force.'

Brother Peter now warmed eagerly to his thesis.

'It depends,' he said, and the words tumbled out like nuts from a sack, 'how that willing consent is obtained. If lies are fed to the people for generation after generation, and never questioned, they become part of the unconsidered background to their mental lives, never truly looked at or examined, hardly even thought of, but controlling everything in the foreground of their thoughts. By these means, as powerful, as all-pervading but as unnoticed as those that cause an object released in air to drop, is the consent of the people contrived and maintained. And anything that threatens to undermine this invisible wall of belief, the way gunpowder can blow down a castle wall, must be treated as anathema, a burning matter.' He sighed, looked around, then up and out of the cloudy glazing of the window. 'It's stopped raining. Wycliffe, the last of our three, was feeling towards all this. But that is enough for now. Let us walk through our garden, admire the rain-drops on the cherry-blossom, then perhaps we'll feed our fish.'

As we walked between the low-cropped hedges, and breathed in the fragrances released by rain and a sun suddenly warm, I attempted a summary.

'Without this...,' I searched for a word and made one up, '*introjection* of belief, on what grounds would a person offer his consent to be ruled?'

'He, or she, would use observation and analysis as nearly mathematical as may be, to work out who or what system, would best suit his own interests and those of his fellow men. By fellow men I mean the men and women he works with. Clearly the people he works for are a different class of person altogether and will think in a dialectically opposed way. He and his fellows would employ a hedonistic calculus. And he would eschew any pre-given Ideas about the Commonwealth of Men said to be based on the Essences that exist in God's head.'

I savoured the subtle sharpness of a needle of rosemary, pinched between my teeth.

'Just now you brought in John Wycliffe, the last of your three Inglysshe Franciscans. There must be more to be said about him.'

But Brother Peter had had enough. Scattering some bread crumbs on the surface of the first of his ponds (the fish recognised his shadow as it fell on the water and came to the pool-side before he threw them), he said:

'You may not not have noticed, dear Ali, that we are now approaching the end of Lent. Yesterday was the day of the Crucifixion of Jesus, which we call Good Friday, a day of fasting which lasts through till the first meal after Holy Communion tomorrow when we celebrate his apparent return from the grave. At that celebration I shall give a talk based on the teachings of Father John Wycliffe, which if you'll forgive me, I shall now set about preparing. You will be very welcome in our church tomorrow at eleven in the morning.'

II *Brother Peter's Sermon*

And here comes his sermon, laid out as it is in Kings of Albion. *No one seems to have noticed that it is presented in the same way as Beckett's (Tom, that is, not Sam) in* Murder in the Cathedral. *Why? To invite comparisons of course!*

Interlude

Brother Peter Marcus *preaches in the church of St Francis, Osney, on Easter Morning, 1460.*

'Everywhere on your road preach and say – The kingdom of God is at hand. Cure the sick, raise the dead, cleanse the lepers, drive out devils. Freely have you received, freely give. Carry neither gold nor silver nor money in your girdles, nor bag, nor two coats, nor sandals, nor staff, for the workman is worthy of his hire.' The seventh to tenth verses of the tenth chapter of the Gospel according to Saint Matthew.

Dear children of God, my sermon this Easter morning will be a very simple one. All I aim to do is remind you of the teachings of Father John Wycliffe, the kernel of his thought at any rate, and suggest how his teaching points down paths we should try to follow.

First, at the centre of his thought was poverty. In this he followed in the footsteps of Francis, our Founder, who heard the words of the gospel I have just read to you at the moment of his conversion. From this, ineluctably, came the certainty that righteousness has nothing to do with power or dominion or possessions or property. To own something is to take it from someone else. He who has a penny more has caused another to have a penny less. Nor does true righteousness confer power or the right to power, dominion or the right to dominion. John Wycliffe believed that dominion and power were the prerogatives of the civil authority, and not of the church or churchmen. But even this he saw was a standby, a provisional thing, until all men and women, all people, should live together in harmony, all equal, and come together as the Israelites did in every Jubilee year and hand back to all, to the people as a whole, all personal property.

Next. Father John believed that the central thing in everyman's life was the immediate dependence of the individual Christian upon God, a relation which needs no mediation of any priest, and to which the very sacraments of the church are not essentially necessary. Indeed he went so far as to assert that round the sacraments, which are but signs and symbols, a dreadful and harmful habit of superstition has grown up, later hardened by the closed minds of the so-called fathers of the church into dogma and doctrine. And by these means, by making the sacraments the prerogative of the priesthood, to grant or withhold as their fallen natures dictated, power and dominion over the gates of heaven and hell were seized by the church. Thus no one can go to heaven unless they have received the body and blood of Christ and only the anointed priest has the power to magic the bread and wine into the body and blood. Brethren, I tell you, following the teaching of our Father John, this doctrine of transubstantiation is a blasphemous folly, a deceit which despoils the people and leads them to commit idolatry. If sacrament there must be then let it be the sacrament of sharing the good things of life, the bread and wine, in good fellowship, as we have just done in our Easter Communion, and remembering as we do so, the teachings of Jesus and his example, as he bade us.

Brethren, these doctrines of the sacraments as laid down by Rome, Avignon or wherever the Pope is these days, deny the true church that is in all of us and especially when two or three are gathered together in His Name. That is the church our lord left us with, the church John lived and breathed for. The true Church consists solely of the community of the righteous and its only authority is the teaching of our lord as left to us in the New Testament. The supreme authority, the only authority, is Holy Scripture and particularly the actual words of our lord as recorded in the Gospels. Which is why John Wycliffe devoted so much of his life to translating and disseminating the Gospels in our own tongue, and it is for these and like reasons that after his death his bones were dug up and burnt for a heretic, as if this mean, malicious act could in any way diminish the power of his thought.

John's wisdom was not a homely stuff woven together on the loom of mere common sense, though there is much of that in it. But it was far more, drawing together the threads left by his two great predecessors, Roger Bacon and William of Occam. The first found truth in what he could see, and feel, and touch and hear and smell and measure. The second showed how the teaching of the fathers and the schoolmen has dragged us away from experience to speculation, from the particular to the general, from fact to essence. John began to see how all this provided the foundations for the tyrannies that spoil us all. It behoves us to continue down the road these three have shown us.

It is my belief, no, my certainty, grounded in experience as well as logic, that we can use their teaching as stepping stones, as stairs to a height from which, looking back whence we have come, we shall see exposed the gigantic fallacy on which our philosophy and morality were built – namely the transformation of facts into essences, of historical into metaphysical conditions. The weakness and despondency of man, the inequality of power and wealth, injustice and suffering are attributed by the Church and its thinkers to some transcendental crime and guilt; rebellion, disobedience against God, became the original sin that tainted us all; and the striving for gratification which is life was stained with the sin of concupiscence.

This departure into metaphysical realms culminated in the deification of time: because everything in the empirical world is passing, man in his very essence becomes a finite being, and death is in the very essence of life. Madness preached: 'All things pass away, therefore all things deserve to pass away! And this is justice itself, this law of Time, that it must devour its children' – thus preached madness.

And again this madness pronounced as doctrine that only the higher values are eternal, and therefore really real: faith and a love which does not ask and does not desire, became the goals to which we should all aspire. And why? By these means the Church seeks to pacify, justify, compensate the underprivileged of the earth, and to protect those who made and left them underprivileged. These doctrines have enveloped the masters and the slaves, the rulers and the ruled, in an upsurge of repression that has caused the increasing degeneration of the life instincts and the decline of man.

Traditional forms of reason, as exemplified in the real thought of Aristotle, the peripatetics and the empiricists of ancient times, are rejected, and experience of being-as-end-in-itself – as joy, *lust* (I use the Teutonic word that combines desire with joy), and enjoyment were thrown out with them. To return to the path we have been led from, to descend on the other side of the mountain, not into the Valley of the Shadow of Death but into the land of milk and honey, to come to ourselves in a world that is truly our own, we must struggle against the dominion of time, against the tyranny of becoming over being. As long as there is the uncomprehended and unconquered flux of time – senseless loss, the painful 'it was' that will never come again – being will continue to contain the seed of destruction which perverts good to evil and vice versa. Man comes to himself only when transcendence has been conquered – when eternity has become present in the here and now.

Before I came here to speak to you I took a turn about our garden. The cherry tree is in blossom, our cherry tree, the only cherry tree in the whole of creation to be just as it is at this very moment. Next to it the lilac tree our brothers in Anatolia sent us is in bud, just about to open buds already white at the tips, and in its branches a bullfinch sang, its black cap burnished so blackness shone almost like the sun and its red breast glowed like fire. No other bullfinch in the world but this one, graced this morning a lilac tree like ours.

'Consider the lilies of the field, how they grow; they toil not neither do they spin.' At this time of Easter, of blossom on the cherry tree, of the scarlet and black bullfinch in the lilac tree, of birth and resurrection, let us remember that if all things pass, all things return; what goes round comes round; eternally turns the wheel of Being. All things die, all things blossom again, eternal is the year of being. All things break, all things are joined anew; eternally the house of Being builds itself anew. All things part, all things welcome each other again.

Eternity, long since the ultimate consolation of an alienated existence, was made into an instrument of oppression by its relegation to a transcendental world – unreal reward for real suffering. Now, here, at Easter, eternity is reclaimed for the fair earth – as the eternal return of its children, of the water-lily and the rose, of the lover and the beloved... The earth has all too long been a madhouse. We must reverse the sense of guilt; we must learn anew to associate guilt not with the affirmation but the denial of life, not with rebellion but with the acceptance of the repressive ideal.

It is no sad truth, but rather a grand and glorious one that this earth should be our home. Were it but to give us simple shelter, simple clothing, simple food it would be enough. Add the water-lily and the rose, the apple and the pear, it is a fit home for mortal or immortal man. Woman. Persons.

III Art and Kindness

(Previously unpublished, but cobbled together for the occasion)

Art

When you make a table you do so for a reason. You will put things on it: meals, flowers, a computer keyboard and monitor, a printer, coffee, a coffee-table book. That's use value. It has commodity value too – you may exchange it for money with which you will buy other commodities. The buyer may sell it on, making a profit or a loss.

It may, however, be a beautiful table. In which case its buyer and such of his acquaintance as visit him will enjoy its beauty. Basically, they will look at it. Maybe they will touch and smell it, even bang things on it and admire the sound, but just now let's subsume all that under the heading 'look at'.

It may have been part of your intention to make a beautiful table. You may have been simply concerned to make the best table you could out of the materials to hand and with the tools you had, and because you were honest about making a good table and your tools and materials were good ones you inadvertently produced a good and beautiful table. One thinks of Shaker furniture and Bauhaus too.

Most of the time the table is a table. But when people look at it it is also art.

This is the fundamental characteristic of art. No matter what use value an object has, or commodity value, it becomes art when people simply stop and look at it. Thus St Paul's Cathedral has use value: it is a good rain shelter if you happen to be passing in a shower; in some people it inspires feelings of awe and reverence to a deity and also a tribe. It has commodity value; why otherwise would you pay to see parts of it, and feel you should pay to see any of it? But it is also a thing set apart for us to look at, from outside and inside it. Circumspice, commanded its creator. It is set apart and we look at it. Duchamp set aside a urinal, called it *Fountain* and asked us to look at it. Both St Paul's and the urinal are set apart for us to look at them. That's what makes them art.

Many works of art serve more than one, indeed often several purposes, of which being a work of art is only one, and not always the most important either to the artist or the looker. Some (say, Damien Hirst's *The Physical Impossibility of Death in the Mind of Someone Living*) say look at me and marvel at how clever my creator is, (that, of course is not all it says by any means but it is certainly an element – as it is in most works of art); others say look at my patrons – how splendid they are (the Medici Tomb); or I love you, as I believe Beethoven's Triple Concerto says to Archduke Rudolf; thousands upon thousands say what Christ suffered on the Cross should make you feel guilty, and almost as many say the Virgin Mother of Christ was as holy as Him and if she prays to him on our behalf we stand a better chance of making it to heaven. People make crucifixes for them, and Mother and Child icons. But look at Andrea del Sarto's Virgin and Child in the Courtauld, the way she looks into the child's mouth, checking out the new tooth that's just come through. It's not about the BVM at all. It celebrates his Andrea's partner and the child they had. But what makes it art (and all the crucifixes and madonnas) is the fact that we have set it apart so we can look at it.

But in some constructions that are thought of as art, which are almost sanctified by their status as art, the message is so dominating that they are scarcely art at all. Picasso's Guernica, Shostokovich's late quartets, The Mastersingers, are all propaganda. *Homage to Catalonia, South from Granada, Memoirs of an Infantry Officer, Seven Types of Ambiguity* have arty strands that say hey, aren't some of the pleasures you get from reading this those you associate with art? – but really their concern to tell the truth overrides any artiness they may have.

'All art constantly aspires towards the condition of music,' wrote Walter Pater, probably before he had heard any Wagner. Outside music Duchamps' urinal is maybe as close to pure art as you can get. Music, the actual sound waves making the tympanum of your ear vibrate and send music to your brain, has no use value, and, in itself, no commodity value either. Contingently it can have both, but not in the way St Paul's has or del Sarto's girl-friend and bambino. Music can be propaganda: patriotic, ideological, though usually it needs a libretto as well to function in this way. And certainly seats on which to sit while listening to it can be bought and sold. And the careers of its most charismatic performers are commodities that sell books, newspapers, films, television and the rest. But all this is contingent. Music itself simply exists to be heard. It has been made, set apart, reproduced, or created as a one-off in a performance never to be heard again, just to be heard. And though music can stir us to dance or march, laugh or salute the leader (whether it's Hitler or Gary Glitter) at its purist, in say the D minor prelude and fugue from the Forty-eight, Opus 111, or the Bagatelles, it is just music and it says just one thing: Listen to Me. That's art.

Very, very few works of art are just art and nothing else. But remember we, both Artist and Looker, make a thing a work of art simply and only by setting it apart and saying: look at it! We take it out of its context, we try to forget that it's worth a million or incites to anti-Semiticism, we take it away from real life. In so far as it manages to shed all of its nature except its separateness, its artiness, it is... a toy!

Art is ludic. I think I am right in saying that no culture or civilisation has existed that did not make music and that did not dance. And then came song, words to the music, and out of song, drama and story-telling. But music and dance came first and are universal, and both depend on setting aside, apart, some time, a length of time, a space of time, separate from getting and spending, winning and losing, reproducing, surviving and dying. Art is a holiday away from all that, even when, often quite extraordinarily when, the material of the art, the stuff out of which it is made, is about, say, loving not wisely but too well, or dying. A real princess dies and a nation mourns. Well, let's say about one tenth of a nation mourns. Whatever that is it is not art. But hear the words come, like the tolling of bells, phrase after phrase: Absent thee from felicity awhile... the potent poison quite oercrows my spirit... the rest is silence... now cracks a noble heart, good night sweet Prince and flights of angels sing thee to thy rest... go, bid the soldiers shoot... and your heart breaks with Horatio's, the tears come, but then, with the applause as the lights come up, that most wonderful euphoria of all, that lightening of the spirit (whatever that is!), that feeling of redemption that you carry away with you through the crowd and into the rainy streets and which lasts, perhaps, for as long as an hour, though it can be recalled as I am recalling it now... that is art.

Art is not serious. But it does have to be made out of something. It has to be made out of time and space. The time it takes, the space it occupies. Sound, materials, ideas, patterns which can be organic, mathematical, abstract. Hans Keller said it must have contrasts and I think he was right. It gets boring, anything on earth gets boring, if it doesn't have contrasts. It has to have a beginning, an end, boundaries, a place where it begins and ends. Otherwise it cannot be set apart. That goes with being set apart. Often it has subject matter, subject matter is part of the stuff it is made of. Often it is communal, shared, as in a concert or when you are part of a crowd singing, say, Abide with Me or the International, or you are dancing a *jota* in the square of a Spanish town during a fiesta. A fiesta itself, the whole fiesta, is a communal work of art, and, yes, it is apart, very much apart from the rest of the year. And, yes, as we have seen, the material, the subject matter can be ideological, political, ethical, to do with religion. But in so far as its creator is truly artistic these are merely the materials, like canvas, paint, clay, vibrating particles of air.

Art is not serious. It is frivolous. It is subversive. It is ludic, it is play, it is Kubrick's train-set.

It's the best thing we have on this squidgy little planet. I mean no disrespect. It's a lovely planet, but not important. Take a look at the images from Hubble. Lost in Space... I'll say! We really should not take ourselves seriously. How can we? Why should we? We are a stroke of luck and we should be very grateful we are and not mess it about, not spoil it, we should make the very best of it we can. The only thing I would rate higher than art is kindness.

I can get very angry. Here are the things that make me angry.

1. All people who take themselves seriously, who think that in any way whatever they may be worth more than someone, anyone else. All such people are immature, inadequate, incomplete. They are half people, less than people, not-people. In most cases what drives them to be headteachers, politicians, CEOs, pundits, journos, talking heads is their inadequacy. I've known exceptions. Not many.

2. Any unnecessary suffering, physical, mental, emotional. Almost all suffering can be alleviated or eradicated. That wasn't always true, but it is true now. Pain that warns you, pain that says take your hand out of the fire is fine, a survival mechanism. But physical pain beyond that needn't exist, not from hunger, severe illness, torture. And psychic pain beyond the separations caused by death can be alleviated: and even the latter – a loved one dies, let's dwell on the happiness they brought us and then seek to fill the place. Other forms of psychic pain are unnecessary, the results of human stupidity, an exaggerated sense of one's own importance, and so on.

3. Puritans of every sort. The work ethic. Meritocracy. Any ocracy, at all, come to that, but meritocracy is the worst. Why? Listen. Aristocracy was basically rule by hereditary land-owners. Now at least there was a blind selfish sort of logic to this: I have land, it can make me rich and fat, but only if I hold onto it and rule the poor buggers who live on it, and make sure they give me the fruits of most of their labours and don't try to take my land from me and my descendants. That's at least honest, and there's a similar snide, slimey, grasping honesty behind most ocracies. But meritocracy? Rule by those who think themselves better, have more merit than the rest of us? And who, pray, decides what constitutes merit? The people who measure it by the tests they themselves set, tests they are rather good at… Oh, bugger off!

For goodness sake, we're here for a short time on a planet that's a squidge, let's make the most of it, let's help everyone to make the most of it or at least mind our own businesses and let them get on with theirs; let's revel in variety, contrast, in difference, in our senses, in the magical, mysterious twistings and turnings of our intellects, let's help others to do the same or at least not ever stand in their way. There is room for all of us. All we need is to learn to be kind to each other. And let's have none of that meritocratic It'd be doing him a kindness… crap from the social or any other sort of ologists.

Kindness

Here's another bit from Trajectories. *It's 2007. Our meritocratic government has decided to make people pay to go
into the Tate Modern. Thomas, nearly seventy-two, has
chained himself to the railings in protest. His son Richard,
lead singer of the enormously successful rock group Evil
Trend tries to persuade him to pack it in. It's raining,
London is about to flood.*

Thursday it had begun to rain. Just a drizzle at first with some
sleet in it before settling in, sometimes a heavy monsoon-like
downpour, sometimes less – but from then on it rained, right
through to the following Wednesday.

The head-lights of the limo picked Dad out through the sweeping
silver chiffon. From the leathery warmth inside, with the lights and the
wet pavements it looked as unreal and as attractive as an arty shot in a
nineties TV serial – say about sahf-London gangsters: the huddled
figure propped like a doll against the two feet of brick wall and the
brutalist square railings, just ten yards along the street from the
surveilled, locked and alarmed double gates.

The big car idled up to the pavement but the gutters were already full
and the wheels rolled a small wave of muddy oily water across the flag-
stones and on to the trailing hem of the doll's mackintosh. Richard slid
out of the passenger door, let it clunk behind him. The car purred away.
Back in four hours was the arrangement. The man on the ground lifted
his head as far as he was able – Houdini-like, like an escapologist, he was
chained to the railings and some of the chains clicked metallically
though most merely tightened their hold on his limbs, torso and neck.

'Rich? Glad you could make it. Nice of you to drop by. Pull up a
pew.'

Over the last decade or so Thomas had lapsed more and more into
the idioms and catch phrases of his parents – much of it dating from his
own father's few but critical years in the RAF during World War II.
Richard never met him – he was run over in 1960, twenty years before
Richard was born. Furthermore, and the archaic way of speaking was
an expression of it, Thomas had also always, but far more noticeably
in the recent past, maintained an ironic distance from his son,
approving, encouraging, yes, but always observing, seemingly
detached. Perhaps another thing he had carried over from his own
father's generation was an ability to love confounded by a reticence in

its expression. Anyway, it wasn't always easy being the father of a multi-millionaire rock icon.

'So, what's new in the great world? Who's in? Who's out?'

His voice rasped, fluids rattled in his throat and probably lower, in his trachea and lungs. He was wearing a once white raincoat, belted, collared, caped and strapped. Taken with the hat, if he had been able to stand up and all had been in good condition, he would have looked like Philip Marlowe in a film noir of the fifties. But in fact he was a sodden wreck, the hat beginning to lose its shape, the rain coat bulging with the extra clothes he had on underneath and black with the water that was soaking in wherever it could.

He took these visits from Richard in much the way a terminal patient accepts visitors in a hospice or hospital – determined, for the sake of the visitor, to show an interest in the world and its doings that was entirely spurious since he was on the point of leaving it.

'Nothing, Dad, has changed a lot in the last twenty-hours or so. Just rain. Flood warnings and so on.'

'But the world turns, it still turns.'

'I suppose so. Else we'd all fall off.'

'Is that really so, Rich? I'm not sure that's so.'

But Richard was not about to get into an uninformed argument about centrifugal force and gravity.

'Dad. It's raining, you're cold and wet and I will be too in five minutes. Tell me where the key is and we'll go to a pub, have something hot to eat, and then you can come back to the hotel.'

Though he doubted the Hyde Park would let his dad in, in the state he was, not even for the lead singer of Evil Trend.

'Nope!'

The chains were tungsten steel, the padlock state of the art, and once he'd snapped it shut Thomas Somers had tossed the key through the grate of the drain in front of him, a drain that was now overflowing, bubbling up a noxious mix of sewage, rainwater, and possibly tidal water from the rising Thames. He'd hidden the second key in a luggage locker at Waterloo with a six button electronic number pad – they'd been installed a month after the Boston Accords were signed and the danger of bombs being left in them had almost completely receded. Only he knew the number of the locker and the number of the lock.

Richard pulled the belt of his butter-coloured kid-skin coat tighter, turned up the huge wings of the collar. He'd always been a dressy lad, spending a large chunk of his first earnings as a kitchen worker in a pub, just ten years earlier, on a deep blue velvet suit.

'The rain will ruin that leather thing you're wearing.'

'No it won't. It's been proofed.'

He wasn't at all sure this was so, but he wasn't going to let his Dad score off him that easily.

'So. How's your Mum?'

'OK, I suppose. Worried sick about you, of course. I was on the phone to her before I came out. She says you ought to think a bit more about all of us, and how we love you, and a bit less about...' His voice faded.

'About what?'

'Making a fool of yourself.'

'And Hannah-Rosa?'

'She too. In a terrible state. Rang up from Sydney.'

'All the way from Sydney. Goodness!'

'She's about to pack in the job and fly back.'

'She'd bloody better not. I'll never speak to her again if she does. And it won't do a bit of good.'

'I know. That's what I told her. I also said that you'll either be off those railings by the time she gets here —'

But Thomas had burst into a prolonged fit of heavy, agonising coughing. Agonising to Richard anyway. It ended with a great gob of sputum most of which reached the pavement though some stayed on the front of the coat. Some was dark – in the rainy street light it was impossible to say whether or not it was blood.

'My right lung's quate gawn,' he whispered. Then managing a shout: 'But m' left one's a stunner!'

'...or dead,' Richard concluded.

Thomas lifted his head as far as the chains would let him.

'"You only know you're in chains when you feel them". Rosa Luxemburg. We called Hannah Hannah-Rosa after her.' He mumbled and fidgeted a little then came out with it. 'Is anyone taking any notice at all?'

'No. Not a blind bit.' Richard added brutally: 'Why should they?'

All that could be done had already been done. Letters to *The Times*. A full-page advert in all the posh broadsheets signed by a hundred and fifty famous arties, including all of Evil Trend except the bass guitarist who was a bit of a fascist, but a good bassist. And on the Sunday a demo where they were now – outside the Tate Modern. Richard had been there. The Director had come out on to the steps and made a statement: he totally agreed with everyone there, charges for entry were all wrong, probably illegal, but since the demise of the Arts Council, and the end of Arts Council grants, there was nothing else for it. The real trouble, which he made no reference to, was that a major sponsor had pulled out three months earlier when they awarded the Turner for an extremely accurate mock-up, blood, bodily fluids and all, of the crashed Mercedes Diana Princess of Wales had died in just over eight years earlier. They then bought it and installed it as part of the permanent exhibition.

Nevertheless, and as a result of the protests, Art Minister Jackson had said on Monday that maybe a special subsidy could be found. On Tuesday *The Sun* demanded her immediate resignation and she backpedalled. Let the Farties pay if they want to – Why should We? had been the leader headline.

And on Tuesday night Thomas Somers moved in, chained himself to the railings and stayed there. He'd spent a lot of money on the chains, and a lot of thought and care on how he had wrapped himself up in them. On Wednesday the experts the police had called in said they couldn't cut the chains without harming him, and the original contractors who had converted the old Bankside power station into the Tate Modern made the point that they had been commissioned to make the rails and wall the outer defences of an impregnable fortress.

For a day or two Thomas attracted some attention. Asked if he was an art-lover he said no, he was a people-lover and art was for people. All people. And should always be free – both of any sort of censorship and any sort of charge or levy on those who wanted to enhance their lives by experiencing it. This was something the journos could not understand so they decided he was an art-lover and, considering the art he loved, a pretty damned weird one at that. The last straw for them was that Thomas refused to say who he was: he would not even give his name. Who he was was entirely irrelevant, he said. He could be Archbishop of Canterbury, CEO of Saintrose or a common or garden dosser, it made no difference. Since by then, after three days, he looked exactly like a common or garden dosser, and there was a difference as far as the media were concerned, they forgot about him.

He was, he said, on hunger strike, not because he wanted to die sooner – in fact the longer he was alive the better, the more likely it was his protest would succeed, but because he didn't want to shit himself too much, and he guessed that that would cease to be a problem after a time if he didn't eat. He had had a catheter attached whose outlet ran into the now-flooding drain, and he took whatever liquids, though in moderation, well-wishers cared to bring him. No alcohol though. Ten years earlier alcohol had damn near killed him.

Richard, on his first visit, had said he would tell the media that Thomas was his father. Thomas had been firm and Dad-like – as firm as he had ever been. 'It won't do me or why I'm here any good at all – and it will do you a lot of harm.'

'Why? How?'

'Oh come on! Pop idol stands by while Dad dies in chains? Don't do it, Richard. Please. Just don't even think of it!'

Now Richard hunkered down over his Dad. Water dripped from the brim of the hat and from the end of his nose into grey stubble. He was hollow-cheeked and his eyes were bright. His fingers shook. He did indeed for all the world look like an alckie dosser on the way out.

'Dad, you must be in pain.'

'The occasional twinge, yes.' He began to cough again but controlled it, held it in. Then, remembering a very old joke that *his* father had been fond of, he wheezed on: 'I only do it, you know, because it will be so lovely when it stops.'

Richard struggled for a moment with a rising wave of pain as intense as any Thomas was suffering, even if it was mostly psychic. It transmuted into anger, fury, rage, but he overrode them too. In fact both men were being terribly British about it all, refusing to become overtly emotional. He straightened, looked down at the bundle beneath him, forced a nonchalant-sounding laugh.

'You look like something by Christo.'

'Yes. I thought of that. Not as big as the Reichstag but bigger than the one they've got in there.' He jerked his head at the building behind him. 'Maybe when I've gone they'll put me in there too. Hirst can pickle me.'

'He doesn't do that any more.'

'Well, maybe he'll change his mind. All in a good cause, eh?'

'Dad, you're not going to last a lot longer.'

'Thought had crossed my mind.'

'Well, what are you going to do about it?'

'Not a lot.'

The anger began to simmer again.

'Sorry to go over it all again but just what do you think you're up to? Killing yourself in the hope a few poor people will be able to look at some art they won't understand and probably not even like?'

'Don't patronise. How many times did you go to the old Tate when you had hardly two pennies to rub together?'

'There are going to be concessions. For students, unwaged, and pensioners.'

'Fuck concessions.'

'It's a lost cause. And even if it wasn't, would it be worth dying for?'

'You could build hecatombs, mountains with the bodies of those who have died for less. Think of the Christian martyrs for a start. Then all the martyrs the Christians racked, hanged, quartered and burnt. And that's just the foothills.'

'For less? You're an arrogant old bugger, you know? Listen. When you chained yourself up here you thought it would work – else you wouldn't have done it. Lord knows why you thought anyone would give a toss for an old tramp who refused to say who he was. But you thought they would. And they're not going to. So let's pack it in and go home.'

The rain thickened from stair-rods into something that seemed almost solid. It swirled across the paving stones, met the rising water from the drain, blotted visibility down to fifty yards through which the street lamps glowed meaninglessly, shedding almost no light beyond their penumbra. It was noisy too, a continuous hiss and clatter backed by rumbling thunder and the distant wail of emergency vehicles. Richard hunkered again, put his face as near as he could to his father's, strove to elicit and hear an answer. He glanced down.

'You're wearing my old Wrangler boots.'

'Mine.'

'Yours.'

Somewhere between them laughter hovered. Ten years earlier they had together bought two pairs, black and brown. The black had been Richard's but he quickly wore them to destruction and then took to wearing the brown ones. But then he got a car, an old Polo, and he found he couldn't drive in the boots comfortably so they had drifted back to Thomas's wardrobe. And Thomas wore them only when he went for a walk on the heath round Thorney Hill – which he did about twice a year. You wear the things you buy as fashion statements far more than those you get for purely practical reasons. Richard put his hands on his father's, partly prompted by the immense sense of loss – of a happy past the memory had sparked off – partly because he could not bear the shake which seemed worse than ever.

'All right. So you're going to stay here and die. Any last messages? Famous last words?'

A croaky whisper. He moved his ear closer to the old man's mouth.

'Kindness and Art, Richard. Kindness and Art. Remember?'

He remembered. He had heard that all before too. Kindness was Anglo-Saxon. *Kynde*. Kin. Nature benevolent and giving, not the *natura* of the Romans that had to be pushed back with Virgil's fork. And Art was creativity, the human soul ranging freely, explaining, exalting, exhilarating, not dominated by technique, the human mind untrammelled. True art included scientific thought too – so long as it was original and strove to be true to itself, not just a means to power or wealth, reputation and self-serving.

'You're serious, aren't you? You really are looking for famous last words.'

'It's what you asked for.' A touch grumpy now. 'I'm trusting you to remember them.'

They stayed huddled as they were for twenty minutes or so without speaking. The rain poured from the rim of Thomas's hat making it look like a weird version of an Australian wideawake. The high collar of Richard's coat acted like a funnel so water slid in a continuous stream into clothes which now clung coldly to the skin beneath. Although it was cold it was not as cold as February had been when Thomas was Richard's age. At last Richard felt pressure returned on his hand.

'I'd die for a cuppa, Rich.'

'Oh shit, of course you would. I'm so sorry.' The night before Thomas had asked him to bring a flask – but he had forgotten all about it.

'Not too much milk and no sugar.'

Diabetic to the very end. Richard stood up, felt the water slip down inside. Tea? Where? He associated cups of tea at night with railway stations. Blackfriars and Cannon Street were commuter stations and surely closed by eleven o'clock. Waterloo, then, maybe ten minutes walk, twenty there and back, but worth a try. And possibly he'd get one of those polystyrene cups with a lid you could clamp on.

'I'll find you one. Give me twenty minutes. Don't go away.'

Head down he pushed across Blackfriars Road, again resisted the temptation to go north of the river, and fought his way on through the rain up Stamford Street with the water often over his ankles and filling his Drakon cordoban loafers, flattening his baggy chinos with their tight cuffs. The kid coat now seemed heavy, less supple, and slapped against his knees. The old man, he thought, had probably been right about that.

A cuppa. He remembered how pleased his dad had always been when, as a teenager, Richard had brought him a cuppa in the morning. Normally Dad got up and made the tea. He always said it was the greatest gift his son could give him – a cuppa in bed. Greater love hath no man than this: that a man bring a morning cuppa to his friend in his bed, was how he put it.

As he reached the ring in front of Waterloo four fire engines, preceded by a police car, came roaring out of the rain across Waterloo Bridge, blue lights flashing, sirens screaming and wailing. There can't, there cannot be, a fire anywhere tonight, he thought. The last four steps of the subway were under water and the IMAX in front of him, and the tunnels that now intersected beneath the new development above what had been Cardboard City, were waist deep. He stumbled back up to street level, climbed through the Wellington Arch and made it at last on to the concourse of the station. It did not have the brightness he had expected but was shadowy with emergency lighting. Limbo. A waiting area. Very few people were about, lost souls they seemed, staring at closed barriers and improvised notices: *Due to weather alert all services have been temporarily disbanded.*

Even the pinpoints of light on the number pads of the lockers were out – so presumably he would not have been able to get the second key even if he had known the number. There was, however, a small queue in front of the one coffee and snack stall that had remained open. He took his turn and got precisely what he wanted – a half pint of hot tea in a sealed cup which still burnt his hands. He looked at his watch – already he had been as long as he had said he would be.

He ran back to the glass doors, pushed through them and tried to run down the steps. Of course he slipped. The base of his spine smacked down three of the steps before he came to rest, sodden, jarred, and with scalded fingers where they had clenched involuntarily and hard enough to crush the polystyrene. He considered weeping. He went back on to the concourse but the stall had closed, the Afro who had been serving putting the last of the shutters into place. 'Sorry mate, hot water failed – no electric see?'

This time it wasn't fire engines crossing Waterloo Bridge, but army lorries filled with sandbags.

They stopped him halfway back down Stamford Street. There were barriers, police, soldiers, and beyond them fire engines pumping water out not in, and human chains passing sand-bags up through the rain to a rising wall he could just make out a hundred yards away. They wouldn't let him through. He argued and they paid no attention. The river's rising they said. It won't top the walls above the embankments but it's coming up through all the drains. He pushed and they grappled him back, told him to go home. He said his father was up there in front of the Tate. The what? The old power station. There's no one up there. We checked. He didn't believe them. He tried walking round the barrier using side streets but two soldiers picked him up again and brought him back. There's a curfew, see? Why? It's dangerous. There could be subsidence. You could get in the way of the emergency services. Some of the plant they're using is heavy. There could be looting. That was more like it. Looting of warehouses, looting of the expensive specialist shops that had sprung up in the area. Looting even from the Tate. He laughed hysterically at the thought of international art thieves trying to carry off that fucking wrecked Mercedes or a pickled cow. Given the chance he himself would have nicked one of the Lichtensteins or a Hockney. Match the ones he'd already bought.

Towards dawn the rain stopped, the tide turned, and the water began to drain away. The smell was awful. There was a thick yellowish-brown slime over the paving stones with panty-pads and used condoms in it and shreds of toilet paper.

Thomas hadn't moved. Of course not. And you could see why no one had bothered. A little heap of old clothes attached to the railings. Anyway, he was dead.

Richard ran and slithered the last fifty yards or so and scooped up him up like a rag-doll, holding him in his arms so the head was on his shoulder. The old hat at last came off and tumbled down his back. And the chains fell away.

The fucking chains fell away.

They looked like escapology chains and they were escapology chains. Pull them most ways they tightened or anyway held fast. But pull them just one way, in the right sequence, and they came apart. Bastard. Fucking bastard.

And his last immortal words?

'I'd die for a cuppa...'

Well, he bloody had.

Five lines in The Sun beneath the headline M-ARTY-R DIES FOR F-ART-Y ART and no obituary in *The Times*.

La Muralla

This, as is obvious, is not me at all but Nicolás Guillén, the Cuban poet. I used it in Zdt (Greenfinger). The narrator is Esther Somers, and the darling she is nursing as she dances, is her four-month-old daughter.

Presently from Minerva's cabin, a hundred yards behind me, there was a guitar, and improvised marimbas. Then singing. I knew the song. The words are by Nicolás Guillén, the Cuban mulatto poet. I suppose Manuel had taught it to them. I danced to it a little, swung round and back and forth and nursed my darling, and crooned the words to her too.

Para hacer esta muralla	To make this wall
Traiganme todas las manos	We must all join hands
Los negros sus manos negras	Blacks with their black hands
Los blancos sus blancas manos	Whites with their white hands
Una muralla que vaya	A wall that will go
Desde la playa hasta el monte	From the beach to the mountain

Desde el monte hasta la playa	The mountain to the sea
Que vaya sobre el horizonte.	Which stretches to the horizon.

Then the rhythm quickens and my step with it and Zena comes off the
nipple and beams her four-toothed smile, pearls in the moonlight, and
flaps her tiny fists and chortles.

Tún, tún, ¿Quién es?	Knock, knock, Who is there?
Una rosa y un clavel	A rose and a carnation
Abre la muralla.	Open the wall.
Tún, tún, ¿Quién es?	Knock, knock, Who is there?
El sable del coronel	The colonel's sabre
Cierra la muralla.	Close up the wall.
Tún, tún, ¿Quién es?	Knock, knock, Who is there?
La paloma y el laurel	The dove and the bay
Abre la muralla.	Open the wall.
Tún, tún, ¿Quién es?	Knock, knock, Who is there?
El gusano y el ciempiés	The worm and the centipede
Cierra la muralla.	Close up the wall.
Tún, tún, ¿Quién es?	Knock, knock, Who is there?
Al corazón del amigo	To the heart of the friend
Abre la muralla.	Open the wall.
Al veneno y al puñal	To poison and the dagger
Cierra la muralla.	Close up the wall.
Al Pay Say y la Hierbabuena	To the CP and apple-mint
Abre la muralla.	Open the wall.
Al diente de Ia serpiente	To the serpent's tooth
Cierra la muralla.	Close up the wall.
Al corazón del amigo	To a friend's heart
Abre la muralla.	Open the wall.
Al ruiseñor en la flor.	To the nightingale in the flower.

Hacemos esta muralla	Let us make this wall
J untando todas las manos	By all joining hands
Los negros sus manos negras	The blacks with their black hands
Los blancos sus blancas manos	The whites with their white hands.

Then slow:

Al ruiseñor en la for	To the nightingale in the flower

Then a huge shout:

ABRE LA MURALLA.	OPEN THE WALL.

An Ageing Adolescent looks at Rubens in the National Gallery

At the far end of the gallery she sat
  Hands in her lap, demure with ankles crossed
  Primly aware, glossy as a cat
Her dark hair bobbed and groomed, her skirt well pressed
As pretty as the pictures, an autocrat,
  A presence in her space so self-possessed,
Yet through her painted lips she softly breathed
Beneath her blouse her bosom gently heaved.

Facing her but somewhere off a prize is traded
  Wisdom, Rule or Beauty for an apple.
Juno storms, Minerva has not made it,
  Venus glows all over though this crap'll
Cause a lot of grief but yet she paid it
  And Ilium's towers'll topple.
That Paris got it right is not disputed
Venus' charms are all that they're reputed.

Although the wispy muslin hides her sex,
  Thighs, nipples, breasts and fold of flesh
Make body-building Paris flex his pecs.
  All men, like Mars, are caught in Vulcan's mesh
And even old ones fumble for their specs,
  Yet although I'm bound her charms to treas-
Ure, my soul remains in thrall to life not art
The living not the painted wins my heart.

 Which leads us, seamlessly, to…

9. EROS AND THANATOS (BONKING 'N' CLOG-POPPING)

It's not easy to do Eros in prose. Music (of course) can do it, and I don't mean Wagner with his horrid Liebestod *nor those excessively extended orgasms in the late Romantics. What I have in mind is almost any baroque to early classical duet between a soprano and a mezzo, probably the latter part being written for a castrato singing the male hero, though not always:* Pur ti miro *from the end of Monteverdi's* Poppea, *through loads of Handel, to Mozart. And in a very different way much of what Beethoven wrote for Archduke Rudolph, especially* Les Adieux. *Painting is good at it, sculpture too, poetry, of course, film and photography occasionally. But prose is… tricky. Either it's flatulent, purple, transcendental, melting stuff or it's pricks, cunts, boobs and bums, which is good fun, sure, but doesn't get that wholeness that is the mark of Eros, that inseparable fusion of tenderness and wonder with physical delight.*

And then there's the fell sergeant – who often seems to get in on the act. But they are like the Weather Man with his scowl and his umbrella and the Weather Lady with her smile and her straw hat. They sit at opposite poles of the same axis and never come out quite at the same time, though like sunshine and showers they can follow each other pretty damn closely. As they do in the first chapter of A Very English Agent…

A Corner of a Foreign Land

This is the first version. In the book it is very slightly bowd-lerised. I'm not quite sure why...

I was fifteen years old, or was it twenty, when I was thrust on to the stage of world history. I remember it well. The thing of it is I don't remember anything before – just tall dark shapes walking across muddy deserts out of darkness. So my most early memory is of a woman, a girl. No, I tell a lie. My first memory is of a butterfly, a fritillary perhaps, at any rate cinnamon coloured with intricately patterned black spots and smudges and dots and wings cut as with scissors almost into a swallow-tail, a diminutive swallow-tail, slowly opening and closing its wings, and occasionally wiping its eyes and its watch-spring proboscis with its front legs. It was sitting on a rounded mound of white skin, just inches from my eyes, a shoulder of perfect marble but for a mole or two and rising and falling almost imperceptibly as the woman whose shoulder it was breathed in and out more easily than I, since my waist was being squeezed by arms that threatened to crush the life out of me.

Maribel was a big girl. And therefore far bigger than I. She had shortish dark hair, crudely cut and the only garment she was wearing was a red scarf with white polka dots, knotted behind her neck. Moments before she had shed a short ochre shift, a coarse black skirt and wooden sabots, after first undressing me.

A prolonged rattle of musketry about half a mile away caused her to move more sharply than before and the butterfly took off. Its weaving, dithering flight took it to a bramble in flower where it settled once more, this time to feed on blackberry-flavoured nectar extracted from the centre of a corolla made by the four pearly petals of a tiny bramble flower. Maribel lifted her head, a curiosity tinged with concern tightening her lips and creasing her brow. Then she smiled up at me, murmured in her coarse dialect, and wriggled a little, repositioning herself so my tautly stiff member could penetrate yet further.

I wriggled too and my knees between her legs squelched in the mud, cow-shit and chalky grit.

The musketry which had distracted Maribel was the British army clearing its throat: that is, in order to clean the barrels of their Brown Besses, each soldier had discharged his piece into the air.

Presently I discharged my piece into Maribel, but too soon for her. It did not matter. Such is the potency of youth I suffered only a momentary and partial weakening of flesh and desire and she quickly resumed her approach to ecstasy.

This was a long time coming. The problem was, she was large and I so small, my whole physique I mean, not my member, and the mounds and slopes of her thighs and pubis were such that even though he was, and is, large in terms of the rest of me, he could do little more than cross the threshold of the door she had opened so wide.

She reversed our positions. Large and huge though she was, she was also strong and healthy. With both hands clasped about my waist she hoisted me above her, much as if I were a pet cat or puppy, and rolling with the slight incline into the bottom of the ditch got me on to my back and her self over me, knees planted in the wet loam on either side of my body, hands way beyond my head, her breasts now slapping my cheeks, obscuring what I might have seen of the sky through the branches of elder and plates of elderflower above us, and attempted to lower her pudenda onto my gallant and manly prick which still stood to attention above my stomach, his still weeping little eye peeping hopefully through my partially retracted foreskin.

The smell of elderflower mingled most aptly with the fragrances of her heated, sweating and leaking body. However, there was holly as well as elder in that hedge and fallen holly leaves prickled my back like a penitential shirt.

Somewhere in the distance fifty thousand feet beat the ground and bands played, but not near enough to distract my Maribel. More troublesome to her were the flies, those bright brown ones that bite voraciously. A yard from her left knee there was a large wet cow-pat that had attracted them initially to sup from the yellowish liquor that lay pooled in its shallow crater, but now, thirst satisfied, they sought meatier sustenance. She took time out from what she was attempting to slap one that had settled on that shoulder that had been beneath my gaze and was now above it. She smeared its corpse from her hand and on to my stomach and then thrust it, her hand I mean, back between us searching him out, feeding him back so I thought she'd swallow him whole, balls and all, and the rest of me behind them.

A jangling of harness, a lot of harness, a clipping and clopping of hooves, many many hooves, and the squelch and rattle as the six foot rye beyond the hedge of holly, hawthorn and elder was pushed aside and trampled. Moving my head as far as I could to the left and peering up through a triangle of light fringed by the hair in her armpit, I could see pennants on the ends of steely lances briskly rise and fall with the motion of the trotting chargers beneath them. A bugle call and all as one wheeled away from the ditch and were gone. But not before the sun had flashed from the rear piece of a cuirass, as bright as a mirror.

There was a sort of down beyond our ditch, a long, low snaking rise above rolling fields of rye tall enough to hide a man, tall enough for a manikin to be lost in, bluey green, more blue than green when the wind ran its fingers through, with numerous partings of deep ditches like the one we were in, overhung with double canopies of elder, alder in the deeper dips, holly, hawthorn and banked with dock, sorrel, nettles, cranebill, bugloss, and Solomon's seal. There were foxgloves too, and clouds of butterflies, small and blue, white, scarlet and black, as well as jet and cinnamon.

The broader of these ditches marked out lots and plots of land and served as conduits for cows, pushed out after the dawn milking, called home at sunset from the pasture that lay along the rises to the south and north, with bloated leaking udders for a second milking. Huge kine they were, beige and cream with sticky stalactites of spew dangling greenly from their masticating mouths.

A distant cock crew, a blackbird sang above our heads, and a league away the wheels of half a thousand cannon, limber carts, and fourgons squealed in unharmonious discords.

Maribel, as I said above, snorted or sighed, hoisted one dimpled knee and milk-white thigh over my body as if dismounting a diminutive hobby horse and exposed for a moment the darkness in her heavy bush, clogged with slime. Then, sitting up on her huge buttocks she slewed herself round, pushing up a little gelid wave of brackish mud, so we were next to each other, side by side. For a moment she sat forward, arms spread across her raised knees, turned her head and shook it again so her black hair, streaked with russet mud, moved lankly across her massive alabaster shoulders. She frowned, pouted, adjusted her polka-dotted scarf, and thought. Then she curled her heavy arm about my waist, and pushing a little and mumbling imprecations until I caught on what she wanted, had me astride her once again recumbent torso but with my back to her face. A heavy hand cradled the back of my head and pushed and pushed until my face was buried where she wanted it to be – between her legs. To get there I had to kneel with my bum in the air, legs spread by her width, her huge breasts beneath me.

Her odours were magnificent. Farmyard shit in the background, sweet musky hawthorn blossom between her swollen lips, and my own semen, a brisk sea-side smell. Then behind me, where the fresh clean, rain-washed breeze (there'd been a terrible storm the night before) played about my raised bum-hole and cooled my heated buttocks, I felt her large hand come, cradling my scrotum, rolling my balls so she almost hurt them, then closing round my throbbing prick. Her other hand thrust into my neck and pushed me down and in and started to pull my head this way and that as if it were the prick larger than I could provide which she so much desired. I suffocated, I gasped, I pulled back, heaved in the foetid air and plunged back in, my tongue probing so the root of it hurt, in through all that tumescent, slippery flesh to find the nodal swelling at the centre of her being.

Now I really went to work, the earth shook, and the thunder roared in my ears, yet through it all I felt my long thick prick swell like a ramrod in her hand, and waves of hot pleasure swept up my buttocks and into my chest. My own hands now squeezed beneath her, through the gluey mud, and as I flattened my shoulders and chest across her rounded stomach I got my finger, then two of them up her bum-hole. This was the trigger. She spasmed, oh God how she spasmed, the muscles beyond the sphincter squeezing and loosening, squeezing and loosening, and my prick went with it, jumping like a live fish in her hand and spewing my spunk yet again right across her navel and into the crevices between my chest and her heaving pelvis.

The rolling thunder went on, and the earth continued to shake.

She rolled me off her, squelch into the mud, and sat up, facing me. Her chest above her breasts was flushed, her nipples as hard now as cased walnuts, her shoulders shiny with sweat. Her head was framed by an oval of light at the end of the green tunnel we sat in. For a moment she smiled down at me, a silly smile, part shy, part triumphant, revealing the natural gaps between her healthy teeth, making twin moons of her apple cheeks.

She spoke, head up and on one side, eyes searching the dappled leaves, blossom and sunlight above us. The sun was almost overhead by now, only intermittently covered by cloud, and when it shone on us directly, benevolently hot. I can't be sure what it was she said, but I'd guess, Englished, it went like this.

'What the fuck is going on?'

'A battle?' said I.

A sphere, iron, a foot or more in diameter, fused with a spluttering string, dropped through the canopy twenty feet behind her, trundled down the slope towards her, the fuse hissed and disappeared and the shell exploded. Fragments of casing and several pounds weight of musket balls screamed through the air, tearing down leaves, twigs and elder blossom. A piece of casing nearly severed her head and four balls smashed their way into her back. She fell forward, over her knees, onto her face. The fact that blood pumped from the jagged wounds for maybe half a minute showed she did not die instantly, though I must hope that the instant of impact rendered her insensible.

I owe her much. Had she not shielded me from the blast, albeit unwittingly, I should have been blown to bits.

This Sudden Growing (Falling in Love Again...)

This patch was reassessed as low-yield land
Burdock and nettle, henbane and black thorn
Flourish where once the thick grain grew.
And cans, scraped to a shit like stain
Lie beneath the tired gorse. No point
In ploughing up. Level it out and let
Contractors come or caravans,
Where cows in heavy summer grazed.

There's use in these. In thickets that support
Rats, feral cats and wireworm in the leaf mould
This sudden growing cannot do much good.
Some harm perhaps. And yet I cannot think
But martins flit in lengthening shadows
Above the reeds, the broom and willow...

Dads Do Die

The first time is the worst, when someone really close to you dies. And it's even worse if it is completely sudden and unexpected. March 1960, I was teaching in Turkey. Two telegrams from my mother: He's gone, he died this morning. The second to arrive: Your Dad has had an accident and is badly hurt. The hospital thinks he should recover. I can't vouch for the actual words but they did arrive in the wrong order, which somehow left a glimmer of hopeless hope until I had managed to phone her.

The effect on me was as profound as it always is for anyone who loses a loved parent too soon, too suddenly, and crept into my writing more than once.

In Joseph *the central figure, then a young man of twenty-two, runs away from the battle of Salamanca to the cottage where he was brought up by the man, a priest and philoso-*

pher, who he thought was his father. He already knows that the old man has died after a fire destroyed part of the cottage, but he has never previously returned to do anything about it.

The heap of refuse at the foot of the stairs was what was mortal of Tia Teresa. The tatters of her black skirts still clung about her bones, and her shawl was wrapped about her head. Beneath it, still attached to her skull her white hair peeped and even stirred in the air I caused to move about her as I stooped. She had not been burnt at all, but perhaps suffocated in the fumes. I mounted the stairs – one, rotten, gave beneath me – filled with dread at what I now felt sure I must find.

The first room was where the chimbley had fallen, bringing in the roof and smashing his clavier to the floor: wind-blown leaves, dust, bird-droppings, and a pool of water from the storm of the night before betokened that it was not shot of the raging battle had brought it down. Many of his books were scattered about the floor – Newton, Descartes, Priestley and Bentham – and the pages that stirred showed signs of mildew; but his brass microscope still gleamed on the table. As I lingered, not wishing to go further, I was suddenly jarred with fright by the swoop and tweet of a swallow, all two-pronged barred tail and red blush of breast, visiting its young, surely by now its second brood, in their mud pellet home in a ceiling corner above the shelves; then it was gone back through the roof to skim and flit above the blood, terror and heat in the valley beyond.

I pushed into the inner room, a dried lath cracked beneath my feet, and I discovered what I had feared – the old man sat up in his cot against a pillow, the sockets of his eyes eyeless, the skin on his brow yellowed and cracked to show the bone, yet some of his straggly beard still there. The tatters of his night-shirt still cased his ribs and did service as a shroud. What was most odd was the ruins of his learning strewn about him – his books open, many with the pages, ripped, as if in frenzy he had tried to spoil them.

I drew nearer and discovered the Will he'd left with Mr Curtis was not his Last Testament – for in his hand, on the coverlet above his knee, he held a framed slate he'd used to school me and then the children of the village. On it three words inscribed:

NADA… NIENTE… NOTHING

But Life Goes On

By the time I wrote Blame Hitler *I was ready, I thought, to confront Dad's death head on. But in the end I could find no better way of doing it than by copying out the report of the inquest, some thirty-five years earlier, more or less as it appeared in the Bognor Post.*

Coroner Criticises of Car *(sic)*

FORMER BOGNOR SCHOOLMASTER'S TRAGIC DEATH

A YOUNG woman told the Coroner at Chichester on Wednesday how she stood in the roadway beside an unconscious man who had fallen off his moped, and waved both arms to stop an oncoming car from running into him. But the car came on.

'I had to move quickly to get out of its way. I did not see it hit the man, but I heard the noise of the car striking metal,' Miss Annabel H. F. Smith, domestic help, of Summertime Bungalows, Felpham, said.

The inquest was on 59-year-old Christopher Richard Tate Somers, retired schoolmaster, of Wroxham Way, Felpham, secretary of the Tithe Barn Club and staff manager for Mr Bob Murfett, turf accountant.

Asked by the Coroner (Mr M. P. A. Winslow) regarding trouble which Mr Somers apparently had with his moped in Upper Bognor Road, east of the junction with the High Street, Miss Smith said that the engine of the machine, which was travelling towards Felpham, stopped.

Deceased got it going again, but had trouble again about 15 yards further on. Then he started 'zigzagging all over the road' and fell off his machine on to his left side. She ran to him and was engaged in lifting the moped off his leg when she saw the car approaching. She stood up and waved to stop it.

CARRIED 39 FEET

Police-Sgt. Jenkins gave evidence of finding two pools of blood on the road, 39 ft. apart. Coroner: 'It looks as if the unfortunate man was carried 39 ft. by the car.' – Sgt. Jenkins: 'It would seem so.'

The Coroner told the jury that the accident occurred just after 10pm on March 17th and deceased died the following afternoon in Bognor Regis War Memorial Hospital.

Dr W. F. Caine, pathologist, said that the left side of the deceased's skull was fractured, but it was not a serious fracture. This injury was quite consistent with deceased striking the roadway with the side of his head when he fell off the moped.

Deceased also had a fractured pelvis, which in itself was not a fatal injury, and also six ribs broken, three on each side, which would tend to increase shock to a substantial degree.

Asked by the Coroner whether, if deceased had only sustained the injuries through falling off his moped and 'nothing further had happened to him', he would have recovered, Dr Caine replied: 'I cannot say so.' He said it was very difficult to assess in connection with the head injuries.

Mr J. Pringle (For Mr Lewison, the driver of the motor car) asked how it could be certain that the fracture of the pelvis was caused by the motor car. Dr Caine replied that a fracture of the pelvis was almost always due to crushing. A pelvis could be crushed from a fall from a height. Coroner: 'Is it consistent with deceased having been run over?' – 'Yes'.

BRAKES INEFFICIENT

PC Blake said that on testing Mr Lewison's car, a black saloon, the brake only acted efficiently on one wheel out of four. At ten miles-an-hour the car took three or four lengths to pull up.

The driver of the car, James Brian Lewison, chemist dispenser, of Rookery Cottage, Middleton, said his car was a 1939 model and he had driven for 37 years.

As he came eastwards along Upper Bognor Road, one of the vehicles coming up High Street went in front of him, causing him to slow down. His speed was 18 to 20mph, gradually increasing to 26mph.

By the light of his near-side headlamp he saw an object on the roadway when he was 10ft to 12ft away.

'I braked a little thinking to avoid what seemed like a sack.

'I never saw the girl waving. She was in a black spot on the road and I never saw her at all,' he said.

CAUGHT THE MOPED

Replying to Mr F. W. Alderson (for the relatives), he said: 'I did avoid the object (deceased) in the road. I turned right immediately but caught the moped and carried it along.'

Coroner: 'Do you not know that it is the duty of a motorist to so drive that he can stop within the limit of his vision?' – 'I didn't know that.' Coroner: 'A great many others drivers don't either – so now you know.'

Miss Anne Frances Docherty, shop assistant, of 1, New Cottage, Middleton, told of travelling on her moped a little behind Mr Lewison's car. She saw something lying in the roadway, but she did not know what it was. A woman was standing in the road waving her arms. Coroner: 'Did you expect the car to stop?' – 'Yes, but it went straight on and hit the object.'

Tony Brown, student engineer, of 'Swallow', Middleton Road, Felpham, said he was a passenger on the top deck of the bus standing in the lay-by. On looking where a girl passenger was pointing he saw a person standing in the middle of the road waving her arms. As the car came up to her she jumped out of its way to the other side of the road.

'I didn't see the car hit anything. I just saw the car suddenly jump up in the air,' witness said.

Addressing the jury, the Coroner referred to the evidence regarding the inefficient condition of three of the four wheel-brakes.

'It is appalling,' he said, 'to find that a man of his age and responsibility should go out in a car such as has been described to you. If Dr Caine's evidence had been that the fracture of the skull had been so slight that deceased would have recovered and wouldn't have died if his later injuries had not happened, Mr Lewison would be in a different position.'

He told the jury that it was not for him but for the police to consider with what offence, if any, the driver of the car could be charged.

As directed by the Coroner, the jury returned a verdict of 'Death by Misadventure'.

Fat Love

Long hours of massive bliss roll through the night
As front to back we fondle soft delight,
Lolloping breasts and lollipop nipples
Invite out tongues and the gentlest of nibbles
The buttocks that dimple, the tummies that roll
The thighs that are highways to our mutual goal.
Mountains of joy offer acres of pleasure,
We roam through them slowly, climb them at leisure,
We Marvell that once we tore through the gate
Ecstacies scant, afraid to be late.
Noon's prick, lunch looms but we lie,
Billows that undulate as Time rolls by.
With all that's between us, we cannot fuck
But, with one big heave, thank god, we can suck.

Waking from an Erotic Dream

That was nice
But not quite anatomically precise.

Fat Mary

Five years ago Steve Jones asked me to have a go at writing a horror story for the annual Dark Terrors *anthology, published by Vista. It's not a genre I'm happy with, either as a reader or writer, but I had a go. The thing was I had just saved my life (with a little help from Alayne and the NHS) by packing in the booze and I was worried that without a stiff snifter to get me going I would not be able to shed my inhibitions in front of the keyboard and the screen. So* Fat Mary *was written in a sort of just testing mode.*

It also marries Eros and Thanatos even more closely than the opening chapter of A Very English Agent. *I'm really not sure about this conjunction which the chattering classes, since Freud, Georges Bataille, et al, seem so firmly to believe in. It's great in literature, and art in general, but does it really work in real life? Anyway, here is* Fat Mary. *Careful though… if I ever have written anything that should come with a warning to the squeamish or the shockable, then this is it.*

It was, I suppose, a small thatched cottage, but you don't see them like that any more – a two-roomed cabin, made of medieval daub – a mixture of cow-dung and fine gravel, terracotta-coloured where the whitewash had peeled off. The thatch was dark brown, covered with blackish moss, roof-tree sagging. There was nothing picturesque about it at all, no briar-roses, no hollyhocks. Thin chickens squabbled over the dusty yard, a white lean rooster with a spare handful of tail feathers racketed amongst them, occasionally flicking them. The hens paid no attention, often just went on desperately pecking at the ground for a grain or seed they might have missed.

There was a shed, a barn and a stable. In the stable, in a stall too small for her, a fat old sow suckled six out of eight piglets. She had eaten the two runts along with all the after-births in order to have milk for the others.

There was a pond, shrunk in July, within a saucer of chocolate-coloured cracked mud, sheeted with emerald green algae and beside it a dung-heap which heaved with thin red worms.

It was all set at the top end of a narrow coombe at the end of a chalky track that threaded the three ten-acre fields she had. The steep sides of the downs were filled with beech and birch woods, but the back end was crowned with an ancient yew forest, planted by Henry VIII to provide longbows. Too late, someone told him about gunpowder so the trees were never used.

We crouched in hiding on the edge of the beech wood, James and I, watched, waited and speculated. We were pupils at Minster Hill, a boarding school that claimed to be a public school. Minster Hill prided itself on its progressive approach to education so, on Saturday and Sunday afternoons, we were let out to walk around the countryside at will.

We were wearing the summer uniform – grey Vyella shirts with sleeves rolled up, grey corduroy shorts, very baggy and loose, wollen stockings, sandals. The sandals were impractical, but there we were, there was nothing we could do about that. I wore a sheathed SS dagger my uncle had brought back from Germany. The hilt was wound with silver wire and there was a swastika on the centre of the cross-guard. I carried it under my shirt when we left the school buildings, but threaded the sheath on to my belt as soon as we were clear.

It was a hot sultry day. The flies were a bother. We headed into the woods and searched out rotten silver birch trees, which, we had discovered, could be pushed over. Often you had to rock them first, then they would begin to crack, and at last they'd topple. Occasionally they would break in three or four places up the trunk and concertina down around us in a flurry of soft umber shards and dust. When we couldn't find any more trees that would go, I took out my SS knife and we practised throwing it at the trunks of the beech trees. These were grey and wrinkled and put me in mind of the giant legs of huge elephants. It wasn't easy to make the point stick in. You could either throw it point first in one sweeping underarm movement, a method which worked over short distances. Or, over five yards or more, we held it by the point and made it turn in the air three times or more, always hoping the point would hit the tree first. Sometimes it did.

After a time, when our throats were dry and prickly and an itchy sweat was building up inside the Vyella shirts, we sat awkwardly on the ground, undid our buttoned flies and pulled our pricks into the warm air. We did it to ourselves, not to each other. There was no passion in this, not even much friendliness. Indeed, back at school James and I were in different forms, different dormitories, kept away from each other, though occasionally we exchanged expressionless, unblinking glances when we met.

James was a dark, saturnine lad, pretty in a sort of Spanish or Levantine way, with olive skin and a mop of black hair. He said little, seemed to live in a world of his own.

When we'd done that we pushed on down the hill, through the trees, to the electric fence that bounded the highest of Fat Mary's fields. And while we waited for her to appear (something which did not always happen) we rehearsed the myths that surrounded her, adding our own embellishments and speculations, and listened to the five second pulse on her wire – enough to keep her three Jersey cows in and the deer out.

'She weighs sixteen stone.'

'More like twenty.'

'The hair on her chin is bristly.'

'So is the hair between her legs.'

'Her bosoms are great fat sacks of pink blancmange.'

'With giant strawberries for nipples.'

In those days even to say words like 'bosoms' and 'nipples' was a thrill, *a frisson*, at any rate.

'Her bottom is huge. Bigger than the two biggest melons you ever saw...'

'Far bigger. And her bum-hole is a black pit.'

'Her feet are rotting and smell like over-ripe Camembert...'

But we weren't that interested in her feet.

'On very hot days she takes off all her clothes and walks around with nothing on.

'On one very, very hot day she made Smithson-Haig go into her bedroom and do it to her.'

'So he says.'

'Don't you believe him?'

'Not really.'

'Nor do I.'

I pulled a long succulent stalk of milky barley grass, easing it from its cellulose sheath. I sucked it, then chewed.

'Would you?' I asked. 'Would you go into her house if she asked you?'

'Yes. If you came too.'

'And do it to her?'

'I don't know about that.'

The distant chug and rattle of a pre-war bull-nosed Morris had us looking back down the track. Changes in the note and speed of the engine and we knew that just out of sight, around the corner of the woods, Fat Mary had got out of the car, opened her five-bar gate, driven through, and closed it behind her. And here she came, driving between the fences, leaving a thin slipstream of chalk dust mingling with the black of her exhaust. A second fence and a second gate, then she half-circled the foetid pond and came to a standstill outside her tumble-down lattice-work porch. Hens and rooster scurried away towards the barn, the cows looked up from their pasture above her, a very large and mangy ginger tom woke up from wherever he had been sleeping and pushed his chin and cheek against the rough lisle of her stockings.

She was huge. And in spite of the July heat she was wearing a tweed suit, the heavy skirt cut long below her knees, the jacket mannish, very sensible shoes on her feet, and a sort of battered felt trilby on her head. She had gingery straw-coloured hair which was probably quite long since it was always bound up in a large bun above her neck, beneath the trilby. Her shoulders were broad and heavy, her back a rounded wall beneath the tweed. Her bosoms, behind a not over-clean white blouse and a structured bra or corset, forced the lapels of the jacket apart above one strained button. Her hands were like dinner plates with pink uncooked sausages for fingers.

Although we could scarcely make out her face, we had seen her in Sherborne on market days and knew that it was broad, once fair, now red with weather, with broken capillaries on the cheeks; small, pale-blue eyes widely spaced but almost lost beneath heavy lids; a spread stubby nose; a big mouth with rubbery lips and discoloured but otherwise large and healthy teeth. She had a large mole beneath the corner of her mouth, and yes, it did nourish bristly hair. Her voice was deep, as mannish as her jacket and shoes, the accent touched with Dorset, but not incomprehensibly broad.

She got out of the car, went round to the boot and hoisted a sack from it, feed of some sort perhaps, or fertiliser, certainly a hundred-weight. Grasping it around its waistless middle she carried it, not with ease but certainly without much difficulty, into the barn. Then she came back, wiping her hands down the sides of her massive hams, and plucked wicker baskets filled with brown-paper-wrapped or bagged shopping out of the back of the car. She put most of it on her doorstep, then reached to a ledge inside the porch for a big iron key and let herself into the cottage.

I batted flies off my forehead, eased my knees away from the coarse grass that had imprinted a network of ridges into them, and ran my tongue across my top lip.

'Come on,' I said, and stood up. 'Show's over.'

James looked back at me, up over his shoulder.
'Maybe. Maybe not.'
'What do you mean?'
'Follow me.'
And, bent double, he scouted along the fence and back into the wood. I followed him, but made a less than elaborate attempt to keep hidden. He pushed on, always near the fence to the meadow, and round to the top of the coombe and so into the edge of the yew forest. This was very different from the wood and I wasn't too happy about going into it.

In the first place it was dark and gloomy and cool – after the heat, almost chilly. Almost nothing grew beneath the low heavy branches, leaving exposed a steep slope of dusty earth, flint stones and chalk. Amongst the dark oily green of the needles yew berries hung like drops of blood. These were obscene – first because they were notoriously very poisonous, but also because of their form. Each was a tiny succulent cup of red flesh nursing inside it a seed. At one and the same time they suggested to the adolescent mind the glans and foreskin of a nearly tumescent penis and some hazy speculative idea of what the parts of a girl might be like. If you squeezed the flesh they exuded a colourless ichor, balanced somewhere between stickiness and slime, which matched exactly the tiny drop of fluid that could hang on the end of your prick when it lost tumescence without ejaculation.

You must remember that all this took place fifty years ago when, for an adolescent boy in a boarding school, anything to do with sex was cloaked in ignorance and imbued with compulsively attractive feelings of deep, dark guilt.

But there was a second reason why the yew forest was a place of very ill omen. Twice, four years and two years previously, boys from Minster Hill had been found hanging from their belts from one of those dark, seamed boughs. The forensic details of their deaths had not been made public, though in both cases it was rumoured that sexual activity had preceded death and verdicts of suicide while the balance of the mind was disturbed were returned by a bemused and horrified jury. On both occasions the school Chaplain had used his sermon on the Sunday following the inquests to attack, in coded terms, the practice of masturbation, dwelling on the feelings of shame that could follow, a shame intense enough to make a young lad take his own life...

None of this seemed to bother James though he did keep to the lower edge of the forest. Presently he edged forward again as far as the fence that overlooked the meadow and, this time, the rear of Fat Mary's smallholding. We were much closer than we had been before, not much more than a hundred yards away, and looking down on a graveyard of agricultural machinery.

An old tractor rotted away on huge flat tyres, the multiple tines of an ancient harrow looked like the ribs of a giant dead fish, the rust-red discs of a plough like saurian vertebrae. Grass and brambles grew through them, willow herb too, in spikes of dark pink bloom, and sorrel already brown and crusted with friable seeds. Long ago Fat Mary's father and brothers had ploughed two of the fields each year and grown rape and flax, barley and oats. The brothers died in Burma, in the forgotten army, Mother hanged herself, Daddy died of drink. Fat Mary survived on and by the animals she reared and let the fields return to pasture.

There was also an ancient pump mounted on a fluted cast-iron column – the only water supply she had... And just then, as we settled down to watch again, the back door opened and she came out.

She had taken off all her clothes.

She went to the pump, worked the long handle, filled a bucket, tipped it over her head. Then she did the same again. Next, she scrubbed herself all over with a huge bar of green Fairy soap, before washing the suds away with a third bucketful. The fourth she took to the lean-to toilet shed at the end of the building. We fancied we could hear her pissing. Then she went back indoors. All in all she had been visible to us for about five minutes.

She was magnificent. In the bright, hot July sun her body glowed pearl and rose and a deeper red where her clothes had been too tight. Her neck was an ivory tree-trunk, her shoulders were like fat rounded hams. As she worked the pump, her huge breasts swung like sacks of cream netted in blue veins and nippled with discs like saucers. Once, while pumping, she straightened and used her wrist to wipe the sweat from her brow which was streaked with her coarse, gingery hair and for a moment, upright, with her huge torso tilted back a little, she was a goddess.

When she tipped the flashing water over herself it slid through the suds, driving them down, and the acres of her skin looked sleek and strong like a whale's. Her huge dimpled buttocks were so pressed together that the cleft was not obvious, until she put her hand between to soap inside, and when she turned her stomach hung like a stuffed hammock and all but buried in shadow the multiple creases beneath and the flattened triangle of straw.

But for all the flabbiness of her body, torso, breasts and buttocks, her limbs, though massive, were strong and round and firm, dimpled again at knees and elbows, but structured by the muscle and sinew deep beneath, the power house that could carry not only her own weight but made nothing or not much of an extra hundredweight, or split the massive logs that were stacked against the wall of her cabin.

The long and the short of it was – I fell in love.

Well, what's your definition of that miserable state?

I had never before seen female naked flesh beyond what the pre-bikini swimming costumes of the late nineteen forties (which included hideous rubber bathing caps) allowed. I had no, or hardly any, preconceptions of what constitutes female beauty or what in a female body might stimulate sexual desire. Even the air-brushed or eclectically posed women in *Health and Efficiency* were plump by today's standards. I had, moreover, been taken to the National Gallery where a visit to Dutch maritime paintings, de Cuyp cows and trompe-l'oil interiors, all deemed to be aesthetically uplifting, could not be undertaken without a hurried passage through the Rubens rooms. And Fat Mary was not that much fatter than the Goddesses poor Paris had to choose between. So, there was no reason to be repelled by her size.

And the attraction? Fantasy made flesh and dwelling, if not amongst us, then little more than three miles away. As soon as the plank door closed behind her I knew I had to see her again. The summer holidays came and that image haunted me. Surreptitiously I drew crude pictures of her and hid them from my parents. I willed dreams of her and sometimes was visited by her in unwilled dreams. By September, when we returned to school, I was obsessed. I haunted the market and caught glimpses of her in her tweeds, which, perhaps oddly, did nothing to put me off. I just stood in front of her, gawped, turned bright crimson, and imagined what I knew lay beneath. Only one thing bothered me and I pushed that away as an absurd irrelevance – I knew she must be at least twenty years older than me, possibly as much as twenty-five. You cannot now imagine how the repression and ignorance of anything concealing sex and the female body poisoned our minds in those days and led to such deep and foetid infatuations.

The weather turned chill, the leaves turned and dropped, and I shivered on the edge of the yew forest whenever I was allowed out, and sometimes when I was not, filled with despair because I knew that even if I caught a glimpse of her, I stood no chance at all of seeing her undressed. I came on my own now, though once or twice I fancied James was maybe behind me in the woods. In school we saw even less of each other than before – with the new school year timetables had been changed, and hierarchies redrawn following the summer end-of-term exams. He was now in the Remove, would be sixteen before he took

School Certificate and did woodwork instead of Latin. I had sold or
bartered my SS dagger in the way boys do, but I had heard that it had
passed on two or three more times and that James now owned it.

But none of this was important. What kept me awake at nights and
patrolling those fences even when the frosts came and the pond below
froze was the obsession, the overwhelming desire to see Fat Mary
naked again, and... And what? I hardly dared imagine. Yet believe it or
not it was not until December, late December, just three days before
Minster Hill broke up, that I remembered that day in July, how we had
seen her let herself in with a big iron key taken from a high ledge in the
porch. It was a Saturday morning again, first light and that cold grey-
ness in the high sash windows that told you it had snowed in the night
even before you looked out. I lay there on my back with my eyes open
listening to the grumbles of my companions as they too woke up, and
then their exclamations of delight as they saw the snow, and all I could
say to myself, over and over again was – 'I can get in, I can get in whenever I want.'

My footsteps squeaked in the bright cold snow as I tramped up her
track, between the fences. The only other marks were the tyre treads
from where she had driven out. The sun was no more than a red disc in
a mauve-grey sky. Everything was still and silent but for the sound of
my footsteps and breathing. Not even the rooks cackled above the
beech trees, nor did the rooster call from Fat Mary's yard. It had been
a heavy fall, covering the patch of sprouts to the left of her door so they
looked like dwarfs or munchkins. It lay thick on the thatch of her roof
though a thin wisp of white smoke rose from the one stove-pipe
chimney. Icicles hung by the wall and from the eaves of her outbuildings. I was cold, desperately cold – a raincoat, a jacket and shoes
instead of sandals, were the only concessions to winter that we were
allowed. We even remained in short trousers. Of course, clothes
rationing was still in force.

Inside the porch I reached up to the ledge that ran along the side just
where the plank roof met the trellis sides and yes, there it was. Suddenly
I realised that part of me had hoped all along that it would not be there.
You know how they say 'his heart was in his mouth'? Mine was. And
my knees had turned to jelly. Almost I hoped the key, black, six inches
long, would not work, or jam, or something. But no, it turned, quite
smoothly, no problem. And yes, the door did creak, indeed, resisted for
a moment before its corner squealed across stone flags.

The first thing that hit me was the warmth, and the second was the
smell. The first was welcome. I was not so sure about the second. It was
a heavy concoction of different things, though predominant at first was

pork fat, sour, heavy, insistent. It seemed to be in everything. Indeed on almost all the surfaces there was a hazy, greasy slime, yellowish in colour, that seemed to be the essence of cooked or rendered pig. But it was undercut by other odours – baking, cooked greens, hot metal, tom cat, all almost as bad, but lavender, stored apples, and warm old age as well, breathed out from the ancient dark furniture. There was no electricity of course, but Fat Mary had left an oil lamp on the large kitchen table – turned low, but to eyes coming out of the encroaching winter gloom, bright enough.

The one room was divided by a beam in the ceiling with heavy brown velvet curtains hanging from it, left three-quarters open. The first room was kitchen and living room combined. Against the end wall beneath the stove-pipe a full kitchen range whose fire glowed behind the ventilation flues in its door was set back in a big alcove that once must have been a fireplace, with another huge black old beam as its mantel. The tick of its ancient clock was marked by a cut-out boat set in the dial in which stood a cowled Death. His scythe swung back and forth with each double tick-tock.

On either side of the range there were cupboards and shelves, and more shelves along the back wall, with a dresser too. Impossible to take in all that I could see, but what stood out were huge greasy jars containing bottled or pickled pig trotters, and, in the largest, a pig's head – boned so it looked like a deflated football. Yet it had eyelashes, and sight seemed to gleam through the dark slits between its lids.

Backing away I found myself in the bedroom which was almost filled by the hugest bed I had ever seen, together with a massive wardrobe, a chest of drawers, and a full-length mirror on a swivel, its glass clouded and blackened where the silvering had dropped away. But it was the bed that I could not take my eyes off. It must have been six feet by six feet at least, piled with blankets, old eiderdowns and grey sheets with a heap of pillows and bolsters against the wall at the far end. Above it, clinging to the rough-cast wall beneath a ceiling of planks, swathes of blackened cobwebs hung like the tied-back drapes of a Princess's bed.

I did, still do, suffer from severe arachnophobia.

At that moment I heard the noise of her motor.

She knew I was there of course – first the footprints in the snow, going one way only, then of course the door, closed as I had left it, yes, but with the big key still in the key-hole. I heard the door slam, the meow of the cat, the crunch of her galoshes in the snow. And suddenly I was faced with a question which had loomed like a thundercloud on the horizon, but which I had refused to face, ever since I had left the school buildings: What was I there for? Why had I come? To see her.

To see her with no clothes on, as I had seen her in the summer... And?

There was only one place to go. I dived on to the bed and burrowed my way in like a worm burrowing into sand, in amongst those heavy quilts, damp but warm sheets, mountainous bolsters. At this point I should say I was small for my age and very thin and I fancy that before she was properly in I was invisible. I could hear her moving about, putting down bags and so forth, and presently I lifted a corner of the foetid mound I was under and managed to peep out.

She had already turned up the wick of the lamp and lit a couple of candles too. She had her back to me, was in front of a wall mirror to the side of the range, drawing a long hat pin out of her hat and hair. As she lifted the hat off her head her hair tumbled down to the shoulders of her rubberised mackintosh. She set hat and pin to one side on a dresser then filled a kettle from a tall jug, enamelled iron, the enamel chipped, and set it on the hob.

'I know you're there,' she said. Of course she did. 'In the bed are you? I'll be with you presently.' And slowly, deliberately, she began to undress.

First the rubberised mackintosh, then a long tartan scarf. Next the tweed jacket, then a moth-damaged woolly that had once been purple. She released the bottom of her blouse from the skirt band, undid the buttons, shrugged out of it. I could now see her massive freckled shoulders criss-crossed with straps and some of her back above a voluminous slip or petticoat. Reaching behind those sausage-like fingers neatly unhooked and unbuttoned (no zips) the fastenings of her skirt. She stepped out of it, then shrugged and pushed at the straps of the slip (which was made of some shiny material, satin perhaps, though stained and grubby) and stepped out of that. She was now clad only in a flesh-coloured corset, bloomers, and thick stockings whose tops disappeared beneath the bloomers.

The kettle boiled, she reached up for a tin caddy, made tea. She poured out two mugfuls, topped them up with condensed milk from an already opened tin, and added a good slurp of brown cooking brandy to each. She carried them towards the bed and put them down on the chest of drawers then, with one swift movement pulled back the covers and looked down at me.

'You might,' she said, 'have taken your shoes off.'

I was shivering, not with cold but fright.

'Here. Drink this.'

It should have been foul, but it was very sweet. The brandy fumes made my head swim even before I tasted it.

'Drink it all.'

I did as I was told.

'Take your clothes off.'

I removed the coats and shoes, then she pushed me on to my back. Her fingers danced like elephants over my shirt and trouser buttons. Finally she unthreaded my belt and put it to one side.

'What a thin little shrimp you are!'

Did she mean all of me or just my not fully mature prick?

And that was all she said. From then on she just grunted or sighed as she pushed me about, got me into the positions she wanted, so she could play out what I soon realised was her fantasy, not mine.

When I was naked, and clutching my genitals out of terrible embarrassment, she pulled me into the middle of the bed, turned me on to my back with my head in the middle of the bed but facing into the room, then heaped the heavy odoriferous covers over me so I was in a heavy black cave of damp warmth. A moment or two later she crawled in at the far end and I could feel her burrowing over me, on hands and knees, her hands on either side of my body moving up towards my head, her knees following her hands. She too was naked now and I could feel the huge softness of her flesh, her great swinging breasts, the floppy folds of her stomach, then the rich farmy odours of her lower parts as they all travelled up over me in the dark until my head was between her knees and then her shins.

She adjusted the covers and for a moment I caught a shadowy glimpse of her mountainous buttocks upside down as it were above my head, then her hands came back between her spread legs and caught hold of my head. And she began to pull. She began to drag me through the narrow gap between her thighs. I thought she was going to pull my head off.

This may seem funny to read, but it was not at all funny at the time. I was terrified, and suddenly in some pain. My shoulders snagged against the backs of her legs, I was suffocating. I pushed my body up and along following my neck and head, using a scrabbling sort of motion with my feet, and then had the sense to twist on to my side so my shoulders could follow my head. I squeezed one hand through that narrow but soft quivering gap, beneath her private parts, and for a moment I could feel the hair, moist, wet even, and breathing honeyed, soured odours, as it rubbed along my cheek and neck.

All this time she was moaning and groaning, puffing and panting. Of course I can see now what she was doing, but I had no idea at the time, no idea at all that she was simulating child-birth.

With my head and shoulders through she straightened somewhat and the covers fell even more away. She got her hands in my armpits, and pushing her knees apart, with one last enormous sigh, pulled me through as far as my waist, leaving only my pelvis and legs still in the gap beneath her. She now had me sitting, with her arms round my back in a huge bear-hug, her bottom spread on either side of my thighs and my face buried in her stomach beneath her breasts so I still had to struggle for breath through all that flesh, and for a moment we stayed like that, and she rocked us both a little from side to side. Her groans and moans had now become cooing sighs which I could hear rumble purringly deep in her chest. By now I was terrified. I cannot say how terrified I was.

With her feet on the floor at the end of the bed she now lifted herself and with one more heave had me free enough to haul my legs out and on to her lap. Gathering her great wrinkled, floppy, vein-laced breast in one hand she thrust a plate-like nipple into my face. Some primaeval if forgotten urge made me suck. There was, of course, no milk, but there was comfort in the floppy saltiness of it which presently hardened a little between my teeth. She pressed my still snorting nose into it with one ham of a hand while the other ran over my head, down my neck and fondled, and squeezed my ribs until I felt they would crack.

And for a moment, perhaps even for a minute or two or more, my fear fell away and I felt warm, happy, secure...

Then, the sow that eats its farrow, she began to strangle me.

She retrieved my belt and with one hand threaded a noose through the buckle. She slipped it over my head, gave the end a twist or two to get a good grip on it, while with the other arm she wrapped me in a bear-hug which pinned my arms to my sides. Then she tightened the noose, slowly.

The first effect was to impede the flow of blood to and from my head and the second was to make me terribly aware of my prick. Until then the experience had not been for me an overtly sexual one. Now it very definitely was. The tumescence felt like a great throbbing hard... I don't know, cucumber or something. And then, as the darkness filled my head, and my lungs at last began to feel they'd burst, something gave and I let myself go in an orgasm the like of which I had never experienced until then. Or since. And with it everything fell apart. Her arms dropped from the killing embrace and I felt, beneath all the fat, how her muscles suddenly tautened into a terrible convulsion. They relaxed as swiftly as they had tensed and a great gout of warm liquid splashed over my head and shoulders before she toppled backwards, taking me with her.

Somehow I knew – from the smell, the iron taste of it, the viscosity – that she was drenching me in blood, her own blood, and that if only I could loosen the belt I might live.

I tried to struggle but she did too, and I could see now the hilt of what had been my SS dagger, which now belonged to James, protruding from her neck. But though the blood was pulsing up around it she still had strength and will and was ready to fight on, but at that moment a dark shadow seemed to flit across the room and there was James himself. He plucked the knife from her neck before she could and rammed it again and again into her neck and breasts until the flow of blood ceased to throb, became a sluggish stream, and stopped.

At last I loosened the belt. Or James did. I can't remember which. I sat up and looked down and across her. She was on her back, half propped up on all those heavy covers and eiderdowns, her arms still twitching convulsively in front of her tortured, fear-filled face, the fingers groping towards the dagger which was again stuck in the crimson tide that flowed across her chest and into the wide valley between her breasts, which were now flopped outwards. For a moment she stared at the two of us, first one then the other, her small blue eyes baleful, filled with hate. Then she pulled in one last huge breath, let it out and blood bubbled with it from her mouth. She gave a long shudder which ended on a croaking sigh, her legs flopped apart and she was gone, as dead as the pigs whose throats she cut each autumn, whose fat she rendered down and whose joints she carved, baked, cured and pickled.

Later the post mortem report said that one only of the many wounds had killed her. The upward thrust of the dagger, whether thrown from close to or administered with a stab, had neatly passed between the central column of oesophagus and wind pipe and the sinew to the side, finding and severing the carotid artery, draining the blood from her brain.

I managed at last to get to my feet. James handed me a large thread-bare towel and I began to wipe myself. The big ginger tom appeared from under the bed and began to rub up against Fat Mary's shin. The door, which James had only managed to pull to behind him, flew open and a flurry of icy snow whirled round the room, hissed on the range. Tom disappeared under the bed again.

'We'd better get back to school,' said James. He pulled the knife out of Fat Mary's throat, wiped it on a sheet. I suppose he's still got it. If he's still around. It all happened fifty years ago, half a century.

'You should wash up as well as you can so no blood gets on your clothes,' he went on. 'There's no reason for anyone to know we were here.'

He was right. It was two days before she was found – the first to call was a gamekeeper drawn by the lowing of cows that had not been milked and the bellows of a sow that had not been fed and whose litter was, by then, too big to eat.

September

How can I watch the steady flow
Of summer madness down the drain?
Only because I unequivocally know
That all that's lovely comes again.
But though I listen to the not so gentle rain
I know I may not pay the debt I'd like to owe.

Snails

Snails like dreams shun the sun
Daylight comes their work is done
They've sliced the leaves with lacey patterns
Turning virgins into slatterns.

Dangerous Games

Perhaps the greatest thrill I've had as a writer was seeing the words Written by Julian Rathbone *on the screen of my TV set. And one of the jolliest things that happened with it all was that though I set scenes very near the end in Gaudi's Temple of the Holy Family in Barcelona (note the correct title – it is not a cathedral) I had no real hope that the authorities would give permission for a shooting match to be filmed there. But they did!* No problema *because, being unfinished, it has never been consecrated. The scenes that follow are set in a tiny square in the medieval Barrio Gotic. Again I imagined that a set would have to be built or an alternative location found, but again it was filmed in exactly the place where I had imagined it happening, and not only the exterior but the interior too. So here are the last pages of the film. One last word, although the whole two by ninety minute mini-series was patchy at times the second half was brilliant: beautifully filmed and acted. Nathaniel Parker played Cranmer, Gudrun Landgrebe (top German actress)*

– Inga, Jeremy Child – Campbell-Myers, Hans Martin Steer
– Brenner, Charly Caine – Winston, Ricardo Palacios –
Estrada, and Mapi Galam – Claret. David Slama was the
wonderful photographer and it was directed by Adolf
Winkelmann. It came out in both English and German
versions.

Note: Cranmer is an English upper-class hitman who has
kept his identity secret from Inga, who calls him No Man.

EXTERIOR, DAY. THE ENTRANCE AREA TO THE SAGRADA
FAMILIA.
CAMPBELL-MYERS and HERZ also go through the turnstiles and
into the church. GOMEZ, near the turnstiles, reports on his RT to
ESTRADA, follows them. More POLICIA NACIONAL move out of
vans in the side-streets and seal off the church. A busload of Japanese
tourists are told to get back in their bus. People already in the information area are asked to leave. A swift, but silent and discreet evacuation
has begun.
Into this come MARTÍN and ARRANZ. Naturally, they are waved on
by uniformed POLICIA NACIONAL into the interior of the church.

EXTERIOR, DAY. THE CHURCH OF THE SAGRADA FAMILIA
HERZ, alone now, appears in front of the inside wall of the east facade,
and heads for the spiral staircase on the right of the main portico.

INTERIOR (THOUGH WITH UNGLAZED OPENINGS TO
DAYLIGHT), DAY. THE SPIRAL STAIRCASE LEADING TO A
GALLERY INSIDE THE EAST WALL OF THE SAGRADA
FAMILIA.
HERZ climbs the narrow, simple, but perfectly carved and designed
stairs. Looking straight up one sees a perfect spiral as the stairs perspec-
tive almost to a vanishing point. HERZ emerges on to a narrow gallery
with a parapet between arches supported on slender pillars. He sees a
small key placed on the parapet and moves towards it. CRANMER
appears from an alcove, behind HERZ, and raises his arm.

CAMPBELL-MYERS' VOICE
Tom? I'd rather you didn't do that.

CRANMER freezes, petrified not with fear but shock and a sense that the invulnerability he has learnt to rely on has suddenly been whipped away. CAMPBELL-MYERS comes into picture from a point higher up the stairs. He is holding his revolver. HERZ turns to face him and CRANMER. At last CRANMER turns too.

CAMPBELL-MYERS
Tom, you've been a very silly boy, up to all sorts of silly games, and dangerous too. Still, all is not lost. If you come quietly with us now, I'm sure we'll be able to work something out...

But CRANMER recovers. Dropping to a crouch he seizes HERZ by the arm and sweeps him in front of him as a shield. CAMPBELL-MYERS fires and hits HERZ in the side, but then restrains himself from shooting again as CRANMER half carries, half drags HERZ a step or two closer to CAMPBELL-MYERS. Then CRANMER heaves the wounded man more or less into CAMPBELL-MYERS' arms, bringing them both to the floor, and hurls himself towards the stairs, grabbing the document case up from the alcove where he left it. CAMPBELL-MYERS gets in one more shot which whines away off the stone work. He gets to the top of the stairs, but of course the spiral is a sharp one, and he will have to get within a metre or two of CRANMER to get him back in view. He turns back, steps over HERZ and picks up the key.

EXTERIOR, DAY. THE 'INTERIOR' OF THE SAGRADA FAMILIA, THE STREET WITH THE METRO ENTRANCE
In one place ESTRADA, GOMEZ, and CLARET, and in another MARTÍN and ARRANZ, respond to the sound of the two shots which echo round the giant stone drum. Pigeons also respond. CRANMER appears in the entrance to the staircase – all attention is fixed on him, so MARTÍN and ESTRADA are still unaware of each other's presence. ARRANZ, automatic out, steadied by both hands and in crouch position, covers CRANMER, and MARTÍN moves forward to make the arrest, but as he does so, GOMEZ moves between ARRANZ and CRANMER. CRANMER fires a short burst from his burp gun and the remaining TOURISTS and SITE-WORKERS scatter, impeding the police so CRANMER can swing himself over crash barriers into the building-site area before they can shoot or stop him. There he hijacks an already moving mechanical digger or earth shovel and uses it to smash through the board walls and out on to the street where he rams the Japanese bus. He abandons his vehicle, and disappears back into the Metro.

Back in the centre of the building ESTRADA and MARTÍN

confront each other. MARTÍN half on the floor above ARRANZ who has been hit and is bleeding heavily from a neck wound. During the exchange between them we see CAMPBELL-MYERS emerge from the left-hand stair-case. Still very much the unruffled British gent, he strides away, unheeded.

ESTRADA
What the hell do you think you're playing at? Cowboys and Indians?

MARTÍN
Estrada, you're a bastard. If he dies... then you killed him, you know that?

ESTRADA
He'll live (Turns to GOMEZ who comes at a trot out of the right staircase entrance) Did you get them? Were they still there?

GOMEZ
Only Herz. He's hurt, shot, but still alive.

ESTRADA
So. Thanks to these wankers, we've still got an armed killer on the loose. (Gestures towards MARTÍN and the GUARDIA URBANA. Then, suddenly very tired...) So what do we do now?

MARTÍN
(Stands up, comes closer) You mean you don't know where he lives? Who he's been living with there?

ESTRADA
And you do? (He takes in the hard half-smile that is now fixed on MARTÍN's face) Shit. You do.

INTERIOR, DAY. CRANMER's ROOM IN THE BARRI GOTIC. LEADING TO EXTERIOR DAY, THE PLAÇA DE SANTA MARIA SEEN FROM CRANMER's WINDOW

A hole in the ceiling. Joists dangle at the edges, beyond them the sky. The table that used to be against the wall is placed under the hole, and a broken chair lies near it on the floor. WINSTON lies on the floor. He has a broken leg.

Key in the lock, CRANMER enters.

WINSTON
Mr Cranmer. Sir.

CRANMER
Smith?! What the hell are you doing here? How...? Ah. Through the roof. And you hurt yourself doing it.

WINSTON
Got in all right. Hurt myself trying to get out. Broke my fucking leg.

CRANMER
Playing silly buggers. Any reason for dropping by?

WINSTON
Came here to kill you. Sir.

CRANMER
Join the club. Most of Barcelona seems to be having a go. But why you?

WINSTON
You shafted Kevin. I know you did 'cos I found what I come looking for – it was you had the second signaller. It was in that cupboard over there. (Shows it) Then you got behind me with a shot-gun and blasted a hole in my back. That's why.

CRANMER
(Thinks about it, shrugs, finds cigarettes and a lighter, lights one, hands it to Winston, lights one for himself, sits on the bed) Shame you see it like that. I'm going to have a coffee. Do you want one?

CRANMER gets up, moves to the gas ring, puts on a saucepan of water, spoons instant coffee into cups. He's about to put a cup on the table by the window...

WINSTON
(Suddenly tense, eyes shut) I'd rather have tea if you've got some.

CRANMER
(Turns back) I think we have. Tea-bag anyway. Hullo. They're on to me quickly…

Responding to crescendoing police sirens outside he goes round the table to the window, looks down and out and we do too. Headlights swing round the Plaça. Police cars arrive in each of the narrow entrances, sealing it. Blue lights spin. Above the din…

CRANMER
Shit. It rather looks as if she's set me up. Tea-time. I think you're right. Tea better than coffee at a time like this. (He closes the shutters)

<u>EXTERIOR, DAY. THE PLAÇA DE SANTA MARIA DEL MAR</u>
POLICE in combat gear, padded jackets etc, cover CRANMER's window with high velocity rifles. A large floodlight is being erected, POLICEMEN unspooling wire to connect it. Two more cars arrive, one Guardia Urbana, the other Policia Nacional. ESTRADA, GOMEZ, and CLARET get out of the second, MARTIN, uniformed MALE GUARDIA and uniformed FEMALE GUARDIA, and INGA get out of the first. POLICEMAN 1 salutes ESTRADA.

POLICEMAN 1
He's in there all right. The woman in the bar saw him arrive.

ESTRADA
So. How do we get him out? As long as he's got that burp gun no one's going to get near him without being hurt. (Pause) I'm open to suggestions.

CLARET
Perhaps the woman can talk him down.

MARTÍN
Apart from giving us this address, she's not said a word since she gave herself up.

CLARET
Maybe she'll listen to me.

ESTRADA
Women's talk? You can give it a try.

CLARET

No. Not woman's talk. You said her name is Mahler. Is she Inga
Mahler, a German?

INTERIOR, DAY. CRANMER's ROOM IN THE BARRI GOTIC.
LEADING TO EXTERIOR DAY, THE PLAÇA DE SANTA MARIA
SEEN FROM CRANMER's WINDOW

For a moment or two it is in almost complete darkness – the light out,
inside shutters pulled to. We sense rather than see CRANMER moving
about, but also pick up on the motionless glow of a cigarette. Suddenly
the room is filled with stark light – from the floods the Police were
erecting outside. WINSTON is lying on the bed, dead from a broken
neck. The cigarette still burns between his fingers. CRANMER is
discovered standing on the table, with the Heckler and Koch from the
document case slung over his shoulder. He is reaching up to the hole
but can't quite make it.

CRANMER

No wonder you broke your leg. Lucky you didn't blow yourself up
since I suppose you were also carrying four kilos of Semtex. It's not
that stable. Jesus, Smith, you really were the king of the nasty little
schemers, weren't you?

While he is saying all this he picks up the chair, puts it on the table
under the hole and reaches up. He can get his hands into the hole. Gets
a grip and hoists himself upwards, but his wound hurts like hell. Then
the joists and plaster give way dumping him first on the table then on
the floor in a shower of debris.

CRANMER

Shit. You broke it on your way out. You found the signaller. You
brought the Semtex and the trembler… You fixed me up a bomb,
didn't you? So where is it? Where the fuck is it?

CRANMER now very carefully checks round and under the table and
chair he has been using, then moves towards the table in front of the
window. He is about to stoop to look under it when a loudspeaker
crackles, booms with feed-back.

INGA's VOICE (AMPLIFIED)

No Man? It's me. Inga. No Man, please listen…

As the voice comes through CRANMER straightens, moves to the
shuttered window again.

INGA's VOICE (AMPLIFIED)
No Man. I don't know how to say this, how to make it work for you...

<u>EXTERIOR, DAY. THE PLAÇA DE SANTA MARIA DEL MAR</u>
Cranmer's window is spot-lit. On the ground, behind a police car with big speakers on the roof, ESTRADA, MARTIN, ARRANZ, CLARET and INGA form a tight little group. INGA and CLARET together hold a microphone connected to the speakers. CLARET has her other arm round INGA, supporting her.

INGA's VOICE (AMPLIFIED)
No Man. Please. No more killing. Not you or anyone. There's been too much, too many. (Voice breaks) They know about Laura, they say she was stabbed... No Man, please stop now. No more killing. Don't make them kill you... (She chokes, then draws breath, for her last effort.)

<u>INTERIOR, DAY. CRANMER's ROOM</u>
CRANMER at the window, as before.

INGA's VOICE (AMPLIFIED)
Tom? (The word is almost sung, high and clear like a trumpet) Do the people who love you call you Tom?

CRANMER
Bitch. You brought them here.

CRANMER's face freezes then he turns, seizes the table with one hand at each end. He hoists the table, and perhaps we just catch a glimpse of the Semtex taped to the underneath.

<u>EXTERIOR, DAY. THE PLAÇA AS BEFORE</u>
Explosion. The window of CRANMER's room billows and his body, burning, hurtles through it, arms and legs spread. Apart from the fact he is now coming out backwards the moment echoes his exit from the plane, and Inga's sculpture.
Fire flickers on INGA's expressionless face. She turns away, head up, tears but not giving in, walks down the street towards the harbour and the sea. The POLICE watch her, then CLARET follows, walks just behind her and a little to the side.

EXTERIOR, DAY. ZÜRICH, THE EURECYCLE BUILDING, THE
NAME CLEARLY VISIBLE AND THE LOGO
CAMPBELL-MYERS seen arriving.

INTERIOR, DAY. BRENNER's OFFICE.
BRENNER standing by the window, CAMPBELL-MYERS in a chair,
very relaxed. BRENNER slowly turns a tiny micro-cassette between
his big fingers.

CAMPBELL-MYERS
Of course, I've had it copied

BRENNER
Of course. (He crushes it, drops it on the floor)

CAMPBELL-MYERS
One can't be too careful.

BRENNER

No. One can't. You mentioned... (He sucks his thumb which he has
cut on the plastic casing) Shit. You mentioned a quite large sum.

CAMPBELL-MYERS
Yes. Not one I'm prepared to negotiate.

BRENNER
Would you accept ERC shares?

CAMPBELL-MYERS

I might if I knew more about you, if I could feel certain that what my
poor nephew did for you leaves you... where you want to be.

BRENNER

We make secret contracts with corporations who are having problems with EC waste disposal regulations. We shift their muck for
them – to Russia mostly, what people still call Russia...

As his voice drones on we follow his gaze down into the street below...

EXTERIOR, DAY. THE STREET OUTSIDE THE ERC BUILDING, SEEN FROM ABOVE.

BRENNER (VO continuing)
…We have deals with seven of the Republics and we are negotiating more. It won't last more than four or five years but we expect to make very big profits indeed during that time…

As he speaks we see a tall, smart and beautiful woman with a large muzzled but equally beautiful Afghan hound. The dog stops to shit on the pavement. The woman clears the mess with a poop-scoop, and wipes the dog's arse with a tissue… Credits begin over the pair as they walk on.

BRENNER (VO)
There's always good money to be made moving people's shit to where they can forget it exists. And that's truer now than it's ever been…

Pull back into a long aerial shot, then in on ERC barges on Zürichsee, maybe a motorway with the exceptional convoy of Part I, a freight train… Or just heavy smog over the Zürich sky-line mixing into the black background of the final credits

BRENNER (VO)
Serious money, you know? I'm talking billions, just for moving shit from one place to another…

END

Pernicious Loves

How did you get those scratches?
Untangling from a rose bush convolvulus that latches.

By tearing down white flowers and red blood roses too?
Teasing out pernicious loves.

Why didn't you use your gloves?
My gloves?

Your gardening gloves.

Intimations

Being eighteen years older than his wife
And she now fifty
The gap begins to bother him

The other day, going into the back garden
Through the arch in the privet hedge
He saw her – digging in the greenhouse;

Unaware of him, new glasses on, she read—
Instructions on a packet of seeds perhaps.
He turned away, back through the arch,

Knowing the space he'd been in will be emptied
Within a year, or five, a decade
But, whenever, on a sunny afternoon

She'll be there
Sitting, reading,
In the greenhouse.

The Difference

Towards the end of Kings of Albion, *Uma, the Indian princess, has a very jolly love affair with Owen Tudor. Earlier in the book she had a fling with Eddie March.*

Contrast and difference. Let's begin at the top and work down. His short white hair that I run my fingertips through and that strange black streak just long enough for me to wind once round my finger. My hair, almost back to its fullest length now, dark but hennaed to a red with occasional wires of bright gold in it and glossy, silky, fragrant. His chin and cheek, bristly with white above, the coppery red, against mine, which has the bloom and colour of a ripe peach. His breath a touch sharp, like milk on the turn: mine like currants and honey. The squareness of his chin and the roundness of mine; the sinews and wrinkles in his neck – well, I have those now, but then… My shoulders creamy and smooth, rounded yet delicate.

His twice as broad and white, with, I have to say, red spots to match the mole or two I have. My breasts like pomegranates, but soft and with large nipples that corrugate at his touch and even leak a sweet drop of ichor; his, massively wide and flat with nipples like pimples, which yet my tongue can raise so they feel hard as grain, and a mat of iron hair between. His arms like the roots of the banyan, strong and sturdy yet capable of grace in their slow yet greedy grasp; mine like the smooth branches of a tall aspen tree. My stomach a shallow dome with a whorled dent in the middle where Parvati pressed her thumb: his hard and six times ridged with muscle.

He has short, strong white toes that, even so, can grip a coin or feather while mine are long, with, when I can get the lacquer, painted nails. His ankles are finer than I would expect, which indicates nobility, but not as fine as mine, which put him in mind, he says, of things as fragile as glass. His calves are twin cords of muscle hazed with hair brindled grey and brown like a cat, and his knees, which he grumbles about at times, but nothing like as often as Ali does, are broad and strong, mine smooth like butter but as firm as apples. His thighs are pillars to support a temple, his buttocks like twin coconuts in a palm-tree; mine are like the mangoes he's never seen.

And our fingers, his short for the width of his big hands but strong with square ends, mine long and thin – what secret joys they find where thighs and torsos meet! His thumb runs down the crease and curves to cup the mound of bone, they part the wiry hair and probe the puckered lips; my thumb and forefinger ring the root of his prick while the other three roll his balls in their wrinkled sack. We play on each other as if on musical instruments smoothing the mucus between the pads on our fingers, teasing the tissue until his strengthens like timber and mine swells like a grape.

And now breath is taken by beauty, beauty of doing not seeing, of tasting and smelling and softly caressing. The longing now is nostalgia for a past that never yet happened, and I pull myself close to him, releasing his sex so I can hold his head and force my tongue and kisses on his neck and mouth, while he rolls us round and with one hand beneath me, in the small of my back, feeling out the cleft between my buttocks, and with the other feeding his hungry pillar into me sends tides of hot joy up from my...

Well. Ali. You and I did it a couple of times, so you know what I'm on about, and you won't mind if I tell you that this Welsh chieftain knew what he was doing, was the best.

Summer drifts into autumn. Here the Welsh hills, which were a dull russet, slowly become lilac-coloured and then purple, spread with tiny bell-like flowers, so many millions of them it's like a purple blanket and springy and soft so that with care, avoiding the bigger branches that hug the ground, one can lie on it and lose oneself in the sweet but light fragrance of it, gazing up into a blue like aquamarine and watch where eagles soar with necks collared in gold. And beneath these low bushes yet another bush hides from the snows and wind that howl across here in winter, blowing fine powdery drifts, but now rich with small black berries, black that is until Owen names them: then you see how they're really blue, a deepest indigo.

These hills are cleft and riven with valleys so narrow near the crests you don't really see them until the hillside suddenly falls away beneath your feet to brown rock and water clear as crystal but brown, too, from the gravel beneath or grey and flat where the water has rounded boulders through the millennia, bubbling and gurgling from pool to pool. Deep in these declivities the air is still and the sun hot. With our ponies grazing on the ridge above us (they'll move and maybe neigh if anyone approaches), we can strip off our woollen cloaks and trousers and, on cropped thyme-scented grass beside the stream, make love again, and yet again, or just lie in each other's arms, backs against a sun-warmed lichened rock and watch the brown fish browse the moss beneath the surface.

Christmas comes, which Owen and his clan or tribe celebrate with some solemnity. Mah-Lo, you will have understood how in those climes far to the north of us and even of your own country, the steady decline of the sun towards the winter solstice is a matter of some significance. All people who live in those climes hope and trust that sooner or later it will be halted and when it is, when by fine calculation, based on careful observation of the sun in relation to tall stones set in circles like giant teeth on hill-tops for this very purpose, they can assert with certainty that the sun has risen at a point a little to the left of where it rose the day before and sets a little to the right, they declare that the goddess has conceived and borne a son, which they call Adonis or Adonaï.

On that day, out of the hills and woods came priests called druids, not Christian. Their leader bears mistletoe, and they enact certain rituals using drums made from oak, which simulate thunder. The leader carries the ancient sword shaped like a sickle and made of gold with which he cut the mistletoe and with which he now guards it.

He personates in flesh and blood the great god of the sky who has come down in the lightning flash to dwell among men in the mistletoe, the thunder-besom, that grows on the sacred oaks in the deepest valleys of Gwalia, by the side of black and fathomless tarns. The goddess whom he serves and marries is no other than the Queen of Heaven…

for she, too, loves the solitude of the woods and the lonely hills, and sailing overhead on clear nights in the likeness of the silver moon, looks down with pleasure on her own fair image reflected on the calm, the burnished surface of the lake, Diana's mirror.

Here, in this country, we call them Shiva and Devi or Parvati.

But Owen is called upon to lead the Lancastrian army at Mortimer's Cross – the Battle of the Three Suns. On the next day...

Candlemas. The day when the year in the north quickens. They take all the candles they will need in the church for the next twelve months and bless them, but really it's for the goddess whom they call St Bride. In the cottages they make straw dolls of her and lay them in a bed and burn candles round her all night. But that Candlemas was ruled not by St Bride, or Parvati, Deva or Uma, for in the evening of the day following the night of Candlemas, in a town called Hereford, they take poor Owen out into the market square. Poor soul, he cannot believe they will execute him. He has led his men for the Queen in the King's name. Surely that queen whose life I saved is Kali incarnate, a true avatar, dragging the deaths of thousands in her train.

Owen's crime, apart from leading an army against this second York, at a battle a few miles north of Hereford, and losing it, is that he is the stepfather of King Henry. An eye for an eye, is what the obscene scriptures of both Christians and Muslims call for, and so it is a case of a father for a father.

Others taken with him, including two young lads, go first and one lad breaks free. The soldiers hack him to pieces, as if he is a steer in the shambles.

Owen turns to the headsman and says, 'I trust you will not handle me so roughly. You have an axe and a block.'

Then they tear off the collar of his red velvet doublet and placing his head on the block he says, 'This head was wont to lie in more than one queen's lap.'

Later, when they have gone, I take up his head and place it on the top step of the market cross and with three ladies of the town I gather up a hundred candles from the church and we place them on the steps around him. I wipe the blood from his face and kiss his cold lips. The air sparkles with frost, and the candles burn all night. As the late dawn streaks the sky with red I feel the presence of another behind me as I sit on the bottom step. The candles, now burnt low, gutter with the first breeze of morning and the smell of beeswax soured by heat drifts about us.

I look up and round and see a tall figure in full armour, blue steel enriched with gold inlay. Behind him two squires carry two shields. On one are blazoned silver flowers on lapis, quartered with golden lions on a field of blood. On the other there are three gold-leaf suns, freshly laid on gesso and burnished to a brightness that catches the light. I have heard the story of the battle at Mortimer's Cross. I have heard how three suns appeared in the sky above the man who would be king and both armies took it as a sign that God was on his side.

He lifts his visor. It's Eddie. Eddie March. Edward Plantagenet, King of England, Duke of York. Behind him, the great black stallion I once saved from a whipping strikes sparks from the cobbles and neighs like a trumpet.

Two Haikus

April

Spring surfs in on a wave-crest of black thorn:
Expect a sloeish Autumn.

Rosemary

Ten thousand lilac stars hold the evening light
Beneath an opal sky.

All About Eve

Maxim Jakubowski has asked me to contribute to his splendid anthologies of short stories on five occasions. Three were shortlisted for the CWA Short Story Dagger, one of them won it. All About Eve *was my contribution to* The Mammoth Book of Historical Erotica *and hasn't won anything, yet. It obviously owes a lot to Elaine Morgan's* The Descent of Woman *in spite of the fact that it is the one book of hers about the Aquatic Ape theory (as well as being about women) that I haven't read.*

Ihave many names but you can call me Eve since I am the mother of
you all. I'm not joking. It's really true. Not only am I the mother of
you all, but there's something of me, just me, something of the
woman I was one hundred and fifty thousand years ago, in every single
one of you. I am you. You are us. We're all sisters and mothers under
the skin, even the blokes. Well, in the skin too, come to that. So, you
needn't be surprised that I can speak out and talk to you every now and
then, that you can hear my voice, feel my presence when I choose. In a
sense when you hear me you are talking to yourselves, we're that close.

Yes, that's it. As teachers say – 'Talk among yourselves for a bit.' Do
that... and listen to me.

I lived in Eden, of course. What was it like? In a word – paradisial!
Imagine – a big, big lake flat and calm and silvery pewter most of the
time, though black when a storm whips up and very occasionally
reflecting the blue of the sky when the almost permanent bright silvery
haze is swept aside or dissolved. On all sides it is fed by tumbling
streams from the mountains, and in the south-west by a large river that
comes to us through rifts and gorges, and, so the young men say, and
the old men remember, tumbles down a giant waterfall a day's walk
inland. Beyond the waterfall and above it are the mixed woods and
grasslands where the men, obeying older and more primitive instincts
than ours, go to hunt. Far away in the north-east there is an outlet to
the bigger lake, the sea.

The mountains are high and steep. Their lower slopes are filled with
forest. The tall thin trees, some of them buttressed, soar from a floor of
forest litter sparsely carpeted with bromeliads which yield pineappple-
like fruit, and, where a tree or two have fallen and the sunlight gets
through, there are plantains and bananas. Many of the trees shed nuts,
monkey-pot nuts, and brazils as well as coconuts. There are plenty of
other fruits which I cannot name for you since they have long-since
become extinct. No doubt the palaentologists have Latin labels for
them.

There are no seasons, though it rains in one half of the year more
than in the other, and so there are flowers always as well as fruits. I like
especially the great vanilla scented swags of purple jacaranda-like
legumes, and the luminosity of pearly orchids.

The canopies are filled with birds mostly with jewelled plumage and
ranging in size from the humming-birds not much bigger than insects
to birds of paradise trailing golden trains behind them. And of course
there are our cousins the monkeys in the trees and our brothers and
sisters the gorillas and chimps lollop about the forest floor or swing
from the lower boughs – though these inhabit the higher areas, rather
than the forest floor. There, where the slopes and protruding rocks

prevent the trees from growing so tall, there are bushes, and scrub, grass and caves.

Inside the ring of mountains there are few predators and none very big. Leopards are the largest, though there are lynxes and smaller cats, also foxes. There are many rodents, some quite large like the coypu for them to feed off, small round pigs, and frogs and toads as well. There are three or four species of forest deer, very small compared with the ones the men hunt beyond the mountains, and difficult for all but the cats to take, and, considering their size, not worth the effort. Anyway, we, the women, love the lithe dappled shapes that flit noiselessly away from us on the rare occasions we actually see them.

Not that we are vegetarians, indeed not. We live on the islands – I didn't mention the islands, did I? – there are hundreds of them in the lake, ranging from rocky pimples to those, up to a couple of miles wide and long, that are forest-clad. We live on the islands and our preferred food is fish, for the most part shellfish of one form or another. There is a huge variety for the water is faintly saline – not as salty as the ocean, but not as pure as the spring-water that gushes out of the mountainsides, and even bubbles up on some of the islands. The result is a happy environment for every sort of edible fish, except the very largest, which you know about, and a whole raft of others that are no longer with us.

Shellfish and crustacea are our favourites. Muscles, oysters, fifteen varieties of clams, scallops, the lot. Chestnut and prussian blue lobsters, many of them clawless, ramble idly across the rippled sandy bottoms, picking their way through the sponges, and a quick duck-dive to a depth of ten feet can bring up the main course for a meal for four in ten seconds. The children love to chase shoals of shrimps and prawns into rocky basins which they then dam. And of course there are eggs galore just after the rainy season peters out – turtle eggs, duck eggs, gull eggs, quail eggs, and if we want a good-sized omelette for four, splayed out on a big flat stone, then one flamingo egg is enough.

Yes, we do cook a little but not much, mainly to set things like eggs that would otherwise be runny and slop all over the place. The men, on their hunting trips, make big fires into which they toss the carcases of the animals they have killed, and I have to say the fatty crisp joints they bring back for us are delicious, though too much meat creates bad temper, constipation and smelly faeces – all characteristics one associates with males, does one not?

Fruits I have already mentioned, but on the islands where again the vegetation is lower than in the forest there are even more varieties – custard-apple fruit, mangoes, papayas, melons, strawberries, guavas, I could go on for hours. Of course many of these are smaller and not quite as sweet as the ones you get in the supermarkets these days, but they have a fresh fragrance you will never know.

Paradise without the serpent? I'm afraid not. There are poisonous snakes in the forest and beyond the mountains, but the islands we live on are free of them because, when we colonise a new island, we simply make sure they are all killed off. But there are still watersnakes and some species of eel too which can do one a severe hurt and even kill a child – some spiders and crabs as well. But fatalities are rare, we know the herbal antidotes, also we have learnt to react instinctively to the presence of any of these at a very early age and indeed infants are born with a phobia for snakes, spiders and scorpions. Still are, are they not?

Crocodiles? In these waters they are so well-fed on the abundance of easily caught fish they almost never bother us – and a good heavy splashing and shouting usually deter any that show predatory tendencies.

So, where are the snags? Well, as you would expect, as it is with every other species that has evolved to fill an environmental niche for which it is just about perfectly adapted, there are, at about seven thousand in all, too many of us. And when the total gets up to about ten thousand, then the elders get together and draw lots between the sixty or so clans to decide on which should leave. They do. Led by their men, who are usually keen to do it since it gives their lives a bit more meaning than they had before, in groups between a hundred and a hundred and fifty, they uproot themselves and set off across the mountains. Of course the men have been there before and think they know all about it, survival in the wilderness and all that.

And that's it. We never see them again because that is part of the bargain. Of course I know now, on the cusp of the year 151,999 and 152,000, what happened to them. Most, nearly all, died out before they'd even crossed what are now the Sahara and Arabian Deserts. But a few made it, especially roundabout the year 80,000 give or take a few millennia on either side. Five tribes in all. No more than a thousand all told. Plus a sixth, the blacks, who never did go. And all of them, every single one of them, descended from me. Eve.

But I'll come to that later.

Copulation with men took place towards the end of the dryer part of the year so the children would be born after the rains had gone away. What we did was this. The men, that is males between fourteen years old and forty, came down to the lakeside at dusk on the night before full moon, and stayed there for three nights and two whole days. We women would swim and then wade from our islands and, keeping in the water, would wade to and fro along the coast-line until we saw a man we fancied.

You remember the first best, don't you? He may not have been the best, but you remember him best.

The sun had dipped behind the mountains to the west an hour or so earlier, leaving the hazy sky blood-red above the peaks and gold then blueish silver above. The green planet was a hole in its fabric. On the other side an orange moon, huge and near, rolled up the crests of the mountains to the east before dragging itself clear of them, launching itself to float like a galleon into the centre of the heavens. Galleon? Not of course a concept I was familiar with then, but, as I said, I've been around, in you, and you, and all the people between ever since, so, I know a galleon when I see one, better than you do.

I wade through the black water with it just deliciously lapping my thighs and pubes, pushing little waves or big ripples in front of me that catch the gold of the moon and which arrow out behind me flashing greenishly with phosphorescence. If I turn and look over my shoulder and narrow my eyes the reflections of the moon turn into a sparkling continuous lacy thread of gold across the darkness of the waters, and I can see the island, half a mile away that I have swum and waded from, a blacker tree-fringed silhouette against the mist that lies between it and the shores beyond.

I am beautiful. Beautiful that is for my fourteen years, but not yet perfect. I have glossy, long, straight black hair that reaches down my back to my dimpled waist and is now wet and stuck between my shoulder blades. I have a broad forehead, somewhat spotted I am afraid to say with the sebiginous pores that make spots and are our inheritance from the intermediary ages when we had fur waterproofed with oily secretions. That was before we developed subcutaneous fat like seals and whales – a far better way of keeping an even blood temperature in water, as well as supplying us with buoyancy.

Fat. Yes I am as fat now as ever I will be, at least until old age sets in. Not grossly fat, but neatly fat, puppy fat you will, quite wrongly, come to call it – wrong, unless you are thinking of seal puppies. I have plumpish high cheek-bones beneath large but slightly oriental eyes which are the colour of dark amber, a small but straight nose, with slightly splayed nostrils, thickish lips. Some of us can pull our top lips back to block our nostrils when we want to stay under water for as long as our lungs will allow, up to five minutes for some, but this is a knack I don't have.

Small neat chin, strong neck, plump white shoulders also, bother it, a touch spotty. My breasts are full and round and firm and creamy, with dark but rosy nipples, my waist thickish by the absurd standards of beauty you have nowadays, my bush a kite-shaped triangle of curly black filaments concealing, at any rate while I am walking or wading upright, the folded lips inner and outer, that gleam succulently with their own moisture as well as with the fishy water of the lake. My anus, when I spread my buttocks, is a tight little flower-bud which contracts and loosens deliciously when I, or one of my friends strokes it. My legs are rounded pillars when I stand, but are happiest and strongest when the muscles are used for swimming, kicking or folding in and pushing out in what you call a breast-stroke. We all swim, almost from birth, and the breast-stroke comes most naturally as it keeps our heads up out of the water. My feet are small and very very sensitive – not that happy when walking on dry land, but fine in water. Some of us are occasionally born with webbed toes – it is considered an incredibly good stroke of luck for those who are, for of course they will swim even better than the rest of us.

Men's feet are larger, flatter, and not so sensitive. They haven't caught up with us. They still like clambering over rocks, arsing about in trees, *walking* for heaven's sake!

Anyway there I am, pushing my thighs through the moonstruck water, with my gaze peering intently over the silvered rocks, sandy beaches, little coves and inlets that fill the space between the lake and the forest curtain. Around me, some closer to the shore, the older or wilder ones, those who have done it before, some further out, even occasionally still swimming, are the other young women of our clan.

We can see the men waiting. A mixed bunch. Some hunker or sit with their arms about their knees on a rock or the shingle where the water laps their feet, some stand. A few are displaying. They cavort, turn cart-wheels, beat their chests and howl or roar like the gorillas, some shake and manipulate their tackle, displaying near erections, cupping their balls in their hands thinking we might be interested in how big they are. Well, it takes all sorts, and some of us do go for this sort of thing. But me, I am looking for someone about my own age, someone as shy as myself, perhaps as nervous as I am, someone also doing it for the first time.

Of course I know, as well as one can without actually doing it, what to expect. What you would call sexual play has been a normal part of life since I was born. Mothers, aunts, grannies, sisters have felt free to play with my cunt, my clitoris, my nipples, and my anus using their fingers and tongues, wrapping me in hot embraces when the urge became overpowering, getting me to do the same to them. Indeed none of this has really been separated from all the other natural things we share – grooming, cleaning, eating, playing, shitting and weeing; it's all part of the same thing, isn't it? All part of being alive.

And there have been males all around too sharing in this, but not men. Infants, with their little button pricks and often empty sacks and rounded chests and buttocks like ours, lads growing thinner and occasionally displaying thin, hard little erections, and of course the old men, growing fat, tired and varicose now after twenty-five years in the plains and the savannahs before we let them back on the islands, caressing us as well, but mainly staying with the grannies, maybe favoured ones they fucked at moon-tide a few times each year and remembered.

Sometimes they get in a sweat trying to get the silly things up again, but for the most part they are happy to play and be played with until they get smelly and silly and we have to push them out into the lake, and not let them land until they sink away to feed the fishes we might eat the very next day.

But that first time. After half an hour I saw the boy I wanted, indeed recognised him. When he was a lad, two or three years ago, we used to play together, fish and so on and I remember once he strung sea-shells on a plait of grasses to hang round my neck. But I only just recognise him. Something about the way he holds his head, slightly forward and to the side, as if listening intently. That was one of the things I liked about him. He listened.

But in other ways, how changed he is! Two years they stay up in the savannah before being allowed down to the moon-tide copulation, until puberty has merged into near adulthood, until the neck has thickened, the shoulders broadened, the torso filled and the arms become rounded and rippled with hard muscle. Indeed, and I mean no joke at all, it is hardness that is the word that best describes the change. Lean he still is, but no longer thin or stick-like, and the muscles when he tenses them are as hard as his bones. He has lost all the softness humans of both sexes have during childhood and old age and has become hard the way only a man, a man rather than a male, can be. Even their buttocks are hard like small unripe melons.

All this is new to me, and even before he has seen me, or at any rate picked me out from the rest, I suddenly feel wave after wave of longing, a great emptiness, a desire for something I have never known before; I have a terrible urge to splash through the shallows, call out, grasp him, hold him...

I stub my toe. On a rock that normally I would have seen or sensed. And the first thing he hears apart from a little splashing, is a whoops! of surprise, then a cry of pain and anger. The pain always comes a second or so later after you've stubbed your toe... have you noticed that?

But now he's seen me. And a moment later he's recognised me too and in a moment I am in his arms, with my fingers in the nape of his neck tearing at the coarse hair which daylight will show is darker and redder than the straw-coloured mop he had, and I can feel that hard chest pressing my breasts so they hurt as well as tingle with delight, and his hands broad and strong lifting my buttocks, and his long middle fingers prying in towards my bum-hole and above all that hard pillar of a prick, a rock, a club pulsing against my stomach.

He tumbles us back into the fine silky sand, rolls us over so I am underneath and suddenly gasping for breath and with one hand tries to push that thing into my groin, my cleft, between my swollen gaping lips, but the poor boy doesn't really know what he's up to, he tries to use his big hand with his strong lean but clumsy fingers, and that does it. The feel of my pubes, of the wetness at his finger tips, and that aching throbbing prick between us, is too much and with a great spurt of the stuff, he comes, a handful of smooth thick viscous come streaking up from my navel reaching to the cleavage between my breasts.

Poor boy. He's fed up about this, very fed up, puts his face against my cheek and I can feel tears mingling with the sweat as well as the pungent stickiness between us.

But his body is still on top of mine. I wriggle about a little, pushing up with my knees between his thighs, trying to get him to take some at least of his weight off me, and then his elbows too between my arms and flanks and as I do I feel it getting hard and big again, not that it had shrunk very much at all, and presently, using my hand between us this time, I manage to wriggle and twist and get it through the front door, if not actually beyond the hall. This wakes him up all right. The little sobs and sighs deepen into pants and grunts, his buttocks rise and with one push he's through and in.

It hurts. They said it would. But not as much as I expected. I get my hands into his hair again and yank and manage to murmur to him to lie still a moment or so, let me get used to that great bruising throbbing thing inside me, and because he is, as I hoped he would be, still the kind nice lad he once was before he was a man, he does so, though not for as long as I'd have liked. Then he's at it again, up and down, in and out, and I try to keep up with him, but he's too quick for me, and I can feel the sudden pulse again and my honeyed cavities fill with his juices.

He stays for a moment, pumping air in and out of his lungs as if he'd done a five minute dive, then rolls off with a sigh of satisfaction and a big grin on his stupid face. The moonlight is bright enough to show it. He's done it. He's got his prick inside a woman, and he's come. *He's* fucking come. Men.

Still, we have the rest of the night, a day, a night, the night when the moon is truly full, a day and a third night, and during that time I intend to teach him a thing or two. And learn.

Towards dawn, after the moon has set, I curl up in his arms and sleep, but when dawn comes he has gone. Not far. He's down at the water edge skipping stones across the gentle heaving opalescent water, skimming them hop, skip and a jump, out into the mist that hangs over everything, so all you hear is the final plop, you can't see it. The mist swirls a little and lifts, and there forty yards away is another man, also standing on the water edge and skipping flat pebbles. He sees my lad, and winding himself up, throws a stone as far as he can to the edge of the now swiftly rising vapour. My lad carefully picks a stone the right weight and size and tries to throw it as far. By the time the mists have gone and the sky which was filled with the rosy glow of dawn is shifting to gold, and the birds are calling and singing in the forest behind us and the flying fish are skimming the waves, and further out the porpoises humping their black backs in and out of the water, as far as you can see in either direction, along the scalloped coast of the lake, men are throwing stones. Who can throw furthest. Who can make the flat ones skip the most often.

This will not do.

I go into the forest, find a pineapple, then a most gorgeous odour tickles my nostrils. I see the signs where a pot-bellied pig has been disturbed by a predator, a cat perhaps or a man, in its search for truffles. I get down on my hands and knees and begin to scrabble in the earth, and soon come up with a beauty, black glossy, multi-faceted, it's exciting enough to make me forget the dull ache of a cunt that has been both abused and left unsatisfied. And then, just as I'm going to get it free of the damp leaf mould that has nurtured it, I sense or hear him behind me and pushing back my sleek black hair look over my creamy shoulder.

He's there. He's followed me after all. Legs astride he's playing with his penis and his balls, pushing the foreskin up and off the gleaming red glans, letting it slide over again and he's getting big. And bigger. I spread my knees even more than before, put a hollow in my back, push my arse up at him. My breasts swing below me, suddenly heavy and throbbing again, the nipples swollen. Come *on* you fool! He'll do it to himself before he gets to me, if he's not careful.

But then he's down on his knees behind me, pushing forward, and this time spread as I am and ready for it it slips in with a musical sucking sound, like a blind animal finding its burrow, while I am all mouth pulling in the loveliest morsel lips ever closed around. Oh, oh, this time it is *sweet*. With a little manoeuvring I manage to get the root of his prick and his balls to bang against my clit, and since he is kneeling almost upright, with no weight on me, I manage to get one hand between my thighs without toppling the whole lovely funny structure we have become, and I can just tease his balls with my nails, then, whooomf! I go off like a whale spouting, whoomf, whoomf, whoomf, head up, shoulders pulled in, back hollowed, and I sing out that great female cry that wakens the woods above me and sets the monkeys off.

It's a bit of a surprise for him too.

That's an end to pebble-throwing competitions, I can tell you.

We do it fifteen more times before he has to go back up into the savannah, and I have to haul myself back to the island, and each time the gap between is a little longer, and each time he takes a little longer, so by the third night I can get on top of him, facing forwards or backwards as the liking takes me, playing with the root of his penis, stroking his balls, getting my fingers up his bum-hole, do what I like while he just lies there moaning, and I come three even four times before he does. And in between we eat fruit and shellfish, I have been told oysters, figs and guavas especially will help him keep going, but by the final dawn he doesn't have the strength left to prise the shells open, he can hardly peel a fig. Sometimes we chat and play a bit... but that's no different from what happens at home with my friends, and right now is not what I want... Nevertheless, I do get to like him and, come the next time I shall wade ashore for the annual copulation I shall be as much on the look out for him as for new flesh.

But that's four years away. In the meantime I have twins, not identical, one like me, one like him, both girls, and there's no point in making the trip until I have stopped lactating.

Now I am eighteen, thinned down a bit but not much, several inches taller, my skin has taken on a deeper creamier look, my nipples are browner, the aureoles bigger. Instead of the spots I have a few little brown moles here and there. My hair is thick and glossy, like a cormorant's wings.

This time I am not in the least nervous, but I am very excited as I wade along the shore peering through the silvery moonlight at the wares laid out for my delectation. I have half an eye open for the lad of four summers gone – I have a nostalgia for him, even feel I'd like to know how he has been faring in the man's world, but really my heart, or quim, is set on something new and different, even strange. And there, even while my mind is dwelling on some great hunk of a full-grown brute of a male, I see him.

You won't believe this, but what I have suddenly spotted, sitting on his buttocks on a high rock overlooking a little bay, with his knees pulled up to his chin, and a thin spear with a fire-hardened point in the crook of his arm, is a thin wiry shrimp of a man with a very dark skin, a top-knot of curly black hair with a golden pheasant's feather stuck through it, big dark eyes, a squashed nose, and thickish lips. Of course I could not see all this at once, but enough to know I'm in luck. There aren't many of these left, a whole tribe of them was sent off into the savannah and deserts a year or so earlier, but my gossipy chums back on the island have said if you can get one, then, well...

I pushed through the water to the edge where the Orion's belt weed wrapped round my ankles and glowed greenly, set my head on one side, arms akimbo, and looked up at him. Take it or leave it. He took it.

He came down off his rock, with very lithe, easy movements, into the water, took my hand and led me on to a patch of very fine shingle. I could see touches of grey in the wiry hair at his temples, and realised he was older than I had thought, quite a lot older than me. Well, I thought, at least he'll know a thing or two.

And he did.

He got me on to my knees, spread them, then lay on his back behind me and pushed his head between my thighs. What the fuck is he up to, I thought. Then his long thin hands rested on my hip bones and pulled me down so his squashed nose was rubbing my clit and his tongue was feeling its way through my lips and finding the juicy recesses beyond. Oh, boy. This was something. I began to squirm and wriggle with the ecstasy of it, but his hands were strong and firm, grasping my waist now and holding me down, so all I could do instead was get hold of the back of his head and and rub and grind his face into my pussy until the juices overflowed and I was off, coming again and again in great surges of pleasure.

It's a wonder I didn't suffocate him. But these dark ones often live near water, even during their manhood, and can hold their breaths for a long, long time. Long enough anyway.

Which brings me to... well that was long too. The longest I ever had, long and thin, longer than the full stretch of my hand from the tip of my thumb to the tip of my little finger, and hard little balls beneath. Hardly any body-hair at all and thin tight hard buttocks that hardly filled my hands.

Long enough to find places no prick found before or after. When I sat on him and moved myself up and up and down and down, ever so slowly up and down the full length of him I could feel the cervix of my womb dilate to fold round his tip and that was a pleasure beyond anything for both of us. And of course long and thin like that he could get it way up my bum-hole while his hands kneaded and pushed and rubbed and stroked my lips and clit and his fingers felt right in, way up my pussy, all this at once.

This time it was he who kept me going with what he brought to eat. He already had cooked cutlets of some sort of mountain goat, wrapped in large leaves, and a couple of gourds of fermented honey that was heaven at first but spoilt the second day a bit with a headache. And he used his spear in the water and got us a couple of big flatfish I guess you'd call them sole. Dover sole. And he made a little charcoal fire to grill them on. He liked caterpillars and crickets too, the last crunchy and sweet, just the thing to end a meal with.

All in all, he was really quite domesticated, and now I look back on it, we probably spent more time messing about with pleasant little chores together than we actually did making out.

Twins again. Girls again. Both dark, but one with my high cheek-bones and almond eyes.

There were three more. A tall thin guy with a heavy beaky nose and a reddish-browny skin, boney face, who said damn all and spent most of the time using a flint flake to scrape the tissue off the inside of a leopard skin he'd brought with him which he finally put on, with the mask of it over his forehead. This was a disappointment too, as I thought he was doing it all to give to me – not that I needed it, it just felt nice, that fur on my shoulder, rubbing against my cheek.

One girl only this time, which was a relief.

Next, when I was pushing thirty and getting on a bit, and felt I wanted a bloke who'd make the running again, I chose another black, but this time a big, strong, really, really dark guy, skin like ebony, muscles like ebony too and a prick which, when it was dangling, came halfway down to his knees. Really. And balls to match. Trouble with those big ones is it takes a lot to get them up and keep them up, which, for all my experience and the gossip amongst us girls, was something I didn't know about or wanted to forget and was a serious disappoint-ment. I spent most of the time giving head and trying to get the thing in where it belonged before it went limp again. Mind, he gave good head too, not that there's a lot of point. I can always get that at home on the Island.

One lovely black girl who grew up straight as a tree and could run and swim better than any of us. She was a bit dippy though, always searching for God. Never found him.

And lastly an oldish white man who was rather disgusting, picking his nose and scratching his bum-hole and then sniffing his fingers. I don't know why I chose him, except perhaps out of sympathy and also perhaps fearing rejection from the young studs who were waiting around for younger flesh than mine. Very little use at all until the last night when I found what really turned him on. He liked me to tie him up with sea-weed and then whip his bum with the stuff. Slowly, bit by bit, his gnarled, old pink prick just about made it to horizontal, and so long as I kept on hurting him, dragging my nails down his back till it bled, and across his scrawny, floppy buttocks, he kept it up, and managed to bring us both off.

My last little girl, and a bit of a pain. Fair hair, blue eyes, not a bit like me, always whining for something.

And that's about it. Seven girls of all shapes sizes and colours and all carrying in every cell my mitochondrial DNA, which is only passed down the female line, and which, your modern scientists will tell you, is so alike in every human being, that it can only have one source. Me. Still alive in you after one hundred and fifty-two thousand years. Say twenty years as an average generation that's only seven hundred and fifty mothers separate you from me. Seven hundred and fifty. It's not a lot, is it?

(She's wrong, by a factor of ten… women! Ed.)

Nina

Nina Murray came to Bognor from Cork in, I think, 1936 to work in the Royal Norfolk Hotel. She married Ron Pullen, son of a local barber, shortly after. I could write a lot about her. There's a good portrait of her in A Last Resort *(and of Ron too). She was admitted to St Richard's Hospital, Chichester, in October 1994 and died on the second of November. All three of her daughters were at her bedside. I am married to her youngest.*

Thin like winter twigs she frets.
Asked what she'd like repeats
What she said as a child to her Mum,
Spells it out like the tired child she is:
All I want is to go down the road
And see the white pony.

Tired and brave
She knows what lies ahead
Will be the holiday she never had.

She gave anything, everything,
But keeps herself whole.
Make do and never want more than you have were enough
For her. She made sure we had more.

With her next to last breath she still scorns
The pretension of those who think they know better.
She rocks and mocks and blows them away
With wheezy laughter.

Brave and giving and laughing...
She loves a good laugh.
And dancing! Given the chance she'd dance
Given the chance.

Chances she gave to others, to us.
What she'll do now is
Dance down the road to see the white pony.

Young Love

*We're back in 1060 or thereabouts, Walt and Erica on
Hambledon Hill in Dorset.*

Perhaps Erica had been talking to her mother. Or an aunt.
Certainly, along with all the other children of her age, she had
watched and laughed raucously at the antics the animals sometimes got up to, how bulls sometimes licked their cows' vulvae, instead
of getting on with it properly, that sort of thing. They drank their cider,
ate wrinkled apples, the last from the previous autumn kept in the hay
lofts above the barns (it was about all they did keep hay for, feeding the
best breeding stock on more nutritious fodder through the winter and
killing the rest for food when winter came). Then, with no more questioning she pulled him down on top of her and made him kiss her face,
her lips, her neck, her shoulders. He lifted her smock over her shoulders
and she shook her head and wonderful hair free of it. For a moment he
was shattered by the soft, rounded, milky whiteness of her, the globes
of her breasts, the nipples like pale raspberries, the rounded tummy and
its blue-shadowed navel, the full hips and the fair reddish brush, redder
than her hair (foxy lady), between and her long, smooth strong legs. He
bent his head, took her nipples between his lips.

After a moment or two of this she sat up to pull at his leggings and jerkin until he was as naked beneath the sun and the larks as she was. She took hold of his throbbing prick with one hand and with the other arm over his lean, muscled shoulders pulled him down but carefully so his member lay between their stomachs. When, driven by impulses stronger than earthquakes and tempests, he tried to wriggle a little lower, find his way in, she seized his buttocks and with nails tearing into them ground her stomach against him until he came before he could get there. Gasping, almost retching with the uncompleted agony of it, he pulled up and back and looked down at her, spread like a universe of potential joy beneath him.

Her hands reached up his arms and on to his shoulders.

'You're not done yet, oh no Walt, you're not done yet,' and shifting a hand to his sweating forehead she pushed him down across her stomach streaked with viscous pearl as it was, right down to where she was moist too and filled with fragrances. She opened her knees and put her legs over his shoulders forcing his mouth into her. His body slipped on the grassy slope beneath them, the wild thyme prickled his stomach and his balls, and he had to scrabble again with his feet to gain a purchase and push himself upwards, and again gather handfuls of grass on either side of her waist.

She pushed with her hands at the back of his head, his neck, twisting them and herself, and once got hold of his hair and yanked his head upwards so his lips and tongue were where she wanted them to be and he felt the small hardness within swell and throb until suddenly she was writhing and moaning as he sucked the rush of wetness into his mouth – sea without the harshness of salt, honey without its cloying sweetness.

And when that was done and the hot flush spread across her breastbone was fading and her head ceased to rock from side to side, when that was over they lay face to face and kissed and gently played with their fingers until it all happened again less urgently but even more sweetly than before. And, of course she found his tattoos. The winged dagger:

'Winners dare'. And 'Walt 4 Erica' inscribed within a heart. That pleased her like anything, because now she knew he had fancied her all along, well before the betrothal.

At last she said: 'Wait here. I don't want to be seen leaving with you.'

And she pulled the smock back on over her head.

He watched her – part walking, sometimes driven by the steepness of the slope to run a little, once slithering and almost slipping on to her backside so she looked back with a grin and a wave. His heart burst with a happiness which enveloped all he could see and smell and touch. The whole landscape from the plants around him, some it must be said a little the worse for being lain on, to the distant hills was hers, was subsumed into her. She was the spirit whose corporeality infused it all.

The grass was a garden, a chalk garden filled with wild flowers, thyme, vetches, clovers, wild flaxes, cranesbills, spurges, borages, mallow, forget-me-nots and harebells. The hawthorn blossom was full and out now and the scent of it, the most sensuous odour that any blossom has and the why of that was something he had discovered first on his tongue and still on his fingers, hung about his head. He looked down and out across a rolling plain framed with the blue hills on which Shaftesbury stood six miles to the north and on the right by downs which lay like a woman upon the earth, contoured so their shape echoed the line that climbs a thigh, dips from hip to waist, then swells into a breast. Below, the coombes were hazed with bosky woods.

Filling the air, making a space rather than an emptiness of it, martins wove cat's cradles of delight so fast all he could follow was the white speck of their rumps above the trees and fields. Higher still, swifts racketed on alternate wing-beats, mewing like kittens as they scoured the skies. A scattering of crows chased a merlin from their rookery, and while a male cuckoo made the air ring his mate slipped in and laid intrusive eggs.

It was all one thing, one living thing, bound into one. Even the farms and enclosures, built from the earth and what grew out of it, mingled with it all, were neither alien nor intrusive, adding harmony to what would have been savage without them.

Again he savoured the hawthorn flavour on his lips and saw how the girl, the woman, yellow hair falling on honey-coloured shoulders above the white but grass-stained shift, crossed a meadow where three horses grazed and came to the fence that circled her father's homestead. One step up and there she was astride the topmost pole. She knew he watched for her and she raised an arm and waved. Wild thing. His heart was singing.

6 March 2003

There will be suicides: not a lot, almost none reported.
A young man scouting through the ruins
May find such human debris he had not thought of.
There'll be Iraqi brides unravelled
By the loss of home, hearth, kids and love.

And here there'll be girls, young women really,
Whose loneliness in front of TV screens in sitting rooms
Where parents come and go and talk of work and friends
Will feed the poisoned lily of despair.

Suicides? A minor haemorrhage
Of affectivity. Collateral damage.

10. LAST WORDS

*Thanks for coming this far with me. I hope you've enjoyed
some of it. I hope some of you will have enjoyed most of it.*

When you're thirty and male a young woman in good health is
like a bowl of fresh ripening fruit.
   When you're seventy and male a bowl of fresh ripening fruit
is like a young woman in good health.
   We hybridise, chill, radiate our fruit and make it conform...
   Not only angst-ridden loonies, but natural scientists, even Darwin
himself in his darker moments, have felt there is something blind, cruel,
unfeeling in the way nature works. In this, at any rate, they are wrong.
The moment when a rabbit feels the teeth of a polecat in the nape of its
neck is the least important moment in its life. The moment when the
last member of a doomed species succumbs to changes of environment,
or its competitors within it, is as nothing to the thousands even millions
of years that went before. What kept the rabbit alive, what kept the
species flourishing for almost all of its span was the fact that life is
worth living. The most powerful force in our lives, without which there
would be no life, is the joy of living, which is as real for a microbe, a
housefly, and probably a rose too, as it is for us. Genes may be selfish
but what keeps them alive is not a drive to avoid extinction, but their
carriers' passion to stay alive, because being alive is such good fun.
There's no need to be hung up about death and dying. What's the least
important part of a sentence? The full-stop, of course.
   Ideas like these will be familiar to readers of thinkers like Richard
Dawkins, who is a star, a hero, but that does not mean I've nicked
them. In the autumn of 1958 I finally gave up on the devotional
Anglicanism that had afflicted me for nearly ten years with an experience that was damascene in its intensity. It was the first truly religious
experience I had ever had. It was a bright frosty morning. I was cycling
across Jesus Green in Cambridge on my way to the secondary modern
school I was teaching in for a year as a more economical way of getting
a teacher's certificate than doing a diploma of education. The chestnuts
were hung with gold beaten to airy thinness. And suddenly I felt deeply
elated, lightning-struck with euphoria. And the words that came into
my mind were: "This is it. This is all there is. And it's GREAT!" And
ever since then that experience has been summonable if and when I had
the sense to ask for it, and often spontaneously it surprises me; not that
it ever repeats itself in detail, it is always a little bit different. Swallows

in flight, especially the first of the year; a lot of Beethoven; a lot of Joyce; Las Meninas; the scent of the rose by our front door or sweet peas; bird-song; sea-song; a cat kiss from our cat; our daughter going through the gate on her way to school; our son on the phone from uni; Beckham scores, yes, even though only seen on TV; Victoria de los Angeles singing *De los álamos vengo, madre...*; and so on, they go on and on until I die, those moments and hours of tearful joy, more now than ever. Are these the experiences that some people call spiritual? If so, there is no duality for I feel them in my veins, in my skin, in my head, in my diaphragm.

The first thinking persons must have been terrified. They had no idea of why anything happened, anything at all. Why, and how they were born; why and how they would die. What made the sun too hot, or the rain too heavy, the wind too cold; where the lightning came from or the moon. They must have believed animals lived with the same understanding as they had, and talked and reasoned in their own languages. A neighbouring troop of baboons must have seemed different only in shape and manners from the nearest tribe of people. Eat one, why not the other? And so on. The only way to make sense of it all was to invent gods.

The god inventors were on to a good thing. Rattle a few bones about, spice it all up with puffs of hallucinogenic smoke, exploit the fact that people who want to get better and believe they will get better quite often do get better. Some, though, don't... ah, must be the devils! That'll be two fish, a couple of eggs and you can throw in a mango for the baby. Thanks. Call again. They had it made.

Next step... agriculture, which means land-owning, which means class society. Kettles boil, classes struggle. Why am I the boss, and you are not? God said so. And if you don't believe me you'll go to hell where the devils are. Thanks a bundle. I'll make you a bishop and you can wear funny clothes, and you needn't do any real work. Especially if you get me into heaven as well.

Women are all slags and blackies trash. How do I know? God said so. Thanks another bundle, you can be an archbishop and live in a palace. Just make sure your girl-friends use the tradespersons' entrance, especially those differently hued to you and me.

If I believe what my senses, my powers of reasoning, and every verifiable fact and thesis science has discovered or proved then we are an unimportant blip in time and space. Is this something to regret? Why? I find it a relief. The only responsibility we have is to us here and now, nothing else. The only reason you want life after death is because you've cocked up the only one you're going to get. The only reason you want a loving, all-seeing, all-powerful daddy is because you're afraid to stand on your own two feet. You're still the brat who was afraid of the dark.

As soon as you infect objects with a value that is other than aesthetic or useful, you betray your humanity and all humanity. Take cars. Cars are a useful way to get from a to b. As soon as you think of buying a car with considerations other than that, apart from your safety, and that of your passengers and other road-users, you are betraying yourself. Why do you buy more seats and luggage space than you will ever need? Why do you buy the ability to drive through deserts and jungles when you never will? Why do you buy a car that will go twice as fast as the legal limit on any road you are ever likely to use? Why do you buy a big fat-arse of a car with bulging curves and flashes of chrome inlaid in its silvery, silky surface? Why do you spend three, four, ten times more on a car than you need to? Because you know other people like you will sneer at you if you drive around in a VW Polo, a Fiesta, or a Seat Ibiza. Because they won't know you ever had that sort of money if you spend the change from a tolerably sensible car on a decent work of art or give it to Oxfam. If you don't have a fat-arse of a car they'll never know that you made it, got there. You won't feel sure about it yourself. Got where? About halfway up the tree.

Why is Fony Blair driven in a black fat-arse car the five minute walk from Downing Street to the House of Commons? It can't be that difficult to make one of the new Minis bullet-proof. There is no answer to this question that does not do discredit to Fony Blair and the way we perceive, or the way he thinks we should perceive, prime ministers.

The first major speech Fony Blair made after he was 'elected' leader of the Labour Party was at the Labour Party conference. The bit I remember of it was when he said: "What this country needs is leader-ship…" I hope you won't think me silly when I say this was the gist of many of Hitler's speeches in the early thirties. Mature democracies do not want leaders (führers). We want servants who will make things work: railways, the NHS, the motorways, that sort of thing, so we can get on with the important things in life. Politicians and civil servants should be lackeys, not the lackeys of the multi-nationals, but of us. They deserve no more respect that anyone else, anyone else at all. Polite gratitude and a wage not obviously larger or smaller than the rest of us is their due when when they get things right. The boot when they don't. A country that wants leadership is a flock of sheep or goats following the bellwether.

I have never known anyone who sought a position of power and authority apart from one headteacher, out of the many I have come into contact with, and Nelson Mandela, for whom I have any real respect at all. Anyone who wants to be looked up to and boss other people has lost or never had a fundamental ingredient of what it is to be properly human: a quiet belief in their own value that does not need to be proved.

Christianity was valuable because central to its faith was the belief that in the eyes of god all people are equal. Humanism goes one better: in the eyes of all of us, all of us are equal and have the same rights as each other. Since this is manifestly not the way things are it follows that anyone who claims to be a humanist must be a libertarian and a revolutionary as well.

How about this? For one year let every Big Issue seller be made a policeman, and let all policemen be required to sell the Big Issue. Go on, give it a try. Dare you!

Say YES.

Very Last Word

I was taught to trust
The poet's song the painter's lust
Furor of music and her lullaby
Ariadne's thread and Orpheus' lyre.

11. BIBLIOGRAPHY

Only the list of hardback or original paperback editions of titles published in England is guaranteed complete. For the rest there may be lacunae and possibly minor mistakes, particularly of dates. Large print and audio editions are not included.

Novels

Diamonds Bid: hdb. Michael Joseph, 1967; pbk. Corgi, 1968; US, Walker, 1968; Italy: *(La Mezzaluna E' Rossa)* Mondadori,1969; West Germany: *(Für eine Handvoll Diamenten)* Kurt Desch, 1971; Turkey: *(Elmas Pazari)* Maceraperest Kitaplar, 1999.

Hand Out: hdb. Michael Joseph,1968; pbk. Corgi, 1970; US, Walker, 1968; Turkey: *(Sonuncu El)*, Maceraperest Kitaplar, 2001.

With My Knives I Know I'm Good: hdb. Michael Joseph, 1969; pbk. Mayflower, 1973; US, hdb. Putnam, 1970; US pbk. Putnam, 1970; Italy: *(Sul Filo del Coltello)* Mondadori, 1970; France: (*A Couteaux tirés)* Libraire des Champs-Elysées – Le Masque, 1973, (2nd edition 197? Or 198?); Germany: *(Der Messerwerfer)* Kurt Desch 1970, Serie Piper Spannung, 1989; Sweden: *(Jagad i natten)* B. Wahlströms, 1974; Holland: *(Het mes erin)*, Bruna, 1976; Turkey: *(Biçak Atmada Üstüme Yoktur)* Maceraperest Kitaplar, 2001.

Trip Trap: hdb. Michael Joseph, 1972; US, hdb. St Martin's Press, 1972; pbk. Popular Press, 1972; Germany: *(Das Geheimnis der Bronze-Stauen)* Kurt Desch, 1973; France: *(le sens de la famille)*, Libraire des Champs-Elysées – Le Masque, 1972, (2nd edition, 197?, 198?); Sweden *(Farligt för turister)* B Wahlströms, 1973.

Kill Cure: hdb. Michael Joseph, 1975; Germany: *(Tödliches Serum)*

Serie Piper Spannung, 1991; Turkey: *(Olüm Ilaci)* Maceraperest Kitaplar, 2001.

Bloody Marvellous: hdb. Michael Joseph, 1975.

King Fisher Lives: hdb. Michael Joseph, 1976, (shortlisted for the Booker prize, 1976); US, hdb. St Martin's Press, 1976; US pbk. Pyramid Books, 1977; Spain: *(El Valle de Las Batuecas),* Jucar, 1988.

¡Carnival!: hdb. Michael Joseph, 1976; German, Serie Piper, 1990 (two editions).

A Raving Monarchist: hdb. Michael Jpseph, 1977; Spain: *(Objetivo: El Rey),* Jucar, 1988.

The Princess A Nun!: The last third only, completing the book by Hugh Ross Williamson. hdb. Michael Joseph, 1978.

Joseph: hdb. Michael Joseph, 1979, (shortlisted for the Booker Prize 1979); pbk. Abacus, 1999; Spain: Title unknown, Edhasa, 2001?

The Euro-Killers: hdb. Michael Joseph, 1979; US, hdb. Pantheon, 1979; US, pbk, Pantheon, 1980; Holland, *(Argand en de Eurokillers),* Van Gennep, 1983; Denmark, *(Argand, den Haederlige Komissaer),* Klim, 1985; UK. Pbk. Pluto, 1986; Czechoslovakia (Slovak), *(Euro-Vrahovia),* 1987; Japan, publisher, title and date to be deciphered!

A Last Resort: hdb. Michael Joseph, 1980.

Base Case: hdb. Michael Joseph, 1981; US, hdb. Pantheon, 1981; Holland, *(Argand op de Virtudes),* Van Gennep, 1984; Denmark, *(Basale Interesser),* Klim, 1985.

A Spy of the Old School: hdb. Michael Joseph, 1982; US, hdb. Pantheon, 1982; UK pbk. Granada (Panther), 1983; Spain, *(Un espia de la vieja escuela),* Argos Vergara, 1983; US, pbk. Pantheon,1984; Denmark, *(En Espion af den Gamle Skole)* Klim, 1984.

Watching the Detectives: hdb. Michael Joseph, 1983; US hdb, Pantheon, 1983; Denmark *(Pas Pa Politiet),* Klim, 1983; Germany *(Vorsicht, Polizei),* Heyne Bücher, 1985; UK pbk. Pluto Crime, 1985; Holland *(Argand en de Stillen),* Van Gennep, 1985.

Nasty, Very: hdb, Michael Joseph, 1984; pbk. Grafton, 1986.

Argand: Denmark, Klim, 1985 – the three Argand books in a collected edition.

Lying in State: hdb, Heinemann, 1985; pbk UK Grafton 1986; hdb, US, Putnam, 1986; Germany *(der Katafalk),* Serie Piper Spanning (2 imprints), 1987; Denmark, *(Lit de Parade)* Klim, 1987; Spain *(De Cuerpo Presente),* Jucar, 1988; UK, The Do-Not-Press (included in *The Indispensable Julian Rathbone),* 2003.

ZDT: hdb, Heinemann, 1986; pbk UK Grafton, 1988; hdb, US Viking revised as *Greenfinger,* 1987; ppb, US Viking Penguin, 1988; Germany *(Grünfinger)* Serie Piper Spannung (2 imprints), 1988; Denmark *(ZDT)* Klim, 1987; Brazil *(Sementes de Violencia)* Editora Best Seller, 1988; Japan *(...?)* Shinchoska, 1988.

The Crystal Contract: hdb, Heinemann, 1988; pbk, Mandarin, 1989; Denmark, *(Krystal Kontrakten),* Klim, 1989.

The Pandora Option: hdb, Heinemann, 1990; pbk, Mandarin, 1990; Denmark, *(Pandora),* Klim, 1991.

Dangerous Games: hdb, Heinemann, 1991; pbk, Mandarin, 1992; Denmark, *(Farlige Lege),* Klim, 1992; Germany *(Gefährliche Spiele)* Serie Piper Spannung, 1992; Poland *(Niebezpieczne gry),* 1997.

Sand Blind: orig. pbk, Serpent's Tail 1993; Denmark, *(Operation Sand Blind)* Klim, 1994; hdb, UK, Severn House, 2000.

Accidents Will Happen: orig. pbk, Serpent's Tail, 1995; Denmark, *(Haendeligt Uheld),* Klim, 1996; hdb, UK, Severn House, 2000.

Intimacy: hdb, Victor Gollancz, 1995; pbk. Indigo, 1996; Denmark, *(Intime Forhold)* Klim, 1996.

Blame Hitler: hdb, Victor Gollancz, 1997; pbk. Indigo, 1998.

The Last English King: hdb, Little, Brown, 1997; pbk. Abacus, 1998; Spain, *(El Ultimo Rey Inglés),* Edhasa, 2000; Germany, *(Der letzte englische König)* Taschenbük, 2003; Poland, *(Ostatni angielski kröl),* 2001.

Brandenburg Concerto: orig. pbk, Serpent's Tail, 1998.

Trajectories: hdb. Victor Gollancz, 1998; pbk, Phoenix, 1999.

Kings of Albion: hdb. Little, Brown, 2000; trade ppb. Little, Brown, 2000; pbk. Abacus, 2001; Spain *(Reyes de Albion),* Edhasa, 2002; Germany *(Die König von Albion)* Europa, 2003; Russia: *(Kings of Albion),* 2002

Homage: hdb. Allison and Busby, 2001; pbk. Allison and Busby, 2002.

A Very English Agent: hdb. Little, Brown, 2002; pbk Abacus, 2003...

As Bad as it Gets: hdb. Allison and Busby, 2003...

The Indispensable Julian Rathbone: hdb. and pbk. The Do-Not-Press, 2003...

Short Stories

As you will see, I don't write many short stories, and normally only when commissioned to do so. Frankly, they are not economical, even when you know you are going to be paid for them, and certainly not when they might never get published at all! That said, it will also be clear that I owe a lot to Maxim Jakubowski for asking for most of the stories in this list. Thanks, Maxim!

Baz, Some Sunny Day, Jack the Lad-Ripper, *and* The Lion of Draksville *all feature Basilia Holmes and her fat sidekick Julia Watson – a contemporary duo who would make great TV, if only someone would wake up to them.*

Baz: New Crimes 3, ed. Maxim Jakubowski, Robinson, 1991.

Some Sunny Day: Constable New crimes 2, ed. Maxim Jakubowski, 1993; Winner CWA Short Story Dagger 1993; The Year's 25 Finest Crime and Mystery Stories, No 3, ed. the staff of Mystery Scene, Carroll and Graf, 1994; The Year's Best Mystery and Suspense Stories

1994, ed. Ed Hoch, Walker 1994; Wide World Writers (as guest author), 1999.

Of Mice Men and Two Women: London Noir, ed. Maxim Jakubowski, Serpent's Tail, 1994; The Year's 25 Finest Crime and Mystery Stories No 5, ed. the staff of Mystery Scene, Carroll and Graf, 1995;Great Stories of Crime and Detection IV, The Folio Society, 2002; Shortlisted for the CWA Short Story Dagger, 1994.

Jack, The Lad-Ripper:; (as 'Jack, der Knaben-Ripper', Neon Schatten, ed Thomas Wörtche, Bastei Lübbe,1994;

Up Your Arse: Crimewave 1, ed. Andy Cox,1998; as 'N Arsch hoch', Möderisches Berlin, ed. Thomes Wörtsche, 1995 (1st publication).

An Illustrious Resident: The Mammoth Book of International Erotica, ed. Maxim Jakubowski, Robinson,1996

The Man who loved Women: The Mammoth Book of Erotica, ed. Maxim Jakubowski, Robinson, 1998.

Damned Spot: Past Poisons, ed. Maxim Jakubowski, Headline, 1998, (shortlisted for the CWA Short Story Dagger, 1998).

Albert and the Truth About Rats: World Wide Writers, 1998.

All About Eve: The Mammoth Book of Historical Erotica, ed. Maxim Jakubowski, Robinson, 1999.

The Lion of Draksville: The Mammoth Book of Comic Crime, ed. maxim Jakubowski, Robinson, 2002; Sherlock, ed David Stuart Davies, 2002.

The Photograph: Thirteen (images by Marc Atkins), The Do-Not-Press, 2002.

Full-length Non-Fiction

Wellington's War: hdb. Michael Joseph, 1984; pbk Ebury Press, 1985; pbk Michael Joseph, 1994.